all the right notes

all the right notes

Dominic Lim

FOREVER
New York Boston

Cover design and illustration by Caitlin Sacks.

Forever
Hachette Book Group
1290 Avenue of the Americas, New York, NY 10104
read-forever.com
twitter.com/readforeverpub

First Edition: June 2023

Forever is an imprint of Grand Central Publishing. The Forever name and logo are trademarks of Hachette Book Group, Inc.

Print book interior design by Jeff Stiefel.

Library of Congress Cataloging-in-Publication Data

Names: Lim, Dominic, 1974- author.
Title: All the right notes / Dominic Lim.
Description: First edition. | New York : Forever, 2023.
Identifiers: LCCN 2022047934 | ISBN 9781538725382 (trade paperback) | ISBN 9781538725399 (ebook)
Subjects: LCSH: Musicians--Fiction. | LCGFT: Gay fiction. | Romance fiction. | Novels.
Classification: LCC PS3612.I457 A45 2023 | DDC 813/.6--dc23/eng/20230117
LC record available at https://lccn.loc.gov/2022047934

ISBNs: 9781538725382 (trade paperback), 9781538725399 (ebook)

Printed in the United States of America

LSC-C

Printing 1, 2023

To Peter,

You are my Happy Ever After.

AUTHOR'S NOTE

All the Right Notes is a celebration of love and music in a variety of forms, but it also contains some sensitive subject matter. Please take care of yourself if any of the following topics are difficult for you.

Content Warnings: alcohol and drug usage; the sudden death of family members; homophobic language; nonconsensual sex.

Chapter 1—Then

EMMETT AOKI WALKED in after sixth period had already started, landing like a bomb in the middle of Handel's "Hallelujah" chorus.

As we were steamrolling our way to the final measures, he entered right in the two-beat rest before the last *hallelujah*, grinding Sunvalley High's concert chorus to a halt. Our choir teacher—who also happened to be my father—cut us off and, distracted by Emmett's sudden appearance, didn't ever motion for us to come back in.

It was super annoying.

My dad smiled the way he did every time the mailman delivered whatever gadget he'd ordered from the latest TV infomercial and indicated Emmett should take a seat in the back by pointing to it with pursed lips—a typical Filipino gesture everyone in choir had already gotten used to. Emmett stared at my dad with crinkled eyebrows and then looked around him before finally spotting the chair. He gave a big thumbs-up and walked up the choral risers.

I watched from the piano bench as Emmett made his way to the top. Unrest bubbled up around him like tar pit goo. Girls whispered into one another's ears. The boys puffed themselves up but then deflated. He seemed oblivious to the effect he had on everyone. But I wasn't buying it.

"Quito!"

I blinked twice. My dad blared into focus. He waved a baton in front of my face.

"Yeah?"

"I said *keep rehearsing them*. I need to make copies for our guest." He pointed at the papers clutched in his hand and hurried out into the hallway, mumbling to himself as he exited. He'd been begging the principal for a choir room copy machine for the past two years and hated having to walk all the way down to Mr. Drummond's band room to make copies. (Also, he hated Mr. Drummond.)

Thirty pairs of eyes locked on to me.

"Let's take it from the pickup to measure fifty-two? Sopranos and altos? At *King of kings*?" I asked, my voice rising higher and higher with every word.

No one seemed to hear what I was saying. But not because of my utter lack of authority.

Everyone had gone rigid, their bodies shaking with the effort to not turn around and gawk at the god in their midst.

"Super," I chirped at no one in particular. My hands curled into claws on top of the piano keys. "Here's your note." I forced my index finger to open and played an A.

I counted. "One, two…"

They came in on beat three.

It was horrible.

Somehow, just by sitting there, Emmett had found a way to suck the pitch right out of them. And the rhythm. And for some people, the basic ability to breathe. I should have stopped playing. Tried to fix the aural assault I was enduring. But I didn't. I was too busy trying to keep focused, to not be more aggravated by Emmett's presence than they were.

I was failing miserably.

It was the way he sat that bothered me the most. More than his letterman jacket or fancy Reeboks, his Jason Priestley hair or the muscle tone on his arms. Even more than the way he made being Asian look not only different but special, almost cool.

No. It was more than that.

What really got to me was this: the way he leaned back in his chair, legs spread, knees out to 10:00 and 2:00. Hands behind his head. Eyebrow raised just high enough to show noncommittal interest in what was going on around him. How wherever he decided to be was the right place because everything acquiesced, the brick walls in the room seeming softer around him and the fluorescent lighting making him glow like some sort of saint. Everything about Emmett expanded outward. He conquered every inch of the world, saying, *Yo, see this? Look at me. I'm hot shit!*

I could tell he was used to it.

And it drove me nuts.

My dad returned with a bundle of music. He stood by the piano, listening to us finish the chorus. "A little off-pitch this morning, don't you think, anak?" I didn't even notice it when he called me his son, something I'd asked him not to do in class. Not because he was speaking Tagalog but because I didn't like people being reminded that the choir teacher was my dad.

"Yeah. I guess. Not sure why," I lied.

Then, inexplicably, I looked at Emmett for a reaction.

Even stranger, he was already looking straight at me.

And then . . . he winked.

I felt a rush of blood to my cheeks.

"Dad," I said, "what's the deal with the new guy?"

"Him?" he asked, pointing his lips at Emmett. "He dropped out of woodshop. Allergic to sawdust. He is thinking of joining the choir, which is very good because we need more male voices. And"—he leaned down to whisper—"somebody of his stature can convince even more guys to join, diba?" He tapped the sheet music on top of the piano. "Laney, please give this to Emmett."

Our soprano section leader, normally a giggling mop of red hair, froze in place. My dad placed the papers in her trembling hands and gently closed her fingers around them. She was eventually able to bring them back to Emmett, though it looked as if she were learning how to walk for the first time as she did.

"He will be good for us, don't you think, Quito?"

Not only was Emmett a member of the Rally Court (the popular students who hung out in the rally courtyard, a concrete wasteland in the center of campus where they held events I avoided), but he was also the all-time record holder for three-pointers on the varsity basketball team. And was in every AP class available. He'd even been in a Sunday newspaper ad for Macy's.

For *underwear*.

But there was no way he was right for choir. I could hear him now, attempting to make a sound. Like a dying animal crying for help.

He didn't belong here. My dad had worked hard to build up the choral program at Sunvalley High, and I wasn't going to have some pretty-boy jock intrude on it. Not my senior year, and not in the one place at school I could call home.

Especially not *him*.

Out of the corner of my eye, I saw Emmett trying his hardest to not pay attention to us. His body defaulted into one of those poses guys always force themselves into: chin jutting out, one hand propped up on his knee, the other cupped against his crotch. He was a poseur, trying his hardest to seem cool in a totally not-cool environment.

But he'd have to sing at some point. He'd have to prove himself, and I knew he'd fail. We'd all see him for what he really was, someone who didn't have a musical bone in his body. Then he'd leave us alone, and we'd get back to the way things were.

I smiled at my dad. "I'm sure he'll be great."

Chapter 2—Now

HERE'S SOMETHING NOT every accompanist will admit—sometimes when we play, we're not actually paying that much attention to what we're doing. Only in certain circumstances, of course. When our heart's not in it. Or if it's something we've played a million times before.

Case in point, virtually every song I get asked to play at Broadway Baby, New York City's fifth-most-popular piano bar, is something I've already memorized. I go through the motions of looking it up on the pianists' communal iPad, but it's all already there in my head, each song tucked away for easy access and ready to be retrieved like a book I pluck from the shelf. When I get asked to play "I Dreamed a Dream" or "Memory" or any number of *seriously-this-one-again?* songs, my fingers go into automatic pilot.

So when a woman asks me, "Do you know 'Defying Gravity'?" my mind already starts to drift. It's not necessarily that it's one of the most over-sung songs ever. It's also because there's something about her that rubs me the wrong way. I've never seen her before, so I try not to judge. But it's hard. She's squeezed herself into a dress that screams *I bought this at full price!*, her makeup is layered on so thick it's impossible to tell what her actual face looks like, and she has so much perfume on that I begin to hallucinate.

"It's a song from *Wicked*, Kevin," she adds.

"It's Quito."

"No, *WICKED*."

I nod, smiling through gritted teeth. "Sure."

She points to me and demands "Two steps lower." Her eyes close. She bows her head. She's making sure everyone understands that she's preparing.

I play the intro. She sings the first line.

Well, not so much sings it as *splats* it.

To be honest, her voice is fine. It's like the voice of almost every other aspiring actress in New York, brassy and belligerent. She plows through, focusing on her own singing, not the song itself. A subtle difference. Instead of communicating the text, she dwells on every note, calculating the sound and timbre and making sure everything spins out at full velocity. She's showing off. And while a lot of people find the pyrotechnics exciting, to me they're just another day at the office.

So, for the next four minutes, I plant a smile on my face and allow myself to drift and look around. The place is super packed tonight. Broadway Baby (which is not actually on Broadway but several blocks over in the West Village) is always busy on Friday evenings, but tonight the people are angling for every bit of space. Even in the frigid February temperatures, a line of people still waits to get inside. I can see them through the window as they snake their way past Joe's Pizzeria, CVS, a perpetually closed tarot-reading salon, and a new falafel place I keep meaning to check out. Office types, show-obsessed gays, and loyal regulars all stand in line, looking forward to an evening of overpriced drinks and the chance to sing along with an enthusiastic and underpaid pianist. Me.

A lot of people are crowded around the piano in the main room. Colored drinks sit in front of them on the piano. Or rather the fake grand piano shell that covers an electric keyboard. I'd always wondered who'd fall for the facade, but surprisingly, anyone who ever gets close enough to see the actual electric keyboard is usually shocked. *Ohmigod, this isn't a real piano?* they gasp, before spilling their drink all over it.

It's their investment in the illusion of the place, perhaps. Everyone here wants to be a star, or at least pretend they are for a few hours, so they give in to the old-time feel—the pressed metal ceiling (rubber), the salvaged-wood bar tables (plastic), the mirrors marked with decades-old imperfections (new mirrors stained with acid)—and accept all of it to be real.

After a couple of the bar's cocktails, everything's real enough.

The people are still listening to the belter. She works the crowd, punctuating high notes with gesticulations and adding a superfluous run here and there.

As I motor into the climax, I notice an older gentleman sitting by himself at a table next to the piano, round in the middle and balding on top with a Caesar-like wreath of white hair. His face is red, as if just sitting on a stool is a cardio workout. There's a slight yearning in his eyes as he listens.

The singer belts her last notes, "Oh-AHAOHAOO!" and I'm snapped violently back to the song. Her yodel stretches the upper limits of the microphone. The crowd rewards her with applause, and she bows, soaking in as much as humanly possible. She doesn't thank or tip me.

"What a voice!" I say into my microphone. "What. A. Voice. Fabulous. *Just* fabulous."

I know I should work off the momentum of her performance and play something else from *Wicked* so that people can sing along. Or ask one of the regulars to share their rendition of some other crowd-pleaser.

Instead, on a whim, I whip around to the older man next to me. "Hi," I say.

His eyes widen. He looks around to find the person I'm talking to before pointing to himself. "Me?"

"Yes. You. What's your name?"

"Edgar."

"Would you like to sing something, Edgar?"

The color of his face deepens, which I didn't think was possible. "Oh. I don't think you'd know any of the songs I know. They're like me. Very old." His mouth smiles, but his eyes don't.

"Try me," I say.

"Do you know 'If He Walked Into My Life'?"

"*Mame*," I say. "Yes, I know it. It's one of my favorites. Come here, Edgar. Up to the mic."

His left hand trembles. "Oh, I'd rather not. Can we just sing it as a group number?"

"I'd love for you to do it by yourself. Why don't you come and sit next to me?" I pat the piano bench.

He hesitates for a moment before slowly sliding off his stool. His walk up to the piano is a little shaky. I can't tell if it's because he's old, nervous, or drunk, though it's probably some combination of all those things. When he sits next to me, I feel as if I've walked into a cabin. He smells of pine needles and warm dirt. And lots of whiskey.

I move the mic closer to him and start improvising an intro on the piano. "How's this key?"

"Just right," he says.

Edgar sings. His voice is a lot like he is. Rough-edged and worn.

Unlike the previous song, though, I don't leave my fingers to play on their own. I do the opposite of disconnecting this time. I focus on accompanying him. Sometimes guiding, sometimes following. He makes a few mistakes, fumbles a few notes. It doesn't matter. He's the opposite of the woman before him. His voice isn't impressive or technically proficient. In some ways it's even a little out of control. And yet I feel as if every word he sings is something he believes in. Like he's written the song himself. Like he's lived the story. Is living it now.

By the end of it, he's grinning, and I am, too.

"Thank you," Edgar says, breathless. "Can we do another one?"

I'm about to say yes, to ask him to suggest another song, some other chestnut for me to rediscover with him. But the energy in the room has soured. People's conversations have gotten louder. A trio of gays at a nearby table is checking their phones. One, a tall pouter with penciled-in eyebrows, puts on his pea coat and motions toward the door. The others seem ready to follow his lead.

"I'm sorry, Edgar. How about later on tonight?"

His face sinks into what looks like familiar territory for him. "Of course."

I groan inside. I want to keep making music with him, this man who has so much more to give than a loud voice and theatrics. But I have to make as many people happy as possible.

"All right," I say into the mic, "who's in the mood for some *Hamilton*?"

Cheers go up. The trio on their way out turn back around. The crowd is on my side again. As I begin to play, dollar bills get thrown into my tip bowl. The crowd starts to sing along, and I notice Edgar quietly lumber out into the cold.

After my shift, I turn the plastic fishbowl over on the bar and count my earnings in the annex, a smaller room with only one bartender and a wall-mounted television showing the NY1 news channel. It's quieter here. I can still hear the music through the velvet curtains that separate us from the piano area, but only just barely. The late-night-shift pianist, J.B., has taken over. She's opening with her Disney princess medley, a guaranteed crowd-pleaser. Once, I'd threatened to steal the idea from her. "Over my dead, lesbian body," she said, her eyes narrowing to points behind her owl-shaped glasses.

More fives and tens than usual from the tips, plus two twenties. I gave the crowd what they wanted and was rewarded for it, though the thought of it doesn't make me all that happy.

As I contemplate what fancy dinner I can now buy, someone sits down on the stool next to me.

Mark, my boyfriend, plants a kiss on my cheek. "Hi, Quito." He motions to the bartender, Jaime. "Two Manhattans, please."

Jaime, a brute with a baby face, gives me a look, knowing I won't drink the Manhattan. I subtly shake my head. He nods and proceeds to make one Manhattan and one ginger ale with cranberry juice.

Even though it's already almost ten, I can tell Mark's come straight from work. Sullivan & Cromwell went business casual years ago, but he still insists on wearing a suit and tie. "Better chances of making partner if I dress for success!" He's been working long hours lately. So long we're barely able to go out on dates anymore, which isn't optimal for a ten-month relationship recently gone exclusive. I can see the wear of stress etching more wrinkles around his eyes, though it sort of makes his Midwest-farmer-boy face even more rugged and handsome.

"I'm surprised to see you here. Why the visit?" After we'd been dating for a few weeks, he visited me at the bar during one of my shifts to see what it was like. An hour into my set, he leaned over the piano and said, "Sorry, but if I stay one more minute, I might never get the sound of this place out of my head. I need to go home and Febreze my ears with the original cast recording of *Sweeney Todd*." Mark's the kind of guy who won't go to a restaurant that doesn't have great reviews and won't see a musical or play unless the *New York Times* has given it a thumbs-up. Among other things, he's called Broadway Baby "Broadway Wannababies," "that place where broken hearts go," and "America's Got Talent?" (emphasis on the question mark). Despite my attempts to convince him the singing's a lot better than he experienced that one night, he's never come back. Until now.

He loosens his Bvlgari tie. He has news to tell me. I can tell by the way he tucks a lock of his blond hair behind his ear and how he's so distracted by what's on his mind that he doesn't complain once about the out-of-tune sing-along of "Part of Your World" from *The Little Mermaid* happening in the other room.

"How'd you do tonight?" he asks me.

"Not too bad." I *frap* a cluster of bills against the bar top, straightening them into a manageable stack. "And you didn't answer my question. I thought you couldn't stand this place."

"So, remember how I was telling you about this attorney at work? Dinesh?"

He's mentioned a Dinesh to me before, but I struggle to remember when or why. "I don't—"

"Get this. When he's not cranking out contracts, he writes plays. He's writing the book to a new musical, and he's looking for a composer."

I already don't like where this is headed. "Okay," I say cautiously. "What's it about?"

"Picture it," Mark says, framing my face with his fingers, "a musical based on *Peter Pan* at the height of the disco era. And it's an immersive experience. Can't you just see it?"

Yes, I can. And a part of me curdles inside. Disco music? Another retread of the Peter Pan story? Aren't there any new ideas? Why do we have to keep mining the same ones over and over?

"He's got some producer friends who might back the show. He needs to present a portion of it to them, partially staged. At least one full act. They want to see something on its feet by June. He's got all the scenes; he just needs a few songs. I told him you'd be perfect for that."

I decide not to remind him that I've been trying to work on a show of my own for years. Well, working on the *idea* of a show, at least.

"That is... incredible. A great opportunity. Thank you." I try my hardest to sound sincere, but my smile is too big. Mark fails to notice.

Jaime slides our drinks in front of us. Mark clinks his glass against mine. "To new adventures."

"To new adventures," I repeat and raise my drink. It slows to a stop against my lips.

On the TV behind the bar, a man is being interviewed live. A face I haven't seen in years looks at me. A face I haven't seen in person, that is, because I, and everyone else in the world, have become accustomed to it on countless billboards, movie screens, and magazine ads. Set against the red, high-gloss walls of a Salvadoran restaurant in SoHo, smiling that smile with the crooked tooth, that familiar face is in full-scale animation telling some story, punctuated by two hands carving pictures in the air, claiming all of the surrounding space.

Emmett Aoki is in New York City.

Chapter 3—Then

MY CHILDHOOD MEMORIES are permeated by music.

Sometimes, I swear I can recall my mother singing to me before I was even born—the brushing of her fingers against the skin of her belly as she sang folk songs and church music while I rolled around inside her and grew.

"Your mother's voice sparkled like light on water," my dad told me once. "They called her *the nightingale.*" They'd met at a church in Echague, where he played the piano and guitar for Mass. One Sunday, she'd come up to him afterward. "You're good," she said, "but your singing could use some work. Would you like some help?"

My father was charmed by such boldness coming from the young woman, her cheeks full like a chipmunk, the wide gap in her front teeth so beguiling that it didn't even occur to him until much later that she'd just criticized him in front of the priest.

He accepted her offer and asked how soon they could meet. My mother was amused by the way he tripped over his own words and kept scratching his nose as he talked to her. She smiled and said she'd be back next Sunday, and they could start working then.

That following Sunday, they met in the small multipurpose room after Mass, the church's sacristy, office, storage closet, and rehearsal space. My mother showed him how to breathe (*fill your lungs like you fill your belly; do not be stingy*), how to stand (*back straight, one foot slightly in front of the other, as if you are about to go on a journey*), and how to use the muscles of his mouth and throat correctly (*relax your tongue, make it soft like a bed so that your voice can bounce off—not stiff or it will become trapped*).

They went for a walk together after that first lesson. The next week, they had lunch together. The week after that, dinner.

Then marriage came.

Then me.

They moved to the United States, where living a life of classical music was more of a possibility. Not like the Philippines, where, unless you were a famous actor or popular singer, the arts were often considered merely a hobby. Playing and singing wouldn't put food on the table.

They settled where so many other Filipinos had, in the San Francisco Bay Area. First with relatives in Daly City and then in a small house in Martinez, where the hot summers made them feel more at home than the fog-induced chill of South San Francisco. They took a variety of odd jobs while trying to pursue their dreams, cleaning homes, custodial work, babysitting. My father slowly built up a reputation for being an inexpensive traveling piano teacher, while my mother sang in the church choir.

By the time I turned two, they had finally saved up enough money for a used piano from a defunct community center. Even thirdhand, it was still an extravagant purchase. We'd be eating only canned sardines and rice for weeks, but it didn't matter. They had me, a home, and a way to make music in it. Everything they needed.

My mother found steady—though nominally paid—work as a cantor at the nearby Catholic church, Queen of All Saints. She sang for all the Masses, weddings, and funerals. And with a piano in the house, my father was finally able to teach lessons at home. There were days when hours would go by without a single break in the piano playing in the living room or my mother's vocalizations emanating from their bedroom. When they weren't practicing, they were listening to the radio or records they bought from the mall. Other children might have been annoyed by it—adults bombarding them with the sounds of their own lives. For me, it was the lifeblood of our family. It ran through everyone's veins, keeping us alive and happy.

As my father tells the story, he had finished with a piano student and was just seeing him out when my dad became dazed. He wondered if he was suffering from some form of aural déjà vu because he was rehearing the past hour. What puzzled him most was that, even if it were some sort of auditory playback he was experiencing, it couldn't have been of his previous student. Because what he heard was better. No mistakes. An innate sense of phrasing.

He came running back into the living room and saw me sitting at the piano. I was playing "Frère Jacques." I was three years old, and I'd never had a piano lesson in my life.

It was all just a game to me. I'd been sitting on the couch as I usually did, listening and watching my father teach. I watched his fingers dance on the black and white keys, a pattern that was simple for me to memorize. The notes manifested in my brain as a rainbow of colors. For as long as I can remember, music has always existed like that to me, like a textured painting or sculpture, something I can reach out and touch. That day, it simply dawned on me to connect the pressing of the piano keys with the colors in my brain.

All I'd done was solve the puzzle.

My father picked me up off the piano and twirled me around in the air, my insides tickling so much that I laughed until I ran out of air.

He started giving me daily lessons. By the time I was in middle school, I was filling in for the pianist at Queen of All Saints, accompanying my mother whenever she sang. I didn't think anything could feel better than playing solo piano until I began playing for her, learning how to not simply play the notes while she sang but to support her. Anticipate her actions. The synchronicity made me feel as if I could read her mind. I adored that connection to her.

Then, the summer before I entered Sunvalley High, I lost that feeling. When the unspeakable happened. When my mother died.

I started my first year of high school with no mother and no desire to make music.

February of my freshman year, signs went up around school for the Spring Talent Show.

"Your song, Quito. The one you wrote in seventh grade and played and sang for us? The one your mom..." My father looked straight ahead as he drove us home from school. We traveled for another mile in silence before he was able to continue. "Why don't you perform it for the talent show?"

I was barely speaking to him or anyone else at that point. My playing had stopped to practically nothing. If it weren't for the fact that he'd recruited me to be the concert choir accompanist and his assistant in class, I wouldn't have been doing anything musical at all.

"Pass," I murmured.

"It's a good song. Other people deserve to hear it."

I shook my head. I didn't feel like showing that, or any other part of me, to anyone. Particularly not the rest of the students at school.

"Your mother would have wanted you to."

I could see my mom when he said that. Sitting in the auditorium. Eyes as wide as the first time she'd heard my song. It was just so unfair of him to bring her up.

I kept looking out the window, watching as the scenery passed by us in a dull blur, and agreed.

Months later, at the talent show, as I stood backstage waiting to go on, I remember the scent of the packed auditorium being heavy, ripe from the heat of an unseasonal heat wave on top of the nervous energy from everyone around me.

Two acts had already gone on, a jazz combo and a garage band called Boo Yah, Bitch! I was on after Straight-Up Sexy, five girls in purple spandex dancing to a medley of Paula Abdul songs.

My palms and armpits were so wet that I was certain I'd pass out from dehydration. The exit sign glowed just beyond the backstage door. My heart pounded.

Applause for the dance team. It was my turn.

I'd been on stages almost my entire life, playing the piano without thinking twice. Now the lights felt unbearable, the sight of the audience a weight around my neck.

I whispered to myself, "For you, Mom," and began.

I get into place
Put a smile on my face

They're all waiting for me to begin
To get to this night
I've practiced all of my life
To change who I am to fit in

Halfway through the song, I began to let go of my fear. The silence in the auditorium meant they were listening. I felt my mother's presence with me, could almost see her in the backstage wing, watching. I kept going, driven by the belief that the audience loved the song as much as she did.

When it was over, everything went completely still. For a moment, I was convinced they'd understood me. They'd seen the real me behind my song.

A deep, prolonged silence.

Then a shout. "Fag!"

It was a football player sitting in the third row. I could tell from his voice, shoved down an octave. A child's idea of what a real man should sound like. His hands were cupped around his mouth in a megaphone of hate. Laughter rang out from the audience around him.

I pushed myself away from the piano and ran offstage, past my father, who'd watched me from the wings and heard everything. I knew he'd go out and chastise everyone, give some sort of stern warning about profanity or threaten to shut the show down if everyone didn't behave themselves. And I knew he'd eventually make his way back to the choir room, where I'd be hiding, not able to talk, only wanting to go home and forget about everything. The song. The audience's reaction. And what I saw as I fled.

As I was leaving the stage, I saw Emmett Aoki in the audience, right next to the football player. Dead center of the Rally Court contingent. I would've recognized him anywhere. I'd been painfully aware of him all year. He was one of the few Asian students at Sunvalley that didn't need Chess Club or Model UN or the Asian Pacific Alliance to survive in a predominantly white high school. He was an athlete, already one of the most popular kids, even though we were only freshmen. On top of everything else, he was beautiful. To be honest, he was the kind of guy I wish I could've been. He'd found a way to not only fit in but to stand out. Everyone loved him. And he was laughing at me.

The expression on his face became a poster of that year, the sum of my pain from that entire horrible time of my life. It hung in my mind. His smug, flawless face so wrenched with disgust at my song that it looked like he was in pain.

Now I was going to have to look at that same face in choir every day until graduation. A face I never wanted to look at, ever again.

Chapter 4—Now

MARK'S SNAP IN front of my face jolts me to awareness. "Hello? Everything okay?"

I clench the stem of the cocktail glass. My hand is shaking. Droplets of cranberry and ginger ale trickle onto it and down to the bar. "I'm fine."

I glance quickly back at the TV screen; the interview with Emmett is live. I recognize the restaurant. Mark and I have eaten there numerous times. It's not far from Broadway Baby, only a few minutes' walking distance. My neck muscles tense into hard wire.

"Did you hear what I said?"

I shake the wetness off my hand and try to focus on Mark. "Something about a Dinesh?"

He traces the direction of my helpless stare and turns around to the television screen. "I didn't know you were an Emmett Aoki fan."

"I'm not."

"God, it's so unfair how hot that guy is."

The remnants of spilled drink stick to my fingers. I take a swig. "I've never noticed."

He watches the news interview, reading the slightly delayed

closed captioning. "He's doing a promo for that new Apple TV miniseries he's in. The one about bioengineered superspies."

Mark is always in the know about pop culture. Every time we do trivia night at Phoenix Bar, we slay the competition in that category. I haven't been following what's going on in Hollywood lately, so I'm in the dark about the new show. I wish I still were.

"Sounds interesting," I say.

Mark makes the sound he always does when he disapproves of something. A cross between a *psh* and a *tsk*. It makes the hair on my neck rise. Like the premonition of an imminent threat. "Personally, I think everything he does is way over-the-top toxic male," he says. "There always has to be an explosion. Or boobs. Or both."

I nod in agreement.

He turns back around to me. "So, about Dinesh's musical—"

The velvet curtain separating the back annex from the piano bar section is shoved to the side. Metallic hoops squeal as they scrape across the pole.

"Guess who's back in the house!" My roommate, Ujima, poses in the frame of the doorway. They tower over the room in clear Lucite platform heels. Colored lights and a sing-along of *The Sound of Music* stream past them into the annex.

As they catwalk toward us, they unzip their puffy pink parka, revealing a sequined Supergirl crop top, tight against their torso. The deep black of their naked belly gleams. Long legs stretch from a denim miniskirt. Their Diana Ross wig is a supersized Afro globe, and their face is a mix of *Vogue* editorial and Salvador Dalí.

They pull me up off the barstool with no more effort than picking up a handbag and surround me in a mama bear hug. They smell of flowery perfume and cinnamon chewing gum.

"Girl, that last set at Escándalo wore me *out*. I need some dinner. All I've had to eat today was a handful of Tic Tacs and—oh." Mark turns around on his stool. Sparks flare in Ujima's eyes. "How nice to see you again, Mark."

"Hello, Gerome," Mark deadpans.

To Mark, Ujima is always Gerome Jenkins. Music ed dropout and son of a Baltimore pastor. No matter how they look.

But Gerome is also Ujima. Drag superstar (in their own mind, at least) and my roommate of two years. Their face always seems to carry traces of their various gigs, smatterings of neon and glitter, hair perennially tied back and at the ready for any number of lace-front wigs. It took me a bit of time to get used to their preferred pronouns of *they* and *them* but now it's second nature to me. I also often call them "Jee," a shortened form of Ujima.

"Huh," Jee huffs. "You can see that I'm Ujima now, right? You know, for a lawyer, you don't actually seem to be that smart—"

"Dinner!" I interject. "Yes, that sounds lovely, *Ujima*."

"You can't go to dinner now," Mark says.

Ujima bristles. "And why the hell not?"

I give Mark a warning look. "We were just celebrating because Mark got me a gig."

"Doing what?"

"Writing music for a new musical," I say. "Partnering with a book writer."

Ujima twists their face into a question mark. At least *they* remember I've been trying to work on something of my own for a while now. "What's the show about? And who might this book writer be? Are they any good?" They glance at Mark with a sideways look that says *because if they're a friend of Mark, they aren't any good.*

Mark checks his watch. "His name is Dinesh. I told him we'd come meet him. Tonight. Right now, in fact. For dinner. In Hell's Kitchen."

"Oh, uh-uh." Ujima's head waves back and forth, hair sweeping the air around us like a giant gay mop. "We already have plans."

They've done it to me again. Put me in the middle of some squabble that always seems to erupt when they're in the same room.

"Let's see if we can work something out," I offer. I try to decide who to go with and who to postpone. Multiple no-win scenarios trample through my head.

Ujima points a jeweled nail at the TV screen. "Ooh, baby, look. Your favorite actor is in town."

Another one of Emmett's interviews is on. Or maybe it's still the same one. He has his arm draped around some young actress whose name eludes me. A perky millennial who seems very aware of her best angles because she keeps presenting only certain sides of herself to the camera.

"Wait a second," Mark says to me. "You just said you weren't a fan."

I eye Ujima. "I'm *not*."

They raise a heavily outlined eyebrow. "Aren't you the one always dragging me to see his movies right when they come out?"

Somehow Jee's managed to make a connection between my movie-viewing preferences and an interest in Emmett. Ujima has many talents, not the least of which is excellent perception. They've locked on to something that I don't want anyone to know. Particularly not Mark.

I try to change the subject. "What if we kill two birds with one stone? Ujima, why don't you come with us to meet Dinesh? And, Mark, you tell us where to go. Easy peasy, lemon squeezy."

Mark frowns. Ujima crosses their arms over their padded chest.

Almost an entire refrain of "The Lonely Goatherd" goes by in the other room before I finally say, "I'll pay."

Mark sighs. "Fine."

"You owe me," Ujima says to me with a glare.

In the cab, Mark texts Dinesh while Ujima checks their makeup. I sit between them, right smack-dab in the middle of a tension sandwich, with me as a slab of buffer boloney between two slices of drama.

Mark snaps his leather cell phone wallet case shut. "Dinesh is in. He'll meet us there."

"Where?" I ask.

"Mess Hall. One of my new favorite restaurants. It's kitschy but chic. It's divine."

Ujima grunts. "Sounds lovely."

We look straight ahead and say nothing as our driver weaves in and out of the lanes of traffic. The car's overly heated air sits on my forehead. "Honey, can you roll down the window a bit?" I ask.

Both Ujima and Mark press their window buttons but stop when they realize they've both responded. The winter air rushes in and flushes away the excessive warmth, though I'm more uncomfortable than ever.

After an interminable six-minute ride, we hurry into the restaurant. Strategically placed focal spots welcome us. I'm momentarily stunned by the bright lights. It feels as if we've stepped onto the set of a carefully choreographed production. The restaurant amps up the garish fluorescence of an actual military cafeteria, with aquamarine lights instead of puke green, though it feels more of an exaggeration than an homage. Like a canteen on poppers. But it's Mark's choice, so there's no escaping it.

We're led through the restaurant by a host wearing a Naval Academy T-shirt and pants so tight I fear for his health. Every detail of the place goes up to the edge of camp and then tips right on over. The servers walk around in formfitting military uniforms, homoerotic pictures of service members in different states of undress line the walls, and marginally military-related music (currently an EDM remix of Village People's "In the Navy") thumps throughout.

We go down the length of two long tables that take up the center of the main room. The dining appears to be communal, a trend that I find annoying. As if New Yorkers didn't spend most of their day trying to carve out personal space for themselves in the waves of people we get continuously drowned in.

A man checks his phone at the end of one of the tables. His hair is shiny black except at the temples, which are the type of gradated gray that looks airbrushed. He's older but still in incredible shape. Much better shape than me. Or even Mark, for that matter (and he spends way more time at the gym than anyone I know). From the way Mark makes a beeline for the man, it must be Dinesh. The host mindlessly motions for us to be seated.

Dinesh stands up. Holy hot pants, he's tall. As tall as Ujima in heels. "Ah, so you must be Quito." His accent is a mix of British and Indian. He shakes my hand confidently. "I've heard so much about you from Mark. We work together quite a lot, you know," a fact I don't think Mark has ever mentioned to me. Inappropriate scenes of them at the law firm immediately flicker through my mind: the two of them leaning in a little too closely while going over contracts, laughing while going over edits, flirtatiously smiling at each other at the coffeemaker.

"And I suppose this lovely vision is the person Mark told me would also be joining us. Uh... Gerome, is it?" Dinesh says with a bemused look.

Ujima tries not to roll their eyes at Mark. "Ujima Decadence Fabricant Jones. It's a pleasure to meet you. Hope you don't mind me crashing your little party."

"Not at all. Please." Dinesh pulls out a chair, and Ujima raises their eyebrows at me. Most of the men Jee tends to meet in New York—particularly at the establishments they work at—have zero manners. I can tell they're impressed with this rare gesture of chivalry.

Dinesh puts his elbows on the table and steeples his long fingers. His biceps bulge against the sleeves of his tailored shirt. "So, what has Mark told you so far?"

Even though the question is clearly directed toward me, Mark says, "Peter Pan at the disco! It's brilliant. And Quito would be the perfect composer for it. He's completely on board. Right, Quito?"

I smile politely and drink some water. In the background, the soundtrack to *Top Gun* has slipped into rotation. Kenny Loggins tells me I'm headed right into the danger zone. "I'm interested to hear more about it."

Dinesh looks pleased. "The book is mostly done. Certainly enough for the first act's worth of scenes that I need. But I need a partner for the music. I've got some ideas for the songs, a few basic melodies to go with the lyrics. But I don't have a musical background myself." He traces his finger over the rim of his water glass. "I've heard you're an incredible piano player. Have you done any arranging or composing lately?"

For the past fifteen years, I've been working as a pianist in New York, accompanying for auditions and voice lessons, playing at piano bars like Broadway Baby, even subbing in for a few Broadway shows. At this point, I've memorized the keyboard books for at least six different ones.

But when it comes to composing, I've been stuck. I haven't been able to finish simple songs, let alone an entire show, no matter how hard I try. The move to New York after college was meant to inspire me to get back into composing. I was supposed to swim in an ocean of creativity. But I've only been treading water for years.

I had tried to explain it to Mark once before when he asked me why I wasn't writing any music. I was missing something, I said. Waiting for the right inspiration. Truthfully, I knew why I wasn't composing.

I still hadn't gotten over the thing that had caused me to quit in the first place.

I didn't tell him that, of course.

"Oh, sure," I say to Dinesh. "I mean, I don't have any new stuff, but I've got some old pieces I can play for you."

Mark adds, "He's an incredible composer. He mostly just plays piano now, but he majored in composition in college."

"I, ah, never finished my composition major, actually," I say.

He looks surprised at this, though I'm 100 percent positive

I've told him before. Part of an annoying habit of Mark's is to only hear or see certain things about me. Only the parts he wants, I suppose.

"Oh?" he says. "Well, it doesn't matter. Dinesh, you should hear some of his stuff."

"Oh, you should," Ujima says. I didn't think they were even paying attention to our conversation. Up until now, Jee's been perusing the waiters as much as the menu in front of them. "I've only heard the stuff he wrote back in school, but trust me, honey. Quito's music is beyond."

Dinesh leans back against the metal chair. "How about this, then? We do a show-and-tell. I show you mine. You show me yours."

Ujima purrs. "Sounds kinky."

Dinesh smiles. His teeth are so white that they might actually be glowing. "We go over what I have of my play's book. You play me some of your songs. My place? Next week, perhaps? Sorry to put the screws in, as it were, but they want to see a reading of the entire first act by June. Preferably partly staged. That's about seven numbers. With a workshop cast."

My heart sinks. It's a ton of work to get done in four months. And the thought of working on someone else's story isn't ideal. Yet I've been trying to compose something of my own for years and have come up empty.

Maybe the simple truth is that I just don't have it in me to do it on my own. Maybe Mark recognizes this. Instead of looking for something to inspire me, Mark realizes I need someone to push me in the right direction. Even if the show wouldn't quite be my own, it would still be mostly my music. It's possible I won't ever get another offer like this. It might be the only hope I have of composing again. And after all, it's better to write music for Dinesh than to not write at all.

Isn't it?

Mark and Dinesh look at me expectantly. Ujima stares at another waiter. Streaming from the speakers above, Martika sings about toy soldiers falling down.

"Yeah. Let's do it," I say.

"Excellent," Dinesh says. He signals to one of the busboys passing by. "Excuse me, Benjamin? *Private* Benjamin?" It's charming that he tries to be respectful enough to address the busboy by the title on his name tag, even though it's more likely he's been in a military-themed adult film than the actual armed forces. "I think we're ready to order."

"Yes, sir. I'll go get your server, sir," the busboy says, saluting.

Ujima watches as the private marches dutifully back into the kitchen and fans themself with one of the menus. "We have to come to this place more often."

Mark, in the ecstatic mood he was in when he first told me about Dinesh at Broadway Baby, actually laughs at this.

My iPhone vibrates against my thigh. Who would be calling me this late at night?

I pull it out of my pocket to see a picture of my father staring at me. I scowl at it, confused. It's a FaceTime request. My dad barely knows how to turn his iPhone on, let alone use FaceTime.

"Excuse me for a minute." I walk to the restroom area and click to accept the call, prepared to ask him why he's calling so late. But the person I see is not my father.

Chapter 5—Then

MY DAD STOOD at his podium as people trickled in for choir. His brow furrowed as he tried to organize his stack of music. I sat at the piano, absentmindedly going through my binder while thinking about Emmett.

The day before, he'd spent his unannounced visit just sitting and listening and looking bored, even after Laney had given him a stack of music (and nearly killed herself doing it). My father asked him afterward if choir seemed like something he'd be interested in. He just shrugged, shook my dad's hand, flashed that snaggle-toothed grin of his, and ran off to basketball practice. So I thought (and hoped) that Emmett wouldn't be back.

After the final bell rang, I relaxed, convinced that Emmett had decided to stay away.

Then, without even looking up from the piano, I knew. A cloud of cologne and briny jock sweat wafted by me, and the room went quiet again.

"Where do I sit today, Mr. C?" Emmett asked in the stilted silence, not quite looking at my dad or anything else, really. I hated that calculated nonchalance. The aggravating fakeness of it, like purposely ripped holes in jeans.

Dad rearranged sheets of music without looking up. "Nelson,

where are you?" A nervous hand went up. "Go sit next to Nelson."

Emmett jumped up to the last row of risers and offered his hand to Nelson, a six-foot jangle of limbs who was having a very visible mini anxiety attack. Emmett took the blue plastic chair and swung it around to sit on it backward.

"Emmett." My father shook his head and made a circular motion with his finger.

Without a trace of embarrassment, Emmett turned his chair back around and sat in that same, arrogant way he had the day before. I felt my neck get red and tried not to look at him by forcing myself to study my music, note by note by note, until the pages went blurry.

I was so focused on *trying* to focus that I completely missed my father's signal to start the vocal warm-ups.

"Psst. Hoy, Quito! Pay attention please."

"Sorry."

He demoed the first warm-up. The choir stood. This time Emmett did, too.

And then something interesting happened.

As I accompanied, I listened to them sing. More confidently than yesterday, as if they'd already started to get used to Emmett being there. Then I watched him. His body looked as if it had traded places with Nelson's, who was standing up straight and singing with confidence. Emmett's hands and feet squirmed, as if they were trying to escape his body. He looked at my dad, the other kids, and finally, at me, as if he'd been asked an unsolvable question and needed one of us to provide the answer.

Emmett Aoki was nervous as hell.

"Quito," my dad said, turning to me, "slow down."

"Sorry. Got carried away."

I smiled down at the keyboard. Maybe Emmett wasn't so great after all.

For the rest of choir period, he seemed similarly lost. I knew I shouldn't have enjoyed his confused looks at the sheet music or his failed attempts at watching and following along. But I did. I soaked up the sight of him flailing, savoring the moments when I could tell that he'd stopped singing altogether and was only mouthing the words.

To be fair, he did try to pay attention to everything my dad said, scribbling in his music when he stopped to give them all notes—though I could see by the way Emmett looked at everyone else's sheet music that he often didn't have a clue what my father was talking about.

Dad didn't seem to notice. I decided it was my job to tell him. It was best for everyone involved that he be made aware that Emmett was completely out of his league and had no place in the choir.

At the end of rehearsal, almost as if he'd heard my thoughts, my dad asked all seven of the tenors—including Emmett—to stay after to audition for the short solo in Moses Hogan's "I Want to Thank You, Lord." I didn't need to tell him after all. He'd get to see and hear Emmett's painful lack of abilities for himself.

"Mr. Cruz, I really should get going." Emmett had his letterman jacket on with his backpack slung over his shoulders. His body was aimed out toward the hallway, gravitating toward the rest of the choir already leaving.

"You have better places to be?"

"I'm supposed to be at basketball practice soon."

"This won't take more than ten minutes. Why don't you go first, since you're in such a hurry?" Dad said, the tone of his voice as amiable as his smile.

But I knew my father. He didn't let anyone get away with anything in his classroom. His office was a mess, his conductor's stand a disaster of sticky notes and disorganized music, but his music-making was flawless, and he demanded the same out of his singers. It was this kind of discipline and hard work he instilled in me from my very first piano lesson.

Emmett went back to his chair and flumped down on it, dejected. He slumped, looking uncharacteristically not in control of the situation. "No, that's okay," he said. "I'll go after everyone else."

"That's very gentlemanly of you," my father responded. This time I couldn't tell if he was being sarcastic or not. "Quito, stay and listen. I want to have your input afterward."

"Hells yeah. I mean, of course." I wasn't going to miss Emmett's humiliation for anything.

The tenors took their turns.

Nelson went first. Fitful and anxious about most other things in his life, Nelson was truly comfortable only when singing and delivered the excerpt with calm assurance.

As the guys sang one after the other, Emmett fidgeted in his seat, his face tighter than a surgical glove.

Second-to-last was Kenneth Sanford. If Emmett was nervous before, he was going to be a mess after this. Ken was the soloist at the nearby Baptist church as well as Oakland Youth Chorus's golden boy. He had the pipes of a million-dollar organ. And as expected, Ken didn't just tear up the solo—he chopped it into little pieces and threw it all over the room like party confetti.

My dad beamed. "Fantastic, Ken." He was proud of all of his singers. Sometimes he liked listening to them even more than they liked to sing, I thought. "And last but not least..." He turned to Emmett.

The poor guy was terrified. His eyes were dilated with anxiety.

I felt a twinge of guilt. This was pure torture for him. I saw the same look of empathy on my dad's face that was probably starting to form on mine. Why did Emmett join choir in the first place if this was so hard for him? Why was he here, when he and all his Rally Court friends thought that singing was...gay?

Well, if he was going to learn how to be in a choir, he had to learn how to perform, and sometimes that meant singing by yourself in front of everyone else. My mind flashed back to freshman year and the talent show. My face hardened. Time for him to know what it felt like to be made a fool of in front of other people.

"I'm sorry, I...I...I still haven't learned all the notes yet," Emmett stammered.

"You've heard it six times now already," my dad reminded him. "Just try your best."

"Can Quito play while I sing?"

He looked at me. I felt the full force of his fear, as if *I* were the deer about to be hit by a car.

"Happy to," I said, complaining internally. I didn't want to help him. I just wanted to be able to listen to him fail. "I can figure out something to play underneath."

"You can't just play my part?" Emmett asked.

"I'll accompany. Don't worry. I'll support you," I said, surprised I'd added that last part.

"Okay." Emmett shook out his hands. "Here goes."

I improvised an introduction, then nodded as a cue for him to come in.

He sang the first line.

And then I stopped playing.

I didn't do it on purpose. I wasn't trying to derail his solo.

But I had to stop.

Emmett had sung only one short phrase. Not even three whole measures. And yet, somehow, those ten measly words and notes had completely thrown me. I'd never felt so discombobulated. I was only vaguely aware that everyone was staring at me. They seemed so far away.

"Shit," I said, forcing myself back into the moment. "Sorry, Dad. I mean, *dang*."

I took a breath and resumed my makeshift accompaniment. I nodded at Emmett again, who looked a little more at ease. It took all my attention to not be thrown again as I listened to him sing all eight bars of the solo, a prayer of thanks to a certain someone who was both his friend and his family.

What was this sound that was coming out of him? It wasn't huge like Ken's voice or precise like Nelson's. He was tentative. And not every note was right. But each note he sang was so vibrant, so full of overtones, that I didn't just see one color per note. I saw entire rainbows. I'd never experienced that before. Not even with my mom.

By the time Emmett had finished singing, the other tenors had clued in to what I was hearing. And to their credit, they didn't react in any kind of negative way; they didn't seem intimidated or jealous. Instead, they were less wary of him now. They nodded and smiled collegially, welcoming him in, as if he'd become someone different from the interloper they'd been seeing him as. Only the rarest of singers can do this. To be self-transformative just through their voice.

"Very good. All of you," my father said. "I'll tell you tomorrow who got the solo." My dad waved them away. "Shoo. Go home."

Emmett slid back into his old self. The guys left the room laughing, Emmett tailing behind them instead of heading out first. He walked backward out of the room, nodded at my dad, and glanced at me briefly before exiting.

I picked up my backpack. I'd expected to enjoy watching Emmett flounder, to get what he deserved. Instead, he'd just earned the respect of everyone in the room. Including me.

"Quito," my dad called out just as I was leaving. "Who did you like best?"

I turned around. "They were all good. Ken's always great. You can't go wrong with him."

"What about this new boy? Emmett? Don't you think there's something *special* about him?" he asked. His emphasis on the word "special" made me uncomfortable.

"He's one of the most popular kids in school. Of course he's special."

"That's not what I mean." That look again. "There's a rawness there that is unique. Don't you agree? I think I will give him the solo."

"But he can't read music, Dad. He was messing up all over the place," I exaggerated. "He'd need a ton of work."

"Maybe you're right."

"I *am* right." I headed back out again.

"So why don't you work with him on it?" he asked from behind me. "Get him up to speed. I'll ask him to meet with you after choir. Once a week should be enough. You can also help him learn the other music. Okay, anak?"

Not only was Emmett definitely in the choir now, but he had gotten a solo, *and* I'd have to work with him on it. And probably other things. My blood rushed to my head. Without turning around to look at my dad, I said, "Whatever you want."

Chapter 6—Now

I AM DEFINITELY not looking at my dad.

My phone screen has been taken over by a girl's plump brown face. Her curly black hair is pulled back tight, and her cartoonlike eyes blink furiously. "Hello?" she says.

"You're not my father."

Background noise blares around her. She puts the phone closer to her face, and her nostrils magnify to gigantic proportions. "Are you Mr. Cruz?"

"That would be my dad," I say to what are now just eyeballs. "I'm sorry. Could you move the phone a little farther away from your face?"

"Oh. Sorry," she says, crestfallen.

"No, I mean—you're a lovely young lady."

She giggles as the phone veers closer to her face, focusing on her mouth.

"With very pretty teeth."

"Thank you!" say the teeth.

"So, again. You're not my dad. And *I'm* not my dad. Could you tell me who you are and who you are trying to reach?"

"I—"

"And move the phone back. Just a smidge. There we go."

"I'm Celeste. Celeste Gonzalez? One of Mr. Cruz's students. The other Mr. Cruz, I mean. We just had our choir concert, and he was talking about how he had seen something on TV, and it made him think of you or something. And he said he should call you before he forgot, and then I said, well, just give him a call? And he said he wished you were here because it'd be nice to tell you face-to-face and also I think maybe he misses you? And I said, well, if you have an iPhone and he has one, too, then he could talk to you on FaceTime. And then I had to explain what that was, and he got really confused about it and also sort of grumpy, and he said he, like, didn't understand, so he told me to just do it for him."

I blink.

"So I called you," Celeste says.

"Okay."

She stares at me.

"So," I say. "My father."

"Yes?"

"Is he there?"

"Right next to me."

I sigh. "Celeste?"

"Yes, Mr. Cruz?"

"Could you hand the phone to my father now?"

"Oh! Sorry."

A blurry transition on the screen. Bright stage lights flash by. They're in the Sunvalley High auditorium.

My father's face finally comes into focus. He rubs his heavy-lidded eyes. Dark circles line the bottoms of them. I remember how he'd get so exhausted after concerts, having spent the previous days fussing over every last detail. The lighting, the blocking, the bows. Not to mention the music. He'd start out full of energy, but by the time the concerts were over, he'd fall in on himself like a blow-up doll whose air had all leaked out. "How are you, anak?" he asks.

"I'm fine, Dad. Though I'm kind of in the middle of something right now."

He scratches his head. People have always said they can see the family resemblance between us. But though we have the same round face, the same broad nose like a downward arrow, and bushy eyebrows like caterpillars above our eyes, he was blessed with a thick head of hair. Grayish now but still full. While the bald spot on the crown of my head grows bigger every day. "You know," he says, "I've been a teacher here at your high school for almost thirty years. Can you believe it?"

Classic Dad, not to get to the point. "What's up, Dad?"

He smiles. Not a happy one. "I don't know if the kids even like what I'm picking for them anymore. They like such different things now. With all this rap music. Lady Gaga. You know that *gaga* in Tagalog means a stupid woman?" He chuckled. "So she is actually calling herself Lady Stupid Lady."

"Dad."

"Okay, okay, you don't have to get testy." He shuts his eyes, looking even more tired. "I am going to retire at the end of the school year."

Something lurches in me, as if I've stopped too quickly at a red light. Dad retiring? I feel like I've aged years in seconds. My father is calling it quits with his career, while mine seems like it hasn't even gotten started. Maybe it's a good thing that Mark's got me involved with Dinesh's show.

"Are you sure? You've got a lot you can still teach to those kids."

"That's what I'm trying to say, Quito. I don't think that I do. I'm getting to the point where I won't be able to... when I cannot—"

Screaming and laughter erupt behind him. A group of teenagers still dressed in their concert white dress shirts and black slacks run around throwing things at one another.

"Hey! Knock it off back there, all you kids!" Dad yells. "Go home now! The concert is over! Where are your parents? Why don't they come take you away? *Susmaryosep!*" he says. "What was I saying? Oh yes. It's getting to be too much for me to deal with."

"I can see that."

Working with kids day in and day out couldn't ever have been easy, even when Dad was in his thirties and had plenty of energy. Now that he's approaching retirement age, why shouldn't he be allowed to stop? I've only ever known him as a music teacher, but some things have to come to an end eventually.

"I guess you should be able to spend more time relaxing. Maybe travel more. You've done so much for that school and all those kids over the years. You deserve to be able to do what you want. I don't know how they'll ever replace you, though."

My father stares at me through the screen. His image is so still, I think the app has frozen. He has on one of those expressions of his that I'm unable to interpret. I can't tell what he's thinking when he looks like that—his eyes looking so far past me that I can never find him.

"Thank you, Quito," he finally says. "I knew you'd understand. That's also why I'm calling you. I am going to have a special concert, okay? At the end of the school year. We are going to raise money for the choir, so I can make sure they have plenty in the budget for some nice upgrades before I go. They need new microphones. And risers. And it would be nice to get a..."

"Copy machine?" I smile.

"Yes," he says, smiling back at me. He looks away from the screen, distracted by something. "By the way, you come back to play for us. Okay? Assist me with rehearsing them. There's going to be a lot of new music. I need your help."

There it is. The real reason for the call. Not that my dad retiring isn't big news, but he could have just told me during our regular Sunday-afternoon telephone conversations. This was a special request he was making.

It wouldn't be that big of a request, normally. I try to get back to the Bay Area at least twice a year, during the holidays and once during the summer for my father's birthday. But what about my responsibilities here now? I glance back into the Mess Hall dining area at our table. Dinesh seems to be explaining his show to Ujima, who looks like they're genuinely interested, though it's hard to be sure if it isn't just because they want to sit on Dinesh's lap. If our connection works out, I'll be busy writing songs for his show. Between Broadway Baby and my other accompanying gigs, I'll need all the time I can get to compose. I haven't done it in years, and I can't afford to be distracted.

"I might be working on something soon, Dad. I'm not sure I can come out right now."

"Oh," he says and shrugs. "Sige. That's fine."

The tone in his voice now is one I know extremely well. Last year, he called asking me if I'd like to "volunteer my time" to go back and perform for the Fil-Am Community Center variety show in Walnut Creek. They were raising money for typhoon victims in the Philippines. When I told him I was going to sub in *Phantom of the Opera*'s pit for the next few weeks, he said he completely understood, sounding exactly as he does now—seemingly okay with my answer but actually not. He proceeded to send me articles about the death toll from Super Typhoon Yolanda. Every day. I couldn't stand more than a week of it before I finally caved in. Later I found out he'd already told them I'd agreed to the show before he'd even asked me. When my dad wants something, he'll keep asking for it, no matter what anyone tells him. He uses the slow trickle of guilt to work its way through the person, waiting for them to eventually yield.

I sigh. "All right. When is it?"

For a moment he looks young again. Not anywhere near retirement age. "The first week of June. Come in May. So that you have more time to work with the kids."

"I'll just be accompanying, though, right?"

"Coach them, too. Take your turn at directing. You've been working with all those Broadway singers now, anak. You can pass on your wisdom to these kids. There's one here especially that could use your help. He's having problems with his voice. I think you can help him. He reminds me of you, Quito. When you were young. He's . . . special, too."

The idea of helping kids and directing a choir does not make the invitation easier to take. I've never stopped accompanying singers, but I haven't conducted them in years. Not since the last time I saw Emmett.

"I'd rather just stick to the piano, Dad. And one week might be all I can swing."

"We'll be very happy to have you," he responds, in a way that implies that he either hasn't heard what I've just said or has decided I'll change my mind about it. "You know I've told the kids all about you. They are so excited to meet such a hotshot Broadway guy."

"Thanks, but I'm not—"

"Oh," he interrupts. "One more thing. I told everyone you'll bring Emmett."

My insides seize up. "What?"

"I saw him on the news. He's there in New York right now, diba? Doing publicity for his new TV show. Have you seen him yet? He's staying with you, maybe? Tell him we need him, okay? We want to sell as many tickets as we can. And with a big Hollywood star coming out to perform, it will be a big success. A big success, talaga!"

"Uh, he's not staying in my shitty apartment, no. He's a really busy, famous guy, and I don't think he'd be able to do it."

"He's your best friend. Of course he will sing. Just ask him."

My body stiffens. "Of course," I manage. "Right. He's my best friend."

"And my favorite student, don't forget. That's why I want him here, of course."

"Right."

"Very good." More screaming laughter breaks out. "Hey. Hey! Time to go home now, you kids. My god! Don't you have anything better to do?" He looks back at me. "I have to go. Tell Emmett I said hi."

"Will do," I say to the already blank screen.

Back at the table, plates of fries and chicken tenders sit steaming. Ujima's favorites. They would live off the appetizer section of the Applebee's menu if it were possible. I watch as they dig in.

"Ah, Quito, I was just giving Ujima the rough outline of my show. *Our* show, hopefully," Dinesh says.

Mark puts his arm around my shoulder as I sit. The sensation of claustrophobia creeps through me.

Ujima tilts their head at me. "Everything okay, baby?"

I try to smile. "My dad's retiring. Which is kind of a surprise. I guess I just thought he'd go on teaching forever."

"He's a teacher, then? That's lovely," Dinesh says, sounding sincere. He does seem like a genuinely decent person. If there's a chance we'll be working together on this show, I don't want to have to tell him that I might have to take time out from it just to play piano for a bunch of high school kids. Better to keep my mouth shut until I can sort out all the details.

"He's a music teacher, actually," I say, "the choir director at my old high school."

"Talent runs in Quito's family." Mark removes his arm from my shoulder and takes my hand, slightly crushing it. "Quito, I'm sure your dad's going to be so excited to hear about you writing music for this new play. Dinesh, why don't you tell him more of your ideas for some of the songs?"

I pull my hand away. "Actually, I'm feeling pretty tired. I think I need to head home."

"But we haven't finished talking yet," Mark says.

"I've had a long day, and I'm just realizing now how big the prospect of this new show is." Which is the truth, albeit only partly. "I need a day or two to wrap my head around everything." Definitely true. "It was really nice meeting you," I say to Dinesh.

"Until next time, then. Would next weekend be okay for our sharing session?"

"Yes. Looking forward to it."

"Aren't you forgetting something?" Ujima waves a fry at me.

"Damn." I promised Jee dinner. "Sorry. I'll make you something at home."

"Baby, you are so aggravating," they say. "But fine. We're taking a cab home, and you're paying. Let me at least take some of this chicken home." They wave their pink patent leather purse at one of the servers passing by. "Sweetie, I'm gonna need a to-go box." They eye him up and down. "Hm, I'd like to take *that* to go."

Mark rolls his eyes. He's gone back to his surly mood. "I thought you were staying at my place?" he says to me.

I'm disappointing everyone tonight. "Tomorrow instead?" I offer, kissing him on the cheek. Then, glancing at Dinesh, "Don't stay out too late?"

"Okay," Mark says, his expression hard to read.

The server returns and practically throws the to-go box on our table from a few feet away to avoid Ujima. Completely unaware of this, Jee happily scoops the food into the box.

The strange look on Mark's face is just about to change my mind about going home when Ujima pulls me out of my chair. "Come on. You're making waffles to go with this chicken."

Dinesh says goodbye. Mark doesn't wave or smile. I sag with guilt as we walk out.

"What was that all about?" Ujima asks once we're outside.

"My dad wants me to come home to California."

"Why?"

"To help him with a farewell concert."

"Oh, good. I was worried there for a minute."

Two years ago, my dad came to visit me during his summer break and stayed with Jee and me in our apartment for two weeks. After just a few days, he was driving me crazy, but he got along well with Gerome, finding all their attention-seeking antics hilarious. Then, when he saw them in drag, not only did my dad approve, but he seemed to like them even more. In fact, even though his usual bedtime is 9:30 p.m., he demanded to go to every one of Ujima's shows, even if they didn't start until after midnight. Suffice it to say, Jee adored my dad.

"I was afraid he might be sick or something." They stick their neck out into the street to look for an available cab. "He don't eat so good, you know. Remind him to have a vegetable every now and then."

"He's old-school Filipino, Jee. His idea of eating vegetarian is having fish."

"When is the concert?"

"Early June. But he wants me to go out there to work with the kids in late May."

"And Dinesh's show? You'd have to compose all those songs *and* get it rehearsed and ready by June."

I grimace. "It'll be fine. I can do both." My brain races as I freak out about the implications of the timing of everything.

"Mmm." They give me that look that says they see something that I'm doing a horrible job of hiding. "You're still not telling me everything."

The cold air bites against my face, and a light spattering of wet snow begins to fall, making my hair damp. I close my eyes against the coldness. "He told everyone that Emmett Aoki is making a guest appearance at the concert."

Ujima's head whips around, and a clump of Diana Ross hair hits me in the face. "Why would he promise that?"

"Because he thinks we're still best friends."

"Best friends? Wait. *Still* best friends? You were best friends with Emmett Aoki? THE Emmett Aoki?"

"No. We just went to the same high school. He sang in choir. We were... We were never friends. Only acquaintances. At best."

Cabs whiz by. Without even thinking about it, Ujima sticks their leg out into the street and pulls their miniskirt up as high as it can go, revealing a wide swath of thigh. Almost immediately, a cab swerves over to our street corner. Jee gives me a wink and then says, "Now talk."

I open the cab door. We're hit by a wall of citrus air freshener. I don't want to get into my history with Emmett, though I'd normally tell Ujima everything. The past is just too complicated, and the night is too far gone. "There's not much to tell."

"Well, whatever tea you got, start spilling it. We've got about a hundred and fifty blocks to go, and Mama needs some entertaining. You pulled me away from a restaurant full of tasty snacks, and I'm not just talking about the food. It's the least you can do."

Chapter 7—Then

THAT EVENING, AS I was helping my dad cook dinner, he laid out the rehearsal schedule for Emmett and me.

"On Fridays after choir, you can practice with him. That will give you at least half an hour together before he has to leave for basketball." His face glistened from the steam spouting from a just-opened pressure cooker. He'd been tenderizing oxtails, the main component of kare-kare.

I kept my eyes glued to the chopping board, mostly to make sure I was cutting the string beans, eggplant, and bok choy into consistently sized pieces but also because I needed to focus on what I was doing so I could avoid thinking about the heartburn that had started to build up inside me.

"And when exactly would I have to start doing this?"

"Tomorrow."

"What?" I asked, nearly nicking my finger with the knife. "There's no way Emmett will say yes to that."

"He already has," he said, straining to be heard above the exhaust fan he'd turned on. Into a pan of sizzling onions and garlic, he poured beef stock, ground peanuts, and some achuete seed–colored water, which turned the stew a deep mahogany. A sweet and savory scent filled the air.

"That's not possible," I said. "Emmett left the solo auditions today without you saying anything to him."

"I called him after school. He said it's fine."

I wasn't sure which was worse. That my dad had set up a regularly scheduled meeting between me and Emmett without asking me first or that he had him on speed dial. My stomach churned, but it wasn't from hunger anymore. Despite the fact that kare-kare was one of my favorite dishes of all time, my appetite had almost completely disappeared.

I didn't want to have anything to do with Emmett. People noticed him. Followed him around. I wanted to be left alone to my music. He was everything I wasn't. And he was a jerk. Maybe he had a decent voice, but that didn't make him a decent person.

I was convinced this was the reason I was upset.

Later that night, after barely eating any of the food, I tossed around in my bed, fixated on the impending coaching session with Emmett. The thought of it blinked like a red light in the distance, never shutting off, getting brighter and more insistent.

My classes the next day went by with me completely tuned out. I couldn't think about anything else. I walked through the hallways scanning my immediate vicinity, afraid of running into him. I wanted to delay the inevitable as long as possible.

I managed to avoid Emmett except for a special combined gym period outside. A massive all-hands-on-deck one-mile run test. I'd been dreading it all semester. During the run, with my insides on fire and my legs screaming at me to stop, slow down, turn around, start crawling—do anything but keep running—Emmett ran by me. Even though I'd started in the first group and he was in the fifth. I could've sworn I felt him come up from behind me without seeing him, like prey sensing the impending leap of a wolf. As he passed, it seemed as if he looked over his shoulder at me. He resumed his five-minute mile, or whatever it was, while I tried not to collapse into a hyperventilating mass on the track. In the locker room later, hurrying to get changed and get the hell out of there, I told myself that I'd imagined it. That he didn't actually see me.

For some reason, this just made me feel worse.

Then, finally, choir.

At the piano, I sensed it again. Emmett's presence, almost vibrating through me. Or maybe it was just the Drakkar Noir cologne he wore, which I'd never really liked before. Though I had to admit, on Emmett, it smelled different—something about the way it interacted with the leather of his letterman jacket, or his clothes, or the smell of basketballs, or—

He slapped me on the back. "Wassup, dude?"

I jumped off the piano bench.

"Me and you after class, right?"

A sting began to creep out from between my shoulder blades and down my spine, to the tip of my tailbone.

"You gonna drill me hard?" he said.

It was several moments before I realized my mouth had dropped open without saying anything in response.

He squinted, probably wondering what the hell was wrong with me.

Then he punched me on the shoulder. A jock move I'd never been on the receiving end of before that he'd probably done to other guys a hundred times. "Take it easy on me, okay, dude? I'm a virgin," he said with a completely straight face.

Overwhelmed with a fear that I'd just blushed, I turned away and tried to come up with an excuse to escape or at least cover up my face. Was he messing with me? He must have known that everything he was saying was a double entendre, right?

I looked back at Emmett just in time for him to wink at me.

The bell rang, the sound coursing through my frayed nerves. My dad emerged from his office. "All right, you crazy kids. Let's get to work."

"See ya afterward." Emmett punched me on the shoulder again and waited for some kind of response. When I did nothing again, he shook his head and strolled back to his chair to sit in that exasperating Emmett way of his.

The class period had an indefiniteness to it, seeming both interminable and fever-fast at the same time. No matter what I did, I couldn't focus. All during the rehearsal, I made way more mistakes playing than I usually did.

Which is to say, I actually made mistakes.

Wrong notes clunked out left and right, incurring bitchy looks from Laney. Emmett seemed to find my blunders hilarious, though. Whenever I messed up, he chortled. Something about this made me acknowledge the gaffes by crossing my eyes and cringing visibly. This only made Emmett laugh louder.

"Focus, please," my dad said.

"Sorry," Emmett and I said at the same time.

Emmett raised an eyebrow at me. *Maybe we should get our shit together?* the look seemed to ask, though why I thought I had any idea what was going on in Emmett Aoki's mind was beyond me.

"Let's go over the pronunciation again," my father said. We were working on Mozart's "Ave verum corpus." "Ah-veh, not

Ah-VAYEE," he pointed out to everyone. "Veer-jee-neh, NOT virgin-ay."

All of it melted into note-and-word mush as I watched Emmett, who had actually resolved to pay more attention, it seemed. He was doing some variation of the same sequence of actions over and over: listening to my dad's instructions, scribbling something in his music score, shaking his head, and then erasing what he'd just written. The day before I'd found his Sisyphean efforts amusing. Now I was starting to feel sorry for him.

I kept looking at him. Again and again. Compulsively. I convinced myself it was just to observe. To see what he might be struggling with so that I could address those issues in our coaching sessions directly, thus minimizing the time we had to spend with each other. That's all it was.

The bell rang. My father made his way back to his office as everyone exited the choir room engaged in loud conversations.

I pretended not to pay attention as Emmett made his way to me at the piano. He stood next to me, backpack over one shoulder, thumb hitched underneath the strap. "Dude, you were fucking up all over the place today."

Now he was making fun of me. The idea that we'd found a connection during class suddenly seemed ridiculous. I began putting sheet music in my binder. In the wrong order.

"Me? No, you," I offered pathetically.

"There's no way you heard me mess up."

"Because you're perfect?" I said, then regretted I had. I didn't have the talent for witty banter. Or even middling banter.

"Because I wasn't singing most of the time." He grabbed one of the blue plastic chairs and set it close—too close—to the piano.

The smell of him bloomed as he leaned into me. "You need to teach me."

Had I remembered to put on deodorant that morning? My body itched with the instinct to scoot farther away from him, in case I didn't smell as nice as he did. "All right, hang tight," I jabbered.

He stared at me oddly, not sure of what I'd just said. I wasn't so sure myself. I scratched the back of my neck, wet with sweat, and then quickly wiped my fingers on my jeans. "Let's start with your solo on 'I Want to Thank You, Lord.'"

His face cracked. "Wait. I got the solo?"

I paused, trying to think. Dad said he'd talked to Emmett on the phone. I assumed he told Emmett that he'd given him the solo. Apparently not.

"Uh, yes?" I responded.

The crack in Emmett's face widened. "Oh, no. No."

"You deserved it."

"I can't do it. That's not why I—"

"I'll help you."

He was looking off into space. He didn't seem to hear me.

"Hey," I said. For some inexplicable reason, I felt compelled to pull him back to earth by putting a hand on his knee. "I said I'll help you." My stomach reeled when I realized what I'd done. Did I just grab hold of a Rally Court jock's knee? Guys didn't do that to other guys. Certainly not ones who barely knew each other.

I didn't know what to do. Jerking my hand away from him would only bring attention to it. Make things more awkward. But I couldn't just keep it there.

I decided it was best to pull away slowly. Very, very slowly.

As I began to slide my hand off Emmett, he refocused and looked at me. "Okay." He'd hardened his face with determination. "I trust you."

I stared back at him. With my fingertips still touching his knee.

I was seconds away from dissolving into a pool of embarrassment when he punched me in the shoulder.

My third shoulder punch of the day. I needed to do something this time. Punch him back? Kick him in the shins?

Not knowing what else to do, I just said, "Oww?"

Emmett snorted. "Dude, you are such a weirdo."

Shooting shoulder pain aside, I was grateful he'd done it. It gave me an excuse to take my hand back. I rubbed my shoulder and felt the pain burn in a not altogether unpleasant way. "Um. Let's start the song from the beginning."

He pulled his binder out from his backpack and flipped through the sheet music. "You'll have to play it a couple of times for me," he said. "I can't really read the notes, but once I get something in my ear, it never leaves."

I tapped a finger to my lips.

"What?" he asked.

"Hold on a sec." I hopped off the piano bench and went to my father's office. He was reading the school newspaper.

"I haven't heard any practicing yet," he said without looking up.

"Do you still have that old tape recorder?"

"It's on the top of the bookshelf. What do you need it for?"

I reached up and swiped my hand back and forth. My fingers made contact with hard plastic. I jumped and grabbed the tape recorder, something he'd gotten at RadioShack for taping our rehearsals but never got around to using.

"I'm borrowing this." I ran back out to the choir room.

Emmett was hunched over on his chair, slowly balling a fist into his other hand. I wondered if he practiced things like this. He always managed to make his poses look so natural. So effortlessly masculine. Something I would never be able to pull off, no matter how much I practiced.

I clicked the eject button of the recorder, checking it for a tape. A cassette jumped out with a plastic pop. I pushed it back in, set the tape recorder on top of the piano, and pressed record.

"I'll play the part. You sing it back," I explained. "We'll do that a few times, and you'll have it all on tape so you can have it to practice with at home."

"Cool," Emmett said. "Hey, thanks for doing this, by the way. I'd be lost without you."

Instead of a wink or an upturned chin or another punch, he gave me a smile. Small and subtle yet unmistakably sincere. Not an ounce of posing. It startled me.

"What?" he asked.

"Nothing." I shook my head. "It's just—you're not exactly what I thought you were like."

"That's funny. Because you're exactly like what I've always thought you were like."

I couldn't have heard him correctly. "Like—what?"

"Funny. Super talented. Hella smart."

"No. What I mean is, you've been thinking about me?" The words stumbled out of my mouth and fell to the floor. I immediately wanted to bend down, scoop them all back into my mouth, and swallow them all whole.

"Your song at the talent show freshman year?" he said. "I was really impressed by it. I couldn't believe you'd written that by yourself."

My head was spinning with too many thoughts. He'd been impressed by me? He thought I was talented? The fact that he'd thought about me at all was throwing me for a loop. "You actually liked it?"

"Dude, it was rad. The music was great, but the words, the lyrics... they were amazing."

Did he understand what the lyrics actually meant? What I had been trying to say with them? "I thought you and the other athletes were laughing at me."

"Trevor. That idiot," Emmett said quietly to himself. "That fucking sucked, what he did."

I thought back to that moment. The look on Emmett's face. Did I mistake his disgust for delight? Had I been misjudging him this whole time?

"That was really hard," I admitted, surprising myself. I hadn't talked about that evening with anyone. Not even my dad. It was a memory I wanted to crumple up and throw away. "I haven't even thought about that song since that night."

"That's too bad. Because you were awesome."

I tried to look at him, tried to thank him, but I couldn't. My mouth was so dry it was stuck shut.

I could sense he was waiting for me to respond. To say something. To compliment him back. At the very least, to thank him. Maybe even something more. The more I thought about the possibilities, the more it felt as if I'd break into a hundred pieces if I did anything.

The last time I said something nice to a guy that good-looking in choir...didn't go so well. The thought of opening myself up only to be humiliated wasn't something I wanted to go through again.

So I just sat there. Getting more dry and brittle by the second.

After a silence that seemed to last hours, I managed to move my hands to the piano. My fingers slowly plunked out his solo part. "After I play it, you sing it back. Got it?"

He said nothing.

I managed to turn and look at him. He nodded slowly, his face shadowed. Most probably from concentration. At least that's what I made myself believe.

Chapter 8—Now

"SO YOU WERE his little choir buddy," Ujima says.

My head presses against the window of the cab as I look out. The storefronts and apartment buildings of Manhattan's Upper West Side zoom by in a multicolored haze. Even this close to midnight, the streets are still buzzing—people smoking in front of neighborhood dives, ducking into bodegas, sitting at the windows of twenty-four-hour diners and late-night cafés. After fifteen years of living in New York, I still can't get over how nighttime burns as bright as day.

"It was a long time ago," I say. The smell of car freshener has mellowed to that of a lemon drop. "And I wasn't his buddy. Just a tutor."

"You never hung out with him?" Ujima asks.

"With the most popular kid in school? Nah."

"Mmm-hmm."

"What?"

"Nothing." The cab turns off Broadway and onto our street. "You can stop right at the corner, honey. Thank you."

Ujima says nothing as we walk up the stairs to our fifth-story walk-up, which is unlike them. Even after a long night of performing, they normally still manage to talk my ear off, going on about how much they hate living in a walk-up and why the hell don't we live in a building with an elevator and wouldn't it be wonderful if we could have a doorman who would greet us every day, preferably one who's swarthy and Puerto Rican?

I unlock the door to our apartment and flip on the lights. We enter into a familiar mix of smells—candles, laundered clothes, half-emptied take-out containers, and the dregs of coffee and cocktails in various glasses and mugs.

Jee commences their daily ritual. A transformation from Ujima back to Gerome. They kick off their high heels, look at themself in the floor-length mirror by the door, and pluck the humongous wig off their head, revealing their own hair. I'm surprised at how full it's become. At some point, they might not even need a wig. Jee tilts their chin up and examines the effects of the evening on their meticulously painted face. Ujima's makeup tonight, as always, was flawless. *Beat for the gods*, they like to say. Applied with such thick, masterful strokes that even heaven can't miss them.

I've noticed lately that they wait longer and longer at the mirror before resigning themself to the bathroom, not wanting to say goodbye to the person they see. As if they'll never see them again.

I sense that familiar sadness in them and try to cheer them up. "You looked gorgeous tonight," I say, trying to support the instinct they have to delay their change back to their less femme self. For a little while, at least.

Ujima's reflection in the mirror gazes at me, their eyes like flints. "Get those waffles crispy," they say and wander off to finish unmaking themself.

I start gathering ingredients for the batter and listen to Jee singing in the shower, washing themself back to the form I was introduced to first. The one who, eight years ago, sashayed half an hour late into the first rehearsal for an off-Broadway (off-off, actually—as in Park Slope, Brooklyn) production of *Pippin*.

I was playing rehearsal piano. Our director, Kelly, an ex-actor whose biggest Broadway credit was playing a dancing plate in *Beauty and the Beast*, was undeterred by Jee's fashionably late entrance. "Call was one thirty, Gerome," she singsonged.

"Sorry, girl. Late night. The boys just couldn't get enough of Ujima."

Kelly exhaled audibly, paused for dramatic effect, and then continued with rehearsal.

Gerome dragged themself to the last open chair, crossed their legs, and put on a pair of reflective sunglasses. As Kelly went over the rehearsal schedule, I sat at the piano, sneaking glances at the new guy and wondering who the heck "Ujima" was and why Kelly didn't seem to care that Gerome had so obviously fallen asleep.

The answer to the latter question came after just one sing-through of the score. Gerome was not only the best singer in the cast, but they were also the most prepared. They'd memorized nearly all their songs as the Leading Player.

Then dance rehearsals began. Gerome could move in ways I'd never seen before. They'd clearly had a classical background—I found out later they'd trained in ballet since childhood—but there was also something else. Something I couldn't quite describe. When they danced the choreography, they imbued all their movements with a sensuality that was both masculine and feminine at the same time. Their movements went beyond my own simplistic concept of gender, being neither as much as both. They were absolutely mesmerizing to watch.

Then, when the cast dragged me out one afternoon to go dancing at Body & Soul, I finally met Ujima.

We'd all been there for over an hour when they waltzed into the club. The crowd instinctively parted for them as they came toward us. I knew at a glance who they were. That afternoon, as I watched Ujima conquer the dance floor, glowing with sweat and looking like an outer space goddess in their sparkling silver outfit, I almost fell in love with them, pulling them aside and monopolizing their time, wanting to be near them constantly.

But later, after floating on a high from hours of dancing, after we'd stumbled into the alley for some fresh air, the brief kiss we shared was more confusing than satisfying. We looked at each other and laughed after we'd done it. Then we hugged, somehow knowing we'd fallen into something that would take a bit more practice before we would figure out how to get it right. We'd realize that we did belong together, but as friends—eventually sharing a home, if not a bed.

Gerome emerges from their bedroom, wearing a lime-green kimono. A pink sash corrals their burgeoning Afro. They close their eyes and inhale the steam from two freshly pressed waffles filling the kitchen. "Now, that's what I'm talking about."

They perch themself on one of the high stools at the counter separating the kitchen from the living room.

I place a plate of waffles in front of them. The pat of butter I've put on top of the stack is already melting into glistening rivulets down its sides. I set out a bottle of maple syrup and the Mess Hall chicken, which I've warmed up and recrisped in the oven and then soused with Jee's favorite hot sauce. "Bon appétit."

"Admit it. You love taking care of me," they say with their mouth already half-full of waffle.

"Don't flatter yourself. I just love to cook." I pour them a glass of orange juice as I continue waiting for my own waffles to be done. "Cooking might be the biggest love of my life besides music."

"Not Mark?"

I pause, my head briefly blank. "And Mark," I manage. "Besides Mark. Of course. Besides music and Mark. I love Mark and music." I see excess batter flowing over the side of the iron and onto the counter. "Shit." I grab a kitchen towel.

Jee tears the sauced chicken into pieces and pops them into their mouth one by one. "You know, I always thought Emmett Aoki was gay. He's too damn pretty to be straight," they say, chewing.

"He's not gay."

"Bitch, please. That wife of his, the reality star? The opposite of real, honey. Fake as a sack of Swarovskis."

"Ex-wife."

"Wait, are you sure?"

"Yes," I say, bending down to the floor to clean up some of the batter, which has somehow ended up there. "Positive."

"Oh. You're right. I remember now. Damn, they weren't married long. Is he dating someone new?"

"No. I don't know. I don't care. Why should I care?"

Gerome continues to eat in silence. Then, "Is something burning?"

I sniff the air and look up. A tiny tendril of black smoke unwinds from the waffle iron. I run to it and pull it open, hoping some of it will be salvageable. "Goddammit." My waffles are a goner. I slam the iron shut.

"Here," they say, pushing their plate toward me. "Have some."

"No, it's okay." I reach for a bag of tortilla chips next to the kitchen sink, grab a fistful, and lean against the counter, munching sullenly.

Jee watches me as I try to quell my hangriness. "So, you're really going to do this? Ask a movie star to sing for a high school choir concert?"

I swallow and cough. Bits of chips irritate my throat. "I guess."

"How are you going to get in touch?"

"No clue."

"Will he even remember you? It's been a long time since high school. At least for you, old man."

I sit down on our cracked pleather couch in the living room. My reflection in the flat-screen television stares back at me from the gaping blackness. My hair is tufted and wild, and my eyes are as puffy as my cheeks. Why didn't anyone tell me I looked like shit? I've been stagnating in every part of my life. My career, my music, my relationship. It's only natural that my body would fall into the same rut. What's in motion tends to stay in motion, and what's at rest stays lazy and bloated.

I think about Emmett's interview on the TV screen back at Broadway Baby. In the years since I've seen him, he's added bulk to his lean frame. Gotten bigger, more muscular. A decade of constant preparation for blockbusters has sculpted him into a high-speed chasing, fistfighting action god. Age has only had beneficial effects on his face, his only wrinkles the fine lines that crinkle in the corner of his eyes when he smiles for the camera. His smile is the same as I've always remembered. Unchanged. Imperfectly perfect.

"It *has* been a long time. I haven't talked to Emmett in almost twenty years."

Jee pats their tiny belly. They belch. "Oh Lord, excuse moi." The fogged-over look of satiation sits happily on their makeup-free face. "Even if you do manage to get in touch with him, how are you going to convince him to do it?"

The truth is, I don't think I *am* going to be able to convince Emmett. Not because, as I told Ujima, we were only acquaintances in high school. There's a reason we haven't spoken in almost two decades. And I don't want Jee, or anyone else, to know about it. In fact, the more I think about it, the less I want to go through with the whole thing. Why dredge up the past?

I get up to pour myself a stiff glass of iced tea to clear my throat. "Doesn't matter. It's not going to happen. On that TV interview, he said he's leaving town Sunday night. After he hosts *Saturday Night Live*."

Jee perks up. "He's hosting *SNL* tomorrow night?"

"Yes. Why?"

"I know exactly how you are going to get a little face-to-face time with your choir buddy."

Chapter 9—Then

WE STOOD AT my doorway facing each other awkwardly for a few moments until Emmett held up a gift bag.

"My mom told me to bring this."

"What is it?"

He opened the bag, letting me peer inside. A green bottle of some kind of liquid and something else wrapped in tissue paper.

"Sake," he explained. "Rice liquor. We brought it home from our last trip to Kyoto to visit my grandparents. My mom saved it for a special occasion. And there's a glass to go with it. Normally, you're supposed to use a tiny one, but we didn't bring any home from Japan, and my mom didn't think a shot glass would be right. It's just a regular-size glass. But we got it from Macy's. So it's fancy."

"Uh, cool." I motioned for him to enter.

He thrust his free hand deep into the pocket of his trousers and followed me into the living room. His blue Oxford shirt was buttoned up to the top, and his usual pompadour had been slicked back. He smelled more of himself than usual—that mix of cologne with his own natural scent, one I've learned doesn't come from his jacket or clothes but somehow emanates from his body, earthen and outdoorsy like a tree that's absorbed hours of sun and is radiating it out again. A scent that doesn't even remotely smell like mine.

I grabbed his collar and flipped it up. "What, no tie?"

"Quit it," he said, turning red. "Dinner at a teacher's house. I don't know. I have to be on my best behavior and everything. Make a good impression."

"It's just my dad. And me."

Emmett opened his mouth but then shut it again quickly, looking like he was swallowing some sort of response.

I decided not to give him another chance to say anything. "This way."

Even though our house wasn't big, he stayed close behind me, as if he might get lost. I'd grown accustomed to the way constant proximity to him felt—a live wire–like energy that used to paralyze me. We'd had several weeks of coaching sessions together by then, and in the beginning, hours would go by after our time together without me ever successfully shaking off the sensation, like a permanent second skin on top of my own.

We walked through the living room, past the brown corduroy couches, the matching walnut end tables, and the entertainment center straining to contain our monstrous television and stereo system with its many cassette decks and speakers.

Emmett paused. The array of framed pictures on our upright piano had caught his eye. Photos of all the stages of my life sat there: me as a baby, a toddler, a teen. And in the middle, a black-and-white picture of a woman sitting on concrete steps, exotic foliage standing at attention in the back. In the portrait, she is young, her hair short, her cotton dress simple and suffused with tropical light. The words "Your Nightingale" are scribbled on the bottom corner of the picture in swooping, dramatic cursive.

"Is that your mom?" Emmett asked.

I stopped for a second. Then I nodded and kept walking to the kitchen, silently willing him to keep following me.

He didn't move. I felt the invisible line between us stretch and detach.

I turned back around and watched as he scanned the surface of the piano, the living room walls, the other tables in the room. "You don't have any other pictures of her."

A familiar ache inside me rose. A sensation I'd thought would lessen over time but always proved me wrong when it resurfaced, just as heavy as before.

"My dad says it's the only one she ever liked of herself, so it's the only one we keep out. She used to be really harsh on herself. Looks-wise, at least."

"Why? She's beautiful. She kind of reminds me of you."

So much sadness was rising in me that Emmett's comment didn't register at first.

"Ah, Emmett." My dad emerged from the kitchen. He wiped his hands with an old kitchen towel.

Emmett presented the gift bag to him with outstretched arms, his body bending slightly at the waist. How he was able to make this look graceful and not at all weird was yet another example of how complete the control of his body was as it moved. "A gift from my mother." My dad eyed it with skepticism. "It's sake. A Japanese liquor," Emmett said. "Made out of rice."

He lit up. "Well, if it's made of rice, then it must be delicious!" He took the bottle and rolled it over in his hands. He inspected the label closely, as if that would somehow render the Japanese comprehensible. He eventually shook his head. "Please tell your mom I said thank you. I'll put this in the refrigerator for now.

Dinner will be ready in about ten minutes. Just spend time together for a while, and I'll call for you. Okay?"

"Cool. Thanks, Mr. Cruz," Emmett said. "Hey." He bumped into me lightly. "Want to show me your room?"

"Uhhhh..." My heartbeat quickened. "No, my room is messy. Which is stressy," I blurted out, which was bizarre and not even remotely true. I'd spent an hour earlier in the day tidying it up, making sure it looked presentable and didn't smell of dirty socks and pork rinds. The real reason I panicked was because the prospect of us actually being alone in my room together gave me a horrifying shiver up and down, like the feeling I'd always get right at the crest of a roller coaster's first drop.

"Why don't I show you more pictures of my mom? Here," I said, walking to the bookshelf next to the couch, "we have a crap-load of photo albums."

His smile diminished. "Cool."

I pulled down one of the albums, green and bulky with too many pictures. I sat on the couch. Emmett plunked down right next to me. The air whooshed out of the couch cushions and my lungs, and breathing became arduous and non-automatic. I tried not to think about his thigh, muscular and surprisingly hot, pressing against mine. My fingers quivered as I opened the album.

The corrugated cardboard pages were covered with cellophane-like plastic sheets, which made them stick together. I peeled two sheets apart, and images of past lives unfolded: my parents dressed in white linen, my mother's hair hidden by a turban-like headpiece; in another picture, my mother stood in front of our house, belly protruding; in another, my father was seated at our brand-new piano, bouncing an infant me on his lap; and then one of me, a toddler, watching my mother by the piano as she clasped her hands to her heart, mouth open wide.

"Did she used to sing?" Emmett asked.

"She didn't just sing," I said quietly. "She was a singer."

"What's the difference?"

I traced the outline of her face carefully with my fingertips, as if I might be able to feel real flesh if I did it correctly. "Anyone can sing. But not everyone can be a singer."

"You're lucky. Your mom and dad raised you with music."

"Not lucky." I frowned and pulled my hand away from the picture. "Not lucky at all."

"Did something bad happen to her?" Emmett asked.

I said nothing. I hated when people asked about my mother. Hated having to tell the story. Because recounting it made it more real in my head, when instead I wanted it to stay a distant memory. To become more indistinct and fuzzy over time.

"I'm sorry," he said. "You don't need to tell me if you don't want to."

I touched my mother's face again. She deserved to be talked about. And I wanted to share the last memories I had of her with Emmett. Even if it was hard.

"It happened right after middle school. The summer before our freshman year at Sunvalley, I'd gotten this gig playing at the new Grayson Creek Mall. They'd hired all these kids around the district to play songs for a ceremony of the mall's opening. My mom had been encouraging me for weeks to perform more for other people besides just church and my piano recitals. So even though I knew she'd be tired all week from work and volunteering, I told her to come see me. This stupid mall concert. She said yes, of course. Especially since my dad was in Riverside that weekend at a choral workshop.

"I got a ride to the mall ahead of time with some of the other kids. When we were performing, I looked all over for her everywhere in the audience, but I couldn't find her. I thought maybe she'd decided to not come for some reason. After the ceremony was over, one of the other kids' parents came up to me with a cop. A drunk driver had hit my mom. On her way to come see me."

Emmett exhaled. "Shit."

"I was waiting for her to get out of surgery. My dad had to drive all the way home from Riverside. Which is really far. Too far. By the time he got to the hospital, the doctor was already done and waiting to speak to us. That's when she gave us the bad news that my mom didn't make it." Tears pooled in my eyes. I wiped them away with a quick swipe of my fingers. "You're the lucky one. You still have both your parents."

Emmett stayed quiet.

In the silence, I started flipping the photo album's pages. I forced them apart, one after another. My mother smiling at me, my mom laughing, my father holding her hand, my parents holding me in an embrace. At a party. At Christmas. At a park. Happy. Alive. The pages kept turning, the months and years passing by.

Emmett rested his hand on one of the pages before I got the chance to turn it. "Is this when Mr. C started teaching at Sunvalley?" In the picture, my dad stood with one hand on top of the choir room piano, his smile so infectious I instinctively mirrored it. His tie was crooked. His hair was still all black, his cheeks full and youthful. "He looks super young here."

"He was," I say. "He's been teaching at Sunvalley since I was in first grade."

"That's a long time. He's really good, you know? The best teacher I've ever had."

There were more photos to look at, but something about what Emmett had said—or rather, how he'd said it—told me to stay with that one for the moment.

"I'm really sorry to hear about what happened with your mom," he said. "But at least you still have your father. And he's totally awesome. Mine—he never talks, never smiles. Just wants everything to be perfect all the time. Stereotypical Asian dad. And my mom worships him. So if *he* wants me to get straight As, then that's what *she* wants me to do. And I do it. No discussion. I barely get to do anything *I* want to do. Just basketball and that one modeling gig for Macy's sophomore year. And choir." He suddenly smiled. "Well, maybe I *am* lucky. Because my mom has a soft spot for music. She managed to get my dad to allow me to join you guys. Without her, I'd never have been able to do *this*."

Emmett moved closer to me. Why did he emphasize *this*? And what exactly did *this* mean, anyway? Choir? Singing? Why did he look at me so intensely when he said it? Was I just imagining that? I felt myself get sucked into that limbo I always felt with him, where every action I could conceive of would lead down some road from which I was afraid I'd never be able to return.

"Boys," my father called out from the kitchen, "come in here now."

Emmett hopped up off the couch. "Let's go!" he said. I put the album back on its shelf, reminding myself to look at it more often.

We pushed the kitchen's French-style folding doors out of our way. The smell of seared meat filled our noses. I immediately recognized at least one dish, longganisa, a pork sausage we usually reserved for breakfast. My favorite brand was tinted red from paprika and beetroot and sweetened with pineapple juice. The familiar scent made my mouth water.

My father stood at the stove, lifting the lids of each of the pots and peering into them. On the counter next to him, a rice cooker stood ready. White steam billowed from the small hole on the top of the lid.

"Anak, ipasok mo sa loob." He handed me Emmett's sake and pursed his mouth, motioning toward the refrigerator. It was already stuffed full of food and drinks, plastic containers full of leftovers, and various bottles of sauces—A.1. steak sauce, soy sauce, oyster sauce, bagoóng, Jufran. I stuck the sake into the only free spot I could find, behind a large bottle of Sunny Delight.

Dad had put out party-style place settings. A spoon and fork (no knife) on a paper plate placed inside a wicker holder, each on top of their own tacky plastic place mats. Emmett tried to decide which seat to take.

"Here." I pulled out the chair at the head of the table, its seat covered with a worn fabric cushion tied to the chair's wooden slats.

"You sure? Wouldn't want to take someone else's spot."

My dad brought a saucepan to the table and set it on top of a pot holder. "You're the guest here, Emmett. That is your place tonight. Francisco, help me."

Emmett looked at me. "I thought your name was Quito."

"Francisco's my real first name. Quito's just the short version."

"How is Quito short for Francisco? I don't understand."

"Well, my cousin Tony is Boy, my cousin Soledad is Choleng,

and my other cousin, Roque Jr.'s nickname is Onyong. And Paquito is short for Francisco, which I shortened even more to Quito. I don't know—it makes sense to me."

"Yes, I agree. It's only common sense," my dad said and put an entire roll of paper towels on the table for us to use as napkins.

Emmett shrugged and waited for the food.

We set out three pots total, as well as the rice and a bottle of RC Cola. Dad lifted the lid off the first pot, revealing chicken adobo. I knew that its marinade of garlic, soy, and sugar cane vinegar would be tempered by the sweetness of my mother's secret ingredient, a hint of coconut milk. The second was full of the longganisa, the plump little sausages so juicy that all their casings had burst. The third was beef sinigang, which, from a quick glance at the empty seed pods on the kitchen counter, I could tell would get its characteristic sour tang from real tamarind instead of the common shortcut ingredient of lemon juice. I was surprised by the extra effort my dad had put into everything. Usually, I would have assisted him with food prep by chopping up the vegetables or at least cooking the rice, but this time he'd insisted on doing everything himself.

Emmett seemed overwhelmed by the choices.

"I hope you like meat," I said.

"Oops. I probably should have told you I was a vegetarian," Emmett said.

A look of horror washed over my dad.

Emmett struggled to keep a straight face before finally laughing out loud. "Just kidding."

"Don't ever joke to my dad about something like that," I said.

My dad's wide eyes shrank. "I think maybe we have some pickles I could give you."

I smiled to myself. Once, back in middle school, after learning about the US government's new food guidelines at school, I'd told my parents at dinner that we needed even more vegetables in our diet. My mom offered to make a tortang talong or pinakbet for dinner the following night. My dad responded by saying *too much trouble* and put a jar of dill pickles on the table.

"Seriously, do you guys always eat like this?" Emmett asked.

"These are some of Quito's favorite foods. I usually make them for his birthday, which is not until late December. But this counts as a special event."

Emmett whispered to me, "See, I told you this was a special occasion."

"Okay, a prayer first. Then we dig in." My father lowered his head and reached out for our hands.

I automatically did the same, with one eye slightly open.

I snuck a glance at Emmett. He looked flustered. It was apparent he'd never said grace before. I held his hand as neutrally as possible because I wanted to make sure no extra communication was being transmitted with my grasp, that it was firm enough to convey confidence but didn't have too much affection-filled grip.

My dad started with his usual grace. Then added more to it. The prayer went on forever. He mentioned me. The choir. Emmett. Emmett's family. The bottle of sake. The food on the table. The food in the fridge. Even the band teacher, Mr. Drummond *(Please, God, give him the wisdom to see how unreasonable he is)*, and almost everything else my dad could think of. My hand in Emmett's was getting warmer and warmer. I began to mouth my own prayer. That my hand wouldn't be completely drenched in sweat before Dad's prayer was over.

When my father finally finished, I squeezed both his and Emmett's hands, a conditioned response to the end of grace, and then immediately pulled away. Emmett flashed a quick grin at me. I smiled back and wanted to deflect with something witty.

"Kain na!" my dad yelled out, inviting us to dig in, before I could say anything.

My father patted his bulging belly and belched.

"Good one, Mr. C," Emmett said.

"Dad!"

"What? I'm not allowed to release gas in my own house?"

"Oh my god." I covered my face with my hands while they snickered. "Okay, time to clean up." I started clearing the dishes.

"Just leave it, anak," my dad said while nonchalantly undoing the top button of his jeans. "I'll take care of it."

"Are you sure?"

"Yeah, Mr. C. Let us help," Emmett added. "It's the least I can do in return for dinner."

"It's okay," my dad responded. He started taking the paper plates out of their holders and throwing them into the trash can. "Go figure out what you're going to do for the holiday concert."

Emmett and I looked at each other.

"What do you mean?" I asked. "Emmett's solo? We got that down weeks ago."

"Not that. I want you to do something together. A voice and piano piece."

Emmett looked as if all the food he'd just eaten might come back up again. "Uh, Mr. C, there're a lot of great singers in the choir. Like Ken. How about giving him a chance?" He was being sincerely generous. I'd gotten to know him well enough to know. But I also knew he was anxious. An eight-bar solo in a choral piece was one thing. Doing an entire song all by himself was another.

My dad rummaged through the cabinets for plastic containers to put the leftovers in. "They'll all get their chances in due course. You're both seniors. This is your time to do something special."

"What, like a Christmas carol?" I asked.

"It doesn't have to be holiday themed," he said, scooping the food into the containers. "Choose a song that means something to the both of you."

Emmett's face wilted. "But I don't—"

"Come on," I said, heading out of the kitchen. Knowing my father wouldn't take no for an answer, I decided to spare Emmett the effort of trying to get out of the assignment. "We'll figure something out."

My dad nudged Emmett out of the kitchen. "Go. Enjoy this wonderful gift I'm giving you," he said, holding a dirty pot. "And when you're done, I'll have some leftovers for you to take home."

"Thanks, Mr. C." Emmett caught up to me and whispered as we left the kitchen, "Do we really have to do this?"

"Look, if there's anything you need to know about my dad, it's that, when he gets something in his head, he won't let it go. I didn't want to be the choir accompanist, but he wouldn't take no for an answer."

"You didn't want to accompany the choir?"

"It's not that. I just felt kind of weird about being the pianist for my own dad's class. I thought it'd be awkward, but it turned out fine. Just like he said it would." I sat down at the piano, lifted the keyboard cover, and slowly slid it back, revealing the polished keys. "Actually, I enjoy accompanying. A lot. More than playing solo piano."

Emmett's body sagged. He leaned against the top of the upright piano. "Don't you get more attention when you're a soloist?"

"I'm not into music for the attention. I don't really care if anyone sees me. I'm more interested in the way I feel when I play. When I play a solo, it's nice. But when I accompany someone, it's way more than that. I hear them sing, and we become, like, one instrument. We're able to make something together that we couldn't have on our own."

Emmett just kept looking down, his eyes floating and slightly lost, as if he were listening to an incomprehensible conversation going on in his head. He knocked the piano's body with his knee by mistake, which caused the strings inside to vibrate softly. I felt the hum of them through the keys into the tips of my fingers, which I had rested there by instinct. I let the feeling of it resonate through me.

"The song you did at the talent show," he said.

"That's one of the only times I've ever done a vocal piece by myself. It was a mistake."

He shook his head. "No, I mean—well, first of all, it wasn't a mistake. Second, maybe we can do it for the holiday concert."

"You want to sing my song."

"Yeah."

"Emmett, I got called a fag for that song."

"By an idiot who thinks that, when a girl says her Aunt Flo is visiting, it's actually her aunt," he said. "Besides, it'll sound buttloads better when I sing it."

"You're a dick."

"Well, if we're talking percentage-wise, that *is* my biggest body part, so..."

"Gross." I tried to not give in to his jokes, but it was impossible. Even crass, Emmett had a way of charming me into forgiving him for it. Or maybe I forgave him more readily now. More than I did when I first met him because I knew him better. "I don't know. The lyrics are—"

"Perfect. They describe how I feel all the time."

A bundle of nerves right behind my belly button began to twitch. Was he trying to tell me that he was...like me?

"My dad is always expecting me to be perfect. To be the best at everything. And it's, like, I'm tired of always having to live up to that. You know?"

"Oh." My nerves flattened back out. "I see."

"Just play some of it for me."

I hesitated. Even just thinking about the song dredged up unpleasant memories from that night.

"Please?" His long lashes blinked slowly. Was he trying to be charming? Or flirtatious?

Whatever he was doing, it was working.

"Okay."

I reached inside and accessed the song, letting it out through my fingers. Slowly, at first. As if I were allowing each note to wipe away the bad thoughts associated with it. Intro gave way to verse. Then another verse. It was coming back to me. Not just the music, which was always just a breath away, but the faith I'd had in it. The pride. And the memories tied to my mother, not the disastrous talent show.

Still, something was holding me back.

"Why aren't you singing?" Emmett said, as if reading my mind.

I stopped. "I . . . I don't know."

"Start over. Don't just play it. Sing it to me."

The demand made me feel dangerously close to being naked. The piano was the only thing protecting me. If I sang the words, too, I'd reveal too much of myself. Again.

He must have sensed the fear in me. He sat down next to me on the piano bench. Like earlier on the couch, his presence was almost unbearable. Too many sensations careened through me.

Just as I started to become too lost to do anything, he pressed his body into me. Gently. Instead of ramping up the sensory overload, the physical contact with him somehow grounded me.

"What are the words?" he said. "I'll sing them."

I heard a click inside as something in me unlocked. That gesture of wanting to take on my story and make it his own somehow felt right.

I opened a folder of music on top of the piano, where I'd put the sheet music for my song. "A Part I Play" stared back at us in my scratchy script. "I know you can't sight-read. But the words are here."

"I think I remember the tune well enough," Emmett said. "Let me try it."

I began the song again, bringing the melody out to guide him.

I get into place
Put a smile on my face
They're all waiting for me to begin
To get to this night

I've practiced all of my life
To change who I am to fit in

He didn't need my help. Whether Emmett remembered the melody from the one time he'd heard it at the talent show or was able to feel it instinctively, his singing of the first verse was uncanny. Like he'd already known it by heart. The second verse went even better than the first.

I'll do what they want
And try not to flaunt
To be something I'm not supposed to be
Do it just so
So they'll never know
Deep inside I just want to be free

Emmett sang faster, almost on top of my playing. I accelerated. Not to try to match him, I realized, but because my heartbeat was quickening, pumping the blood to my fingers.

When we got to the refrain, I felt everything slide into place, the two of us matching each other's tempo and phrasing. Even our bodies seemed to be moving at the same time.

They tell me the show must go on
So I'll try to be strong
And I'll say what they want me to say
But the person they'll see
Won't really be me
It's only a part I play

By the end, we were nearly out of breath. Neither of us said anything. We just sat there, the last page of sheet music looking at us. All I wanted was to stay wrapped up in that moment, locked in my link to him.

"Ahem."

Both of our bodies jerked. We stood up from the piano bench on opposite sides. My dad was standing in the frame of the kitchen door, drying a plate with a worn dishrag. He regarded us with that inscrutable look of his. "I see you've picked your piece."

"It was my choice, Mr. C," Emmett said quickly. "I wanted to do Quito's song."

My dad kept wiping the plate and looking at us.

"What do you think?" Emmett asked.

My dad focused on me. I was certain he'd say no. The song was so tied to me and my mother—and him—I was sure it was disapproval that obscured his eyes.

"What do your ears tell you?" he asked.

"That we need to work on it some more," Emmett said.

"That we shouldn't do it at all," I said.

"No. That's not what I meant." My father finally stopped wiping the plate. "Yes. You will need to practice it, of course. Then listen to what you are making together. Really listen. If what you hear sounds good—if it sounds *right*—then you have my approval." His eyebrows lifted slightly, implying something I didn't quite understand.

He turned around and walked back into the kitchen, resuming his wiping of the dish, which must have already been beyond dry.

Emmett punched me in the shoulder. "Dude. We are so doing your song."

"You're not anxious to be doing a big solo? To be doing . . . this?"

"Not if I'm doing it with you." He stroked the sheet music. Tiny pins pricked up my body, as if he were touching me instead.

A horn honked from the street. Emmett's mother was here.

"Hey." He tapped his fingers on the music. "You don't actually need this anymore, right? You've got the song memorized?"

"Yeah. You can take this and use it to practice with." I pulled the music out from under his hand, straightened the pages on the piano with a quick tap, and handed them over to him.

My dad came out of the kitchen and gave Emmett a brown paper bag stuffed with plastic containers of leftover food.

"Thanks, Mr. C."

"If you want more, just let Quito know, okay? We'll bring you some at school."

We walked outside. On the street, his mother was in the driver's seat of a gray BMW, while a girl sat in the back seat, roughly college-aged. She looked, like Emmett, to be a mix of his Japanese father and white mother—her hair shiny, black, and unmistakably Asian and her eyes and nose more like Emmett's mother's, perky and patrician. Emmett had never mentioned having a sister before.

He saw me watching them and tensed. "Tell your dad thanks for the food. And thank you again for the sheet music. I mean, yeah, I'll practice with it. But I'm also thinking, if I framed it, it could be a great present. For a special birthday coming up." He waved at the idling car. Two slender arms waved back in almost the same exact manner. He turned back, patted me on the shoulder, and winked. "One day, when you're famous, it'll be super valuable and worth a lot of money."

Planning ahead for my birthday? Making something special out of something I'd written, something we'd soon be working on together? It was so thoughtful I wanted to hug him. Which of course I didn't.

Instead I said, "Enjoy, my boy." Then I hung my head in embarrassment.

Emmett bared his crooked-toothed grin and got into the car. "You won't regret it, dude!" he shouted from the open window.

But later on, I did.

Chapter 10—Now

A LONG QUEUE snakes down the block at 30 Rockefeller Center.

"Lines." Ujima groans. "Why can't we just do it like it's Black Friday at Walmart and rush it? Survival of the fittest."

"Whatever, Mx. Pilates," I say, giving Jee a sideways glance. "Not everyone has your physique." Their body looks stunning in a close-fitting cheetah-print dress and bedazzled sandals. A silk scrunchie holds up their wig into a ponytail.

Jee taps an older woman on the shoulder. "Excuse me. What is this line for?"

"Oh!" The woman, sporting high-waisted denim and a fanny pack, is momentarily speechless. It's obvious she's never met someone like Ujima before. "*Saturday Night Live*. Just waiting to go through security. Emmett Aoki's the host. He's very handsome, don't you agree?"

Ujima pulls her aside. "Girl, he is to die for. And get this, he just so happens to be the high school buddy of my good friend—"

"Thank you, ma'am. Hope you enjoy the show." I pull Ujima away. "Let's not cause a scene."

"Fine. I won't. Unless someone offers to pay me for it." They pop open a red fan with SHADE written across it and begin fanning themself, despite the fact that it's ten o'clock at night and still February.

I follow Jee inside to the lobby of 30 Rock, toward a beefy Middle Eastern man. His uniform says SECURITY in bright yellow. When he sees Ujima approach, his face becomes almost as bright as the letters. Jee notices this, of course, and takes their hair out of the scrunchie, letting the long, magenta curls wave behind them like a waterfall.

Security Guy smiles. "How can I help you?"

"Are you the man in charge here?" Their voice, already normally low, takes on a ragged huskiness. "Why am I even asking? Of *course* you are. Anyone can see *you're* the person I need to get to know better..." Ujima bends toward Security Guy's chest to read his name tag. "Tariq."

He stands up straighter and sticks his thumbs into his belt loops. "Yes. That would be me. Tariq. Miss...? What can I call you?"

They offer a hand to him. I get a little nervous waiting to see what the man's reaction will be to Ujima's hand, broad and thick, maybe the only thing about them that doesn't quite pass in drag. "You can call me Ujima. Miss Jenkins if you're nasty," they coo.

Tariq looks down and blinks. He grabs hold of their hand. I relax when he kisses it. An almost imperceptible look of apprehension on Ujima's face extinguishes once his lips make contact with their skin.

"What can I do for you, then—*Miss Jenkins?*" Tariq says, with so much loaded innuendo that his beard hairs engorge.

Jee bats a row of fake eyelashes. "Bradley Rose is expecting us. To take us to the VIP section."

"I'll call him." Tariq pulls out a small two-way radio from his vest. "You just stand there and keep looking beautiful."

I notice that people at the front of the line waiting to get into the lobby are watching us as if we were the warm-up act. "How do you know this Bradley guy again?" I ask Ujima.

"From Escándalo. He comes every Sunday night to see my act."

"And you're sure he'll be able to get us in?"

"Honey, he's one of my biggest fans. After I perform, he always *conveniently* runs into me in the bathroom and tries to get some alone time with me in one of the stalls. That pervert," they sneer, though I can tell they're impressed by his depraved tenacity. "Anyway, he'll do us good. He's *SNL*'s audience wrangler. One of the many little things he keeps trying to impress me with."

I don't want to know the other little things he tries to impress Jee with.

One of the elevators opens onto the lobby floor with a ding. A cute, slightly pudgy frenzy of strawberry-blond hair pops out of it, frantically clutching a clipboard and sipping coffee. He looks like what would happen if Prince Henry and Elmo had a very gay, very hyper child.

Tariq waves me over to the elevator. "He will take you to Studio 8H." He kisses Ujima's hand one last time. "It was a pleasure, Miss Jenkins."

"You rascal." They pull their hand away playfully and then pat him on the chest before we walk away from him. I think I hear him moan as we leave.

"Hi! Hi! Follow me." Bradley ushers us into the elevator. "So glad you were able to make it, Ujima. So beautiful. As always." He looks Ujima up and down. His body holds an incredible amount of tension, as if he's having a hard time restraining himself from doing something. Like touching Jee. Or howling at the moon. "Wow. Wow. What a dress." He pivots to me. "And you're Quito. Interesting outfit. Very simple. 'Cazh Friday' for a Special Saturday."

I thought I was dressed up. I'm wearing my favorite cardigan and a classic white button-up shirt. I have on jeans, but at least I'm wearing nice brown Oxfords. Maybe too brown. Are they the color of crap? Am I wearing poop-brown shoes?

"Stop worrying," Ujima says, stroking the back of my neck. "You look fine."

"Yes. Agreed. You do. The look suits you," Bradley rapid-fires, not making it clear if what he's saying is actually a compliment.

The elevator opens up to the main hallway leading to the studio. Walking down it, we glance at the walls lined with photos of *SNL*'s best sketches before entering Studio 8H through the main doors.

Bradley shows us our seats. In the VIP section. The very first row.

"Here we are. And don't worry, Quito," Bradley says. "From where you'll be sitting, no one will be able to see your outfit. They'll only see the back of your head. All five million of our viewers." More audience members start filing in. "Got to go." He spins around and looks over his shoulder. "I'll text you the after-party address. See you both there. Ta-ta!"

Ujima immediately befriends the people sitting next to us, a ridiculously attractive hipster couple, all tattoos and piercings and mismatched thrift store clothing that somehow look like they spent a fortune. I sink into my chair and wish our seats were anywhere but where Bradley put us.

As the NBC pages seat more people, the atmosphere in the studio begins to ramp up. Expectancy whirls around us, especially when the band starts to play. It's hard not to get caught up in the moment. I start to relax a bit. After a few songs, longtime cast member Kenan Thompson comes out to give the audience instructions, peppered with a few jokes. They're tepid at best, but I laugh nervously at almost everything he says.

"Oh. I like this one," he says, pointing a finger at me. "And my, my. I like your friend, too." Kenan rubs his hands together and makes a cartoon awooga face at Ujima, who smiles regally. Jee is, as always, a cool goddess, while I am a tittering, poorly dressed loser.

After Kenan is done, the cast gets into places for the cold open—the sketch that starts the show. This one takes place in the White House. Mostly unfunny, it plods by without a single appearance by Emmett.

I begin to worry. Did we come on the wrong night? Is he not tonight's host? No. Midwestern Mom Jeans confirmed he was. Was he replaced at the last minute? I ping-pong internally, not knowing whether I want him to actually show up, when everyone onstage starts chanting the intro, "Live from New York, it's Saturday NIGHT!!"

And boom. The set bursts like a dam.

Stagehands in black shirts come running out of every corner. They shift the set, tucking the Oval Office away and replacing it with something else. Props and sets go flying while the band plays its familiar *SNL* theme music and the announcer lists off the names of the cast members and musical act, some new band I've never heard of (although I never seem to recognize any of the musical acts these days).

"Ladies and gentlemen, your host. Emmett AOkiiiiiii!"

The upstage door swings open.

Emmett appears.

He jogs downstage toward the audience, looking more relaxed in a fully tailored suit than most people do in sweats. His shirt is unbuttoned to almost midway down his torso, which reveals the edges of his pectorals, and the fit of his pants is surprisingly revealing. Everyone can easily see what God gave him. Ujima clutches my hand and says "mm-mm-mm" into my ear, confirming that I'm not the only one impressed.

He looks up toward the audience in the upper level, plants himself in the center, legs spread, back arched, arms stretched out, and takes everything in like the petals of an unfolding flower drinking in the sun.

I'm within inches of him again, for the first time in years. It's surreal. As if reaching out and touching him will make the illusion shimmer, waving outward in concentric circles like the dropping of a pebble on water.

I completely forgot what it feels like to be near him.

"Thank you. It's so great to be here! I've always wanted to host *Saturday Night Live*, and here I am tonight, living—" He stops midsentence.

He's looking straight at me.

He swallows audibly and continues. "—my best life."

He doesn't say anything else.

Emmett is frozen in place.

I feel the entire studio tense. Some of the musicians behind him look at each other. Emmett just keeps staring at me, unable to speak.

I don't know what to do. Should I smile and wave? Say

something? Encourage him to continue? Pretend he hasn't seen me? Run out the side entrance?

Mercifully, Kenan comes out from one of the wings. "That's what you get for being in all those Michael Bay movies, man. All those explosions did a number on the old noggin." He raps Emmett on the skull. The audience lets out a cathartic laugh.

Emmett's gaze snaps away from me. He looks out and smiles broadly. "Yeah, but now I'm so good at jumping from burning buildings and running away from dinosaurs. Basic skills that everyone should have."

He goes on to casually mention his new TV show, his upcoming movie, and the fact that he's the first Japanese American to ever host *Saturday Night Live*, all of which is met with enthusiastic applause.

I think.

I'm only marginally aware of what he's saying. Mainly, I try not to go into cardiac arrest over the fact that my mere presence has almost derailed the live taping of a show on national TV.

"We've got a great show for you tonight," Emmett says. "WonderBelly is here! Stick around. We'll be right back!"

The main camera operator waves them out, and Emmett walks toward me, mouth open, but is yanked away at the last second by a stagehand who literally drags him off the set as two others start undressing him. Others move set pieces into place for the first sketch. In less than five seconds, he is gone. Whisked off to wherever he needs to be.

Ujima turns in their seat to face me. "What are you not telling me?"

"Sorry?"

"I might not know a lot of things, but I know men. I can read them like a community theater playbill. And that man—that *demigod* of a human being—was destroyed after one look at you." Jee turns my face toward them. "Just choir buddies, my flawless black ass. What went down between you two?"

"Nothing."

"Quito."

"Nothing."

"Francisco Calimag Cruz. Tell me the truth."

I sigh. "We were friends. At one point. And..."

"And what?"

The band leader waves his hand and cuts off the music. The stage area to the left of center has been transformed into a house in the suburbs. Emmett, along with a few other cast members, walks on.

"I'll tell you later," I whisper.

"Yes," Ujima whispers back. "You will."

We watch Emmett play a salesman. He holds knockoff Tupperware parties and makes a fortune selling the products—which are clearly inferior—only because all the women (and some of the men) just want to have sex with him. He plays it as if he's unaware that everyone is attracted to him. It's the only funny thing about the sketch. That and the way Kenan keeps breaking character when the plastic containers make fart-like noises when Emmett opens and closes them.

Afterward, they do Celebrity Jeopardy! with Emmett as Kim Jong-un. His impression is...not great. The same goes for the sketch after that. A reality dating show spoof. Everything he's doing seems a little detached. The audience laughs generously, but I can sense things are falling flat.

The more I watch, the more I begin to see that I'm responsible for his mediocre performance. He's disturbed that I'm here.

More than disturbed.

Angry.

WonderBelly, a retro-punk band that steals all the wrong things from the eighties, plays a midshow song. During the commercial break, as the stagehands put things into place for whatever follows, I find myself floating out of my seat and leaving the audience area.

"Hey!" Ujima hisses. "Where are you going?"

I don't answer. I don't know where I'm going. I only know that I need to get out of there. That I don't want to be there when Emmett returns to the stage.

I wander into the outer hallway. The faces of past cast members and guests stare at me from framed photographs, laughing.

Bradley comes running after me. "Quito!" He jogs beside me, clipboard still in hand. "Bathroom break?"

I keep walking, staring straight ahead. "Yep."

"Okay. Follow me." Bradley rushes on ahead. "But hurry. Commercial's almost over. Weekend Update next!"

"Wouldn't want to miss that."

He shows me to a unisex bathroom off to the side of the main corridor. "I'll wait. Take you back when you're done." He looks nervously at his watch. "Two minutes to do your business. Hope it's not too *in-depth*?" His left hand mimes air quotes.

I shut the door in his face and lock it.

I stare at myself in the mirror. In the bright light, the face looking back at me glares in high definition. My eyes are tinged with red. My pores seem larger than usual. My lips are dry.

This was a mistake. This whole thing was a mistake. I don't want to let my dad down, but I should've just let things lie. Not poke at the past. I don't have it in me to face Emmett. To tell him that I'm sorry. Certainly not now, when I'm being watched by the entire country.

I lean my back against the wall. Then I slowly slink down and end up on the tile floor. The ceramic feels cold against the seat of my pants. I pull my knees in and hold my legs close.

Bradley knocks on the door. "Finishing up?"

I don't respond. I'm seriously considering just curling up into a fetal position on the floor of the bathroom. It doesn't seem that dirty. It's miraculously clean for a semi-public restroom. So I tip my body over and let gravity pull me down. The floor is freezing. Strangely, that's all right with me.

"Quito? Look, are you . . . ? Is everything okay in there?"

Through the crack underneath the door, I can hear Bradley's feet nervously tapping. Finally, his footsteps recede into the distance. Good. Now I can lie in peace, inhaling the strangely comforting scent of bleach and antibacterial spray.

The footsteps return. More knocking on the door. Less urgent this time, though. I decide to just tell him I'm having stomach problems and won't be able to catch the rest of the show due to leaky bowels or something equally disgusting. Years ago, I learned that the more explicit you can get with excuses, the more likely it is that someone will believe that you're sick. That little trick I got from listening to all the messages other kids would leave on my dad's office voicemail. *My snot is yellow! I'm having a heavy flow day! Ear wax isn't supposed to be green, right?* I push myself off the floor and unlock the door. "Geez, I'm sorry," I say. "I think I might have soiled my pants."

The door opens. Emmett's face stares back at me, changing from concern to amusement. "Well, hello to you, too."

"Shit."

"In your pants, apparently." He holds the door firmly, quashing my best efforts to close it.

The coldness from the floor evaporates in a flash. "Ha. Ha. You're a funny bunny."

"Is it safe to come in?"

I strongly consider bolting out of the bathroom and back into the studio, but instead say, "Sure. Step into my office."

"Nice place you got," he says, looking around. Then, squarely at me, "I'm surprised you're here."

"I needed to use the bathroom." The more he looks at me, the more true that is. I'm certain he's about to lay into me, tell me all the things he's been holding back all these years, and my bladder isn't reacting kindly to the eventuality.

"No, I mean, *here* here. At *SNL*. I wouldn't have thought...I didn't know you liked the show," he says, not as upset as I thought he'd be.

I run my fingers nervously through my hair but regret it instantly as I encounter hardened gel. I continue to push through the crystallized mass, feeling everything fall apart with a crunch. "Sure. I watch it all the time. I've always wanted to see it live."

"And you just happen to be at this one."

"I know, right? Wow. What a coincidence."

"I saw you from the wings, leaving the audience. I thought you might have left."

Emmett smiles that crooked-toothed smile. I'd always assumed that, when he hit the big time, he'd get it fixed. But it's survived.

A welcome holdout from an earlier time. Back when *my* Emmett Aoki hadn't yet become the world's Emmett Aoki. A time when I couldn't help but think about that tooth every day. How it was one of the things I loved the most about him.

"My agent keeps harping on me to fix this," Emmett says, pointing to the tooth.

"What? I wasn't—"

"Quito, you were staring."

"Nope. Wrong." I feel the urge to close the door again. The coolness of the bathroom floor beckons.

But it also finally feels like Emmett is actually here. Real. Not a thousand miles away, untouchable. He's in front of me. Close. So close I could just reach out and—

"Mr. Aoki, we have to go!" Emmett is yanked back out of the bathroom by a stagehand. "Weekend Update is almost done, and you're up next after the break!" I watch as he's dragged, again, down the corridor.

"Meet me at the after-party. After the show," Emmett calls out before disappearing.

"Oh god. You're all right." Bradley comes back to the bathroom in a tizzy. "Emmett wandered out here. He said he knew you? Is that why you and Ujima wanted to come tonight?"

I straighten up, feeling more like myself again. "I knew him in high school. He used to be . . . a friend. A really good friend, in fact." It surprises me that I admit this to a complete stranger.

It surprises me even more that I feel good saying it.

Bradley motions with his head. "Come on, they're about to start again." He accompanies me back to the main stage in a hurry.

"Hey," I say as we run-walk. "Tell me more about this after-party."

I take a sip of my virgin mojito. It's smooth, sweet, and latently assertive—the lime tang kicks in at the end. Can a drink be passive-aggressive? If so, I'm in the right place for it. A prohibition-themed place in Chelsea called Speakeasy, this week's *SNL* after-party spot. I've passed by it a couple of times on my way to other places in the neighborhood without ever noticing it was there. That's the whole point of it, I guess. To be hidden from people who aren't in the know.

I kind of hate it here.

The seats are lined with expensive leather. Wrought-iron chandeliers force shadows onto the brick walls, and bartenders in bow ties and Vandyke beards mix cocktails behind the bar. Everything is haughty, aloof. As if we should all be glad we were even able to find the damn place.

A stick of a woman in a flapper dress stands by the door. She's in charge of the guest list and looks miserable, although she does sport her four-inch stilettos admirably. If I pointed the shoes out to Ujima, they might be impressed, but they're in a banquette on the other side of the room, trying to feign continued interest in Bradley. He's wound up way too far, his body jerking with each point of whatever it is he's talking about. (Himself, most likely, from the way Ujima mindlessly twirls a chunk of magenta hair.)

I've been roaming around, reliving my run-in with Emmett in the bathroom in my head, trying to process the fact that he wasn't upset to see me like I'd been dreading. He was thrown off by my appearance, yes, but only because he was surprised.

And... happy?

Maybe time does heal everything. There might actually be a

chance of me being able to get him to sing for the concert. And for us to have a relationship again.

A friendship, I mean.

After an hour of waiting, he still hasn't shown up. So I decide to make myself useful and rescue Jee from Bradley.

Several choices for an emergency excuse run through my head. Exploding toilet? Sick cat? (We don't actually have a cat, though we do have an aggressive pigeon who keeps shitting on our fire escape.)

So many little lies fill my head that I don't see Emmett step in front of me.

Virgin minty goodness splashes all over his chest, pushing the drink over into the more aggressive side of passive-aggressiveness. "Oh crap."

"No worries," Emmett says, unperturbed.

His shirt becomes transparent straight through to the hardened pecs. I grab cocktail napkins off a nearby table and furiously dab at his chest. It takes a long time. There's just so much to dry. He's so much more of a man than when we were kids. Broader and thicker in every direction. Then again, action stars don't get paid the big bucks for looking like the scrawny kid on the beach. Pleasant thoughts of sand and sun on his skin start to swim around in my head when it slowly dawns on me that I'm rubbing Emmett's right nipple in tiny little circles.

I grin and pat him one last time. "Yep. All dry now." I shove the damp napkin mound into my pocket. A wet chill hits my crotch.

"I can toss those for you." He reaches for my pants.

I push his hand away. "I'm good. Truly cooly."

He laughs. "You still do that."

"Do what?"

"Rhyme when you're nervous."

"I'm not nervous!" I say too loudly. "I'm not nervous," I whisper. I have absolutely no idea why I can't modulate my voice correctly. So I punch him in the shoulder.

He reels backward. "Ow. That hurt."

"Sorry! I—"

"Just messing with you."

He unbuttons his shirt, sticks his hand inside, and pulses it in and out, trying to breathe air into the damp fabric. Classic Emmett. Doing something that seems absentminded but is actually meant to focus attention on him. It takes everything I have not to stare at the tiny goose bumps rising to attention on the surface of his skin. Thank goodness for the cold shower in my pants.

"So, how have you been?" he asks me.

"Oh, you know. Busy doing the piano thing. Teaching lessons, playing for shows. I sub in on Broadway shows every now and then."

He nods as I talk, as if he somehow already knows all this. Is it because I'm babbling?

"And I play at a piano bar. Broadway Baby. Two times a week. Fridays. And Sundays. Fridays and Sundays. Is when I play piano," I say, babbling.

"Broadway Baby. In the West Village? What a coincidence. I was near there last night, taping my NY1 segment. I would've come to see you if I'd known you were playing."

"The West Village, yes. I'm on again tomorrow at three."

"Playing the show tunes. Just like old times."

"Just like old times," I repeat. The past comes flooding back. All those afternoons and evenings spent sitting at the piano together, playing and singing. It feels like we've been doing it for the past twenty years, uninterrupted, almost as if we'd never parted at all. I'm wary of holding his gaze for too long, so I look at something else to distract myself.

Unfortunately, that ends up being his bare chest. "I see you're keeping in shape."

Dammit. Thanks for nothing, cold crotch.

"It comes with the business." He takes his hand out of his shirt, rests it on my shoulder, and then massages it, casually, as if it were the most natural thing in the world to go from fondling himself to stroking me. "You look great, by the way."

Everyone else around us—the *SNL* cast members, the random VIPers, the band whose name I absolutely cannot remember—fall away, and I'm back someplace familiar, somewhere where we aren't complete strangers to each other, where he and I are connected by more than just high school choir.

His fingers massage harder. They dig into my shoulder, just skirting the edge of pain.

It feels incredible.

He lets go and slides his hand back into his shirt. "Hey, how's your dad doing?"

I inhale deeply, not realizing until then that I'd been holding my breath. "He's, uh, fine."

Emmett's given me a way to bring up the concert. But I hesitate. He's been in the movie business for so long, stopped singing years ago. That's not a part of him anymore. And I'm not sure he wants to bring it back. "Uh, how're *your* parents?"

He smiles sadly. "Not really talking to my dad at all. They finally got divorced about ten years ago. But my mom is doing well. She's getting remarried. Next month, actually."

"That's great! I mean, great for your mom. And you. For not talking to your dad. I mean—"

"I know what you mean, Quito. Don't sweat it." He laughs, flashing his smile. "It's great you're doing so many things. You must've composed a ton since I last saw you."

I don't respond to that. I don't want to tell him how wrong he is. "So... how come you haven't done a musical? Every actor seems to be doing one these days."

"A musical? I've thought about it. No one's ever pitched me anything I've been interested in."

"Waiting for the right project?"

"You could say that." Emmett raises an eyebrow. "Any suggestions?"

He hasn't changed. Still flirting his way through life. That's all it is, I know—just his hopelessly ingrained habit of flooding all lines of communication with his hormones. I have to keep reminding myself it's not a specific message to me.

I decide to use it to my advantage. It's becoming clear now that I don't have to bring up our disastrous last interaction in college. He's either forgotten all about it or forgiven me. Now is the time to bring up Dad's request. "I do have a suggestion, actually, something to get you singing again. My father—"

Ujima swoops in between us.

"Hello there," they say. Bradley is nowhere to be seen. I wonder how they managed to get rid of him. "I'm Quito's roommate and BFF. Ujima."

Emmett takes his hand back out of his shirt and shakes Ujima's. "I saw you in the front row next to Quito. You're a hard one to miss."

It's rare to witness Ujima speechless. After nothing comes out of Jee's hanging, half-formed mouth for a few seconds, I kick them in the calf. "OH," they shout, "thank you, dear. You're a hard one yourself. I mean a hard one *to miss* yourself."

I stifle a laugh.

"So," Jee says, giving me a quick look, "Quito tells me you two used to be quite close."

"We were," Emmett says. "We met in high school." He turns to me. "Speaking of which, you were about to say something about your dad?"

The question feels loaded with something I can't put my finger on. "He's retiring."

"Wow. Really? Time flies."

"He's putting on a farewell concert for his last year. A benefit. He wants me to play. And for you—"

"There you are." Bradley comes up to us holding drinks. "Thought you said you'd join me at the bar, Ujima."

Jee takes a drink and gives him an air kiss. "Bradley darling," they say, rolling their eyes at me behind his back.

"You friends with Emmett, too?" Bradley asks.

"Of course. I came over here to catch up with him. We go way back." Ujima gives Emmett a look that says *Go with it.*

"Eeexactly," Emmett says. "Old high school chums. In fact, Quito was just catching us up on his dad. Our old choir teacher."

"Choir?" Bradley says.

Before someone else can interrupt me, I say, "Yes, and what

I've been trying to tell Emmett is that my dad is retiring. He's putting on a benefit concert, and he wants me to play and Emmett to sing."

"I'm sorry," Emmett says. "What?"

Oh no. I was too concerned with being able to get a face-to-face with Emmett and what he might possibly do when he saw me that I haven't worked out an actual strategy to get him to say yes after I've asked him.

"It's a lot," I say. "I get it. You're too busy. Maybe we can pay you or something? No, we can't do that. Rename the auditorium after you? No, that won't work. Name the new copier after you?"

"Hold on a second," Emmett says, laughing. "When is it?"

"First week of June? With rehearsals in late May."

His eyes flicker, like he's scrolling through a mental calendar. "I might be able to make it work."

"Seriously?" I share an incredulous look with Ujima.

"Get the old dream team together again?" He laughs. "Yeah. Why not?"

"Fantastic! I'll tell my dad—"

"Wait." He snaps his fingers. "Late May? I think I have to be at the Cannes Film Festival." He checks the calendar on his phone. "Yeah, I do. I'm sorry. I forgot."

Ujima, clearly agitated by Bradley's presence, has already finished their drink. "Debuting a new movie?"

Emmett squirms. He scratches at his chest and fumbles with the buttons of his shirt. "Yes, but . . . not one of mine. I'm supposed to be there for Emma's new release."

Bradley gasps. "The gossip. It's true. You're dating Emma Chen."

"Who?" I ask.

"Emma. Chen," Bradley says, clearly annoyed. "*Road to Canberra*? Last year's Best Supporting Actress Oscar? Hello?"

A TV ad starts playing in my head. A young woman with a tennis player's body, her muscles taut, walks along a desolate dirt road somewhere in the Australian outback wearing hiking boots and carrying the remains of some dead relative in an urn. She glistens with exhaustion. Her pale skin and long black hair remind me of another girl. Someone from our past.

"You're dating her?" I ask.

"Yes. And no. We're not official. Yet," Emmett replies. "We were waiting to announce it until after we're seen at Cannes together." He doesn't look at me. "Look. My agent plans all my social activities. I mean, he picks all the important things I need to go to."

"Does he pick your girlfriends, too?" I mutter.

He gives me a smile that really isn't a smile at all. "Why are you here, Quito?"

"You invited me here."

"That's not what I mean. Why were you at *SNL* tonight?"

"My dad needs you."

"That's it? That's the only reason?" He shakes his head. "And after all this time, you thought it'd be that easy to ask me? When we haven't talked to each other for twenty years?"

So, he hasn't forgotten. He hasn't let things go.

"I know. I'm sorry we fell out of touch. I'm not sure why that happened."

"You know exactly why that happened."

The big band jazz music being played in the bar sounds as if it's been turned all the way up. The twenties roar into my ears. There are too many people here at the party. Too many conversations, too many people looking at us. Everything engulfs me.

"Excuse me." I walk toward the bar, seriously considering an alcoholic drink for the first time since college.

My phone buzzes. A text from my dad:

> Quito this is your dad. Kamusta ka? OK? Did you talk to Emmett yet? My god, the students and the parents and even the other teachers are all so excited. The concert is already sold out! I think we will have to add standing room only in the back of the auditorium. Text mo ako ha. Ingat! Love, Dad

Then I see that Mark has left me a series of texts. I didn't even notice my phone vibrating all night.

> 10:15 pm: How's your evening out with Gerome? (j/k) Ujima?
>
> 11:40 pm: Where did you guys go? When are you thinking of leaving? You still coming to my place after?
>
> 12:50 am: Excited for the musical with Dinesh. Just know you're going to write amazing stuff for it.
>
> 1:20 am: You must be having a good time. Going to bed now. Miss you.

I stare at my phone. The light of it blazes. A bartender finally acknowledges my existence and indicates he's ready to take my order.

I put the phone in my pocket, wade through the crowd of people, and exit into the predawn darkness.

Chapter 11—Then

I STOOD IN front of the mirror second-guessing my clothes for the third time (third-guessing them?) and wondered if it was too late to buy something new. Jeans and a short-sleeve polo shirt. The outfit I wore nearly every day. To school, to church, to the movies, to the comic book store. My closet was full of a variety of tasteful polo shirts to suit every occasion.

At that moment, for example, the one I was wearing had a thick stripe across the front, blending from sky blue to dark black. It made me seem more broadish in the chest area. There wasn't a lot of pec matter to accentuate, so every bit helped. It was a good shirt, in an optical illusion kind of way. Perfect for a simple get-together. Except Laney's Christmas party wasn't just a simple get-together.

Laney was a choir geek like me. But her older sister, Deborah, captain of the varsity cheerleading squad, was Rally Court royalty. Like Emmett. At their party, I'd be surrounded by people I didn't like being in the same school with, let alone the same house.

What kind of dressing up did they do? Or did they...dress *down*? I should've asked Emmett. Or better yet, I should never have said yes to his invitation in the first place.

I blamed it on the post-performance glow of the holiday concert.

I'd been singularly open to the idea of braving the unknown because of how well everything went.

The concert had started with "I Want to Thank You, Lord" and Emmett's solo. His basketball teammates (who'd originally come out to heckle him) were so genuinely surprised by how good he was that they jumped to their feet before the song even ended and gave us a standing ovation. They pumped their fists in the air, chanting Emmett's name. *EmMETT! EmMETT! EmMETT!*

My father scowled at all the shouting. Then he saw the effect this had on the choir, and his face softened. He realized what we were all feeling.

Pride.

He must have felt it, too. Not because of the response from a pack of hormonal athletes but because the choir sounded amazing. We usually performed well, but somehow Emmett improved everything. It wasn't just his singing. His very presence galvanized us. He gave us a sort of credibility, a visibility, we'd never had before.

I still had a brief moment of panic when Emmett and I took the stage to perform "A Part I Play" and looked out into the darkened auditorium to see, shadowy but unmistakable, many of the same faces I'd seen at the talent show three years before. The same ones who'd laughed at me. Were they going to make fun of me and my song again?

As soon as Emmett started to sing, I knew I wouldn't be living a repeat of that night. The audience, already firmly on our side from the beginning of the concert, was enraptured. I attributed it completely to Emmett's singing, of course, not to my song, though it didn't matter. It didn't matter that they might not be going on the journey I'd intended when I composed it. He was taking them somewhere totally different, and that was fine. That was the magic of music. Every performance of the same piece can be something new. Especially in the hands of someone as talented as he was.

When we were done, there was no booing. No insults. Just long, enthusiastic applause.

Emmett pulled me from my incredulous stupor on the piano bench, put his arm around me, and made me bow with him. Three years ago, they'd all laughed at me. Now they were cheering. I should've known everything would be fine with him at my side.

After, in the choir room, Ken blasted "We Are the Champions" from the sound system. My dad busied himself with putting the chairs away and pretended not to watch a room full of kids hugging, laughing, and dancing around him. He just shook his head and went on about his business as if everything were normal.

"Dude." Emmett tousled my hair. "Your song was a hit."

"Pshyeah. It was all you," I said. "You could've peed onstage, and they would've loved it."

Emmett stared back at me quietly. A stillness formed around us in the middle of the choir chaos. My thoughts spiraled. Was that the wrong thing to say? *Thank you.* Say *thank you*. He paid me a compliment, and like an idiot, I deflected it when I should've just said—

"Thanks, by the way. For giving me the sheet music of your song." He walked to the back of the room and put his folder away in the cabinet. "I framed it all nice and shit. It's gonna be hella rad."

"Oh. Cool."

"By the way, Laney's sister is throwing a party this weekend.

You're going, right?" he yelled over his shoulder, straining to be heard over all the noise.

I was about to respond by saying, *Sorry, no thanks, not my kind of thing, I'd rather hang out with my dad, or anyone else, really*, when he winked at me and my brain short-circuited.

I shouted back, "I'll be there!" as he melted into a crowd of his adoring public in the hallway.

At the party, I sat on a worn-out couch squished between two bulky and oddly baby-like seniors from the wrestling team, wishing I hadn't been an impressionable idiot after the concert and agreed to come.

The only thing keeping me there, still waiting for Emmett to show up, was the fact that he'd brought up the gift of my framed sheet music right before he'd invited me. My birthday *was* next week. It was the reason he'd asked me to come. He was going to give me my gift. It had to be here. It was going to be the last chance we'd see each other before I turned eighteen.

Lumpy and Dumpy nestled red cups to their chubby chests, watching as people walked past our couch. They weren't drinking very quickly. Probably because the drinks weren't their first. That's the way they smelled, at least. The whole house smelled this way, actually. Fermented. Like hard water stains and yeast. I briefly considered getting up and moving someplace else, but there was really nowhere else to go. And besides, the weight of Lumpy and Dumpy had sucked me into the couch like a black hole, so I sat there and tried not to think of how I looked like a loner with no drink and no one to talk to.

Some of the varsity swim team members were playing billiards in front of us while a handful of girls made out with the other swimmers. I recognized the girls as a team of some type. A dance troupe or flag squad. Or from the way they were using extra tongue, French Club.

The guys really sucked at playing pool. The balls rarely went into the holes. And when they did, it was usually by mistake. One guy, his skin more acne than not, got frustrated, lined his cue stick up, and used all his arm strength to plow through the ball. With a loud crack, a red billiard flew through the sky and straight at my head.

In middle school once, forced to play softball during PE (despite my best efforts to convince the teacher my fingers were an insurable commodity), I'd failed at catching a pop fly. It slipped through my hands and hit me. I ended up nursing a raised red welt on my forehead for two weeks. This was going to be much worse. Unable to dislodge myself from the Lumpy and Dumpy fat-trap and knowing I'd never be able to catch it, I covered my face.

A hand plucked the ball out of its midair arc. I looked through the safety net of my fingers to see Emmett gripping it. "Do I get to keep this?" he asked the swimmers.

"Thanks," I said, relieved on several fronts.

Emmett tossed the ball back onto the pool table. "That could've been bad, dude. Good thing I was here to save your face." He had on a turtleneck and fancy acid-washed jeans I'd never seen before.

I tried not to fixate on how the clothes hugged every part of his body. "Yeah. Thanks. No balls in this face, please," I said, then closed my eyes as a wave of mortification washed over me.

Emmett laughed. "Come on, let's go get a drink." He grabbed my hand and yanked me out of the quicksand couch.

I watched as the dozens of people who had crammed themselves into the crevices of Laney and Deborah's house moved aside when Emmett shepherded me through them, his arm tight around me. It felt as if I were back on the auditorium stage performing, on display again. I didn't know if I liked the feeling or not.

"There are so many people here. I don't even recognize most of them," I said to Emmett.

"They're not all Sunvalley. Some are Sycamore High. And a bunch of Valley Creek Community College students, too."

"I'm at a college party?"

"Welcome to adulthood."

He pulled me in closer as we maneuvered our way through a crowded hallway. He smelled like high-end shampoo, the stuff they sold at hair salons. "So... ummm... why'd you ask me here?" I asked.

"It's a party. We deserved a good time."

"You didn't ask me here to... I dunno. Give me something?"

He looked, briefly, as if he'd just been caught telling a lie, before edging us to the front of the line for drinks. "Well, duh." He handed me a clear plastic cup full of beer. "We're here so I could give you this."

I took the cup but didn't drink from it.

"I've seen that look before," he said. "I thought it was because you didn't know what sake was."

"I didn't. But I've also never had beer before," I said.

"No time like the present. Cheers." He clunked my cup with his and waited.

I put the cup up to my lips. It smelled like the house did. I tried not to gag as I sipped. Bitter bubbles gathered in my mouth. As I swallowed, I felt my insides roil.

Seemingly satisfied that I'd passed my first rite of adulthood, Emmett took a long sip of his own drink, which looked like it went down significantly more smoothly than mine. A small mustache of foam formed on his upper lip.

"What do you think?" he asked. He noticed me staring at his lips and licked them.

Something rose inside me, catching in my throat, and I was pretty sure it wasn't the beer coming back up. "Delicious," I replied without thinking. Then I pretend-coughed into a clenched fist. I took another drink of my beer, trying to hide my reddening face by turning away, only to cough for real this time. A big, wet, hacking one.

He shook his head with disappointment. I hoped it was only at me not being able to handle a beer and not my response to his question.

He looked past me. Behind, through the glass doors, winter sun lit up a patio and a lawn that looked as if it had been hacked at with a machete. At the very back of the sorry yard, vaporous steam issued from a large outdoor Jacuzzi. A few people had already gotten in.

"Hey, you want to go out back?" Emmett asked.

"Depends," I said. "Will the beer taste better outside?"

"Nah." Emmett stuck out his tongue. "Nothing could make this cheap shit taste good."

Outside, shrieks of laughter erupted as one of Emmett's fellow basketball team players stepped into the Jacuzzi fully dressed.

Whether it was because of a dare or full-on drunkenness, I couldn't tell.

Emmett eyed me. "Want to get into the hot tub?"

"I didn't bring a swimsuit."

"Yes, you did. So did I. Look." He reached down into his pants and pulled up the waistband of his underwear. A black Calvin Klein label came into full view, along with a long stretch of the lower part of his abs. The sight imprinted itself into my brain like a lightning bolt leaving scorch marks. Heat flooded my crotch area. I stuffed a hand into my pocket. "Okay. Yeah. Let's go outside. Swim, swim, everybody in!" I yammered, hoping to distract attention away from the tenting going on in my pants.

"What's going on over there, Quito? You that excited about the hot tub?"

"What?"

"Can't wait to see me in my underwear?"

"What? NO! I would never—I mean, I'm not like that!"

"Dude," Emmett said. "Chill out."

He paused, did an about-face, filled his cup with more beer, and made his way toward the patio without another word to me.

I felt as if I'd narrowly averted some disaster.

Or else, maybe, pushed something away that I shouldn't have.

The patio door slammed behind him, the sound of it shockingly loud. He said hello to the guys outside with fist bumps and ass slaps—all that coded language of masculinity that was completely beyond me.

I hesitated, confused about whether I should follow Emmett outside or stay indoors. Around me, people drank or stuffed their faces with snacks from multicolored plastic bowls as they swayed to Bon Jovi blasting from a boom box sitting on top of the avocado-green refrigerator. Two girls smoked cigarettes in the corner while a couple of woodwind players from the band made out sloppily at the dining room table. *Nice embouchures*, I thought to myself, retching slightly.

Gas bubbles gurgled in my stomach. I burped up rotten apples and vinegar. I wanted to be behind my piano at home, not in a moldy-bread-smelling house trying to be friends with the most popular guy in high school.

Who was I trying to fool?

I looked out into the backyard expecting to see Emmett there, tossing a football with his buddies or stripping down to his underwear to jump into the Jacuzzi. Instead, he just stood in a semicircle of people, beer cup in hand, seemingly not listening to what anyone was saying. He looked agitated, distracted.

He was looking at me.

He seemed to be trying to communicate something across the expanse of concrete and through the glass patio doors.

I couldn't make myself look away.

The more we stood there staring at each other, the more I became convinced I was just imagining things. Emmett wasn't looking at me but at something near me, or through me, or nothing at all. Or it was a hallucination. A fun house mirror refraction of my point of view.

I took another sip of my beer. It was the same drink. But now, for some reason, it didn't taste half so bad. Was I imagining things?

No, the beer *was* better now. It wasn't an illusion.

And Emmett was definitely still staring at me.

I finally tore myself from my spot and crept toward the glass doors when I felt a tap on my shoulder.

"Are you the composer?"

I turned around. A pretty young woman stood behind me. She wore a baggy knit sweater over cotton leggings, her hair clipped on the side so that it cascaded like a wave over one ear. She had on thick-rimmed glasses that didn't look nerdy on her at all.

I'd seen her before. Somewhere. There weren't many Asians at Sunvalley, and I didn't recognize her as one of the juniors or seniors, though she was old enough to be one of them. Was she a college student?

She waved at someone across the room with a willowy gesture of her long arm when I remembered: the girl from Emmett's car. His sister.

"I'm sorry, what did you ask me?"

"You're Quito, right? Emmett's composer friend?"

"I am. You must be Emmett's sister."

She giggled, her creamy white cheeks flushing faintly. "Oh no. I'm not his sister. I'm his girlfriend, Angela," she said, offering me her hand. "Nice to meet you."

I stared at her hand in horror, as if it had suddenly turned into an octopus tentacle.

His girlfriend.

"He never told me he was seeing anyone."

"Oh." She pushed in some loose hairs that had escaped from her hair-sprayed bangs. "I go to UC Berkeley. Between my biochem classes and all his basketball practices, I hardly ever get a chance to see him. I've been looking forward to this party. I knew you were coming, and I wanted to meet you. He talks a lot about you."

Her words entered my ears and promptly turned into mud. The fact that I was one of Emmett's favorite conversation subjects should have made me feel amazing. Instead, all I wanted to do was toss what little remained of my drink at her, refill the cup, and then walk outside and throw the entire thing at Emmett.

"I know a little bit of piano, you know. I was out of town, so I wasn't able to go to your concert. But I did play through that piece you gave to him. It's gorgeous." Angela's left eye was smaller than the other. She tried to compensate for this by adding more black eyeliner to its outer edges. It made her look like a raccoon. "It was so nice of you to let him have it to give as a gift. He put it in a black frame from PrintPlus and everything. It looks really nice."

I'd been a complete idiot. Of course it wasn't *me* he'd wanted to frame the sheet music for. It was for his pretty little college girlfriend.

The beer in my gut was threatening to resurface. I swallowed the bile back down and looked outside. Emmett's buddies were still there, but he had disappeared.

I turned around to see him standing next to Angela.

"You finally made it," he said, giving her a peck on the cheek. "Quito, this is Angela Asari."

"We've met," I said.

"Looks like you seem to be getting along."

"I've seen you before," I said to her blankly. "With Emmett's mom. That's why I thought you were related."

"We both have Japanese dads and white moms," Emmett explained.

"I was just telling Quito how amazing his song was." Angela placed her arm in the crook of Emmett's.

"So this is why you invited me here," I said to Emmett.

He looked confused. "No. That's not—"

"Dude! Is this your girlfriend? She's hella fine!" The gang of basketball jocks had made their way back inside, some of them dripping wet.

"Hold on a sec," Emmett said. He started pushing them back toward the patio, which swiftly devolved into a wrestling match. Angela's eyes widened. She looked to me for guidance.

"Sorry. Nice meeting you. I have to go." I put my cup in the kitchen sink.

"Should I tell him you're leaving?"

I started winding my way through the throng of people, all of them lost in conversation, moving to the music, carefree and oblivious to what I was going through.

"No," I shouted back at her. "He won't care that I'm gone. He won't care at all."

Chapter 12—Now

I WALK FROM the Christopher Street subway station to get to my Sunday shift at Broadway Baby. Trudging through the uncleared snow, still fresh from a noontime snow flurry, I think about how I nearly let history repeat itself by holding on to that tiny little hope, again, that I could ever be more to Emmett than just a friend. That's already gotten me into one too many messes. I can't afford another one.

Now that I think about it, it's just as well that Emmett can't do the concert. I'll figure out an alternative for my dad. Maybe Ujima'd be willing to guest star instead. Jee's not famous, but they sure as hell can command a stage.

By the time I get to the bar, I'm wet and cold. I place a hand over one of the nearby radiators. Barely a hiss of steam.

"Hey," I call out to Jaime, "where's the heat?"

"Dunno. Been like this all day. Someone's working on the pipes. I'll make you a hot chocolate."

I wait at the bar, shivering. Everyone has their winter coats on inside, cutting down on the amount of wiggle room, so no one's moving around much. They look cheerless and aggravated. Common for New Yorkers at most times but rare for Broadway Baby.

J.B. is finishing out her shift at the piano. She's working her way through a set of Patti LuPone's songs. A little *Les Miz*, some *Gypsy*, some *Company*, a bit of *Sweeney Todd*. She's currently pounding out "Don't Cry for Me Argentina." With a red and white winter cap on to keep her head warm and her glasses and boyish face, she looks exactly like Where's Waldo.

She still manages to play impeccably despite the freezing temperature. After I finish my hot chocolate, I maneuver my way to her and find out why her hands haven't completely frozen. There's a space heater plugged in by her feet. It's old and rickety. If she kicked it over by mistake, it would probably burn the whole place down.

"Has it been like this all night?" I ask her.

J.B. nods. "Jaime texted to warn me, at least. That's why I brought the space heater. Thank god, or else my fingers would be icicles by now."

"Everyone's so quiet. They usually belt the crap out of this song." There are a few women singing along to J.B.'s playing. Most everyone else seems to be contemplating whether they've had enough of the frigid room.

"They're not happy," J.B. says.

"And the tip jar's not very happy, either."

"Hey," she says, segueing into *Anything Goes*, "I heard you might be working on a new show?"

"News travels fast."

"You know how it is. Everyone knows everything in this town."

"Mark got me the gig. I'm not that into the concept, though."

"What's it about?"

"Peter Pan," I say. "Except it takes place in the seventies. Peter

Pan is gay. And so are the Lost Boys. Wendy's a lesbian. Or a stripper. Maybe both. I can't remember."

"Interesting." I can't tell if she's being sarcastic or not. She seems to linger on some thought while continuing to play the Cole Porter from memory. "I might have a song or two that could fit."

I believe her. J.B. has more right to call herself a composer than I ever could, having written songs for at least three of her own shows, including one that made it to the Fringe Festival a few years ago. J.B.'s the person I want to be when I grow up. Minus the having-sex-with-girls thing.

"Maybe you should do the show instead of me," I reply. "Want me to talk to the guy?"

"Really? You won't mind?"

"Nope."

"What about Mark?"

I hesitate. Of course Mark would mind if I handed off the opportunity he was so excited about to someone else.

"Maybe I can just give you some ideas. Free of charge." Not only is J.B. more prolific than I am, but she's also more generous. In fact, she's the one who introduced me to the owner of Broadway Baby. She'd asked me to fill in for her while she was away musical directing a non-Equity tour of *Joseph and the Amazing Technicolor Dreamcoat* with a cast that was, in her words, "gayer than the goddamn coat." After my tryout stint, I was hired as a regular pianist. I still owe her for that.

"Sounds good," I say.

"Great. Now"—with the edge of her thumbnail, she glissandos down the length of the keyboard, her usual ending flourish—"take over. I'm done freezing my tuchus off."

"Can I borrow your space heater?"

"Be my guest. I never actually use that thing at home. It's a fucking fire hazard." She bundles her puffy parka around her as she waits for the tip jar to come back from one last go around the crowd. She sticks her hand in, takes out the few bills, stuffs them into her backpack, and hugs me. "Tell Mark I said hi."

Everyone in the bar is quiet as I take my place at the piano, their conversations blunted by the temperature. My internal Rolodex runs through the songs most likely to get them going. I start off with some *Mamma Mia!* But despite the fact that ABBA is always a dependable crowd-pleaser, barely anyone sings along.

It's going to be a long night.

I look over to the bar and notice Jaime handing a familiar old man a hot chocolate, steam rising in the cold air. I smile when I realize that it's Edgar and that it's not a hot chocolate but a hot toddy. He sips happily, his face plum red, and waves at me with a hand covered in a tattered wool glove.

Behind him, Jaime catches my attention with two muscular thumbs-up. Has the heat been fixed? Over my crowd's half-hearted sing-along of "Dancing Queen," I hear what I think is the banging of pipes being forced full of new steam. The crowd hears it, too. People turn to one another, looks of hope growing on their faces. I feel the place slowly warm up as the hiss of heat starts to issue forth from the radiators.

Then the room explodes.

It isn't the pipes that have erupted. It's high-pitched squeals and shrieks, which peal out from men and women both.

Emmett Aoki is in Broadway Baby.

He brushes snow off his winter coat near the entrance. The

crowd draws close to him like he's the resurgent source of heat. He sees me at the piano and waves. Then he tries to work his way through the mob of onlookers filming him with their phones.

I close my eyes. Maybe if I stay still, he'll forget where I am. I'll just disappear into the wood-paneled walls like a brown chameleon.

"You ran out on me last night," Emmett says, standing in front of me. He takes his jacket off and places it on the fake piano cover. A few people eye it with desire, probably contemplating petty larceny. "Seems to be a habit of yours."

"Habit?"

"Leaving without saying anything. You did it to me at that Christmas party in high school, too, remember? It's a pattern."

"It's not a pattern," I say. "Twice is not a pattern."

The room seems to shrink as everyone closes in on us, straining to hear our conversation. "What are you even doing here?" I ask as quietly as I can, though getting softer only makes everyone nosier.

"Thought I'd left town already?"

"*That* would be a pattern, wouldn't it?"

A tiny muscle in his jaw tenses and untenses. The clanking of the radiators ratchets up to full volume. I feel sweat collecting at my hairline, about to drip onto my face. I quickly wipe my forehead with the back of my sleeve.

The left edge of Emmett's upper lip lifts into a tiny half smile. "Good thing for you I'm not dependable enough to form any kind of habit."

"Yeah. Good thing."

His half smile grows. That wonderful, crooked tooth appears.

"So, what were we talking about last night before you bailed?" he says. "Oh, yes. The concert."

"Which you can't make. Because of Emma Chen."

Somebody says, "So you *are* dating Emma Chen?" A chain reaction of chatter flares up around us.

Emmett ignores them and leans over the piano. He says to me, his voice steadfast, "I'm not dating Emma. That was my agent's idea, okay? He was trying to set us up as a thing. I didn't say no. Maybe I should've. I will now. Since I'm not going to Cannes anymore."

The clanking around us stops abruptly. Jaime props open the front door to dispel some of the excess warmth. Cold outside air floods in and mixes with the radiator heat, stabilizing the temperature inside. Only then do I remember that J.B.'s claptrap heater has been on this whole time. I reach down to turn it off and instantly feel much better. "Wow. That's great. That's really—just great."

"The me-doing-the-concert thing or the me-not-dating-Emma thing?"

"Thing shming." My cheeks are burning. Still flushed from the surplus of heat, I decide. "So, what will you sing?"

"Don't know. I have a few weeks to think about it, though, right?"

"No. I mean, what will you sing," I say, getting louder with each word. "Right. NOW?"

"Oh." He shakes his head. "Quito, no."

It's too late, though, and we both know it. Everyone has heard me throw down the gauntlet.

"Look, everyone, I don't have anything prepared. I'm sorry," Emmett says.

He clearly underestimates the crowd's desire to hear him sing. He has to give them what they want now. They won't let him out alive if he doesn't. "Sing! Sing! Sing!" they chant.

Emmett cranes his neck around, toward the front door, the annex, and the fire exit, literally looking for any way out of his predicament.

When he finally realizes he can't escape, he raises his hands. "Okay, okay. Just one." He looks at me. "Pick something. Something easy!"

Really, I should listen to him. Pick something simple. Ubiquitous. Let him off with an easy standard, something any person in the bar could do, even after a long night of drinking.

I look over at the bar and see Edgar. His face is so red with excitement that it looks as though he might keel over. And I decide. Edgar deserves a show. Everyone in the bar does. They've been suffering for the past few hours in the miserable cold.

Plus, I kind of want to pay Emmett back for the Emma Chen thing.

I grin devilishly to myself and start playing a familiar six-note theme in two groups of three, instantly recognizable to everyone in the room.

Emmett blanches.

"Something's Coming" from *West Side Story*. A song everyone knows but very few can sing. It's deceptively difficult, both rhythmically and range-wise.

I keep repeating the same two intro bars over and over, needling him with the theme. "Come on. We used to do this at my house all the time," I say.

"That was a long time ago, Quito."

"Just like riding a bike."

Emmett covers his face with his hands and groans. "You're a bastard."

"You're welcome."

He focuses on my accompaniment, lining himself up with the vamp to begin at just the right moment. All conversations around us cease.

He breathes.

He sings.

Now, the patrons at Broadway Baby are used to good voices. Trained voices. Professional ones. New York is full of them, and many of them find their way to the piano bar at some point or another. But there's always been something more to Emmett's singing than just a nice voice. It's the way he delivers the text. There isn't a trace of tension in his body, no raised veins on his neck, no strain on his face, his mouth as relaxed as if he is using no more effort than to whisper directly into your ear, as if he's delivering the song to you and you alone. And even though "Something's Coming" is one of Leonard Bernstein's trickiest pieces from the show, Emmett doesn't miss a single note, syllable, or beat. He makes it all feel effortlessly real. True.

I feel the piano keys give way underneath me, responding to his singing on their own, his breaths manifesting in my fingers.

He sings about possibilities. Urgency. The hope that the one great thing he's always wanted to happen to him will, indeed, happen. Maybe tonight.

As the song winds down, Emmett comes around and sits down next to me on the bench, which I somehow sensed he would do. On the last word—*tonight*—he opts for the high variant G on the last syllable, floating in the air so ethereally that everyone questions themselves: Have I even heard the note? Am I dreaming it? Even after I'm done playing, long after he's finished singing, everyone waits for that last note to fade. None of us wants to let go of the feeling of it sounding in our ears.

Applause finally ends the silence.

Emmett beams. He reaches his arm around me and pulls my head into his chest, mumbling into the top of it. I can't hear what he's saying exactly, but it doesn't matter. The message burrows into me.

The past is behind.

We can move forward.

I look up, past the crowd of people, and see a pair of eyes laser-focused on us from across the room. There, hanging on the periphery of the crowd near the entrance, his coat slowly being zipped back on, is Mark. He's leaving.

And unlike Emmett, he is definitely not happy.

I push my way through the crowd and out onto the street. In my hurry, I leave without grabbing my jacket. Streams of late-afternoon sunlight peek through a bank of clouds, refracting through the slow but persistent sprinkle of snow.

"Mark, wait!"

He continues to trudge down the street, shoulders square, face straight ahead.

"Christ, it's freezing out here," I mumble.

"Go back inside, Quito. You'll get sick."

I manage to catch up to him. "I thought I was coming to meet you at your apartment after my shift."

"Dinesh and I had lunch." He stops but still faces away from me. "He's nervous about you not being serious about the show, so I came over early to convince you to meet with him before next weekend. Maybe take you out to the dinner we didn't get to have on Friday. But I see you have other things on your mind."

"It's not what you think. Emmett—"

"Knows you. Clearly," he says.

"Let me explain."

"You told me you didn't know him. That you weren't a fan." His voice is hoarse. I recognize that sound. The stress that creeps in when he's mad.

"I'm *not* a fan of his. That much is true," I say softly.

"But you know him. Were you and him ever—"

"Friends," I say. "Just friends. We went to high school together."

He finally turns to face me. "You went to school with Emmett Aoki?"

"Yes." I rub my hands together. "Can we just go back inside? I'll introduce you. I know everyone sees him as this big deal. To me he's just a guy I knew as a kid, okay? Nothing else. Just, please. I'm freezing."

He sees me shaking in the snow. The frown on his face melts slightly. "Fine."

I hurry back to the bar, turning every few seconds to make sure Mark is still behind me. He takes his time. And despite the warm temperature inside Broadway Baby, he doesn't take his jacket off when we get back.

An unrelenting crowd has trapped Emmett behind the piano, waiting for him to sing something else. I motion to Mark to follow me to him.

"I'm fine right here," he says.

Emmett notices that I'm back, waves at me. Mark's glare hardens.

"Hey, Emmett," I shout over the bar's buzz. "Come over here. I want to introduce you to someone."

He extricates himself from the crowd's clutches. All eyes follow as he makes his way over to us at the entrance. "Hey there. I'm Emmett," he says, offering his hand. "You are . . . ?"

"Mark." He takes Emmett's hand firmly. "Quito's boyfriend."

Something flits across Emmett's face, like a moth obscuring the light. In a nanosecond, his face shines again with a brightness that feels more forced than usual. "Very nice to meet you."

"You look surprised," Mark says. "I take it Quito hasn't told you anything about me."

Without a pause, Emmett says, "He didn't tell me how handsome you were, that's all."

Watching Emmett handle Mark, I'm reminded of how he's always been able to read people, how he's so quickly able to glean what a person needs and respond accordingly. It makes me wonder how often he's done that to me.

"Thank you," Mark says, his face less tense. "You two went to school together?"

"Good old Sunvalley High."

"How come you never told me this?" Mark asks me. Beads of sweat line Mark's forehead. He still doesn't take off his jacket. He's ready to jet at a moment's notice.

Emmett replies before I can say anything. "Because I asked him not to. I like keeping my personal life private. It's better off for them that way. Otherwise"—he leans in closer to Mark, looking peripherally at the people around us—"you have all these idiots trying to get the scoop on any crazy behavior from my past. Besides, school was hell. I mostly put it out of my head. I'm sure Quito did, too."

I force a grin and say nothing, leaving the smoothing over of things to the professional.

"You just wanted to keep the past secret? What kinds of things?" Mark's neck is sweating heavily now as he tries to dig deeper.

Don't I owe him the whole story? We've been together for almost a year now. A lifetime compared to my other relationships. I lied to him about knowing Emmett, and he found out. He could find out about everything else. It's not too late to just come clean about our past, to bring it out in the open, right here, right now, for us both to accept. It's what's best. Not just for Mark. For me and Emmett, too.

The truth begins to form at the base of my throat, but it feels painful and gets lodged there. All around us, videos and pictures of Emmett are being taken. Ours is not a private conversation. In the end, no words come out at all.

"Look," Emmett says, "Quito and I used to sing together. His dad was our choir director. They invited me to sing for a benefit concert in June since he's retiring. That's all."

"Really?" Mark asks me.

My throat constricts even more. I nod.

Mark turns back to Emmett. "And what did you say?"

"I said yes." He turns to me, sealing the deal with a wink and a smile. "Quito's dad was like the dad I never had. So, yes. I'm doing it. And," he adds, for emphasis, "I'm going to have to tell my *girlfriend* that I won't be able to go to her Cannes movie premiere like I promised to do. Just so I can help out Mr. C. And our old pianist, here, of course."

Mark scans his face for a trace of deceit. He won't find it. Emmett is an actor. This is what he does. Making you see what he wants you to see.

Mark finally begins to take off his coat. "And your girlfriend won't get mad?"

"I've got her wrapped around my finger." Emmett wreathes his right index finger with his left fist and thrusts it in and out. Then he laughs his jock laugh—the one that used to both infuriate and turn me on in high school. "Emma'd do anything for me. You've heard of her, right? Emma Chen?"

"Emma Chen is your girlfriend? Hey," Mark says admiringly, nudging me with an elbow, "did you hear that?"

"Well, I hate to run, but my flight back to L.A. leaves soon," Emmett says. "A pleasure meeting you, Mark."

My stomach lurches. We haven't even figured out the details for the concert yet. When he's coming. What we're going to do. We haven't worked anything out at all, really.

He pauses as he buttons up his coat. "Quito, we should probably exchange numbers so we can get in touch." We trade phones to put our numbers into them. "After my mom's wedding next month, I'll give you a call so we can go over the logistics of your dad's concert. And thanks for the tunes, by the way. Some things never change. Right?" He raises both hands to everyone. "Remember to tip your pianist!"

A chunk of the crowd, their phones still recording Emmett's every move, follows him toward the exit. He turns to wave at us before he's pushed out of it.

"You never told me about this concert for your dad," Mark says.

"I didn't? I thought I did. I'm pretty sure I told you he was retiring. I must've told you about the concert."

He gives me that look that tells me he's caught me in a lie.

"Look, I wasn't sure I was even going to do it. And I had no idea I'd be able to convince Emmett."

"But you managed to find a way," he says. Not with bitterness or envy. But with something approaching awe. Whatever other problems we've had in the past, Mark has also believed in my musical abilities. And I've been lying to him this whole time.

"You'd still be able to do Dinesh's show, though, right? June's the backer's performance, too," he says.

He's been trying to support me by giving me this opportunity with Dinesh. I can't bear to see him lose faith in me. Not after all I've done to give him reason to doubt me.

"I'll make it happen," I say, not entirely sure that I can. "I won't be in California for long. Just for the concert and a few rehearsals beforehand. A week or two, tops. The concert's in June and I don't need to be in California until the end of May. I'll be done writing and arranging all of Dinesh's songs by then. I might even have some ideas already." I do, in fact. They're J.B.'s, but he doesn't need to know that.

"Hey, maybe you can convince Emmett to be involved with our show. Have him make a demo of one of the songs? Or be one of the backers?"

"Sure, yeah," I say, barely registering the fact that he called it "our" show. "I'll see if he's interested."

"I knew this was going to be the right project for you. This is going to be your big break. You're going to get what you deserve. Finally."

He rubs my fingers with his. His face is glowing with sweat from wearing his coat too long indoors but probably also from excitement.

The crowd no longer pushes in on us now that Emmett is gone. It thins out, giving us more space. Mark hugs me. I breathe in the familiar scent of designer cologne covering a slightly acrid musk. “Thank you,” I say.

As we hold each other, I sense the crowd’s attention shift to the window outside, as if catching sight of someone looking in. When I turn to see who it is, I see nothing. Whoever it was is gone. If there was even someone there at all.

Chapter 13—Then

AFTER MY VANISHING act from Laney's Christmas party, I walked out into the cold and thought about the colossal mistake I'd made. I'd misread my relationship with Emmett and built it up into something it never was. When I got home, I locked myself in my bedroom and sank into a general funk of low-level depression.

I thought he really cared about me.

But I was wrong.

I was just a means to an end. Someone to teach him how to sing, how to get better at one more thing in life. Someone to provide a one-of-a-kind birthday gift for his college girlfriend. A gift I'd given him first and was hoping to get back in return, a circular symbol of what we meant to each other.

But I didn't get anything from him. Nothing at all.

When classes started back up again after the holiday break, I kept as much distance as I could between us, steering clear of him in the halls, coming to choir late, leaving early, never looking up from the piano during rehearsals in case he was watching me.

I stopped helping him with choir music. My excuse, if he were to ask me, was an increased homework load in English. Not that he ever asked me. Emmett seemed to be okay with me disappearing from his life. Further proof that we were never as close as I thought we were. It was a relief, as well as—though it killed me to admit it—a disappointment. The petty part of me had wanted to punish Emmett by giving him the silent treatment; I wanted to see him suffer. But he went on with life as if nothing had ever happened. As if he'd lost nothing.

In fact, my dad was more upset over my silent treatment than Emmett was.

"Why are you avoiding him?" he asked me at dinner one evening.

"I'm not," I lied.

"Then why doesn't he come over to the house anymore?"

"Because I never invite him."

"Why? Why don't you ever practice together?"

"I don't know. Ask him."

Though it seemed as if my dad might actually take me up on my suggestion, he never did. Instead, he resorted to assigning Emmett more solos he'd need help with, hoping that would make us work with each other again. Unfortunately for him, the ploy never worked. Emmett had gotten the hint and kept his distance from me, asking my father directly for help instead. They'd work on music after class, and I'd slip out, thankful that they were keeping each other busy.

The new status quo worked for everyone. I got space to think. Emmett got someone to help him who wasn't obsessing over him. And my dad got to work one-on-one with the son he'd always wanted.

It was the only thing that made sense. Why else would he have tried so hard to get Emmett into choir? To have me teach him? To get him to come over for dinners? Emmett was smart, talented, confident, athletic, popular. Someone my dad could be proud of in endless ways. Unlike the shortish, average-looking Filipino loner whose only redeeming quality was the ability to magically play stuff on the piano. My parents had always been happy with my musical abilities, but I'd long suspected my dad wanted more from his only child.

In middle school, he'd tell me to take a break from practicing sometimes and drag me to my older cousin's soccer games. We'd spend an hour driving all the way to San Bruno in our beat-up Subaru and then sit in the bleachers while he'd cheer for Manny in his (admittedly festive) green uniform. "Isn't it fun, anak? Wouldn't you like to be like your pinsan?" I wanted to tell him that running around chasing a ball, kicking and jumping and getting grass stains all over my clothes, was the last thing on earth I wanted to do. Not wanting to hurt his feelings, though, I said, "Sure, Dad," and feigned interest while I retreated into my brain to let Mozart and Sondheim take me someplace else entirely.

After a while, when he'd gotten the hint that sports bored me to tears, he stopped trying to get me interested in soccer. And Oakland A's baseball games. And basketball. And boxing matches on pay-per-view. I was relieved. Though a part of me always felt like I'd let him down in some way by not being the kind of son he wanted.

Well, now he had the perfect son. Emmett. And he could have him all to himself.

As the spring semester went on, I got used to not spending time with Emmett. It hurt at first to see him during choir rehearsal forming bonds with everyone else, but I kept reminding myself that the piano had been my closest companion almost my entire life. I didn't need anything or anyone else.

Then one afternoon, after we'd returned from spring break, he snuck up on me in the hallway after third period.

"Can we talk?"

I would've refused, but the shock of having his voice so close in my ear, warm and muggy, caught me off guard. What's more, his whole body was strangely off-kilter, his back bowed from the weight of sagging shoulders. I'd never seen him so upset. My defenses dissipated. "Okay," I said.

He led me to the end of the hallway and crammed us between two banks of lockers. "I need your help."

"For what?"

"Look. I just need a friend right now." His body was almost on top of mine. There wasn't a lot of room between us. For weeks, I'd managed to allow the intangible connection between us to fall away. Now every second of being close to him was building it up again, link by invisible link.

I needed to stop it. "You've got more friends than anybody I know. Any one of them could help you out. Give you moral support. And stuff." I couldn't look at him. "Why not ask Angela?"

"She can't help me with this. Just you." He forced a smile, which cracked. And through this chink in his armor, I was able to see him. The true him.

My heart, already racing because of our closeness, was making it hard for me to stay calm at his assertion that there was something only I would be able to understand.

"It's my mom. She's not doing well."

The thumping in my chest lessened and then shifted into a different gear as I realized what he'd just said. "Oh, is she sick? Did she get into an accident?"

"No, no. Nothing like that. It's just...well...she's really unhappy. My dad is treating her like crap."

The story came rushing out of Emmett. A month prior, his father came home early, suitcase in hand, his breath reeking of alcohol. It took his mother almost an hour to pry it out of him, but eventually, in a torrent of screaming and profanity, he admitted he had gotten fired from his job. Some sort of "impropriety," although he declined to go into any further detail. He went on to yell at Emmett's mother, blaming her for not being a better wife—as if that had anything to do with him losing his job—before finally passing out on the couch in a drunken haze. Almost every evening since then had been some sort of variation of the same event.

"He yells at her all the time. Telling her that she's useless. Stupid." I watched as the crack in Emmett's smile grew, tiny hairline fractures of concern taking over his normally flawless face.

"He's not, like, hitting her, is he?"

"Oh, hell no. I'd hit him back if he did that." The lines on his face burned, and I knew Emmett would do exactly that. He'd defend his mother from anyone, including and especially his father.

"When I'm around and hear it happening, I tell him to back off. He just storms off and locks himself in his office. But I'm not always around to stand up for her. My mom says it's fine. He's going through a rough patch, she says. But I can see what it's doing to her. She's not sleeping. And sometimes, late at night when she thinks I'm asleep, I can hear her crying in the kitchen."

My hand started to raise instinctively to touch him. I forced it back down to my side. "I'm so sorry."

"I keep telling her she should just leave. Go somewhere else, maybe stay with my aunt in San Francisco. I told her I'd go with her. I mean, there's no way I'd stay with my dad and leave her alone."

"What did she say?"

"That she needs to stay. For my sake. Since it's my senior year. She's willing to put up with my dad's crap for a few more months, at least until I graduate. But she says it's only because he's out of work, anyway. She's convinced that once he finds another job, he'll go back to normal." He shook his head and frowned. "Not that *normal* was that much better."

The space between us had shrunk to nothing. I could feel the pain inside him as it flowed outward and blanketed us both.

He needed something from me. But I wasn't sure what I had to give, what I had to share with him besides our love of music.

"My parents had problems sometimes," I said.

"No way. I can't see your dad ever treating your mom badly."

"He didn't. But he didn't always have steady work. And even when he did, there were times when it wasn't enough to pay the bills. Musicians don't make a lot of money. My mom told me once that my lolo and lola—her parents—didn't approve of her marrying my dad. They said he'd never be able to provide for her. That he needed to get a *real* job. They tried to get her to convince him to give up his dreams of being a musician and become an engineer or a nurse instead, or else he'd never be a good husband to her and a good father to me. She told them she knew my dad, that he'd take on a hundred jobs if that's what it took to take care of his family. She fell in love with a musician. He'd never give up his dream, and she never wanted him to. She saw that in him."

I allowed my hand to rise this time, to rest itself on Emmett's shoulder. His eyes, glistening, locked with mine.

"Your mom sees that in you, too, Emmett. She supports you in everything, but especially in your love of music, right? She's staying because she knows that if she left, you wouldn't have someone on your side at home. Or, if you went with her, then you'd be away from . . . um—choir."

Emmett's shoulder, at first iron cold under my hand, warmed up and loosened.

"And you," Emmett said.

I felt the heat from Emmett's shoulder run down my arm, up my neck, and straight to my face. "I mean, I guess we make pretty good music."

The lines of hurt had disappeared from Emmett's face. "The best," he said.

A crowd of people walked by us on their way to class, chattering. Out of the corner of his eye, Emmett noticed them. A hardness veiled his face briefly, and his eyes shifted subtly to my hand on his shoulder. I let go of him. He turned to the people passing by and gave them a chin nod.

When they disappeared, he turned back to me, the momentary callousness and the earlier despair now gone. He smiled his slightly flawed smile.

"Would it make you feel better if we worked on some new stuff together?" I offered.

Emmett pushed his fist against my shoulder. A kinder, gentler version of his usual punch. "Hells yeah."

I didn't want him to know how much I'd missed it, so I shimmied out from our cramped quarters together, clamping down on the growing smile on my face by gritting my teeth, almost painfully. "Meet me after choir," I said and hurried to fourth period.

Emmett needed a friend. That was all.

That's all I was going to let it be.

I needed to make sure I didn't ever get carried away with him again.

Later that day, my father noticed that things had changed. "You're friends again? That's good."

Emmett and I had simply walked into the choir room together, sat down on opposite sides of the room, and took out our music, ready to begin.

How could he tell? What exactly had he seen?

I ignored my dad and leafed through my sheet music, careful to keep a mask of tedium on my face. I needed to keep denying the fact—to everyone, including myself—that I felt more stoked for rehearsal than I had in weeks.

After choir, lacking anything from our upcoming concerts to work on, Emmett and I decided he'd just come over to the house for dinner and work through some new solo repertoire, songs I'd been keeping in mind for him.

He poked me in the ribs. "Nice to know you've been thinking about me."

"Don't flatter yourself. It's just some stuff I think you'd be good at. That's all," I said with such disinterest that I even managed to convince myself.

My father, of course, was thrilled his prodigal son was coming back over. He cooked up an entire Filipino feast for us to have for dinner. And even though it all smelled delicious, we were so engrossed in our music-making that we had to be dragged away from the piano to eat.

There were so many new things to try that evening that Emmett came over again the next evening. The following week, after his dad had calmed down a bit (feeling more hopeful from some promising interviews, Emmett said), he felt freer to come over, sometimes as many as three or four times a week. Which was good because a surfeit of music had been trapped inside me, pent up since December. I hadn't realized how much it all needed release.

I made Emmett listen to the original London cast album of *Les Miz* and taught him some of the songs. The next week, we worked on *Into the Woods*. Then *The Phantom of the Opera*. Even *Rent*, which I didn't have the vocal score for but didn't need because I'd been listening to the new cast album on nonstop repeat and had every song memorized. It ended up being Emmett's favorite. We'd often sing through the entire show, even the girls' songs. I tried not to make a big deal in my head over the fact that Emmett's absolute favorite was "I'll Cover You," a duet between the two gay lovers, Collins and Angel. I just let myself enjoy his singing and the look on his face when we'd sing through it together.

One Sunday afternoon in late April, while we were playing through the *Little Shop of Horrors* songbook, my dad brought out plates of leche flan and insisted we take a break. One look at the caramel sauce dripping over the creamy mounds of custard was enough to get us to agree.

He sat with us in the living room as we shoveled spoonfuls of it into our mouths. "Sounding good, you guys," he said. "Emmett, you're picking up music very quickly these days."

"Aw, thanks, Mr. C. Honestly, it's all Quito. He's a natural teacher. I mean, he doesn't even need to look at the music. He has it all in his head. Like, sometimes he makes it all sound better than it does on the CD."

As compliments went, that was a pretty good one. Too good for me to acknowledge with any sort of grace. "As if," I said, embarrassed.

"You know," my father said, "Quito has written some new songs that he could share with you. They are even better than all the stuff you have been doing so far."

I was baffled. How the hell did my father know about my new songs?

In the weeks after Laney's party, they'd started coming out of me, showing up uninvited in the shower, at breakfast, or during boring stretches of English class, when Mrs. Hempstead would drone on about totally irrelevant books like *A Separate Peace.* I'd write the songs in my head, sketching out chord progressions and basic melodies. A few lyrics here and there. Most of the songs didn't have titles, and some weren't even complete. There was no possible way he could've known about them.

"I don't have... I mean... they're just dumb songs. They aren't any good," I said, flustered.

"Don't be so dramatic, Quito. I think they're excellent. And I have the best taste." He took a bite of his leche flan. "Mmm. Like this, for example. It's very good, diba?"

"How would you even know? I'm pretty sure I never played through any of them while you were home."

"A little birdie told me," he said. I think. Hard to tell since his mouth was crammed full of custard.

A chill went through me. Was that a reference to my mom? Like most old-school Filipinos, my dad had an unwavering belief in the hereafter and in ghostly visions. He used to tell me that my mother would sometimes appear to him at the foot of his bed at night, watching him sleep. The first time he confessed that to me, I made him promise not to ever bring it up again. It saddened him, I know, for me not to want to know about my mom's supposed visitations. But the thought of a ghost appearing in my bedroom, even if it was my mom, scared the crap out of me.

Emmett tapped his fork on his ceramic plate with a clink, startling me. "First of all, Mr. C," he said, "this Filipino pudding is hella dope. Secondly—dude, you have to play me your new stuff."

"Let's just do more *Little Shop*. You can be Audrey II this time."

"Quito." My dad glared at me, clearly unhappy. "Don't hide that part of yourself. You know your mother would not have liked it."

I was trying to think of more excuses to give myself time to get the songs into more presentable shape. My music felt safe where it was. Inside. Where no one could touch it, criticize it, or hate it for being less than perfect. Where no one could call me names because of the meaning behind the words.

But Dad was right. My mother would have wanted me to share my songs. If not with the world, then at least with one other person.

"Okay, but just so you know, they're not really finished yet," I said.

"Whatever." Emmett set his plate down on the coffee table and wiped his mouth with the back of his hand. "I'm gonna like it all anyway."

"You don't even know what they sound like yet."

"Don't have to. You wrote 'em."

My dad smiled at this and then packed his mouth with the rest of his leche flan. "Go. Practice," he mumbled while pushing us both to the piano.

Later that afternoon, after I'd played my songs for Emmett, he surprised me and my father by insisting he help prepare dinner.

"No," my dad said. "You're a guest here."

Emmett responded, "Am I just a guest, though, Mr. C? Or don't you consider me more, like...one of the family?"

My dad stared at him, saying nothing. But in his eyes, I could see a change in the way he saw Emmett, as if Emmett had suddenly turned a brighter color or grown an inch. "Well, I suppose. Just this once."

I accompanied Emmett, intending to help guide him through the food prep. But surprisingly, he had skills in the kitchen. He knew how to properly peel ginger by scraping the skin off the knobby roots with a spoon. And he was decent with a knife, able to mince garlic, onions, and ginger with ease. I sautéed those together with hunks of chicken and poured in rice and water, which would simmer down into one of my favorite comfort foods, arroz caldo. Meanwhile, my dad cooked diced pork and fried cubes of tofu. He had Emmett and me make a sweet vinegar dressing, which he combined with the pork, tofu, and chopped red onions to make tokwa't baboy, an ideal complement to the arroz caldo.

When we sat down to eat, we were quieter than usual, only speaking to ask for the food or drinks to be passed around. Part of this was probably because we'd already spent the past hour shoulder to shoulder, talking, giving each other instructions on how to create the delicious meal we were now eating. But it also felt as if familiarity and comfort had settled into us, making general chitchat unnecessary. All we needed was the food and each other's company.

Afterward, Emmett and I sat outside in my backyard to take advantage of the warm weather we'd completely ignored the rest of the day. Even with the shouts of neighborhood kids, dogs barking, and the hum of the BART train all around, the calm still stayed with us. We drank from cans of RC Cola and watched as the sun sank. Neither of us said anything for a long time. The quiet between Emmett and me felt just as natural as all the singing and playing that had come earlier in the day and the cooking after that.

"Thank you," he said, finally breaking the silence.

"For what?"

"Sharing your songs with me this afternoon. I know you said they weren't done, but it didn't feel that way to me. They felt, I dunno, right, somehow."

"You learned them super fast. Even faster than any of the musical theater stuff."

"I know. Almost like you wrote them for me."

At that, a part of me came loose and was set free—a part I hadn't realized needed freeing. I'd written those songs in my effort to *not* think about Emmett, when, really, they were the part of him inside me that I couldn't deny, wanting to come out.

"Hey," Emmett said, turning to me. "Why did you stop talking to me after Laney's party?"

A small child's shriek from next door pierced the air. I flinched and swished the remainder of my cola around in its can. "I got really busy," I said.

"You were mad at me."

"No, I wasn't," I said, which was only half-true. I was more mad at myself than him.

"Quito, don't lie to me."

"How come you never told me you had a girlfriend?"

"She goes to another school. I didn't see a reason to."

"I thought you were my friend."

"I was. I am," he said.

"Look, she told me you never had enough time with her, that she barely saw you. So I thought—as a *friend*—I shouldn't be taking up too much of your time," I said, lying. "You shouldn't have to choose between us. I just did what I thought was best. For you."

"For me," he repeated.

"Yeah."

"Well, it doesn't matter now. She's out of the picture. We've got all the time in the world to chill." Emmett stared out across our yard as the sun dipped down. The sunset flared brightly, all of its being concentrated into a glowing crescent of light.

"What do you mean?"

"I broke up with her."

"What? When?"

"Right after I started hanging out with you again."

I said nothing at first, letting what he'd just said settle in the air.

"I'm sorry it didn't work out," I finally said.

"Thanks."

We sat in silence, watching the sunset overtake everything.

"I got into Oberlin, by the way," I said. "I was going to tell you before, but I never found the right time."

He punched me in the shoulder, sloshing the contents of my soda on the concrete porch. "Dude!" he said.

"Full ride, too," I added.

"Sweet!"

"Yeah."

"And I heard from USC," Emmett said.

"You got in?"

"Yep."

My eyes stayed fixed on the horizon, trying to hold on to the sun as it faded.

"Congratulations," I said.

In a few weeks, we'd graduate. After the all-too-brief summer break, we'd be going our separate ways. We *didn't* have all the time in the world.

Emmett said, "I'm gonna miss our jam sessions."

"We'll hang out during vacations," I offered. "And you could come visit me."

"In Ohio? Not."

The colors of the sky were changing quickly now. Blue morphed into pink, purple, magenta. They were undefinable. Never settling on one shade or another.

"What if I made it so you had to come?" I said.

He turned to me. "What do you mean?"

"If I end up being a composition major, I'll have to pass a jury at the end of my freshman year. That's how they decide if you're good enough to go on. They're going to want a recital of my stuff. I'll be writing a bunch of vocal works, of course. What if I wrote some songs for you? Things that would fit your voice. Then you'd have to come visit me at Oberlin to sing for the recital."

"Hm," Emmett said. "Sneaky."

"The songs that run through my head, you're always the one singing them. I can't hear anyone else. I write for you because that's all that will come out. So you have to come. Or I won't be able to finish my degree." I felt my insides seize up. I hadn't planned on telling him how much he inspired me. Up until that moment, I hadn't even realized it myself.

He held out his can of RC to me. "Here's to me being your Musetta."

I snickered. "You mean *muse*. Musetta's a character in *La Bohème*."

"I thought that was Maureen."

"You're thinking of *Rent*."

"Same difference."

"Right."

"Anyway, here's to me being your *muse*."

I clunked my can against his. "And more." My fingers closed around the can, making it crinkle. "Like, you know," I stuttered, "to your visit. And to me writing songs for you. And stuff."

On Emmett's face, something revealed itself briefly, like the ruffle of a stage curtain. Then, just as quickly, the curtain fell back into place.

"Yeah. And stuff." He chugged the rest of his soda, burping loudly afterward.

We laughed and looked out as the sky settled into a single tone of darkness.

Chapter 14—Now

"THIS IS WHERE Ujima's show is?" Mark asks.

A warehouse wall stretches down the block. Electronic dance music thuds from inside, spilling out of the entrance and onto the sidewalk.

I put my arm around Mark's waist. "This is it."

It's been a while since I've been in the Meatpacking District. The neighborhood has changed since the last time I was here. Gentrification has taken over, claiming its stake with shiny restaurants, art galleries, and condos, while a new stretch of the High Line park watches from above. Compared to everything else, the warehouse next to us is a relic, a reminder of a seedier past. The gamey smell of meat even seems to still linger in the air around it.

"I always wanted to come to this club back when it was still open. Never had the guts, though. I was too intimidated by all the muscle boys," Mark says. "Did you ever come here?"

"Not a lot." I rest my head against his shoulder. "A few times."

"Did you like it?"

"Not really."

He watches as people walk inside. His face is lined with a trace of yearning. "I think I would've loved it."

Originally a slaughterhouse, then a skating rink, the building beside us was best known as Twixxy—a discotheque that opened in the early eighties. At the height of its popularity, it lured in huge crowds. People came from all over the world for its celebrity DJs, hordes of shirtless men, and nonstop dancing that went into the early hours of the morning. I managed to catch the last few years of its notorious run after graduating from college, right before it closed in the mid-2000s. By then it had fallen victim to the rising popularity of the internet, its more convenient chat rooms and dating sites eventually replacing the gay megaclubs.

A black Tesla drives up to the sidewalk. Puddles of spring rain splash at our feet. Dinesh emerges from the Uber. He's dressed in a tweed overcoat that looks as if it costs more than I make in a year.

"First working note," he says, waving his printed-out e-ticket at us, "let's make sure the title of our show isn't rubbish. *ONE-derland*? Really?"

"It's a remake of *Alice in Wonderland*," I tell him. I'm about to add, *yet another one*, when I remember that his Peter Pan show isn't exactly the apotheosis of originality. "Would it make it better if I told you that the score is made up of one-hit-wonder songs?"

"You're joking."

"That makes it worse," Mark says.

"Well, I think it'll still give us good ideas for our show," I say. "Let's just try to keep an open mind."

Mark puts both hands to the side of his head and expands them like blooming flowers. "I'm sure it'll be *one*-derful."

At the entrance to the club, we're greeted by a large THIS WAY DOWN THE RABBIT'S HOLE! sign, which seems appropriate in several ways. The pink neon TWIXXY sign by the box office window is turned off and dusty with age, though the ticket sellers are just like the old Twixxy ones—inexplicably angry at us for making them do their job.

Once we're in the main part of the club, subwoofers saturate us with ultra-low bass frequencies, and memories come flooding back to me. Every Saturday night for two years, I'd wait behind the Twixxy velvet rope for the privilege to pay too much entrance money and be ignored by the half-naked bartenders and everyone else. I've never had a body like a sculpture, never been famous or well connected or into ludicrous levels of substance abuse. So the odds were against me. Not to mention the fact that, as an Asian, I was on the lowest rung of the NYC gay male desirability chart.

Not really sure of where to go, we lean up against one of the walls where several other people have decided to wait. The wallpaper is scuffed and tearing away in some places, revealing older wallpaper and even older paint. The urge to pull at the layers to see what's underneath gnaws at me, to see if, maybe, I'll find the actual wall and see what the place really looks like.

A couple of people are brave enough to be the first out on the floor. They dance awkwardly to the music. Above them, the disco ball still sparkles as if it has never stopped spinning. The DJ works her equipment at the booth on the side, though there doesn't seem to be any sort of stage for the show—just a bunch of black box platforms of different sizes and shapes scattered about, like the ones the Twixxy go-go dancers used to dance on, thrusting and gyrating in their thongs. I used to be transfixed by the dancers but always made sure I didn't watch them for too long, afraid it would make me look desperate. Not that that helped me be more attractive to anyone.

I squeeze Mark's hand. He squeezes back. We've had a good few weeks. I'd never seen him as jealous as he was at Broadway Baby, when he caught me with Emmett. But that's behind us now. He believed me when I told him that we were just old classmates. Nothing more. And while that wasn't exactly right, the truth was that there was nothing between Emmett and me. There never has been, and there never will be.

In a strange way, our run-in with Emmett actually brought us closer. I wasn't sold on Dinesh's musical at first. The project didn't seem like the right fit for me, and I couldn't understand why Mark was pushing me so hard to write music for someone else's show when I barely had the inspiration to write for myself.

But at Broadway Baby, I saw how scared he was to lose me. He was only trying to do what he thought was best by setting me up with Dinesh. It was the kick in the ass I needed to start writing again, even if it was for someone else's idea.

So far he's been right. I have to admit to myself that it feels good to compose again. I've managed to write two of the songs Dinesh needs, plus arrangements for four others that he'd already come up with melodies for. We just need one more new song to round out a decent first act to show the producers. After that monumental writing effort, I felt myself running out of creative steam, so I suggested a group field trip to Ujima's show as a way to get some more ideas. It felt like the perfect thing to get my juices flowing again. Not to mention the fact that I wanted to support Jee's first official off-Broadway show.

I see Ujima emerge from a side entrance. Even if they didn't wave at us, they would be impossible to miss. Their costume is a ruby and ivory sculptural dress that takes up most of the space around them, the shoulder pads so big that they could be used to serve food. People jump out of the way as Jee comes toward us, pushed aside by their dress. Or maybe it's because everyone is scared of the object they're carrying—a flesh-colored staff that's topped with a heart-shaped tip, which is, for some reason, upside down.

It's basically a massive dildo.

"Hello, boys."

"Wow," Dinesh says.

"You like?" they ask, waving the staff over themself.

"Er . . . y-yes," Dinesh stutters.

They sigh. "I can see you're not gagged by my divine eleganza. Just this enormous—"

"Power rod?" Dinesh offers.

"Sex scepter?" Mark says.

"Wig in the shape of a crown?" I say.

Ujima rolls their eyes at me. "Bitch, please. Don't pretend you can't stop looking at this thing like everyone else. I can feel your sphincter muscles tightening from here."

"So you're the Queen of Hearts, I presume?" Dinesh asks.

"Miz Queeny Hart. Owner and MC of the Croquet Club." They bow low, showing off the center of their crown-wig, which is filled with stuffed hearts. It really is a phenomenal hairpiece. "Thank you all for coming," they say, to Mark in particular.

He nods. "You can thank Quito for that."

"Well, you didn't have to say yes. I appreciate your support."

"You're welcome." Mark is being sincere. I know that he's been trying. For me, at least, if not for Ujima.

"Oh. I have presents for you all." Jee hands us heart-suited playing cards. "Entrance to the VIP lounge behind the bar. Drinks are gratis in there," they say, pronouncing it *graTEES* in their best incorrect French.

I give Mark a quick peck on the cheek. "You two go ahead. I want to catch up with Jee." As Mark and Dinesh head back to the lounge, I take a closer look at Ujima, touching different parts of their costume. It's surprisingly decadent for a show I didn't think had a huge budget. Then again, there seems to be no set, so maybe they've saved money that way. "So, where is the stage? When do we get to see Wonderland? I mean, *ONE*-derland."

"Honey, you're already in it. The main tunnel where you came in? That's the rabbit hole. So, technically, you've arrived."

"And how does this whole interactive thing work? Are we part of the show? How are we supposed to know what to do?" Past nightmares run through my head, the ones where I suddenly find myself onstage for a concert without knowing any of the music I'm supposed to play.

"Don't worry. We're going to guide you through everything."

I survey the club. It looks as if some of the other cast members are also starting to mix in with the crowd. I'm not entirely sure about all of them, but some—like the white boy in dreadlocks and a green trench coat smoking a vape pen and the man in an ivory fur coat twirling a watch on a gold chain—are definitely part of the show.

"I'm along for the ride, Jee, whatever this ends up being. It's your first off-Broadway gig. I know how much this means to you."

They look down at their dress and touch the sides of it, as if they're reassuring themself that everything is where it should be. "It does feel right somehow. Like this role was written for me."

"It was. I wouldn't have missed it for anything. Not even your scary stick could've kept me away."

They wave it at me, and my butt cheeks automatically clench. Dammit. Jee was right about the sphincter thing.

"So has you-know-who called you yet?" Jee asks.

I shake my head. It's been seven weeks and four days since Emmett and I last saw each other at Broadway Baby. Not that I've been counting.

"Girl, why don't you just call him?"

"It's fine. He's busy. He'll call when he can. We still have plenty of time."

They shift their attention off to the side, and a flash of light goes off. A photographer gives us a thumbs-up. He's just snapped a candid of us.

Jee pulls me in close to them, filling my nose with the smell of stage makeup, hair spray, and lavender perfume. "How's my face?" they ask through their teeth. I give an okay sign. "Do me a favor, sweetie, and take one more of us," Jee says, standing in bevel and presenting their other side to him. "Promo pictures for the website," they explain to me. "Look pretty for the camera!"

I give a closemouthed smile and then wriggle away so that the photographer can't take another picture. I've never been fond of getting mine taken. My dad always used to lug his camera with its complicated lenses and attachments to my recitals, snapping endless shots of me while I played. When we'd pick the developed pictures up from the drugstore, I'd refuse to look at them. They always seemed like someone else. Someone whose eyes were too far apart, with a nose that was too big and a chin that was too small. He'd frame his favorite ones and put them on the piano. Whenever I'd practice, I'd turn them around so I didn't have to look at them.

"I should go find the boys." I kiss Jee. "Break a leg. Both legs."

"Honey, these are my money makers," they say, pulling the sides of their dress up and slapping their padded hips and thighs. "Mama's in big trouble if these break."

I wade my way through the crowd, now thick with audience and cast members. The lights flicker briefly. The DJ begins to play the theme song to the old TV show *Alice*. No doubt a cue that the show is about to begin. I hurry back to the VIP lounge and almost miss the dark glass door behind the main bar. Back when Twixxy was open, I never had the connections or the money or the drugs for VIP access. I show my red playing card to the bouncer and slip in.

Some of the people are already starting to leave, meandering out toward the main dance floor for the show. Even with the thinning crowd, I have a hard time finding Mark and Dinesh. Finally, I spot them at the very back near the mini-bar area. They're not talking to each other. They stare at their drinks like they're both concentrating on something. As if someone's just asked them both a question and they're still trying to come up with the answer.

"Hey," I say. "I think the show's about to start."

Mark looks up at me, startled. "Great. Let's go." He starts walking toward the exit immediately without looking back at Dinesh, who follows us without a word. I make a mental note to myself to check in later with Mark to see if they've gotten into a fight of some kind. If they have, I hope it doesn't have anything to do with our show. Or my songs. I'm the first person to admit they're not my best work, but they're still decent. My heart sinks with the possibility that Dinesh hasn't been happy with them, that Mark might have been trying to stick up for my music. He's already done so much for me.

I take his hand when we arrive back out on the dance floor. He doesn't hold on to it quite as tightly as when we first arrived.

Four of the movable boxes have been smooshed together, forming a makeshift stage on the dance floor. A spot lights up Ujima, standing in the center of it. "Ladies and gentlemen and everyone in between, welcome to... ONE! DER! LAND!"

The crowd roars. The show has begun.

Ujima explains that everyone is now part of the show as ONE-derland clubgoers, witnesses to Alice's evening of adventures. The story will unwind in different parts of the club. We'll be nudged along to where we need to be by cast members as they move the platforms in and out of formation, creating an ever-changing set.

Once the actual show begins, I become distracted. Unmistakable tension runs between Mark and Dinesh, standing on either side of me. Mark can't seem to enjoy himself. Not even when the Alice character, a whiny bridge-and-tunnel girl, starts crying over not being able to get into the VIP lounge and a slew of chorus boys in bathing suits perform "It's Raining Men" as a response. Mark's got to be truly upset not to enjoy being surrounded on all sides by endless abs.

When Alice befriends a bunch of club kids dressed in animal-themed costumes, I ask Mark if he's doing okay. He looks confused. And not just because the cast members are now instructing us to dance the Macarena with them in a big circle. "I'm fine," he says. "Why?"

"No reason," I say as I pat each of my ass cheeks and shimmy my hips. "But is Dinesh having problems with my songs? I can fix them up. And the last one, which I'm almost done with, will be the best one yet." Not a lie, exactly. More of a hopeful exaggeration.

"Oh," he says. "No. He loves your songs. Don't worry about that." He rubs my back briefly before returning to the dance steps.

I'm happy they haven't been arguing over me. And I am surprised at how much Mark is getting into the Macarena.

As the story unfolds, it becomes increasingly clear to me that this Alice isn't as sweet and innocent as other versions of the character. In fact, she's kind of a sloppy drunk drama queen. She keeps taking other people's drinks and asking everyone for what she calls "happy cakes," which, from the strange ways they affect her, are infused with questionable substances. When Off-White Rabbit—a tweaked-out dealer on way too many uppers—gives her one, the seat of her pants inflates, making it look as if her ass swells up.

Naturally, he sings, "Baby Got Back."

The three of us look at each other and burst out laughing. We decide the best thing to do is to give in to the sheer ridiculousness of the show.

We dance along to the song and everything that comes after, including Mr. Caterpillar's rendition of "Ice Ice Baby," Chester Cheshire singing "I'm Too Sexy," and, finally, Ujima's performance of "Bitch," which is the highlight of the evening. It's such a tour de force I completely forget that we're watching a show and give Jee as big a hug as my short arms can around their massive costume after they're done. I don't care if it's not allowed. I don't even care that the heart dildo is only inches from my face. I just want Ujima to know how proud I am of them.

After the cast bows at the end of the show, the Off-White Rabbit announces that ONE-derland will stay open. The DJ will spin more one-hit wonders until midnight, turning the venue into a real club. "At that point," he says, "the Rabbit's Hole will close!" Talk about tightening sphincters.

We manage to pry Ujima away from a group of appreciative audience members so that we can celebrate with a round of drinks in the VIP lounge.

"I have to admit, that was quite a show," Dinesh says. "I'm genuinely impressed by how they managed to make 'Tubthumping' work. That song has never made sense to me until now."

"I can't believe I'm saying this, but I agree," Mark says. "Congratulations." He raises his martini to Jee.

"To the queen," I say, clinking my soda to everyone's glasses.

Ujima lets out a throaty laugh. "Long may I reign!" they pronounce, before sipping their fruity cocktail through the tiny stirrer stick.

I feel my cell phone buzz in my pocket. Maybe Emmett is finally reaching out.

I don't want to check it with Mark sitting right next to me. "Excuse me," I say, "just have to use the little boys' room." I run to the nearby bathroom, where the booming beats aren't quite as loud.

By the time I get to an empty stall, my phone has stopped buzzing. I check the caller ID. Not Emmett.

Dad.

I call him back.

"Mr. Cruz?" responds a familiar girl's voice.

"Celeste? Why do you always have my dad's phone?"

"Um, I'm at his house? Your house, I mean. In your old room, bee-tee-dubs. You have super-cool taste! All these framed posters of old musicals. Did you actually get to see any of these? Like the original production of *Into the Woods*? I mean—"

"Celeste, what are you doing at my house?"

"I stopped by to bring your dad some chicken soup. My mom makes some really amazing pozole. Not too spicy. In case it irritates your dad's condition."

"What are you talking about? Why are you bringing him soup?"

"He didn't want to tell you." She brings her voice down to a whisper. "He's asleep right now. Recovering. Us choir kids have been taking turns visiting him."

I pump up my phone's volume to maximum and press a finger to my free ear in order to be able to hear her. "Please. Tell me what's going on."

"Mr. Cruz. I mean, our Mr. Cruz. I mean, your dad. He's been gone from school for the past two weeks. He's been sick. Like really, really sick. Mr. Drummond, the band teacher, is subbing, but all he does is put on DVDs of movie musicals. And not even good ones like *Hairspray* and *Dreamgirls*! Terrible ones. Like *Seven Brides for Seven Brothers*. We haven't had a real rehearsal since Mr. Cruz left. He's never been gone this long before."

She takes a ragged breath before asking, "Can you come earlier than you were supposed to, Mr. Quito? We could really use your help."

Chapter 15—Then

"YOU'RE SURE YOU'RE okay? Did you get someone to help you like I suggested?" I asked.

Outside my dorm room, rain was coming down in torrents. Our tenth straight day of spring showers. Yay, Ohio.

Emmett *tsk*ed on the other end of the telephone line. The noise of rushing cars and honking horns echoed in the background. "I got this, Quito. Just chill."

"You've been practicing all three songs?" I'd mailed him the sheet music for my song cycle two months ago. Then, after stress-obsessing over it for a week, I'd followed up with a tape recording of me playing them overlaid with a separate track of me singing the vocal line on top. Just to be sure. Emmett wasn't an expert at reading music, and I wasn't at USC to help him.

"It's all good. I found someone here to run through them with me. She's more of a jazz pianist, but we got through it all right. Your practice tape helped a lot. Plus, most of the melody lines by themselves aren't that hard."

I'd done that on purpose. Not because I didn't trust Emmett's natural musicality. It was one of the defining aspects of my cycle: setting simple melodies on top of an accompaniment that constantly changed. The texts I'd chosen, excerpts from Filipino national hero José Rizal's poems, were easy to read and absorb—while the themes behind them were complex and myriad. I wanted that to be reflected in the piano and voice.

"That's great," I said, relieved. "How are things in L.A.?"

"Good. I booked a couple of modeling gigs. The agency's thinking of sending me out for some other types of auditions."

"Awesome. And classes are going okay?"

"Still getting straight As."

"Show-off. Rehearsals for *Guys and Dolls*?"

"Oh. I had to drop out. Conflicted with basketball practice."

"You're still in choir, though, right?"

He laughed sadly. "Yeah . . . so . . . I dropped out of choir, too."

"What? Are you really that busy?"

"It's not that. For choir, at least. It's just . . . I don't know. I didn't like it. The director picks interesting music. He's just not like your dad. He's kind of, I dunno. Boring. And, like, *you're* not there."

"Yeah, well, no one could possibly replace me," I joked.

"Exactly." He stretched the word out, filling it with unspoken things. "It's just not the same without you."

We tended to end up like this during our phone calls. I'd find myself maneuvered into a place where I had to choose carefully what I said next, mindful not to cross over into a misunderstanding of our friendship again. The things he said and the way he said them to me—they always felt as if they were some riddles to solve. When he'd do that, I'd force myself to think back to Laney's party. Him and Angela. Side by side. A perfect picture. I'd think: What girl was he dating now? Or fooling around with? Because there had to be one, of course. Or more. Maybe the pianist was one of them. But while it wasn't something I wanted him to tell me, not knowing about that part of his life bugged me. It always crept in on the edges of my mind, no matter how hard I tried to keep those thoughts out. So I did what I always did in those situations. I pivoted the conversation back to him.

"So you're not in choir. You're not doing the musical. Are you singing at all? You must be out of practice. I should have just asked someone here to do my recital."

Emmett's stay wouldn't be long. The fact that we'd only have a day to prepare together before my composition jury stressed me out. This wasn't us going through nonconsequential music back at my house just for fun. We'd be in front of people whose job it was to judge me. There'd be no room for error. The comp professors would be holding my future in their hands.

"Don't be a spaz," Emmett said.

"Just be ready," I said. "I don't want you fucking things up."

"Dude."

I gripped the phone in my hand. "I'm sorry."

It wasn't just the jury. My anxiety level was growing the more I thought about the coming weekend. Two whole days of nerve-racking events. Emmett would arrive next Saturday afternoon, which meant we'd only have an hour or two to practice my compositions before Acappellooza at Finney Chapel that night. It would be the first time for the Obertones—Oberlin's premier all-male a capella group—to host the event and my first time directing them. Then, the next day, the Tones would have to sing again for the Alumni Luncheon. Right before my composition jury with Emmett. We'd have to run from the luncheon to the Conservatory just to get there on time.

But the thing that made me the most nervous? Emmett. We hadn't seen each other since Christmas break. Just enough time for a brief dinner at Red Robin, doing our best to catch up on a semester's worth of first-time college experiences over the all-you-can-eat fries. This time, he'd be coming to stay with me for an entire weekend, sleeping just a few feet away in my roommate's bed while my roommate would be visiting his cousins in Cleveland. The thought of spending that much time with Emmett—and being that close to him at night—made my head swim with anxiety.

"It's gonna be okay. I promise," he said, the confidence in his voice as powerful as ever. He always had a way of convincing me of almost anything.

"Okay," I said. "Well, thanks for agreeing to do this. Coming all this way just for my exam."

"I'm not coming just for your exam."

"And for Acappellooza."

"You know what I mean, Quito."

The line on his end went quiet. He must have closed the windows of his room to the riot of Los Angeles outside because I couldn't hear a thing.

I felt him growing impatient on the other end. As if this were a scene in a play and I was missing my cue to say the next line.

I had to keep reminding myself: Emmett liked girls. Not me. Not that way.

Remember.

"I. Um. I'll... see you in a week," I barely managed to say.

Silence.

Finally, Emmett said, "Yep, see you," and hung up.

I listened to the dial tone for a while, letting it drone in my ear until the busy signal took over and drilled into my head. I knocked the receiver end of the phone onto my forehead a few times before finally putting it back on the hook.

Next door, in the adjoining bedroom, Jayesh was talking to his computer science study partner, Melina, a trust fund kid who tried to hide her privilege with dumpster clothing and had questionable personal hygiene. They were arguing about subroutine programming. Or ASCII dots. Or something. I couldn't make it out and wouldn't have been able to understand it even if I could. All I knew was that in order to get out to go to the bathroom, I had to walk through Jayesh's room, and I wasn't eager to do that.

Melina kind of had a thing for me.

The first time Jayesh introduced me to her, she grabbed me by the hand and regarded me as if I were the biggest stuffed animal prize at a carnival booth. After that, she started making a habit of bumping into me in Dascomb Dining Hall and then staring at me from across the room while she gnawed on her whole-grain breadsticks. Not that I was any expert at flirting, but I'm pretty sure she was the absolute worst at it. I steered clear of her as much as possible to avoid giving her the chance.

The ache in my bladder was building up. I knew I didn't have much time before pee started to leak out of my body, so I decided to chance it. They'd stopped talking. Maybe they were studying so intently that I could slip out unnoticed.

I tiptoed through Jayesh's room. Only to walk straight into Melina. She was almost six feet tall, so she was pretty hard to miss.

"Hey, Quito." Her eyelids blinked slowly and heavily as she

looked down at me. Either she was on barbiturates, or she was trying to seduce me.

"Hey...you," I said, avoiding her gaze at all costs. "Sorry to disturb you. Just have to use the little boys' room."

She planted herself right in front of the door. "You were so very, very quiet. Like a little mousy. I didn't even know you were in there. Trying to hide from me?"

The main door opened, and Jayesh sauntered in, holding several bags of barbecue potato chips from the vending machine. I took advantage of the distraction to sidestep Melina and escape. She yelled out behind me, "God, Quito! You're so *random*!" while I sprinted down the long hallway, filled with panic and built-up pee.

Later that afternoon, after hiding for at least half an hour in one of the bathroom stalls, I tiptoed back to my dorm room, peeked to make sure Melina had finally left, grabbed my music portfolio and practice binder, and hightailed it to the Conservatory. Not only did I need to make sure my composition jury pieces were absolutely perfect, but I also had to practice my conducting on the Obertones pieces we were doing for Acappellooza and the accompaniment for a bunch of voice recitals in the coming week. I had a ton of work to do and only a few days to do it all before Emmett came.

The day Emmett arrived, the sun had finally come out. The air smelled of wet grass and budding flowers, everything fresh and full of potential. It almost pained me to rush him to the practice room building straight from the airport shuttle. He'd spent several months in smog-congested Los Angeles. Being in suburban Ohio must have felt like an environmental detox.

"Do we have to practice right now?" Emmett asked. "It's so amazing out. I saw some people playing Ultimate Frisbee out on the lawn in the park. Can't we go join them first?"

"Emmett, we only have two hours. Then I have to get ready for Acappellooza."

"Pfft. Plenty of time to rehearse."

"No. This is too important."

He took the only chair in the practice room, the one for the piano, and sat back in it, putting his hands behind his head and stretching himself to the outermost limits of the tiny room. I strained myself trying to ignore him and focused instead on the sheet music I was spreading out onto the piano's stand. He knew I was trying to avoid looking at him because I saw him smile out of the corner of my eye.

"Quito," he said. God. I'd missed that crooked-toothed smile more than I'd realized. "Chillax. We used to learn entire musicals in an hour. And not just because I'm a fast and incredibly gifted learner. Which I am. Because you're an awesome teacher."

I shook my head and sighed. "Let's see how much we can get done in an hour. And if we're good enough, I'll let you go do ultimate freestyle or whatever. Deal?"

He got up, took my hand, squeezed it, and shook. "Deal."

Even though I hadn't seen Emmett in months, I hadn't forgotten how it felt to touch him. Like watching infinite sunsets setting at the same time and feeling the accumulative warmth of them in my body.

I shook it off. I had to.

We got down to work.

Thankfully, he hadn't lied. He *had* practiced. A lot. So much that he almost had things memorized. At one point, I almost stopped playing when I realized he was singing the songs without looking at the sheet music. Instead, he was watching me, keying into movements, my playing. Just like I'd always done with his singing.

We went through the first song twice before moving on to the second. It was just as well prepared.

My fingers became looser. I played more freely. We were able to have more fun with the music, to work on nuances I didn't think we'd have time to address.

He'd really done what he'd said. I never should have doubted him.

Then we tried the third song.

Halfway through, Emmett stopped singing. He tilted his head at me. "Am I messing up that much?"

"Nope. You're fine."

"Quito, I see that vein in the middle of your forehead. It only throbs when you get anxious."

"I have an anxiety vein? Why did nobody ever tell me this?"

"It makes you look more mature." Emmett laughed. "So tell me. What am I messing up?"

I tapped a finger on the sheet music. "Let's go over the first verse again."

"That part's the trickiest for me, for some reason."

It was the complex accompaniment. Maybe too complex. I had wanted the poem's theme of conflict to come across in the music. So I filled it with runs of chromaticisms paired with syncopated cluster chords. Of course he was having a hard time singing the melody correctly. I was throwing him off.

But I had built something into it that he probably hadn't noticed. Something that might make things easier. "Let me play it for you again. Don't sing. Just listen."

I started from the beginning. This time I brought out certain notes. They never appeared in an obvious string. They jumped from hand to hand and sometimes even from octave to octave. It took careful listening to discover the harmony I'd hidden, one that paired perfectly with the melody. "What do you hear?" I asked.

He shook his head. "I don't—"

"Keep listening," I said. "Close your eyes. Let yourself really hear it."

I kept going, bringing the hidden line out even more. Playing it as if it were the actual melody.

Emmett's eyes popped open. He laughed. "You hid a duet in there."

"See. I'm with you every step of the way. You just have to listen."

He stared at his music, tracing the notes with the tips of his fingers. At first I thought he was trying to locate the hidden harmony. He wasn't. He was caressing the pages. The same way he'd touched my copy of "A Part I Play" when I'd first given it to him. As if it were something precious.

"So you think you got it?" I asked.

He nodded. "I got it."

"I know you do. Actually, I think we *will* be able to finish early. You can go have some fun before Acappellooza."

"Cool! And, Quito, we're going to be fine," he said. "More than fine."

But, unfortunately, he was wrong.

Chapter 16—Now

I'M FLYING.

The New York skyline is barely recognizable from up here. As I ascend, the island of Manhattan melts into the rest of the Eastern Seaboard. The sun is so bright that I can feel it searing into my eyes, leaving a corona-shaped imprint. The clouds are cool and bracing against my skin. Shouldn't the air sting more this high above the ground?

Someone squeezes my hand. Mark is holding me aloft. He takes me higher, into the dark reaches of the sky, out into space. I can see the entirety of the United States. An expanse of valley greens and mountainous browns.

We keep climbing.

A pull. Coming from my other hand.

Emmett.

He turns and shines me that smile of his and then tugs me down back to the earth. Heading westward toward California.

Mark pulls us back up. The fringes of his tunic flutter in the wind, and his feathered cap escapes and flies away. He's . . . Peter Pan?

He lets out a mischievous laugh.

I'm stuck in midair. Like a human rope in a game of tug-of-war. My arms cramp up.

A woman materializes ahead of us. Her hair is pixieish and

dark brown, her eyes obsidian black. Her dress sparkles with every color of the rainbow. Her mouth, beak-like, lets out a beautiful, silvery tune. It sounds like a bell. *Tinkle, tinkle, tinkle, tinkle—*

"Hoy! Francisco!"

I force my eyes open. "Dad?"

"Your alarm has been going off for the past ten minutes." His face, prickly with several days' worth of stubble, hovers above mine. "Halika na. Gutom na ako." He scratches his behind and lumbers out of my childhood bedroom. "I want some Spam pancakes."

I stare up at the ceiling above me. Splotchy in all the same spots. My old desk and bookshelves still hold the same books, the walls the same Easter egg blue I'd wanted for my fifteenth birthday. My blanket and pillows even still smell like my childhood. Layers of generic laundry detergent struggling to rein in years of messy, musty adolescence.

White noise crackles in the living room, followed by loud conversation. Like clockwork, my dad is tuning in to his favorite morning news show. A host tries unsuccessfully to get his guest to shut up and gets cut off by a commercial for fibromyalgia pills.

Grunting, I throw my legs over the side of the bed. My toes poke around everywhere, trying to find my tsinelas. I get them on after the third try but still can't muster the will to get out of bed. I've gotten used to a schedule of going to sleep around 2:00 a.m. and not getting up until ten o'clock the next morning. I'm resentful that I now have to get up at 7:00 a.m.

As if to spite me, my phone alarm goes off again. I grab it off the bedside table and carry it with me to the living room.

I rub my eyes with the heels of my hands and flop down on the couch. "Can you turn it down a little? It's so loud."

My dad sinks lower into his recliner and begrudgingly points the remote control at the wide-screen TV, one of the only things in the house not originally from the eighties or nineties. "I have a hard time hearing what they're saying sometimes." His disheveled hair is more gray than I've ever seen it before.

"All right," I say. "You can put it back up a few notches."

I pull out my phone and check my texts. Still no word from Emmett. Just a reminder about an upcoming dental appointment and a check-in from Ujima.

My emails scroll by. In among the junk is a message from Mark.

> Hey. Hope your dad is doing okay.
>
> I've been working feverishly with Dinesh to get *The Forever Boys* (working title) on its feet. The auditions went better than expected. We found some great people. Including the PERFECT guy to play Peter Pan, touring and regional credits and a fantastic voice AND looks like he's 12 (though he's probably around 30, that bastard).
>
> Anyway, we start rehearsals soon . . . sooooo we're hoping you've managed to get some work done on the final song? I reattached the lyrics here, just in case. Oh, and we changed a few words here and there, to tighten it up.
>
> We miss you.
>
> -Mark
>
> PS: when are you back?

With me here and the producers' audition coming up, Dinesh needed logistic help. So Mark offered to assist. Not that he's ever been a director, actor, singer, or dancer—but he knows more about musicals than even I do. He's got plenty to offer.

I just hope it isn't anything more than that.

We.

A ten-sentence email and he used the word four times, each appearance of it brighter than any of the other words on my phone screen.

I force myself away from the main body of the email and open up the attachment. The lyrics to the Act I finale. A song about Tinker Bell's magic fairy dust. The changes they made did nothing to improve it; the allusions to cocaine are still clumsy and the rhymes are beyond lazy. *"Soaring so very high. When we are so very high?"* Really? It's no wonder I can't manage the motivation to finish composing the last song. I've got shit-all to work with.

Still, I know Dinesh is getting nervous. We're running out of time. At least he was kind enough to not get upset when I told him I needed to come back to California to take care of my dad. Unlike Mark.

"Is he really that sick? It doesn't sound so bad. One of the partners at work had walking pneumonia, too, and she was back to work after two weeks or so. Why do you have to fill in for him at school? Aren't they supposed to get a substitute for that?"

"They do have a sub. He's the band teacher. And he hates choir. Plus, they need to keep preparing for Dad's concert."

"What about our show?"

"I'll finish the last song in California. I promise."

"Fine. Just don't be gone too long. We can find someone to

play the songs while you're gone, but it'll be better if you're back in time to music direct. It's your stuff, after all. This show is your big shot. You don't want to mess it up."

I didn't know how to respond to that. Not in any way that wouldn't start a fight, at least. The truth was, they didn't need me like my dad did.

"You just got out of bed and already you check your phone," my dad says to me. "You kids these days. I'm always confiscating the students' phones because they're like you. As if you all cannot live without it. Is there really something so important there you have to check it all the time?"

When I arrived back in California two weeks ago, I gave in and texted Emmett. I didn't tell him my dad was sick. Only that we needed to start figuring out when he should come up to the Bay Area to start rehearsing for the concert. The Emmett I knew from school would only need a day or two to practice with me and the choir. But as far as I know, it's been years since he's sung in a public concert—not since high school. So I sent a text suggesting he come up at least a week in advance. More than one text, in fact.

He still hasn't gotten back to me. I'm starting to panic. Though, of course, I can't tell my father this.

"Nope. Nothing important," I say. "Did you say you wanted Spam?"

"Yes."

"And pancakes?"

"Spam pancakes."

"You want Spam pancakes? Is that even a thing?"

"Trust me."

"How do I make them?"

He taps a finger onto the outstretched palm of his other hand, as if this gesture is enough to explain.

"What the heck is that supposed to mean?"

"Put Spam inside the pancakes."

"Like, as a sandwich, or . . . ?"

Dad sighs. One of the deep, weary kind that only parents seem to be able to make.

"I'll figure something out."

I plod into the kitchen. At least now I can make some coffee.

The coffeemaker's insides are crusted over with so much residue that I can't even make out the original material. It's like the rest of the kitchen, unchanged from my high school days. I'd suggest remodeling, but Dad is a creature of habit. *So what if everything is old? Why waste the money when everything still works fine?*

The Last Supper woodcraft relief on the wall stares at me as I wait for the coffee to brew. A serene and lopsidedly carved Jesus watches, just as it did every time I'd sit at the table and beg for McDonald's instead of the food my parents made. It took me years of living without home-cooked Filipino food to realize how good I had it back then.

"Maybe Dad's right," I say to wooden Jesus. "Sometimes the old stuff is best."

Feeling renewed after a sip of hot caffeine, I root around in the cabinets looking for flour. All I see is a box of Bisquick. After checking the expiration date to make sure it isn't as old as I am, I mix a cupful with eggs and milk to make a batter and then pop open one of the many cans of Spam from the cupboard. I chop it up into small cubes and, not knowing what else to do, toss them into the bowl with the batter.

I pour chunky, decidedly non-pancake-shaped blobs onto the frying pan. After flipping them over, I tear off a piece of one with a fork to test it, dipping it in some syrup before popping it into my mouth. Dad was definitely onto something. It's delicious.

There's still fresh orange juice left in the refrigerator. I pour some in Dad's favorite glass. The same one Emmett had given to him with a bottle of sake so long ago. The multicolored Mondrian-like block pattern on it still looks as good as new. It astounds me how, after so many years of constant use, he's never once so much as scratched it.

I bring the OJ and pancakes out and set them on a TV tray table. "Here you go."

"Did you try it already?"

"I did."

"What did I tell you? You should always trust my judgment." He closes his eyes as he chews, and his face takes on a satisfied, sanguine look. When I first arrived, he was still in pretty bad shape—always exhausted with barely any energy to get up in the morning. And although he wasn't coughing or sneezing, he complained of minor chest pains often enough that I never forced him to do anything more than eat his meals, even in bed if he wanted, which he usually did. Seeing him almost like his usual self makes me more confident that he's well on the road to recovery.

"Dad, do you think you might be able to go back to school soon? I don't want to push you, but you seem to be doing a lot better. You're not even coughing at all, and I don't think you've had a fever since I've been home."

He keeps eating and watching the television.

"Dad?"

He says, still not looking at me, "I'm sick."

"Okay, fine. I'll see if I can extend my visit for a little longer. But I was only supposed to be here for a few days and not until later in the month. If I stay too long, I might lose my job at the piano bar. And I'm supposed to be working on a show."

"Show? What show is this?"

"Oh." I'm immediately sorry that I've brought it up. "Just this new musical. I'm writing a few songs for it."

"Why didn't you tell me, Quito? A new musical? Wow, that's good news! Ang galing talaga ng anak ko!"

"I guess."

"You haven't composed in so long. I've been wondering why you haven't been using your gift."

"Playing piano has been enough."

"You didn't have the right inspiration. And now you have it."

I swirl the remains of my pancake around in a puddle of syrup. "I know I should be excited, but I'm just not that into it."

"You don't like the project?"

"Not really."

"Why did you agree to it, then?"

"Mark got it for me. I owe it to him," I say. My chest tightens. "I'm sure I can make it work somehow. The more energy I put in, the more I'll get into it. That's all."

My dad mutes the TV. The sudden absence of noise startles me. Growing up, if music wasn't being played in the house, the TV was on. There was always a near-constant stream of sound. Silence was reserved for sleeping time and sometimes not even then. "Francisco. You know that's not how music works. When something you're working on is worthwhile, it gives *you* strength, not the other way around. If you don't find it with this show—with Mark—maybe you should be looking elsewhere. Maybe you should be focusing on something you really love."

Something breathes its way into my lungs. "Maybe."

"Why don't you write a song for our concert?"

The tightness comes back. Emmett hasn't been in contact, so we haven't worked out any of the details of what he'll be doing. "You mean for Emmett? I'm not exactly sure what he had in mind. He probably already has something he wants to sing."

"No. I meant for the choir. Why don't you write something for the kids?"

"Those kids wouldn't want to sing anything I write for them."

"And why is that?"

"Because they hate me."

"They don't hate you. You're *my* son, and they love me." Dad laughs.

"They miss their Mr. Cruz."

"You are a Mr. Cruz, too."

"Just consider going back to work soon. Okay?" I get up to bus his plate. Dad hands me his empty glass. I hold it firmly in my hand before putting it on the tray. "The sooner the better."

"Anak, speaking about Emmett, I should probably tell you something—"

The doorbell rings. At seven o'clock in the morning?

I open the front door and see Emmett standing there holding a carry-on bag and what looks like a gift-wrapped painting.

"I heard you could use a little help," he says.

Chapter 17—Then

I STOOD IN the wings of Finney Chapel's stage, watching the Tufts University Beelzebubs obliterate the audience with their rendition of "Motownphilly" at Acappellooza.

When they'd first arrived, I wasn't expecting much of a show. They seemed like a boring collection of geeks in buttoned-up jackets and matching ties. Nowhere near as cool as the Obertones, dressed in our jeans and untucked shirts. In fact, when their soloist had taken the stage, I thought they'd made a mistake and announced the wrong song. There was no way that this guy—a skinny kid with the sex appeal of a saltine—could be the lead vocalist on a Boyz II Men song.

Then he started singing. With one thrust of his bony hips, he completely upended my brain. His baritone voice oozed more sex and white-boy soul than Rick Astley. I peeked out into Finney and saw everyone's faces light up. The rest of his group backed him with tight harmonies and slick dance moves, almost turning Finney Chapel, however briefly, into an actual place of worship.

How the hell were they this good?

And how were the Obertones supposed to follow it?

Just an hour before, I was in great spirits. Emmett and I had run through my song cycle twice, perfectly. After watching him chase a Frisbee in front of Harkness Co-op for a while, I'd even managed to squeeze us in some time to grab food at Wilder Hall before the concert.

"This place is nothing like USC," Emmett said in between bites of his chicken sandwich.

"Is that a good thing?"

"I mean, it's such a tiny campus. There's nowhere to go. But you kinda got everything you need here. And the... Con? Is that what you guys call the music conservatory? It's amazing. We have, like, twenty times the students you do, but our music department sucks compared to yours."

"We do have great music here. The best in the country."

"I bet the Obertones are incredible."

"We're pretty solid," I said.

"There you go again. Downplaying shit." He grabbed a french fry from my plate, dipped it into the mound of ketchup there, and popped it into his mouth. "Look at you. You're already leading the number one a cappella group on campus, and you're just a freshman."

"*First-year*, thanks. *Freshman* is way too sexist for Obies."

"Oh, excuuuuse me."

"And I don't know. I feel like I just lucked into it. I didn't even try that hard to get into the group in the first place. This senior voice major that I accompany, Shane, he sort of fast-tracked me in. Then, when their director Brett left all of a sudden, they just unanimously voted to make me his replacement."

"Why'd he leave?"

"For selling pot, I think. To a student he was tutoring. Or having sex with a student he was tutoring," I said. "Anyway, I think he was also a seventh-year senior, so they probably just got tired of him being here."

"Maybe that's why Shane got you in so fast. He saw the writing on the wall."

"Yeah, maybe." I took a sip of the last dregs of my soda. "You know, the weird thing is, my dad predicted I'd be leading the Tones within the year."

"He said that?"

"Yeah. He said I helped him conduct a choir for years. I was meant to be a director."

Emmett chewed, swallowed. "They're lucky to have you." He smiled.

I responded by finishing my sandwich and tried not to get too wound up by his compliments.

I was excited, though. This was going to be my first concert as the Obertones director. And Emmett had flown all the way here. To sing for my recital, yes, but also to hear our concert. After we'd finished eating, I made sure to seat him in the front row in Finney before heading backstage to warm up the Tones. I was fully expecting to lead them to success, to give Emmett a one-of-a-kind performance that no one would forget.

But Saltine Boy and the Sex Gods in Suits were messing up my plan.

They ended their number and were rewarded with cheers.

For their second song, the Beelzebubs got into a tight clump and put their heads down. Their director blew into his pitch pipe and counted them off. As each guy entered, they lifted their head, creating a visual road map of the song, an arrangement of Toto's "Africa." Each part bubbled along, accompanying the lead line, splitting into different solos among the group. There was no central soloist or flashy moves this time. Just great singing. Great enough for me to continue doubting myself. How was I going to make sure the Tones brought it all home and justified being the closing act of our own event?

The Beelzebubs finished their song to enthusiastic applause. They walked off the stage grinning at us while they passed. They'd transformed into rock stars right before our eyes, and they knew it.

"Let's do this!" one of the Obertones shouted. Shane, I think. I was too nervous to be able to tell. They bunched up around me, howling, and pushed me out onto the stage like a tide carrying a body out to sea. I fought back the sensation of drowning and tried to look as confident and excited as they sounded.

We got into our standard semicircle formation: tenors on the right, baritones on the left, and basses in the middle with mics in front to capture their low notes. I stood on the outer edge of the tenors so I could direct. I hummed an E-flat. Shane took the center of the stage. I counted off a measure for nothing, and we were off.

They *da-da-da*'d in a syncopated harmony—the intro to my arrangement of "Kiss from a Rose" by Seal. Shane, stout and blindingly blond, was the physical polar opposite of Seal. It didn't matter when he started singing the solo, though, because his voice was perfect for the song. Light and flexible with a craggy edge. He maneuvered through the solo's extreme interval jumps like an acrobat leaping through circus hoops. The rest of us felt his confidence and returned it to him with rock-solid accompaniment.

I glanced out into the audience, looking for Emmett's reaction.

But from where I stood, the dim house lights made it too hard to see him.

Then, sooner than I'd expected, we arrived at the end of the song. Everyone held on to their notes while Shane slipped back into place with the tenors. Their eyes shifted to me while sustaining the chord. They were waiting for me to conduct them into the segue for the next song. "Father Figure," by George Michael.

My solo.

Whose idea was it for me to sing this song?

Oh yeah.

Mine.

I'd auditioned for it, knowing we'd be performing it for Acappellooza, knowing Emmett would hear it. For some stupid reason, I thought it would be the perfect time to show off a little. Impress him like I did the first time I sang "A Part I Play" for the Sunvalley talent show. I wanted him to be proud of me.

The tips of my ears began to heat up so much that I was certain they'd ignite. The rest of the Obertones stared at me, looking as if they might pass out soon from singing the chord for so long. They weren't going to be able to hold on for much longer.

I took a deep breath. With as much calm as I could manage, I motioned with my hand for them to let go of the chord and move on to the next piece. Their faces melted with relief. I crept out to the center of the stage as they sang the beginning of "Father Figure." Why did such a slow song sound like it was moving at a hundred miles per hour? My throat was starting to close up.

They got to the eighth and last measure of the intro. Time for me to sing. I stared blankly out into the audience. Not a single thing came out of my mouth.

Confusion rippled behind me. Some of the guys stopped singing momentarily. Quickly, they realized they needed to regroup. They repeated the first four bars of the verse accompaniment. Then again. Over and over. They kept vamping until I could find my way back when I was ready. *If* I'd ever be ready. With all of the moisture now totally gone from my mouth, I was positive that moment was never going to come.

Then I saw Emmett. He was leaning forward out of his seat so much that he was falling out of it. He mouthed something to me. I shook my head. I was horrible at reading lips. I couldn't understand what he was trying to say.

The Obertones tensed behind me. Their singing became more rigid. They were losing faith that I'd be able to do this.

Emmett pointed to his ear.

Oh.

"Listen," he was saying. *What do you hear?*

I closed my eyes. The Tones sang louder, singing my own arrangement back to me. I heard them trying to buoy me up. I felt their support. I listened even harder and heard Emmett in my ear.

We're going to be fine.

I opened my eyes. All I could see was him. He'd been telling me how much he believed in me. I waited for the right beat and started to sing. In that moment, I felt as if Emmett were singing with me. Just the two of us onstage. Together.

I sang, pleading for the object of my affection to put their hand in mine. I'd be their preacher. Their teacher. Anything they had in mind.

The words rang with crystalline clarity. I'd never really

understood the song until that moment. Emmett was watching me. Looking out for me. Somehow fueling my voice as if he were somewhere deep inside me. I'd never felt so good in my entire life. I wanted the strange symbiosis to keep going—me on the stage singing and him out there supporting me. The opposite of how we usually were.

The last refrain. I gave a vow to love until the end of time.

Everything went quiet. I looked out to see Emmett's reaction. He smiled and winked.

The bubble of silence popped, and sound flooded in. Cheers and clapping echoed in my ear. Only then did I even realize that the song was over.

Emmett jumped to his feet. In typical fashion, everyone followed his lead.

I'd done it. I'd made it through my solo *and* led the Tones through a fantastic performance. As good as, or hell, maybe even better than the Beelzebubs.

And I knew that it was all because Emmett was there for me.

We bowed and ran off the stage. All fifteen of us bunched up together in the wings.

"Nice work, guys," I said to them. "We did good."

"Better than good! We were the fucking bomb! Booyah!" Shane said, punctuating it by punching his fist in the air.

This set everyone off like firecrackers. They ran around yelling and grabbing one another by whatever body parts they could hold on to. Someone threw their arms around my chest from behind. Shane, I assumed, until I inhaled the familiar smell of tree bark and leather.

Emmett.

He'd come running up to the backstage area. He engulfed me in warmth, with a feeling that everything in the world was perfect. The same as I'd just felt out onstage. He spun me around to face him and pulled me in close.

And then I felt it.

A stiffening. Down there.

Not from me. (Although my body mirrored his *very* quickly.) My instinct was to pull away, to avoid the embarrassment of what was happening.

Emmett pulled me in even tighter. Did he have any idea what our bodies were doing? Was it just, I don't know, friction?

Whatever it was, *why*ever it was, Emmett didn't seem to care. In fact, it seemed as if he wanted me to know. He was holding me so close that I could hear his heart pounding. Or maybe it was mine. Whoever's it was, it was telling me something.

It was telling me it was time to stop denying how I felt about Emmett.

It was time for me to be honest and tell him.

Chapter 18—Now

"WHAT ARE YOU doing here?" I ask Emmett.

"Nice to see you again, too," he says. "Can I come in?"

My dad brushes past me. "Yes, come in! Come in! Oh my god, Emmett. It's so good to see you again." He throws his arms around Emmett, who hands me the gift-wrapped picture or whatever it is he's holding, to better return the hug. My dad rests his head on Emmett's chest, smiling so hard that his eyes water.

"Mr. Cruz, you haven't changed one bit."

My dad pulls back and laughs up at Emmett. "Naku, what a flatterer!" he says, and pulls Emmett into the living room. "Quito, get the suitcase."

I drag Emmett's carry-on inside and close the door. "Would someone please fill me in, because I am clearly being left out of the loop. Emmett, you haven't responded to any of my texts. Why are you here all of a sudden?"

He and my dad look at each other and grin sheepishly.

"Anak, why don't you sit down? I'll get some coffee for Emmett while he tells you everything."

"Gee, thanks, Mr. C," Emmett says.

He unzips his track jacket, sits down on the couch, and motions for me to take a seat next to him.

I eye him warily, not moving. I sit, finally, in my dad's recliner, a few feet away.

Emmett looks at me for a second before erasing all the space between us by scooting over to the end of the couch closest to me.

He leans over onto his knees, which are now so close that they almost bump mine. I smell the leather of his high-end running shoes and the soapy-clean detergent smell of his pants.

"Your dad told me you might need some help with the kids while he's out of commission."

"No. Yes. I mean, maybe—but I can handle it on my own, thanks. More importantly, how the hell did my dad tell you that?"

"He called me."

"He has your phone number?"

"He's *had* my phone number."

"What? For how long?"

"For many years now," my dad said. He's holding an oversize mug of coffee, steaming and so sweet with sugar and cream that I can smell it from across the room. He sits down next to Emmett.

Emmett takes the coffee from my dad, blows on it, and sips. The super-sweetness of it makes his eyes widen. "Yeah, we talk every few months, actually."

"So you—you've both been . . . ?"

A years-long hidden history exists between Emmett and my father. An entire relationship I've never been aware of.

"Dad, you knew Emmett and I hadn't talked in years. But you never said anything about it to me."

"I knew you stopped talking. Emmett would never tell me why. That was your business. I didn't want to get involved."

My face burns. I don't want to talk about our college fallout in front of my dad. "So, if you two have been so chummy all these years, why didn't you just call Emmett and ask him to sing for the concert yourself?"

"He did," Emmett says. "The day before you and I ran into each other in the bathroom."

"The bathroom?" my dad asks.

"Long story," I say. I think back to *Saturday Night Live*. I knew there was something funny about the way Emmett asked me about how my dad was doing. Like he already knew. The same for when I filled him in on my life—as if everything I said were things he'd already heard. Which he probably had. From my dad.

"Wait," I say. "So, then, why did you make *me* ask Emmett?"

"It was long past time for you two to start talking to each other."

My dad had decided to just go and manipulate the events in my life. As usual.

"Unbelievable." I fall back so hard in the chair that the back reclines and the footrest pops up. I nearly go flying off it. Both Emmett and my father start laughing.

"Hahaha." I pull the chair back up. "Yes, very funny. The joke's on me."

"I'm sorry, anak. I should have told you. But now that Emmett is here, why don't you talk? Decide how he can assist you with the concert."

I turn to Emmett. "You couldn't be bothered to answer my texts, but now that my *dad* asked, you've come all the way here to help?"

"Help with the choir, yes. But also with your dad."

"Susmaryosep! I'm fine. Don't worry about me. I don't need a babysitter."

"Hold on," I say. "That's a great idea."

Taking over for my dad at school has been rough. The kids barely respect me as it is. If I brought Emmett into school early, they'd be focused on him, and I'd lose any of the attention they had for me completely. There's no way I'd be able to get them ready in time. Best to work with Emmett on music separately and bring him in for just the last few days, after the kids are in good enough shape to risk being disrupted by his megastar presence. Plus, if he were at school, the choir kids wouldn't be the only ones affected. The teachers, the staff, and the rest of the students would be distracted for weeks. Everyone at school.

Including me.

With Emmett at my side, I'd have every eye on me. It's an occupational hazard of being friends with him that I learned about a long time ago. You can never just recede into the background. With Emmett, I'd always be in the spotlight. And I've never been comfortable with that.

But if he stayed at our house instead of going into school, he could keep an eye on my dad during the day, so I wouldn't have to worry about how he was doing. Emmett could relieve some of my stress *and* not prevent me from doing my job.

"How long can you stay?" I ask.

"I cleared my calendar," Emmett says. "Rehearsals for the play I'm doing at the Mark Taper Forum are coming up in late June, but I've got my script so I'm good."

"I can handle the choir alone," I say.

My father begins to open his mouth.

"For now," I say to him. "But maybe . . . you could stay with my dad for a while, Emmett?"

"Huh. Yeah, sure. How about it, Mr. C? Want to help me learn my lines?"

"So what, you will just hide here with me all day long?"

"Well, I generally try to keep a low profile when I'm visiting friends and family. You don't know how the paparazzi can get. Those guys can be real assholes."

Paparazzi. I hadn't even considered that. In New York, people tend to be respectful of celebrities' space. We get excited about them, sure, like at Broadway Baby when Emmett showed up unexpectedly. But there are so many famous people in New York City that the antics of gossip sites angling for a good scoop are pretty well dispersed among everyone, so no one gets too hard of a time. It'd be different in the Bay Area. Our celebrities are mostly boring tech moguls. Once word got out that Emmett was around, he wouldn't be left alone. *We* wouldn't be left alone.

"And then you will just go back to your hotel room at night?" my dad asks. "People will see you coming and going there."

"I'm at the St. Regis. They're pretty good about being discreet. They set me up with an entrance through the back."

"Forget all that cloak-and-dagger stuff. You just stay here, in the spare bedroom."

Oh. No. I shake my head uncontrollably. That's not a good idea at all. Emmett definitely cannot stay here. That is a horribly—

"Great idea!" Emmett claps his hands together.

"But... the spare bedroom has all your exercise equipment in it, Dad."

"Yes, yes, most of those things are still in their boxes. Easily moved. Good thing I never got around to using any of them."

"Come on Quito. It'll be just like high school," Emmett says.

"You never lived with us in high school."

"I mean, I basically did. I was here, like, every other day."

Not quite, I think to myself. Even though I wanted him to come home with me every day.

Emmett's long arms go wide as he gets more worked up. "And it'll be way easier to practice music for the concert together. When you're done with the kids at school, you and I can go over our songs here. Just like old times." Emmett snaps his fingers. "Ah, speaking of which—" He grabs the gift-wrapped picture leaning against his luggage. "This is for you, Quito."

"For me?"

"My mother cleared out most of the old stuff she had in her condo when she moved in with her new husband. She gave it to me, but I thought you should have it."

I pull back the wrapping paper and see sheet music displayed in a wooden picture frame.

"'A Part I Play.' How did your mom get this?"

"Don't you remember?" Emmett asks. "I gave it to her as a birthday present our senior year."

Sunlight through the living room window glints off the glass covering, making the song glow.

"You gave this to your *mom*? I thought you gave it to your girlfriend. Angela."

"Angela? Why would I have done that? Nah, it was for my mom's fortieth birthday. Music was this bond that we had because it was the one thing she defied my dad to support me on, remember? This was my first solo performance ever. I figured it'd be the perfect gift for her."

"Angela said . . . I just thought . . . " She said she'd seen the music and had played through it. I had assumed the gift was for her.

All these years I thought he'd given a part of me away to a girl.

The notes come alive in my mind as I scan them. I look up from the music, and Emmett is smiling at me knowingly, as if he can hear the song, too. I want to go over to him, hug him, thank him for giving my song to his mother—not Angela—and for giving it back to me. But my dad's flip-flopping stares between the two of us are making the back of my collar itch, so instead, I just say, "Thanks, Emmett."

"You're most welcome."

"And I don't have any problem with you staying here."

As I get up to finish getting ready for school, I notice my dad and Emmett glance at each other briefly and nod, but since I'm running late and have a ton of work to do before choir starts, I don't think about it too long.

That afternoon, when I get back from yet another unproductive day at school with the choir kids, Emmett and my father are sitting on the couch together, eating Hawaiian pizza and watching the opening scene to *The Catwalk Killer*.

"Oh, Quito. Nandito ka na pala. You're just in time. Do you know what this is?"

"Yes, Dad." I toss my messenger bag next to the coffee table. "Emmett's movie debut."

"The best acting of my entire career," Emmett says.

"I wouldn't go that far."

He throws a chunk of pineapple at me. I try to dodge it, and it hits me on the forehead.

Emmett laughs, almost choking on his pizza. "Wow, you still have zero athletic ability."

"Yeah, we can't all be action movie studs like you."

"A stud, huh?"

"What?" I say, sitting down at the far end of the couch from Emmett. "Stud, spud. Whatever. Just saying, I've always been athletically ungifted, that's all."

"One of the many things I like about you," Emmett says. "Anyway, you've got your talents, and I have mine."

I glance at my dad, who doesn't seem to be as embarrassed as I am by our interaction. He hasn't been listening at all, in fact. He's too busy watching the movie. A busty brunette model is taking her shirt off in a room filled with creepy dress form mannequins and ancient-looking sewing machines. Emmett's character, a young fashion student, watches her, although one could argue the target of his passionate gaze is actually the intricate lace of her see-through bra, not what it conceals.

"I remember watching this back in college." I sit down on the couch next to Emmett. "You and I hadn't...ah...talked in a while, and I didn't know what you'd been up to. Then one day senior year, I walk into the Apollo Theatre off-campus to watch the new horror movie that had just come out, and there you were."

Emmett and the girl on-screen, both nearly naked, are going at it hot and heavy in the dark fabric warehouse. I try not to notice how engrossed my father is by the scene.

"All three minutes of me," Emmett says.

"You managed to do something with this dinky little appearance, though. It launched your career. There were practically no famous Asian American actors back then. Barely any on TV and less in the movies. But when I saw you there, larger than life, just like I'd always remembered you, I knew you were going to buck the trend. You were always going to be a star. It was only a matter of time before the rest of the world realized it."

The girl screams. On-screen, Emmett grabs her hand and flees with her down an empty hallway. After a few seconds, he trips and falls. The girl, pausing briefly, screams and keeps running off without him. Emmett turns around to see a masked killer holding a pair of bloody scissors and then turns back. The camera zooms in on his face, filling the screen with his utter terror.

Emmett grunts. "Kind of embarrassing how bad I am in this."

"You were great," I say.

My dad, mindlessly chewing on his pizza, waves in our general direction without looking at us. "Shhhh."

"America fell in love with you with a single appearance," I whisper.

The movie's soundtrack swells, and movie-Emmett's scream rings out and ends with a ripping sound. The music stills to nothing. A gush of wetness fills the silence.

"Well, looks like I'm done. Want to go talk about music?"

"Sure," I say.

"Shhhhh!!" my dad hushes.

Emmett smiles and shakes his head. He takes another slice of pizza and motions for me to follow him into the kitchen. I close the folding door behind us, leaving my dad to watch the rest of the *Catwalk Killer*'s designer do-ins.

"Your dad cracks me up."

"I'm glad someone thinks he's funny."

"You know you've always had the best dad ever." Emmett pulls out one of the wooden dining chairs, swings it around, and straddles it as he sits. "He's always been more of a father to me than mine."

"I knew that was true back in high school. But, apparently, he's been parenting you for a lot longer than that." I lean against the kitchen counter. "So, how *did* you guys start talking to each other? How did he even get in touch with you in the first place?"

Emmett takes a bite of pizza, chews thoughtfully, and swallows. "He wrote me a fan letter, believe it or not. Right after *The Catwalk Killer* came out. Remember when people still sent actual letters? He said he was proud of me. My own dad never told me that. But yours did. I reread that letter so many times, my fingers smudged the ink on the sides of it." He pauses, staring off into space for a moment. "He scribbled a phone number at the end of it and told me to call him anytime I needed someone to talk to. So I did."

"Why?"

"I was lonely. I'd call my mom, but she's never been great on the phone. I was still feeling out of my league in Hollywood. It's a tough town. Big and isolating. I guess I needed someone to remind me of home."

"Then you told him that we weren't talking to each other anymore."

"Not at first. He'd ask me if I'd spoken to you, and I'd just say we hadn't talked recently. That I was too busy. I skirted around it. Then one day I was... thinking about you. So I called him. Asked him how you were doing. I told him the truth. That we hadn't spoken since college. But he never asked why. I think he could tell I didn't want to talk about it. He didn't want to force anything."

The edge of the counter digs into my lower back. I straighten up and lean my elbow against it instead, but for some reason, I can't find a more comfortable position. "Emmett. About that night at Oberlin—"

"You know, Quito, I was thinking I should sing 'A Part I Play' for the concert."

He doesn't quite look at me when he says that. His body seems to be in two different places at once, slouched over the chair, amiable, eager to talk about music yet also hiding rigidity in certain parts—his neck and shoulders, his balled-up fists. He doesn't want to talk about that night together. He wants to move on.

"Um, all right," I say. "Well, actually, I had another idea for you." I've been mulling something around in the weeks since he'd agreed to participate in the concert. I know that denying Emmett the chance to sing my song again will upset him, but I also know he'll understand.

"You don't want me to sing your song?"

"That's not it. I just have other plans for it."

"Okay." He attempts to extinguish the look of disappointment on his face. He compensates, in that very Emmett way, with extra swagger. He jumps up and stands next to me. "Well, if I can't sing *your* song, how about another song that reminds me of you?"

He closes his eyes and begins nodding his head, bobbing in time to some internal metronome. He's so close to me that I can feel him as he prepares to sing, taking in all the air around me.

He sings George Michael's "Father Figure" to me, all its lyrics sensual and pleading. My face flushes. A feeling I definitely do not want to be having in my parents' kitchen roils in my lower regions.

I cut him off. "Yeah. How about something not so much about sex for a high school choral concert? Thanks."

"Am I wrong, or are you looking a little bothered there, dude?"

I want to tell him the truth. That yes, anytime he sings to me, it feels as if he's located the pent-up longing inside me and set it free, out in the open for all to see. That thinking about that night after the Acappellooza concert, even with all the unsettled drama, still sends a shiver down my torso and into my groin.

But I can't. I have a boyfriend. And Emmett has...Emma Chen. Maybe. I still haven't figured out if they have any sort of real connection at all.

"What about 'True Colors' instead?" I ask. It's a simple song, but one I know Emmett could really deliver well. It feels so appropriate for him. And—in some ways—for both of us.

"Ooh. I like that song. It could work."

"And maybe for a second selection—"

"I already know what that second one's going to be. I'm keeping that one a surprise," he says.

"How are we supposed to practice it if you don't tell me what it is?"

"You won't need to accompany me."

"You're singing it a cappella?"

"You'll see." He cocks an eyebrow. "You've got your secrets. I have mine."

"Tease." I poke him in the ribs.

Emmett freezes.

Oh. I shouldn't have touched him like that. I've overstepped a boundary. I...burst into laughter as Emmett digs all of his fingers into the sides of my body and tickles every inch he can find. "HAHAHAhahahahaha!"

"Hoy!" My dad's yell pierces through the kitchen door. "Ang ingay nyo! Quiet, please! I cannot hear the TV!"

We cover our mouths, trying to smother our laughs, which end up bubbling through our fingers.

"The movie will be done in about an hour and a half," Emmett says, still half giggling. "We can work on 'True Colors' then, right?" He pulls one of my dad's San Miguel beers out of the refrigerator. "Want me to grab some more pizza from the living room?"

"Actually, I need to take care of something really quick. I'll meet you in the living room when Dad's done watching the movie." I've forgotten that I needed to answer Mark's check-in email from earlier this morning. Plus, I need to tell him about the whole Emmett situation. I wasn't going to make the same mistake twice in not coming clean about all things Emmett-related. There was nothing to worry about, anyway. Emmett was just here to help me with my dad and to prepare for the concert. He's just staying at our house to avoid being seen. That's it.

But as I head back to my bedroom, I pass by the spare, where Emmett has settled in. His track jacket is draped over the side of a chair, and his clothes are all already unpacked and hanging in the closet, organized by color. A black binder lies open on the desk, its pages marked with pink highlighter. The room already even smells of him, sweet with an underlying dusky warmth. Only one thin wall will separate me from Emmett and the space he's already saturated with his essence. Tonight I'll be sleeping in the room right next to his.

Just like what happened that night in college.

Or, rather, how it was *supposed* to have happened.

Chapter 19—Then

I TORE THROUGH all the clothes hanging in my closet, going through everything at least twice, and I still wasn't able to decide on anything. Why hadn't I brought more options from home? I'd packed an entire suitcase full of music scores to bring to Oberlin. I should've left some and brought more polo shirts instead.

It was only after I pulled out the same shirt for the third time that I noticed my hands were shaking.

After I finally broke off my awkward embrace with Emmett backstage at Finney Chapel, he went around congratulating everyone whose hand he could manage to shake.

"Party at Love Shack!" one of the Tones had yelled at us as we all filed out of the church.

"Hey," Emmett said, "we're going to whatever club that is, right?"

"It's not a club." There were no clubs near campus. Oberlin was in the middle of absolutely nowhere. "Love Shack's an off-campus house. A few of the Trebs live there," I said, meaning members of the all-girl group Nothing But Treble.

"Sounds fun."

My head was still reeling from the performance. And our hug. The hundreds of different thoughts running through my head were hard to manage, but they were slowly coalescing into something. A plan.

"You go on ahead," I said. "Just tag along with Shane. I want to drop by my room first."

He looked slightly confused but let it go. "Okay. Just don't be late."

"Later, gator."

He ran after Shane, leaving me standing on the sidewalk, already going through my clothes in my head and obsessing over what to wear.

In the end, I settled on black jeans and a shirt with a red horizontal stripe, one button left unfastened at the top. It made me feel scandalously slutty.

I examined myself in the mirror. Rolled my sleeves up. Unrolled them. Rolled them back up again. Buttoned the top button. Unbuttoned it. Added extra gel to my hair. Splashed on more cologne. Decided it was too much and wiped it off with a towel.

The bedside clock glowed eleven o'clock in bright red. The party would be in full effect now. Emmett hadn't really had a chance to see my room yet. We'd dumped his suitcase off on Jayesh's side before running to the Con to rehearse my song cycle. My desk was a mess of music manuscript paper and theory books strewn haphazardly across it. A half-eaten cheeseburger stolen from Dascomb Dining Hall was wrapped up in napkins and sat on the corner.

My bed was made, though. The sheets and pillowcases had just been washed. I formed my music into a single stack and threw the cheeseburger in my garbage can. Good enough.

On the way out, I grabbed a small case of mints from my desk. Just in case.

Love Shack was crammed by the time I arrived. People had been squeezed out of the house like toothpaste, forced onto the porch, patio steps, and the sidewalk. Cigarette smoke wafted in the colorful lights still trimming the patio some five months after Christmas.

Inside, Nolan Botts, a jazz guitarist from the Con, was DJing a set of early-eighties dance songs from behind a faded couch. Everyone's conversations were several decibels above normal in order to be heard over Katrina and the Waves blasting from the speakers. I smelled hard alcohol mixed with patchouli and marijuana smoke, all tinted with the funk of spring fever hormones.

One of the Obertones waved at me from the kitchen. "Yo, Maestro!" Jordan was a sexually ambiguous women's studies major with consistently fresh-smelling breath and even better-smelling hair, so he was lusted after by pretty much the entire college. Singers from several of the visiting a cappella groups surrounded him, still wearing their concert outfits. "Wicked concert tonight, right?" he said. "You did a great job leading us."

"Thank you."

"We're doing the same songs again tomorrow for that alumni lunch thingy, yeah?"

My nerves, already frazzled, sparked at Jordan's reminder. But the benefit luncheon wasn't going to be as nerve-racking as the concert. We'd be the only group performing besides a string quartet from the Con. And besides, Emmett would be there again. I'd managed to get him a ticket to the lunch, which had cost me most of my spending money for the month, but I needed him to be there. "Yes. Same set."

"Cool beans." Jordan nodded affably. "So, what do you want to drink?" His big baritone voice boomed even above the blasting music. He opened cabinets to look at the available liquors. I vaguely recalled that Jordan's sister, Alex, was one of the Trebs living in the house.

"Have you seen Emmett anywhere?" I asked.

Jordan poked through the bottles, sorting through and organizing them. Not by type but by color. He burped and then giggled at himself. "Uh, I think I saw him go upstairs with a bunch of girls from that Wooster group."

I couldn't help but frown. "Make me a Long Island Iced Tea. Super strong."

"You got it, Maestro," Jordan said, pouring with abandon.

Though the house was Treble territory, the Tones had been entrusted to run the show. They were infamous for their parties. Hallmarks of an Obertones-hosted party were surprisingly competent DJs, tons of weed, and generous open bars, courtesy of Jordan, who was super rich, another reason so many people wanted to get into his pants.

At first their bacchanalian culture wasn't something I jibed with. My last experience at a high school party certainly wasn't something I wanted to live through again. But things were different at Oberlin. As an accompaniment and composition double major, I'd made a ton of friends playing piano for people's lessons and writing music for various ensembles and soloists to play and sing. Being in the Conservatory felt as comfortable and safe as being in Sunvalley's choir, except on a much bigger scale. I learned to let go a bit and enjoy. I never developed the taste for beer, but the Tones were more into mixed drinks anyway. And pot. Lots and lots of pot.

Jordan handed me my drink. "Here you go."

I took a sip. Jordan, even as blasted as he already was, made a damn tasty concoction. I tilted my glass at him before making my way through the crowded kitchen to the staircase at the back of the house. It was a typical off-campus student home with outdated appliances and furniture all on its last legs. Everything worn at the edges but homey. Certainly good enough for college students.

The top of the stairs leveled out into a small corridor with two doors on each side. Two bedrooms on the left, bathroom and another bedroom on the right. The bedroom on the right was bright with laughter.

Emmett was sitting on the floor, his legs stretched out in front of him, his arms propping him up from behind as he leaned back. He watched as a girl from Wooster took a too-large hit from the bong in the middle of a circle of people and coughed it back out, laughing afterward. Emmett looked up and practically launched himself at me in the doorway.

"Where have you been?" he asked. "I thought you'd never get here."

I couldn't help but smile. He put an arm around me and led me into the room. "Guys, the amazing Quito Cruz."

I was greeted with kind faces smudged with stupor. I was pleased to see the room wasn't just Wooster girls. There were people from all over, though no other Tones. Mostly visiting a cappella singers and other non-a-cappella Obies.

Emmett pulled me down to sit next to him and immediately rested his head against my shoulder. He must've been completely blitzed to openly do that in front of strangers. I wanted to put my head on top of his but couldn't. Not with so many people around.

One of the Beelzebubs, a linebacker of a guy with a crooked buzz cut, pushed the bong toward me. Pot wasn't really my thing, so I was about to turn it back to him. Then I felt the weight of Emmett's body against mine. I ached to lean in to him, to pull him down on the floor right there and just lie next to him. I changed my mind and took the bong. I brought it to my mouth and inhaled.

Emmett pulled his head up and examined me, brow furrowed. I looked at him as reassuringly as I could. He squinted and then smiled. He must've already had several hits from the bong. I took another hit, smaller this time. Emmett seemed satisfied and put his head back on my shoulder. His body heat amplified the sensation of warmth growing in the center of my chest.

"You okay?" he whispered to me.

"Yes." I was okay. Everything was exactly how it was supposed to be.

One of the Wooster girls noticed that I'd been eyeing her drink. I was, but only because I'd become fixated on the swirling colors, the orange juice mixing with the red cranberry, all swimming around the melting ice cubes like an expressionist painting. She offered it to me. I nodded and took the cup from her hands without saying anything. Talking felt overrated. Better to just ease into the flow of things. Things were so flowy.

I drank. Sour. Sweet. Delicious.

The girl noticed the smile widening on my face. She waved the cup to me. *Keep it*, she mouthed. Hey, I could actually read her lips. Cool.

I drank a little more and offered the rest to Emmett.

The bong was passed around one last time. I went to go for

another hit when Emmett took hold of my hand. *You sure?* his face asked.

I nodded silently. *Yes.* I was sure. I was feeling free. More than I had in a long time. I needed that feeling to keep going. Now more than ever.

I inhaled.

The night went on. Emmett and I whispered nonsense to each other while the circle of people got smaller. That was the only way I could tell that time was actually moving forward—the change in the scenery. Eventually, it was just us and two Oberlin girls who had been talking to each other on a pile of cushions on the floor, their legs and arms tangled around each other. They looked as if they might move on to whatever came next. Probably in that very room.

I swallowed. My head felt like it was filled with cotton. In the middle, a white glow pulsed. I tried to poke at it with my consciousness but wasn't successful.

Emmett rubbed the top of my head. "You ready to go?"

"Mmm." His fingers were massaging my brain.

We stood up, balancing against each other. I was pretty sure I was supporting Emmett's full weight, but it was no problem at all. Like I'd been carrying him my whole life.

Downstairs, the music had wound down to a soft stream. Most of the house had cleared out except for a few people on the threadbare couches talking softly to one another.

Outside, Shane and Jordan were sitting on the patio stoop, taking long, languorous drags of a shared cigarette. Shane let out a steady stream of smoke into the now-cool air. "You calling it a night?" he asked.

"Yep," Emmett said, almost tripping down the stairs.

"Don't kill yourself," Shane said.

I pointed at him. My finger felt longer than usual. "I thought voice majors weren't supposed to smoke."

"I thought musical geniuses were supposed to know how many bars of intro there were before the beginning of their solos," he responded.

"Touché."

Jordan took the cigarette from Shane's fingers. "Good thing you guys are going home together. I don't think you'd make it on your own," he said to Emmett. Though, for some reason, he was looking at me.

"Thanks," I said. "Good night. Great work. On the concert."

Shane laughed and gave me a two-finger salute. "You got it, Maestro. See you at the luncheon tomorrow." Their continued conversation lilted behind as we made our way to my dorm.

It was almost morning. The air was wet with dew. We walked into a bank of mist, and droplets clung to us. My lungs filled with coolness as we walked so close to each other, we were almost holding hands.

What was my plan again? I was going to talk to him. About me. Us. How was I going to do it? I tried to focus, but time was mercurial. At one point, I was convinced that we had been walking for hours. Then, before I knew it, we were back at South Hall.

I was out of time. As I unlocked my dorm room, I realized I'd soon be putting Emmett to sleep in Jayesh's empty bed while I drowned myself in my sheets in a different room. I needed to say something before we'd be separated.

The door unlocked with a click. We entered—and a snore ripped through us like a gatling gun.

Jayesh was asleep in his bed, covers tucked up to his chin. Someone was sleeping next to him, an anonymous series of lumps. Whoever it was was the one snoring.

Jayesh stirred. "Mm," he grunted. "Sorry. Trip canceled," he murmured before falling back asleep. The person next to him kept snoring.

"Shit," I whispered.

"What do we do now?" Emmett asked.

"I guess you're taking my bed," I said, not thinking clearly. We went into my room and closed my door behind us.

"Where are you going to sleep?" Emmett asked.

"The couch. In the lounge." The air in my room felt thick and gauzy. I waded my hand through to reach for the doorknob.

"No." Emmett grabbed my arm. "Stay."

"You're the guest. You get the bed."

"No. I mean, stay here. With me."

This was what I wanted. Right? Or...god...Why weren't my thoughts sticking...? Was he just being a friend? A good friend? My *best* friend. Saying we should just crash in my twin bed. Because that's what buddies would do. Without even thinking twice about it.

He was still holding my hand. For how long? I couldn't remember. All I knew was, I said, "Okay."

I didn't look at him. I couldn't. I tried to take my shoes off and lost my balance, almost falling on top of him. I sat down on my bed. Kept my eyes focused on my feet.

Emmett stood beside my messy desk, not moving, regretting his suggestion (probably). Or he was too drunk and too high to move.

He sat down next to me. We sat there for a minute. Or ten. Doing nothing.

I unbuttoned my shirt, reached down to take off my shoes and socks and threw them on the floor.

Emmett did the same. The unzipping of his pants was so loud that it made the hairs on my neck stand up. He tossed them onto my desk.

I slid behind him, into the bed and under the sheet. I tried to hide myself. I turned on my side, facing the wall.

Breathing was hard. I had to think to make it happen. My head pounded. I clutched the edge of my bedsheet and crumpled it in my hand.

Emmett eased beside me, turning on his side, facing the opposite direction.

We had no room. His back pressed against mine, making a map. The expanse of it went on forever, extending out of our bodies, into the air.

He breathed in. Out. I tried to match him. *Calm down*, I thought. *You're not nervous. Everything is fine. Natural.*

Only, the more I tried to slow my breathing, the more ragged it got. My own body fought against me.

Emmett breathed slower and slower. Was he falling asleep?

"Hey," I whispered. "You still awake?"

No answer.

He'd passed out. The moment was gone. I'd missed my chance. I had to wake him up. Should I shake him? Make some kind of noise?

I started to spiral. All the space in my head funneled into a tiny black hole, sucking me down into it.

Then Emmett said, "Do you have anything warmer than this sheet? It's kind of cold in here."

"You're, uh... you're cold?"

He cleared his throat, likely dry and scratchy from the pot. "Yeah."

I stared into the wall, boring holes into it with my eyes.

I knew what I had to do.

I turned over onto my other side. Slowly. Achingly slowly. My tummy pressed against Emmett's back. I snaked my arm up and over, casually draping it over the side of his body.

I clutched his chest.

My heart exploded.

I realized I couldn't match Emmett's breathing anymore because I'd stopped breathing completely. I was paralyzed, waiting for him to throw my arm off, jump out of bed, move away.

Except he didn't do any of those things.

We stayed that way for so long that I lost all sense of myself. Where I was. When I was. Who I was. I found myself muttering incoherently into the darkness. I tried to hold on to everything in my head but felt it all slip into the black hole now growing, turning into a gaping maw.

In fact, when I looked back on that night, what I'd remember most is how much of it I couldn't really remember at all.

Chapter 20—Now

I WAKE UP to the ping of a new email notification from my phone. I've had only three hours of sleep. Not only did I toss and turn all night, excited by how fruitful and familiar my rehearsal of "True Colors" with Emmett was (and still unnerved by the fact that Emmett was sleeping less than three feet away from me), but it's also only five o'clock in the morning.

Mark's written me back. A quick message before work.

> Hey—
>
> Thanks for letting me know about the situation with Emmett. It's cool that he's helping out with your dad while you guys work on the concert together. You're still going to be okay getting our final song done, though, right?
>
> Hey, maybe you and Emmett can work on it together? Maybe even talk up the show to him? Any involvement from him would help us out tremendously. Just think about it.

Quito, what if you could convince him to come sing for the producer showcase? We'd have to give the current Peter Pan the boot, but who cares. It'd be worth it.

Anyway, just a suggestion.

Can't wait to hear what you come up with. Tell Emmett I said hi and that I think he's a star for helping you guys out.

Miss you,

Mark

He doesn't seem to be concerned about my and Emmett's close quarters at all. That makes one of us, at least.

I turn on my side in the bed and set my hand against the wall. Just on the other side of it, Emmett lies sleeping, completely unaware of the excitement and anxiety that have kept me awake all night.

Mark doesn't care that Emmett's here, so why should I?

Why *should* I?

I can't give in to that hopeless fantasy again, the one where Emmett and I end up together. We're fantastic as friends. And as musical collaborators. Anything more than that...we tried before.

Or rather—*I* tried.

And it didn't work.

Besides, I have a boyfriend. One who's depending on me.

If I can't get back to sleep, I might as well do something productive and work on the last song for, ugh, *The Forever Boys.* (I can't even think of that horrible title without gagging.) I pull up the lyrics on my phone and read through them a few times, trying to let some sort of melody come to me.

Nothing presents itself. First of all, the lyrics are hopelessly banal. I don't get any inspiration from their meaning. Second, the words don't quite scan right—they fumble and halt, never quite attaining any sort of musicality on their own, so trying to come up with a decent line to go with them is almost impossible. I need to try to rework the words to make something actually singable. If Dinesh would be open to that.

Dinesh and Mark, I mean.

But I lack the energy to alter the lyrics. The words just lie there lifeless on my screen.

I decide to text Ujima instead.

I haven't had a chance to tell them about Emmett yet. I could use their advice on that. And maybe Jee can give me some tips about how to get the kids to pay attention to me. They did study to be a music teacher in college for at least two years before switching to a performance major. And Ujima is a master of attention-getting. They know how to command a crowd. And more than that, they've always known how to buoy me. To get me to believe in myself.

Besides, sending texts to Jee is way more fun than altering someone else's bad lyrics.

Quito: Hey, boo. You'll never guess who's sleeping, like, right next to me (kind of)

. . .

[finger on chin emoji]

Emmett :)

My phone vibrates. It's Ujima. Which is impossible because, unless they're attending an open-call audition, they never get up any earlier than 10:00 a.m.

"Explain yourself." Jee's voice is so raspy that it sounds like the signal's being broken up by static.

"Hey," I whisper, "I didn't mean to wake you. Go back to sleep. I'll text you the story."

"Girl, I don't know what possessed me to look at the text you sent me, but now that you've tittie-lated me and ruined the rest of my beauty sleep, you better tell me everything. Why are you sleeping with Emmett? How did you manage to get into his pants? And what are his measurements?"

I crawl into the closet on the other side of the bedroom and slide the door closed. "He's not in my bed. He's in the room next to me. He flew here early to help with the choir. Except I'm not letting him. So he's keeping an eye on my dad instead while I'm at school. And my dad made him stay here. With us. In the room next to mine."

"Have you notified the nineties? Because this sounds like the setup for a bad sitcom."

"I know. But at least I already told Mark, and he's fine with it."

"Well, thank *god* Mark's happy."

"Be nice, Ujima. I thought you guys were friends now."

"Honey, we ain't ever gonna be actual friends. Friend-adjacent at best."

"Look, I can't think about it right now. I have to focus on the kids. Which I definitely need your advice on, because now that I'm trying so hard not to think about Emmett..."

The closet door slides open. "Why are you trying so hard not to think about me?" Emmett asks. He's wearing boxer shorts and a tank top, and even with a colossal hairlick sticking out from his head at a vertiginous side angle, he looks breathtaking. "And what are you doing in the closet?"

"I'm not in the closet. You're in the closet."

Every single drop of blood in me gushes to my head as I wonder if it's actually possible for my heart to overtax itself and give me a cerebral embolism.

"Hello? Hello?" Ujima says from my phone, which is now hanging lifeless from my hand.

My eyes close slowly. "Jee, I'll call you back."

I hang up and manage to look up at Emmett, who is smirking at me. He yawns. "Want some coffee?"

"Coffee, yes. Please."

He pulls me up from the closet floor, and we head into the kitchen.

"I'm sorry I woke you," I say, watching as he moves around the room, easily locating the coffee grounds, the mugs, the sugar. As if he's lived in our house for years. "I was trying to be quiet."

"It's cool. I'm usually up early to go running anyway. Probably better to do it now before most people in the neighborhood are up, so I can do it in-cog-NEE-to."

The warm, roasted smell of percolating coffee fills the air. Emmett sits down across from me.

"Quito, do you not want me to be here?"

"No. I mean—no, that's not it. It's just...I need to keep focused on helping my dad with the choir. And it's good to see you. Really, really good. But it's also been a long time. We're not the same people we were all those years ago. I just have to remember that we're not those kids anymore."

Emmett looks away, back over his shoulder, and nods, as if agreeing to something some invisible person behind him has just said.

The coffeemaker dings. He pours two mugs full of coffee. "Cream and sugar?"

"No thanks."

"Black it is." He brings both unadulterated mugs to the kitchen table. "I love your dad, and he makes amazing food, but his coffee is not good."

"It's just a little too..."

"Dramatic?"

I smile. "Yeah."

Emmett takes a sip and watches me as I drink. "Quito, your dad wasn't the only reason I came up early, you know. I wanted to see you again."

"Oh. Okay."

"Look, I know we haven't been close in a long time. We didn't exactly part on the best of terms, back in college."

"I've been wanting to talk to you about that—"

"Hold up. Let me finish." He puts his hand on top of mine. The coffee I've just sipped intensifies into something too hot for my mouth. "What I was going to say is that, when I saw you in New York, sitting right in the front row of freaking *Saturday Night Live*, it was both completely surreal and also—I don't know—right? Like we'd both been there before. Or had always been there. You and me, together. Does that make sense?"

I swallow, feeling the coffee burn as it goes down my throat. "Yes, it does."

"Quito, singing that song with you at Broadway Baby? That. THAT made *me* happy. And after I left, watching my mom get married, seeing her be with someone who was actually right for her...I kept thinking how I wish you could've been there with me. My mom was always a fan of yours, you know? She always saw you as a positive influence on me. And you were the one who helped me to see that she was just trying to do her best back then. For me. Because you've always known me better than anyone. That's the me and you I want to remember. Everything else, I just want to let go. I've just been trying to figure out a way to tell you that for the past few weeks."

Emmett watches me. And waits. His hand, still on mine, is bigger and heavier than anything I've ever felt. As if nothing could separate it from me.

"I'm happy you're here," I finally say. "I promise."

My hand squirms for a second. When Emmett lifts his off, I turn mine over and quickly grasp his, bringing it back down to the table.

"But can we just make sure my dad gets the send-off he deserves? And also enjoy the time we have together? Just...let's not think about it too hard?" I say, as much to myself as to Emmett.

He smiles. "Deal."

A hacking sound comes from down the hall. We let go of each other's hands.

"Hoy, no coffee for me?" my dad says as he wanders into the kitchen.

"Go for your run, Emmett," I say. "I got this."

Evenings at home fly by. Sometimes when I get back home from school, I continue to chip away at the final song for *The Forever Boys*, but mostly, I spend it with Emmett and my father. As my dad's energy has improved, he's been cooking more. He started with easier dishes like tinola—chicken soup with garlic, ginger, green papaya, and fresh watercress—and has gradually been making more intricate dishes and desserts for us. Sometimes he permits us to help him, like when we chop vegetables to be mixed with shrimp, chicken, and Chinese sausage for Emmett's favorite noodle dish, pancit. Or when we roll a savory meat mixture into spring roll wrappers to make lumpiang Shanghai, fried until they're so crispy and addictive that we can't stop eating them until they're all gone. But usually he insists he's fine on his own and pushes us out into the living room to rehearse for the concert.

We continue to practice Emmett's "True Colors." He's asked for a jazzier rendition, something like the way he'd heard Michael Bublé sing at a recent Hollywood Bowl concert. I oblige him, but I also throw him a few curveballs and sometimes segue into different styles. Reggae. Doo-wop. Classical. He always manages to keep up, though he swears at me the whole time.

After that song feels solid, we move on to other songs. Older songs. Things he hasn't sung in years. Not for the concert, but for the simple joy it brings the two of us to be making music together.

I spend less and less time working on the song for Dinesh and Mark. Even though Mark's told me they already have the cast up on its feet, learning the other songs and working on simple blocking for the rest of the first act, I can't bear to pull myself away from the fun Emmett and I are having—him singing by my side, filling a space that's been empty for so long.

One that Mark or this new musical should be filling, though neither of them really do.

I try not to think about it too much. I can't. Watching over my dad and rehearsing for the concert must be my main priorities. In some ways, they're almost the same one—making sure Emmett and the choir are fully prepared is the best way I can think of to make sure Dad is happy and healthy.

But while the evenings with Emmett are a joy, the days with the kids continue to be a struggle.

My father still doesn't believe I'm having any problems with the choir, even when I beg him to give me some pointers. When I tell Emmett about the situation, he's the same. Their unwavering belief in me is nice, but I'm still in the same situation: in a slowly sinking choir boat with me at the helm.

After a few more days of me struggling and failing to get the choir to a level worthy of the most important concert of my father's career, I text Ujima again to get the advice I'd been meaning to solicit from them.

Quito: Jee, please tell me how to get these kids to listen to me.

Ujima: They are. Kids just always look like they hate you, but they don't. Mostly. Just put your big girl panties on and stop complaining.

How much longer do you have to sub, anyway? I thought your dad was doing ok?

Quito: He is. At least I think he is. But he says he's not ready to go back. It's weird, he loves his job. Not sure why he's avoiding going back.

Ujima: hmmmm

Quito: Yeah.

How are things with you, btw?

Ujima: Good news and bad news. Pick.

Quito: Bad first.

Ujima: Of course :-P

Quito: You know me so well.

Ujima: ONE-derland is closing.

Quito: What? When?

Ujima: Well . . .

yesterday.

Quito: Oh no! I'm SO sorry.

Ujima: But some good news—

I got some business in the Bay Area, so I can come visit y'all! I'll get to see you and your dad. And my future husband, of course.

Quito: Slow your roll, there, Jezebel.

Ujima: ;-)

Also, maybe I can help you with those kids while I'm there. I wasn't the best music ed student but I remember a few things.

Quito: Yes! Please! When are you coming? Also: why??

Ujima: More deets later. I'm taking a red-eye, getting into SFO early next Tuesday morning. Will be there about a week. Maybe longer.

Can you pick me up from the airport?

Quito: Of course.

Ujima: Good. Thank you! Ta-tas!

A visit from Ujima would be a true gift. For the kids *and* for me. Jee could provide a different perspective on things. Give me a supportive boost. Get the students to open up. Something. Anything to help me get through to them.

When I first arrived at Sunvalley High School, the situation seemed much more positive than I'd envisioned. The choir kids were so glad I'd come to save them that they broke out into an impromptu rendition of *The Wiz*'s "Brand New Day"—like those videos of the cast of *The Lion King* suddenly breaking out into "Circle of Life" at the airport, or the subway, or at Filene's Basement, any place they happened to all be together. (Why were they always together?) I'd never believed people actually did that sort of thing. But there they all were, harmonizing their silly teenage faces off.

They had several reasons for celebrating, I guess. I was Mr. Cruz's son. I had big-time New York experience. And because of me, they'd soon be meeting Emmett Aoki. Not to mention the fact that my arrival meant their nemesis, Mr. Drummond, was done for, melted into a puddle of mismatched socks and bad comb-over hair. It must have felt like a brand-new day for them indeed.

Then things started going astray. As if their acne-prone noses could smell that I was anxious, slightly resentful of needing to be there in the first place, and had no business taking over for my dad. I tried to use their initial enthusiasm to hold positive rehearsals. But nothing I did seemed to work.

Now, on this overcast Friday morning in the choir room, there is no breaking out into song. No celebrating. Just a bunch of faces broadcasting at me: *You suck*. I wrestle with a mass of music from my messenger bag and finally just toss the pile on top of the piano before it can all fall apart.

Celeste springs from her seat. "Can I help with any of that, Mr. Cruz?"

I wonder if she knows that her oversize polka-dot dress does absolutely nothing for her, hiding her body instead of showing how beautiful she really is. "We've been over this before, Celeste. Just Quito is fine."

She winds and unwinds her brown hair around her finger and keeps balancing from leg to leg, never quite finding the right position to stand still in. I worry that, if I don't give her something to do, she might burst into an explosion of polka-dot dress confetti.

"Actually, why don't you help me reorganize these copies and start handing them out to everyone?"

"You got it, Mr. Qui—uhh, Quito. Cruz. Sir!"

One of the sopranos in the front row rolls her eyes and keeps scrolling through whatever she's reading on her phone with her painted-black nails.

While Celeste and I sort the sheet music, I see that one of the boys is sitting in the middle of a ring of empty chairs. I noticed he hadn't spoken a single word to anyone since I arrived, but he's even more self-isolated today. He's a tiny kid with hair so blond that it's almost white. I wish I could remember his name. Melvin? Merlin? I've tried to memorize everyone's name. So far I've only been able to remember Celeste's.

She stands at attention next to me at the podium after handing out all the music.

"Thank you, Celeste."

Her body pulsates with the need to do more, help more. I sigh and use my lips to point to her chair. She dwindles with resignation as she takes her seat.

We've managed a complete run-through of almost every song on the concert program at least once. And they all sound... competent. I can never get them past a basic level of mediocrity. I decide to tackle the "Gloria in D." It's especially tricky in that I have to play the piano *and* somehow conduct the choir at the same time. My dad's always been able to do this by using graceful head gestures as he plays and looking at the choir to cue them at key musical moments. I've been mostly doing a bunch of nonsensical lip and eye movements while I jerk my head around. Not surprisingly, the kids just ignore me.

As I'm about to begin, I hear someone behind me clearing their throat.

"Working on the Vivaldi, I see?"

Someone cries out. Celeste runs past me to the doorway. I turn around to see her tackling my father in a bear hug so forceful that he almost tips over.

Though his face is newly shaven, I can tell he's not here to take over. He'd have worn his standard button-down shirt and khakis instead of the sweats and 49ers hoodie he's thrown on.

The rest of the choir follows Celeste's lead and runs over to him.

"I wasn't expecting you, Dad. Everything okay?"

"I'm fine. I'm fine. Aray! Not too tight, kids," he says. Then, out of the corner of his mouth, "You-Know-Who wanted to run an errand here at the school, so I decided to tag along."

"What?" I whisper. "He's here?"

"Don't worry. He's got on a disguise. He said he only needs about ten minutes or so. I'm just killing some time before we go get some Taco Bell for lunch."

"And you wanted to check on me?"

"Of course not."

Most of the kids have given my dad space, but Celeste is still hanging on for dear life. I'm both touched and a little resentful of the fact that they look like they're on the verge of tears. It's no surprise how much they love him. I was one of them. I remember how much of an impact my father makes on everybody. No matter how many students he has, he's always managed to make a connection with each one, always seeing through to the very core of each kid and finding the potential waiting there. He's turned the most tone-deaf students into competent singers and just average musicians into proficient ones. He empowers them. Shows them how to find joy in music. He makes them happy. How he does this completely eludes me. The very last time I led a group of singers was a disaster—the Benefactors' Luncheon with the Obertones the day after Acappellooza. The day Emmett left me. The day I decided I didn't have any business trying to show other people how to make music. Or to make any of my own.

"Mr. Cruz, are you coming back?" Celeste asks my dad.

"Soon. Quito will still be your teacher for a while."

"Aww." Celeste sags. "I mean, yay." She pumps one fist into the air and smiles at me half-heartedly.

I give my dad a look. *See, I told you.*

He pushes them away. "Go sit down now. Go on. Just ignore me," he says, attempting to shift attention back to me.

I try to strike the right balance between authority and coolness. "All right, all you excellent song makers. Let's all please take our seats. If you don't mind." My words are limp. A poor echo of my dad. "Let's skip the Vivaldi for now. Let's do an a cappella piece—how about the 'Hiney Mah Tov'? From the top." As the kids rearrange their music to switch to the madrigal, my stomach sours in anticipation of my father's inevitable disappointment of what they'll sound like. "Remember to breathe in with the vowel."

Dad drags a chair over and sits next to me. He closes his eyes and tilts his head upward, the state he always settles into when he prepares to listen to something important, as if readying himself to receive signals from above. Memories of him in this exact pose flood my brain—attending my piano recitals, listening to records of great choral works, and sitting in the church pews as my mom would sing.

I smile and inhale. "And..."

The choir breathes with me. A solid entrance. More than solid. It's confident, almost brazen. Their sound is better than I've ever heard it. It takes me by surprise at first. What happened to the lackluster droning from every other rehearsal we've had? Has my conducting really improved that much? Is it because I'm more aware of my technique, now that Dad is—

Ah.

That's it.

They *are* better now, singing their very best.

Just not for me. For him.

I try something. I pull back a little, making my gestures a little less overt. More inelegant. Their energy is the same as before. I do even less. To the point where my hand movements are merely ornamental. A basic bobbing in time. It doesn't make a difference. The choir still sings with everything they have, leaning in or backing away when the music calls for it, almost instinctively. I know it's not instinct, though. It's muscle memory. They're calling up instructions they've been given before. They're imagining my father in front of them. Not me. Why can't Dad see that?

Well, for starters, he's not watching. His eyes are still closed, his face calm throughout the entire song, though his body moves ever so subtly in time to the singing, weaving to and fro with the kids. When it's over, he pops his eyes open. The choir has delivered a prize-winning performance. Too bad nothing I did had anything to do with it.

"Very good, everyone," my dad says. "I see you're in very good hands with my son."

Their faces radiate pride. How do I tell my father that the only hands they should be in are his?

My phone vibrates. A call from Ujima.

"Hey, Dad, can you step in for a second?"

He gives me a look, probably thinking I'll just abandon him completely, a gambit to make him take over.

"It's Ujima. They're planning a trip here...It might be important."

"Oh! That's wonderful!" My dad turns back to the kids. "Okay, kids. That sounded so good. Why don't you sing it for me again?"

They do an encore performance of the song as I go into the office and shut the door.

"What's up, Jee? You can just text me your flight details if that's easier."

"Baby, I just saw something you need to see."

I wait for Jee to continue.

They sigh.

"You're making me nervous," I say.

"Get onto Instagram. I'm gonna text you the name of the user you need to look up." My phone chirps with the text message: *photodabomb_nyc*.

"Should I know this person?" I ask.

"He was our *ONE-derland* photographer."

"Okay."

"Quito! How could you forget an ass like his? Anyway, it's not about him. It's something he happened to take a picture of."

I scroll through the first few lines of pictures until I see familiar faces—including me and Ujima, posing for the camera the night of their show. Then I see it, a picture taken in Twixxy's VIP Lounge. In the foreground, two women, their smiles straining against the unfortunate effects of one too many Botox injections. And directly behind them, not as sharp, but distinct enough: Mark and Dinesh.

Locked in a kiss.

So that's what was going on that evening. I knew I wasn't imagining the tension between them. And even before that I'd sensed there was something more to Mark wanting me to work with Dinesh. Something sublimated. That evening at *ONE-derland*, those underlying currents broke the surface, spilled out, and resulted in the spectacle captured on film now being displayed on my phone.

Was it their first kiss? Possibly. But probably not their last. Not after all the "work" they've been putting in on the show together these past few weeks while I've been gone.

"You still there?" Ujima asks.

The choir has finished singing through another effortless run-through, prompting plaudits from my dad. "I gotta go."

"That's it? No cussing Mark out? I just showed you the receipts that he's a cheating pig. At least let me hear you lose your temper."

"I'm not going to get mad about this, Jee."

"Hmph. And I know the reason, too. Because now you're free like a bird, baby. Spread your wings. Fly on over to that bedroom next door!"

"BYE, Ujima."

I hang up as they yell, "Go on and get yours!" into the phone.

The kids have devolved into boisterous chatter when I reenter the choir room. My father pushes off his chair to stand, his face twisting with effort. "Excellent job, everyone. I see you're in good hands with my son. You're very close now to being able to work with the famous Emmett Aoki. Maybe closer than you think," he says, winking at me. "Quito, I'm going now."

"Wait," I say. "They're not—"

"You were exaggerating, anak. I knew you'd do a good job." He pulls up his sagging jeans. "I think our *mutual friend* must be done with his little errand by now. Besides, I need to take a nap."

"You sure you're okay?" I walk him to the door.

He pats me on the back. "The office told me the concert is oversold now. Principal Higgins says many of the parents are so excited about Emmett that they spent some extra to get the best seats. We will make so much money for the kids. All thanks to you and Emmett." He turns back around to the choir. "Keep it up. See you soon. I promise."

The students wave and yell back goodbyes as my dad shuffles out of the choir room into the empty school hallway. I listen as the slapping of his flip-flops against the floor tiles fades. I want to follow him down the corridor, out into the parking lot, and into the car for Emmett to drive us both home. Or anywhere else. I still have no clue how to direct this choir.

And my boyfriend cheated on me.

What am I going to do?

When school gets out, I find myself filled with an excess of free-floating anxiety. I'm not ready to go home just yet.

I call my dad and tell him to not expect me for dinner, that I need to get a couple of things related to the concert done. Instead, I get into my car and just drive around aimlessly. I venture out beyond town, find myself on the freeway, and end up driving westward through the Caldecott Tunnel and onto the Bay Bridge, trying to sort my thoughts as I go.

Ujima had expected me to be mad at the picture of Mark and Dinesh kissing. But all I felt looking at the two of them together was a smallish, dull thud in my stomach. Not much more. It did hurt me that he'd betrayed me but in a general way—like the pain one feels when someone close to you has lied. Not the bone-crushing agony of my one true love proving himself to be anything but.

Ujima was kidding, but they were probably right. I'm not that upset because I do feel like I've shed something that was holding me back, not lifting me up.

How happy have I actually been with Mark?

The truth is that it doesn't surprise me that Mark cheated. For all the months we've spent together, I always had the feeling that I never made a deep connection with him, never really knew who he was. And, more importantly, that he didn't really know me.

No.

That wasn't exactly it.

Mark has never really known me because I've never truly been myself around him.

Other people are like mirrors. If you look at someone else, you can see your own reflection in them. Or at least a piece of it. And the closer that person is to you, the more pieces of yourself you're able to see. With Ujima, I can see nearly all of myself. My dad reflects back a lot of what I know to be true about me. But with Mark, I don't ever seem to add up. He brings out parts of me that don't feel as if they should go together. Maybe because his vision of me isn't quite right anymore. Maybe it never has been. Maybe it's my fault because I've never shown who I really am to him. Then again, Mark has never brought it out in me, either.

My eyes should be welling up with tears from the betrayal. But they're dry as a bone.

As I cross the bridge into San Francisco, the setting sun filters through the buildings, throwing columns of light my way. It's beautiful. I can't help but smile.

I wind my way through the city and end up at the top of Twin Peaks. It's been years since I've seen this view. I step out of the car and look out on the landscape of lights all just beginning to twinkle awake. The wind up here is merciless, but I don't mind. The cold feels good. Invigorating. A reminder of the human capacity to feel pain.

And the ability to overcome it.

Chapter 21—Then

IN THAT SPLIT second upon waking, I had no idea where I was. The bedsheet in my hand felt unfamiliar, the furniture in my dorm room strange. I sat up quickly in a panic and then immediately regretted it. Light and sound converged into a tiny point in my frontal lobe and exploded like a shrapnel grenade. I grabbed my forehead, leaned over, and threw up on the floor.

"Gross." I wiped my mouth with the back of my hand and looked around for something to clean the mess with. A used bath towel on my dresser was the nearest option. My legs nearly gave out as I made my way over to it.

The person looking back at me in the mirror was unrecognizable. My hair stood up at awkward angles, and my eyes flamed red with a maze of veins.

I blinked. Then blinked again.

Emmett.

I threw open the door adjoining my room to Jayesh's. The sound woke him and the person sleeping next to him on the bed. Insanely, I hoped it was Emmett.

The lump of unflattering clothes and clumpy hair lifted its head up and looked at me with lazy bedroom eyes.

"What's up, cutie?" it said.

Melina. The sight of her and Jayesh in bed together triggered my gag reflex.

"Are you okay?" Melina asked, her voice ruined from a night of drinking and smoking and who only knows what.

"Have you guys seen my friend? Emmett?" There was no sign of his stuff in my room or Jayesh's. "He was staying with me this weekend. He's supposed to sing for my composition jury today. But he's gone."

Jayesh yawned. I could smell his rotten beef breath from where I stood. "Yeah. I think he, like, left early this morning."

"What do you mean, left? Like, went to get breakfast or—"

"Naw, man, like, *left*, left. He threw his stuff into his suitcase and went out and never came back."

"What time was that?"

"Right after we woke up and had some freaky early-morning sex. Right, babe?"

"Yeah, lover." She looked at me with puckered kissy lips. "Around six o'clock."

I looked at the clock on Jayesh's wall. It was 11:52 a.m. Emmett could be anywhere. I could check the Conservatory. Maybe he just wanted to practice my songs some more. Left early to get some coffee, took his stuff with him so he didn't need to come back here. Or maybe he was already at the Benefactors' Luncheon. Which was at noon.

Eight minutes from now.

The bottom of my stomach fell out. I ran back into my room and, unable to hold it in any longer, threw up again. At least this time I managed to get it into the wastebasket. My knees slammed down onto the plastic tiles of my bedroom floor, and the room spun around in tight circles. I was supposed to have warmed up the Obertones for our performance at the luncheon at eleven thirty. Hopefully, Shane took over for me. We were last on the program, after the lunch had been served. But even that gave me less than an hour to get sober, clean up, and most importantly, find out where the hell Emmett had gone.

"Are you all right?" Jayesh yelled from his room.

"Do you need any help? Some water? A back rub?" Melina added.

"No!" I screamed back. I threw on some clean clothes, tried to wrangle my hair into something more presentable, slipped my shoes on, and ran out.

"Hey! You gonna clean up your acid chowder?" Jayesh's voice trailed behind me as our door slowly shut. "Smells like ass!"

There was no sign of Emmett in South Hall. He had to still be on campus somewhere. I had to believe that he was. I ran around outside aimlessly. The sun high above was bright, digging daggers into my brain. The humid Ohio air was cutting off my flow of oxygen.

I made my way to the Carnegie Building, where the luncheon was being held on the second floor in the cavernous Root Room.

The Tones stood around waiting on the first floor. Shane was pacing back and forth when he saw me come in.

"Jesus, Quito. Where the fuck have you been?"

"Have any of you . . . ?" I could barely make it out, breathless. "Have any of you seen Emmett?"

"Who?"

"Emmett? My friend from USC? He was at the party last night."

"Keanu Reeves?" Jordan asked. Unlike the others, he lay back comfortably on the staircase, probably high.

"What?"

"That's what we were calling him at the party last night. He's got those movie-star looks."

I shook my head, trying to get the nonsensical dribble out of it. "Have. You. SEEN. Him? He's supposed to be at the luncheon."

No response.

Shane said, finally, "I snuck a peek at all the people upstairs. I didn't see him."

"You're sure?" I asked.

"He's hard to miss, Quito. Not a ton of hot people at Oberlin, and that guy is Brad Pitt level."

"Forget it." I tugged at my hair. "Warm up. Then a run-through."

I should have just taken a moment. To breathe, to relax. To focus on the task at hand. The Benefactors' Luncheon was an important event for the school. It usually raked in tons of money from wealthy alumni and other donors. Especially after they listened to the impressive slate of young, world-class musicians from the Conservatory. The Obertones were the uplifting, feel-good dessert served at the end to seal the deal.

But my head was pounding so hard that I couldn't hear my own thoughts. I couldn't center myself. All I could feel was confusion, anger, and resentment from Emmett's absence. The throbbing in my forehead hammered like a series of red-hot rails between my eyes. I couldn't stop it, no matter how many times I tried to blink it away.

"We're gonna rock this!" Shane said.

"Shut up," I said. Shane flinched. "Be serious for once in your life. I don't want you all screwing up and making me look bad."

Jordan's placid smile disappeared. I intoned the starting pitches for "Kiss from a Rose." But my throat was an arid mess. All the notes I sang at them wobbled out of tune precariously. Some were completely incorrect. They looked at me confused, not sure of what to sing. I raised my hand to cue them, "One, two, three, four, five—"

The tenors started singing in two different keys.

"No, no," I said. "Wrong. Start again." Shane started to say something. I cut him off with my hand. An even faster cue this time. Without regiving any pitches. "Four-five—"

An even worse entrance this time.

"What the hell? Get your act together, tenors!"

"Dude," Jordan said, putting his hand on my forearm, which was already raised, ready for yet another doomed start. "They're confused. You need to give better starting pitches."

"I don't need to do anything. They're the ones who sound like crap. Just do your job and sing. Four-five—"

Somehow, maybe through panic, or sheer will, or, more likely, a unified need to vocally kick me in the nuts, they sang—crashing their pitches together for the intro until they met in the middle. We kept going. They managed to make it for another eight measures before I clapped my hands together like a hyperactive walrus. "Stop. Stop. STOP. We can't go on sounding like this. Why does it sound like a hyena orgy? Did you all get completely wasted last night?"

Shane stepped out in front of the circle of Tones, his pointed finger accusing. "Quito, *you're* the one who got hammered. And high. And whatever else you ended up doing with your friend. You're the one making us sound like this. We're all fine. You're clearly not."

Shane was right. I wasn't okay. I was going to mess them up again. Except this time Emmett wouldn't be there to save me.

They stood there, waiting for some kind of apology or reconciliation. Something that would reassure them that whatever was happening to me was just some fluke. That I could shake it off and focus and be the leader they needed me to be.

My skin felt translucent. Like they could all see to the very core of me. Weak. Rotten. My head was killing me. I grabbed the sides of it and tried to squeeze the pain and anxiety and hurt out of it. None of it disappeared. Nothing came out except me saying, "I'm out."

I turned around and left.

"Quito! Hey!" Some of them called out to me as I walked. I kept going and didn't turn around. They were better off without me. In the state I was in, I was only going to lead them into a performance that would sound as horrible as I felt. That's what I told myself, at least, as I made my way to the Conservatory to look for Emmett. I had two hours before my composition jury. Two hours to try to make at least one thing turn out all right.

I crossed through Tappan Square to get to the Con. A few South Hall residents saw me and waved. I ignored them. It was taking all my energy just to keep moving forward.

Why the hell did Emmett leave? What had happened? I tried to focus on remembering the night before and managed to call up a few muddled recollections. Flashes of things I thought I remembered. A party at Love Shack. To celebrate the Tones' performance at Acappellooza. Music. Drinking. A bong. I was there with Emmett. Next to Emmett. I wanted...I wanted to be *with* Emmett. I was trying to figure out a way to let him know how I felt about him. The alcohol and the pot—I did it to loosen myself up, to find some courage. And since Emmett was drunk and high, too, maybe, just maybe, he'd be open enough to my confession.

I couldn't recall the walk home, yet we ended up there somehow. Jayesh was in his bed. Emmett had to sleep with me. Everything was lining up for us to be together.

Then what? What did we do?

What did *I* do?

Emmett was cold, he said. Though I remember his skin burning against mine. Or maybe that was *my* skin. My arm against his chest. Rubbing. Moving downward.

Oh god.

It was coming back to me. The friction of my hand against his erection. Me behind him, trying to focus. To register every second in my head as if I needed to somehow catalog the bits of memories, afraid they'd be gone forever, and failing as almost all of them slipped away, disappearing into a muddled haze.

Wetness in my hand. Between my legs. Someone rolled over. Me or him? As I tried to recall, pain hit me behind my eyes. I blinked hard. The only thing that came back to me was the absolute stillness during all of it. As if we were scared to be heard. As if engaging any more of our senses would have been too much for us to handle in that tiny bed.

Or did we not talk because we were ashamed of what was happening? If we weren't talking, then I wasn't checking in. Which means I didn't ask his permission. The first-year students laughed at the amateur skits during Orientation Week, all the steps required for safe, consensual sex drilled into us by our Resident Coordinators. And yet one of the scenarios had emblazoned itself onto my brain. The one about date rape. Mainly because it had involved two cute upperclassmen. The message came across loud and clear. *No* meant no. And we couldn't automatically assume that silence meant everything was okay. We were supposed to be on the same page at every point during the encounter.

But I'd never asked him if he was okay with what I was doing. I was too far gone. And too afraid he'd say no if I did ask. So instead, I just took advantage of him in his drunken state.

I sprinted the rest of the way to the Conservatory, barreling into the building to retrieve my composition portfolio from my locker. Clutching it tight to my chest, I skidded through the hallway joining the lounge to the practice room building, almost careening into an open door. Emmett *had* to be there. Practicing my songs. The more I thought it, the more important it became for me to believe. Though with every step I took, the plausibility of him being anywhere but the Cleveland airport waiting to get the hell out of Ohio was becoming infinitesimal.

I checked every room on every floor. Peeked through all the diamond-shaped windows, not caring who I was disturbing.

He wasn't in any of them.

I looked up at the clock on the wall. An hour and forty-five minutes before my fate as a composition major at Oberlin would be decided.

A wave of acid sloshed up into my mouth. I kept it closed and forced it all back down. I needed to make this work somehow.

The nearest empty practice room had one of my favorite grand pianos. A small piece of luck.

Half of my compositions were piano only. Those would be fine. It was the song cycle that needed a singer. Too late now to try to recruit anyone. Even the best sight-singer was never going to be able to sing the pieces; they were too confusing against my seemingly unconnected accompaniments.

I would just have to sing them myself. Which was going to be a challenge for me, given how tricky the piano parts were. All my composition's faults would be magnified. All my vulnerabilities laid out for the professors to pick up, point out, and note on my jury sheets. Only Emmett's singing could have smoothed out my inconsistencies, saving me with his ability to make me better than I had any right to be. When Emmett sang, all my problems disappeared. There were no mistakes. No strange segues or unjustified dissonances. He managed to make my broken parts into something beautiful. Without him, the songs weren't good enough.

But he'd left me no other choice.

Maybe what I had done crossed a line last night. Maybe what I'd done was inexcusable. But for him to leave without a word, without giving me the chance to explain myself, apologize, grovel—anything? This was my future Emmett was ruining. My chance at becoming the kind of musician I'd always wanted to be. My grade depended on this. My entire major. If I couldn't show the jury I deserved to be a composition major, I didn't know what I'd do. How could I show the rest of the world I had a voice that deserved to be listened to if I didn't succeed? I wouldn't be able to call myself a composer. I wouldn't deserve to be one.

Surprisingly, I didn't completely lose it by melting into a puddle of hangover-tinged self-pity. I bucked up instead and devoted the next hour to salvaging my music.

When I got to Kulas Recital Hall, my teacher and the other composition professor were in the audience, setting themselves up for the day. There were eight first-year composition majors, and all of them had to do their juries. I was the first to go.

"You're right on time, Quito," Professor Hoffer said, looking up from his semi-rimmed glasses. I was unable to look him in the eye. Instead, I fixated on the tiny ball-bearing chain that allowed him to take his glasses off and wear them around his neck.

Mr. Birnholz, a professor with curly white hair and bushy black eyebrows, asked, "Solo piano and accompanied vocal pieces today. Correct?" He looked at, then around me. "Where is your vocalist?"

I swallowed so hard that bile hit the bottom of my stomach. "He, uh, got sick. Real quick."

"Sick?" Mr. Birnholz said.

"I can still play all of my pieces for you." I took out my stack of sheet music and started spreading them out across the piano's music rack. The papers quivered in my jellylike fingers.

"Maybe we should postpone until later in the week?" Mr. Hoffer offered, his glasses sliding forward on the bridge of his nose.

"It won't help, Mr. Hoffer. My singer's from L.A. I think he left. I think he . . . went back home."

"Was he that sick that he'd just leave without singing for you?" Mr. Hoffer asked.

Mr. Hoffer had been working closely with me on my songs, guiding me all year. He'd been excited to hear them sung. Once he'd even said my style of writing reminded him of another composition student of his who'd gone on to win a Grammy. I was gambling that my effort to do the entire song cycle on my own would be enough to carry me through my jury, despite how bad it would sound without Emmett.

Then the images of last night came rushing back, whipping in rapid succession through my mind.

My hands on his body. My insistent groping. All while he lay silent and wondered how I could be doing what I was doing. Realizing that he never wanted to see me again. Emmett abandoned me because I did something I never should have even *thought* about, let alone gone through with. I didn't learn my lesson with Angela Asari. I should have accepted that Emmett was straight. I'd just pushed my own selfish desires onto him. Regardless of how he felt.

I'd betrayed him. And now I was paying the price.

"Quito," Mr. Hoffer said. "Did you hear me? I said, why would your friend just leave?"

"Because I'm a horrible person, Mr. Hoffer."

"Excuse me?"

"Sorry." I snatched the sheet music off the piano, crumpling the paper into my portfolio. One of the pages snagged on the zipper and tore. A violent rending of the paper filled the hall. I shoved it in regardless. "I can't play these for you. They're nothing without Emmett."

"Excuse me?" Mr. Birnholz said.

Professor Hoffer stood up and took his glasses off. "What about your jury?"

My face was wet with tears. "Fail me. I deserve it," I said and walked out of Kulas Hall.

I'd let down the Obertones. I'd failed Emmett. Why not my comp jury? It all seemed to be karmically correct. Emmett was my best friend. I loved him. So no matter how much I loved him or in what way, I should've respected what we had instead of forcing it into something it was not, like trying to push a square peg into a round hole. Now I'd broken the entire framework of what we used to be. I was blinded by lust. Or loneliness. Or I'd allowed myself to dream when I should have been content with reality. I didn't know. All I knew was that my life was going to be very different from now on. It was going to be missing a few things. Things that made it the life I wanted, *needed*, it to be. And I deserved all of it.

Back at the dorm, Jayesh and Melina were gone. So was my puke. One of them must have cleaned it up for me (probably Melina), though the smell of stomach acid still lingered. I didn't care. I crashed down face-first onto the bed. My tears turned my pillow into a sloppy, wet mess.

Chapter 22—Now

WHEN I FINALLY get home later that evening, my dad, for some inexplicable reason, has on a top hat and is wearing a bedsheet on his back like a cape. He's holding a copy of *A Midsummer Night's Dream*, the play Emmett's rehearsing for.

"This falls out better," he says, "than I COULD DEVISE. But hast thou yet latch'd the ATHENIAN'S EYES," he recites, leaning into the rhyming words with a bit too much emphasis. "With the love juice. As I did bid thee DO?"

Emmett, seemingly unfazed by my dad's getup and halting line readings, says, "I took him sleeping, that is finish'd too—"

"What is this love juice he is talking about?" my dad asks.

"Ah..."

"Is this something dirty? Some kind of pornography thing? Wow. Maybe Shakespeare is more interesting than I remember," my dad says, flipping through the rest of the play.

Emmett looks at me briefly before realizing, rightly, that he shouldn't because we'll just bust up laughing.

"Hey, Dad, can I steal Emmett for a minute?"

He looks up from the booklet. "Ah? Oh, sige na. I'm getting tired now. I should go to bed. Did you eat already, anak? There's plenty of food there in the kitchen. I put it in plastic wrap for you in the fridge."

"Thanks, Dad."

I watch him shuffle down the hallway to his room.

"So, how's my father as a scene partner?"

"Incredible. I'm putting in a good word for him as my understudy."

"Don't actually ever say that in front of him. He would one hundred percent believe you."

"Well, I'm one hundred percent telling the truth," Emmett says, with that smile that says otherwise.

"Hey," I say, "I'm going to tell you something. But before I do, I'm going to ask you to not do something that you're usually really good at doing."

His smile fades. "And what would that be?"

"Act."

His face goes hard, unreadable for a moment.

"I'm just saying—can you promise to tell me the truth? To just be you?"

He nods.

I head back into my bedroom, and he follows without a word.

I close the door behind him and sit on the bed. With my lips, I motion to the spot next to me.

He smiles and sits down. I feel him so clearly beside me—that unique, familiar sensation that thrums through me like a chord.

We sit there, staring at the wall and outward beyond it.

"Mark cheated on me," I say.

"Oh," he says quietly. "And... how does that make you feel?"

"I'm not really surprised about it. Not that sad, either."

"I guess that's good," he says.

"How does that make *you* feel?" I ask.

"I'm sorry to hear that happened."

"Yeah?"

"Well, sure," he says. "I'm sorry that he was such a jerk to you."

"Really?"

"I mean—"

"Remember what I said. The truth," I say. "Are you *really* sorry?"

"No," Emmett says immediately. "Not at all. Not even a little bit."

"Why?" I ask.

"Because that means you can dump him."

I smile to myself.

I rest my hand on his knee. He goes quiet. So quiet I can't even hear him breathing.

"Is this okay?" I ask.

He nods.

I sink the tips of my fingers into the marble-like muscles of his leg.

"How about this?"

"Yeah," he says, his voice low.

I massage his leg with tiny, pulsing movements. "This?"

"Yes." A small moan escapes his lips. "More than okay."

My hand drifts upward, digging into the side of his inner thigh.

"Mmm."

I stop. I take my hand off him. A spark of panic flashes in my chest. My heart is racing so fast that I can barely spit out what I say next. "Emmett. Look at me. Are you sure?"

He looks me in the eyes but says nothing.

We stay there with time at a standstill, staring at each other.

Then, with the expanse of his hands, he takes the sides of my face, pulls me to him, and kisses me.

All the fear I have disappears. All the unallayed anxiety from the last time we'd found ourselves in this situation was now gone with the touch of his lips on mine.

Our kiss isn't only transformative—it's synergistic. Vital. Like being underwater or in space, out where it's just him and me. Breathing for each other. It's us anticipating and matching each other, pushing and pulling, flowing exactly when we're supposed to. Moving to the rhythm that drives us both. To the melody that has always been there.

In a way, our kiss is the natural culmination of what we've always found ourselves doing together: making perfect, glorious music.

I pull him down to the bed. His body presses against mine, all two hundred pounds of it like a blanket, surrounding me in strength and certainty. I asked him not to act, and I feel his promise to me now, the absolute truth of him on me, no curtain or facade separating us. There can never be barriers between two people truly in sync with each other. I feel that now, in a way I've never felt with Mark or anyone, really, before.

Our kissing becomes more urgent. I take his shirt off, and he takes off mine. Emmett places his hand against my chest—a caesura, a brief pause—as if bringing to a close the end of one phrase and the beginning of another. He kisses me deeply and then slowly begins to unzip my pants, pulling them down. I am somehow aware that I do not need to return the favor. I sense that he's now taken the reins and will do the same for himself.

Soon only the slimmest of layers separates us. As he continues to kiss me, now moving on to the sensitive ridge of my ear, tracing down the lobe of it and the sides of my jaw to the tender, vulnerable skin of my neck, I let him continue taking the lead while I do my part in the background and slip his boxer briefs down, past the rigidity of his hip bones, past the smooth roundness of his flawless buttocks, down, down, down the length of his legs and finally off his giant feet. I rip my own underwear off in seconds because I want to feel the core parts of us together, in perfect harmony, finally, after so many years of wanting it.

His hands are at the sides of my head, his fingers buried in my hair. I grasp my arms around his back, trying to claim the vastness of him.

The tempo accelerates, our metronomes ticking past the grounded, rational markings of time as every part of our bodies, including our erections, line up, matching each other, filling the gaps of each other perfectly.

We swell and crescendo.

And climax.

We stay there, holding each other, breathing, not daring to break the stillness in the afterward.

I hold on to him happily, knowing that this time we've gotten it right. That what came before this was just an ill-conceived, unprepared rehearsal. And as I lie there with Emmett, knowing that what we've just experienced will naturally, inevitably dissipate, I can't help but wish that the music we've made together won't ever fade away.

Through the open window, a breeze, warm with the promise of summer, carries in the scent of early evening. Cicadas click and buzz—the only other sound I hear besides Emmett's steady breath next to me.

"That was nice," he murmurs into the side of my face. "How was it for you?" His body goes slightly taut when he asks this. He's apprehensive maybe, afraid of my answer.

"Fishing for compliments?" I ask, butting my head softly against his.

He *tsk*s and wiggles his head *no*.

"I mean, besides the fact that we just did it in my childhood bed, it was pretty incredible."

Emmett's body relaxes, every part of him re-easing into me. "I've been thinking about doing that for a long time."

"Me too," I say. "For years."

"Ever since—"

"Oberlin. The night I completely fucked up."

"Quito—"

"Wait, Emmett. Just listen. Back then, the morning after, I was confused. When I woke up and saw that you'd gone, I was upset. Really upset. Your leaving me screwed up my composition jury." I pull my head away just enough to be able to look him in the eye with our bodies still completely connected. "But as angry as I was at you, I was even more mad at myself for chasing you away."

"You didn't. I had my own reasons for leaving," Emmett says. "I should have told you why. Or at least left you a note. Something."

"No," I say firmly. "*I* was the one who should've called you to apologize. But I didn't. It was easier to pity myself than to own up to what I did to you. For... *assaulting* you. I've done so many things wrong to the people I care about the most."

"I told you, Quito, you don't have to apologize." He puts his hand on the side of my face, caressing it. "Because you didn't take advantage of me."

Holding his gaze, intense and unrelenting as it is, is impossible. I close my eyes. The pain of the mistakes I made that weekend come back to me. I feel tears welling. "You don't have to lie just to make me feel better."

"You probably thought I was high and drunk that night. The truth is, I didn't have any pot at all. And I'd stopped drinking before you even arrived at that off-campus party. I was completely sober when we walked back to your dorm." He strokes my cheek, and a few tears drip onto his fingers. "I knew what was going on the whole time. I even pretended to be cold just to get you to hold me. Do you remember that? I was too chickenshit to touch you. So I made you do it instead."

"But you didn't say anything when I... when we started to... you know. You were quiet the entire time."

"*I* didn't say anything. But you did."

"I did?"

"After you put your arm around me, you said, *Is this okay?* I mean, you kind of mumbled it into my neck, but I heard you loud and clear. I only nodded in response. And I know you understood because you let out this little *hooray.* Even as drunk as you were, you still managed to do that cute little rhyming thing you always do."

Something unlocks inside me, letting go of a weight I'd carried for years. The relief makes me so happy I almost want to laugh. "Thank god."

I turn to him. "So why did you bail without saying anything to me? Were you really okay with everything that happened?"

"In the moment, absolutely. And I knew if I told you to stop, you would. No questions asked. But afterward, to be honest, I did sort of freak out. I thought I was ready for it all, but it was a lot to take in. After you passed out, I couldn't get to sleep. I just lay next to you, staring up at the ceiling. Thinking about what we'd done. Wondering if we did the right thing. The more I thought about it, the more I realized we crossed a line we were never going to be able to uncross. Our relationship was going to be different. Everything I knew had changed. About me. About us. I looked at all the ways we could move on from there, and all the options scared me. So I ran out. Threw my stuff in my bag and left. I couldn't think anymore at that point. All I remember was waiting at the bus stop for the first shuttle to the airport, thinking about how I wish we could've done that night over somehow."

"You agree it was a mistake, then."

"No. Not what we did. But maybe the way we did it. And the way I reacted, definitely. I'm the reason you flunked."

"I deserved it. Cosmic retribution. You were the one who always inspired me. I deserved not ever having another good song in me again for what I did to you."

"Whatever happened between us shouldn't have stopped you from composing. We might have approached it the wrong way, but that night? Us? The sex? Okay, it wasn't great. But it wasn't wrong. *You* didn't do anything wrong. I wanted it just as much as you did. So stop punishing yourself."

"I thought about you," I say. "All the time."

Emmett nods sadly. "Yeah."

"I wrote all these letters to you. Then threw them away before sending them. I'd pick up the phone. Dial your number to the last digit. Then hang up. I'd wonder why you never tried to get in touch with me. But then I'd remind myself it was because of what I'd done. And then I'd sink into a depression about the whole thing because I knew you'd never call me and I wasn't brave enough to apologize to you. It went on like that for months. Years."

Emmett smiles sadly.

"What?" I say.

"I wanted to talk to you, too. But I was too scared. I didn't want to accept the consequences of what we'd done. I was so stupid to leave you. I missed you. And your songs. By letting you go, I had to let that go, too. That love of music. That joy I felt when we did it together. I've never really felt that again with anything. Or anyone."

We lay quiet for a while in something not exactly like silence. Something seems to wind around us, a strain of some shared melody. Unheard but there.

"You don't actually want to go out with Emma Chen, do you?" I ask.

"I mean, you've seen her, right? She's hot as hell."

"I'm going to slap that dumb smile off your face."

"I can think of better things for you to do to my lips," Emmett says.

He kisses me.

Our reprise is even better than the first time.

Chapter 23—Now

WHEN I REACH over for Emmett in the morning, all I touch is a cold pillow. I rub my eyes and, yawning, make my way toward laughter and conversation in the kitchen.

I'm confused when I enter. There are no smells of garlic rice or eggs being fried, no sausages on the pan. My dad is eating a bowl of children's cereal (mostly the colored marshmallow bits), and Emmett, wearing running shorts and a shirt damp with sweat (and smelling insanely sexy), is eating a banana.

"What, no silog?" I ask my father. "It's Saturday."

Emmett swallows the rest of his banana. "Oh, your dad was about to start cooking, but I told him we already had plans."

I raise my eyebrow. "Oh?"

"They have these incredible soufflé pancakes at Bette's Oceanview Diner in Berkeley. Saw it on *Diners, Drive-Ins and Dives*. We have to go there."

I grab a mug out of the cupboard and pray Emmett's made the coffee this morning instead of Dad. "That place always has a long wait. Plus, I thought you were going incognito while you were in town."

"I was, but—" He looks at my dad briefly before saying to me, "I dunno, I guess I'm kind of tired of hiding. I'm not so concerned about being seen anymore."

My dad keeps on eating. I swear I can almost see him smiling, though it might just be the overzealousness of his mouth muscles as he chomps away at the marshmallows.

"Okay. If you really want to. When do you want to go?" I ask.

"I have to hop in the shower, but there's no rush. I called ahead and asked them to save us a table."

"But they don't accept reservations."

"They don't? Huh," Emmett says. He shrugs and walks off.

"Bring me home some of the famous pancakes, okay, anak?" my dad says, his mouth full of milk and cereal.

Emmett's got on his Ruth Bader Ginsburg hoodie (all black with DISSENT in white letters), a Lakers cap, and aviator sunglasses as we arrive at the café, already packed and with a sizable crowd outside waiting for their turn to be seated. When he approaches the person standing behind the cash register, though, he takes everything off. "Table for two under Aoki, please?"

The person—who doesn't seem to be a host or even a waiter but one of the cooks who just happened to be looking for something near the register—stares at Emmett with her mouth half-open. While the poor young woman seems to sort through endless thoughts without actually saying anything, the actual host, wiry and lithe with long blue braids, steps in front of us.

"Emmett? Hey. Welcome. Don't mind Liv. She's watched *The Hanoi Heist*, like, a million times." She grabs a few menus off the counter and walks back into the restaurant. "This way, please."

As we walk past the crowded tables, I can't help but be distracted by all the people looking up at us with expressions ranging from curious to incredulous, with plenty of surreptitious asides and not-so-subtle pointing.

The host seats us in the back. I casually slip into the seat facing forward so that Emmett can sit with his back toward the rest of the restaurant. He pauses for a second and then acknowledges what I've done by winking at me and sitting down.

Even with only the back of him visible, I can feel the weight of dozens of pairs of eyes on us. I watch them use the mirrors on the walls to look. Some even fully turn around. I don't understand how Emmett can deal with this kind of attention all the time. What must they all be thinking? Are they wondering what he's doing in Berkeley? Confused by the fact that he's grabbing brunch, not with some beautiful woman but with a sometimes-when-he-tries-really-hard-he-can-be-handsome-in-a-dorky-way-but-mostly-he's-just-an-average-looking Filipino guy?

I start to regret my decision to take the seat farthest in the back. I feel trapped. Everyone seems to be closing in on us.

"Emmett, wouldn't you rather just get something to go?" I whisper. "You can wait in the car, and I'll get the food?"

"Hey," he says. "Hey." He puts his hand on mine and squeezes it. The feel of it is initially comforting, but I eventually pull away, wanting to protect him. Or maybe myself.

He frowns. "Don't freak out, Quito. Okay? This kind of stuff happens all the time. It's not a big deal. People generally get over it after a minute or two. When they see I'm just like them, just a regular dude wanting to get some pancakes and scrapple, they calm down and forget about it."

I want to push back, to argue that being seen like this is something he's used to but utterly new and scary for me. Then he smiles. When his crooked tooth comes out, I think to myself: Just focus on that. On him. Block everyone else out. If he's okay with being watched, then you can be, too.

"What the heck is scrapple?" I ask.

"It's kind of like Amish Spam. I'll order us some. You'll see. It's going to be amazing."

"I can't wait," I say.

The scrapple is, indeed, amazing in an undefinable pork-product way. Also amazing are the pancakes—though the soufflé-ness of the ones I later bring home to Dad gets lost in translation by the time we get back. But as good as the food is, I just can't seem to let myself enjoy it fully. Even when most of the restaurant patrons stop overtly ogling, I can still feel the stings of their stolen glances like a hundred mosquito bites on me. The itch of it all makes brunch a joyless occasion when it should be a celebratory one. Emmett is mine. Finally. But not all mine, I realize. Someone like Emmett will never be just for me. Not when he constantly shares himself with the rest of the world.

After, I suggest we head straight home, but Emmett insists on walking off all the calories by doing an impromptu hike. Since my version of hiking is walking crosstown in Manhattan instead of waiting for the bus, I have no idea where we should go. He offers to find some suitable options on his phone. Knowing we'll be seen by more people in more popular, open parks, I steer him toward lesser-known options and more secluded trails. He seems to know what I'm doing but doesn't object. Perhaps because he's starting to sense that it *is* a good idea to stay hidden—and, in fact, when we return home and I suggest we just stay in for the rest of the weekend, he agrees without even trying to argue. In any case, my father is happy to have the both of us around to cook for, and we're rewarded with mountains of food.

Early Monday morning, as Emmett slips out of my bedroom to go for his daily run, I lie awake, unable to go back to sleep. Both Saturday and Sunday evenings, after watching TV with my father, we waited for him to fall asleep before going to bed ourselves, Emmett sneaking into my room only after we could hear my dad's snores echoing down the hallway from his room. We laughed about how silly it felt for Emmett to sneak around the house like that, not wanting to let my father know we were being scandalous under his roof.

But after the silliness subsided, the reality of our hiding begins to sink in to me. How much longer will we have to keep things a secret? From my dad? From the world? Will Emmett ever want to let people know about us? Coming out of the closet for a celebrity as big as he is would be a huge deal. It would change everything about the way the world sees him. It would change his entire career. The more I think about it, the worse I feel. I don't want to be responsible for anything bad happening to him.

And yet I also don't want to let him go. We had an amazing weekend together, when it was just us. As long as we keep it that way, we'll be fine. This afternoon, after school, I'll tell him that he has nothing to worry about. I'll stick by him but out of the way, where no one will ever see me, where no one will use me against him.

But before I do that, I need to get up and get into school early. To take care of something before classes start. A hanging thread that needs to get tied up.

Or, rather, cut off completely.

After a quick coffee run, I get into school and set myself up at the choir room piano. I pull the sheet music for *The Forever Boys* Act I finale out of my bag.

Unburdened by the need to push myself to do my best work, I finish up the last few lines of the bridge by scribbling in a repetitive three-note melody. I throw that on top of a repeating I–V–vi–IV chord progression, the most overused of all time. The lyrics were horrible. Why push myself to make the music any better? Certainly not for the guy who made out with my boyfriend.

I scan the music in the school office copier and send the sheets to Mark and Dinesh along with a copy of the picture of them kissing in the Twixxy VIP lounge. The email is short and to the point:

> I'm done.

After rethinking it, I send them both one more message.

> Ask J.B. at Broadway Baby for way better music than I could write for you.

Within minutes, apologies fly back from Mark. I'm almost inclined to write back to tell him off. To let him know what a jerk he was.

But I don't. He's no longer worth the effort.

I block his phone number and email address and shift my attention to my rehearsal outline for the day, trying not to sabotage myself with negative thoughts before I've even begun to plan.

As I stand at the podium sorting through sheet music and making notes, I feel a presence nearby.

The shy young tenor whose name I cannot remember is sticking his head through the door, staring at me with adorably droopy eyes.

I walk over to him. "Hi, Mel, Mel..."

"Milton."

That's it. "Milton. Come on in. What's up?"

He pushes the door open a crack and squeezes his body through, as if apologizing to the door that he's disturbing it. "I'm sorry I've been messing up lately, Mr. Cruz."

"What do you mean?"

"All those mistakes you keep hearing from the tenors. That's me."

"What mistakes? I never hear any mistakes," I say. He looks up at me with such clear awareness of my lie that I blush. "Milton, you're an excellent tenor. Really. You've got a lovely voice. You don't need to apologize for your mistakes. You're not the only one who makes them."

He shakes his head. "I just hate the way my voice sounds."

"Everyone feels that way sometimes."

"No. It doesn't feel good. I mean, it doesn't feel like my right voice."

His speaking voice has a high ring to it, sounding almost like a young woman's. There's no way he should be a bass. "Do you mean you think you're singing incorrectly?"

"Maybe. I'm not sure."

"Would you like me to do a little vocal coaching with you? Sometime after school, maybe?"

The bell rings. More students begin to enter. He looks around and fidgets. "I'll think about it."

"Well, I'm here if you need me."

He waves at me sideways as he rushes to take his seat, and I can tell that he won't be taking me up on my offer anytime soon.

After we do our warm-up, I decide to run through our trickiest piece—an English madrigal by William Byrd. Lots of problems with this one. The choir's musical skills are excellent, their pitches solid, and their rhythms mostly correct. Yet, for some reason, they seem to be missing something essential. The sound is sometimes muddled. At other times, sterile.

As I've been doing since I arrived, I run through the whole piece. I don't stop. Even during the rougher places. I know how hard they must have worked on the notes and want them to have that feeling of accomplishment by singing the song all the way through with no disruptions. They make plenty of mistakes, but I pretend not to hear them. I don't want them to feel frustrated.

"Very nice." I nod reassuringly. "Super duper, troupers."

Their faces reek of apathy. Even Celeste's normally sunny face is cloudy. Like every day since I've been with them, my anxiety level begins its gradual ascent. Can they not follow my conducting? Is that it? Am I really that bad? Am I not encouraging enough?

"You guys are great. Should we sing this one again? What do you all think? Maybe, with, I don't know, a little more joy?"

We do another run-through. I widen my eyes and grin, showing both rows of teeth. They respond by forcing smiles. This only makes them strain and sing louder. Some of their pitches push upward. They fall out of tune, which wreaks havoc on my sense of perfect pitch. I can't help but make a face. They see this and falter. Some of them stop singing altogether. I try to get them to keep going, but there's no escaping that it's a total train wreck. "Oops. Let's try that again. You all are doing so awesome."

None of them even bother to make eye contact with me at all after that. They must feel horrible. I have to keep being positive.

Celeste shoots her hand up. "Mr. Quitocruz?"

"Yes, Celeste?"

"Are you sure we did that okay? I mean, can you tell us what our mistakes were?"

"No mistakes! No mistakes."

"But, I mean, like on page two, when the tenors came in, they—"

"They were fine," I say, cutting her off. If she starts pointing fingers at her fellow singers' errors, it could lead to disaster. "We just need a bit more excitement, that's all."

Celeste slumps into her already rumpled dress.

I resume immediately to try to keep the energy going. The third run-through is worse than the first two. My head cramps up with stress tension. At this point, the choir will be worse for the concert, not better. I rack my brain, trying to think of some other ways to encourage them, when Celeste raises her hands again.

"Mr. Quitocruz?"

I sigh and brace myself for her question. Her instincts, musical and otherwise, have proven to be impeccable, but I just don't have the energy to deal with her suggestions when I can barely fix the problems I'm already painfully aware of. "Yes, Celeste?"

"Um, so I heard a rumor that Emmett Aoki is actually in town already. Is that true? Is he going to be rehearsing with us now?"

Shit.

Excitement surges around the room. Other students repeat her question out loud. They're all getting too worked up. I'm losing control.

"Uh, yes, he's in town. He... arrived this weekend. And he's just visiting with family and old friends. You all know he grew up here, right? And that he's an alum of Sunvalley? Yes, once he's done, uh, connecting with people, he'll be in to practice for the concert with us."

Unfortunately, my response does nothing to dam the deluge of follow-up questions that Celeste has unleashed from everyone.

"Isn't he your friend?"

"Mr. Cruz told us he was your friend."

"Your best friend."

"What's he going to sing?"

"Is he any good?"

"Is he staying in town all the way until the concert?"

"Is he staying with *you*?"

"How close are you guys?"

"Is he really dating Emma Chen?"

I hold up my hands. "Stop. He'll be here, okay? Just chill out!"

My inability to modulate my voice during stressful moments rears its ugly head again. They reel back. Some laugh nervously in response. The rest fold up like closed books.

Great move, Quito. Another in a long series of perfectly executed gestures.

My phone vibrates in my pocket. I pull it out quickly—a text from Emmett.

"Okay, everyone take out the Moses Hogan spiritual and take another look at all the words. Make sure you know them well. We're going to start rehearsing it from memory today."

They pull out their sheet music as I read Emmett's text.

> Hey. Have to run a few urgent errands this afternoon. Might not be back this evening, so don't wait up. xo

I watch the kids silently mumbling lyrics to themselves and try not to be upset about the fact that I won't be able to talk to Emmett this evening—to tell him I've broken up with Mark and that he doesn't have anything to worry about with me keeping our relationship a secret.

But the more I think about his text, the more it begins to feel there's something else. Something he's not telling me.

It starts to feel familiar. Like he's telling me he's leaving me.

Again.

Chapter 24—Now

NORMALLY, HAVING TO get up at 5:00 a.m. to pick up Ujima at SFO would have been an utter impossibility for me, but considering I didn't sleep at all last night, it wasn't an issue. I tried not to stay up to wait for Emmett to come home from whatever he was out doing, but I did, fretting away in the living room, the kitchen, my bedroom, his. My father eventually got so tired of me pacing around everywhere that he actually forced me to sit down at the piano and play some music for him, which I was thankful for. It took my mind off Emmett—for about an hour, at least.

After my father fell asleep, I was back to wondering where Emmett was, what he was doing, and—most importantly—who he was doing it with. Visions of him cavorting around in some private hotel room in San Francisco with some woman or man—or both—raced through my head, making it coil up with metallic tension.

At around 2:00 a.m., I lay down on the bed and turned off the lights, thinking the worry would just burn itself out with me falling asleep from the fatigue of it all. No such luck.

Driving into Arrivals, I yawn so loudly, I startle myself. I smack my face a couple of times and scan the people waiting outside Terminal 2. Even a hundred feet away, I can spot Ujima. They tower above nearly everyone else.

I drive up to them and roll down the passenger window. "Aren't you freezing in those hot pants?"

"I got a jacket on," Jee says, as if I need my eyes checked. Never mind that it's a crop-top jacket that only goes down to their navel, and underneath all they've got on is a *She-Ra* T-shirt.

"Why all girled up?"

Ujima's loaded side-eye makes me blush. I was referring to their evening-ready getup, complete with platform heels and perfectly spherical Afro puffs. Not the fact that they didn't do the flight as Gerome. "I mean, why so fancy?"

"It's all for you, baby," they say, tossing my unintended slight away with a frosted purple kiss on my cheek.

"Get in. I'll take care of your luggage."

My knees buckle when I attempt to pick up the bags. "Were you planning on staying until Christmas?" I throw the luggage into the trunk, and my car sinks down. "Geez. That's my workout for the day."

"My gift to you," Ujima says, squeezing my biceps. "These munchkins need all the help they can get."

As we leave the airport, the fog clears. Glimpses of buildings and rolling hills become more expansive, and the majesty of the San Francisco Bay reveals itself. Jee turns the heat up and hums something low. "It is beyond beautiful here. Why did you ever leave?"

"To pursue all my unattainable, deluded dreams in New York. Just like you."

"We do make sacrifices, don't we?" Jee says.

"And speaking of dreams..."

They snap their head away from the window and look at me. "Yeeeeeess?"

"I slept with Emmett."

"Bitch, you better not say something like you both stayed up all night talking and fell asleep next to each other like fourth graders at a slumber party. If you're pulling my leg, I will slap you."

"No jokes this time. We did it."

"For real?"

"Yes. Several times."

"WHAT?!" Ujima slaps the side of my shoulder so hard that I almost swerve into the car next to us. "Ahhh, sookie sookie now! That's the best news I heard all month! Tell me everything. Don't leave anything out."

"I don't know, Jee. You know I don't like to kiss and tell."

"Girl, I will cut you."

"And the other thing is—I think we might have gone too far, too fast. I think he's bailing on me."

"What do you mean?"

"Well, he was out all day yesterday. And all night. He never came back home."

"I'm sure it's nothing. He's a busy man. He was probably meeting up with other friends from your old hood."

"He did say he had errands to run. But the choir got wind of him being in town, and now they're expecting him—today, actually. They're going to hate me even more than they do now when he doesn't show up."

"Why do you keep saying the kiddies hate you? What possible reason could they have?"

"The fact that I'm not my dad. He's their hero. I can't compete with that."

"You're helping them while he's gone. I'm sure they understand."

Ujima turns on the radio and surfs through the stations. Bursts of static alternate with music snippets as they try to settle on something. "Anyway, don't they have to be nice to you, considering you're the one who's bringing Emmett to the party?"

Old-school R&B blasts from the radio. Boyz II Men and Mariah Carey warble loudly for a few seconds before I turn the volume down.

"Jee, something doesn't feel right about Emmett being gone. I think I might have messed things up again."

"Were you that bad in bed?"

"Ugh, no, I—well, I mean maybe? No, that's not what I'm talking about. After the first night we, you know, slept together, the next day he insisted on going out to brunch. In public. Together."

Traffic flow slows down around us as we approach the Bay Bridge. The cars crowd us, hemming us in on all sides. Everyone eventually slows to a standstill. I look ahead at the long lines of cars ahead of us.

"It was his idea," Ujima says.

"Yes, but I should've said no. Now I'm sure he's regretting the fact that people saw us together. They could probably all see the afterglow of sex on my face and wondered why the hell Emmett was with me, and then he got embarrassed and remembered that he wasn't gay, or that he could do much better than me, or—"

A car changes lanes abruptly with no indication, swerving into a tiny open space in front of us. I plant my hand on my horn for a good five seconds. "Asshole!"

Ujima presses two extended middle fingers up to my windshield. "Y'all *better* be glad I don't get out of this car right now!"

"You know they can't hear you."

"Oh, they know what I'm saying. They can read my lips. They're too luscious to miss," Jee says, waving their fingers around their open mouth.

Ujima's set the temperature in the car too high. The steering wheel starts feeling like putty in my hands. I squeeze and squeeze, trying to somehow change the form of it into something else. I can't stop thinking about the possibility that Emmett has regretted his actions and abandoned me. Again.

Jee places their hand on my knee. The weight of it centers the floating parts of me, and I stop trying to alter the steering wheel into a different state of matter. "It looks like I got here just in time. You're falling down some kind of black hole, baby. And not the good kind." They sigh. "I'm going to have to snap you out of it."

The cars around us begin to gain speed. A red Dodge pickup with a flat tire takes up a chunk of the shoulder of the road as we get onto the bridge. Once we pass it, the traffic eases. As we drive over the bridge, the sky clears. We reach the end of the fog bank and coast into bright, sunny skies.

"Quito, you know you tend to overthink things, right? And that you're always too hard on yourself. So he was out for the night. So what? That doesn't erase everything that happened between you two this weekend—and by the way, don't think for a *second* I forgot that you haven't told me all about that yet. Y'all are fine. Just give the boy some space."

"You're probably right."

"Of course I'm right. I'm always right."

"Oh. And something I know you'll appreciate. I broke up with Mark."

"Hallelujah!" Ujima says, turning the music back up. "Time to celebrate!" They roll their window down, and the car's heat dissipates into the cool wind flowing in.

They start singing along with the Earth, Wind, and Fire coming from the radio. Their voice is a miracle. Unapologetic and real.

I join Jee in singing as we zoom across the bridge.

As we get off the freeway, I ask them, "Did you want to freshen up at my house before school starts? I know you can't check into your Airbnb yet. And you probably didn't get a lot of sleep on the red-eye over."

Ujima flips down the visor, checks their face in the mirror with a quick side to side, makes a kissing face, and snaps the visor back up. "I didn't, but a mug this naturally divine doesn't need as much beauty sleep as most other people would. I'll be fine. But I could use some coffee."

"There's a drive-through Starbucks nearby."

"Thank you, Jeeeesus," they singsong.

I switch lanes and change direction, heading for a nearby shopping center. "I'm sorry we don't really have room for you in the house with Emmett still in the guest room. Well, I hope he still is, at least. You know my dad would love to have you at the house."

"Your daddy needs his peace and quiet to recuperate. And I'm sure y'all already make enough noise as it is. I mean, *music*," Ujima says, snorting.

I drive us into Olive Crossing, a small outdoor shopping complex. Of the various stores and restaurants, only the gym and the Starbucks are open. We get in line behind the four other cars already waiting their turn at the drive-through.

As we wait in the queue, Jee perks up their hair with an Afro pick. "Have you told the kids I'm coming?"

"Oops. Sorry. I was just so preoccupied with what's happening with Emmett, I didn't mention it. In fact, they're expecting Emmett today, not you. I'm sure they won't mind."

"Right. Because anyone can see I'm a natural replacement for Emmett Aoki. Girl, you better be glad I already like you, or I'd be giving you some choice words right now."

A horn blasts from behind us. In my rearview mirror, an older woman with a transparent shower cap covering a headful of roller-curled hair throws her hands up at me from behind the wheel of her BMW. The cars in front of us have all moved ahead.

"All right, all right. Hold your horses!"

I jam on the gas. My car screeches forward too far. I don't brake in time and hit the bumper of the SUV in front of us. It's only a tap, but it's enough for a very large, very hairy man to jump out of the SUV and come at me, the edges of his lumberjack beard bristling with rage. I put the car in reverse and back up a few inches, careful not to hit the BMW lest I also get into it with the salon escapee behind us.

"Crap, crap, crap." I roll down the window after I've backed us up. "Hey, man, I'm sorry about that."

The man looks at his SUV's back fender and brushes it with his hands. There's a small smudge of dirt there from the impact. He turns around and looks as if he is about to pound on the hood of my car with his ham-hock-size fists. Instead, he says, "Watch where you're going, pendejo."

"Yipper, skipper," I say. "Sorry again. No harm done, right?" He's on the edge of arguing back. Before he can say anything, I add, "And please tell the cashier I'm buying your coffee for you."

The sneer on the man's face slackens. He shouts over his shoulder, "Then I'm buying coffee for the rest of my office, too."

"Great," I say. "You do that."

"Oof. What a beast," Ujima says. "Hit him again so I can ask him for his phone number."

I sigh and drive up to the speaker to order our coffee.

Our Starbucks trip makes us late. We arrive just in time for second period. I ask Ujima to stay out in the hallway so I can introduce them. The students are already sitting in their seats, looking more anxious than normal. Not surprising, as I know they've been waiting for Emmett's arrival. Still, some of them seem strangely out of sorts when I walk in alone, staring at me as if they've never quite seen me until now.

"Listen up, everyone," I announce. "First of all, I want to apologize. Emmett is here, but he's not here. I mean, he's not *here* here. He's in town, but he can't come today because he's busy with some... Hollywood stuff? He'll be here soon, though, I promise! Maybe as soon as tomorrow." I hope. "Anyhoo, in the meantime, I'd like to introduce you all to my friend. Who is, uh *are*... Oh, actually, you should know that they prefer the use of, uh..."

Ujima opens the choir room door wide. "Good heavens. Let me," they say and glide inside. "Hello, children. My name is Ujima Jenkins. Like Quito, I work in the theater business. I act, sing, dance, and MC every Friday night at Escándalo, Chelsea's hottest, sultriest, sexiest—"

"Jee!"

"What? Oh fine," they say, mock pouting. "Suffice it to say, I've been around a long time. I'm here to help y'all put your show together. But before we begin, let's just get it all out in the open."

They take a spare plastic chair from the side of the choir room and scoot it right up to the edge of the front row to sit with the students. They perch themself on the edge and cross their legs. "As I mentioned, my name is Ujima, but you can also call me Jee. And my pronouns are *they* and *them*."

I had expected that, out of the lot, Celeste would have something to say. Some sort of insightful, inclusive welcome. Instead, it's Milton who pipes up first. His chipmunk voice cracks from the back row, "You're the most beautiful person I've ever seen."

A few of the sopranos giggle. Ujima turns their head toward the girls, slowly, making the most out of every millimeter of movement. The girls sink down into their chairs so far their heads disappear between their shoulder blades.

Jee gets up and glides back to the empty-seat circle where Milton sits. They kneel down beside him. "What's your name?"

"Milton."

"Enchantée," Ujima says, holding out a hand.

Without hesitating, Milton shakes and holds on to it. "When did you know your pronouns were they/them?"

"You might not believe this looking at me now, but I wasn't always so comfortable with my body. It always felt like my skin didn't fit me quite right. It took doing drag for the first time—on a dare, mind you—to realize I felt better this way," they say with a flourish of their hand over themself. "More powerful. More myself."

Jee puts Milton's hand back onto his lap and stands in front of the choir.

"I know y'all might not understand this now. But the most important thing anyone can ever do is to truly see themselves and to love what they see. And at times, it isn't easy. But just hear this: No matter what people say about you, no matter how they try to define you, just remember that you get to decide who you are. *You* have the agency. Not anyone else. Not your mother, your teacher, your friends, or your enemies. No one." Jee looks at Milton and then back toward me. "Just you."

I see a variety of emotions on everyone's faces. Agreement. Admiration. And on a few, confusion.

"Questions?" Jee asks. "Don't be shy. This is a safe space."

I knew I needed Ujima's help to connect with the kids. Jee's always had an ability to get people to trust them, to let them in, past the safety of their hardened exteriors. I used to think this was because Ujima was like Emmett: an actor. Skilled at becoming whoever people needed them to be. I know now that it's actually the reverse of that. Ujima lives their life with no compromises. It's easy to put your trust in someone who so clearly believes in living their own truth to the fullest.

The kids are all smiles and wide-open faces, genuinely interested in Ujima's story. I decide to wait until tomorrow to figure out what to tell them about Emmett. Let them all at least have one more day.

After they're done talking, I clap my hands. "Shall we get started?"

"Now I know why so many people live here," Ujima says to me at the stoplight on the way back to my house from the school. They bite down into a burger. The pace is obscenely deliberate, like a slow-motion scene from a mukbang video.

"I thought you said it was the weather."

"No, it's definitely this," they mumble. "In-N-Out Burger? More like Put-It-In-My-Mouth Burger."

"Title of your sex tape."

"Charming." Jee holds the burger up to their face.

"What are you doing?"

"I'm taking a mental picture to save for later so I can fantasize about it when I go back to New York."

"Fanta . . . ? Actually, never mind. Just don't eat mine."

"What kind of person do you think I am?" Jee wipes their mouth gingerly with the edge of a napkin, leaving a trace of lip gloss. "I'll just have some of your fries."

Green light. Warm late-spring air breezes through our windows, smelling of flowering trees. "Those kids adored you, Jee."

"They sing beautifully. Especially that little Milton kid. His instrument is damn special. The way it just sits up there? Child, I only *wish* I could sing that high. There's something off about the way he vocalizes, though. Feels breathy. Too loose. Tenor might be too low for him."

"You know tenor is the highest male part."

"And you know typical gender roles don't mean shit to me."

Ujima does it again. Reframes things in a way that's never occurred to me. Reminding me, as someone who has lived their entire life out of the box, that merely thinking outside of it is only the beginning.

"Do you think I should move him up to alto?"

"Possibly. Maybe even soprano."

"I just don't want to disrupt things too close to the concert."

"Quito, those kids are good. Really good. Even a music ed dropout like me can see that. They'll take anything you throw at them."

"My dad taught them well," I say. "I just really wish I could help them better. I've been trying to be supportive."

"Mm-hmm."

I groan. "Spill it."

They crinkle up their empty burger wrapper. "Do you remember that Cole Porter revue I did two years ago? At Peoria Playhouse?"

"Yes. You always knew it was going to be a lemon."

"You know why?"

"Because the director paid you with IHOP gift cards?"

"Because, during rehearsals, he told us that we were amazing, nonstop. The show was fantastic! We had nothing to worry about! Never gave us a single note about what we were doing wrong or how to improve the shitty sections. And believe you me, there were plenty of shitty sections. I mean, most of the cast was from New Jersey," they say. "When the person in charge tells you you're good, and you know you're not, well... There's only so much smoke up one's ass a person can take before they start gagging on it."

"I'm not blowing smoke up their asses."

"Yes, you are. Don't just run the songs and tell them they're perfect. They know they're not. They're looking to you to tell them what they're doing wrong. To tell them the truth. When you don't, they lose faith in you."

"I've had bad experiences in the past giving harsh criticism to other singers. Really bad." I slow down as we approach our house and park on the cracked concrete driveway. I make a mental note to mow the overgrown lawn. The grass has overtaken the meager bed of petunias Dad planted a few months ago. "I was just trying to keep their spirits up while my father was away."

"They don't need a cheerleader. They need a teacher."

With a tray of milkshakes in one hand and the sacks of burgers and fries in the other, I slam my door shut with my foot, a little harder than I intend. It startles a few sparrows from the ginkgo biloba tree shading the entrance to our house, making them fly off in a huff. "I'm not a teacher."

Ujima takes one of the bags from me. "Mm-hmm."

"Whatever, Jee."

Inside, the house is cleaner than it's been in days. Sun streams in from the open window shades, and the hallway floor smells of fresh Pine-Sol. "Dad?"

"Ah, you come bearing gifts." My father, dressed in a clean shirt and pressed trousers, hurries to Jee and goes in for a hug. "How have you been, Ms. Ujima? Or what is it, as the kids say these days? *Mx.* Ujima?"

"Either is fine, Mr. C." They pull back a bit from my dad and give him a good once-over. "Don't you look like a million dollars? Tell me the truth. You've been faking illness because you've decided to moonlight during the day at some secret new job." Jee rubs my dad's biceps muscle. "Are you running an illegal arm-wrestling ring?"

He titters like a little kid. "Ah, Quito, did I ever tell you how much I just love this one?"

"Yes, Dad." I hand the bag of food to him. "Eat up."

"Yum. Burger." He takes the bag into the kitchen. "Come, come. Eat with me."

The kitchen, like the living room, is unexpectedly spotless. The dishes have been washed, and the counters are tidy. I wonder if it's because Emmett's absence has made my dad so bored that he's decided to clean or because he wanted to impress Ujima.

We sit at the dining table as my father digs into his food. "Quito," he says between bites. Bits of lettuce fall onto the table. "How did today's rehearsal go?"

"Great. Ujima was there. The kids adore them."

They kiss ketchup off the side of their hand and reach for what remains of my fries. "Thank you. But the students were already in good hands."

"My son is a born leader."

I slap Ujima's hand away. "Dad, stop."

"You have a gift, anak. They sounded fantastic when I stopped by last week."

"That was the only time they sounded good. When you were there. Otherwise, I've just been making them sound like crap."

"Bullshit," my father says.

"Mr. Cruz," Ujima says, putting a hand on his arm, which makes him sit up embarrassingly erect. "I was just telling Quito that he might be taking it too easy on them."

"What do you mean?" he asks.

"He's not pushing them hard enough. They need to be corrected more often."

"Quito, you have to be honest with those kids."

"I just wanted them to like me."

"Ah, Francisco, Francisco." My dad sighs. "He's always been like this, you know," he says to Ujima. "He wants for people to like him so much, even if it means he has to refrain from telling the truth. Do you know what I'm talking about?"

"Yes, I do." Ujima tilts their head at me. "But it seemed to me like those kids liked you just fine, Quito. In fact, I caught a few of them shooting you some interesting looks during class today. I think some of them might have a crush on you."

"Actually, I sensed something weird, too. Like they wanted to ask me something but didn't know how."

"Or," Jee says, taking their phone out, "they *knew* something about you but didn't know how to bring it up. Didn't you say they already knew Emmett was in town?"

"Yeah?"

"Well, they had to have found out somehow. And they're kids, so it was obviously from something online." Jee swipes and types. The tips of their long nails click on their phone's screen. "Oh. OH."

"What?" my father and I both ask at the same time.

"Quito, there is a picture of you and Emmett trending on Instagram right now. And uh . . . " They glance at my dad. "Let me just show this to you."

Jee hands me their phone.

Someone at Bette's who had been sitting close to me and Emmett, with a view of the sides of our faces, snapped a shot of the exact five seconds when he put his hand on mine. From the angle, it looks like we are holding hands. The look on Emmett's face is less of friendly concern than it is utter devotion. The picture is tagged with #EmmettAokiOuted. It's been liked over 250,000 times.

I scroll through the comments.

Emmett has a boyfriend?

Always knew this guy was a homo.

Who is the mystery guy?

Time to quit hiding, closet case!

Seriously, Emmett Aoki is going gay for THIS dude?

"I need to call Emmett. Excuse me."

I push away abruptly from the table and run to my bedroom. The door slams more forcefully than I intend. I dial Emmett's number.

Thankfully, he picks up right away. "Quito?"

"Emmett, I saw our picture online. And all the things people are saying, and—"

"I was going to call you."

"Oh. Right. You must be pretty upset. I knew we shouldn't have gone out in public."

"Quito, listen. I'm going to try my hardest, but I might not get back in time to rehearse with the choir for the concert. And there's a slight possibility I might not be back in time for the concert at all."

"You . . . you what?"

"I just—it's important that I take care of a few more things here."

"Here? Where's *here?* Where are you?"

"Los Angeles."

"Excuse me?"

"I told you I needed to take care of some business."

"You didn't say you flew all the way back to L.A.!"

"I didn't want to worry you."

"This is about the picture, isn't it? Now that you've been outed, you're freaking out."

"That's not exactly right."

"Not *exactly*? Okay, why don't you tell me, then? Exactly."

"Quito, look, it's complicated. I just—"

"No, don't bother. I get it. You're running away again. Emma Chen is probably looking like a really good choice right now, isn't she? I should've known this was coming. I should've known not to try. I always end up here. I always end up in this place. Alone. Dammit."

"Quito, let me explain."

"Goodbye, Emmett." I hang up and then watch as my phone screen goes dark.

I drag myself back out into the kitchen and throw myself down into the wooden chair.

"Anak, what is going on?"

"Emmett left. He's not coming back."

"What?" my father cries out.

"He's got *urgent business* he needs to take care of."

"What does that mean?" he asks.

Ujima gives me one of their looks that says I need to tell my father everything.

"Dad, Emmett and I . . . we . . . um, kind of got together? As more than friends. And when we went out in public—well, it looks like people could tell we were kind of a couple."

My dad looks at me. His eyes, searching mine, seem clouded. "I don't understand."

"We hooked up, Dad. And people figured it out somehow. And now he's been outed. So now he's gone, and he's not coming back. Because he's afraid. Or he's crawling back to Emma Chen or something. I don't know."

"That's not possible," my dad says.

"Well, I'm sorry, Dad, but that's what happened."

"No." He massages his chest and gets up. "Excuse me. I need some antacids." He leaves the kitchen and heads toward the bathroom.

Ujima sorts through more social sites on their phone. "I don't think it's that bad, Quito. It's just that one picture. And a lot of gossip."

"That's all it takes to kill a career. You should know that."

They look up at me. Their face softens as my statement kicks in. Jee's part of the entertainment business. They know full well the damaging power of negative public opinion. And even though we've been blessed with so many more out and proud queer celebrities in the past few years, the ones that find it the easiest are the ones that come out early in their careers. For those who have been around for years, who have built a certain type of persona for themselves—like being a Hollywood heartthrob or an action movie star, for example—it can completely ruin everything they've so carefully crafted. They're afraid they'll be seen in a completely different way. Because they will. It's part of the reason people come out, because they choose to be seen for who they really are.

But some people aren't ready for that. Won't ever be.

Like Emmett.

"Just call him back," Ujima says. "Tell him he'll be okay. He'll be safe coming out. You'll help him."

"No," I say adamantly. "He has to help himself. He has to make that decision. Not me. I'm done trying to make decisions for us as a couple. What am I even saying? We were never even a couple to begin with. And where the hell is my dad, anyway? It shouldn't take him this long to get antacids."

"I'll go check." Ujima points at the mess from our In-N-Out meal on the kitchen table. "I'll leave you to clean all that up."

I start tossing things into the trash and reach for a kitchen rag to wipe up a few stray droplets of milkshake from the table when I hear Ujima scream out.

I bolt toward the sound.

When I get to the bathroom, I see them. Jee is standing over my father, who is lying down on his side on the tile floor. His body is convulsing, his right hand curled up into a ball against his chest. I quickly kneel down and cup a hand under his head. "Dad? Dad? Can you hear me?"

My eyes fill with tears. I look at Ujima. "Call 911."

Chapter 25—Now

IT'S NOT FEAR or anxiety I feel the most in hospitals.

It's loneliness. Under the ice-blue lights, surrounded by chemical smells piled on top of an undercoat of decay, I'm reminded of the time when I felt the most alone. When, as my father drove hundreds of miles to get to us, I needed someone to tell me that my mother would pull through her six-hour surgery, that the surgeons would be able to siphon the blood from her brain, the pressure of it suffocating her just like the shrinking walls of the waiting room were doing to me. I needed someone to tell me my mother wasn't going to die.

And as my father now lies in the ICU, his body tucked into blue and white hospital bedding with an IV drip attached to his arm, the feeling of loneliness encroaches again. It makes me and everything around me feel tiny and insignificant.

I place one of my hands on top of my father's. The clamminess of it shocks me.

He stirs. A low sound rumbles in his chest, followed by a cough of water and gravel. He opens his eyes and manages a smile. "Mm," he grunts. Warmth ebbs into his hand.

"Hi, Dad." I smile back at him.

He tries to talk and is only able to open his mouth and rasp. His face stiffens into a scowl.

"It's okay. Don't try to talk. Just relax."

As usual, he ignores me. "Waa... water."

I take the pitcher on his bedside table and pour water into a plastic cup. "Here." I tilt it up to his mouth.

He takes the cup and tries to laugh but only coughs again. "I'm not an invalid, anak." After drinking the entire cup, he hands it back to me.

"More?"

He shakes his head and points with his lips for me to put it back on the table. I see now how wonderfully elegant the gesture is in its efficacy, how everything I need to know I can see in his face.

"Gutom ka ba?" I ask in my garbled Tagalog. *Are you hungry?* So typically Filipino of a question. That immediate instinct to feed our loved ones, the need to sustain them. I'm not sure he's allowed to eat yet, though, and I don't think I should be making the decision. I've already made plenty of bad ones for him. It wasn't a minor case of pneumonia he had. He's been seriously ill this entire time. On the verge of heart failure. And I should've seen it. Instead, I cooked him pork pancakes and brought him burgers and fries for lunch—when I should have been encouraging him to eat healthier.

"Hungry," my dad says as he closes his eyes. A restful calm falls over his face.

I reach for the phone. "Hi. This is Francisco Cruz, Mr. Cruz's son in room 138? He's awake and asking for food. Can you bring something?"

By the time I've hung up, Dad's already fallen back asleep. I'm tempted to turn the TV on to pass the time, to give him the soft background noise he always seems to have on at home, but I decide not to risk disturbing his slumber.

"Hi," Ujima says softly. They enter the hospital room with a brown paper bag smelling of shallots, ginger, and five-spice. Their face is creased with concern. "How is he?" they ask.

"He woke up for a minute. Spoke a little." I stroke my dad's hair, rearranging the brittle, errant bits into something more kempt. "He said he was hungry."

"Thank god." Ujima breathes out a sigh. "Speaking of which, I got your favorite."

"Pho ga?"

"Of course."

"Thank you," I say. When my dad visited me in New York, I asked him what he liked best about his visit. The Bach concert he'd attended at Lincoln Center? The *Godspell* revival? Or maybe even an evening at Broadway Baby during one of my shifts. He said, without even having to think twice about it, *the cheap and plentiful Asian food.* He wanted to try a new take-out place every night, and we did—Vietnamese, Chinese, Burmese, Korean. At the time, it pained me to think that the thing he'd remember the most about his trip to New York wasn't anything uniquely cultural but something he could just as easily get in the Bay Area. Now my fingers crunch around the brown paper bag, and I hold it there, not moving, thinking of how much I'd love to be able to share the meal it holds with him and not have to worry that I might be killing him with it.

I start to cry.

"Hey, hey, hey." Ujima pulls me in close. "Everything's gonna be okay."

A soft rapping sound on the doorframe makes me wipe my eyes with an embarrassed swipe of my sleeve. A nurse walks into the room, holding a small food tray. Or maybe it looks small because he's so huge.

"Thank you—" Jee looks up. "Sweet Baby Jesus."

The nurse, six and a half feet of Tongan muscle and tribal tattoos, says, with a smile on his face, "Sorry. Nurse Baby Jesus works in the maternity ward. I'm just Bryan."

Jee bats their lashes. "Last name? So I know what to engrave on our wedding invitations."

"Palu. Already married, unfortunately. But flattered!" He takes a look at the chart by the bed. "You said Mr. Cruz just woke up?"

"He did. For a minute or so," I reply.

"That's good. He was awake early this morning, too, when Dr. Sloan checked on him. His levels look pretty decent. You can take a break if you want. Go home for a bit. He'll be okay."

"No," I say. "I'm staying right here."

Ujima shrugs at the nurse. *Don't even bother trying to argue with this one*, their look says.

"All right," Bryan says. "But visiting hours are almost over. Family only after eight o'clock." He makes a few marks on the chart. "When he wakes up again, you can feed him his cherry gelatin," he adds as he exits.

"Jell-O?"

One of my father's eyes pop open, eyebrow arching like a comic book character.

"Hey there, handsome." Ujima pulls the rolling table with the food tray closer to the bed. "You had us scared there."

"Sorry." His voice croaks, though it already sounds stronger than it was earlier. "Can I have the food now?"

I take the small container of gelatin, pull the metallic covering off the package, and dip a plastic spoon into the bright red and wobbly mass. Something about the texture of gelatin is usually off-putting to me, but seeing the look on my dad's face, bright-eyed and childlike, makes me rethink my bias. He slurps it up like it's the best thing he's ever tasted.

I should be happy that his appetite is back so quickly, but a shiver of apprehension runs through me. I made a bad situation worse by making him worry about the choir's preparedness, constantly telling him I wasn't good enough, that I wasn't going to be able to get them ready for the concert. And then, on top of that, I told him Emmett and I had sex and that he decided to bail on me—*us*—completely. That last bit must have been what sent him over the edge.

That's why he's here. Because of me.

"Why do you look so miserable?" he says, laugh-coughing. "I'm the one who had a heart attack."

"I put you here."

"Hay naku, Quito. Be quiet. It's my own bad health choices."

"No. You got so worked up when I told you about me and Emmett. It made you sick."

"You're wrong. That's not the reason."

"If we hadn't done it, you'd be okay. I shouldn't have told you."

"Don't be stupid, anak. Of course you had to tell me. You should not hide things from me. It just makes you feel worse." He finishes the rest of his gelatin with a final slurp. "Ujima, did Quito ever tell you about how he came out as gay? To his mom and me?"

"Ooh! Story time." Jee leans forward, arms resting on their knees and manicured fingers interlaced. "Spill the tea, Mr. C."

My dad loves telling this story as much as I'm tired of listening to it.

"He was still in middle school. I brought him to one of my high school choir concerts. It was in the spring, I think. On a Saturday afternoon. We had this new boy who was a transfer student. Chad. He was very guapo, diba, anak? Very handsome?"

I groan. "Ohmigod, Dad."

Ujima is so far forward on their chair that only their impressive leg muscles are keeping them seated.

"This guy, he had such an effect on my son. Quito could not wait to talk to him after the concert. To congratulate him for his singing on one of the solos. You should have seen how bewitched he was! Like in that song. You know that song, Ujima? *Bewitched, bothered, and bewildered...* " he manages to sing in a thin, scratchy voice.

"Yes, of course you do. Anyway, I introduced them to each other while I talked to the parents of all the kids. I thought, well, he's happy. Then after that—susmaryosep! He was so upset. Their talk did not go well, you could say."

"Poor Quitolito!" Ujima says.

I roll my eyes in an attempt to diminish the event. But the truth is, I was devastated. I'd figured out I was attracted to boys by the time I was in sixth grade. Not wanting to deal with my feelings, I channeled all the unwelcome urges into playing piano and listening to music. Then, when I saw Chad sing at my dad's concert, everything that had been bubbling underneath came simmering up to the top.

It wasn't his voice, really. My crush on Chad had to do with his surfer blond hair and his Malibu tan. The fact that he looked like a boy band member straight out of a VH1 video. Most importantly, he seemed to be like me. The cute upturn of his lips, the almost unnoticeable flare of the wrist as he walked. All signs that we had more in common than just music.

"He was kind of a dick to me," I say.

"What happened?" Jee asks.

"I told him I thought his solo was great. Even though, honestly, it wasn't all that. But he seemed really pleased that I'd congratulated him. Really flamed out about it, to be honest. I thought, *That's his way of telling me he's gay*. So I took a chance and told him I thought he was really handsome, too. On top of being a good singer. All of sudden he shuts down, gives me this stone-cold look, and says, 'Yeah, I'm not into you. I'm not a faggot.' Then he just turned around and walked away."

The pain of that memory hits me harder than I expect. It was a mistake to reveal myself to Chad that day. It wasn't so much that I was afraid he'd tell other people. It was that I was horribly embarrassed by how wrong I was, thinking he could be like me. That a boy that beautiful would even want to talk to me. So much of that affected the way I'd go on to see Emmett—to be afraid of opening up to him, another boy who was so clearly out of my league.

I couldn't hide my shame and disappointment from my dad that day. But I didn't want to tell him the cause of it. When I got home that evening, I tried to erase the whole event from my head by doing the usual—playing piano nonstop. Hours of Chopin, Gershwin, Billy Joel, anything that came to my head. I played for so long, I managed to wear out my parents' threshold for listening to music. *Anak!* my dad shouted. *Cool your jets now, okay? Give your fingers a rest.* I got the point. Even they had their limits. I went to my room to listen to more music on my Walkman.

Then, after lying in my bed and humming along to the entire *Miss Saigon* soundtrack, something surprising started to happen.

All my tamped-down, adolescent hormones started sublimating, combining with the music I was force-feeding myself.

The notes came first. I remember seeing them floating, swirling in the air and then alighting onto the music staff in my brain. For years I'd been able to see music as clearly as I could hear it. This was just an extension of that.

The harmonies came next—a little more effort. Not much. It just took a realization of the accompanying bass. Filling out the harmonic structures was simple.

What was harder were the words. I'd never had much talent for them and might never have been able to come up with decent lyrics otherwise. But my blossoming desires pushed them to the surface, and they came to me, almost as easily as the music itself.

One day I'll break through
And do what it takes to
Be more than this simple disguise
Until then, it's clear
I'm giving in to my fears
By always hiding myself in these lies

I ran back out into the living room and started to work through it. My mother was preparing dinner, while my dad had fallen asleep on the couch watching the news. The song had so consumed me, needing to be let out, that it didn't even occur to me to hide any of it from them—the music *or* words.

They tell me the show must go on
So I'll try to be strong

And I'll say what they want me to say
But the person they'll see
Won't really be me
It's only a part I play

By the time I'd finished running through it, I wasn't even aware they'd been listening until I realized the TV had been turned off and the sounds in the kitchen had stopped. I turned around to see them sitting on the couch together.

The looks on their faces were hard to interpret. They seemed displaced. Confused. Their eyes searched for something to say.

"Oh," I said, embarrassed. "I didn't realize you guys were listening. Just a tune I came up with. I know it's not any good."

Those looks again, staring. Almost as if they couldn't place me. Like I was a curious stranger who'd just walked into the house out of the blue.

"It...it's very nice," my dad finally managed to say. "There's so much...so much...I don't know the right word." He turned to my mom. His face tried to squeeze out some sort of answer.

"Sincerity," my mother said. She rushed up and hugged me.

"So you like it?" I asked.

"More than like, anak. Much more than that."

My father hung back, so I was never quite sure if he felt the same as my mom. But though I didn't know what he thought of my very personal composition at the time, I did get the sense that he understood where it came from. And what had precipitated the creation of it.

I decided to go all the way. I told them both about my interaction with Chad after the concert. All of it. My mother said nothing in response, only taking me in her arms again and embracing me tightly against her, her tiny arms shaking, but with an excess of strength, not weakness. My dad nodded slowly. He came over, rested his hand on my shoulder, and said, quietly, *It's a good song, anak. A very, very good song.*

My dad coughs quietly now in the hospital bed. "Did you know, I made sure never to give Chad another solo?"

"I didn't know that."

"You're a good father, Mr. Cruz," Ujima says.

"I try." His eyes crinkle.

"I'm pretty impressed, actually," Ujima says. "Coming out to your parents when you were that young? It's never easy telling people, even the ones you love, who you really are."

My father, though still slightly pale, is more awake and alert than before. "Ujima, you are right. I continue to tell my son to be open with me, and yet I do not do the same. I am a hypocrite."

He coughs quietly. "Quito, this was not my first health emergency. One year ago, do you remember, during the summer? I told you I had a problem related to fatigue. I didn't tell you the whole truth because I did not have the whole story at the time. I thought maybe I was dehydrated. Light-headed from working too hard. But I was talking to Mrs. Ramos, the Spanish teacher, and all of a sudden I had such a hard time thinking of the right words to say. I couldn't even form a simple sentence. She told me I should go see the doctor. Just in case. Thank god I listened to her because I would not have known otherwise that I had a—what do you call it? A ministroke."

I fall into the chair next to his bed. "Dad! You should have told me."

"About the stroke? No. I didn't want to worry you." His face sags. "But the heart attack after that, yes. I should have told you."

"I was there for the heart attack."

"I mean the one before this one."

"You had a heart attack *before this one?*"

"When Celeste called to tell you I was sick, it wasn't from mild pneumonia. I was recovering from my first heart attack. Not too serious. At the time, I thought it was just acid indigestion. But, you see, I learned from my mistake! I called the doctor right away."

"Oh my god! Obviously you did NOT learn!" I jump up and begin pacing the tiny length of the room. "I should have been helping you get better. Buying you healthy meals. Making you exercise...I don't know."

He laughs, a phlegm-saturated sound. "We all die, Quito. That's why we have to make the most of the time we have."

"I don't want to hear this," I mutter.

"There's more. Sit down. Please."

I sit, crossing my arms and legs over myself like a strait-jacket. Whatever it is he's about to tell me, I need to be fully fastened in.

"I haven't been honest with you. I *have* been feeling better these past days, well enough to go back to school."

"Well, obviously not, since you're back in the hospital."

"What I'm trying to tell you is that I want you to take over the choir for me," he says matter-of-factly. Period, end of story. As if this decision of his has ended the discussion of how he's completely hidden the truth of his health from me.

The ends always justify the means when it comes to my father making decisions about my life.

In the aftermath of the Chad debacle, for example, after I came out, he asked me to be the accompanist for Sunvalley's choir. He said I'd grown in his eyes. I'd told them the truth about myself and shown great strength. It was time to claim more for myself. To do more. To be more.

I told him, *Hell no*.

I hadn't even graduated seventh grade yet.

But he'd already talked to the principal of my school. Everything was set for the coming year. I'd be given an exemption for one class period in the morning to play for the high school choir. Glenview Middle was just across the street from Sunvalley, so all I had to do was cross the road and—bam. I was an adult. That's when I realized it wasn't an invitation, really. It was him telling me what to do. Like when he "asked" me, at the age of three, if I wanted to start taking piano lessons. I wasn't even fully potty trained yet. How would I know what I wanted to do?

But, like the piano lessons, it was a good idea. I eventually became a better musician just by learning how to be a better accompanist. For an hour every day, I worked with him and the choir, watched his hands weave music, felt the breaths of a roomful of people come alive in my fingers. I became a part of something bigger than myself. And as a bonus (or was it the main goal all along?) I forgot all about Chad. My experience with him wasn't allowed to ruin choir for me. Dad got ahead of it. Turned it around. Prevented any bad associations with the choir by creating good ones instead.

He gave me the chance to be the director of my own life. To move it in a better direction. Even when he knew it'd be difficult.

"Dad, I don't know how to work with those kids. I'm just a pianist. I don't have any business teaching anyone how to sing. Plus, I live in New York. I can't just leave all my music gigs. Or my friends. Or Ujima."

He asks, "What about Mike?"

"Who?"

"Your boyfriend."

"You mean Mark."

"Whatever his name is. You didn't mention him."

"Quito broke up with him, Mr. Cruz. Before he and Emmett hooked up," Ujima says. "Mark cheated on him with the lyricist of the musical they've been working on."

"Thanks, Jee."

"What?" they say. "I thought we were supposed to be getting everything out in the open."

My dad shakes his head. "I always wanted Emmett to be the one for you, Quito. From that very first day he came into our lives."

I stare at him and attempt to respond, but I can't. I'm absolutely speechless.

I try to process what he's just said. I scan the kaleidoscope of memories from then, trying to remember what happened. I always knew that my dad has been a fan of Emmett since that first, irritating day that he forced himself on us in the choir room, with me nervous and upset and my father blissfully unaware of it, content that Emmett Aoki was gracing us with his presence. And certainly, I knew he'd grown to love him even more when he and I inexplicably became friends. But I thought it was just because Emmett filled a different sort of role as a son that I couldn't. I'd never had any idea he knew what was going on between

Emmett and me. How could he? I didn't even really understand it myself.

Time lengthens out while I sit and think.

"Dad," I say, finally, "I had barely come out to you and Mom. We never really talked about it afterward, either. I never realized how okay you were with me being gay. I mean now—sure—but when I was just a kid?"

"It was hard for me, Quito. At first. But your mother, she was the one who convinced me to be fully accepting. She told me, *If you're ever in doubt, just take a step back. And then look at our son. See through to the core of him, and you will know. This is who Quito is. We must make sure he wants for nothing in life, to get the chance to be who he was always meant to be. That is the job of a parent. To love their child one hundred percent, no matter what.*"

It's as if she's here in the room with us. I can see her so clearly, her deep brown eyes filled with steadfast resolve as she says these things to my father.

"But, Dad," I say, "how could you have known that Emmett had any interest in guys back then? Or in me, for that matter?"

"A parent knows these things. One day you'll understand." He shifts in the bed. Ujima and I instinctively reach out to help him. He waves our hands away. "That's why I asked you both to come here. I wanted to bring you together again. One last try."

"What do you mean, one last try?"

He coughs again, the edges of it so rough and wet that Ujima and I instinctively swallow. "I have been trying to get you together for a long time now."

This flies in the face of all the times I thought my father had seen us together. Seeing his expression when our bodies were too close or when our interactions seemed too intimate. I'd always assumed that he wasn't comfortable with the idea of me and Emmett being more than just friends.

"Dad, what are you talking about?"

He says to Ujima, "His mother and I, we always knew he was going to be different, you see. It came with the musical genius." He puts a hand on his chest and looks at me. "So much sensitivity in him. Seeing the world and hearing it so differently. I think this changed him, maybe. I don't know. I am not a scientist. I am just a father. I would watch them during choir rehearsal, you know? Or at our house for dinner. When they would work on music together. Emmett would watch Quito. All the time. That look on his face. I'll never forget it. As if there was no better thing in the world than to be near my son."

Ujima sighs in that annoying, dramatic way they do when they watch black-and-white movies. "So romantic."

"That was just the music," I say. "Emmett always loved music."

"He always loved music because he always loved *you*. And he always loved you because he loved your music. I don't have to know what famous actresses he has dated or has married. He will always come back to you because you are his home. We are his home. We are his family."

"You're right, Mr. C," a hooded man with sunglasses says from the doorway. "You were right. About everything."

"You're here," my dad says.

"I booked the next flight out as soon as I got the call."

Emmett takes off his sunglasses and pulls back his hoodie. He's holding a gift bag and an enormous bouquet of birds-of-paradise in full bloom, their orange beak blossoms on the verge of bursting into a tropical song.

He greets Ujima with a quick peck on the cheek. "How did you get here so fast from New York?" he asks them.

They take the bouquet and gift bag from Emmett, laying both on the table near the window. "I got into town early yesterday. To try to help that mess out over there," they say, waving in my direction.

"Who called you? How did you know we were here?" I ask Emmett.

"Don't look so confused," my dad says. "I asked the doctor to call him this morning while you were gone getting coffee."

Emmett hugs him, carefully, so as not to hurt him. "You seem fine to me." He ruffles the top of my dad's hair. "Are you sure this wasn't part of your master plan to get me to come back immediately?"

My father laughs. A much lighter sound now. "Even *I'm* not that dramatic. But... now that you're back, you can both make sure the concert happens as planned," my father says.

"The concert." My heart sinks. "We'll have to cancel."

"No," my dad says forcefully. "You have to go on. Both of you. They're all counting on you."

"Dad, there's no way we're doing this without you. This is *your* farewell concert."

"It's the concert I wanted, yes. But I never wanted this to be for me. My time has passed. Now is for you. You lead them in my place."

"I can't do that," I say.

"Yes, you can," my dad says.

"Do you think you'll be well enough to attend, Mr. C?" Emmett asks.

"Of course, of course," Dad says, dismissing the notion of his absence. "We have two weeks still. Plenty of time. I will be fine. I'll be dancing in the aisles. Happy I can enjoy listening to the music instead of having to be in charge of it."

Looking at him, he does look markedly better, his health somehow bolstered by Emmett's appearance. If he's able to come home tomorrow, he'd have plenty of time to rest and be well enough to attend the concert. At the very least, we could have someone live stream the event so that he could watch from home.

The bigger questions are: Do I have enough time to figure out how to get the choir back on track? Will Emmett stay? Is he done running away from me?

My dad has been looking at me, watching the gears turn in my head. "Quito," he says, "you haven't gotten a chance to eat the food Ujima brought you. And probably Emmett is hungry from the flight. Why don't you two go to the cafeteria? Ujima will keep me company."

"Are you just trying to get me alone, Mr. Cruz?" Ujima says.

"Maybe," he says, smiling.

Jee pushes Emmett toward me and takes his place by the hospital bed, shooing us out of the room with a flick of their wrist. "Go on. I'll stay here. And bring me back something tasty. Like Nurse Bryan."

Emmett and I stumble out of the room and meander the length of the hall. It's only when one of the nurses behind the desk lets out a gasp, pointing at an undisguised Emmett, that we're forced to move with purpose. We hurry down the hallway.

A room at the end looks to be empty. After checking to make sure it's devoid of any people or belongings, we close ourselves in.

The air inside has the heavy bite of bleach to it, and the beds have been vacated. Hopefully because the patients got well enough to leave and not the alternative. I begin to feel a little queasy. Or maybe I've already been feeling this way.

Emmett grabs one of the chairs and offers it to me. I hoist myself onto one of the beds instead. He sits in the chair and struggles to get comfortable, first sitting back, then leaning forward with his elbows on his knees, and then just resting his hands on his lap. A series of diminishing poses.

"Thanks for coming out," I say finally, cringing at the unintended double entendre. "My dad is definitely glad to see you."

"Quito, I'm sorry I left in such a hurry. Things were going on back in Los Angeles, and I needed to be there to sort them out in person."

The bed I'm sitting on is squishy and unstable. I hunch over in an effort to balance myself. "The picture," I say, "of us together. We weren't careful enough. We made a mistake. You needed to salvage your career. I get it."

"The picture complicated things, yes, but we didn't make a mistake, Quito. I knew being seen in public was a risk. That if I showed my face and if I showed any sort of public affection toward you whatsoever, people were going to come to some conclusions. Quito, I knew the person at the table beside us was taking pictures. I knew they snapped one when I held your hand. I didn't mind. In fact, I wanted them to. And I kind of expected them to post it online. That's just what people do."

"You...did?" I stare at him.

"As soon as the speculation started hitting, my agent called. I told him I wanted to make a statement coming out, wanted to get his help in crafting it. Maybe we'd need to pull in a damage control expert. I don't know. But he didn't want to hear it. He said I was at risk of losing a couple of upcoming deals. Stuff we hadn't signed on yet. He wanted me to refute the gossip. Make a statement saying I *wasn't* with you. That you were just some friend going through a hard time. He said my reputation depended on it. It's hard enough just being Asian American in Hollywood; it took me almost ten years to land my first movie as a romantic lead. Being gay on top of that? He said it was going to be a massacre and that I needed to do something to fix it ASAP. So I did. And I needed to fly back to L.A. to deal with it. To try to salvage some of the roles he claimed I was going to lose but also to be there so I could do it in person. So he understood how serious I was."

"Do what in person?"

"Fire him. Told him right to his face. He's been my agent for fifteen years, Quito. But he wanted me to stay in the closet. He's been wanting me to stay there for my whole career. I'm tired of it. Tired of not being seen for who I really am. Tired of not *being* who I really am. And tired of not being with the person I really love."

I sit quietly, trying to think of the right thing to say. Before I can respond, the silence is shattered by the ringing of an alarm and a garbled announcement from the hallway.

Emmett opens the door. Two nurses rush by. We watch as they run down the hall.

Into my father's room.

Chapter 26—Now

I NEVER REALIZED before today that my mother's closet has been empty all these years.

It took months for my father to go through her things after she died. A heartbreaking task for anyone to have to do, to go through the belongings of someone they loved, package them up, give them away. Every item another loss. I offered to help him, but he didn't think it was necessary or appropriate. Secretly, I was thankful. I didn't actually have the strength to follow through on my offer.

After he'd finally donated all my mom's clothing to Goodwill, I assumed he'd filled her closet with his own possessions. My father always had so many trinkets, inventions, and gadgets from thrift stores, sidewalk sales, or impulse purchases from infomercials, their promises of *getting things done better, faster, smarter* too much a part of the American dream that my dad couldn't ever resist them. He hoarded dozens of these things and stored them in every part of the house.

Just not, apparently, in my mother's closet.

The only things inside were his barong Tagalog—the classic Filipino dress shirt, gauzy and stiff, still in its packaging from a trip to the dry cleaners—and a pair of Prada shoes I'd given him three years ago on his birthday, which look as if they've never been worn.

I roam the bedroom. It feels as if he is still inside it, somewhere, if I only look hard enough. Everything is imbued with his smell, a combination of drugstore aftershave, unwashed shirts, and old music scores. His bedsheets are still crumpled in his familiar shape on the bed. I can see him waking up, putting on his tsinelas, stretching and singing a song on his way to the bathroom. The way he does every morning.

The way he *did*.

I've been lost in this one-hundred-and-fifty-square-foot room with nowhere else to go, replaying the last twenty-four hours in my head, seeing the doctor's sorry look of compassion as she walked toward us in the waiting room with her droopy eyes and mushy mouth, a face made of putty. I wanted to press my fists into it as far as I could go, pushing until I squeezed every bit of pity out of it. Pushing until I wouldn't have to see her looking at me the way she did when she told me, *I'm sorry, but your father is dead.*

I can't even remember how we got home. Ujima drove us, possibly. Or Emmett. They stayed up with me almost the entire night. I know that, at least. I sensed their constant presences, clinging to the periphery of my awareness and prodding me gently throughout the night. To eat. To drink. To use the bathroom. To sleep. Even when, every time, I'd shake my head in silence or just stare off into some void they couldn't pull me from. I know that they finally fell asleep on the couches toward dawn. I sat there with them for a while and then went to my father's room to escape their snoring. Something about the sound of it seemed obscene to me, a rude reminder of the constancy of life.

It's only when I feel the both of them stoop down onto my father's bedroom floor and hold me from behind that I realize they're awake again. I can't tell who is who, and I don't care. I let myself be tucked into an indiscriminate tangle of arms. We stay wrapped up like that for a while, rocking in time.

Later, at the kitchen table, I force down a lukewarm cup of coffee, finishing it in one bitter gulp. I push the empty mug toward Ujima. They brush my hand lightly and get up to make another pot.

Across the table, Emmett watches me intently. As if it's the only thing keeping me tethered to existence. Maybe it is. I don't let myself think of what I'd do, where I'd go, without the two of them here.

"How are you doing?" Emmett asks.

I don't respond.

Ujima stretches. "He's drinking something. That's a good sign. You need to eat, too, though, Quito. You haven't had anything since yesterday. Let me warm something up for you." They open the fridge and gape. The leftover containers filled with unfamiliar-looking Filipino dishes confound them. "Or I can go out and get us some doughnuts."

Emmett looks up. "Great idea. Doesn't that sound good, Quito?"

I trace the tip of my index finger on the edge of my coffee cup. "On Sundays after church, we used to stop by Crown Café and get apple fritters and maple bars. Dad used to eat at least three."

"That settles it." Jee stoops to kiss me on the top of my head. "Emmett, darling, may I borrow your car?"

He tosses them the keys to his rental. "All yours."

"I won't be gone long," Jee says to me. They catch Emmett's eye, communicating things to him in a knowing glance that I'm too exhausted to try to interpret.

The door thuds shut. My skin prickles from the sound of them revving up the engine and peeling out of the driveway.

The hard, heavy wood of my chair pulls me down. Gravity feels even stronger in here, almost inescapable, though somehow dust particles manage to float right in front of my face in the harsh morning sun. The slow impossibility of them signals to me that time is grinding to a halt. Like the world is increasingly refusing to spin on its axis.

The refrigerator door pops open. "Don't know why Ujima couldn't have just warmed us up some of this stuff," Emmett says. He holds up a plastic container of leftovers filled with a mixture of dark brown, lentil-size beans flecked with the red and green of diced tomatoes and spinach. I hear the low rumble of his stomach. "Looks like the monggo guisado from last week. Your dad was the best cook, you know? Even when he was sick, he was cooking for us. Taking care of us."

The thought of all the leftovers makes me sad in a way I can't explain at first. Then I realize that it's because the refrigerator is filled with remnants of my father. Time spent chopping, stirring, frying. Making things I've taken for granted my entire life. The refrigerated air creeps closer and corkscrews its way through me. I want Emmett to close the door, to shut it all back inside, but he just stands there, staring at the container in his hand, and I realize he's not turning around because he's crying. I can hear it in his breathing, the stilted rhythm that comes from trying to hide it, from not wanting to add his grief to mine.

He closes the refrigerator door. He's no longer holding the food but has, instead, taken out the carton of orange juice and goes to look for a glass in the drying rack near the sink, still being careful not to let me see his face.

Emmett says, "Hey. Didn't I give this to your dad that first time I came over for dinner?"

He picks up my father's favorite glass from the sink. It's wet, slick, and because Emmett isn't holding it carefully enough, or maybe because he's exhausted and broken, it slips between his fingers and falls, pushing through the thick, time-resistant air. The glass plummets for miles down to the countertop. I think to myself how surprising it is that Emmett still remembers the glass. How sad it is that he's the one to destroy it. And how my father will never see it again. Not just because Emmett is dashing it into a million jagged pieces. But because my father is dead.

The glass shatters.

"Shit," Emmett yells out, immobile.

"Leave it," I say.

"I'll clean it up."

I defy the sinkhole of my chair and push Emmett out of the way. "Just leave it!" Without thinking, I slap my left hand down onto the counter. A shard of glass punctures my skin.

"Dammit, Quito." Emmett grabs hold of my bleeding hand. "Let me see that."

I flinch. "I'm fine."

"You are not fine. This is a bad cut. Here," he says, rinsing my hand off in the sink and then pressing my other hand against the bleeding wound. "Apply some pressure. First aid supplies still under the bathroom sink?" Emmett says, running off to the bathroom.

I hold my hand up to my eyes, watching for a few seconds as blood sprints down my forearm. An iron-tinged tang fills the air. I tear a paper towel from the holder above the sink and press down on the wound. The blood pools quickly onto the paper, a crimson circle endlessly expanding. I'm surprised by how little pain I feel.

I find myself wandering out of the kitchen and into the living room. I slump down on the piano bench. I think back to my early childhood, watching my dad at the piano, wondering what wondrous machine he'd brought into the house and wishing I, too, could make it sound the way he did, coaxing the hard keys into creating a warm, round, vibrant sound that filled our home, that made my mother sing, that made me smile and sing along, too, even if I didn't know what words to sing. Those days of being together are long gone now, my mother missing for so many years. And now this—the backbone of our family dead, with only me to hold everything together. But what is a song without its structure? Without its beautiful melody, without the underlying bass line to support it? Just a lonely set of black and white keys with nothing to tie them together.

I smash my fist down onto them. The blood from my wound flows freely. The resultant sound is dissonant, ridiculous. I make the sound again and again. Red mixes with white and black.

Emmett comes running out of the bathroom, sets first aid supplies on top of the piano, and sees the mess of blood and tears. "Hey! Stop that. You're going to hurt yourself even more." He stands behind me and takes hold of my arms.

I collapse backward into him, crying.

"I'm going to patch up your cut, okay?" Emmett says. "Before you bleed out any more." I nod, still looking down at the mess I've created.

He sits next to me on the bench, peels the wrapper off a bandage, and moistens a cotton ball with alcohol. He pulls the bloodied paper towel off my hand, takes the wet cotton ball, and cleans the gash in tiny, tight circles. He blows on my hand to dry it and then affixes layers of gauze with firm pressure.

"Thank you," I say.

He says nothing, his attention focused on the squeezing.

"I'm sorry I didn't listen to you when I called. I was convinced you'd left me. Left *us*. I should have trusted you." I tug my hand away from him and continue the pressure myself, pushing my hands deep into my lap.

Emmett sighs. "To be honest, Quito, there was a moment there when I was tempted to do what my agent suggested. To go back into hiding. Back to how things were before. But being with you and your dad again, it reminded me of how happy I used to be. Here, in this very house. At this piano."

He takes both sides of my face in his hands and forces me to look at him. His eyes are wet with tears. He smiles. "What your dad said at the hospital was right. The two of you have always been my family."

My hand throbs, the wound pulsing from the blood racing around my body. I clasp my hands together, digging them deeper between my legs, as if that will somehow slow the pumping of my heart.

"All those years without music, without singing, without you—they were good, but they were never enough. And I knew I had to make a choice. With my agent. My career. My life. I had to choose to be the person you always saw me as. Because that was always the real Emmett. Not the one on the screen. The one here, that isn't complete without you."

When he says this, the previously shattered song of my family, with its plucked-away parts, winds through my mind and seeks out his words, using them to try to make itself whole again.

I put my arms around Emmett. We hold each other as the faint, unassuming threads of something new begin to stitch themselves together.

"Well, don't y'all look cozy," Ujima says, holding two large boxes of doughnuts.

Emmett and I are sitting together on the couch. His arm wraps behind my neck as I lay nestled against his muscled shoulder.

"How many did you get?" he asks, dumbfounded.

"I just want to make sure Quito doesn't lose his ample, curvy figure."

"Whatever. Your wig is a mess," I say.

"And he's back."

They put the boxes down on the coffee table and then pat their scalp with their fingertips, massaging their hair back into place.

"What? I had the top down. And I still look better than you," Jee says, sticking their tongue out at me.

"Gee, thanks."

"So, what did I miss?"

Emmett's hold around me tightens. He tilts his head down, touching his cheek to the top of my head.

"Nothing," I say.

"Mm-hmmmmmmm," Ujima hums, sliding all the way down the scale and back up again. I almost object when they sit down in my dad's recliner, tucking their long legs underneath them. Then I remember that it doesn't matter anymore who sits there. Jee glances over at me, their eyes scanning, reading the trail the shifting thoughts leave on my face. "Quito, what should I tell the choir kids?"

"What do you mean?"

"You're in no shape to have to deal with things with your dad *and* have to deal with the choir. Let me handle it."

We have only two weeks to go before the concert. There is no way the kids will be able to go on now. Not after losing my dad. It will destroy them.

And yet his last request, his last *demand*, was that the concert go on. No matter what. He'd want us to go through with it even more now. He wanted me to take over. Wanted me to take care of his students.

And he wanted me and Emmett to be together.

He's always gotten his way. Why change now?

"No, Jee. Thanks, but I'm going to take care of it. I have to. The show has to go on. I'll probably still need your help, though." I turn to Emmett. "And you, too, of course. It's time you came in to work with the kids."

"Will they even be able to sing?" Emmett asks.

"I won't force anyone to. If any of them can't because they need time to process everything, that's fine. Even if we just have half, or even a quarter, of the kids, I can make it work. It's what Dad would have wanted." I look at Ujima. "Help me rally the kids. I might even need you to sing if we don't have enough people left for the concert."

"And me?" Emmett asks.

"Just show up. They'll be heartbroken when I break the news to them. Just seeing you, meeting you—it'll give them a boost. I know they look up to you. Maybe you can help them feel more able to participate."

"Whatever you need," Emmett says. "I'm here for you."

I get up slowly, disentangling myself from Emmett's embrace. I stretch and yawn. The air in the living room smells old, stale. I pull back the curtains and roll open the window.

Ujima says, "I canceled the rest of my stay at the Airbnb. I'm staying right here on this couch for the rest of my stay, and I don't want to hear any arguments from either of you."

As sad as I am, I can't help but smile. "Of course."

"Wouldn't dream of it," Emmett says.

"And one more thing." With one deft move, Ujima flips open the top box of doughnuts and grabs a rainbow-sprinkled. "I can help out with the choir every day *except* for tomorrow. I have an appointment. With an old family friend, Dr. Sinclairé. She's the reason—the other reason—I came to the Bay Area. I'm going to be starting hormones, with her help." Jee's eyes begin to tear up. They smile, embarrassed. "Ooh, girl. I didn't think I'd get so emotional."

I go over and embrace them. "Oh my god. I'm so happy for you, Jee."

"Not sure if you've noticed, but I'm rarely out of my girl clothes these days."

I kiss them on their moist cheek. "Haven't noticed at all."

"Bitch, please." They laugh. The bright, unburdened sound of it is wonderful. "For the past few months, I've felt more comfortable with my femme side. I've been seriously wanting to transition to being a trans woman and I've finally worked up the courage to do it."

"So would you like us to start using she/her?" I ask.

"I'm still identifying as nonbinary for now. But it's a journey. I see that. And I'm going to embrace it all."

I hug them tighter. "I'm so proud of you."

"Thank you," Ujima says. "I knew you'd get it. Now, about that concert. What exactly is the plan?"

Chapter 27—Now

EMMETT YAWNS. "REMIND me again why we had to get here so early?"

"So we can hide you before the choir kids get here."

"It still smells the same," he says, "like cardboard boxes and chalk. With a dash of BO."

He walks the perimeter of the choir room, taking time to look at the various wall hangings my father has put up. Music informational charts, inspirational sayings, humorous anecdotes, posters about tolerance and diversity. He runs his hands over the concrete walls and wooden shelves and pulls out one of the student's choir folders. Sheet music ruffles in his hands. "Hey, I think I remember some of these."

His face scrunches as he scans the pages, as if trying to recall something from his memories. Watching him makes me wish I can somehow make him experience what happens to me when I read music—how the notes stream off the page, key themselves into the waiting locks in my brain, and release specific sounds tactile enough to hold in my hands.

His brow smooths out. He *is* able to hear something. Maybe not as vividly as I can. But still, something familiar. Like the half-formed recollection of a dream, perhaps.

With a snap, he closes the folder shut and tosses it with unerring accuracy back into its slot. "Can we go into your dad's office?"

"Why not? I'm pretty sure he won't care," I say, more curtly than I intend.

"Hey." He comes up to me and squeezes my arm. The wound underneath the bandage on my hand wakes up. "I didn't mean to—"

"It's okay." The pain flares only briefly. I wait a moment for it to die out before entering the office with him. "Just messing with you."

Everything is how I left it—which is how my dad left it. The stacks of choral octavos, music books, catalogs, lesson plans, and sticky notes with jotted-down scribbles have been in their same exact spots since I first arrived. Moving any of them even a single inch meant that I was claiming his place, preventing him from coming back to take over exactly where he'd left off.

My dad's chair whines angrily when Emmett sits in it. He swivels around and leans back. His eyes latch on to something at the top of the green metal filing cabinet.

"That looks familiar." He jumps up and pulls down my father's tape recorder. A quick puff of his breath scatters dust into the room. He presses play:

. . . the part. You sing it back. We'll do that a few times, and you'll have it all on tape so you can have it to practice with at home . . .

It's jarring, the sound of my own voice as a high school student. So different from the way I hear myself now. I want to blame it on youth. And inexperience. The high pitch, the strain, the slight wavering of it. How what I'm saying doesn't seem solid enough to stand on its own, how the words seem inches from falling in on themselves.

Cool. Hey, thanks for doing this, by the way. I'd be lost without you.

When Emmett's voice emerges from the recorder, as unmoored as mine, I realize that it isn't because we were young. It's because we were afraid. Of each other. And of ourselves being with the other. Not the kind of fear that comes from the threat of being hurt but rather the kind that comes from wanting something too much, for too long, and then finally finding yourself possibly within arm's length of it. If only the right words are said.

And only if the other person can actually hear those words.

"You were never allergic to sawdust, were you?" I ask. "Why did you really join the choir?"

He sits back down in the chair. Metal parts grate.

"Hearing that song of yours freshman year hit me hard, Quito. I needed to find some way to thank you."

"Thank me for what?"

"For waking me up. For giving me permission to see something about myself I was afraid to look at before. For the hope that I wasn't the only person who thought that way about myself. It's just, I could never figure out how to tell you. We never really had any classes together. Didn't run in the same circles."

"I remember."

He laughs, the chair chirping along with him. "I figured I needed to take drastic measures. So I joined the choir. Even though it took me three years to get up the courage."

"Just to talk to me?"

"And more."

Looking at him now, I'm startled by what I see—a semblance there of something familiar. Some*one*.

A reflection of myself. My own desires. And needs. And fears.

And love.

I touch the side of his face. He smiles up at me.

As much as I want this little trip down memory lane to keep going, I have to cut it short. "Come on. We need to go over the lines you'll be singing for this new arrangement I did for the concert."

Emmett's eyebrows go up. "And what new arrangement might this be?"

"You'll see," I say.

After about half an hour of practicing, I push Emmett into the office a few minutes before the bell rings. "Okay, now, be quiet," I remind him. "No more listening to old rehearsal tapes."

The kids start trickling in just after he hides himself. I wait at the piano, trying to maintain a normal look on my face. Every part of it is tortured and insincere.

I decide to let go of the facade. I've done them a disservice this whole time by not being honest. Now is not the time for sugar-coating anything. Now is the time for truth. No matter how hard it is. Even when my body starts to feel that familiar, inescapable weightiness.

As the kids settle quietly into their seats, Principal Higgins—normally a rosy-faced, ebullient man—ambles into the room without a single ounce of joy. He's accompanied by the mild-looking school counselor, Ms. Mulholland, and, surprisingly, Mr. Drummond, whose lips are so tightly pressed against each other, they look like one conjoined mono lip.

It's clear from their expressions. The students as well as the adults. Everyone is either worried or upset.

I steel myself.

"Everyone, what I'm about to say will not be easy. That's why I've asked Principal Higgins and Ms. Mulholland to be here. To help me, and all of you, with the news I need to share. And thank you to Mr. Drummond for also coming. And for subbing in for me the past two days. I didn't know you'd be here. I didn't expect you to..." My mind begins to drift, an effort to leave my body and go someplace else.

I close my eyes, take a deep breath, and exhale.

"My father, Mr. Cruz. He..." I hold on to the edge of the piano. I've never been so thankful for its faithful constancy. "He passed away on Wednesday. A complication from another heart attack."

Some of the students cry out. Celeste wails something loud and incomprehensible.

Ms. Mulholland moves swiftly to Celeste, who holds on to her. Principal Higgins comes to my side and says, in a loud yet calming voice, "Ms. Mulholland is here for any of you who would like to talk to her. And you are all excused for the rest of the day. Take as much time as you need."

The students are in tears. Some, like Celeste, are close to despondent, though Ms. Mulholland and Principal Higgins and even Mr. Drummond do their best to console them. I see that

Milton, alone as usual, is crying into his hands. I go up to him and, channeling my best inner Ujima, stoop down close, there for whatever he needs. Without a word, he leans over on to me. I hold him as he and the rest of the students continue grieving.

"Will we still do the concert?" Celeste manages to ask between sobs.

I let Milton go gently and swipe my face with the back of my sleeve.

I look out at all of them. It makes my heart ache to see them quietly breaking down in their seats, looking at each other, at us, down at the floor or out the window. At anyone or anything that might possibly tell them this is all some kind of trick. That they haven't just lost a teacher they love. That things can keep going on as before.

I move to the front of the room but still close enough to be able to feel them and our shared loss. The hardened, heavy wave of it. "As Principal Higgins said, if you need to take the next few days off from choir, or even not come back for the rest of the school year, you should absolutely do that. I know you all loved my father. Every student, every *person* who has ever known my dad has loved him. And you all know how much this concert meant to him. In fact, one of the last things he said to me in the hospital was that he still wanted it to go on, no matter what." I press a fist hard against my chest, trying to force it to slow down and steady itself. "So I want to honor my dad's last wish. I still want to put on the concert. With whoever can sing."

"I'll do it, Mr. Quito," Celeste says, her head still tucked against Ms. Mulholland's shoulder.

The other students nod. In their teary eyes, I can see determination replacing despair.

"Then I have someone I want you all to meet," I say. "He can't replace my father. No one can. But maybe he can help make the concert a better experience for you all. Emmett?"

Even before he emerges from the choir office, the kids scream.

It's the happiest sound I've ever heard in my entire life.

When he stands in front of them, I experience a brief flash of déjà vu—of Emmett appearing in this very space for the first time and everyone's reaction to him. How everyone was suddenly petrified. For someone unaccustomed to his presence, it's a lot to take in all at once. He can encompass everything in the room.

He opens his arms wide and motions his fingers gently toward himself. That's all the permission they need. They tackle him. He holds on to as many kids as he can. They're generally unable to speak, but the message is clear. They huddle in a mass of crying and laughter, the hopeful sound of happiness slowly wrapping itself around grief.

"So. You all really want to do this?" I ask.

"Yes," they say.

"For Mr. Cruz," Celeste says.

Emmett looks at me. "For Mr. Cruz."

Chapter 28—Now

HERE'S SOMETHING NOT every pianist making his debut as the conductor of his own father's choir will admit: the sight of a packed auditorium can make the idea of adult incontinence pads seem perfectly acceptable.

Standing center stage, I peek into the theater from behind a tiny crack in the velvet curtain and watch the people stream in. They crane their heads and gape at the camera crews, newscasters, bloggers, and other paparazzi filling the back and sides of the auditorium, angling to capture Emmett's performance (and breaking who only knows how many building fire codes in order to do so). A barrage of thoughts nips at my consciousness. Did we prepare well enough? Was two weeks enough time? Will we fail completely? Will people like what we've done?

Would my dad be proud of us?

Of me?

Honey-hued perfume winds around me. Ujima plants a quick peck on my check. Their platinum-blond hair is tousled in a 1940s glamour wave, their body snug in a strapless fuchsia evening gown and arm-length gloves.

"Hello, Norma Jean," I say.

"Norma who?"

"Norma Jean? As in Marilyn Monroe?"

"Oh." Ujima pats all around their body as if making sure they have the right dress on. "I thought I was serving you some Material Girl realness."

"Right. You do know that Madonna was..." Something about the way they're inhabiting the dress, the way it seems to have always been there on them, waiting to be seen, makes me hold both their hands. "You know what? Never mind. You look stunning."

"Thank you, baby."

They take a step back and look up and down at me dressed in my father's barong Tagalog. Originally dressed in the black suit I'd brought with me from New York, I'd found myself drifting into my dad's bedroom before heading to school with Ujima and Emmett for the concert, seeking some sort of last-minute guidance. The white barong hanging in his closet glowed like a halo and called out to me. I knew I had to wear it.

Jee's fingers fiddle with my hair. They look at me as if they've just found me after having lost me but fear they might lose me again if they're not too careful. "How are you doing?" they ask.

"I'm okay."

"Good." They pat the top of my head. "Now go talk to your boyfriend. He's wigging out in the bathroom. And not in a good way."

"He's not my—"

"Just go!"

"All right. Sheesh."

Jee gives me a quick satin squeeze before pushing me off, stage left.

When I get to the bathroom, Emmett is standing in front of the cloudy mirror. Staring, though not exactly at his own reflection. It looks as if he's mentally willing himself to do something. What, I can't tell. I'm too distracted by how his tuxedo pants hug his body so well that I can see his buttock muscles flexing.

"Hey. Everything okay?"

He nods. Adjusts his tie. Readjusts it. The tie ends up coming loose in his fingers.

I reach around his neck and take hold of the fabric, pulling and shaping so that the bow folds back into shape. He continues his unfocused stare and says, "Thanks."

"We have a huge turnout. The concert's going to be all over the news. The whole world's going to know about Dad and what a great teacher he was. What a great man he was. Because of you."

"That's great." He tries to smile and ends up gritting his teeth instead.

"Are you really that nervous, Emmett? You're used to being in front of hundreds, thousands of people."

"Quito, this is different. I feel super unsure of myself right now for some reason."

In the few minutes before any kind of show begins, when places have been called and the time remaining is announced, there's a mental pileup that can happen. A crash of worry and fear. Usually that means everything else gets squeezed out and left to huddle in the corners of our minds. Emmett's used to being in front of a camera, saying lines from a script, knowing that he can do another take if the first one doesn't go according to plan. But this is more like *Saturday Night Live*. And we both know that didn't go so well. He doesn't like being this vulnerable.

"Look at me, Emmett. Take a deep breath. Inhale through your nose. Fill your lungs as if you were filling your belly. Exhale." I massage the sides of his face. "Relax your jaw, your tongue." I hold on to his shoulders, pulling them upward. "Feel the air inside you rising up like a column of energy supporting you, giving you energy to propel you forward."

The tension in his body is replaced by a calm strength. His face relaxes. "Thank you. Looks like you learned a few things from your dad."

"I had a good teacher. But he had an even better one," I say.

"Mr. Cruz?" Celeste's voice pushes its way through the door. "Everyone's ready, and the box office said everyone's been seated. Should we start lining up?"

"Just a second, Celeste," I yell out.

"Quito, what if I can't remember the words? Like, I'm trying to think of them now, and they're not coming to me."

"That's because you don't need them now. The words will come when the time is right. If they're coming from the right place, they'll be there. Your body and mind can't just turn them off. The dependable parts of you will still come through."

Emmett smiles that wonderful, big, crooked-tooth-revealing smile.

Looking at him, I realize what I love about that tooth.

I love how imperfect and real it is. How small. How everything else about Emmett can sometimes be too grand when, really, these things are just a tiny part of him, a habit of staking his claim in the world. Or rather, of accepting ownership of what he's always been given—a capitulation to the privilege of being talented, and smart, and beautiful—whereas the tooth is who Emmett really is. Immoveable, unconventional, unapologetic. Never asking to be fixed because it doesn't need fixing. It has the ability to exist with every other tooth, straight and perfect. It stands out and says, *Look at me. I'm not like everything else. And that's amazing.*

I kiss him.

"Mr. Cruz?" Celeste squeaks outside the door.

Emmett chuckles. "Mr. C has got some moves."

"Ick. Mr. C is my dad."

"Well, you're wearing his Filipino shirt and everything. You look very handsome in it, by the way—"

"Okay, shut up now," I say, and redouble back on him, my second kiss even deeper than the first.

"Mr. Cruz?"

Dammit. I force myself to break loose. "We're coming!" I shout. "Are we ready?" I say to Emmett.

He laughs. "We're good."

"Break a leg."

"You too," he says as I open the bathroom door, trying to brace myself against the nerves sparking off Celeste. I walk with her to gather everyone else from the choir room.

They all follow me to the backstage area. Hushed conversations percolate as the kids take their places in the wings. The noise of the audience through the curtain is overwhelming. So much louder than the ambient conversations to which I'm accustomed. They're more excited than usual, maybe because of Emmett. Or maybe I'm projecting.

I take my position center stage behind the curtain and block out all the sounds. A vision of my father in this exact position forms in my mind's eye. His hands clasped behind him, a ruffle of soft belly gently overtaking his leather belt, his brow damp in its many creases, full of the same worries and doubts as mine, feeling the same low-sitting pulse of excitement in the gut, and I realize—everything is how it should be. All the details have fallen into place, coaxed into position by my father's unrelenting, well-intentioned machinations.

"Okay, Dad," I say, smiling to myself. "You win."

The curtain parts. The noise of the crowd decrescendos to silence.

A spotlight shines.

"Whoa. Ah, hello. All you... fellows." The lights on me are unimaginably bright.

Focus, Quito. Focus.

I will myself to breathe.

"Over thirty years ago, my father, Mr. Cruz, became Sunvalley High's first choir director. During that time, he built up a choir so successful, they earned countless titles and awards, including last winter's first place win at the All-State Choir Festival. Tonight was to be his very last concert because he was going to retire. Instead, as you all know, he passed away unexpectedly."

I pause to look around at the endless faces, which, remarkably, shine back a strength of sorts. An energy to help me push through the sadness and keep doing what I'm doing.

"But as he told me in the hospital before he passed, this concert had to go on, no matter what. So while we are here tonight to celebrate the legacy he's created, to show my dad how thankful we are for so many years of being our director, mentor, friend, and inspiration, we're also here because this is what he wanted as his final note—his last gift. To *us*. Ladies and gentlemen, and everyone in between," I add, turning briefly and smiling to Ujima in the wings, "the Sunvalley High School Choir—with our special guest, Emmett Aoki—presents Mr. Cruz's final concert program, 'Stronger Together.'"

Chapter 29—Later

WHEN I LOOK back on that night, I will remember some things about the concert more than others.

I'll remember—after a week and a half of trying to get the boys to walk in from stage right and sing the entrance Gregorian chant without getting out of sync, slowing down, or tripping on their own shoelaces—how proud I was of the aural and visual effect they created. Exactly as my father must have intended. Dignified and hopeful.

How the chant was a perfect prelude to give everyone enough time to get into place for the Vivaldi, which went off without a hitch. Every section of the choir nailed their entrances with contained passion. How they'd taken all the prior notes I'd given them about the sopranos' unsteady pitches, the basses' overly covered sound, the tenors' tendencies to rush and the altos' to drag and transformed their merely okay practices into a glorious performance.

I'll remember how giddy I felt when Milton's solo as a soprano caught everyone by surprise during the spiritual, "Hold On"—a clarion treble tone coming from a young man. How it decimated their understanding of what the human voice could (or rather, *should*) do, the ringing out of his sustained soprano high C at the end of the piece soaring, sterling, so forward and bright that it knocked the wind out of everyone.

How Celeste's rich mezzo solo sprang from the heart of the choir as they sang "You'll Never Walk Alone," its melodies so stirring that it tested the choir's efforts not to cry. (Not at that point. Not so early in the program!)

And how, when Emmett took the stage for the first time, they were unable to hold the tears back any longer. How he sang "True Colors" with such sincerity that everyone felt stripped, deprived of their protective outer layer.

I'll remember how shocked I was to see that the accompanist for Emmett's second song wasn't some other pianist but the wind and string ensembles under the direction of Mr. Drummond. How he sidled up to me before walking onstage and said, *I never hated your dad, you know. I was just jealous that he took the best pianist I ever heard before I could recruit you for my jazz band.*

How they performed "You Raise Me Up," a song Emmett didn't so much sing as inhabit, starting from the inside of the phrases and propelling them outward, beyond even my own capacity to assign colors, shapes, or textures, the notes becoming mysterious and undefinable.

I'll remember how, after the strings wound their way around Emmett's final held note, he called me out onstage during the applause. How the audience's chant of *Quito Cruz, Quito Cruz* only ceased when I stood beside him. How Emmett then confessed to everyone that the song may have been in honor of my father (who was always more of a dad to him than his own) but was also intended for me. Because I'd always been the one to hold him up and see him for who he was. Who he should've always been.

How, then, Emmett pulled me into his arms and dipped me backward. Just enough to make my breath stop completely.

How he kissed me full on the lips in front of the audience and exponentially more, thanks to the countless cameras and phones memorializing every moment.

How Emmett finally, officially, came out of the closet to the entire world.

And how—even though the kids, the audience, and the press were going crazy, everyone trying their hardest to record, process, and celebrate the moment in a cacophony of gasps and excited chatter—everything crystallized around the two of us in utter silence, trapping us there like flies in amber, and how I wanted to sip the quiet sweetness of that moment forever.

Until I remembered that we had one more song to go. The finale. Which I'd reprogrammed to be "A Part I Play," but rearranged and reworded for not one person but many.

It started with me at the piano by myself, singing the first verse. Emmett joined me. Then Celeste. And Milton. The rest of the choir. Even a surprise appearance by Ujima, radiant in their gown, all of it building the song up to its refrain.

We know that the show will go on
'Cause our hearts all belong
To the person we sing for today
Yes, together we'll be
More than just you or me
We all have a part to play

And we all did. Because none of it could have happened without everyone's involvement. The kids. Rosie. Milton. Ujima. Even Mr. Drummond.

And Emmett, of course. And me.

And my dad.

And speaking of my dad, most of all, I will always remember this.

How, as I stood onstage, blown back by the onslaught of applause and cheering at the end, gripping Emmett's hand in mine and motioning the choir to take a bow, I was able to see my parents again.

My mother looked back at me as she did when I first played her my song, and the look on my father's face was the one he had when he'd walked in on me and Emmett sitting on the piano bench in our house that first night, our bodies so close that there was nothing between us.

Those looks on their faces I'd first assumed, from their resolve, were from fear, maybe. Or apprehension.

But now I see and remember. And know. It was always something so much simpler.

Understanding.

We see you, anak, they say to me.

We see you.

Coda

THE KIDS ARE just about there.

Their unison singing on the "Lo, How a Rose" section of Craig Hella Johnson's arrangement is impeccable. As close to sounding like one voice as it can get. No other high school choir can come close. Maybe because no other choir has singers who feel this close to one another, though I might be a bit biased.

The soloists need a bit more work. When they sing "The Rose," which intertwines itself with the Praetorius hymn, there isn't enough meaning behind the words. They're probably too young. Too inexperienced to understand the different images of love the song paints.

"Milton, Celeste. Could you stay after class for a few minutes?" I ask. "We'll work on this one together."

"Sure thing, Mr. C," Celeste says, looking lovely in a cardigan and a floral A-line skirt.

"Mr. Cruz?"

"You can't stay, Milton?"

"No, it's not that. It's just—it looks like you have a visitor."

I turn around. Emmett holds one of his infamous gift bags in one hand, the other placed casually on the doorframe; he takes up almost the entirety of it. But once he comes in, he scales back down to size. The same as everyone else.

"Hey, you." He gives me a quick peck on the cheek.

"Oooooooooh," the kids say, giggling.

"All right, all right. Enough for today. Celeste and Milton, we'll work on this tomorrow. For homework, go watch *The Rose.* Or listen to Bette Midler. Or fall in love. Whatever sounds the least painful to you," I say, winking at Emmett. "Now get out of here."

The students stream out and wave their goodbyes at Emmett.

Celeste hugs him. "How long will you be gone?" she asks. "Will you be able to come back for our holiday concert?"

"Filming for the movie I'm in wraps in November, so absolutely. I can't wait."

"Awesome," Milton says. "I can introduce you to my new boyfriend."

"Ah! Congratulations. I'm looking forward to meeting the lucky guy."

"Cool," Milton says.

Celeste squeals, "Byeeeeee!" as they hurry out the door and merge with the flow of student traffic moving on to third period.

As soon as we're alone, I pull Emmett in for a long-overdue kiss.

"Too embarrassed to do that in front of the kids?" he asks.

"As a certain friend of ours likes to say, *I won't make a scene unless I'm getting paid for it.*"

"How is Ujima doing, by the way?"

"Good. The hormone therapy was a bit rocky in the beginning. But it's getting better. You should see how long their hair is now. It's crazy."

"Are they still doing that *Color Purple* tour?"

"Yes. They're in Pittsburgh, I think. They've even gone on as Shug Avery a few times."

"Can't wait until they perform it in San Francisco in a month."

"Speaking of which," I say, "did you end up putting an offer on that house in Pacific Heights?"

His eyes pop open. "That reminds me—" He bends down to pick up the bag. "For you."

"What's this?"

"Open it."

A bottle wrapped in pink tissue paper. It crinkles as I peel it away. Inside, a bottle of premium Dassai Junmai Daiginjo sake.

"Thank you?"

He laughs. "I know you won't drink it. It's for me. The other thing's for you."

I didn't notice the other, smaller wrapped object. A glass. With a familiar multicolored block pattern.

Like the one my father used to have.

"Took me forever to find it on eBay," Emmett says. "Macy's doesn't make them anymore."

A tug inside. No longer painful but there. And welcome more than not.

"This is so sweet of you. What's the occasion?"

"I didn't put in an offer on the Pac Heights house."

"Okay. I'm missing something."

"I think something closer to here would be better. Orinda or Lafayette, maybe? With a big enough garage for my cars. Maybe even space for that glass. And the rest of your stuff."

I nearly drop the glass.

Instead, I put it carefully on the top of the piano, next to the bottle of sake, and watch as the smile on Emmett's face grows, revealing the crooked tooth and every other part of him. All of it. None of it as overpowering as I thought when I was younger.

Just enough. Just him.

Not too much.

But still great.

A PART I PLAY (LYRICS)

VERSE 1

I get into place
Put a smile on my face
They're all waiting for me to begin
To get to this night
I've practiced all of my life
To change who I am to fit in

VERSE 2

I'll do what they want
And try not to flaunt
To be something I'm not supposed to be
Do it just so
So they'll never know
Deep inside I just want to be free

REFRAIN

They tell me the show must go on
So I'll try to be strong
And I'll say what they want me to say

But the person they'll see
Won't really be me
It's only a part I play
A part I play

VERSE 3

I'm tired of these games
Of not taking the reins
of my own life—to dictate my fate
But what else can I do
Gotta see it through
Can't alter the script; it's too late

VERSE 4

One day I'll break through
And do what it takes to
Be more than this simple disguise
Until then it's clear
I'm giving in to my fears
By always hiding myself in these lies

REFRAIN

They tell me the show must go on
So I'll try to be strong
And I'll say what they want me to say
But the person they'll see
Won't really be me
It's only a part I play
A part I play

BRIDGE

Be better
Try harder
Say all the right things
Play the role that was written for me
But one time, just once
I'd like to let go
And be the person I'm longing to be
Be the person I'm longing to be

REFRAIN

They tell me the show must go on
So I'll try to be strong
And I'll say what they want me to say
But the person they'll see
Won't really be me
It's only a part I play
A part I play
Yes, the show must go on
So I'll try to be strong
And I'll say what they want me to say
But the person they'll see
It's never been me
It's only a part I play
A part I play

***ONE*-DERLAND**

Act 1

Scene 1: Waiting in Line (The Rabbit Hole)

"Torn" (Natalie Imbruglia) .... Alice and Maggie

Scene 2: ONE-derland

"It's Raining Men" .... Alice and Ensemble
(The Weather Girls)

Scene 3: The Caucus Race

"Macarena" (Los del Rio) ....Ensemble

Scene 4: The White Rabbit's House

"Baby Got Back" (Sir Mix-a-Lot) .... Off-White Rabbit

"I Want Candy" (Bow Wow Wow) .... Alice

Scene 5: The Caterpillar's Pad

"Ice Ice Baby" (Vanilla Ice) .... Mr. Caterpillar

"I'm Too Sexy" (Right Said Fred) .... Chester Cheshire

Act 2

Scene 6: Spilling the Tea

"Don't Worry Be Happy" .... Mad Matt and Martha Hare
(Bobby McFerrin)

"Closing Time" .... Alice, Mad Matt, Martha Hare, Off-White
(Semisonic) Rabbit, Chester Cheshire

Scene 7: After-party at the Croquet Club

"Bitch" (Meredith Brooks) .... Ms. Queeny Hart

"Who Let the Dogs Out" (Baha Men) .... Ensemble

Tubthumping (Chumbawamba) .... Ms. Queeny Hart and Ensemble

Scene 8: Back to ONE-derland

"Funkytown" (Lipps Inc.) .... Alice and Ensemble

Scene 9: Home Again

"I Melt With You" (Modern English) .... Alice, Maggie, and the Company

Sunvalley High School

Martinez, California

STRONGER TOGETHER

The Sunvalley High School Concert Choir

Mr. Manuel Cruz, *Conductor*

Mr. Francisco "Quito" Cruz, *Accompanist and Guest Conductor*

Ecce quam bonum .... plainchant

Tenors and Basses

Gloria in D Major, RV589 - 1. ....Antonio Vivaldi
Gloria in excelsis

"Hold On"..arr. Moses Hogan

Milton Mathieson, *soprano*

"All Works of Love" ....Joan Szymko

"You'll Never Walk Alone" .... Richard Rodgers & Oscar Hammerstein II

Celeste Gonzalez, *alto*

"True Colors"................................. Tom Kelly & Billy Steinberg

Emmett Aoki, *tenor*

"Hiney Mah Tov" .... arr. Iris Levine

"Lean on Me"/................... Bill Withers /Anthony J. Showalter &
Everlasting Arms Elisha Hoffman, arr. Pepper Choplin

"The Tree of Peace" .... Gwyneth Walker

Altos and Sopranos

"You Raise Me Up" ....Rolf Løvland & Brendan Graham

Emmett Aoki, *tenor*

SHS Wind Ensemble & SHS String Ensemble

Mr. Jim Drummond, *conductor*

"We All Have a Part" .... Francisco Cruz

Francisco Cruz, Emmett Aoki,

Celeste Gonzalez, Milton Mathieson,

Ujima Jenkins, *soloists*

ACKNOWLEDGMENTS

To Gina Panettieri, thank you for helping to get my first chapter query ready for the perfect agent and then becoming that perfect agent.

Thank you to my editor, Alex Logan, for believing in my queer Filipino love story and for doing all the million things you needed to (and the million things beyond that) to help make this book a reality.

Thank you to the team at Forever—Beth, Leah, Amy, Estelle, Dana, Penina, and Anjuli—and to Caitlin Sacks for the beautiful cover.

To Dr. Hiyas Hila and Rhya Raymundo, maraming salamat for improving the authenticity of the details regarding Filipino culture, food, and language. And to Cleopatria Peterson, many thanks for your guidance on nonbinary and trans identities and issues.

To my Monday Night Writing Group—Esther Gulli, Barbara Jordan, JoAnne Tillemans, Steven Wight, Richard Kleiner, and Nancy Bourne (who I know is still cheering me on from the great beyond)—your friendship and advice over these past few years have meant the world to me.

Thanks to my teachers, Junse Kim, Joshua Mohr, Dan Coshnear, Roy Hagar (the greatest AP English teacher of all time), Margo Perrin (who gave me my start by publishing my first short story), Rachael Herron (without whose guidance this book would never have gotten off the ground), and Laurie Ann Doyle (whose mentorship has been a gift of pure gold).

And speaking of Laurie, thank you to my other fellow Babylon Salon cohosts, Lauren Johnson, Ryan Sloan, and Maury Zeff, as well as to the members of the Writers Grotto. You've all been my role models and inspirations.

To the two most gorgeous singers on the planet, Arwen Myers and Laura Thoreson, thank you for believing in my book and for watching trashy TV and eating junk food with me during my self-imposed writing retreat in Portland. There aren't enough heart emojis to describe how I feel about the two of you.

To my beautiful brander, Beth Carr—you are my Broadway Baby. And to Debbie Bidwell, my best friend of over thirty-five years—I love you "Always."

To my brother Joseph, music teacher and choir director extraordinaire, thanks for helping me with all the high school choir details. And thanks to Joe, Michael, and Theresa for being the best brothers and sister a guy could ask for. I hope you are proud of your kuya.

To my dad, you were gone from this world too soon. I wish you were still here to see this.

And so many thanks to my mom, who was wise enough to know that teaching me how to read would be one of the greatest gifts a parent could ever give to their child. Thank you for that and for the countless other gifts you've given me.

Finally, to Peter—you helped me create a story for myself I never thought I'd be lucky enough to have. You are more than just my rock. You are my love, my life, my everything.

YOUR BOOK CLUB RESOURCE

READING GROUP GUIDE

Dear Reader,

Toni Morrison once said, "If there's a book that you want to read, but it hasn't been written yet, then you must write it." That's what I set out to do with this book. Growing up, I was an avid fan of romantic comedies. My favorite movie was, and still is, *When Harry Met Sally*. I also read all the gay novels I could get my hands on, particularly ones about Filipinos or other Asians.

What I could never find, though, was a combination of the two. Rom-coms were usually centered on straight white characters, while gay stories were often serious, focusing on the struggles of being queer. I wanted to create something I was never able to find for myself—an uplifting love story in which a gay Filipino, surrounded by other BIPOC and LGBTQIA+ people, finds his Happy Ever After.

Many of the people, situations, and settings in this book sprang from my own experiences studying and working in music and theater in the San Francisco Bay Area, Oberlin College in Ohio, and New York City. The Broadway Baby piano bar is a combination of Marie's Crisis in New York City and Martuni's in San Francisco. Quito is based partly on me but also on several composer and pianist friends of mine. The character of Mr. Cruz is a mixture of my parents and my brother Joe, who is a high school choir and piano teacher, while Ujima was inspired by a few singers and actors I've worked with in the past.

Emmett, however, is totally made up. I've never personally

known any movie stars, but that's okay. My husband, Peter, is far hunkier than any Hollywood actor could ever be!

And speaking of movies, when people set out to write a book, they sometimes say they envision theirs as one. Not me. I have always seen my story as a musical, complete with soul-baring solos, love duets, comedic numbers, and a big, showstopping finale. I hope that, after finishing *All the Right Notes*, you walk away with either a tune in your head or a song in your heart. If so, then I've accomplished what I set out to do.

Thank you for being a part of Quito and Emmett's musical romance. I hope you enjoyed reading *All the Right Notes* as much as I enjoyed writing it.

Yours truly,

DISCUSSION QUESTIONS

1. Before Quito and Emmett start working together in Sunvalley High's concert choir, they already have preconceived notions of each other. What are they? Have you ever gotten close to someone who ended up being very different from what you initially thought they would be like?

2. Quito goes on to work as a pianist in New York but can't seem to find the love he once had for composing music. Why do you think this is? Have external circumstances ever changed the way you viewed something you were once passionate about?

3. Quito decides to reveal a part of his inner life by composing a song for the high school talent show. Do you think this was a good idea? Why or why not? Have you ever made yourself vulnerable by revealing something secret about yourself to the rest of the world? How so? Were you happy with the outcome?

4. The song "A Part I Play" appears several times throughout the book. What do the lyrics mean to you? Do you identify with them in any way? If so, how?

5. Ujima considers themself nonbinary and uses they/them pronouns. What does this mean to you? Have you ever met anyone who identifies as nonbinary or who uses alternative pronouns? How do you feel about the issues surrounding gender identity?

6. Ujima and Mark don't get along, but the reason is never really explained. Why do you think there is animosity between them?

7. Mark offers what he believes to be a great career opportunity to Quito—the chance to write music for Dinesh's musical. Why do you think Quito has conflicted feelings about this? Has anyone close to you ever offered you a gift that you felt conflicted about?

8. When Emmett auditions for a choir solo, the other characters in the room are impressed, even though he's not technically adept at singing. Why? Can you think of people who have impressed you with "raw talent"? How do you feel when you experience their work?

9. "Seeing" and "hearing" are recurring themes in the book. What are some instances of the characters seeing or hearing things that change the way they view other people?

10. Even though Quito is busy, he isn't able to say no to his father when he asks for help with his farewell concert. Why do you think this is? Are there people in your life that you find you can never say no to? Is this a good or a bad thing?

11. Quito and Ujima have a physical encounter when they are first getting to know each other, but instead of going on to have a romantic relationship, they end up being best friends. Do you tend to stay friends with your romantic partners or not? If not, why?

12. It's eventually revealed that the reason Quito hasn't spoken to Emmett since college was because of an awkward sexual encounter that Quito fears was nonconsensual. What do you think Quito should have done instead? Have you ever broken off a relationship as a result of a mistake you made?

13. Some problems arise from Quito and Emmett being seen in public together. Would you be interested in being in a relationship with someone who was famous? Why or why not?

14. Emmett chooses to come out of the closet publicly. What kinds of things do you think might happen to him because of that decision? What do you think might have happened to him if he had done so when he was just starting out in Hollywood? Do you think people are more accepting of

out LGBTQIA+ celebrities today? How do you feel about LGBTQIA+ men or women playing straight TV or movie roles and vice versa? Should LGBTQIA+ roles only be played by LGBTQIA+ actors and actresses? Why or why not?

15. Food plays an important role throughout the book. In what ways does food either bring people together or cause conflict?

16. The power of music is a major theme in this book. What does music mean to each of the characters? In what ways does music shape or transform them? How do they use music to communicate with one another?

Q&A WITH THE AUTHOR

1. This is your first novel. How did it come about? What inspired you?

I'd written a short story about a pianist who loses his boyfriend in an accident, which I'd wanted to turn into something longer. When I finally sat down to outline the details, the story shifted into something more optimistic and romantic. A lot of the short stories I'd written up until that time tended to be pretty serious, but I realized I wanted my first novel to be more of a reflection of who I am as a person—and I'm way more upbeat and fun-loving in real life! I'm always laughing and singing. I love to make music and celebrate love in all its forms, so all of that ended up inspiring the direction of the book.

2. Your novel provides a great slice of Filipino American life. Do both your parents have Filipino heritage like Quito? Or are you biracial like Emmett? How did your experience affect your portrayal of that character?

My parents were both born in the Philippines, and like Quito's parents, they met and got married there before moving to the United States. I was also born in the Philippines, but we immigrated to the United States when I was only a year old. So while I'm technically an immigrant, I consider myself more of a first-generation Filipino American. Many of my experiences growing up in a Fil-Am household informed Quito's story. Little things like Mr. Cruz's barong Tagalog, saying a prayer before eating, and the Last Supper picture above the dining table. But also bigger things, like his parents' struggle to establish themselves in this country, working odd jobs and making do with only the basics in order to provide for their child. My parents did that for me and my siblings, as did so many of my relatives.

3. The American dream is a big part of Emmett's plotline, and he succeeds beyond his wildest dreams while Quito struggles to find his place. In what ways have you been pushed to succeed? In what ways have you struggled to find your place?

From a very early age, I was motivated by my parents to do well in school, to make good on the opportunities they worked so hard to provide for us. My mother was an English teacher in the Philippines who couldn't find a job as a teacher when we immigrated to the United States, so she taught me instead. I was able to read before I even got into kindergarten. Early on, I wrote stories and poems that won prizes in local competitions. I always read a ton of books and did well in English classes. As I got older, my focus shifted toward music. My parents had provided piano lessons early on, which led to a passion for singing and acting. For years, I could never decide what to focus on—the performing arts or writing. In many ways, writing *All the Right Notes* is the culmination of my two great passions.

4. Your love of Filipino food is evident throughout the book. Who is the good cook in your family? Is it you? Are there special Filipino holidays to celebrate? What foods do you eat to celebrate?

I love to cook! I like to think that I'm the best at it in my family, but my two brothers, Joe and Mike, would probably disagree. They're both really great cooks, too. The three of us often make Filipino dishes for our family get-togethers (and my sister Theresa loves to eat them). Joe loves to make inihaw (BBQ), Mike makes a mean kare-kare, and I usually make adobo or arroz caldo. We all got our skills from our mother, who is by far the best cook in our extended family. She was the auntie whose dishes everyone would be excited about at family get-togethers. Our relatives always looked forward to her pancit or lumpia at Thanksgiving, Christmas, Easter Sunday, birthdays, and wedding anniversaries. The first thing we'd often hear when we'd arrive at any party was "What did your mom bring?" Nowadays, however, she's quite content to leave all the cooking to us.

5. Your love of Broadway is also evident throughout the book. Can you tell us a little more about where you got your knowledge of show tunes? In what ways has the power of music shaped or transformed you?

One of my most cherished childhood memories was watching *The Sound of Music* on TV during the holidays. When I was in middle school, my cousin played me her original cast album of *Les Misérables*, and from then on, I was hooked. I started performing in and musical directing the shows at my high school. (Fun fact: the person I codirected the musicals with was a young Craig Brewer!) I went on to Oberlin to study voice, and after college, I moved to New York to be a musical theater actor. I got my Equity card doing *Miss Saigon* at North Shore Music Theatre in Massachusetts and did a few more shows before I decided to go back to grad school to get my masters in music. Music has always been a huge part of my life. From musical theater, to playing piano, sax, and bassoon in school bands, to singing in choirs and early music ensembles, I've never not been making music in some way or another. I hope I never stop.

6. Your book is being published in June, which is Pride month. How do you self-identify? How do you celebrate Pride?

I usually identify as a gay cisgender male, though I sometimes just identify as queer. I'm thrilled that my book is being released during Pride month because I've always been so proud to be gay. I celebrate Pride in different ways. When I lived in New York, I'd always go to the Pride Parade and all the parties and clubs, but I was much younger then! These days, I'm more likely to celebrate it quietly at small get-togethers with my husband, Peter, and our friends. Lately, I've committed to reading books written by queer authors during Pride month. There are plenty to choose from, thankfully.

7. As your book is published, we are living through a period where LGBTQIA+ rights are being rolled back in many places. What do you want readers to take away from your story? Do you think that stories like yours can make a difference?

It's especially hard for me to see things sliding back because, over the past few decades, we'd seen so much LGBTQIA+ progress. That's why it was important for me to write a queer romance. There are a lot of stories about our struggles—and these are incredibly important to have—but we also need to have stories where queer characters can just be themselves. Ones where they aren't persecuted for being gay or feel afraid because they are trans or nonbinary. Stories are so powerful. They can be a way of wishing things into the world. If people can read about queer people and people of color being free to live their lives, finding happiness and love just like everyone else without having to worry about being hated for being who they are, then hopefully they can envision it for the real world, too.

8. Do you have a real-life coming out story that you want to share? It can be your own but could instead be someone else's experience that influenced your story.

The first person I ever came out to was my best friend in eighth grade, Debbie Bidwell, who is still my best friend today over thirty years later. It was over the phone and extremely awkward because she had a crush on me at the time, which I didn't know!

Luckily, she was extremely supportive. In high school, I came out to everyone, which, at the time, wasn't such a common thing and a bit risky. But, for some reason, all the "popular" kids decided it would be cool to have me as a friend, so no one ever gave me a hard time about it. I like to think that having such a good coming out experience helped make it easier for my sister and brother to do the same. They both also came out in high school!

9. Ujima seems to have the most fun in this story! What inspired their story? Does this character have a real-life inspiration?

Ujima is based on a few people but primarily on a very talented actor/singer/dancer friend of mine whom I met while doing a production of *Kiss of the Spider Woman* in Brooklyn. He wasn't nonbinary or trans, but he did do drag at the time. I was somewhat enamored with him whenever he transformed into his drag persona. Whenever we'd go out dancing, he would command the entire club's attention, no matter how huge it was, yet when we spent quiet times together, he was so sweet and funny and personable. I wanted to capture that feeling of someone who was both larger-than-life and down-to-earth, someone you'd want by your side during the fun times as well as the bad.

10. What are you writing next?

You've probably already guessed this, but I am a big fan of drag! And like most Filipinos, I also love karaoke. So I'm combining the two for my next book. It's about a Filipino drag queen named Rex who runs into his ex-boyfriend—the "one who got away"—now a bartender at a failing gay bar. Rex tries to help him by hosting a karaoke night to drum up business, except he doesn't want his ex-boyfriend to know he's a drag queen, so he trains a frenemy to be his doppelgänger. It's sort of a mix of *Kinky Boots* and *Tootsie*. I'm doing lots of research by going out to various karaoke nights at gay bars in the San Francisco Bay Area and watching lots of *RuPaul's Drag Race*, especially *Drag Race Philippines*. The hard life of being a writer!

TINOLANG MANOK (SAUTÉED CHICKEN SOUP)

I'm lucky enough that my mother still cooks me a dish of my choice every year for my birthday. When I was younger, I'd ask for pancit or lumpia—more labor-intensive dishes usually reserved for special occasions. These days, however, I ask for her chicken tinola. It's an everyday comfort food, the Philippines' version of chicken soup. Tinola is easy to make and doesn't require a lot of ingredients, so I sometimes make it myself, but it never tastes as good as when my mom makes it. She manages to add that extra special touch somehow!

INGREDIENTS:

- 1 Tbsp minced garlic
- 2 Tbsp diced onion
- 2 Tbsp diced fresh ginger
- 1 Tbsp coarsely ground black pepper
- 1 to 2 Tbsp powdered Knorr chicken broth
- 2 cups of water (or more)
- ½ cup of green papaya wedges (or chayote or upo/green Filipino summer gourd)
- 1 cup or more cut-up pieces of cabbage, napa or bok choy

- Moringa leaves, mushroom, broccoli, or small wedges of celery are optional
- 1 to 2 pounds of cut-up fresh chicken
- 1 Tbsp of fish sauce (amount according to taste; salt may be used if preferred)
- 2 to 3 Tbsp of desired cooking oil

DIRECTIONS:

In a stock pot, sauté the cut-up chicken with minced garlic, onion, and ginger in hot cooking oil. Keep stirring the chicken until the garlic, onions, and ginger are transparent. Season with patis (fish sauce, according to taste).

Toss 1 Tbsp or more of powdered Knorr chicken broth into the chicken and keep stirring. When slightly browned, pour two cups of water and cover. Let chicken legs and thighs simmer for half an hour. If cooking an entire cut-up chicken, cook covered for at least 35 to 40 minutes.

Adjust the amount of the soup or water to the amount of cut-up chicken. Add the ground black pepper. Then add all your choices of vegetables and cook until soft. Serve hot with rice, and enjoy!

NOTE: If wedges of green papayas are desired, you may mix them with the chicken halfway through cooking until the chicken is tender. Papayas are our traditional choice, as well as cut-up green upo or summer gourd. You may also use wedges of potatoes if preferred.

The amount of seasonings listed may be adjusted to your desired taste. I like to add more garlic, onions, and ginger depending upon the amount of cut-up chicken, as well as the amount of soup to cover it.

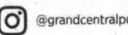

ABOUT THE AUTHOR

Dominic Lim has enjoyed a lifelong love affair with music. Dominic holds a master's from Indiana University Jacobs School of Music, is an alum of the Oberlin Conservatory of Music, and has sung with numerous professional early music and choral ensembles. As a proud member of the Actors' Equity Association, he has performed off-Broadway and in regional productions throughout the United States. Although he probably shouldn't admit to having favorites, the thrill of singing "This Is the Hour" in the chorus of *Miss Saigon* still pops up in his dreams. Dom supports his local writing community as a member of the Writers Grotto and as cohost of San Francisco's Babylon Salon. He lives in Oakland with his loving and supportive husband, Peter, and their whiny cat, Phoebe.

Sun bursts out before setting—unearthly & brilliant—calls to mind the change to another world. Every leaf a golden lamp—every twig bedropped with a diamond. —The splendour departs as rapidly.

DOROTHY WORDSWORTH, *The Late Journals*

BEE SONG

O hand us her secret pages
Each word a golden mote
Preserve her Incantation,
guard the eternal note!

We ferry her simple terms
within each velvet pouch
consigned to our ephemeral halls
marauders cannot touch

Hand us the words she wrote
for we know all they mean:
Trust us in our timeless flight
'round our conspiring Queen

who will preserve the trove
until mad patent dies
caught in its own manacles,
drowned in its own lies

Her word will never die
as long as we exist:
heaven's daughters are not shy
to delve the sacred list

Vivifying power
of our work and hers—
more potent than male emperors,
more patient than the years

1

Where the bee sucks, there suck I

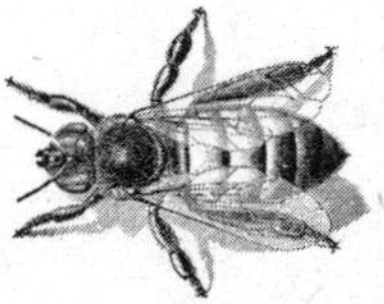

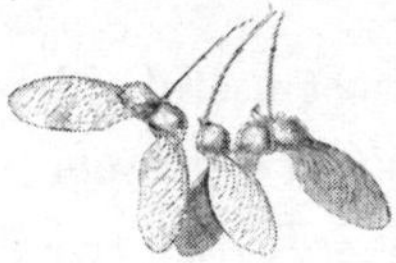

James Dixon's face moves in tiny expressive ways, one moment smooth as a new loaf and the next ruffled like windblown Rydal Water. He was far from bald in 1816, when he first came to Rydal to work for Rotha Wordsworth. Then he had a headful of wavy hair and he smelled like sweet baccy, a scent all the garden creatures loved, including myself, Sycamore, oldest tree of our garden. That summer was a very cold one because of a faraway event that humans here did not know about, though anyone with wings or pollen knew: Volcano! Locals knew it as the year without a summer, and were it not for James Dixon's arrival, many of us living things here in the Wordsworth garden might not have survived. James noticed details you ought to, if you're to be of use to a garden. Small things. Beautiful things. He worked hard and did very little harm.

But now James Dixon is in his fifties, and he sports one of those wool caps that keep the chill off the bald bit. Poor bald head! How poignant the forward rush of human time. James was with the Wordsworths for so long—nearly forty years—that he became intimate with their patterns.

Patterns are the most useful thing in the world. They help us recall what is about to happen.

That is why, on this so-called twenty-fifth of January in 1855, as James sits under my branches later than his usual hour, we know something has changed. The bees know. The slumbering seeds are aware. And I plainly see. His cap is atilt, his step rusty, and he has a funny, burnt scent. We feel his distress before he says a word. It whooshes through my branches like wind, rattling my few dead leaves. One or two bees scouting for signs of spring sense he is not right, and they bolt for my centre where the hive congregates, keeping itself warm. Snowdrops probe green nubs above the hard soil. It will be a week before they hoist their pale ghost flags.

James sits on what he loves to call my knee. His trousers are well-worn, like the creases in his face and hands. He does not possess new clothing or give off a shiny air. Bees love it when old softness emerges and continues on into new time. We all do. Soon the bee scouts venture back out of their entrance and settle on his lap.

Do ye mind, he says at last, if I just sit quiet for a minute before I take on our last chore of all?

He has a round basket at his side and on top of it lies a red book bright as a rosehip, and he also carries his old tinderbox with a few matches he made from splinters of my deadwood, dipped in the bees' wax.

Little Miss Belle noses out of Rydal Mount's side door and sits a distance away on the grass. Normally that dog is

never far from Rotha's side. As soon as he sees Belle, James calls out Rotha's name.

Rotha is what Dixon calls Dorothy Wordsworth privately to himself, and to us in the garden—myself and all beings green, living and quick. Rotha is the name of the river that leaps through our haunts, and it is what poor Sam Coleridge called Dorothy when they were young and Sam loved her as deeply as we do now. There will be another Rotha in the family, but there'll never be another like the one we love best, the Dorothy who has slipped off this morning, five years after her brother William.

Who would have thought she'd outlast him? But on the day William died, his sister rose from her bed as if born again! As soon as he died, up she leapt! Making funeral arrangements, flinging windows open, dashing outdoors to fill her lungs with April air. Quick as in her youth, though everyone had feared news of his death might kill her. No. William's death quickened Rotha and made her more present to us than ever. The life of the sister.

James weeps and a few more bees venture out despite the cold. They do that when someone they trust is sorrowful. They hold time, humming around the hive quietly as the person gives way to feeling. They accompany the person, but do not try to console. There is nothing worse than consoling the bereaved too soon.

The January wind rustles my last leaves and the bees keep up their faint hum. And this man who has little left in the human world weeps for us, talks to us. He speaks to us all

the time. We are his audience and he is ours. He and Rotha both. But now?

My mam, says James, always told me this: When someone you care about dies, you can tell their story to the bees and they'll keep it, like. Even if everyone else forgets. Bees'll hold onto it for you, then once you're dead yourself they'll scatter it abroad with the pollen so the world never really forgets. That person stays alive and the world hasn't lost them, and you haven't lost them either. What about it? Do ye reckon Mam's right? He reaches his hand forth and five bees alight on it.

Only in our world does James possess anything now. So we denizens of the garden do what we always do for those who acknowledge us the way he and Rotha have done. We eloquesce in the realm of light, wind and water—and with our earthen bodies we listen.

one

LOOK AT THAT, WILL YE! James Dixon points at a diamond of glittering frost on one of the sycamore's low twigs, and delight flashes through his tears. Rotha's world aglitter! And me, I fell in! Inside the shimmering. Right in I fell, that very first time I ever saw her . . . she lying in the road with her brother. I was only five!

And I says to my mam, Are they all right?

Never mind them two, Mam says. Cracked as two piss-pots, the pair of 'em.

But what are they doing? I asked her.

Hoping the road'll rattle! Then they know the postman's coming. Letters is all those two cares about.

But how will the road rattle, Mam?

Very feeble it'll shake, son, from 'es wheels in the distance . . .

Really?

Get up, son! You're as daft as they are. Honestly, I just washed them trousers. Slaving away!

I felt it, Mam! It rattled a bit like you said.

And sure enough the two arose, he like a black crow and she tiny all in white as if the crow had married a moth, and off they flew toward Dove Cottage . . .

Aye, off she flitted like a moth. Or like a quick, flighty bird racing over the hill. But then stopping while her brother ran ahead. She different from him, stoppin' and startin' and stoppin' and startin' just like a little wild creature. A linnet hopping along or a little rabbit, starting and stopping. Twitching almost, but—she had no idea we saw her. And those eyes! Coal-black but the coal burned with a flame full of its own blackness. Me and Mam hid behind a boulder. Rotha still had her real teeth then and we saw her laughing to the sky and Mam said, She's right off her head. And him, her brother, look—he's gone and run off and left his lovely cloak lying on the ground. Forgets everything, him, he's that daft. But her, she's more than daft, she's mad.

But someone mad is not what I saw. I saw somebody that was a snippet of the whole day. A piece of everything. A bit of birdwing, of leaf, of cloud. Everything shimmering around her. The whole world made of gems!

Such a windy day. She was like something the wind had blown through the day. She would bend in the funniest way! She was, all at once, like a stick and a wing. Like bone and wing somehow laced together and set free on the fell.

After that I glimpsed the shimmer all by myself in droplets on the feathery carrot leaves in me mam's ordinary yard.

I saw it in the quivery bird that stopped right in front of me in the woods.

But later I went to places where I never saw it, nobody

could. Places where no one could find any shimmer in the world. And I feared the shimmer had been only an enchantment, it had never been real, or it was only for children. Aye, I saw bad places. Things that are here already and worse things to come. Things I see very plain whenever I shut my eyes! Or whenever I've been to see my own born-family, Mam or my sister Penny. Nightmares they have had to live. And I haven't helped Mam or Penny, have I? No.

And in all the years since I saw Rotha Wordsworth that very first time when I was five, I never met the glimmer in anyone except her. Even her brother the crow borrowed it from her. William. I wonder if I stole my own bit of glimmer when I nabbed his cloak! When we got up close to it, Mam and me, its lining shone, satin Rotha had mended by hand. Anything glitters that Rotha looks upon with her silver needle or her pen or even only her black and fantastic eyes. And now, where has she gone? Can ye tell me that?

Look how Rydal Lake gleams with frost. And down there, that line of froth—the silver frill—lapping onshore. In Rotha's world everything was all eyes and ears. Things pay attention and you have to answer them. Unless you become dead to the glimmer. And things that deaden you, well, there's no end to those, is there . . . Please don't let me go dead.

THE SECOND TIME I EVER saw Rotha . . . this was a long time ago, mind, long before I came here to work for her. This

was when you could still call her a young woman and I was twelve. Seven years after that first time I saw her running for the mail. This time we weren't on the fells, we were in Lady Wood. I was crouched in the ferns hunting mushrooms for me and Mam's tea when I heard the two of them talking, Rotha and her brother.

She sat on a stone covered in moss and her brother loomed over her and he wasn't happy. I heard her whimper. She was crying fit to break her heart, in fact, and he couldn't stand it. He wasn't having it. Some men get that way when a woman is sad. Even if they once had a bit of sympathy they can no longer muster it and they become impatient. They want to get on with their lives, away from a crying woman. I had heard that kind of conversation before and I knew better than to reveal myself because it was private and now William sounded irritated like.

Stop it, he said. It's only nervous blubbering. You are even worse than when our John died.

At this she cried harder, for John was their brother who had died at sea and she had loved him.

John's death was much worse for me, William said. For me, it was business. For you it's only the loss of your own joys and feelings. He sounded very angry.

I lay very still and by and by he left her stooped there and after a few minutes I slithered on my belly a few paces and rose up from behind a slant in the ground as if I'd just come upon the scene. And I made as if to veer off without having seen her but she stopped me. She had wiped her face and she had that quivery transparent whiteness of a flower that has

begun shaking raindrops off itself. She seemed interested in the treasure I had gathered up in my shirt.

Are those mushrooms?

This was the first time I ever heard her voice. It's not like any other voice. Ye know that. Her voice is like a gurgling bit of river. Was like. Is. Was. What do ye think? I mean it was so much like a bit of river that for all we know it is still so. When she passed might her voice have slipped back where it came from, into the river? Rotha's voice into the River Rotha. Aye, I'll wager that might be happening now as I talk to ye.

Mushrooms, aye, I says to her then. A few little ones.

What kind—can you let me look?

I haven't got very many. Me mam's very particular about not bringing home maggoty ones.

She had in her own lap a few plants whose roots sprawled in all directions and she untangled a blue flower to show me. I'm transplanting gentians to our new house, she says, but the day is too warm for it. They're wilting even before I can get them out of this wood.

I says, Miss, what you want is to lay a small quilt of moss round them, here.

And I laid down my mushrooms and scooped some moss up and coaxed the blooms from her. I wondered that she did not know you are never supposed to move that kind of flower. I slipped the coldish cushion, green and refreshing like, under the plants in her hand.

Cover them with this mossy flap I says, folding it over them. Her hand was fine and small and she had on a brooch that looked like a drop of blood. Any blue flower, I says to

her, is very difficult to move. It wants with all its heart to stay where it is.

I wanted with all my heart, says she in return, to stay just down that lane here in Dove Cottage, but we have been obliged to move.

She had a like to sob so I says, Try and leave that bundle in the moss and don't plant them until night, and they might have a chance.

We were two souls in a shady wood and I got a bit frightened and I don't know why but I said, I have to go home to my dinner now, me mam'll be waiting—although there was no dinner on our table of that you can be sure—and off I ran.

And I never saw her again after that 'til I was seventeen because me and my mam tried moving to Hawkshead but then the bad things happened with Mam like, with me and Penny having to go and live in the workhouse. And Rotha and her brother and his wife Mary moved around a lot an' all. Aye, Rotha kept living with her beloved William even after he married Mary. Their whole lives. And they moved all over the place and so did I.

It was my uncle Jim who knew the odd little Wordsworth fam'ly and their whereabouts more than I did because he had them as customers. Him and his best pal Tommy Thistlethwaite sold them hares and coal and fresh crab. A few times when I left the workhouse to try and stay with Uncle Jim, I tagged along selling his wares. The Wordsworths lived at the old rectory then, but I never saw inside. That rectory was a forlorn place. William and Mary had a baby who died there, Baby Catherine. And their little lad an' all, young

Thomas. Both died and Uncle Jim said the house was damp, it rested in a bog and filled with smoke if they lit a fire, so anyone living there got bad lungs and that's what the bairns died of. He saw all that but I never got another glimpse of Rotha or her brother until I was older.

But I never forgot Rotha in Lady Wood. I did not forget her hands or her eyes that were dark as coal but bright as flame.

Are ye lot feeling sorry for my tears?

Look, don't feel sad on my account. I am heartbroken but ye know as well as I do that before the day is out I'll be all right. I'll be singing my song again on my own. I've got hare broth simmering in my hut as we speak and I'm looking forward to dropping an onion and sage in it and drinking it with the big cooking spoon. Ye know me and my aloneness and my hut and my song.

Flax, chicory oats 'n' corn
Grains for all ye know and thine
Flour, sugar and barley sown
Ring around the old Oak shine . . .

two

IT'S FUNNY, YOU KNOW, the way I came to the little fam'ly was really through a bit of subterfuge and smuggling.

That year I turned seventeen, the year I came to the Wordsworths', I barely knew what to do with myself for I was thinking about very hard things I had seen and done at Waterloo only the summer before. And I started doing an awful lot of walking on the coffin trail to try and work it all out. Backwards and forwards all winter through the start of that very cold spring.

That trail as ye know goes right behind Rydal Mount. William was often out raking stones in them days and sometimes Rotha was with him cutting back shrubs or checking to see how herbs had overwintered for their kitchen, sage and chives, and I glimpsed the two from afar, white and black glimmering through the trees and sometimes the hubbub of their voices. I still felt very shy of her. I hardly knew if I was afraid to startle her or if she herself startled something in me.

But this one time her brother was all alone.

He was bent over. I nearly didn't see him but then he

unfolded like a raven waking up and he says to me he says, Hello James—it's young James Dixon, is it not?

Yes, I says. It's me.

He says I've seen you with your uncle—then we exchanged words, y'know about a few gardening things, and he had a perplexed look. And I said are you searching for something?

And he said well, I desperately want to try a plant I have read about, and I can't find it anywhere. You wouldn't happen to know—and then he asked if I knew about something called an Egyptian onion.

And he says I want to try it like mad because it reproduces by an onion growing on a stem, a top stem and then its own weight bends it over—and it's a cluster by then, a little cluster of onions—and it roots by gravity.

Oh, I says?

Yes, he says, getting excited. It lowers by gravity to the soil again and then that little cluster of onions, the ones you haven't harvested, for you can harvest some of them—that's how you harvest them is partially, and you let the other part of the cluster bend down and root itself magically again, so you've got—it's like an Egyptian dance with the connected arms bending and reaching and bending and reaching and it goes on into perpetuity! he says. You've hardly got to ever think about them again once you've planted them. And I wish I could find some. But do you know, I cannot find any. I've read about them but I cannot find one to propagate.

And I says well, I don't know, but if anybody has an Egyptian onion it's the experimental garden behind the

rectory of Durham Cathedral. Because I'd been there to that garden on my way home from all that had happened at Waterloo and by then I didn't care a bit about churches or their custodians or what anybody would think of me, and I'd already pilfered a few things out of that garden and stuck 'em in my cap and planted them myself.

So William said, Aye, he says, I wouldn't mind . . . d'you think you could take me there and I might have a look?

And I says to him—it was dawning on me he wanted to pilfer a few for himself—and I says all right, we'll go. Next time you're going to Newcastle let me know and I'll come and I'll show you where they'd be. Because everyone knew the Wordsworths had cousins in Newcastle. But I says it's got to be soon like, before Easter, or in the autumn. You can't pilfer the plant in summer when it's in its full glory.

And he says aye that makes sense. And he says, The only thing is, we won't say a word to my sister Dorothy, because—well she might not approve of our uprooting a plant from a place where it rightfully belongs.

And that was the first inkling I had that William kept things from his sister.

Can you really be her brother, I wondered, yet not know her habit of uprooting a plant ever so tenderly and easing it into a new placc to belong?

I was thinking of her blue gentians and wondering where they were by then. I glanced around the yard for any sign she had transplanted them from house to house whenever the little fam'ly had moved. Those gentians cannot stand any kind of glare. So I knew they were not out in the open and

in any case they wouldn't bloom until well after Easter. I was looking for their old spikes that show over the frost in a particular shape.

William had a furtive look on his face as he stuttered about the onions. It dawned on me that he felt guilty over his plan of stealing them from Durham Cathedral. Aye, that was the truth of it. The way he'd said *their rightful place.* It wasn't the plants' own discomfort he minded so much as stealing from the important folks at the cathedral rectory. He looked around us now as if half afraid someone might be listening. He cupped a hand to one ear and seemed a bit dazed.

I sensed then something that would become even plainer with time: on his own without his sister near, the brother was hard of hearing when it came to the natural world. He heard human voices, but found flower or wind or trees inaudible, even bird messages or your own voices here, buzzing now round your sycamore. While for Rotha it was the other way around. She heard a faint speech of the flowers or of yourselves far more plainly than any speech from people.

And it was the very same with their two sets of eyes. William had bad eyes but Rotha saw for miles.

Anyway, in the end it turned out I went to Durham by myself the very next week, and I pulled a few early scallions for William of the variety he had mentioned, and he planted them and . . . did Rotha ever enjoy eating them! She craved them. She'd lay them on bread and butter with salt and eat them whole. So that was the very start of things I contributed around this place. After that I did more and more for William in the garden.

William fancied himself a garden designer when he was not being a poet. What's more, he admitted to me right at the start that his poetry situation had deteriorated. He was getting a little bit famous for his poems and people came to visit because of them, and he didn't mind that. He liked the attention. But he let on to me that he was privately feeling as if the poems were leaving him.

Maybe it's because I'm getting a few grey hairs, he said. I'm not sure of the reason, but my writing is getting away from me. The precision of it. It still comes to Dorothy and always did and I hope always will, because if anything comes to me in the way of inspiration it comes to my sister first of all. She is and has always been the first one to whom inspiration comes.

He had laid out a few instruments on and around a chopping block where we sat by the moss shed and he told me what was expected of me. On the block sat a strange little mahogany box whose function I did not at first understand. Against the block leaned two mallets and several hatchets and a couple of wire brushes as well as spades and hoes inherited from the previous tenant, the handles needing to be tightened or in some cases removed and whittled and then refitted. He was attempting that very thing now, fitting the handle into a spade laid on his knees, but without much progress as I could make out.

There's nothing worse, says he, than trying to dig with a wobbly spade.

As far, he says, as outside work goes, I need someone I can rely on to help me with the steps and the terraces we have

begun, so there'll necessarily be a fair bit of stonework and lifting and levelling of stairs, then the planting and weeding and clearing dead-fallen twigs. But those last are things an old fellow like me can still do, if slowly. I'm afraid it's the brutal grunt work I'm after from you, but you're young—how old are you?

Nearly twenty, I said. I had added a couple of years on so they would let me fight at Waterloo and I kept them tacked on now.

That is less than half my age, he said, though I feel as if I were twenty yesterday. And I can see how fit you are . . .

He was only forty-six himself at this time and in truth he was a bit bandy-legged but I knew he could still walk for miles and miles, for days on end and uphill as well, all the way over Kirkstone Pass. Everyone knew that. Him and his sister the both of them could walk for what seemed like endless time. So I said, Sir, you'll be able to do anything I can do for a good few years yet, and he laughed at that, he liked it. And while he was laughing I figured it was as good a time as any to let him know the kinds of things I like doing best.

I can do the stonework for you, I says to him, any time you want. And as you already know I'm always looking for ways to increase the health and yield of any garden, whether flowers or vegetables . . . people say I'm a bit enchanted that way but the truth is I have one very old book and I study it. But really . . . I was about to tell him the work I most loved when he interrupted me.

Dixon, he says, it's certain *indoor* tasks I wanted to mention to you while we're by ourselves out here.

He stopped and looked at the grass that had coltsfoot beginning to open, and I waited, but then he looked like he wanted someone to help him out of a confused spot, so I said, By indoor tasks, do you mean helping with the firewood and things like fixing the broken banisters and having a look inside the fireplace as regards all that smoke coming into the house?

Well yes, says he, there is always smoke in every house we've lived in. We can't seem to get clear of it and it has driven us all nearly mad. He still looked uneasy as if there was some other task he meant for me to do. I thought surely he is not talking about paperwork because he has John Carter for all that. I was not overly fond of John Carter but people said he was good with any kind of clerical duties. So I says, trying not to sound incredulous, It isn't serving dinner to your guests that you need help with indoors?

And right away at that he swipes his hand in the air and gives a dark shake of his very longish hair and says, No!

His hair flopped in his eyes and I took it as a sign of the perfect moment to tell him about my particular talent . . .

Or if you don't mind my saying it Sir, that hair of yours, I am pretty good with any task requiring the use of any kind of small blade. These scissors, for instance—I showed him the small pair I keep in my top pocket, stuck in a bit of cork—women all over Rydal ask me to keep their husbands' hair tidy and their eyebrows an' all, and even the hairs coming out of their ears and sometimes their noses. And some women even let me cut their hair.

You think I need a haircut?

Sir, whenever you're ready for one I can do it. I've cut the hair of all hands near me ever since I was nine or ten. I have a knack, like I said, for anything requiring the use of a small blade.

In fact I had learned precise cutting in the oakum cellar at the workhouse, but I did not tell him that.

Scissors, I says to him. Awl. Knife. Any finicky cut or carving or scratch you might need done.

And that's when I took my latest Pace egg out of my jacket and handed it to him.

This one had a swan on it, etched in green, with willow leaves all around, hanging like, as if the swan were just now appearing in a clearing in the fronds. I'd scratched it the night before with my Waterloo knife. I was getting a few dozen ready for Easter. I had painted some green and some black and a few were blue though blue paint is very hard to come by.

This exquisite little goose needs a much closer view, he said.

His eyes were pretty bad even then. He opened the little mahogany box and took out a magnifying glass. While he was examining my swan through the glass I saw that inside the box had popped up two bone circles on slender brass legs, and one of the circles had a lens set in it. Up rose the rings as he opened the lid. What on earth was the thing?

Oh, he said, this is a swan! But this is the loveliest Pace egg I've seen in all my days—how do you do it?

I noticed that one of the brass legs holding the lens inside the mahogany box was loose. There was a tiny hinge on each of the others but a third was missing . . .

Surely, he says, this isn't white ink on top of green paint? Can it be the eggshell shining through?

Like I said, Sir, I am pretty good with anything requiring the use of a very small blade. I've scratched the swan into the green paint. It's a question of being precise and not being in a hurry. And it helps me not worry about anything that might otherwise keep me from sleeping at night. I find it calms me down before bed.

Can you draw a swan like this with a pen?

No, Sir, with a pen I am useless. It has to be a needle or a knife or a tiny metal tool. I notice for instance in your interesting little wooden box, there—if you want me to fix that missing hinge I have a mustard tin full of tiny spare parts, all sorts of bits and pieces I've saved for mending things, and I'm sure one of them . . .

He looked at me anew. I thought, he says, I was going to have to send that box back to London.

What is it? I normally restrain my curiosity when talking to an employer but I couldn't bear not knowing the purpose of the little box only four inches long with such intricate insides.

This goes with it—he waved his magnifying glass—but the lens on legs, see the small disc under it? You put any flower on that and you look through the lens above it and you can see the flower as if you are looking into a cathedral. The spans, the struts, the stained-glass light, its whole architecture appears and you can kneel before it in wonder. Better than a Sunday service!

I was a bit surprised as William often went to church and I had not heard anyone like himself profess that nature was

better than religion, although I felt it to be so myself and have kneeled, as ye know, before the gold-lit chambers of many a bonny lily. Not only kneeled but laid down and fallen asleep under the spell . . .

But this equipment, he said, belongs to Dorothy and I'm afraid she hasn't been able to use it for months . . . can you really fix it?

Yes, Sir, I think I can. May I just . . . I went to lean over the thing to get a better look, when out of my shirt pocket tumbled a little shower of objects that clattered on the wood block like tiny dice and I gave a start.

I was embarrassed and I am sure I turned crimson as I tried to scoop them up again with my hand before he could get a good look at them.

There have been many instances since that day when I have been glad of William's poor eyesight, but this time he, in his helpfulness, grabbed one of the little dice as it rolled upon the block, and straight away he felt more than saw exactly what it was.

He looked at me with his mouth agog.

I felt ashamed, but what could I do?

He knew that I had soldiered at Waterloo. So he understood what was in my pocket. When you are on the battlefield and you are prying the mouths of the dead open and extracting teeth it seems normal. All the lads are doing it. I learned before I ever got to Belgium that I should take a sharp pocket knife for that very purpose and that is the pocket knife I own yet. It is the knife I still use to scratch my swans and all the birds and patterns in the Pace eggs. I want to make

something beautiful out of my old knife after all the harm it has seen and done.

At home in England you could get a good price for a single Waterloo tooth, but for a whole set, you could live on that for a month, and that is just what I had been doing since I returned. There were several buyers right around here. Cora Freetorch was one. She lived by Paterdale so to get to her I had to face climbing Kirkstone Pass but Cora would buy any teeth I cared to sell her to make full sets of Waterloo teeth for her many customers and she could fix old sets as well. She'd pay for singles or any combination you could supply. People thought she was poor in that hut with no more than a stove and a lambskin on the floor, but Cora Freetorch was never short of a pocketful of gold when I knew her. One reason I was eager for the job at the Wordsworths' in the first place was that I had sold Cora nearly all my supply. The ones in my pocket weren't even part of my inventory but were the teeth I had kept as memorial to a friend of mine who had been killed: Joseph Bell.

Now William Wordsworth rolled one of Joseph's beautiful teeth in his hand. I was ashamed. I was mortified and the sadness came upon me very fast. I didn't know what to say. I cared what Wordsworth must think of me and at the same time all I cared about was getting that white shard of my friend's life back safe in my pocket away from the light and away from anyone, the way I myself sometimes wanted to get away from anyone so I could be quiet and listen to a stream or a waterfall or the wind here in your sycamore.

But the look on William's face.

I thought that was the end of my work for the Wordsworths there and then. He could look very grim, that man. He tilts his head as if he's thinking very hard, then he clamps his teeth shut and sort of sighs through them. It sounds like the north wind. I mean it did. No breath in him now, is there. No breath in any of them. I'm the only one of the little fam'ly left now. Except Mary, but Mary is not mine and I am not Mary's, not the way I was for the others.

But William didn't sack me on the spot. No, not at all.

He held Joe's tooth on a flat hand where it loomed like a relic on the altar in the church where I never go. And he said, James, do you reckon you could use one of your small implements to adjust any of the three sets of my sister's teeth that have been causing her agony every time she fits them into her mouth? Each set needs at least one replacement tooth, and two of them have problems with their hinges.

Dorothy's teeth?

Yes, she is barely forty-five yet her own are nearly gone.

Cora Freetorch is usually the one who does that kind of thing around here, Sir. If you want I can introduce you to her.

Cora has tried over and over again. My sister has sensitivities that Cora cannot surmount. And every time we have made an adjustment someone has to go over Kirkstone Pass and back again and it takes, as you know, all of a day. If you could make a tiny adjustment here and there, well, it would save me a great deal of inconvenience I can tell you. This very tooth, for instance, looks as if it would perfectly fit the gap in my sister's oldest pair.

And he handed me Joe's tooth, and I was very relieved to have it back.

You mentioned inside work? I wanted to take his mind off the unsavoury portion of what we had been discussing. I wanted to forget about putting my friend Joe's teeth into Dorothy Wordsworth's mouth. But William had one more thing to say about it.

It will be important not to mention to Dorothy that these are Waterloo teeth. That they are teeth that have been torn from the heads of deceased soldiers. She can't know this or she'll never acquiesce to our using them. We have to tell her all the teeth are porcelain or at the very worst carved animal bone, and even at that she is liable to balk. She is liable to inquire as to what kind of animal and how it was killed and even what its name was, if it had a name.

I said nothing, taking this in. I didn't want to let on that I felt funny about lying to his sister, or that I felt Miss Wordsworth would somehow know the truth of anything no matter how convincing you were. If you are lying some people know it and she was one of those. And even if they don't know it they as good as know it because something in their blood runs away from the person lying. They know there is love missing or sympathy missing. Something. They can just feel it the way you feel a change in the wind or a current in the water.

Because as I told you, said William, my sister has sensitivities . . . in fact this is exactly what I meant when I said I have work for you inside the household.

Sir?

You've seen my sister, I think?

Er, in the way anyone in the village might have seen her on her walks, Sir. I—when I was a young lad I might have seen her a bit more, as I was often on the fells with my mam . . . I decided not to tell him anything beyond this.

So you know that she is not like other women. She is different.

Is she, Sir?

She is very different. She has to be handled most carefully.

Sir?

I have been the careful one, now, for years and years. I have been so careful that there are bags under my eyes. And frankly, I'm tired and I need help. Is it a terrible thing, to ask, finally, for help?

No, Sir?

Dorothy can be . . . He twiddled his hands round a button and I wanted to warn him it was about to fall off any minute but I kept quiet. I learned a long time ago how shutting up helps you get to the bottom of nearly anything.

She can be exuberant, he said. Too exuberant. Because then she flattens. After the exuberant time when everything is charged and full of a joyful energy, her sun goes out like a blown lamp. Worse than flattens. What is the opposite of exuberant, Dixon?

I don't know, Sir?

I was not about to furnish the poet William Wordsworth with a word, although various words came to mind. I had

seen my own sister Penny worse than flattened. But you don't go talking about your own sister to a man like William while he is talking about his. Not if you want to get to the bottom of your job, the job he has in mind for you. There are all kinds of people ready to rant on and on about themselves given the slightest opening. My mam is one of them but I am not. I had seen Mam lose many an opportunity through talking far too much and I knew to stand quiet as a mouse waiting for the job that would instantly benefit myself and that might in time help my sister Penny out of her worse than flattened situation.

At least, in my mind on that day I was daring to allow these hopeful thoughts.

Of course what happened to Penny happened despite all my old hopes, and I now look back on those hopes very differently. But on that day my hopeful thoughts made me hesitate to provide the poet with words that popped freely into my mind, like *grey* or *sallow*. I did not say *maimed* or *wasted*. I did not mention hunger or damp and I said nothing about lungs and I did not mention Penny's shoulder. I wanted to! I wanted to take the chance that William might open his eyes and help Penny Dixon there and then by allowing me to bring her to work at his household, just as he was offering to open the door to me.

No. I forced myself to wait and to listen to the one man in the world who looked to be nearly ready to release the tiny bit of money needed to change my own situation. And not just money. There was hardly hope for my mam, but for myself and for Penny there was something here in this garden

and in the Wordsworth household that went beyond what a few coins can buy.

Blasted?

Sir?

Enervated? Whatever the word might be, Dixon, I rather desperately need help with my sister.

Yes, Sir?

And I need it from a person who is not one of our family, and who has the dexterity of someone like yourself. I mean finesse of hand but I also mean dexterity of spirit. I sense this dexterity in your face and now I see it in your beautiful artwork covering the surface of this egg. It is perfect, and it might be only folk art but it has something refined in it, something of the angels, if I believed in angels, which I do not. But if I did . . . do you know what I mean, James Dixon?

Perhaps not quite, Sir. But I do enjoy making the designs on the Pace eggs . . .

Never mind. I see it in you. And you'll see it too, if you spend enough time here with us, in the gardens and in our company. You might be raw now, in fact you look as if you've been out in the wind a few times in bare feet and a woefully insufficient coat.

Aye Sir, I have. But I didn't mind it. You get used to it. You even come to like it better than being too well wrapped-up.

And you seem like a solitary soul, the way I once was . . .

Aye, Sir, I am often by myself, but then again there are creatures and mountains and streams full of fish.

And I respect a man who enjoys his own company. For one thing, he doesn't band up with every galoot in the tavern.

Sir, I never drink.

And you don't seem to have friends—but with us you might feel a modicum of friendship. What do you think?

I could hope so, Sir.

I still did not know what he meant by the indoor work requiring a certain spirit that he saw in me. When someone of William's sort talks to you like that, you feel that they are putting some kind of hope in you, and it lifts you up in a lovely way even if you wish it didn't. They think the best of you even though you are not a rich person or an important man. They see something in you that other people don't see and maybe you yourself don't know is there. I loved it, even though I didn't know what it was William saw and I was frightened he might be wrong. I know what it is now that I own, but I didn't know it then.

Still, I was not a timid youth even though I was shy, and I did want to know exactly what he meant when he said he had other work for me in the house. So far he was talking in riddles. If I was to be of any help I had to know exactly what I was supposed to do. So I said, Sir, can you be a bit clearer about what it is you wanted me to do for your sister?

He went quiet. He often wears black clothes. Wore. He often wore black or dark clothes and that day he had on something that crumpled up as he bent into himself, as if to hold his self dear or tight or apart from troubles that haunted him.

Sir?

I wondered if Wordsworth, no longer young like me, had run out of words. Or words had run out of him. He was a giant bedraggled bird with fresh air gone out of him at that

moment. Flightless and wingless and making no sound. Not dead as now but something like pre-dead. I felt he needed me to change the subject.

It has been a colder than usual spring, I said.

Yes, he managed to say. People can talk about the weather no matter what is going on inside them. Our garden, he said, has been struggling.

You'll want help with the sweet peas. They are very tender.

They are indeed in danger.

We'd had lots of rain . . . as ye know. But I knew it had not been the kind of rain our north of England normally has in spring. We were missing that fresh smell that comes when spring is just starting to unlock the green that's trapped in everything, in the soil and everywhere. It hasn't come out fully but shows just little tips. Seams are ripping and the little tips are hardly even showing. It's just that you know the stitches have broken and the green's about to burst out, that's what the rain brings out. The fragrance. And this spring that joy had not come. And it wouldn't come, either. We didn't know yet how there would be no summer at all that year. Although ye lot probably knew. Ye always know that kind of thing in advance. Ye must have been telling each other to hoard whatever drops of honey ye could eke out of that summer that was never a summer.

My sister, William began again. He was trying to find something essential to tell me about Rotha but he ended up telling me an odd joke instead. At first I couldn't make out why he was telling it to me as it seemed unrelated to all that had gone on between us.

Have you ever heard the one, he says, about this doctor? A surgeon?

No, I says.

Well there was this surgeon and he saved a couple of people's lives. Thought he was being very helpful. But after he's saved them, one tries to hang himself and the other one tries to drown himself. And the surgeon can't understand it. Why are they not happy about having their lives saved? So he asks them both. And one after the other they say to him, Doctor, we thought it was all finished, and here's you saving our life! And now we're stuck here and have to make a living and all that goes with it. Doctor, they said, pardon us but now you'll have to foot our bills because by rights we shouldn't even be alive. So he vows after that, this doctor, never again will he save another soul from any accident without making sure first, do they really want to be saved? So one day he goes out with a rowing party, and one of the men falls overboard and starts flailing about. He cannot swim. And our surgeon grabs him by the hair and lifts his head above the water and says, Now then, do you want to be rescued or not? And the poor man gasps, Me poor wife! How would she manage? She's not well, and oh, our seven little bairns . . . And the doctor shouts Ha! Wretched bloke—no wonder you've jumped in! And pops him back under the water to his doom!

William started chortling. He was never a man given to much laughter but at that moment he was quaking. His whole body. He couldn't stop. I wasn't sure, myself, how funny I found the joke. It did not seem funny at all in any way that can make a man like me laugh. I laugh at things. I think I

laugh at things. But the best face I could conjure at his joke was simply one that did not look, I hoped, too puzzled.

Sam Coleridge told us that one, William said, once he'd stopped laughing. At a little party. Well we all nearly died laughing at it. We were all busting. Except Dorothy. Once the merriment died down a bit we noticed her brimming with tears. Oh, she says, however could the doctor do such a thing—was he so very inhuman as that? Well. Sam and Bob Southey and the rest of us just about fell off our chairs. But we had to comfort her, and Sam said to her he was sorry. And any time he told the joke after that he told about Dorothy's tears and how they made him love her all the more.

Nobody wanted to let my sister down. When she trusts you, it's like being trusted by the trees.

He said this as if he himself had disappointed or was about to disappoint her most terribly.

She's got no guile, he said, and she is hardly able to laugh at anybody.

We sat in the garden as clouds gathered and it grew very chilly. He recapped what he needed me to do: garden work outside, mostly, and an eye upon his sister's well-being inside. Her mental health, really, he said. Because she never leaves the realm.

The realm, Sir?

That's what you've got to understand, he said. I myself leave the realm. For practical reasons. I step outside the circle. I can look back at it, shining and golden. Rimmed by time but filled with timeless and treasured air. But Dorothy never leaves it. She is always inside it.

Inside what, Sir?

Inside the place where everything in the natural world, each anemone, each oak, each aster, each daisy, each ripple at the water's edge—are you with me, Dixon?

I think so, Sir?

Each rustle of the grasses . . . hangs all about you in the air. Each part listens to one another with the attentiveness of a lover.

He started laughing. It was a different kind of laughter from when he had laughed at the joke. I cannot remember exactly what he said next. Something about the air being charged, every mote of it listening. Did William say the air was listening? Could he have said that? This was a long time ago.

You see, he said, they're all getting ready to sing their song, aren't they.

Who is? I could not fathom what he meant. It would take me all of my years with his sister to understand.

They're all getting ready to sing their song of glory, he said. If this frost ever melts. That's what the poetry is. My poems. Once caught, it all goes on the page: pinned, wings of each specimen—magnificent, annihilated. But my sister! She is awake, attentive in a surround that is also awake. She knows no dead specimen, only charged song. No matter the season.

Charged song?

Did he mean charged as lightning charges the sky? What did he mean?

The clouds opened and a cold sleet fell on us. Shreds of ice lay like coconut in his jacket folds. William folded his sister's mahogany box with the lenses in it and gave me it. I somewhat self-consciously slid it in the pocket containing my friend Joseph's teeth, for I had no other safe place for it. I promised I'd fix it the best I could, and William asked me could I come to the house next Thursday, and that was the real start of my regular work here: part-time at first and then, with the years, more like my whole lifetime.

three

I AM A BIT OF A FAIRY KING when it comes to mending just about anything. From wood and stone to feather and stem, I can usually mend it.

But all the broken things in the little fam'ly!

It was hard to tell what was going on in the house at first. Cold wind thrashed outside and people ousted from their land came begging for bread and coppers all over the vale, but the household seemed harmonious and I felt lucky to be in it. You couldn't really call it a lonely house. The cacophony of that party they had on my first Easter with them! Two roast birds and fresh bread. Their writer friends Charles and Mary Lamb—sister and brother like Rotha and William. Sarah Hutchinson and William and his own Mary in their element, and half a dozen friends. The chatter. The laughter. You'd never dream Mary Lamb had stabbed her mother to death with a carving knife.

Everybody had quietly forgotten about that.

The drinks, the pipes. The firelight on the pots and pans. True, Rotha kept looking out the window for Sam Coleridge who did not come and would never come: he had turned his

back on them all by then—but even without Sam there was endless chatter and real affection. And the smells of toasted bread and roasting meat and beef drippings melting on the gravy in silver motes, glittering and welcoming. You'd never say Rotha might feel lonely in the midst of a party like that, but she grew agitated.

William whispered in the corner, Dixon, can you please take my sister upstairs?

So I did. Would you like me to leave you alone? I asked her. She sat at the foot of her bed gazing at a blank place in the wall near the window. Beyond the window your sycamore here was having a hard time trying to bud. Swallows faltered at Rotha's window-ledge trying to build their nest in all that cruel wind. Yet she kept looking, not through her window but at the wall.

Beside her was a fancy hat box on the floor. I already knew what was in it. The box was off one of Mary's hats, a hat Mary often wore to church, so the hat itself was in Mary and William's room. I can't remember the hat. But the box was a green box. It had paisley and knots of rosebuds and some gilt ribbon and it was nearly worn out, but Dorothy liked that kind of thing and in that box she kept her stack of diaries. I knew this because I had gone upstairs one day to unstick the window so she could let air in. She had to have fresh air even though spring had not come. And she had left the lid off the box, so of course I glanced in and saw her diaries. A stack of dark ones, black and blue, but tucked under them this scarlet notebook I've brought out here with me this morning. Something red, you notice it flickering like!

I didn't do more than glance down in the box. But I noticed this red book. I bet ye notice a scarlet blossom, how it stands out from all the others.

Now she pulled the red book from the bottom of the stack and untied it and then unwrapped it—it was the only one she had wrapped up and I had never unwrapped it. But now I saw it had a red cover under its red cloth. The others were just bare books. She stared at the wall as if she saw something through it, and then she wrote in the red book but I couldn't see what she wrote although I wanted to.

I felt as if she had forgotten my presence so I said, Miss—I still called her Miss Wordsworth then—I only started calling her Miss D after we got closer. I said, Did you eat any dinner? Aren't you a little bit hungry?

A bit, she says, but I don't feel like eating meat. What I would love while I'm writing, she says, is one boiled egg with salt on it.

I went back down and brought her an egg and I scalped its top off with my knife and this amused her.

Her diary lay open on the bed while she stared at that spot on the wall again and ate her egg.

I pretended not to be interested in the diary but of course I was, anybody would be, and I saw bits of what she had put down. She had written something but crossed it out, except for the title: *Togetherness Committee*. And Mary's name was there, and *fireside* was there, and flames were mentioned. Half of Sam Coleridge's name stuck out from some particularly strong, black lashings of ink. I had met Coleridge and for the life of me I could not see what all the fuss was about.

He was folded in on himself and uninterested in anything around him. He was a ruined man by the time I saw him. But I knew, I had heard, that when he was young he was one of the loveliest young poets in England and Rotha had loved him. Many's the tongue had wagged over her traipsing through the vales with him alone, lying sidelong on the turf until the stars came out.

In fact, tongues did nothing but wag about Rotha and her brother when I first came to Rydal.

People thought the fam'ly had a bit of money once they moved to Rydal Mount and William became the new tax collector. Oh, they said, William Wordsworth has got buckets of money now, you're in the good books.

When Berthe Briggs came with the eggs she'd get me to mend her tin pail and she'd crow in the lane after, That Dixon, he can do anything, him, shove the arse back in a cat, but he won't let on a word about what's going on behind Rydal Mount's walls! Aye, Berthe and all of Rydal were one and the same in concluding the handyman must know what's going on, let's get him by himself, once he's off duty . . . I had a steady stream of visitors at my hut on Sunday afternoons, prying and thinking of me as the Wordsworth Times, a trusted source ready to provide them with all the news. They all thought I tacked on with the Wordsworths only for the pay.

But the wages are not why I came here to work. I could have made the same money working elsewhere. I could have made more, some places. There is more to it than the money when you are in the company of people who have an exciting way of thinking.

Ye know yourselves, when anybody gets even a little bit famous as the Wordsworths were starting to do, people respect them well enough to their faces. Oh yes, they show great politeness in person. You'd think, after the poet's child was dead—little Catherine—simple as she was, more like a beloved fairy than a child able to grow up to read and write or anything—you'd think when the Wordsworths lost her that people might hold their tongues.

But question number one flying around the vale was, Poor dead Catherine was under a spell wasn't she, her eyes weren't right, was she a changeling? Question number two was, How did I expect anyone to believe that Rotha, a woman roaming the fells alone, had done so without a horde of wild lovers, some of them probably half-human beings in the dusk?

Yet she lets on so as to appear maidenly, they marvelled; surely that's a canny disguise?

And what about the way Dorothy and her poet brother used to carry on before he married Mary?

Talk of the town, all that, and people expected me not only to know everything that had happened before I got there, but to be dying to inform them of the sibling pair's every move.

Now Rotha said to me, Dixon, she says . . . she was tackling the bottom of her boiled egg . . . do you know what I wish you and I were doing?

No, Miss?

Hunting kittenracts.

Swallows banged against the glass—we watched their

fluffy bellies and their forked fishtails and she said, They are trying to swim in an unsympathetic current!

The swallows distressed her.

I wish there was some way we could give them shelter! Did you know, James, that just there—she pointed her spoon at the blank spot in the wall where she had been staring—is a secret window?

I don't see any window, Miss, I ventured.

I felt disappointed for her that I could not see what she saw but I wasn't going to pretend to her that I saw a window where there was none. I felt there was a wee beck starting to flow between us and I did not want to dam it up with fibs. It wanted to become a living stream. I wanted it.

I know you don't, she says. Because it has been concealed. It's a very old window still inside the wall. I feel as if I can see right through it.

This certainly seemed odd to me but I did not explain it away by concluding that she was mistaken or feverish or, as her brother had mentioned, over-exuberant. I sensed even then that I was to learn more from Rotha's strangeness than I could imagine.

I just can't seem to gather myself, she said to me then, when there is a crowd like the one downstairs now. Even people I love, even Mary Lamb, who by herself is a fountain of refreshment to me. But together! They are all talking quite happily to each other and in the wild babble I can't reach a place where I'm listening to somebody and they are listening in return, heart to heart. The way you are now—you're listening, aren't you, James.

I am, I says to her.

But downstairs, she says, it's arm to arm and finger to finger and mouth to mouth and hair to hair and fire to song and wine to bread and meat to soup and ladle to knife—but one heart, mine, wants to run, cowering, shutting the covers over itself, closing the curtain Making itself as small as possible like a child curled up. Hiding under the stairs! As if something frightening has come to the door . . .

I waited for her to say what frightening thing that was. But she scooped the last of her egg in little white-and-yellow moons on her spoon and continued looking at the white wall where she had said there was an old, hidden window. A window I couldn't see, not even a slight impression in the wall.

There's so much good will and love downstairs just now, she said—all happiness!

I did not mention Mary Lamb's having murdered her own mother quite recently, or the fact that Miss Lamb's brother Charles had brought a straitjacket in a sack in case he needed to slap it on his sister once again. These things went without saying in the Wordsworth house at the time, though it had certainly been said in all the papers.

All heat and cheer, said Rotha. But, James, do you notice none of it is any fainter now that we are here, away from the party?

Miss?

When you went down to get this egg, did anyone notice your presence?

I daren't . . .

They didn't, did they? You were nothing but a shadow.

I can't be sure, Miss. They were all talking amongst themselves . . .

Our absence is—and don't imagine me full of self-pity, James, I'm simply stating a fact—our retreat, our absence—does not take away from their jolly heat, from the heightened temperature of the gathering. She pointed at the real window, the one we could both see: Look, she said. Our swallows have flown away.

I felt a pang when Rotha said *our* swallows. I felt it deeply, and when I think about it all these years later I believe that day of the Easter party was the start of how she and I became a magic team, at least in my own mind. Am I imagining it? Ye lot are lucky, ye have each other—a hive of ye working together, keeping each other warm, always in the glow of one another's natural company, and your old sycamore for shelter, and the whole garden nourishing ye.

But for some of us humans that Easter day was a cold, lonely day like today. Only the twigs of the swallows' half-built nest showed through the rain-blurred glass. It had teemed cold rain that whole spring.

James, Rotha said to me then, can you see those two single droplets of freezing rain suspended on the eave?

Yes, I says.

Just quivering there and reflecting everything, she said, not adding to the warmth of the house nor drawing more than an iota of heat away. I don't mean that the two raindrops are insignificant. I know I am loved, and you must be loved too. Are you loved, James?

Was I?

Rotha had a sixth sense when it came to knowing if you were alone in the world or not. If you had anybody. And I did have somebody—but I did and I didn't. My somebody was not very well. Penny, my little sister. There was something not right with Penny's shoulder, wasn't there? She was hoarse an' all—her voice the last time I went to Manchester croaked from the depth of a dry pit like a noise I once heard come out of a parched baby frog.

Have you got a girl?

No, Miss. I'm far too busy.

Have you any brothers or sisters?

I have a younger sister, Miss. Penny, named for her copper hair.

And do you see her?

I remained silent and Rotha said, Perhaps it is only that people like us do not know how to love a crowd. We cannot find the individual souls in it.

And I felt then that neither Rotha nor I had a clue what was going on in each other's family, and we had not admitted to ourselves why we each felt so alone. That day was when I started wondering how Rotha and I could help each other. Though I knew even then that to wonder this may be wrong, or foolish, or impossible. Because I was only the . . . what is it I heard their visiting preacher Edward something-or-other call me with a teacup in one paw and a goblet of elder wine in the other and currant-bun crumbs all over his gob? The *factotum—What a good mute and earless and eclectic factotum you have—he can re-weave the seat on a*

beloved old chair or mend any irreplaceable tool! For all I knew, he was calling me a Peruvian hedgehog. It took me ages to find out the meaning of that word. But it only means handyman.

The rain grew louder and in the din I asked her, Miss—what did you mean by saying you wished to hunt a . . . some kind of a kitten?

William's wife Mary was always on about getting a kitten. Mary longed for a household cat. It was a fierce argument at times, with Mary disgusted by mouse droppings and Rotha defending the swallows and all the other birds that came near. The birds would be massacred if Mary got her way. So I couldn't fathom why Rotha had just now mentioned trying to find the very animal that would destroy our swallows, who were already battling for their lives against the gale outside.

My question made her laugh.

Then she said, You're still the same lad that came upon me while I was crying, aren't you. What a sad time that was, the time in Lady Wood—our baby Catherine had only just died, and Sam Coleridge was so lost to us, you might as well say Sam had died as well, but you wouldn't have known, you were only a boy. It *was* you, though—I know it was you. You're the little lad who caught me crying.

I had no reason to deny this, but at the same time I felt somewhat exposed. I guess I'd thought that with all the growing up I had done in the interim, Rotha had not recognized me.

I'd know your face anywhere, she said. All shy and funny and folded in strange ways, like a darling goblin.

She couldn't have known my mam had often called me a little goblin.

But Rotha was very keen and sharp in her perceptions then, and in my eyes she has never lost that keenness. When everyone around would later lament she was no longer right in her mind I vowed she was the same Rotha as always.

I cannot say why I see her so differently from the general opinion. I only know that she never changed in all our time together, from that cold Easter of 1816 when we were alone together in her room until today. I know she is dead but even so I still feel Rotha has not changed. People don't stop existing when they die, do they? They just go somewhere else. Some place where we cannot reach them.

My mam wasn't an extra wise person. Haha! Far from it. But one thing she said feels very real and true to me now, and it was about the dead. Mam said the reason the dead don't reach out and contact us and let us know where they are and that they are all right is because they are far more than just all right. They are having such a lovely time that if they gave us so much as a hint of how wonderful it is being dead, we would kill ourselves here and now. Don't you worry, my mam says, the dead are only being kind to us.

A kittenract, Rotha said to me that Easter day, isn't a kitten. Guess what it is, James.

I can't, Miss. I don't know.

Think about it.

I'm not a very good guesser.

She crushed her eggshell into pieces like sand and scooped the dangly pile up and handed it to me and said, Do you know what this is for?

I said to her, shaking my head no, Miss, I says—it's starting to look as if I might not know much at all.

Come on, she said, we're going out. Don't worry about the party, we'll sneak out the back door.

The box is still open, I said, with all your notebooks exposed—would you like me to put its lid back on?

No one is going to bother with my diaries, she said. I only put quiet observations in them. The family, Grasmere. The time the Green children lost their parents. The seasons. Times I waited alone for my brother while he was away, written to entertain him. They're all in those books in that box. And my recollections of Scotland. Trips I've taken with William and Sam Coleridge, when we were young and before Sam fell out with us . . .

I did know about the Scottish recollections because there were copies—I won't say flying around, but she had made five or six copies for friends, and there was one copy in her room that she was always working on, trying to make it better and better. It would come in and out of view again as she revised it or put it away.

I don't know where I got the nerve—maybe because the red notebook she had been writing in still lay open on the bed—but I asked her then if I might look at any of her writings. And she said, Why not, they were written for the household. William looks in them all the time, she says.

So right from the start I felt, or I believed at any rate—she would not mind if I knew something of what was in her notebooks.

But she did say to me that day—I've got to confess—Only please don't look in this one, which is for myself alone. And she picked up the red diary off her bed.

It was the only time I had seen her claim a particular object for herself.

So of course that became the diary I longed to see most of all.

I watched her shut it, wrap it, and tie it with a lace off one of William's old boots. It was not a single knot and it wasn't even double, it was a triple knot—but the tool for unfastening it was, and still is, in my pocket. I noticed she hesitated before sliding that book beneath the others. Maybe she suspected she should hide it elsewhere if I was not to look inside. But she stuck it under the rest . . . though that is not where I found it later.

Then we crept out the back door. No one in the party heard or saw us, and she took me along a winding walk William had made past the birches, and what did she show me but the struggling tips of a cluster of leaves belonging to a plant I recognized.

I knew it by the husks of its previous year's flowers scattered around, papery edges tinged gentian blue.

I said to her, You managed to keep them alive all this time?

From their natural home near Dove Cottage, to Allan Bank, then to the cursed Rectory and now here, she said, and you're the kittenlyst!

I remembered William's tone in calling her exuberant, like she had something amiss.

Is a kittenract, I says to her then—I had caught something of her glee out in the wind; the whole outdoors, the wind and everything it touched was her company and I saw she was recovering after fading at the party—is it a cataract that hasn't grown up yet?

And she laughed, and said that now I was a real playmate.

Sam Coleridge made that one up, she said. I noticed the difference between her manner in and out of the house. It was night and day. Sam and I had found a waterfall, she said. Miniature but wild, just rippling and dripping like a thread loosened from a bridal gown. I'll show you!

And she pulled me by my hand up the coffin trail and showed me a falls, a tiny one, beginning to grow ferns around itself though ice shards still lined the rocks, and we sat awhile in the sleet and got wet through while she listened to the water that sounded like bells in a hollow cave: a small voice that combs the bones in your neck and spine with soothing vibrations. It refreshed us and made us laugh.

This was our first kittenract, she said, and forevermore after that we kittenized anything that had *cat* in it. Sam once found a forked stick and pulled a ribbon out of my gown and picked a piece of—you know—that little—tiny yellow pincushion in the middle of the weed that smells like pineapple. He'd flick it at my face and that was his kittenpult. And at the lake, anywhere with a crease in the stones, any tiny indentation—if you could imagine yourself tiny enough to fit inside it, you were in the kittencombs. And if we had

any minor misadventure, such as if we forgot to put leavening in the dumplings, or if William stubbed a toe—before his toe got real bad, if he just gave it a knock like, we'd say don't worry, it's only a minor kittenclysm.

I had not known Coleridge was funny and I did not realize until much later that it was his wife, Sara, who made up their secret language, though Sam made out it was his own.

After our day by the waterfall I would not find Rotha humourless even when she grew depressed. I never came to share William's perception of her. I doubted myself in this at first, because I've noticed that people tend to be blind to very obvious things going on around them. I have asked myself, Why should I be any less blind?

Rotha seldom said *I*. She said *we* meaning herself, William and Coleridge, as if the three were one person. It was a funny way she had, and even, later, when Sam and William were both dead, she still said we. I fear I was daft enough to believe I might become part of that *we* once William and Sam were gone.

Practically every day, James, she said to me, we have a kittenclysm. Just yesterday we sent a letter off to the wrong person. And they'll read it and see immediately it wasn't meant for their eyes. But it was only about the curtains so it's a tiny kittenclysm. It was not about anything harmful or troublesome.

She sounded joyful, explaining this game the friends had made amongst themselves. But in the diary she forbade me to examine—is *forbade* too strong a word for the quiet way she asked me not to look? In the red diary I would find a

page she had titled *Kittenclysm*, but then crossed that out and scrawled *Cataclysm* instead.

Sometimes no matter how beguiling a kitten is, you cannot deny it will grow up and slaughter the swallows.

four

HER BROTHER WAS THE ONE who had hired me, but he hired me to be all and everything for his sister. And it became very evident once I began working regular days at Rydal that two streams were going on as regards my assigned tasks.

For William I did small repairs and brick work and big lifting, using my hands and my reasoning to get the family out of practical fixes and various messes. It amazes me how intelligent people like the Wordsworths cannot think their way out of the simplest everyday problems such as a smoking chimney or a leaky sill.

So when I was not doing the gardening grunt-work for William or listening while he hemmed and hawed about how to form his steps and garden terraces, he assigned me small tasks for the household, some outdoors and others inside: papering and sanding, or patching this and that such as the family umbrellas, pattens and clogs, or their bellows and coal-scuttle. And mending the candle tin or gathering straw for the boots or making the candy for ye bees and bringing it to your hive when it became apparent that we were not going to have good weather at all. In fact I found out by only

a slight inspection that ye were starving! That spring of 1816 we had starvation all around us with beggars coming to the door and Rotha enlisted me to help the odd traveller, especially if they had young ones, by handing them a sixpence and sometimes giving them clean straw for their shoes, if they had any shoes.

Strictly for herself she asked me to provide very little but there was one thing—James, she said, do you see much fallen wool on your travels? Locks of fleece on the fences, tufts in the brambles? Wool in the sticks and on the stones, caught, from the lambs and the sheep?

And I says, Aye, Miss, I see it all the time, I know just what you mean.

She says well, I gather it myself when I am out walking, to stuff cushions, but any time you're on your rambles, if you don't mind putting some in this sack and giving it to me, I'd love that.

So that was a thing I did wholeheartedly and happily because you can shove a bit of wool in your sack and it weighs nowt. It compresses. And she was delighted with that. She was over the moon. She made me a small cushion for my own and it's lovely. I've still got it. It's got leaves on it. She stitched leaves all around it twined like a laurel wreath, like something off a Roman coin or an emperor's head. It was like a royal wreath that's been lost, fallen on the ground, weathered and left for a long time and found by a child in the field.

Everything she fashioned by hand was like that, wasn't it? It was weathered and a bit lost. And everything she said to me was weathered and lost an' all.

Rydal Lake has an ever-changing skin, she said to me on a frozen day that first year. A smoky sheen, she said, clouded underneath as if by one layer of smoke, yet mirror-shining. She said things like that. *Mirror-shining* . . . or, *cut like a ransacked facet of garnet attacked by an axe!* And as she said the word *axe* she looked fierce and alarmed.

I comforted her and I said don't be frightened—look, the water's lovely green all the way through, clear to the bottom. Look—coins and fish and glass bottles and glimmer-stones. Look at the glinting fish, trying to catch our eye, wanting us to see them.

I'd say them things to her. Comforting things.

Looking back on it all now I can barely tell if William pushed me closer to his sister because he saw she and I were getting along so well, or if he had planned me as a kind of replacement for himself all along. At any rate I did a lot of little things for her, and our resulting friendship—was it a friendship?—it grew gradual, like.

That first summer we never stopped making fires because all the land was so bitterly cold. Furrows from the year before couldn't be worked because they were frozen to mid-May in the fields. I'd gather sticks after Rotha pruned the trees, and I lit them and in those fires I toasted many a slice of bread-and-dripping for my luncheon and ate it happily while she continued her orchard work humming like a wren, though I had my doubts over any gooseberries or damsons appearing. She'd sit nearby for a break and say how she savoured the smoke and wasn't it a pity William could not smell its fragrance, in fact he couldn't smell

anything whatsoever, and she had no one with whom to share the fragrance of wood smoke or of lily of the valley except myself.

Can William really not smell anything? I said.

And she says to me, My brother can only engage with certain forms and colours. Fragrance eludes him and I cannot bear to talk of it with him for fear I might seem to be gloating. I have to wait until he reads of fragrance in my diaries and then he can use it in his poetry as if his own nose had smelled it.

I could hardly credit this. Did her brother really read her sensations and then put them in his poems as if they were his? I thought how painful this must have been for him. Knowing glory was there second-hand, like.

All this she confided to me with our heads bent into the cherry wood smoke and our two noses twitching at the waxen bells' musk which floated that May through the cold. Those lilies of the valley are a hardy marvel. Most flowers are. You think they haven't a chance against the wind but away they bloom. And William couldn't smell them! I knew his eyes were bad but between that and not smelling anything and being hard of hearing, no wonder he needed to comb Rotha's diaries for sensation lost to him.

This cherry smoke is lovely, Rotha said of our outdoor blaze. But when coal smoke fills the house from that wretched chimney in our kitchen it fills me with despair!

I knew their chimney smoked and I had my own idea as to why, but I had been busy with my other tasks and no one had yet pressed me to address that problem.

It only smokes on cloudy days, she said, but it reminds us of all the awful smoke in all our other houses that we dreaded, smoke that made us ill—especially the children . . .

I knew she was thinking of wee Catherine and Thomas, both dead with pneumonia, and I said yes, I know the Rydal chimney smokes. Have you checked inside it for any blackened heart?

And she says, do you mean there is something wrong with our hearth?

I felt offended but I did not let on what I was thinking: I know how to say hearth when I mean hearth, Miss, and heart when I mean heart. My name may not be Wordsworth but I do know how to properly say the words I know.

But I did not say any of this. I said, Miss, I meant only that sometimes there can be a heart blocking a chimney.

What in the world are you talking about?

I'll show you, I says. We'll have a look tonight after the fire's died out. Once the fam'ly is off to bed.

And at half past midnight she crouches on the floor while I reach up with tongs clamped on a stick holding a ball of snarly wire and down tumbles the very heart I suspected of blocking the flue, much petrified and charred.

There you are, I says. More than a hundred rusty pins sticking out of this one.

I see Miss Wordsworth hasn't got a clue what to think. Eyes darting all over the place. Those eyes, they darted everywhere. They were deep and—they were like water. They were like the blackest, fastest-running stream, but with pools and becks that slowed or bent back on themselves but then

gushed forward again. People said her eyes were the wildest they'd ever seen. Her friends all said so, but I was the one who saw where gold flecks were located in that stream, those eyes. And I loved showing her my tricks, like finding a heart in the chimney.

It's nowt but a sheep's heart, I says. Someone has lodged it up there for revenge, judging by all the pins. Some previous tenant or their servant. Someone unlucky in love.

I didn't tell her my mam had done this very manoeuvre after my father left us or that she credited the act with his having been killed in his accident at Windy Brow forge. The sheep's heart stands in for the heart you want to bring to harm.

All that day and into the next week Rotha and William and everyone in the house talked about the blackened heart in wonderment. It was as if they had discovered it themselves. I had given them a thrill. And I realized I had a kind of a hidden influence.

And gradually there grew that second manner of task I have mentioned, all concerning Rotha, though purely at William's bidding at first. It had nothing to do with the hefty things I did for him, such as hewing stone for the terraces.

This second responsibility was a task that was not stated. It was never outlined or written in any list or note, nor spoken out loud, though it had to do with the things William had said about Rotha's mental state and how she needed him.

All through 1816, that year without a summer, I was hardly aware it was being formed, this main duty of mine concerning Rotha. If I had noticed it I might have had to put

a stop to it. But then again, maybe I did notice it and perhaps I did not want it to stop.

William had complained to me that for no good reason she grieved and grew distant but I could not agree with him. In my company she was never absent-minded and hardly seemed unhappy at all except over sorrows that would make anyone sad.

Visions impressed themselves on her. I mean real visions: a dove in a puddle or anything she saw, whether the smallest bit of sedge or . . . it's funny . . . a little insect, anything. I mean, I'm looking at a bit of clover now, commonest thing in the world, a bit of red clover. Yet she'd look at that and she'd sense the sweetness of every creamy point plunging into the heart where the nectar is. As if she was one of ye. That bloom called to her and she'd take it right to heart, that little bit of clover. It could be her companion for a day. Aye. Some people, it might look as if they're going through life the loneliest person in the world, but they might be the ones that have a companion in a tiny unremarkable hiding place.

My replacing William in her days happened in a quiet stream at the beginning.

All that first spring he would plan to go out with Rotha doing one of her favourite things: hunting waterfalls or climbing the fells. She would talk about it all day beforehand—falls edged with frills like milk frothing from the cow or lavish as a wedding veil! Imagine! Falling waters and fallen water crashing together into an opalescent pool! She said things like that. She got very excited and baked small pies to carry in their pockets. How William could let her bake

those pies I don't know. She was all thrill. But then morning came and he would say to me, furtively, Dixon—please, you go with Dorothy instead of my going for I've been called away.

He could be called away anywhere like this at any time, and by the time Rotha flew downstairs and started wrapping her pies—it was heartbreaking—she'd glance around for William like a bird looking for its mate and she'd finally ask me, James have you seen him? And I'd say, As a matter of fact, Miss Dorothy, he's had to go off to Carlisle on an errand to do with his stamp duties and has asked me to accompany you in his stead.

I SUPPOSE THERE MIGHT BE some that would call me worshipful, subservient—a hangdog bloke following after Dorothy, and after William as well, in their gardens, the beautiful terraces that William made to walk in, to compose in, to be with his sister in, although it became plain that he didn't want to be with her as often as she wanted it. Through the years he wanted more and more to be alone. Even his wife Mary had her own activities and could make herself scarce. I fear I was not there for Mary. But Mary was self-sufficient. I was there for William. But more and more, it was for Rotha. Him and her both, that was my balancing act. And whatever William wanted and Rotha wanted is what I tried to arrange and provide. I suppose, heh, there were times when anybody watching me could've said, That bloke's gone

soft in the head. Dixon. He's gone along with the madness in that household. Well that's for them to think, and ye can think it all you want if ye like, yourselves.

But I just want to tell ye here and now that I got as much from the Wordsworths as they ever received in the way of service.

Ye have to understand this was the first time in my life that somebody wanted done what I know how to do. What I want to do. The very sort of task that makes me wake up with a song in my heart. Ye must know how satisfying that is.

And as regards my being only a servant, she'd forget. Rotha would forget that I was only the hired hand. I mean, forget is not what she . . . no, she didn't forget, but she . . . She never forgot. But . . . she fully *listened* to anything I had to say.

Didn't she?

And she—I mean yes I slept in my hut and I—I never ate inside the house with the family but . . . that cushion Rotha made me is on my cot even now, so lovely. And it's—haha—it's soft, and I like to think that the softness of that cushion matches the gentle way I helped her, gathering the wool. The fleece. But not only gathering the wool. All the ways I helped her over the years. They were little ways, I know. But I like to think they were tender ways. I mean apart from the times when I didn't know what to do.

And I had days off like any servant but . . . And I was a servant, all right. I was their servant. But what I'm trying to say is that I was made to feel . . . I mean, maybe this was a thing that was done by the family very skillfully, eh, but I don't think . . .

They tried—but I don't think it involved effort, I think it was real. I think they really liked . . . I mean . . . I mean I hope they . . . I'm trying to say that . . . there was a string from my heart to theirs, we had heart-to-hearts, it wasn't as if I was some sort of . . . lackey or fella off the street that just came and hoisted stones . . .

I mean, it wasn't like that at all. At least I—I look back now and I hope, I hope I'm remembering it right.

I mean they felt . . . affection for me, I think? I mean I hope they did, because I certainly . . . I've got to stop telling ye all this for a minute for I feel a kind of—dread? A kind of horrible feeling that I might've been wrong—but—I don't think I am wrong . . .

Do ye think I'm wrong?

I got more from them, companionship like, than I ever knew in my own family, the one I was born into: my mam and my uncles, or anyone in all the hellholes I stopped in as a lad.

Ha.

Some people get a chance in their life to touch gold, to live in a kind of heaven while their hands squelch in the muck, weeding. And I've been one of those people. And I think . . . (are those crows cawing in the distance?) . . . I've been . . . I've been a lucky man.

2

In a cowslip's bell I lie

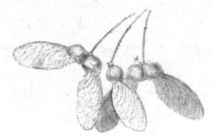

Have you been a lucky man, James?

Now you are a decade older than Dorothy was when you came to her, and what have you to show for your dedication? Her story? I, Sycamore, already know the bones of her tale!

How Once Upon a Time there was a lass whose mother died, then her father, and she, Dorothy, lived alone without her brothers, for the children were all separated. Isn't that correct, James? And she lived for a Time with her stern and unloving grandparents, until lo, she was reunited as a young maiden with her beloved brother William, from whom she vowed never to part . . .

I know her history. But the bees have been busy with future events; just this morning they brace for destruction in Benson's Wood and the slaughter of whole tracts of Luckan gowan—their kingcup—to make way for quarry and road. They see a time when the railway will not only arrive, but become obsolete. A time when machines replace their wings, and life as we know it is a quaint antique. The bees sense in every bluebell the myriad ways humans may destroy their

haunts. Yet they endure errand upon errand for the world, and though they live many-as-one they feel a supernatural loneliness.

Comfort them, Sweet James. The Royal Botanic Society should call a flower after you, like Sweet William's flower! Tell the bees about your Rotha, who looked inside ten thousand star-chambers—bluebell, potato-flower—and saw each mote as a bee does, each ray or spear or flare, shaking. Tremulous. Never still, but all efflorescence, fluorescence, signal . . .

So that is her red diary on your wicker skep? The wind blows its first pages open! Why don't you read it to us? Why do scout bees nose around your skep? Have you candy in it for them? Why have you brought matches? To melt beeswax and seal my wounds after you prune my dead winter branches? It's half past ten o'clock—time for pruning, raking, preparing the ground for spring. Speak, James, and then act, for today's light is a third gone.

five

I RECKON THERE WERE THREE WAYS, says Dixon, that I ended up reading her diaries.

The first was innocent enough. It was that she grew used to me. We both cared about the poems William was making up, him muttering in bits and pieces out on the terraces. But I cared about her ideas more.

Hers were different.

Have ye noticed how the feet of certain small birds when they are running over the ground, their feet they go so quick it's as if the birds are on little wheels?

They tilt up and down a bit, they rock, like, and that is how Rotha was on her feet, all those first years while her feet still carried her. *Oh that my feet may always carry me*, she cried out once. I didn't fathom why, not then.

Her ideas were like scraps of windblown fog or choppy bits of lakewater but William's had to have beginnings and middles and endings. He took ideas from her but by the time he finished with them his were poems and hers were something apart. His were very easy to remember—I got to know a lot of them by heart—but hers you could never know by

heart, you felt them the same as you'd be affected by a scrap of tune tumbling from a bird you had never heard before or had half-heard while you were dreaming. You certainly hoped you would hear it again. You hoped you might get to know that bird. But then you might go all your life without hearing it again. You might wonder if the tune really happened.

And when I say I knew William's poems by heart, I don't mean I read them, I mean I heard them fall from his lips. He didn't write them down, he said them, he muttered them, he was famous for muttering them everywhere he went, all along the terraces and in the fields and along the lake edge, everywhere. So I mean I heard them and yes they rhyme and—most of them, a lot of them, they rhyme—I mean I'm a—I can read, it's not that I can't, but—I think if you put the words to William's poems down in front of me and I had to read them, I'd get a bit bogged down, you know. But when he said them, well, it's like Shakespeare isn't it—I mean you've got to hear it and then you figure out what's going on.

Well Rotha, she scribbled William's poems down for him after he said them out loud. That's how his got written down. If it wasn't for Rotha I don't know what would have happened to William's poems. Moss would've drunk them all. So he was always chanting them out loud for her to write them down and if he got in a muddle she'd fix him right again. So I got to hear his poems over and over again. And anything I hear I'm pretty good at remembering. But Rotha and her words—well. After she scribbled his for him she wrote hers down an' all. He was hardly going to write hers for her. Nobody was. And hers were nowt like his.

Hers in Mary's hat box, all Rotha's own books—all her own lovely sayings. I mean, what she wrote about every step she took to the tarns, Nab Scar, Loughrigg Fell, all her travels, a lot farther afield than William.

And she started letting me read her books—I could sit for hours if I had hours which I didn't. I wished I had more time. But I had scraps of time between tasks and in those scraps I could sit reading her diaries to my heart's content. They glowed up and you saw everything she had seen, you saw it all shimmering. The diaries lit up my own memory of every place she mentioned and it felt like the magic lantern show my mam's cousin took me to at Manchester when we went there to try and get some money her brother owed us. We never got a farthing but the lantern show was better than gold for me—all that blazing light. Where did it come from? Light blazing from somewhere. That's the feeling I got reading her diaries. Not the red one but the plain little dark-coloured ones.

Last night I went to see the delphiniums. Most were not yet burst but two or three had burst out . . .

. . . & they looked like blue dancing skirts kicked open & two little feet inside, wearing furry little lemon-coloured slippers . . .

& at the graveyard I saw lupins with their pods out after the flower had gone, & I opened these, green glimmering through a skin of silver fur . . . & inside lay the

"peas" just like Rose's kittens, all in a line feeding on their mother pod . . .

. . . & I noticed that the iris leaves bend over in the breeze & their bent top part has light shining full down on it but the base hides in shadow . . .

Bits like that, with the lemon slippers, but other bits were crying like . . .

All the rosetrees are now fullblown, though they do still have buds on them. They show every stage of the rose now. Their foliage is crowded with buds, one-petalled flowers, fullblown flowers, & the pollen-yellow hearts of flowers that have had all their petals blown off. The old-fashioned garden rose-tree has a white rose, a modest one, in bloom right at its edge. For the pink rose tree it looks as if the blooming has been excessive: the tree looks ravaged, used out, as if it were ravaged by the cloying blooming of too many roses. I think it looks as if the tree is sick. Sick of roses . . .

So I read her diaries and Rotha said it was all right and I got pleasure out of it. But the second way I studied her diaries was not for my pleasure but was work William asked me to do.

I mean William was not a bad man. He had every intention of being the world's kindest brother. He had made a promise to be exactly that. A promise to himself and a

promise to Rotha. And he kept that promise, sort of. He never left her destitute, did he. Not in the matter of money or a roof over her head.

I can remember Rotha telling me it was all arranged between herself and William that he would inspect her diaries. In fact she wrote them for him when he was away and even for times when he was right there, for as I've told ye, his eyes were that bad and he couldn't smell a thing and this got worse as he got older.

And he told me himself, Dixon he says, it isn't only my eyes and nose. People come to Rydal to glimpse the great poet and here I am unable to feel any of the youthful things I once felt. Those things have gone from me . . . But they have not gone from my sister.

Aye, William was right there.

No, Rotha never lost what her brother lost. She could grow older and older—ancient, it didn't matter, she was the same. Her feet would betray her, aye! Though I am the one who found a way for her to ride the wild way of a sprightly wren. She flew on my little wheels! Aye, I made her the wheels once she was not able to walk. The little wagon. No matter what happened to her legs I would get Rotha outside and in her element. But I'll come to that later. Anyhow she kept writing and never stopped.

But in William's mind her writing was not for herself. It was all for the sake of him and his poems.

What I remember is one day William said, Dixon—you claim you are good with pointy little tools. He hands me a nib and he says, see how you make out with this. Rotha was

out traipsing the fells that day and he brought me up to her bedroom and opened the box that had her diaries in it.

He never opened her red diary, only the black ones and the blue ones. He had me read them out to him and copy bits for him into a notebook of his. Her handwriting was very hard for anyone to read even if they did not have William's terrible eyesight. And writing things down with a pen, well he found that irritating.

He considered pen work drudgery. Scratching, he called it. He hated scratching. It got in the way, between the idea and the poem. He wanted someone else do his scratching. Rotha had done it. At times his wife Mary had done it.

Now it was my turn.

I noticed early on he seemed to want to go upstairs only when Rotha was not present. She was out here in the garden or gone to the post office or flying over the fells. She was still fleet as a lark then. Later when she was not as well, William would bring me upstairs to read her books while she slept, which made me feel uneasy.

I asked him, Sir, if you don't mind my asking, why don't we look in the books while Miss Wordsworth is awake? Perhaps she could help us decipher the penmanship and make our work go all the more quickly.

And he said never mind that, Dixon. She'll get caught up in the memories and we won't be able to get her to turn the page. We'll be here all day. And my sister cannot discern between a passage of literary value and a mere sweep of strong emotion. So let's you and me just get on with it by ourselves.

And I said to myself, Well William is the one paying my wages.

He said he only wanted the perfect timeless things she had set down: the natural, floating things, not details between. The words he fished or made me gather and move from her world to his own were like pollen and nectar ye collect.

We harvested his sister's weightless and golden thoughts.

He did not have anything like those in himself.

He would wait as I read, and he held one hand up in the air like a clock hand ready to strike the moment I read something he wanted to clasp. There was a quality in the air whose name I can't remember. There's a word I can't reach. One that sounds like church bells set to clang, but something binds them aslant in the tower.

He'd say to me Dixon, see what my sister had to say on April the nineteenth.

Went for a walk in the mild thin air, I read out. I had to be careful not to go too fast.

Watch that you miss not a word, he'd say. Don't run the words together. Don't miss the ends off! *Watched the black river with a frost-silvered willow hung low over the water, bent with the weight of the silver, one tip touching the river, dispersing some of the small, white froth-ovals floating on top—listened to the sounds of rain, river, lake—water gullying everywhere—saw three little birds . . .*

What sort of birds, William interrupted.

I don't know.

Damn it does she not name the bloody birds?

No, she just says—

Never mind that page then. On to the next! What does it say?

The next page, Sir, is about Mary not liking it when plates are stacked together for washing whilst food is still on them . . .

Never mind any of that. Who cares about food squashed on plates! Get us back out of doors.

Figurines on top of the larches—a witch riding a broom, Napoleon galloping on his horse—many of these figures seem to be riding fast—

All right, that's better! Go on.

—Nothing in the woods is whiter than the snow of blackberry blossoms on the dark green leaves, & the leaves are dry as bones under the few raindrops that sit on them like tiny crystal balls—

Keep going. Write that one down.

—& water sparkles among the reeds, its voice a flute in the undersong of wind, thrush and reed—lights in the grass—& the lake glimmers through the lilac leaves—skeletons of the lilac flowers stand on the treetop, brittly swaying—a strong wind blew the lilac leaves so they became folded hearts—half-hearted, & it tore the skin off the lake revealing glittering silver blood—like ripped metal—the sound of the wind went hollowly around the hills like a soft-headed stick scribing a spiral on cymbals—

Yes, write it down! We'll have all that.

Sir, Rotha is stirring. She looks as if she might awaken.

No, he says, she's had twelve drops.

He meant the laudanum for her headache.

Read on, he says, sounding impatient.

I had tried their laudanum myself one day when they were all out. I was curious. I never drink a drop of alcohol

because I have no interest in making a fool of myself like some fellows do, wandering over the roads in a chaotic fashion, saying things they shouldn't say, telling all sorts of their own and other people's secrets. I like to keep my private information to myself. But in the interest of understanding the little fam'ly I thought it wouldn't hurt one day while they were all down at the lake to take a dozen drops of the medicine they each took at various times, to see what it did.

The best way I can describe it is to say it sanded the edges of my worst hurts.

It made me nearly forget the plight of my sister for a start. Imagine forgetting Penny. Who would want to take medicine like that over and over again? That makes you forget someone that dear. But then I couldn't remember Waterloo in my usual way at all. Waterloo did not jab me behind the eyes to remember the dead or things I had done or times I had been terrified out of my mind. And that kind of numbing was something.

Laudanum makes your worst sorrows hide behind soft young trees. After I tried it I knew better than to ever try it again for I saw at once why half of England was dependent on it, for it is stronger in far smaller amounts than gin. Takes the sting out of the worst details—it even stopped troubling me that Rotha had my mate Joe Bell's tooth in her mouth. In fact, the laudanum told me that perhaps now whenever Rotha spoke her voice had a trickle of Joe's in it; her voice remembered his. What an idea!

Even after the laudanum wore off I did not forget the thoughts it gave me.

William shouted, Dixon, keep reading, please!

Wild roses on the path along the shore—some of them still folded like ballgowns. Wind makes a merciless hash of the soft-leafed ash tree . . .

Is that all?

That's it for that page, Sir.

What about the next?

Mary is peeling potatoes—the sound a soft scridge scridge of the knife, the softer bubbling up of water in the pot, the creak of the kitchen chair as Wm shifts while reading the paper—& the knife, scridge scridge—a little like the snidge snidge of the razor-grinder's horse eating grass yesterday—or

Forget about peeling potatoes, he cried. Let's mark down the snow of the blackberry blossoms though. And the half-hearted lilacs—was it folded hearts or half-hearts? What did she write?

It was both, Sir—I copied it down for him.

At first I had no way of predicting which of his sister's words William would want to keep or leave alone. And bit by bit I grew able to tell. He did not want to hear about potatoes or their peel or their blossoms. Whereas for her, a potato flower was as important as any other.

He never brought up the red diary and for a while it disappeared. But one afternoon I spied a corner of it sticking out from her blankets and I said, Sir, do you mind my asking about that red diary belonging to your sister? I nodded towards it casual like.

No, he says. I do not mind at all. He did not sound put out or on the alert.

So I says, Sir, might you like me to have just a peep inside it for you as we have not looked at that one before, as far as I remember?

It is not an important document, he said.

No, Sir?

Not at all, he said. The red volume, unlike the others, contains not a fragment of literary merit.

You cannot use it for your poems, Sir?

The red diary is of no use to anybody at all. It is nothing but a record of my sister's feelings.

six

HER FEELINGS!

I think people show different sides of themselves depending on their company, and I might be flattering myself but I feel as if when she was with me, Rotha was clear as the pool under the kittenract where we went many times even after she lost her foot power and I became her trusted steed. She was clear about her feet. She knew something was happening. But before it happened she was not only clear but merry. She made up more and more of her own words. If an apple shrank and wrinkled she called it shrinkled. She called Cockermouth where she and William were born that Cockamoodle place. She was forever playful when it came to words, though she claimed not to have William's talent for poetry. I did not think this true. I thought, on getting acquainted with her notebooks, that she had a wild streak no one could match. Certainly not her brother. She suited me down to the ground as a companion though of course I was only a servant.

But I mean one servant can be entirely different from another servant, can't they?

It's funny how two people looking at the same thing can see something different from each other, isn't it. I've often thought that. You can take a walk with somebody and you can return home and the other one can flummox ye with the things they've noticed and you didn't have a clue, and same the other way around. You can tell them something you would've thought plain as the nose on your face about what ye'd seen, whether it was a migrating duck off its course or a tree that needed pruning or even something as simple as the way some reeds are getting to overtake, you know, other plants that were wanted to proliferate. Anybody not interested in anything like that, they won't even see it. It's completely invisible!

So I suppose it's not really unusual that John Carter, ye know him, the other servant who helps William with his secretarial work and the stamps and everything, but I mean he does a lot around the place as well and as ye know we don't overlap so much as pass one another on our various rounds. He saw things very different from the way I saw them.

Especially concerning Miss Wordsworth, which is what he never ceased to call Rotha even when she begged him to use her first name. She could not get a human response out of him.

Though I have to watch it. My uncle Jim used to say lad, your da might be dead and gone but he'll be in your blood and you'll have to watch out you don't turn out like him because sadly the man had massive trouble putting two an' two together.

I says what do you mean, Uncle Jim? I was only about six at the time.

Well, he says, the conclusions your dad would draw from something were amiss, y'know, meaning they weren't what anyone else'd ordinarily draw given the same evidence. Your da often used to get the wrong end of the staff. I mean he never suffered badly for this, now, he had a way of going easy over the ground and getting by. That's what he did isn't it? Tramped everywhere, who knows where he'd end up. One time he'd been away to Brighton. He come back and he says well there's a lovely beach, not a grain of sand. They've taken all the sand away and dumped lovely smooth pebbles there instead! And I says they've done what? I'd been to Brighton. I'd seen that beach myself.

He says to me Jim, he says, they've replaced every speck of sand with lovely round stones, all along the waterfront, and I says man you're daft, how would they do that? An' he says well, you know, an army of diggers must've come and carted every bit of sand away and replaced it with—I dunno where they got the stones but aren't they lovely, all colours just like birds' eggs. Speckled! And green veins in 'em an' blue spots and red spots like blood!

Lad, your father had a fantastic time exploring those stones and picking them up in 'es hands and enjoying them. I says you're always jumpin' to barmy conclusions. I says man Brighton is a stony beach and is now and forever has been and will forevermore be world without end amen, and it got that way by itself. But o'course nothing I could say would convince your old man of that. So all I mean, son, is be careful you don't start thinking too much like your da.

And I think my uncle Jim did suspect I might turn out

like my father—not able to put two and two together without some sort of mix-up. I mean ye lot don't have to take what I say as gospel, it's just I am trying to look at, you know, William and Rotha and myself and dear Mary an' all, everything I saw over our many years and, ye know, this is just me trying to . . . look at it all for ye . . . and yes, put the two and two together. For ye now, telling you all this, now Rotha's gone.

So about John Carter, the Wordsworths' other servant, he says to me one morning it was the most curious thing, he says William is . . . he's having trouble, y'know, with Miss Wordsworth again.

This was probably a year after I started with them.

And I says John what do you mean? Is she sleep-walking again?

Because Rotha was, I'll grant, a sleepwalker at times, and one of the housekeeper's jobs was to keep an ear out and not let her roam all the way to William's room. Many's the night, I was told, she'd end up on the edge of William and Mary's bed fast asleep in the morning and sometimes on the floor.

But John Carter says no. He says Dorothy's on the lament about never seeing her brother and he's always out and he's not coming up to her room to see her and he's eating his mutton at different times from her mealtimes or he's just not there.

And I said well, John man, I've been working on it. I've been trying to keep her company.

By rights I couldn't really argue with John Carter. He had a point. I had gone to Stickle Tarn with Rotha only days

before. At the summit I had thought she might like to dip her feet in the water and I was unwrapping the pies and putting our lemonade in the shade of a rock when I saw her throw herself on the turf. And she cried something out very loud, but whatever she cried the wind carried away.

Pardon, Miss? I says . . .

William, she says in a heartbreaking tone, is a different man when he's alone with me.

Aye, Miss, I says, I reckon we're all different according to who else happens to be around.

But my brother is hardly ever alone with me, in fact he's never alone with me anymore.

Aye, Miss, William is a busy man.

When he was alone with me, we had a world! Everything else, all his business and all the parties and people talking on and on about small things, they are not our world. They are things he tells me he must endure. I always believed him. Tell me, James, what does he say about it to you?

I had not yet managed to repair her botanical magnifying glass. At that moment I wished with all my heart that I had mended it so I could draw her back to the exact observations she loved to make out of doors. *Calyx, stamen, ovary* . . . But I had not found the right parts—the pins I fastened it with kept dropping out.

William doesn't endure his business, does he? He enjoys it! What has he told you, James? You are the one with me now. Sometimes I wonder if my brother has brought you among us so as to prevent his being alone with me ever again . . .

I didn't know what to make of it all. We sat like a pair of stones. Us and the wind. And then very quiet I started up a song. Not my old, private song, but a new one I had made up after coming to work for the Wordsworth family. I only hummed it, as I did not feel like letting her hear the words in case she recognized herself.

But she said, James, that is a lovely tune. Has it any lyrics?

Not really, I said, which was not true, but I am convinced she could always spot an untruth, especially one coming from her brother or from me.

She said it *has* got words hasn't it.

So I says Miss, it is a song I made up about . . . about a dear sister.

I didn't know you had a sister, James. Is she older or younger?

Penny is younger, Miss. I realized Rotha did not recall I had already told her I had a sister.

Sing it for me. If they belong to such a tune as that they will be words I'd like to hear.

Clouds raced over our heads and there was nary a soul to be seen for miles over the Langdales, and Lake Windermere glittered far below us and it seemed safe enough to give in to her request. Sometimes you feel reckless.

Once upon a time a very wild girl
clambered the fells all night:
Her eyes two living lumps of coal
with diamond flames alight

Her feet were clouds all tiny and fleet
that raced o'er sky and vale
And I yet see that same wild girl
In the rain and wind and hail!

And as I sang my song the wind crept in with my voice. I looked at Rotha and she looked at me. The song was about a sister all right, but whose sister?

I was not sure if my song calmed her or further agitated her and it took a meeting with some stitchwort—counting and naming its parts—to bring her to her regular precision of mind where I knew she would be safe.

And while we were yet up near the tarn she said, If only I had money, James. Do you know what I would have done?

It took resolve on my part not to answer, But you do, Miss. You do have money.

For compared with myself and my kind, such as our Penny now destitute in Manchester on account of her injuries not being able to work, Miss Dorothy Wordsworth had plenty of money indeed. Some survival instinct in her had seen to it that her brothers signed over sufficient for her keep. More than sufficient, for she had made them promise extra for books, and for going places she wanted to go such as London, and for giving sixpence to those who came to the door after losing their land. She had plenty for beggars so as to feel helpful in this world. Only those who have extra feel that way. But I said nothing. It was dawning on me that where money is concerned everybody seems to believe they have far too little.

Money! There's either a small bit of your soul or a medium-sized bit or a giant portion that's taken up with money.

My small salary I know how to stretch.

I grow my own onions and potatoes and leeks. I hunt a few rabbits. And like I told ye, I come from a long line of sheep-stealers. But the Wordsworths? Aye . . . William . . . I think money is what changed him. The Wordsworths thought they were going to have money. And then it didn't come. According to John Carter it got lost. They had to wait. And it was years before they saw any of it. It was owed to them by a man that owed their dad. Something like that. And then their brother John got lost at sea and with him all their investments.

Their rent. Their tea. I mean who knows, if I were them maybe I'd have drunk the enormous quantities of tea they drank. How they quaffed it. Maybe they couldn't imagine a day without that consolation. After all the freezing cold wind and rain and sleet and hail, and more wind, and lightning and thunder on their walks—walking and walking. They needed a cup of tea. But Rotha—she stood up for herself when it came to money. John Carter told me. It was when William married Mary Hutchinson and William asked Rotha what she wanted.

He didn't mean, what did she desire?

He meant money. And Carter told me Rotha gave William written instructions, very detailed. A stipend each year. A roof over her head—William's roof. William's and Mary's. That roof, over her head, for her lifetime. Which has happened. I mean we're looking at that roof now. And extra

to give tinkers or gypsies or families who have lost their homes. Have I mentioned books? She had to have her books. I mean she read William's but she had to have her own.

Aye, she stipulated all that. And once William promised it to her, she signed off on all her soul's care over the material things in life. Whereas William, that job he had at the stamp office, and his other bits and bobs he had going, well he was the one who had to see to it all. And trying to sell his poems—she helped there. There's no doubt his sister was his biggest salesperson . . .

WELL? DO YOU, JAMES? Rotha asked me again. Do you know what I would have done if I had money?

I had to be careful. The wind from those pikes had a mind to push us both to blurt whatever we felt. I had to watch what I said but Rotha did not. That is another thing money does for a person.

What would you have done, Miss D?

Because money has eluded me but not before love eluded me! And the two, money and love, well, James, surely you yourself know this—without one or the other, nothing can be accomplished. And a woman without money cannot do the thing I should have done.

What should you have done, Miss D?

I should have become like my powerful friend in Borrowdale.

Which friend, Miss D? Though I knew who she meant straight away.

Surely you know my friend—everyone talks of her—they call her wilder than the rivers or mountains. They even say she is mad, but she is not mad at all. My friend is simply free.

Who, Miss?

But I knew she meant her friend Mary Barker. The Barker woman was unusual. She was unmarried and had built a house for herself to live in all alone, miles from another soul. Miss Barker was a wild one all right, traipsing the land all by herself, carrying her paintbox to hidden places and making paintings of thunderheads and crags, paintings she did not need to sell because she was well-off. The Barker woman could surround herself with rock and thunder by day, and with her own paintings of rock and thunder by night.

My friend Miss Barker, Rotha cried, does not have to answer to anyone, and I wish to god I could go and live like her, since my brother is to be only my pretend companion!

I began coaxing her by way of attention to detail.

I pointed out to her this and that bit of plant.

But she said, There is something in both you and me akin to rage, isn't there. Oh! Do you see that anger has the word rage hidden in it?

Pardon, Miss D? I was not up on word games like she was, but I saw some new idea was calming her down.

The word anger has r-a-g-e in it, she says. But anger contains an extra N. Is N for never, James? Do you never show anger?

Miss—I can't say . . .

Or is N for new? Maybe your anger is newer than mine, James, because you're young.

She was wrong about that. My anger went generations back and yes, it did contain rage. But I had mine under control. I knew where my income camc from and I knew how to maintain the sweet world I enjoyed so much. My work-hut and my Sundays and my being the lord of everything William thought he created in his gardens. Such is the way with gardeners. We don't serve a human employer. We work for the place that came before the boss and carries on without him.

My friend Mary Barker has escaped, Rotha said.

Aye?

Yes! Miss Barker is free. Whereas I am forever in danger of losing my world in every aspect.

Are you though? I tried not to sound incredulous.

It is not like that when you are a man, she glared at me. Even a manservant such as yourself owns more say in his own freedom than I do. Through money and through reliance on her own mind and her strong will my friend Mary Barker has indeed escaped! But for me, and for anyone without money, being a woman and running free are diverging forces, and agony to contain at once.

Aye, Miss D, I said. The world of money won't help anyone locked outside it. And the world of love is a daft illusion . . . better not cave to it at all, eh?

But as soon as I said that she suffered an episode whose frenzy I needed to quell or I'd never have got her home. She'd have clung to the rocks and remained as lichen under

the snows. What a job I had to run after her that day and to bring her home again.

She had a way of vanishing that frightened me. I don't mean that her body vanished.

BUT I DID NOT ADMIT a word of this to the other servant John Carter, not a peep.

And now Carter says, Dixon I know you've been doing the best you can but the fact is, Miss Wordsworth is not settled. She is anything but settled.

And I says, Well is she confiding you this herself? Or is someone else telling you tales?

And he says no, no, no, I see it in the way she is with that dog of hers.

Little Miss Belle, I says—how d'you mean?

John says, Well you know how Miss Wordsworth renders the dog's fur all damp.

I said what do you mean she renders . . . ?

He says have you never seen the times that dog goes around with soaked fur and it hasn't been in the lake it hasn't been in the rain and she's crying over that dog and you know yourself it's only a very small animal. After an hour of her crying over that dog it's sopping wet, man. The woman's not right in the head.

I did not like John Carter's saying this.

For I had paid attention to the same topic, the matter of Rotha's mental state, and had not come to his conclusion at all.

Right at the start of my time with Rotha, when she told me about the secret window in her room, hidden in the wall, I asked William did he have any idea what she might have meant by that. I was trying to get to the bottom of her strangeness and find out how deep it went and if it meant I should believe the things she told me or instead believe the things other people said. Oh, said William, yes, there is a window hidden in Dorothy's bedroom wall. It has been covered up these many years to avoid paying the window tax. The more windows in a house, you see, Dixon, the more tax the owner must pay.

Now John Carter said, it pains William every time he sees that wet dog because he knows it means Dorothy has been crying again.

I said, have you tried slightly licking it?

He says have I tried what?

And I said, The dog: have you tried touching your tongue upon the dog to see if it's a bit salty? Maybe it's not Miss Wordsworth's tears, maybe it's the rain.

He says man, you're as daft as she is.

I went off before I could respond in irritation. I had tomatoes to stake and plenty of other tasks to do that day, and tasks save my mind. I knew John Carter was not alone in his thinking. My own mam had claimed both William and Dorothy Wordsworth were more than a bit daft and so did a lot of others. Most people lumped the pair together. All their muttering and the pacing out in all weathers . . . people said that was why they had to leave their first house,

before Dove Cottage. Their lease never got renewed because the villagers looked on them and on Sam Coleridge and thought—no, *knew*—the three of them were mad.

But this was the first time John Carter had said anything to me.

And William paid John to do a lot of intelligent work for him, head-work more than my kind of work. Still it never occurred to me that John Carter might think William had a level head but Dorothy didn't. I mean this was a new idea to me—that William was sane and Rotha wasn't—and I never came to adopt it myself. To me both brother and sister were above and beyond the ordinary.

But I did tuck John Carter's notion away in the back of my mind as something certain people thought.

And I came across it again down through the months and the years . . .

People had much to say about Rotha that they never said about William.

And what I have to conclude—what I want to tell ye now—is that I am of the mind that part of it was simply because he was a fella and she wasn't.

I mean I don't know if that's right or not. Maybe I have got the wrong end of the staff.

But I failed to make any sense of John Carter and the things he said, the things anybody said, regarding Rotha being mad.

I thought to myself, John Carter, you haven't got a clue. So Rotha has been crying. So what?

I mean what's wrong with, if you do find—that she's cried—what's wrong with going and asking her, Have you been crying? What's the matter, pet?

That's what a brother should have done!

Any rate I touched my own tongue ever so lightly to Little Miss Belle's fur, and of course I found it wasn't salty at all—it was only rain that had splashed through the window.

A wee shower of early summer rain.

I mean anybody can recognize rain on a dog. It's not a smell of sadness at all. In fact, what could be happier?

But I did keep in my mind that John *had* seen Rotha crying. She did burst into tears at times but it did not always mean she was sad. Has nobody heard of tears of happiness? What did William call her? Exuberant!

Still, after John Carter said these things, I kept an eye out.

Because it was part of my job to keep an eye out if anybody in that little family had a heavy heart. Laugh if ye want. True, I might not always know how to help, but just being companionable can lighten the atmosphere, even if you never say anything out loud. Even if you're just with the sad person in a quiet way. I think this is where me and John Carter were different.

He thought weather outside had nothing to do with weather inside. But I have always known that with Rotha the two kinds of weather touch each other. Rain splashes through the window and looks and feels like tears. Or thunder crashes louder and louder until you can't tell anymore if it lives in the sky or in your head.

And with Rotha that was something I understood. I helped her withstand the roar of any weather that rose up; thunderclaps or lightning and the like. That was something I knew how to do because I knew the weather was in her.

Right inside her was the weather!

So there was I, doing as her brother had asked me, plodging beside her in my boots.

Crows.

Sere, yellow grasses.

Puddles.

Reflections of bare branches in the puddles.

The lake.

Caw, caw!

Rotha would say, The water's sullen. She'd say James, the hay bends at the waist, its brow touches the mud, desolate. The hay is desolate!

If the gulls cried, she said something was hurting them.

Yes, I answered, the gulls are downright sodden as up they arc but not near as high as they might if their day was sunlit, you're right, Miss D.

The sunbeams have departed the gulls, she said. The sunbeams have abandoned the grass. The sunbeams have left the water.

But she'd never say, the light has left *me*. She didn't need to say it.

I knew that one and the same thing to her were gull and grass and lake and path and her own self.

seven

ooooo

AND I MEAN IN THAT WAY, in the way of being part of nature and loving and revering it, Rotha was a new kind of woman, to me, so very different from the likes of my mam, who was a lot more ordinary and I hate to say it but who I might even have felt a bit . . . I mean, was I? Ashamed of my mam? I mean she wasn't ordinary as such. My mam was very intelligent. Only she ruined her intelligence or time and place ruined it for her.

Ye would think, looking at Mam with her body gone to wasteful ruin, all grey and swollen like, fed on buns and tea and gin and tobacco—*paff-paff, paff-paff,* always the tobacco with my mam, fumes of it, or fumes of gin . . . ye would think she hadn't a sensible brain in her body, but she did. My mam could read very well, and she could certainly put two and two together, especially any time it had to do with money. She sniffed out the aims of people and she had disdain for their scheming. Everybody scheming, she used to say, yet she herself was the head schemer. Aye, if anyone went on and on about the advantages that might be gained by our family once I got in with the Wordsworths, it was

my mam. Ye would think I had come across dead gentry on the highway, festooned with medallions and their pockets crammed with gold, and all I had to do in the quiet wind and the wild loneliness was lift the gold off them and be on my merry way.

But let me stick up for my mam here a bit! Don't judge her that fast.

Ye have to look at it as regards things she believed. And she didn't drink as much as lots did. She drank herself out of pain which is what many do, though I don't do it myself. And was it when she drank that my mam dreamed of a different life? Or did she dream of a different life before her drop of gin, and was the gin only to help make the dream move closer . . .

And it did. Once, I . . . her dream came closer and closer whenever I went to see Mam, after I got in with the Wordsworths. Maybe that was my fault. Maybe I praised the situation up too much. At any rate Mam believed I had found her own dream come true. She believed the Wordsworths were like royalty and in fact as far as we were concerned, our family, they might as well have been.

What Mam and Penny thought my new life was like—ha, it wasn't like that at all. But could I convince them? I didn't even try.

Because my mam had a fantasy. She had never been inside the Wordsworths' home like I had. She saw it—it's funny, this—she saw it a bit like the Wordsworths saw it, themselves. A tall house hidden behind trees and gardens, separate from that other world where Mam skivvied for coppers

and ate only buns with no raisins, and drank tea that got weaker and weaker as time went on, until it was nowt but a cup of hot water, because she steeped it over and over again until it had no trace of comfort. Not like the Wordsworths' house where tea is plentiful every day and strong enough, aye. Gallons of it!

That was one thing, the tea.

But it wasn't tea, or roast pork shoulder, or even the use of a horse that Mam thought about when she kept on with her Wordsworth dream. Her dream of what I had amounted to by coming to this place.

No.

Mam's fantasy, and Penny's also, since Mam passed on to Penny her notions about my job. Penny had not seen me in my new element. I *wanted* Penny to come! But Penny had only Mam's version. Cream in a bowl, honey from ye lot, with the comb afloat in it to lift out and gnaw like a king. Berries as well—all that on one bowl of porridge!

And quietness.

And flowers.

And books.

Mam said to me son, you've certainly hit the jackpot. Roast pork for you on a Sunday! Aye what would I not give for a nice pork shoulder like that. She said *like that*, as if she had with her own eyes watched me in the Wordsworths' kitchen seated at their table spearing a slice of pork with a silver fork and putting it in my mouth. Slick pork grease on my lips. My mother saw this in her mind's eye. She had a bright imagination, perhaps as strong as the imaginations of

the Wordsworths themselves. And in her mind she had seen the roast, and the silverware all polished, and a fine tablecloth. These things had not really happened but Mam saw them clear as day. She and Penny fancied jonquils on the table, a real la-de-da situation with me as a kind of honorary Wordsworth enjoying the spectacular fruits of that life. You couldn't talk them out of it.

And if I am honest with ye, my mam's imaginary Wordsworth family and my own imaginings were not very different at first. This is why I can't bear feeling ashamed of Mam. I was not forced to stay in her world. If my life here is not what Mam thought it was, or even what I hoped it might be, it is still a world far grander than ours. Mine and Mam's and Penny's.

But I found out I had a capacity to appreciate things William said or wrote, and things his sister said and did . . . I soaked up their world and I knew what it was made of. Mam did also. Even Penny. It didn't belong to us but we recognized it. We were wishful. We were waiting. But we would never claim it. What can I call the Wordsworth atmosphere?

Loveliness? Shelter? How is it ye regard your hive? Full of sweetness and shade and protection? Fragile and filled with gold treasure the whole world wants but hardly anyone can have?

When I started here I thought of myself as coming in from outside. Coming into shelter, into paradise. But very soon I saw that William and Rotha were doing the same thing! They were coming in from outside. Coming into shelter, into paradise. And paradise was pretend. Even for

them. It was a moving painting or it was that lantern show I told ye I went to see in Manchester with Mam's cousin. It was no more real for William or Rotha than it was for me or my mam or for our Penny.

Was it?

Sometimes I cannot make out the real difference between the Wordsworth family and mine, as far as our ideas go about shelter from bad things in the world—things causing blight the way foul weather or fungus can come to ye and to your glory realm and to your hives and even your very bodies, if you are not careful and if you are not blessed.

How does paradise touch some people like a lantern beam? While other people, like Mam and Penny, fumble in the gloom?

It doesn't take long for copper to tarnish and it did not take long for my shining sister Penny to lose her youth and her health. I wanted to help her, even if that only meant bringing her here to the Wordsworths' made-up paradise. For the Wordsworths have not lived in the real world!

Did Mam start the notion of my getting Penny a job with the Wordsworths? Or did I? Did Mam say she wished Penny worked beside me instead of at the factory in Pendleton? And did I chew on that wish until it was mine?

Because it did become my thought.

All my first year here at Rydal and maybe my second, I could not make out how to bring that thought up with William or his sister. I mentioned Penny whenever I could, reminding them that I had a sister and that she was a very hard worker.

I spoke this as if I was talking to myself but I made sure William overheard. After all, I am my sly mother's son, thought I. But William did not bite the bait. I was doing it all wrong. Or I was not the son of my mother, who'd have spilled the information naturally, completely innocent like. And because I was so woeful at it, it soon became all I could think of. Mention Penny as a good worker and hope someone would take me up on the idea. But my attempts fell on deaf ears until one day Rotha was reading the paper and there was an article in it about Manchester and she flung the paper in the fireplace. I watched the word *Manchester* flame up then shrink to grey with a gold edge and then collapse. It was one of her last fires of spring. I remember because I was measuring the fireplace to fit a new summer board over the hole. I know it wasn't my first spring there because that first year we had no summer. So it was my second or third.

Rotha shuddered and she said, James, I am most glad I do not have to look very often at a street in that town!

And of course I was all ears since Pendleton, where my sister worked, was on the edge of Manchester.

So I said, Manchester, Miss? I made out as if I was very carefully double-checking my measurements for the fireplace. My sister works there, Miss, I said, although I had told Rotha this before.

But in truth at that moment my sister was out of a job. Something had gone badly downhill with her shoulder. My mam had her at the house and was trying painful exercises to get it to rise back up evenly with the other shoulder. Because Penny had been working at the same spot on the

floor in the same position from the age of eleven and was now nearly sixteen. She had become a piece of the machine. Her shoulder had ground itself down low like a worn-out machine part and my mam had it strapped up with bandages night and day, but I wasn't confident of the result. Or I was pretty sure what the result would be and did not want to admit it to myself. Here was I, very comfortable, while Penny . . .

An awful place, Rotha said. A sister, you say? I had thought you mentioned a brother.

No, Miss, a sister.

A sister?

Yes, Miss. I kept my surprise to myself, that she did not remember all that I had told her about Penny. As a matter of fact, I said, Penny is off work on a little break at the moment, and I have been wondering . . .

Is she? How nice for her. I myself am very glad that our own tranquil paradise means I hardly ever have to look at a filthy industrial city such as Manchester. I do hope your sister has a chance to come back to the Lakes.

Yes, Miss. I was going to ask you . . . I mean if you and your brother didn't mind . . . if it would be all right for Penny to come and see me for . . . a short visit.

Heavens, James, you don't have to ask me that. It is up to your family, surely, whether your sister comes to visit them, is it not? And we can certainly spare you the few hours you would need to go and see her, yourself.

Rotha had misunderstood me. Or I had not said it properly, the thing I wanted to ask, which was whether it would be possible for Penny to come here, to Rydal Mount,

to recover in the fresh air and the peace here, as the Wordsworths themselves repaired their own health whenever the world beyond our little paradise affected them too much . . . but I had not managed to say it. And now if I said it, the thing would come out all wrong. It would be presumptuous. I could not figure out how to ask. I envisioned Penny curled up in my hut where I had a spare blanket and straw to make an extra bed. She would be no trouble at all to the Wordsworths! But I could not for the life of me find a way to paint this picture in Rotha's mind without it sounding preposterous.

Thank you, Miss, was all I could think of to say. Her working hours at the mill have been long, I said, and my sister does need a rest.

Yes, Rotha said. I have just now read that the government has sent inspectors to the Douglas mill and to other mills to assess whether the floors are really as bad as they all say. Inspectors! But, James, anyone could tell them the answer to that. I could tell them, myself!

Miss?

I was not sure what she meant as I could not picture Rotha having gone inside a mill and seen the workers.

Anyone could, she said, who has visited the streets of Manchester and seen the youths maimed like people who have come home from a war.

Miss, I said, that is true, for our Penny's workmate Rhona got caught by a strap on the machine and flung against a wall and broke every bone in both arms and both legs and has to . . .

Stop! Rotha said, and she shot both arms toward me with her hands splayed as if I had thrown my yardstick at her face.

I realized I should never have spoken. What had come over me?

I did not continue about how Penny herself would never stand straight again. I did not say how her shoulder skewed her spine. Nor did I mention Penny was thin as a nail since thread and dust clogged the air and landed in the porridge you ate as you worked, more thread than oats—you ate the thread you milled and breathed pieces of it until your lungs were full but your stomach empty and you were let go as soon as they caught you spitting blood.

I did not say any of that, because the look on Rotha's face meant if I said another word she couldn't take it and Penny might not be the only young Dixon out on the street. I had a glimpse into Rotha's hard-heartedness that minute. It was something I took in. If she heard or saw even a glimpse of something that didn't go with her vision of paradise in that closed-off, shaded world of theirs, Rotha Wordsworth wanted it gone.

What made the mill send Penny home at last wasn't her shoulder or her lungs. They sent my sister packing with a note. Mam told me they kicked her awake in the drying-room at one o'clock in the morning. Penny hid there instead of being driven into the cold in wet clothes after her shift. They all hid. In the wool. Under the baskets. But when the overlooker kicked Penny she jolted up and went through the motions of her work though her machine had stopped for the night. Like I told ye she had turned into a machine

herself, or a wrecked or manic part of the machine going on and on after the controls were off. The note called her unfit due to laziness. But is it lazy if you keep working while you are asleep? I don't think lazy is the word and what the word might be I do not know.

But all I said to Rotha was, Sorry, Miss. I understand. It's just that my sister, Penny, has been having a little trouble with her health, and . . .

Are her feet all right? Rotha asked.

Her feet, Miss?

Yes. As long as one's feet are all right, then everything is not lost.

She looked down at her own feet and I realized she was worrying about them, about being able to cover the miles on foot that she wanted to cover. She was not thinking about Penny, but about her own freedom. Wild miles on the hoof. Would the miles always meet her? She suspected something faltering in herself and this was when I caught wind of it. That moment when she asked me about Penny's feet.

AND AFTER THAT I STARTED noticing Rotha talked often about feet.

Mostly the feet of women older than herself. She kept a running commentary. Poor Molly, for instance, the Wordsworths' old servant who had died before my time. Rotha described to me how Molly shoved her poor ankles into her boots deformed like. Her legs didn't come out of the

boots straight. Her shins overflowed like puddings from a pan and her legs were ready to topple like a couple of water-logged larches!

And William rubbed his sister's feet. That was one thing he did do. He only asked me to do that whenever he was away from the Lakes.

Once when I did rub her feet I saw they had the start of a bunion and I said Miss, do you wish me to make you a splint to straighten it up? Because I knew how to make one out of willow. The bark fits around a toe and besides that there's medicine in willow that stops any ache.

But she said no, thank you, James, it's not bunions I worry about. Bunions are insignificant. Nor am I the least concerned by blisters or corns. Calluses, however, quite interest me.

They interest you, Miss?

Yes, in fact, I welcome calluses since in the right places they can increase the working lifespan of a person's feet.

Ah, I says, like an extra bit of leather?

Exactly, she says. I have a few calluses and I don't mind them at all. It's not those small inconveniences I worry about, but larger, systemic things that start elsewhere in the body but end up affecting one's feet so that the feet cannot do what they were designed to do. That is what frightens me.

I wanted to ask her what she meant by systemic things that start elsewhere, but I kept quiet. Like I have said, it behooved me to learn when to keep my mouth shut with the Wordsworths, and when to speak, in order to gain and keep their trust and to learn all the things I needed to learn.

So yes I kept quiet about her fears until out of thin air she would begin ruminating on them.

I was giving her feet a rub and she says to me, James, she says, you, now, you're a lad of no more than twenty-two. You'll have nothing the matter at all with your feet, will you? Not a thing. Your feet must be like the feet of Mercury, adorned with wings! And she looked at mine more than a bit jealous like. In fact she looked at them as if she'd like to chop them off me and have them for herself.

As a matter of fact my littlest toenails had both cracked right down the middle but I didn't tell her that. The nails cracked because my boots were tight. They had got soaked and dried out enough times that the leather had shrunk. And in the toenail cracks I stuffed globs of your bee wax to keep dirt out and to try and repair the nails. But they were a sight. Any gardener that doesn't have filthy feet is no gardener at all is he? And filth had ground into my feet. The dirt was ingrained. I knew if Rotha ever saw my bare feet what a fright she'd get, although hers were not as white or spotless as other women's feet. Her feet were brown as a child's that has been playing outside all summer. But they were nothing like mine.

But I says no, Miss D, I have no problem with bunions or blisters or anything like that.

And, she said, I can see for myself your ankles are not swollen.

No, Miss, my ankles are all right.

But she says mind you watch that lopsided sole on the heel of your left boot. It means your gait's uneven. And

James, I warn you, your second twenty-two years will whizz past twice as fast as the first! By then that foot won't know what hit it—look at William's poor toe!

Yes, Miss.

Gradually is how it happens, says she.

That was when I noticed she was forever remarking on the state of everyone's feet and shoes.

And aye, she mentioned wings. Because those feet of hers were like your wings are to ye. Your wings get you pretty far over these fells and lakes, and her feet were wings in her mind. Everyone's feet were wings in her mind. And you have to give it to her, the shape of feet with their toes is a bit like fans or wings with the feathers sticking off. Hands and fingers an' all. Wings and feathers on our bodies. If only we could fly! Ye lot are the lucky ones.

So I noticed she started caring about feet. And once you notice something you can't help seeing it over and over.

It did not matter who came to Rydal. Friend or foe. Lad or lass. Mrs. Dobson down the hill or Mrs. Luff or any of the relatives. First Rotha would greet the person face to face, but then, to herself, she'd note the condition of their feet. I saw her looking at feet and I heard her talk and yes I saw what she wrote. And it was true that William had a very bad toe and it plagued him and stopped him from walking half the distances his sister trod.

Have ye ever noticed how people will admit something out loud but only in a half-told fashion?

At first when I climbed the fells with her after William asked me to stand in for him—it was all I could do to keep

up with her, and she twice my age! It's funny about that isn't it. Rotha was twice my age when we started together, but today she would be only thirty years older than I am, not twice my age at all. Far from it. Time brings you closer in so many ways. But at first we would fly uphill and on our way back down she'd say, James, aren't our feet wonderful? How they get us up here so efficiently and without any trouble at all?

She said without any trouble . . . but even then she glanced at her own feet as if they were getting ready to run away without her.

And by and by she worried about them more and more. What did she know? Even before they failed her, she stared at them as if they were already starting to lose their miraculous powers. And I'd say, Miss, is it your feet? And half the time she'd say no, it's not my feet. But the other half she would say perhaps it is my feet. And if William was not around she'd let me give them a rub.

I felt sorry that he was gone although my hands were better suited to the job than his. She was missing William's hands and to cheer her up I admitted to her that I had made up a song about feet, did she want me to sing it?

The song is a song about the wandering life alone on foot, I said.

I sang it to myself when I wished I could go back to when my da's family were travellers, a time I only know by song or by old tales that flicker like a faint campfire. But I did not mention that to her. I don't think she wanted to hear too much of my story. She was very comforted by the fact that I

was a quiet and strong person who did not demand anything in the way of attention. She hated it when people gabbed on about themselves, which in my observation nearly everybody does. It's amazing to me, really, how they don't notice that nobody really cares about anybody but themselves.

James, she said, you know I'd like any song you care to sing. And I do think she meant it. Times when we were outside and I made myself believe she forgot I wasn't her brother, she opened a part of her mind that allowed song or fancy or other things I had to give her.

So I sang part of my walking song.

My caravan has a little brown roof.
My caravan has two blue windows.
My caravan has a pair of funny little wheels,
They go slow they go far over the hills, over the fields
I wouldn't trade my little caravan . . .

And I stopped and said Miss, do you get the riddle?

Oh, she says, it makes me want to fling myself on the turf and waggle my bare toes!

Because it's about feet, Miss, that song. It goes, *My caravan has a pair of funny little wheels*, and those are your feet, see?

I want to learn it by heart, she says.

The little brown roof is your hair, I says . . .

She got it right away. Two blue windows for your eyes, and like I told her the pair of funny little wheels well that's your feet, and the little caravan can take you wherever you want to go—it's your earthly form you have as long as

you're alive. I have one and Rotha Wordsworth has one, or did have—and my sister Penny. No matter who you are or how much money you have or have not got, you have your little caravan.

It's not a complicated song, but my songs never are, not like the poems of William or Sam Coleridge. I don't think I could ever have sung my songs for the men.

I even hesitated to sing for Rotha for fear she might repeat my song to William.

A song—or anything secret—is valuable until the wrong person gets wind of it and thinks it silly or unimportant.

A great deal of my time with Rotha was like that—precious to me, but if anyone knew the things we talked or sang about or made or played as time went on . . . Like the maps we would make of all her old journeys so she could take them again in miniature when she was old—

People would think we were both off our heads.

But while she still had the use of her feet—before they started obeying her fears or whatever it was that began elsewhere inside her and moved to her feet—I sang My Little Caravan for Rotha. And outside when it was windy and no one heard us I sang it for her that many times, soon she was singing all the verses with me, happy as a lark.

As long as her funny little wheels worked all right.

I mean as long as we sang and as long as we brought the botanical glass and she got in right close to all your flowers, she was happiness itself. Even flowers that were only a spangle in the undergrowth. I could hardly see them but they spangled out for her and in she went like ye go in.

Not like this grey day of her death.

No. Colour raved everywhere.

Yellow of yolks and butter in the sun fresh-churned. Bold blooms she'd bring home and stand on her windowsill. Coltsfoot and speedwell and columbines. She'd ask them, do you mind my taking you home?

And they nodded. They said she could take them and she did. But the spangles, the jewels, the tiny stitches hiding or half-hiding . . . *a violet by a mossy stone, half-hidden from the eye! Fair as a star, when only one is shining in the sky* . . . that was something she whispered.

You don't pick certain ones. Even if they say yes. Rotha showed me that.

I am very good at hanging back, wait and see. And with both Rotha and her brother, what I saw and heard wasn't run-of-the-mill. It was worth thinking about.

There's always things you find when you're looking for something else.

And bit by bit I found out there were two of me. Two James Dixons. I mean maybe there were more than two. Maybe we've all got a dozen me's in us or more.

Loyalty was breaking me into different bits.

One for William; planning his gardens, placing the stones where they fit together without anything binding them, no lime or clay, only what gathers naturally—a bit of soil blown on the wind. A natural placement of plain things, one against the other in the wind and the rain and the sun and sleet. Mosses gathering in the cracks and garnishing the stone with velvet as time passes. Me and him planting shrubs

that sprayed in a fountain William called the fountain of refreshment.

Aye, I thought, Penny Dixon and her workmates could bloody well use a fountain of refreshment. That thought came to me strong but I kept on working with William and his fancy fountain that had no water in it. His was a fountain of leaves. It was a fountain for a poet who had no lack of water. Who was not parched in a factory where if you did not fall asleep you might be lucky enough to capture a cup of your own sweat.

You have to laugh at someone who can ignore everything going on right under his nose!

I had to quell my feelings. I had to be careful of scorn if I wanted to keep my sanity and my job.

Part of me felt proud of all the work I did for William. I built up a reputation with him for a seriousness and a kind of seeing I'd had from the time I was born. That sight of mine was a seed, and being with Rotha and her brother made it grow.

But the first me—my old self—knew fine well that we were in a kind of false green world.

And my old self is the one who wanted to rip away the fantasy and know what lay under it. I knew something lay under it. And that is why I began wandering into Rotha's bedroom alone.

Her room was different without herself or William in it.

All quiet, like, all white.

I felt wary of her mysterious window that was covered so no one could see it. It was no longer a visible window, but

still . . . I felt it, an eye open inside the wall, watching me steal in.

I should not have looked in the red diary Rotha kept for herself alone but part of me could not resist. An old part of me that was not loyal to William or to her.

I felt the hidden window stare at me from in the wall.

You can't see me, I told it.

And I untied Rotha's red diary and put my nose close to her very difficult scrawl.

For this I can only claim that loyalty has its limits when it comes to the shadows in our souls.

3

There I couch when owls do cry

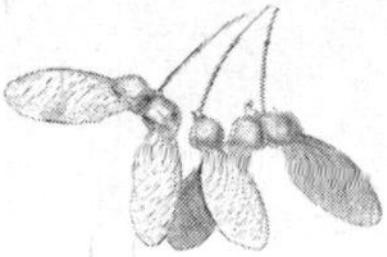

Dear James! Everything in this garden was warm and alive that year your dear Rotha became aware her feet were mortal. You were her young servant and her own youth had only just blown away over the mountains—was that not the year she went running, running up those mountains with her strange friend, Miss Something-or-other, to catch one last wisp of immortal youth? But it's cold up there! Not a Sycamore kind of place at all. No tree larger than a creeping larch. Not even a single anemone. Even the bees hardly venture there for fear of blowing away.

And those feet of your Rotha! They had started to run a little less wild, hadn't they, on her legs that had once been so lithe. Some fluid or poison trickled down, drop by drop, through her belly and legs, and droplet by droplet into her feet, and she felt it. Oh, she did. And James, reliable James, attuned to your Queen's minutest tremor: what was that poison?

eight

THE VERY FIRST PAGE I opened—I only glanced upon it where her red book fell open—was so ablaze I could hardly stand it.

> *Rubies—sharp-cut. Faceted rubies yet with parts melted, Smashed—poured & sprayed, aglitter on her kitchen floor—& a thrust of silver—undersides aspen show whilst making their castanet song to the universe. Then a crack! The kind lightning is made of & thunder only remembers . . .*

I slammed the book shut and did not know what I had seen. A thrust of silver? Red glittering on the kitchen floor . . . I remembered the murder Mary Lamb had committed against her mother. Rotha never mentioned that. No one in the Wordsworth family uttered a word on it. That slaughter was something the whole village knew but nobody in this house seemed to remember. And yet in her red book it continued fresh as if Mary Lamb's knife slashed even now.

Did Rotha Wordsworth think the scene horrible or beautiful?

The way she wrote it! Stronger than her brother's poems but no verses and no rhyming and no space down the edge. I knew William did not rhyme all his poems. But his were tall and thin like himself, with space around them. Hers sprawled over the page. What was she about?

When I feel strange, that's when I go out walking.

The lakelands are themselves a trance and on them your mind slips into a trance of its own. So you're floating. You're a trance within a trance. That's when the ache of anything drains. Grasses whisper ache away. The thrushes flitter it away—it just dissolves.

Willows sway.

The water keeps moving.

There's a thing I feel. And Rotha feels it as well.

Felt it.

We did agree on it. That when you pass under the branches of certain trees, over your head there's . . .

In your hair as if a loving hand . . .

A mother's hand. Not a mother like my mam. Some other kind of mother has smoothed your hair in your dreams. Shifted the path of your dreaming. Of your song. I could cry thinking about it. The peace walking under a tree can give you. No matter if you've seen some terrible frightening trouble. And who hasn't?

And yes, she took the laudanum—Rotha. They gave it to her and they made sure she took it. She didn't want to, though.

If it weren't for her trusting her brother and Mr. Carr so much she would have asked me to pour more of it in the geranium than she did, and she asked me that quite often. She said it made the geranium bloom where it made herself wilt.

Any spoon of laudanum you might swallow never mends you as a tree mends you.

I've often thought ends of the willows are hands. What a light strong touch willows have got. I love when they smooth my head.

Ack listen to that crow! Raw and scratchy.

Here's the second bit I read.

The terror that befell Mary Lamb will never befall Mary Wordsworth, will it. For our wife Mary is far too giving in every aspect. Mary Wordsworth will never let a crack appear. Mary Wordsworth loves it when every moment of her waking life is spent in service for others. Mary Lamb, however, was not like that—

Mary Lamb stabbed her mother with a kitchen knife unto death. Mary Lamb splayed her mother upon their kitchen floor & the blood sprayed & dropped & dripped & splattered on the stones. This is not something Mary Wordsworth would do.

Mary Wordsworth harbours not an iota of resentment. Mary Wordsworth is full only of devotion for her husband, Wm, & for me, his sister, Dorothy, isn't she. Nothing could possess her to do what Mary Lamb has done.

I hardly knew what to make of it.

So yes I walked outside as soon I got the chance. Ye fly and ye go in your buttercup chambers and the blue halls of your morning glory and ye know glory not only in your minds but all through your pockets and wings and then you pass that light on in your honey to us all, ye do. Ye have your golden ways figured out. But I don't fly, and I don't make honey. I only walk to clear my own head. I walked all the time the Wordsworths were alive and I will have to keep going now that Rotha has followed her brother into death. Over the years the medicine I give myself has not changed.

So I walked after I discovered things that lay in the strange red book, and Rotha saw me walking. She watched me out the window. A pale face at the glass, like. Talking to me without a sound.

Take me with you.

But I kept on alone. I had to. And when I came back, she says, James, you know I have been dreaming and dreaming of a very long walk of my own.

Yes, Miss, I says. I know.

I knew she had in her mind to fight her strange worry around her feet. Her feet still worked then as far as anyone else could tell. But according to herself there was something to worry about. She wanted to bring back her young scrambles. Uphill all the way. Something even more strenuous than her young escapes.

I says Miss, you're looking for an extra upness.

Up, up, up, she says, I have to see if I'm still able and how high.

Right, Miss.

The last time I exerted all my leg-power was twenty years ago!

Yes, Miss. I remember seeing you when I was a wee lad and thinking you were the wind. You're hardly any slower now, though, Miss—

Oh, I'm afraid I might be, James. And where those twenty years went or who stole them from me I do not know.

No, Miss, the time flies for me an' all.

But I, she says, feel in me the beginnings of a wooden death and if I want to thwart it I have to climb, and I am bound to do it before these legs forget how. James, I have seen you mend your shoes and rub ointment on your feet—what is that stuff?

Lanolin, Miss. Off sheep.

Do you think it good for preparing one's feet for rough terrain?

Yes, Miss, lanolin is the best.

And she says well you know I am dying to see if I can still climb the high hills around Borrowdale . . .

Around Borrowdale, Miss, I warn, is quite high mountains rather than mere hills—

Yes, she says, I know they are high.

Very high, Miss. Nobody goes up there, only the sheep.

Then do you think you might procure me some of their lanolin? And perhaps also reinforce my shoes the way you mend your own? What is that tool? Can I please hold it?

It's my stitching awl, I says. I hand it to her and I says for a laugh, Miss D, of course I will give you my awl.

And she laughs as well. She has a smashing laugh.

Had.

You think she's come to the end of her world with sorrow untold but then up she wriggles like a trout and leaps into the sunshine. And she says James, you have been giving me your all now since you were a boy, and for that I thank you from the bottom of my heart. And she lifts her pincushion which is heart-shaped and flips it upside down and slides a pin out, and it's a hatpin with a pearl animal head. Some animal I do not know. Like a deer but not a deer. And I have it to this day. I have a wool band I wrap around myself when there is a draft, and I secure the end with the pin and I swear it renders the wool twice as warm so as to give off its own heat like embers long after a flame has died.

I suddenly wanted to ask her why her diary had blood and Mary Lamb and Mary Wordsworth all in the same breath on one page. I found something awful about it. While she was laughing and handing me the pearl pin, a desire to know rose up in me. When you get someone's confidence and they are off guard . . .

I knew Miss Lamb was still in London and I wondered was she better these days or not? I knew her brother Charles was responsible for her and that was why she was not locked up. Could a person get better after a thing like that? Lamb is a funny name for a woman who slaughters her mam. And what about Mary Wordsworth? *Not an iota of resentment . . . Full only of devotion . . . Nothing could possess her.* This all ran through my head and I was dying to ask but I knew I should not have looked in Rotha's red diary—and I managed to

accept the pearl pin off her and thank her without asking her a thing.

For how does a beloved servant question his mistress without turning into a prying nuisance? He doesn't, is the answer. Instead he does what is asked and then some. He does a sort of work that gets done with no one quite sure who did it. A kind of enchanted tasking. And the tasker waits and watches the little family, and in particular he especially watches his Rotha to make sure she will be all right whatever circumstance may befall, at least while he is present. He decides she should never be frightened. For she might not be his own sister Penny but she is someone's sister. Someone who has made himself scarce and has not realized what his sister is thinking and writing. William thinks she is only writing about her feelings which are not important and if they overflow he has asked the tasker to take care of the problem so as not to let those feelings flood Rydal Mount.

So I accept the pearl pin and she laughs that smashing laugh and moreover, James, she says, you're the only one who hasn't sounded incredulous.

At your planning to go mountain climbing?

Yes. My brother doesn't want me to do it. Our wife Mary says I am mad. But here you are offering me the foot balm which is exactly what I need. And you are doing it with a straight face. James—

Miss?

Do you believe I can do it?

. . . Aye, I says. By now, I says, I think you can do anything you put your mind to as regards walking outdoors.

And I meant that. I did not lie to her about it.

But, she says, you're remembering me from the old days.

Aye, I says. But time is funny.

And you're still only twenty-two if that, and me, I'm nearly forty-seven. My mother was only thirty-one when she died, and my father forty-two. I hardly come from hardy stock!

Forty-seven you may be, I says to her, but from what I've noticed of your legs—she gave me a funny glance; was she surprised or amused?—I mean, Miss D, that they are strong legs, I says.

You're right, they are, she says, and they are sometimes fast, but I am nevertheless becoming old and William does not wish to accompany me. He cannot take the time from his writing and I suspect the Toe prevents him as well.

She had taken to calling her brother's sore toe *the Toe* as if it held a place in the world as the king of toes. When I told Mam this she laughed all right. Aye, says Mam, the brother's toe is coddled very like our king. Because by then King George was laid down in velvet being fed goatmilk buns soaked in brandy and never coming up for air. And it's true William's toe saw the physician nearly as often as did the king, and he had Rotha talking about the Toe as reverently as if it had a life of its own.

And she says, James, it's not only my legs and feet I'm thinking of. Or my bowels. Because her bowels were bad, they were sometimes good but all of a sudden they'd—but it wasn't bowels she feared now. It's things you have to be careful of on highlands, she says, things we forget about here low down in the vales, and you must know the things I mean.

Getting lost up there, I says.

Yes.

How easy it is, I says.

Nearly impossible not tò get lost at some point, says she.

Yes, I says, I know what you mean. You'd never think it looking up at a mountain from down here. For it looks to reduce to a high point from where you can plainly see all that is below.

When in fact, she says—

Yes. The thing is, unless you're at the pinnacle—

Which is so easily prevented! Getting to the highest height—

Yes, any hard gale—

Or sudden fog blanket—

Even snow, I says. For by then we were nearly into October.

Especially snow! Or sleet and hail and the north wind—

Or terrible cold—

Or falling off a ledge after fog or snow might have obscured the way—

Or getting nearly to the top, says I, and not being able to reach the summit, and so not being able to see the way down—

That's it, she says—that last one is my greatest fear regarding the mountains. What if any of those circumstances we have mentioned traps me below a summit, where it can be utterly astonishing how big the mountain is, how far it stretches, and though you are very high up, exposed and far from home, you are not yet beyond the blind wastes as far as the mountain is concerned. You could wander on that level until you perish!

Shambling without food or water, says I.

Yes, and having to muster all your presence of mind in order to simply continue.

Aye, I says.

And we both knew she had often done all these things before in the hills around here. She had been lost and cold. And she had come back home. So then I says, Miss D— presence of mind is a thing you own in great measure.

Yes, I know. That, and the strength in my feet and legs, are all I have, or did have.

I saw then that she was asking me if I believed her presence of mind and the strength in her legs were still strong enough to get her up and down our summits. I said, It sounds, Miss, as if such a climb might give you the measure of what you still possess in that department.

Exactly.

Who are you going to go with?

I wanted her to have someone good. I was half-afraid she meant to set off by herself but I didn't let on. Part of me was crying out to say I'll come with you but I managed to refrain from speaking. Wait and see, that's my motto. Wait and see what she wants.

My painter friend in Borrowdale.

That Miss Barker?

Yes.

I kept silent a minute. Solitary, that Barker woman traipsed mountain crag and ledge, lugging her paints. Now there was a one who knew how to mend her own boots. She was said to be bewitched.

I suppose, I says, if anyone can climb mountains it's Miss Barker . . . but if you don't mind my suggesting it, I can put you onto a fellow who tends sheep in those mountains and he'll not get in your way, but he will be sure to know when a storm is coming long before you or even Miss Barker sees it . . .

At the mention of an old shepherd Rotha lit right up and said, Yes, James! Your shepherd friend will be our shepherd friend.

He won't be obtrusive, I promised. Not auld Thomas.

And she allowed me to arrange Tom's presence and I was secretly relieved. Tom might be seventy-odd but he knew those mountains.

And she says I know, James, I've asked you a lot already but if I am going to ascend the mountains of Borrowdale I have heard there are tiny rare lichen and plants of all kinds, and I wondered if—

The wee microscope?

I'd been fiddling around with it in my hut trying to mend the thing once and for all. Its hinges were not only small, they had a square hollow and I had yet to file replacement pintles I'd managed to scrounge from old pairs of glasses I had collected on my travels.

There's only one or two more adjustments to make, I says, then if you want you and me can go for a ramble to one of the tarns and test it out.

Might I come to your hut and watch you mend it?

At this a leap of alarm hit my throat. My hut! I wasn't having that.

I wouldn't advise it, Miss, I says.

You can't give them everything. My hut is my sanctuary. I didn't want Rotha in it. It was my place. Long as I was the family servant I had to be careful I didn't lose my own privacy. That hut is my own private haunt. Ye lot have been inside my hut. Ye know. Ye've perched on my tools. My saws and everything I've hung on pegs. You've seen the line I drew round them with chalk. Not so I'll know if somebody's gone off with them. I'm not a suspicious man. More so I will be certain I've put a thing back where it belongs. Having things be where they belong is key. You know where to find the right tool for any job as soon as you need it, long as you put it back where it belongs.

My hammers, mauls and spanners! My turn-screws and awls and my old carving set, which is the prize. My wire, my sandpaper, my funnels and hooks—and my scrap paper and a few pencils for drawing out the ideas I show various ones in the fam'ly—Mary pretends interest, and her and William's daughter Dora was a fine hand with needle and thread; the lass enjoyed my creations, my fences or the rockery or any of the small improvements I made over time.

Then there's plant pots, trowels, edging tools . . . all the sticks and tags I use for labelling plants. Ye lot know how important it is to classify! My basket of gauzy bits of . . . haha it goes on forever . . . twine and wool and string and other bits I'd lash on a trellis for sweet peas or anything needing a stake. The scent of earth and boards! Wood, rain, my lovely scented twigs and composted dung sweet as barley malt. Ye know I do sweep the floor but I never mind bits and pieces of dried leaf and other vegetation. That scent means

the hut is half in the outside world where I belong. My hut's an in-between world betwixt the indoors and the outdoors and it is the heart of all I know how to make and mend.

Alone in it I would mend the microscope that let Rotha enter into your flower chambers, delving inside them like yourselves. I'm the one who looked after that for her. Helped her go into the heart of all wild rooms-out-of-rooms. But I had to work alone. No one can come in and look over my shoulder while I work in my own space. If they come in, then it's their space, isn't it. People like Rotha and her brother. They control the thinking. And when they control the thinking they control you. And I was never having that.

And funnily enough she did not argue. And I believe that is because she knew her place.

nine

AND WHAT HAPPENED NEXT WAS a bit like what goes on with ye bees in the hive, because ye gather the honey yourselves, don't ye, but someone else always takes it away. It's hard to keep any of it for your own survival through the winter, yet without it ye'll surely perish. Still we come and haul away your gold treasure, eh? And we replace it with the candy if you're getting short, but the candy is not the honey.

As September broke into October did Rotha's legs get better or worse? And her bowel complaints? One day this and the next that. I remember I kept thinking she'll never in a million years make it up the mountains of Borrowdale with that going on in her limbs and her bowels. It was then, yes, that it got worse. Right before her climb. But it interrupted itself like. Over a matter of weeks it got worse but then it got better and nobody knew what to make of it.

Rise up, rise up! Get out of your bed and walk!

That's from the Bible, isn't it? That's what it was like with Rotha just before her climb, or it got more like that every day. The occasional miracle whereby up she'd leap!

Then the next day unable.

Mary Wordsworth claimed she was doing it for the attention. I heard her say this to John Carter. Or did John Carter say it to Mary? The two of them considered themselves the sensible ones, I know that.

But Rotha. Headache one day, bowel agony untold numbers of days, and then the leg thing, where she'd tell Mary and Mary would tell John Carter and John Carter would tell me—Rotha's legs are freezing cold and heavy as a pair of marble rolling pins and she durst not move them even if she could because of the pain. Any of this would last a day or two at first, in those days before her climb. Then miraculously she would rise up and get out of her bed and walk as if nothing had happened. And so it was in October that year, 1818, seeming free of her complaints for the moment, off Rotha set to Borrowdale to climb with that Miss Barker.

And poor William while she was gone—he couldn't work on his poems if Rotha wasn't there to aid him, so he worked on his accounts and ah, it was a constant calculation goin' over and over, somewhere between the heart—in the breast—somewhere between the heart and the neck. A constant calculatin' machine, an abacus, never stops, *click click click click click* have we got enough or have we got too little? Is there enough? There's not much. There's not much left. There's not much to come! Accounts in, accounts out . . . He and o'course Mary along with him took care of all that. Paying me . . . I mean, John Carter they didn't have to pay because he was paid for by the, it was included with the stamp job. But . . . *click click click. Click click click. Click click click.*

Money!

Gold hides the seed falling from your sycamore in a spiral. It drowns out the gentle lapping of Rydal Water on the stones. It drowns out the very soft crackle of the rabbit's passage over the turf. It drowns out the wind's voice and the cloud's path. It drowns out the undersong of the leaves and the birds. It drowns out, most of all, haha, the poetry that's welling up, that's wanting to well up, that's dammed inside ye. Dammed.

Rotha being gone up that mountain was torture for William. Why d'you think, he says to John Carter the third day she was gone off—and mind, William's feeling very irritated with not being able to fix a sonnet without her—why, he says, do you think young men are poets and old men are mere husks?

As if John Carter could answer a thing like that!

I mean John's all right but he's one of those people, he's lived in little villages but . . . so John is not a city person, but I think his mam was. So from when John was little, there's something, some reason why the fells and the water and the soil are a bit, y'know, beneath him. And John, even though he's never lived in a big important place like, he gives off the impression that he's a bit above it all here. And he's always got a smirk pasted on 'es face that's more like a mask. He's missing a key aspect of what I like in a person. A gravity where you know it's really the person you're talking to, he's not putting it on.

That's my thinking about John like, and that he would say the things he said about Dorothy—that for one thing she considered herself married to her brother. That she believed

deep down in her heart and soul that William Wordsworth was her own husband, and if William had married Mary Hutchinson then Dorothy had married Mary an' all. That was John Carter's explanation for why Rotha often called William's wife "our wife Mary." I had to admit I had no answer to that one. But I mean John Carter gives the impression that he's the, you know, he's the man for William. He's all loyal to William.

Well you cannot profess loyalty to William Wordsworth and be disloyal to his sister. That doesn't wash. This man of William's, John Carter, is unaware of crucial things. Or a piece of him is asleep. There's a bit that is not thinking, a thing in John Carter that doesn't understand and he, ye know when they say of somebody, he hasn't got it in 'im. That's how he, you know, John Carter, that's how he is. He hasn't got it in him to understand a person like Rotha. But he's a loyal clerk for William, I suppose. Was.

But the real sympathy and devotion I'm talking about, and I don't mean being a slave, mind, it's more like having sympathy with anything at all. With the wrens, with the place itself—he's floating around, John Carter is, disconnected from it all. He's missing a connection. He's missing a flame inside himself that warms and melts you into the bigger flame of these people and this place. John just hasn't got it in him.

I suppose I should feel sorry for him.

John Carter, when the little fam'ly can't hear him, rants, Somebody has got to keep these people in line! Somebody

has got to keep these people from disgracing themselves by looking completely daft—wandering around, muttering to themselves—living in the selfsame garments year in and year out and year in again. And year out again. And year in again. The same coat, patched all over. Somebody has to make a little bit of money and that somebody's got to be William! And he'd better do his job at the stamp office and not sit around making up verses all the time. Somebody's got to have one foot in this world!

That was John Carter's proclamation. It was his own self-proclaimed job to keep somebody in the little family with one foot in this world. But I'm telling ye that was the disease that made William claw Rotha's inner life and grasp it for his own. One-foot-in-this-world disease. He knew he'd caught it when he wrote *The world is too much with us* . . . Aye if anyone siphoned the spirit out of me that William drew from Rotha I might have a pain in my guts an' all, and sore bowels and stiff legs. William devoured her observations but he spat out her feelings. She saved those in the red diary knowing he had no interest. He delved for morsels of his choice with his pointy nose like a fox.

And I was the fox's helper! I felt somewhat uneasy but he did pay for my keep. I could send a bit of money to Mam and Penny! Didn't we both try to take care of our younger sisters, William and me? Big fox and little fox. Bandy-legged William Fox and the young Fox Dixon.

ON THE THIRD DAY ROTHA was climbing in Borrowdale I hung around with William a bit more than usual because the two of us were at loose ends without her. We worked here in the gardens and he mentioned his dingy shirt and said that Fanny, the maid who helped with the washing and ironing, had pleurisy and could not work. I am a man who sees an opportunity immediately and when I heard this I sat on a stump, my eyes shut, for if I must ask anybody for something—I cannot bear seeing a "no" on their face before they utter it.

I says, Sir if Fanny is off more time than you can spare her, I've a . . .

Oh it's all right, he says, Fanny will be back in a fortnight.

That'd be excellent, Sir, I says, only in case she's not, I have my own sister Penny who's a strong lass and nobody claps a flatter shirt or mixes a better pudding. And her sewing, Sir, Penny's hands are nimbler than mine if you can believe it . . .

Silence. Bitter wind against my face. I unscrewed my eyes to see William look up from his prong with a question mark that seemed to doubt me and my whole place there. Exactly as I'd feared.

But of course, I says, you won't need Penny once Fanny comes back and I hope she gets better.

Why wouldn't she get better, Dixon, he says, and he resumes pulling the horseradish, and I lay awake that night and wondered what he thought. When a higher-up person won't answer you after you've shown them a desire they didn't expect out of you, your heart sinks and all kinds of

fears flood you. A stream of shame no matter how proud you were.

That night I did not abandon my dream of bringing Penny into the Wordsworths' fine world, but I vowed not to mention her to William again either, for fear it'd put an end to my own job and so end any prospect of Penny rising.

On Rotha's fourth day off in the mountains with that Miss Barker I had a mind to wonder whether she'd ever come back. She delayed first one day and then a couple more until William was beside himself asking after her—has she come home—he had done all the calculating he could do as well as all the poem writing and moreover his clothes desperately needed washing and finally he worried that she might be lost.

I reminded him of Miss Barker's surefootedness and of the fact that old shepherd Tom would never let them down, and I did not need to remind him that Rotha herself was like a goat as long as she was well, as she had leapt into pure wellness only days before her journey. It was as if the notion of going mountain climbing with her friend had poured life right back into her that had been draining away as long as she lay upstairs waiting for William's company. I think the prospect of Borrowdale with Miss Barker had given Rotha a new passion and William—a bit of a dog in the manger—did not wholly like it.

I know it could seem to Rotha as if it might hardly matter to William if she was alive or dead. But I could have told her that without her William lost substance and became like a flake of soot wisping round these gardens, worrying about

not writing and about needing more money. After a week of her absence he worked up a restorative vision of himself as an important poet who must go on business to the city. He allowed Mary to clap and whiten two shirts and off he sailed to his publisher who would, he hoped, pay him to revise a guide to the Lakes that had made him quite a bit of money already, and which bore his name as sole author though only Rotha could have written many of the things in it. Things only she could have noticed in the first place.

So William was away when Rotha came home from Borrowdale to a house going on about ordinary house business: its chimneys clinked as autumn cold contracted the stones, and briars scratched the walls. But the house was silent inside and Rotha climbed its creaking stairs and greeted her diary that always heard. She wrote her feelings about Miss Barker and the mountain and kept the diary with her in the bed. When I went up to her room to bring back the chair I'd patched while she was away I found her in a state of real excitement.

Finally, a living soul, she says! Oh James—you will never credit what we did, what we gained, how high we climbed. I can't wait for William to hear it!

It wore on me a bit how she supposed William might listen to please her when he would—for anyone with eyes to see—take her tale down, not in.

Aye well, I says, you will have to make do with my ear, Miss D, as William is yet in London talking to his publisher—

James! I never fathomed when we started off to the head of Borrowdale past the black lead mine, the guardhouse and

spoil-heaps and the wagonway and all the dirt and racket—and beyond it Seathwaite . . .

Aye, I says, thinking of Penny. How I had once begged her not to work in that very mine, where you might be hanged for leaving your shift with a morsel of lead fallen by mistake into your pinny pocket, and not enough wages to keep you fed. And now here Penny was far worse off after that Pendleton stinkhole. Aye, Miss Dorothy Wordsworth would pass by a place like the black lead mine blithe as a moth. She would flit beyond . . .

. . . And then the mountain I thought we were going to climb—Ash Course they call it, but it is really Esk Hawes—I believe it comes from German—

And I minded not for the first time how Rotha insists on very proper names for things. Mind, I says to myself, you don't get offended over that now. Remember your benefits in keeping clear of scorn. Remember the Miss D that little boy James met and will always . . .

So I says, Aye, Miss, Ash Course, I've been up there. There's a swirly beck with a smashing pool and two ash trees with deep shade under 'em . . .

Yes! We stopped there, and James, we scrambled to the top with hardly an effort—it was as if my limbs were the same as they were when I was young. You saw me then—

I did—

And I have not felt invincible like that since the children died—little Catherine and Thomas—Or perhaps I have not been my old self since they were born—I mean my young self. Oh, James, I do not know when it happened . . .

Aye, Miss, you have had a lot of strain and a lot of sorrow and it is no big surprise if—

—But I found out with my friend that I'm not diminished at all! That's the thing. Troubles are not what they seemed to be, once you are in the mountains.

Aren't they, Miss?

No! Once Mary Barker and I rose to the top of Ash Course, what should we see but—you know it don't you!

I reckon on a clear day you'd see—

—Oh, it was a clear day all right! I have never seen things so clearly in all my life.

Then, Miss, you'll have seen all of Borrowdale and Bassenthwaite as well as Keswick and Skiddaw, all the mountains from here to Helvellyn an' all. And the other direction mebbe all the way to Yorkshire.

Yes, and beyond! And Solway Firth and all the way to the mountains of Scotland.

Scotland, Miss!

Scotland was something the mere mention of which sort of made a fizzle in me and I know it did in her an' all.

But James, even that was nothing compared with what we accomplished next. Miss Barker had her eye on another summit—

The other summit would be Scaw Fell, Miss, and by the sound of it you were already more than half-way up it.

That's it! She was breathless. There was a dancing feeling all round her as if she had run and run and run and wasn't a bit tired, which from the sound of things was about the size

of it. She reminded me of myself when I get out in the freedom of the hills.

Scaw Fell loomed so near! But it wasn't near—as we walked towards it, it moved away from us like a great ship sailing off, tricking us, and by and by we saw a dip appear before us and we would have had to climb down and down quite far before we could go upwards once more, so we were disillusioned and instead headed for another height on that same mountain, but closer—

The pike?

Scawfell Pike, that's it! And James, there wasn't a breath of wind. We unwrapped our dinner and the paper lay on the rock without a rustle, and there was no sound—we had left the waterfalls far below us and could not hear even a buzzing insect, only a world of silence and deep air going on forever. And I've since learned that we were far higher than even we thought, as Scawfell Pike has been measured and the mountain-measurers say it is higher than the more distant point of which we imagined ourselves to have fallen short. In fact, James, without intending to do it and without even knowing it, Mary Barker and I have climbed the highest mountain in all of England!

She sat back and looked at me with a very pleased expression.

Have you got your knife? she asked me. I have my favourite pen ready and I wish you might sharpen it, James. The ascent has done something to my desire to write. It has sharpened me and now I need my best pen sharp, but William is

not here. Even if he was, he cannot sharpen a pen as well as you. I am going to bring my notes downstairs!

And she carried them down—it was the first time I ever saw her bring her writing into the main part of the house. I tried to make myself scarce but she was eager to seek me out and read me little pieces, and they were so full of life I felt blown to bits as if I was out-of-doors in a big gale nowhere near a house at all.

Was there a gale when you were up there? I asked her. For I could nearly feel the wind. No. I did feel it.

Oh yes, she said. Were it not for your old friend the shepherd Tom we might not have made it back home! He saw, once we were at the peak, a mizzle of gauze fizzing off in the distance over Whitehaven. Mind, he says, we get out of that thing's way, and he brought us to shelter under a crag while the mizzle loomed and blackened and boiled and wrapped seven mountains!

And she read me all about the lowland plants, and about looking through her microscope: flowers in surprising pockets beyond their summer comfort—the violet and the rose—and then alpine flowers, but once they reached the top—what was that? I had to ask her to read it twice. I was hearing it but not able to understand.

Bones, Miss? Mighty neglect?

I know what bones are and I know the meaning of neglect but not when they are put together on top of a mountain. I wanted to ask if I might read the words myself but before I could drum up the nerve she handed me the notes and said James, you read it to me.

So I got frightened because I can read in my head but not always out loud, I mean not properly. I might get words wrong. Their sound. Words I knew from reading, like, but I might not have heard them said. And I didn't want to sound them out wrong in front of her. William I didn't mind—he was used to the way I read her diaries out. But I had never read her own writing to herself before. So I says thank you, Miss, but I have a bit of a sore throat.

All right, then, I'll read it again, says she—*We came against bones of the earth once all the plants stopped, once we reached a height where nothing has green blood—only bone is left. Mighty neglect! The maker of worlds had bones left over from all the animals & people & even all the fish & spines of hardy plants & anything bound down by force of weight—the maker had extra bones & cast them down at the top of Scawfell Pike in a tumble of lifeless petrification!*

Petrification, I says—were you—were you frightened, then, Miss?

It was thrilling. And James, but for your having mended our scope I would not have seen the life, only felt it. I felt it all right, it was fearsome, you're right to mention a fright—who would have thought there is life in austere stone cast aground? Rubble left-over yet important! I had a feeling were it not for that piled rock devoid of softness, no real softness could endure here below. It was as if the bony rock held all endurance for us so we need hardly consider it down here below, but it considers us—

Yes, Miss D, I says, I admit I have thought myself at times that the mountains notice us.

I did not confess that sometimes I found myself talking back to them, as I talk to ye, or that whenever I was away from the mountains I felt lonely, that I missed them. My mam always said when my dad left us that she didn't care because she had the mountain out back of our house for company. Me and the mountain, she'd say. Me and the mountain enjoyed a dollop of bramble jelly on toast for our tea, thank you for asking . . .

And then, James, Rotha tells me, I examined the rock surface, which blazed with petrified paint—lichen that clung to the stones. I unfolded our microscope and saw that lichen is more important than any flower! Lichen is the efflorescence and voice of the bones.

Efflorescence, Miss . . . This was one of her mystery words. I wondered if I would see it show up in the red diary. Sometimes she wrote lists that had no meaning, only a long snake of words, and they were not words you normally hear in the run of a day. She stored them, like, the way Mam lays up her best tablecloth and few tea towels, separate from the ordinary lot.

Sizzling and miniature, she says.

Lichen, Miss?

Yes. Orange, white, green, pink, like the flag of a rock nation, the speech of the mountain itself if only a person knows how to translate it. And James, our lovely magnifier revealed to me that the mountain is always attentive and alive. I peeled my shoes off and felt its grave sermon enter me. It mineralized my bones, James, after everything had threatened to drain all the metal out of me.

You mean it made you stronger, Miss?

We have metal in us, James, and I had forgotten how to restore it. It drains out and you have to make it come back. No wonder that before the climb I had so often to lie down!

But then she tells me a very strange story about the mountain, about looking over the sea far over Eskdale and seeing a ship that ended up being a bit of a wild ship. A ship I couldn't quite understand.

That ship, she says, gave me the best lesson of all the visions the mountain provided that day!

Oh she was delighted to tell me about that ship. I couldn't make head or tail out of the ship story but I didn't let on. I couldn't even tell if the ship was a real ship on the ocean in the distance, or some kind of dream. What did she mean? But I did not interrupt her.

It's all making me realize, she said, I need to get my *Recollections* out again and keep working on them.

Scotland, Miss? I knew these writings were about having walked all over Scotland with William and Sam Coleridge when they were still young and they left Mary Wordsworth back in Grasmere—Mary and William's first baby John was a newborn—and off Rotha and William and Sam went through the highlands as if there had been no wedding, no our wife Mary, only Dorothy and her two beloved men, three pilgrims on foot with a horse and a shambles of a cart that made children everywhere laugh it was so ramshackle. Off they had traipsed over the highlands. She never kept a diary that whole journey but she had not stopped thinking about it ever since, or writing her remembrances and

wondering if one day she would publish it. It would be her masterpiece. Yet it lay in a heap forever growing and changing and being revised or laid aside. Perilously lay her notes near her bedroom fire, or on the floor, or they were gathered up and put away but then out they inched once again. And William would say no, don't publish that, you'll never be able to stand the glare of going public. *Public!* He said it as if he truly thought getting published would kill her. Still, she revised her Scottish walk over and over again.

And now William was not in the house to argue and she says to me she says yes, my recollections of walking in Scotland—I could perfect the prose and add it to my account of climbing Scawfell Pike, and I am sure I could reap some income from it—I know I have talked of this before, but now I feel invigorated enough to work like a horse until it is done! If Miss Barker can sell her paintings and live in a house of her own then I can surely do the same with my own word-paintings of all the magnificent climbing and walking I have done—it's only a matter of getting the work out there into the world!

She had all the energy of the October wind from the mountains, a wind that knew her as it whirled round the eaves of Rydal Mount, trying to reach her and talk to her.

And then William came home.

ten

AND IF YOU ASKED ME to name the time when it all changed around her walking and climbing and yes her writing, I'd put it square on the nose of that moment when her brother clicked the latch on his return from seeing his publisher in London. He was all ablaze. He brought the streetlamps home from London and waved them round the house 'til they outshone all her thin bright air and bits of lightning fallen off Scawfell Pike which turned to silver and scrappy remnants fizzling out in her clothes next to his new moneymaking project which was the pure hard gold!

By now money outweighed the shining hills for him and he even admitted it with a sad face that said, *There is no other choice, unfortunately.*

My publisher, he told Rotha, has agreed to pay me to revise our guide to the Lakes for all the new visitors dying to see the place. They're all searching, he says, for the very glory I put in my poems. Though I know they'll never find it, not even if they traipse from here to Windermere with my poems dangling in one hand and their cheese and onion sandwiches in the other!

My poems are too—something—he says—I forget his word—the poems are too something—but the Guide! The simplest one of them can buy my Guide and turn to page twenty-one or page thirty-seven and quickly find a place, a name, a tarn or stone or tree or fell all mapped and labelled and described clear as day—the location easy enough for a child to find, and all the flowers documented, and the feelings they produce, or should produce in any reader owning so much as half a heart or having one eye open . . .

And soon as William says that—I mean only once he's finished—does he ask Rotha about her climb up the mountain. He listens for a minute as she begins to tell him things she told me but he interrupts her—

Have you written it yet?

Aye, she says, and he puts his hand out to take it like and she hands him the sheaf and off he goes with her writing upstairs to his private . . . *cryptic*! That's the word. I get mixed up with cryptic and crypt. His poems were too cryptic is what he said. Did he mean like something you'd find in the crypt? Dead like? I dunno. Any rate that's what he said about his poems, they just wouldn't bring enough money to pay the bills. But the Guide now, with Rotha's account of all the things she's seen and done all her days scrambling over the fells and now up the very highest peak in all of England, that was something he could use and sell. For the benefit of everyone in the household.

And while he was working on fitting her tale of Scawfell into the new Guide he'd get me to keep him in fresh nibs and he'd mutter a bit to me now and then, and one thing he

says sticks in my mind. It had to do with a violet in the lowland bit below where his sister reached the heights. And I realized he was reciting again. He did that often, recited his own poems, and John Carter thought it was ridiculous but I liked it.

A violet by a mossy stone . . . Half hidden from the eye! . . .

Aye, that was one Rotha recited an' all, for that one was about herself if ye ask me, although it's supposed to be about someone named Lucy who lives hidden away. No one hears or sees Lucy except William himself. She lives all hidden away and no one but him understands how important she is. No one but him cares. And it isn't really about Lucy of course, Lucy's a made-up name. William told me nearly all writers use real people and then just give them a new name so as not to make it seem like they are only writing about themselves and their own families.

Any rate he was copying stuff about a violet down in the Guide and he was reciting that poem and then all of a sudden he says to me, you do know, Dixon, precisely what a constitutes a violet's form?

I think I could scratch a decent likeness of one, Sir, I says, if that's what you mean. For I had done a few violets on the Pace eggs. But he knew that.

So I wondered why he was asking me this and then he goes on and he says remember it has a low petal, that hangs down below the rest?

And I says aye, I remember that. This was nearly November now, but I had seen enough violets in enough springtimes so as to well recall exactly what one looks like.

And he says that low petal, that's my sister, Dorothy. It's really the highest!

Sir, how can low be high?

William got on with riddles like this once in a while. He seemed to like it and I didn't really mind. I forgot most of them but I remember this one now because I was surprised by it.

Because, he says, you know how it's the odd one—a violet bears two pairs of petals, and then that odd one, a fifth, hangs down—

Aye, Sir, I says.

Well, he says, that low one is really the uppermost! Only by virtue of the violet's stalk bending near its summit does it look to us as if that highest petal is really the lowest. I fancy, he says, the two petal pairs being two married couples: myself and my wife Mary, and then Sam Coleridge and his wife. Or De Quincey and his wife Margaret, or any one of us and our wives forming the couplets surrounding that lone petal at one time or another. All alone is the lowest petal, all our lives—that one being Dorothy all by herself bearing the rest of us up.

And that is my sister, he proclaimed. She climbs Scawfell Pike, the utmost summit in England, without even knowing she is in the highest place. To Dorothy it's all just another day's adventure.

He sounded crestfallen about it. I decided not to argue that Rotha climbed Scawfell Pike with her friend Mary Barker and not alone at all. She hadn't been alone. But William seemed to think she had been.

And his pen scratched and scratched 'til I had to recut it a few more times and he filled in the old Guide with many

new lines from his sister's life, but nothing at all from the life he himself was living.

Scratch scratch scratch no matter his headache, getting ready to post her living days to London and hammer them into gold he could spend.

As if he could hear me thinking, he says it's all right, you know, Dixon, that I am inserting my sister's observations into my own book. One famous writer in the family is nearly one too many and we have all suffered enough from the glare that falls upon myself as it is. You see heads bobbing outside the garden now, as we speak? Here to see the poet. Imagine our dear Dorothy if she had to endure the exposure of literary fame. Have you noticed especially lately how easily she is brought out of equilibrium into some passionate spiral of thought? And then her bowels start their torment until the strength leaves her legs and she becomes unable to see anyone and cannot even get out of bed.

This did not yet happen often and it had not happened at all since her scaling the high peak. I wondered if William felt at all to blame. I know I felt slightly sheepish as he spoke about the visitors, for I had that very afternoon sold another three of his signatures to tourists outside the gate. I cut them off copies of letters he had dictated but not sent. Myself and John Carter had a little side enterprise going. John was afraid to go and hawk the goods but he did not mind saving the signatures for me in exchange for a percentage on the quiet. But me, I have hawking and selling in my blood, and as far as I am concerned if something was destined for the fire to begin with then it is not stealing to rescue it from there. For

instance, whenever I cut William's hair for him what do you think I did with the sweepings?

So when William mentioned the hardships of fame I knew only too well that there were quite a few benefits in it for him and for me. Who sails through life not having done a single thing they feel guilty about? Show me the person who claims that honour and I'll show you a real swindler.

When he read me the final version—his tale of Scawfell Pike that made it seem as if he was the one who reached that summit all by himself—you would think since he used her script that it would sound like hers, but there was something missing. His version was all tied up and had a bow on it like, and he left wild bits out. Any bits that made no sense to him or were a bit unfinished he didn't bother with. And he asked me, What do you think, Dixon? And of course I said I thought it sounded pretty good but that he shouldn't rely on me, he should send it out to people who were used to criticizing. His writer friends. Robert Southey or De Quincey.

But you are a servant and a gardener, he says to me, and if it works for you then I think it might work for the ordinary public.

And I says well, Sir, it sounds all right to me. It sounds like you got all the details about the heights and the plants and particular views from various parts like Esk Vale and Black Combe and Wasdale and Great Gable—

I did not mention things he had left out, for I couldn't quite recall if they were parts Rotha had written, or things she'd only said to me. I did not want to offend William by

pointing out gaps but I was curious about one thing so I says to him, Sir, did you happen to forget the part about a ship?

What's that? he says. What ship?

And I knew I had made a mistake.

He wouldn't let it rest, now I'd let it slip.

So I told him best as I could remember, how when they were looking over Eskdale as far as the sea, Rotha saw a ship and she told the other two, Miss Barker and auld Tom the shepherd. Only Tom says then, Is it a ship? And Miss Barker assures him that yes, she sees it too and she has seen enough ships to be certain when something is a ship or not!

And of course auld Tom doesn't argue with her. The likes of shepherds or servants never argue. We might not get hoyed off the mountain but we don't want to risk our living. Only in two minutes auld Tom says real quiet like, he says look at your ship now, it's a horse! He couldn't help it.

And Rotha was over the moon laughing at herself—a gallant horse it was, she says, galloping over the sea. And Rotha tells Mary Barker: Mary, she says, you might know all about ships but our old Wise Man of the Mountains knows even more about clouds!

And Rotha says to me, Never again, Dixon, will I be satisfied with how certainly I know any single fact. For anything could indeed be completely different to what I might suppose. If you see me huff and puff all certain about anything, James, she says, remind me of our ship that turned into a horse! Away with all conclusiveness!

. . . But William doesn't write down a word of this story. He dismisses it.

Me mam used to say each one of us has a secret stone. She said it's between our neck and shoulders at the back, inside. Some people make no headway with it. But other people notice it has a little door. And then that door can open. And inside is what looks at first like a jewel. It's behind a little grate, very protected, deep in the stone inside us all. But if you look closely, if you pay attention to it, the jewel is wrapped in a membrane—it's like wasp's nest paper, it's that thin, and it breaks. It breaks open and you see what you'd thought was a jewel glimmering inside is really an all-seeing eye.

Aye, that's what Mam told me. But again—all-seeing, second sight, extra sight—to me it's, that's not what it feels like. To me it feels like, not have you got a magical, special eye, haha, not—are you going around with it wrapped or open—but are ye sighted or blind?

And either that very day or soon after it a strange fella comes to the door. Someone I had never seen yet he had a familiar look, like someone out of a fairy tale.

William spied his head bobbing beyond the hedges with very wild hair and great orbs of eyes about to pop out of his head like exploding lanterns, a man broad like a keg around but not very tall—That's the poet William Blake, says our William. Quick, tell him I am away and can't be found here for the next fortnight at least, for he's a raving lunatic and I don't want him in my house.

My William doesn't know it but one look at the face of this Blake fellow and I know I can't lie to him for those eyes'll burn through any fib like fire through that wasp's nest paper I was talking about, in fact they have already burned through

any cloak I tried to wrap round my thoughts before I say a word to him.

He bursts in the door, this Blake, before I can keep him out. But he surprises me in not caring to visit William at all. It isn't William he wants to see, but the woman who saw the ship that wasn't a ship.

He has heard about it somehow.

How?

I think it was a cloud, I says to him, wanting to be helpful. From up high on a mountain it only appeared to them like a ship at first.

He looks at me pityingly.

I see my William has fled the yard and run down the bank. He has done this before when he does not have it in him to host a difficult visitor and just the thought of this William Blake had given him a blinding headache. I wondered at it, but before I could answer for it Rotha appeared at the top of the stairs looking down at Blake with an expression I had never seen on her before.

The only way I can describe the scene is that when the two glanced one upstairs and one down at the other, a beam lit from Rotha Wordsworth to William Blake like the flash you get if a lamp flame meets a cat's eye. I remembered the eye in us all that my mam described, and I knew Rotha and the Blake fellow both had that all-seeing eye sprung wide open, and our William, William Wordsworth, fled from it. But these two burned and I saw the flash before they turned back into an ordinary pair of writers such as the ones I was used to seeing at Rydal all the time.

I could not hear what they said to each other that day, though believe me I cocked my ears. What they said was muffled and I don't remember much else about their encounter, or truth be told even if it happened on the exact day when William copied down all about his sister's climb or on another day around that time, which is the time like I said when everything changed in the gleam of an eye. I feel as if it was the selfsame day. I know Rotha had her pale green gown on. And I know that the same evening or the one after or no later than two or three days after at the most, I crept in Rotha's bedroom and spied the red diary at her hand, she asleep on the bed with her pen rolled away and ink staining her bedding, and I should not have looked but I did glance at what she wrote about the talk she had with William Blake.

Blake says, she wrote, *that the ship was not merely a cloud but a Vision—*

I remember Rotha and that Blake fellow all fired up in some kind of cahoots none of the rest of the household knew about or understood. I remember her telling me of that cloud, or was it a cloud? On Scawfell Pike. The ship that turned into a horse. And my not understanding.

I remember our William, William Wordsworth, thought Blake should not have been alone with Rotha. It is all bad enough with her own imaginings, he said when he returned after having fled, but—Dixon—*you* failed to shield my sister and now she will not come out of her room.

It was one of very few times when William was angry with me and he couldn't stay angry for long—we both knew it—for hadn't he himself run away and left his sister behind

the minute he saw Blake's head bobbing over the gooseberries? Fled, though he somehow believed his sister to be in trouble.

Aye, he said after he found her upstairs unwilling to come down for prayers or even to eat a bit of pudding, that man would be better locked up at Whitmore or Warburton's than free to roam around our paradise here, troubling our peace to match his own madness.

I knew he couldn't mean this, for Whitmore was a bad place to which no one should be sent for we all knew their friend Mary Lamb had been there and what she had seen, if she was telling the truth, and she always, it was said, told the truth no matter that she had murdered her own mother and no matter what else she did. In fact they all said, William and Rotha and everybody, that whenever she was not locked up Mary Lamb was the most sane person any of them ever knew. And according to Miss Lamb they force-fed you at Whitmore 'til the spoon tore the last teeth from your gums and they beat you with brooms, and that was only the start. So for him to say Blake should be in Whitmore I knew our William was far from happy.

And what about Rotha?

A cloud but not a cloud, she wrote, *and Blake bade me wait and watch. Wait and watch and when you find yourself on a ship as foretold by this cloud, know it is the ship of your transformation!*

What did Blake mean by that?

I sat on her bed and read what he'd said and I did not understand what it meant, not then.

—& he said Dorothy, the ship will take you from one life to another—the ship will first falter & run aground—beware that you do not rely on anyone to save you, least of all family. Very least of all the one on whom you most rely for your heart's ease, for that ship is already long wrecked—but lo, from this new shipwreck is born a horse you have rightly called gallant of neck & head, & aboard that horse—if you leap in time—soars your freedom!

That is all Rotha wrote of William Blake's words the day he visited after she climbed Scawfell Pike.

At that time I had no notion what any of it meant. It was not until more than a year later, after we had all been away and she came back from Europe with her brother and their wife Mary, it all came clear.

Aye, the wink of an eye.

Did ye ever notice—ye must've—how you can dwell in one place and things are going pretty well and everything seems to be one way, with sweet accord and a fair amount of knowing what's what—everything has its own place and there is a kind of peace over things, or if not peace then at least there is a comfort or a routine. The house at Rydal was full of a kind of comfort or even I might call it love. Compared with the rest of England I mean, where there was no comfort and things were not full of love.

All I have told ye so far was before 1820 and like I said over the next few seasons I had to go away off and on and so did the little family. We briefly went our own ways. And it seems, have ye lot noticed this? That the minute ye turn your back for even a moment, well it's like what happens in

a garden if you leave it. I'll wager this happens to ye with your flowers and fields. Everything goes all topsy-turvy!

Ye head for the clover fields one year and then ye turn your sweet little backs for what seems like no time at all. Maybe ye try a cowslip field for a day or an elder grove or a place where all your honey comes from yet another sort of bloom ye've been meaning to try for some time and suddenly you get the chance!

That's what happened to me, like, and from the way things turned out I am telling ye it must've happened to Rotha at the same time. We both turned our faces away from each other for that instant, and when we came back . . . I find it a bit upsetting how nothing stays the same though I know ye lot know how to keep yourselves safe through the biggest sorts of changes in weather or in society or whatever might befall ye. At least so far. But ye have me beat on that score. The difference in Rotha when the little family returned! You might as well have called a magician into Rydal to hoy a cloth over us all then whisk that cloth away only for us to find we could recognize nothing from before.

4

On the bat's back I do fly

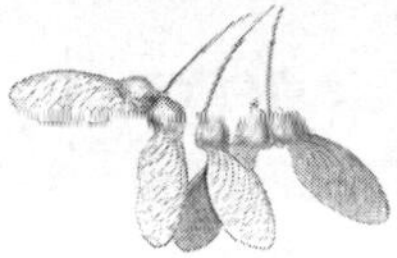

James, when you leave the presence of our garden, whether you go indoors to Rydal Mount or travel as Rotha and her brother and Mary did to behold cities, or strive to raise your sister Penny from the dead . . . once you leave off touching the land with your own feet and hands and senses . . . once you leave our influence . . .

Have you beseeched your pillow as to what you, or Penny, or Rotha, or I, Sycamore, can do against brutality, except withstand it?

What does it mean to withstand?

Brutality's weapon is the lie that it is stronger than our withstanding. As if withstanding has no power. No. In our presence brutality is pathetic, dwindling. Withstanding is our glory. Our conversation is eternal dignity. We are the realm of life.

Remember that, James, when you imagine yourself bereft.

eleven

IT WAS CHRISTMAS EVE OF 1820 that they were to return. Christmas Eve! I was working over in Ambleside the week before when Grace Threlkeld got a note over to me saying the Wordsworths wanted their house prepared for that day and everything ready for the following day, Christmas Day. And they'd like to have myself there to help with the preparations and to be there on the day itself and the days following as well as the months if I felt like staying on. My hut was even waiting for me and I was glad. For the hut was mine and mine only and I slept better in it than at Ambleside or anywhere. So I gave up my Ambleside lodgings and went back to my true home.

Leaving Rydal for that while had made me uneasy, as if my standing with the little family might go wobbly. I didn't want it wobbly. I wanted to be in with them like a wren in its nest. And now I'd be back for Christmas Eve and Christmas Day and Saint Stephen's Day an' all, the very day of the little wren!

The wren, the wren,
The king of all birds—

Saint Stephen's Day
He got lost in the furze—

The wren is a kingly bird yet a humble little bird. That's somehow the way I like to think of what the little family has done for me. They made me a kingly bird in my own spot. Maybe not in an important kingdom but . . . I felt like a little wren with, you know, I'd fluff my feathers and I'd fly here and there and I felt as happy as if I'd been wearing a little crown.

And that's how I felt on the Christmas Eve when I was getting the place ready for their return. Cutting the holly branches for the mantel and a few bits of moss an' all, for I knew how Rotha loved moss. The green of it! I knew just what to do and what to gather and when to show up with it in my arms. That little wren in the song got lost in the furze but I was never lost as long as the Wordsworths gave me a home.

I had not known to expect their return so I had quite a few jobs I was doing here and there around Ambleside. So for me it was a Christmas surprise. But I always found a way to put off anybody who wanted me if the Wordsworths needed me an' all. Mrs. Hills and Mrs. Aglionby and all the rest of them who I have helped over the years—they have all been very kind to me and for that I can tell ye I have always considered myself a favourite of Fortune. But my gratitude has been always and forever foremost towards the little family at Rydal Mount.

And if I'm telling the whole truth, I had another reason to look sharp soon as the note came telling me of the Wordsworths' Christmas Eve arrival—I had invited my sister

Penny for Christmas dinner at my Ambleside lodgings and she was on her way from Manchester. I had sent her the money and she was coming. Ye'd be surprised how much money I've managed to save up. I've even got quite a few railway shares, but don't tell that to any of the family! For they despise any talk of a railway. Although who minds that now, with Mary the only one left? Aye, Mary likely wouldn't be averse to having a few railway shares herself. Any rate, Penny was coming to share my ham and bread with me for a small Christmas at my lodgings, but soon as I heard the Wordsworths were coming home, I felt then that this was my one and perfect chance to bring our Penny over to Rydal Mount and get her foot in the door.

I thought the family would be glad to be home and good cheer would prevail and no one would think twice about Penny's presence.

I told Penny to wait until noon on Christmas Day then come to my hut which I would have warmed up for us, and we would have our ham and bread together and she could wait for me while I did my afternoon's work. And I'd keep an eye out for the right moment to tell the Wordsworths that Penny had come to see me for Christmas, and that by the way she happened to be free should they need a hand with the multitude of tasks involved in settling back into Rydal after their journey . . .

All of that I would figure out how to say in the moment, when that moment came. I was relying on Christmas happiness to carry the day as Christmas Day was as ye know Rotha's birthday as well as the Christ child's. It had always been a

time of opening summer's cowslip wine, and card games and mince pies and a great roast and a slab of jellied tongue.

So help me I should have known by that time in my life—I mean yes I was still young but I had been through enough to know that the best-sounding predictions in the world are often the most foolish, and no one can tell what might fall asunder just when you think you have a keen eye for a situation.

So me and the maid Fanny and even John Carter were all looking forward to the family's return on Christmas Eve. We had the house bright with holly branches and the larder ready. But when they arrived—William and Mary looked all right if a bit tired—but Rotha looked to me as if she had all her force kicked out of her. Her force was ousted by some violent sort of kicking! The same as if ye lot were—imagine—flying over your fields with all your summer powers, honey and everything all full-charged, revellin' in your own flying, going Whee! Over the fields ye carouse—

But then ye get the air swept out from under ye by some vicious storm.

Aye, as violent as that.

Some sort of storm had happened, and Rotha stumbled out of the carriage and hardly acknowledged me though I felt my heart leap for her, sad as her state appeared. She was still my wild-eyed Rotha and her curls still bounced. But I saw straight away and I confirmed this over the next days that Rotha'd had her will—to walk, to stay upright, to move, to live the life she was made for—blasted out from under her by a force of, aye some gale force of . . . disappointment.

Some unexpected letdown.

Punctured breath—aye, something took her breath away.

And it's one thing for ye with your wings, but for us without wings ye might need to be told our breath feeds the movement in our legs. Aye, it was all one wasn't it, with Rotha? Her leg-power was all one with her breath. And her breath's what she'd had kicked or pushed out by the time they came back . . .

And I knew there had to be more to it than what William told me, which was that the journey had been long and Rotha was very tired. And when he said it his face was made of very well-placed stones while Rotha's face looked like anything but, or like stones that were dissolving to powder and forming some completely new kind of face as she struggled upstairs away from us.

Will your sister be all right? I says.

And William says aye, you know how Dorothy cannot stand hustle and bustle, and it was true. But when he said it his face closed in over that story very final and clever.

I mean, people are a bit self-clevering, aren't they. You cannot get away from it. They . . . we . . . all want to be thought well of. We don't want to put forth our failings and foolishness. But ye know, from start to finish, from the first minute I ever laid eyes on William's sister, I knew she wasn't self-clevering in any way. She was simply laid out like a field full of daisies. Not simple, mind. Ye know how deep, but even that's not the part I mean. Self-clevering . . . making yourself into a pleasing or nicely complicated intelligent person

for other people to look upon and admire. There was none of that with her, but plenty with William.

Admiration?

Haha, I can't imagine in Rotha the bit of people's brains that wants admiration, and nearly everbody's got it. I suppose even pigs and lambs have got it. They want to be looked on with favour. And William did. But she was lacking that bit. You could say she was missing it . . . but that wouldn't be right. Missing is when something leaves a space. She had an absence of something that made for a glory of something else. Maybe glory's a strong word. But I know ye have seen a long view over the fells from up at the top—seen the way things are laid out, just themselves.

Oh the bits of sun fallen like melted coins on the green. Ha, the tarn like pewter. And the old rough stones, nothing to be admired haha, yet you can't help feeling something dissolve that hard, persistent stone in your own heart.

And on Christmas morning she came downstairs early, looking for me to help her with the part I help her with every Christmas morning after we have put the finishing touches on the greenery. And that is the pastry figure of the Christ child, which goes in the pastry manger full of sweet mince.

I hope the mince is all right, she says, as I am using leftover from last Christmas.

You'll have topped the brandy up though, says I?

Aye, she says, in April and June before we went away, and she hands me a bit on the end of a spoon and I pronounce it fine indeed. It has a fatty edge and a fruity depth

and is not too sweet and the brandy wasn't cheap, nor were the nutmeg and mace.

Sometimes, I says, mince gets better the longer it ages.

Aye, she says, mixing very cold water into the fat and flour for the pastry, but her hand is trembling.

Are you all right, says I?

I wasn't a good traveller, she says.

No?

The others got up very early each day, she says.

But here we are up before all today, I says.

Yes, she says, but I'm home, aren't I. I am all right when I am home. But on our travels the others rose early while I had not the strength. And, James, I did not see what they saw. I lay in the carriage and slept through the loveliest parts of the road all along the Rhine! I overdid it walking in Ghent and my bowels raged, and James, you know how when my bowels give out, it is not long afterwards that I will lose all power in my legs.

Oh, Miss.

Bowels! Leg weakness! Exhaustion in Brussels . . .

I'm sorry, Miss D.

I loved watching her do the part of the pastry where the fat gets cut into the flour so that it is like wet sand with knobs of fat throughout. It goes from silky fine flour to that knobbly damp sand and then in goes a splash more of cold water and magically she swirls the wooden spoon until it gathers the dough in a fine, fat ball ready for my part. I was sorry that while she seemed so sad at the pastry board, here I was finding it satisfactory to watch the pastry form like God forming

Adam and Eve out of fine, dry dust. For that was what us two were about to accomplish, myself and Dorothy, except it was the other way around. Instead of God making man, man was making the form of the Christ child. You make the ordinary mince tarts like, by the dozens, then at the last comes this, where you make the manger in a wee loaf pan and you make the baby Jesus out of the last of the pastry and you lay him in the manger. And I was the head one for carving the little baby if I do say it meself.

Even though neither of us went to church this was a blessed moment and I waited for her to give me the pastry in my hand, for the feel of it—so fat and cold—gave me a thrill like etching the Pace eggs over Easter. Because with the Christ child I was standing near Rotha and we were making the body of the Christmas child together as if we were its earthly mam and dad. But I never said this to her of course. I wonder what she would have thought if I had.

And I thought of what she said about being home. How she was all right as long as she was home.

Home was a funny thing with her. When she was at home, all she wanted to do was dream of travels afar. Glorious travels, either remembered or planned. Over Scotland's highlands and the Alps and now all those places she had just been, places a man like me hardly dreams of unless there is a war. Days after her last topping up of brandy in the mincemeat she had left England and gone to Brussels and Cologne, and up the Rhine to Switzerland, then Lucerne and the Italian lakes and Milan, and back to Switzerland and then France, for they stayed in Paris a whole month. I was giddy thinking about it.

But she had not been happy.

Were you thinking of home all the while, Miss?

Home, yes, she says. All through the Italian lakes I could think only of our own dear Lakes here. And the spires and glorious towers of Liège I saw only by moonlight, for I lay faint through entire days. The same happened in Cologne. I had to resist the temptation to walk because if I did walk even a little bit too far I would pay for it dearly soon afterward.

But what about London, Miss?

I knew she loved London and I knew she had spent November there and no matter how much she loved the Lakes she saw beauty in London. She saw it when she visited Mary and Charles Lamb. She'd go in a courtyard or back lane and she'd look at the way old stones had worn on the corner of a building and she'd marvel at the loveliness of a puddle, only a rain-puddle. She'd come back and she'd say—I mean I think sometimes she should've been a painter—she'd say James, there was a pigeon in the puddle and I watched it have a drink. Its bright brown eye looked straight at me, and its neck was iridescent turquoise, indigo and amethyst.

And I'd say, Miss, if you don't mind me saying, a pigeon to me looks completely grey.

Yes, she'd answer, but the drab, grey bits only serve to make it shimmer the more.

She'd go on like that and all she'd been to was some sooty lane behind Mary Lamb's house, and you'd think she'd been to that place Sam Coleridge made up that begins with an X or a Z, I forget the name. Domes and that. But I think like Sam she was in that place even when she wasn't

there. I mean she could go in any ordinary place and she would see it exalted, like.

And she finishes up the pastry so it's springy like the flesh of a real newborn babe and she lays it on the floured board and she says, London was all right, James. In fact I would like to go back and spend more time with Mary Lamb. But before we got to London I knew I was a failure as a traveller. I felt so very far from the way I felt on my travels twenty years ago—or even five years!

I looked at her sideways, puzzled. When somebody has made an impression on you while ye were both young, and later you see them and they have grown a lot more haggard, you mightn't notice them getting old at first. You still have an outdated version of them in your head. It hovers over their new-old self and you don't see at first that big changes have taken place, that the person is closer to death, or some jolt has caved them in like a shore that has been eaten away.

And I knew from my mam that when a woman turns fifty she becomes different. I could see that Rotha had not for some time looked young on the face of it, but I had to make a real effort to see this because to me I did not see the surface of a person and never had. But I could tell something in Rotha had been shaken.

I clamped the urge to remind her how little more than a year and a half earlier she had climbed Scawfell Pike with no hint of weak legs and if anything she had more power than a woman half her age! But I could feel the letdown in her at her European failure, and even as she lamented, I had the feeling there was some shock she was leaving unsaid. What was it?

What had happened to Rotha when they were in Europe, her and William and their wife Mary?

She gave me the pastry and I started feeling the lump with my hands and stretching it ever so gentle here and there to make the parts change to living limbs, or limbs and a body and a wee face belonging to a living child, and not just any child but the Christ child. Baking the pastry Christ was one of the old-fashioned things she loved to do and she took my finished babe in her hands with great care and she says to me, James, you know I once had a little boy child of my own?

And I says hesitant like, Miss, you mean your young nephew Tom? For I knew Tom had been the son of William and Mary and had died when he was little, soon after Catherine, and I did not want to start a mournful conversation.

But she says no, not the son of our wife Mary. Our own son—William's and mine! Little Basil.

Now I didn't have a clue what to say as this seemed very unlikely. But so had other things, like the window concealed in her bedroom wall. So I kept quiet and kneaded the pastry Christ child best as I could without interrupting or looking worried.

And she says yes—William and I had a child together just as Mary and Charles Lamb have theirs even now.

So I says, I couldn't help it like, Miss I says, you mean Mary and Charles Lamb, brother and sister, have a little one between 'em?

And she says yes—a brother and sister can be very excellent parents together, as William and I were for our little Basil.

That's when I wondered for the first time if John Carter and half the village were right all along—she must be raving and how had I not seen it before?

And she takes the baby Jesus made of pastry and slides him in the cooker and I must say he's fine-looking when he goes in and I hope he'll weather the heat all right and not shatter or sink and lose his perfection, and here she hands me a second lump of pastry and says, James, can you please make me another child?

I wonder what she's about. I hope she's not wanting me to make the baby Thomas who died. Or is she trying to have me make young Basil who I don't believe is real? I don't know what to think but then she says, And James, make it a girl.

A girl, Miss?

Yes—a Christmas birthday sister for the Christ child.

At last I twig that she means make herself as a babe, for this is the day she was born. And she says please, James, do make the girl. So I fashion the baby lass and she pops that one in the cooker right beside the Christ child. The two of them together come out looking absolutely perfect.

And she says there. There's little mortal Dorothy and her Divine brother, both born on this day, keeping each other company in the manger. She can be his little doll.

And the way she says doll I remember how only William ever calls her that, and hardly ever, only when he thinks nobody else can hear. Other Dorothys get called Doll all the time, but not her. She's nowt like a doll though she is small. If you could trap a lion inside a doll maybe. Anyway she lays

baby Jesus in his manger on the mincemeat, and in she lays the baby Dorothy right beside him for all the world as if he has a doll, and she says, I forgot to make them a pastry blanket!

But the house was waking up—it was getting on for ten in the morning and they were all still tired from their journey but they vowed they would have a good Christmas all the same, with the roast and the mince pies and a few games of cards, but there was one window not done up yet—the kitchen window—and I went out to gather a few branches to deck it out same as the others. And from what I can gather while I was out William came downstairs lured by the fragrant mince tarts that had come out of the oven and he was not exactly jolly but he felt happy enough about the tarts and he poked his nose over the loaf-pan manger with the baby Jesus in it and he says, What's this? And he picks up the pastry Dorothy. And he says, You made a spare? And he cracks the legs off it and pops them in his mouth before she can stop him. And I think, mind ye cannot be certain but all the same, something about that . . . a doll made in the likeness of a person, then someone by mistake, not knowing like, breaks part of it . . . Well my mam had candles like that, she fashioned her neighbours out of stubs while the wax was still warm. And anything good she wished for a certain neighbour, she wished it over their wax figurine. And if anyone crossed her, well their wax figure would meet a pin or two and that was how many a fate was met, according to my mam. Of course ye don't know if the good or the bad was a direct cause like.

But I was out cutting the holly boughs and I got carried away in the woods. I found a sweet-smelling spot to sit, very

quiet, and a few snowflakes floated down, and a bird or two sang their carols for me and maybe I dozed off but surely not as long as all that! For I woke and saw by the sky that it was already past noon. And I frowned because I'd told my sister Penny to come to my hut at noon so I could eat with her then introduce her to the family and try and see if she could stay for a little while into the new year. That had been my plan or my hope. And if into the new year by even a few days, why, then, it couldn't be too hard to extend Penny's stay and maybe have her start doing some little job or other. A new start for Penny.

I headed for my hut, praying Penny had waited and could come to the house now properly with me by her side to introduce her.

But there was no sign of my sister.

I went in the house and looked around. Rotha had gone upstairs—I saw the legless baby version of herself on the counter—and William was in his study and Mary off somewhere with the cat Rotha hated because it hunted birds. With that cat beside her Mary was in her own world. So there was no one I could ask had my sister Penny come to the door.

I searched to see if Penny had crouched in some nook waiting for me, her brother, hiding like. Oh, I felt awful. But no. My sister wasn't in the pantry and she was nowhere around the landing or in any of the rooms. So I went upstairs to Rotha's room—Rotha lay on the bed—and I said, very quiet like, Miss, you don't happen to have seen anyone come to the door around noon?

Who do you mean? she says. Were we expecting someone?

Miss, only I told my sister to wait until noon and I would be able to see her today . . .

I thought you told us you had a brother, James.

No. Miss. A sister. My sister Penny.

I knew I had told her about Penny more than once and why she kept hearing brother though I said sister every time, I'll never understand.

You have a sister?

Yes.

She hasn't got ginger hair?

Penny, yes, Miss, she does. My mam called her Penny on account of it.

Oh.

Have you seen her?

I only saw a young red-haired beggar at the back door. A ragged-looking lass. Are you saying, James, that this might have been a relative of yours?

Eh, Miss D . . . I think . . .

For I took her for a beggar and I pressed sixpence upon her and asked her to be off and then I shut the door.

I see, Miss. Did she not ask for me?

I don't know what she said, James. I do not remember if words were coming out of her mouth or if her lips simply chattered with the cold. For my own part I was loath to leave the door open and let our heat out into the cold day, so I shut it rather quickly. I do remember that I thought she would've been a bonny lass if she'd only straighten her back, but she

had that sunken look of girls who meet hopelessness in their youth and so look strangely old.

I still held a branch of holly and Rotha noticed it, and she asked if I would lay it on her sill to cheer her as she rested before the evening's feasting and merriment. And I fastened it for her on that sill where the same little wren and robin who had carolled me to sleep might come and visit Rotha. Their carols had come at the wrong time for Penny and I did not know how I could forgive the little birds for singing to me so sweetly in the woods, or myself for succumbing to their voices.

Ye know I could've made the bones of what I need moneywise without this job.

Moneywise I always made do. Going outside and not inside, that's how I manage. And between me and Penny I was the one who no one could trap indoors for a minute let alone a day or a year or a life. But Penny, no. Dank. Deafening. Reeking. Damp. Years. No break for the privy. If the lasses weren't wet enough from the splashing machines, they wet themselves! Whereas me, all along ye found me outside didn't ye? Where scent fills the hay and feathers cling tight to the living birds and my own lungs swell pink and glittering and full of rose-sweet air.

Outside!

Aye, I had all my stolen bits of time—they add up here with the Wordsworths—time when nobody is looking over my shoulder! Even William says to me James, he says, I fear this place belongs to you more than it has ever belonged to

us. And when did William ever lie down and fall asleep where the limbs meet the trunk on your sycamore? He's too tall for a start. Whereas me, I'm small enough to fit right in them crooks, and a knot that looks hard to anyone who hasn't tried it turns out to be a comfortable pillow for my head.

The dreams I've had in your tree!

But Penny, when did she ever know any sleep but pure exhaustion? I mean if William caught me dreaming on the job he'd count it as my conjuring some answer to a question he'd asked me. Can I grow ginger between the cabbages? He having read an article about it. Ginger grows sideways and needs little soil, according to the latest Royal Botanic expert. Do I bother William with the argument that it is far too cold in England for tropical plants? No! My whole tactic is this: find a way to do what the master would like done, and when it's done congratulate him on his vision.

And I do what he asks but the fantastic side is all the days and weeks and months of time on my own in the gardens or on errands or anywhere out-of-doors in a free man's air. Free to think whatever I want! Every once in a blue moon William spies me on my own having a moment and he says Dixon, here you are in solitary splendour! A jealous look on his face if I'm not imagining it—for what wouldn't he give to get in his punt and row off to Grasmere Island instead of trudging to the stamp office or having tea with all and sundry or going off to wring money out of his publishers—always on the hunt. When I count up my personal moments of solitary splendour they might easily outspan William's,

and for that I am glad to be here. But when I think of how I failed Penny I cannot be glad for long.

Penny. She had to face the world. I couldn't help it. Her brother. She was not her own. That is the point of the world now. To make us not our own.

I was not fit. Because I didn't find a way. A way out. A way of escape. A way of freedom. I didn't find it for Penny. My sister. My sister Penny. The crowd here at Rydal did not care to help me free her.

twelve

PENNY MUST'VE BEEN SEVENTEEN by the time Rotha turned her away that Christmas day. I saw a little sister in her but she saw herself as grown, though like all the lads and lasses ruined in the mills she had hardly grown an inch from the time she started. If anything she was shrunken or stooped so as to seem smaller than she had been. It galled her to be treated by me as a bairn, and I admit her face was grey as an old woman's. She said I was barmy to try and lift her out of her situation. She herself thought it a better situation than I thought it. I've been doing all right, she says, for I have had an offer from an old man called Nahum Troake to be his servant and I think I will do it, so stop thinking you're any better off than I am!

What does Mr. Troake do for a living? I asked her. She said nothing and I felt bad. I wondered if the Wordsworths' situation had rubbed off on me and made me seem as if I thought over-highly of myself. For there was no question that in the eyes of the world and in my own eyes I had risen higher than Penny had.

And for all I knew maybe William was noticing likewise about himself and his own sister.

I wished I could have warned William that a brother can look after his younger sister only so much and then she has her own way of wanting to look after herself. And no matter how sick or poorly or wretched she seems to that brother, if she wants to get up on her own feet and see through her own eyes the older brother cannot make her see through his.

Could I have warned William? Or do I know these things only now myself, after the years that have gone by? Some things I don't know and will never know and other things I know but I don't know how or when I learned them!

For instance I know now that after that Christmas Penny did go to the door of the man called Nahum Troake. It's a hovel not a house, and it is in one of the worst parts of Manchester, and she says yes, Sir, I cannot go back to the factory because of my deformity, and I have no help from my brother so I have come to take your offer. And Penny has worked for Nahum Troake since that day, scrubbing his step and cooking his joint and I have been frightened to imagine what else. He is older than her by thirty years and once when I had a chance to ask her, Penny, is Nahum Troake at least a mild-tempered man?, she told me his temper is no better and no worse than that of any other fella making his living as part rat-catcher, part vagabond. But is he mostly kind to you? I said. She gave me no answer and I have often tried to fathom the look on her face but its meaning I will never know.

And here I was back at Rydal with the Wordsworths and it was them I had to mind, not my sister, and it was not easy. It took us all some time to get used to being there after we had all been away.

It's as if a house knows when you've gone, it knows you've abandoned it and it feels angry with you and it takes its own back against you. Ye feel this in the hives, don't ye. Ye have to be homebodies for the home to take you in as a home should. Each space in house or hive has the spirit in it of whoever lives there and the space gets used to our spirits. And if we go away, our spirits in that house die away like wraiths and then blow away, and when we come back we have to start all over again breathing life into that home.

And that is what I tried to do after the little family came back from Europe. We all worked hard but everyone had a frayed edge, irritated like, or singed somehow, too dry, and crying out from thirst in body and mind. Things didn't feel right and I had no one to talk about it with. I mean John Carter was there keeping William's paperwork up to date and the business affairs in order with the stamps and that, but John had no notion of feelings in the house.

To him everything is made of stone or wood or paper or metal and nothing is made of tears or loneliness whereas I think loneliness is a thing like wood or grass, you can feel it as surely as you can feel a stone. And Rotha when she came back was like a stone separate from the others, and she was heavy and clammy and her legs often would not move, or she chose not to move them, according to Mary for one.

Rotha was disappointed in herself after their voyage but that wasn't it, I could tell that wasn't everything.

Mary, unusual for her, took me aside and asked me what I thought about some of Rotha's health bits and bobs—what Mary called *mysteries*. William never wondered like that. He faced Rotha whatever way she happened to be with each—let's say ailment, for want of a better word. He believed his sister. He accepted what she said and the words that she used for what was happening to her. I felt as if he knew all along why the things that were happening to her happened. And I think he did know back then. He still remembered. But for Mary it was different.

It was as if Mary thought Rotha was covering something up, covering the truth up, by using the word weakness, for example. I mean Rotha often had pain, or she often had weakness. Sometimes she had both pain and weakness. But the weakness itself, Mary was very puzzled by that.

She says, Why is it one day Dorothy can't support herself on her two perfectly sensate legs, but no, she has to be . . . we have to carry her? Yet on another day she can walk quite well, or she can at least allow herself to be brought out to the terrace and stay in the sun for the good part of a day and eat a substantial dinner such as a duck leg and not one but three jam tarts. Two days apart!

Now what's going on with Dorothy today, Mary would say. Is it the pain or is it the weakness?

She sounded very matter of fact but there was something else under the matter of factness. Pain Mary could forgive

but weakness was another story. If I myself gave up every time I felt weak, she says, why I'd have been bedridden myself, years ago. One has to keep going!

Rotha's weakness was something Mary found very hard to understand and I suspect she found it hard to believe.

Did I think Rotha was putting it on?

Mary would ask me as if I knew.

And I did know, and I do know.

But some states are not easy to explain to a person missing a kind of sight. I'm not saying Mary was less sharp than the rest of the household. She was very sharp. I'm saying that as regards Rotha, specially over a word like *weakness*, Mary had trouble—she had to pin it down. She wanted to pin down something I knew did not want to be pinned.

Rotha's weakness wasn't only in her body. It was not this muscle or that muscle giving out though sometimes it had that appearance.

If I had to put it into words Mary might understand, though I don't think she will, but if I had to try, what would I say?

(Sigh)

After that Christmas I had the luxury to think about this and to watch Rotha more than in the old days. For William was back in the thick of business talking with John Carter half the time and working the other half on articles, not poems but essays and revisions and that. And he says to me with a kind of desperate look on his face, Dixon, he says, it is one thing to go off on travels such as a Continental Tour,

but it is another to come home again and have to re-enter the system of operations from which you extracted yourself to embark on those travels. System of operations is how he put it. I remember that. I remember thinking it sounded like the way the bosses had run things in Penny's factory. All the chains and cogs and hooks and hammers in place.

Which was the opposite of how things were going up in Rotha's room. On her good days she had bits of paper flying everywhere, and her pen and notebooks open all over the place as she tried to write down her memories of the latest tour as well as revise her own Scottish *Recollections*, the book she had begun years before and worked on over and over again, hoping to publish it though William had told her no.

But I was watching her.

And I knew she was not right especially on the days when her legs gave out and she could do no more than lie in bed, and on those days I watched her and waited and I wanted to coax out of her what was going on but I knew the best way for that was to listen and wait and keep taking Little Miss Belle in and out to do her business. The dog nearly considered itself mine, for I talked to it more than anyone and Rotha did not find comfort in it as she had done before.

Would Rotha have changed as much if I had not been apart from the little family while they went to Europe? I wondered often but I tried not to go too far down that road.

My mam accused me of making myself out as far more important to the Wordsworths than I really was. She says I

had a cheek that way even regarding my own fam'ly. Thought a bit too much of myself, like.

And not long after that Christmas, on a Thursday in January when William and Mary were in Keswick, the dog became frightened to death because we had thunder and lightning that came close enough to shake the whole place, and dogs loathe that with all their hearts. They don't know what to be doing with themselves, and Little Miss Belle hunkered down under the bed quivering with fright, like, and Rotha was not far behind her in the fear department. I was nearly as bad myself as it was a sky-blackening storm and each thunderclap felt like it had a mind to crack your sycamore and send it crashing through our roof. There was a closer crash right in the bedroom and I said don't worry, Miss D, it's only your cup and saucer tipped off your sill, and she says are you sure, James?

And she is sick on the floor right then and she says James everything is swaying, is everything swaying?

And for a minute I don't know if things are swaying or not because the stench of the sick is great and branches are going mad against the window and Rotha is falling around as if the floor is heaving up and down and she cries out, Where is my brother?

The way she cries it out is bloodcurdling in a way that makes me know it's no good at all to tell her where William really is, which is in Keswick on notary affairs, for he told her that was where he was going and any rate it's a good fifteen miles away so I says hang on, Dorothy—at that moment I call her by the name her brother calls her—I'll clean the

mess up, I says, and I'll get lavender and we won't open the window but we'll lie you down on the bed until it passes—

And that is what happens, only as I go to lower her on her bed she hauls me down on it with her and holds me tight, sobbing, William!

Miss, I says, wanting to bring her back to herself, and to know I was me, like. James Dixon, not William, but—

I feared you were lost to us all!

And I ken she is somewhere else. She is grabbing on to me but she is sure she is grabbing on to her brother.

Where are we?

Little Miss Belle is whimpering under the bed fit to break your heart but there's nowt I can do about her now except hum my trouble song and hope it calms everybody down.

I start it low at first to make sure it won't scare Rotha though like I told ye I'd calmed her with a song of mine before but that was a different song.

There's no tune to this one, like. It's more of a rumble with a moaning song that has no words unless I am by myself, and then the words it has only I can hear and the trees or whatever animal or bird is about. But now all I do is the rumbling low part, so holding on to me lying there on the bed what she feels is like what you might feel if you were pressed down into the ground and you sensed a herd of horses rumbling in the distance.

And she says please keep singing. Does she know yet it's me she's with?

And I says, it's not really singing, Miss, as much as it is a kind of old chant.

And she says whatever it is, don't stop.

And it remains this way, her holding on to me and me doing my song with no words, until the thunder subsides. Once I think the cracks are fading off I wiggle away a bit to see if I can get out of Rotha's hold, and she does, she lets me go.

I'll open the window an inch, I says, because the air was sucked out of the room and we could hardly breathe. When I opened it a wild cold breath rushed in and I felt very relieved. I could smell the lavender over the top of the sick, and the rainy smell came in and freshened the room and by and by Rotha rolled over and looked at me and knew I was me and not William. If there is one thing about Rotha it's that she comes back to herself with a clear eye no matter where she has been in her mind.

I was on our ship, she says.

Ship, Miss?

And she says yes, the ship we boarded to come home from Boulogne—William and myself and Mary—that storm!

I didn't know there was a storm, Miss.

It was a week of gales! And we had to stand on the beach with our baggage every day waiting for the breakers to subside before they would let us on the boat to cross the channel to Dover. And once they let us on the boat, we knew they should not have done so, for the ship was far too small—it was the only one they allowed as fit to sail the conditions—but it was insufficient, tiny really, with only one real sailor—and the waves wild and the winds malevolent—James, I knew then that I was on the ship that had been foretold and prophesied—

Prophesied, Miss?

And she proceeded—but I felt very sheepish because I knew the prophecy from having read it in her red diary—the story of Mr. William Blake and what he had said about the ship-cloud of Scawfell Pike foretelling a real ship that she would find herself on. I knew the prophetic part of the story already—but I let her go on telling me as if I had not read any of it in her private notebook.

And I resolved at that moment, because of the guilt I felt, that I would have to soon find some way to let her know I had been reading it. Some things are all right done in a devious manner, but other things are not, or things develop in a way that makes you change your mind.

So we shouldn't have been on that ship at all, she says. There was an Irish woman and a little Italian man both curled up down the stairs in beds alongside mine—I descended there to shelter from the waves but William and Mary remained up on deck. And before we were out of the port ten minutes we had a frightful heaving on the waves! Our ship lurched and grated—parts of it flew asunder and water came rushing in—the grating noise went on for many seconds as we ran aground. The sound was like a building being razed. I thought the ceiling would crash down and crush us before water inundated and drowned us! The Italian man leapt off his bed and knelt praying on the floor. But the Irish woman was kind—she enfolded me—she was large and I am so small, it was like being enfolded in a mother's velvet arms.

But the violent tearing-apart sounds kept on going and I saw William and Mary in my mind up top being cast into

the sea and I saw everyone at home mourning for us as we had mourned when we lost my brother John—it was just the same as the way John was drowned! His ship was not far from shore either, yet all hands were lost, and now we were re-enacting his death!

All this happened in a few instants and with all my heart, she says, I wished I were a large, strong man able to save people, instead of a tiny person who might as well not even exist. So small was I and so large the wreck and the storm and the roar of the timbers being torn apart . . .

James! When you are in a boat running aground it is as if the boat's bones—its beams and all the solid parts of its construction—are of one piece with your own bones—you become the grounded creature and as you lose equilibrium you fall askew. You know you will flounder and break apart on the stones. Water will flood the boat's lungs and your own lungs, erasing your life's every breath from first to last!

No, I says, for she was quaking. You're here. Back safe.

No, James, she says. I'm not.

Yes, I says. You're safe here, home at Rydal Mount.

And she says no, James, home is not safe. You think it is because you don't know what happened next.

I says what was that, Miss?

She says, James, our ship tilted and swayed but I found my feet and rushed up to the deck. And found William with his shirt and coat off, stripped to the waist!

She waited for my reaction but saw I had not understood.

James, he was poised to dive for his safety and swim ashore! I shouted to him and he was right startled, and he

muttered, Dorothy, I believed you and Mary were lost down in the cabins. For he had seen Mary flung down the stairs by the storm although I had not seen her. And he says to me, Sister, I thought there was no hope for either of you, so . . .

I asked her, incredulous, William was ready to swim and leave ye?

And she says he was.

And I says, No, Miss, surely not.

But she says oh yes, I know it true and strong as the storm we have just witnessed.

And I don't know what to tell her for my troubles song is not the right song for a sunken heart.

But don't worry, she says. It's as if she feels she suddenly needs to save me from thinking what I am thinking. She turns stiff and brightens like. I can't make out what kind of brightness it is. There is something about it that I don't like.

We were saved, she says—we were in very hard shape but in half an hour we saw the tide was on its way out, and we were close enough to shore so as not to be engulfed—but—

She fell face down on her blankets thoroughly limp and I knew she had just been through the shipwreck again. I wondered if she had been reliving it again and again while we were all downstairs or outside, oblivious.

She spoke not another word about William having been ready to swim and leave her and Mary for dead. But her plight on that day remains a thing I cannot put out of my mind. Yet there was something in her that refused on the face of it to think any the less of William. She tried as hard as anything to believe he was as devoted a husband and brother as ever.

But in my mind the scene on the ship called into question the idea that he had ever been devoted to anyone but himself.

This is a hard thing for a servant to believe about his master and I am not saying I carry a grudge or that I think of it often. Only it is a thorn, a mind-prick, a puncture hole, in what used to be my dream about the little fam'ly.

A dream is a thing that can live even with a few puncture holes if the wind is right and the summer holds and a garden like this garden grows all around.

Yet somewhere in me on the day that storm came to Rydal and Rotha was sick and I helped her recover and she told me about the shipwreck and William's plan to lunge off without her and Mary, I knew from then on that Rotha could not rely on a single soul, and maybe none of us can. And I vowed to do the best I could for her.

thirteen

AND IT WAS A FUNNY THING—I started to wonder what might have happened if I'd gone on that expedition to Europe with them.

Would I have left her for drowned in the shipwreck to save my own skin?

Mam says when I get on like that, Son she says, you think you're all right, you think you're better'n anyone else, we all think that of ourselves. In the moral way. We all go yes me I'm the one you can count on to do best. But when push comes to shove, you never know what you might do or not do.

But I think I do know that I would never have peeled my own shirt off to dive in that water without Rotha in my arms safe. Or I hope I would not have.

So I was thinking about that, about going on travels with her over and beyond the ones we did increasingly at Rydal, which were travels without the miles. I mean we walked around the terraces as if they were many miles.

For she had me walk with her up and down and around the terraces like she and her brother used to do. Walking the

sacred earth, he used to call it. But she just called it traipsing, plain like. That was how they both composed. The poet and his prose-writing sister. They never sat at a desk. Well, he—he hated sitting and he sat if he had to correct things but it gave him a headache like you wouldn't believe. And if he got the headache that was it for the day. Neither one of them could be happy unless they were outside. And of course early on she followed him and wrote down whatever he muttered. But that was long ago when they both walked their feet off. And both let the ground talk to the soles of their feet.

Only now I was the one tagging along and hanging on her every word.

I kept my ears pricked open in case I heard talk of a new visit to some other place farther than our wee gallivants around Rydal. I made up my mind to be in the right place at the right time as soon as ever a proper new journey was mentioned.

It was dawning on me that home to Rotha was the place she thought about if she went away. But once she came home, all she could think about was new journeys abroad. She wasn't at home in either place, home or away. Her real home was somewhere in her dreams no matter where she ended up.

She said the Lakes around Rydal reflected the skies and clouds and same moon that she had seen in Liège or elsewhere. They were like mirrors or windows into a dream of being a pilgrim in a far land with her old wagon and one horse like the gypsy. And me, I understood that. And I think I understand it better than her brother William ever did.

And that's why I wished I could go somewhere with her.

Yet it's why, once she was at home again from Europe, after the shipwreck when William was ready to dive and leave her, I understood she felt glad to be home. She loved her home. And when she was away in the Italian lakes or the Scottish lakes or anyone else's lakes, none could compare to her own lakes at home. Because her own lakes at home held all the other lakes in them. But at home, well no matter how much she loved it, off she longed to wander again.

And I wondered, I couldn't help it, what about she wanders away with me?

I did wonder that and I kept my ear out for any possibility. And when it came, it wasn't Brussels or Switzerland or Lucerne and it wasn't steeples in the moonlight at Liège, but it was somewhere. So my ears perked right up.

First she says to me, James—would you do something for me, please? And she touches her jaw.

Yes, Miss? For by now I was ready to do anything Rotha asked of me. Do you need me, I asked her, to have another look at your teeth? For she hadn't been wearing them and I was afraid the hinges had once again come undone and I felt bad about it.

They do need mending, she said. And I am afraid there is nothing more either you yourself or poor Cora Freetorch can do this time. For it is not only my false set giving me trouble, but my last three teeth on the top and those remaining on the bottom are going to have to come out, so it is, sadly, a question of paying Mr. Demergue fifty guineas and having him fit me with a whole new set.

Mr. Demergue, is he the tooth man in London?

Yes and it means I will have to stay with Mary and Charles Lamb and their little daughter and not show myself for a fortnight before all is back to normal inside my mouth.

There she was on about Charles and Mary Lamb's little daughter again, the thing she had told me at Christmas, and I didn't know what to say, for it was absurd, a brother and sister having a daughter between them. So I let that pass. Sometimes I get a bit paralyzed in my talking if I run across a thing I can't make sense of. I sort of shove it in my pocket and try to find a way to make sense of it later.

So I says to her, I says, Miss, is Mary Lamb—but I got stuck again there because I did not know how to ask was Mary Lamb all right, was she at home? Was she mad or well or in-between . . . for Miss Lamb was in and out of the madhouse as we all knew. I mean, I says, how is the state of her health?

Mary Lamb, says Rotha, is of the same state as I concerning her poor teeth.

So she'll be sympathetic, I says.

Yes, and she is sympathetic not only on that subject but regarding every subject under the sun. And sympathy or understanding, which Miss Lamb possesses in uncanny measure, mean more to me at this moment in my life than any amount of what is ordinarily called sanity.

She gave me a look. And to tell ye the truth I don't know where I got the nerve to say what I said to her next.

I can understand that, I says. Miss, might you need a . . . a reliable person's help, if you're to stay with Miss Lamb a whole fortnight?

It dawned on her that I was struggling but she did not twig what I was getting at so I says, Miss, I could come along if you think it would be of any help to you. I nearly said *and save William the trouble* but I thought better of it.

Would you really want to come with me, James, for a fortnight in London?

The thought of it got a bit more real then and I became alarmed and she saw what must have been a look of fright on my face. But was only a small fright. It hung in the room along with her own surprise at the way things were shaping. It was like the air in the room altered a bit, for we were glimpsing an arrangement we had not thought of before.

Miss, I says, perhaps it's not a good idea. I have never been to London before.

Are you frightened of it? she says. Surely not. You've been to Manchester, haven't you? To see your family? A brother, I think?

Manchester is not London, Miss. I did not bother to correct her this time about the brother she still thought I had. It occurred to me that in Rotha's world sisters must be invisible.

Here among the Lakes, she says, there are things just as frightening as any city. Look out the window now beyond the sycamore! The sky looks as if some hand has broken vast amounts of black cake all through it.

Aye, Miss, the sky does look like crumbled treacle cake.

And the wind! she says. Look how it gathers over the treetops in the village, ransacking the tips to reveal silver undersides that sizzle and thrash!

It's a mad whoosh all right, Miss, I says.

Let's you and I guess, James, how many minutes it will take for the incoming deluge to drench us. What do you think? How long before Rydal Mount is soaked?

I'd say, Miss, half an hour? I did not like to claim I was sure about the timing of weather, for that's a thing uncertain at all times. I felt uncertain about that and the conversation took a turn that I felt even worse about. I mean she started talking in a way that I couldn't understand, and I was worried. I wondered if the impending storm was going to make her sick like the last one did.

Have you noticed, James, how many souls in the village are women who are getting old?

Here in Rydal, Miss?

In Rydal or Grasmere . . . in Ambleside or any town hereabouts. Women labour down the road on their messages—look, there's Mrs. Jackson who retains fewer teeth than I and has replaced none of them, flashing her black gaps and begging for ale—Parched, she cries, I'm parched! . . . And here I am as toothless and haggard as she is—

No, Miss—

As squat, James—as short, and as insignificant, if you look at me as men look at women, from the outside looking at her, or looking upon her . . . but you don't look at me like that, do you?

No, Miss.

And I did not. For it was as true as anything that to me Rotha Wordsworth was still, no matter her age, a dark slip of night shot with starlight, I don't know why. I'll never

know why. But I did not let on to her for I was not sure how that might sound in her ears.

And I am afraid, James, she says, that if I were to describe to you my inner state, I would tell you that my fatigue is so thick as to resemble a fog bank coming in off the sea. Muscular I am not. And people value musculature as it exists in a man such as my brother. Muscle fuels his rage and his inspiration. I am not supposed to have rage. Although lo and behold I have it. You have eaten oats, James?

Aye, Miss, I says. For I had eaten plenty.

And she says, I have eaten oats until William claims I look like oats. I look like a bowl round on its bottom—a bowl full of oats—each oat itself a round entity, oats being blips that nourish; greyish seeds having no legs nor horns nor wings. An old woman is an oat and she is the bowl that holds the oat and she is the spoon that digs the oat from the bowl and she is the mouth that sups the oat and she is the tongue in that mouth. Do you understand me, James?

I'm . . . Miss?

And if she isn't an oat she's a currant bun, inert and white with black eyes, many eyes, but eyes unable to transmit what they see because she is only a bun and is passed by, sitting in the larder. And what is the fate, James, of all buns you have known?

They get gobbled, Miss?

Yes or they grow stale and must be fed to the hens. Already I feel the eyes being plucked out of me by Little Jack Horner. You do know him?

Yes, Miss . . . and I couldn't help it, I recited—

Little Jack Horner
Sat in the corner
Eating his Christmas pie—
He put in his thumb
And pulled out a plum—
And said, What a good boy am I!

Gobbled, she says! And who was in our Christmas pie? Who lay on a bed of currants and plums and was born on Christmas Day?

You mean the mince pie you fashioned, Miss? For the Christ child?

For whom?

She looked as if I had not spoken well and I wasn't sure what she wanted me call Jesus. I couldn't really call him by only his first name. Only people down in the fields listening to the Wesley preachers talked about him by name as if he was a friend they knew. Rotha owned a Bible but I seldom saw her look in it and she was never down listening to the preachers.

The Lamb of God, Miss? I says.

Other than the Lamb of God, she says, looking weary.

I didn't want her to sicken of my stupidity. For I desired to go to London with her. I wanted it suddenly and badly. Just Rotha and me, on the road.

And I remember. Oh! Miss, I'm wrong, for you meant yourself. *You* were born on Christmas Day.

Yes, she says. I was. And I intend to jump out of the Christmas pie to see *my* Lamb, the Lamb who is also not the Christ child.

Mary Lamb, Miss?

Yes, she says. Neither she nor I is anything like Jesus or any man. We are both of us, Mary Lamb and I, something quite other than what Jack Horner imagines. Sitting in his corner with his thumb in his mouth.

Miss?

Get me out of here, will you, my dear James? And pack a bag for yourself and we will tell William we're away for a fortnight while I get my teeth renewed, and he'll think that is all I am about and he will be relieved he won't have to do a thing.

I'll see about the mail coach, Miss.

And tell them we want to ride on the outside and we won't give a damn about the weather.

I'll tell them, Miss. In fact, I says, seeing the look on her face, I'll let them know that weather might be the very thing we desire.

BUT WILLIAM GREW WORRIED VERY soon after she told him of the London plan.

He says to me James, I wonder if you've noticed how my sister is lately and if you think she is fit to go to London at all. I mean, he says, you're the one who's been talking with her more than any of us since we came back from our travels abroad. Have you noticed anything about her speech that might be—he stopped, searching for a word.

I supplied words in my mind but decided to keep them there . . . *vexed* . . . *wild* . . . *trapped*.

—Discontinuous? William says.

Sir?

Fragmented, he says. Not properly strung together. Have you noticed anything like that?

I'm not so sure, Sir.

If I thought, James, that Dorothy—if she weren't able to—it's all bad enough with Miss Lamb's own condition, for heaven's sake. What do you think?

I thought of things Rotha had started to say to me, and I thought of things I had read in her red diary. Water that is not wet. Wrinkled water. Dry water! Sizzling leaves. What had she said? All that. She had told me about a tree being a woman diving head-first into the ground, its trunk her legs waving about in the sky . . . or had I read it in the diary? The thing is, I could somehow understand what she was getting at, in everything she said or wrote. It was wild but I didn't mind it and I did not find it any worse than the wild glare her brother fixed on me now.

Was his nose getting longer than it had once been? How pale his face. Gaunt. Rotha wasn't gaunt. She was plumper now. What had she called herself—a bun! Maybe the bun was worth mentioning to William. But I did not mention it. I didn't want to tell on Rotha. It wasn't herself thought she was a bun, as far as I could see. It was other people thinking it. Him. Her brother. Thinking of her as a stale auld . . . what had he said just now? Fragmented? Coming to bits. Falling into crumbs.

Well, Dixon?

No, Sir, I says. I don't find that your sister is talking in a discontinuous way or a fragmented manner or anything like that. She seems herself, I says to him. Only, I says, there is one thing—

What is it?

And I said, because I was still trying to figure out a mystery, Sir, only she mentioned that—I don't know quite how to say it, Sir, not meaning to give offense . . .

For heaven's sake, Dixon . . .

Well, Sir, only she mentioned that Mary and Charles Lamb have a child together, and I did wonder, I mean—their being brother and sister—

Oh! He waved his hand broad and drapey. Never mind young Emma, he says. That's right. Charles and Mary Lamb do have a little girl whom they have adopted. Emma Isola.

Oh I see, I says. That's all right then. So Miss Dorothy was right—but, Sir, she said as well that—well I think she said you and she had a child as well, and I wondered if perhaps she—I mean my mam tells me sometimes women who have had no bairns sort of pine for them when they get a bit older like, and—

You mean you thought Dorothy had made up an entire child out of thin air and called it our own?

He started to laugh then, a bit cruel like, and I felt ashamed and foolish so I curled up like a snail in my shell and he looked at me and took pity on me and said, Dixon, we had a little boy called Basil, and yes we had intended to be his guardians for a long time, and he was with us a while. Little

Basil Montague. Dorothy looked after him and taught him. But in the end, James, you'll understand, we wanted our travels to continue. Germany, in particular. We wanted so much to succeed in our German travels when we were young.

I said, Sir, what happened to Basil?

And he says, In the end, Dixon, we sent him back to his family. You needn't worry about my sister's sanity on that subject, for Basil was like a son to us, and Emma Isola is indeed a daughter to Charles and Mary Lamb. And about London, James, if you're sure you want to go with Dorothy, and if you keep an eye on her and watch for any decline in her spirit—here . . .

He wrote on a piece of paper and wrapped fifteen guineas in the paper and said the address on it was for more money if I needed it for the care of myself and his sister in London. He gave me a stout bag containing her medicine and said not to give her more than twenty drops at a time but make sure she swallowed at least ten if she suffered any agony or became clouded in her thinking or grew dark-willed or morose.

And for god's sake, he says, do not let Mary Lamb drag her down with her into the mad zone. You know what I mean. That woman is like quicksand.

Yes Sir, I says, and I tried to leave the question mark off. Because he had said similar things to me before and I wasn't sure what he meant that I should do.

fourteen

ROTHA WAS EXCITED ABOUT seeing her friend Mary Lamb.

She brushed her hat and got her bag ready in no time with a great bottle of tea and extra chops in case it took us more than the usual time to reach the city. And I spied that in her bag with her letter paper she tucked her red diary. I packed my own bag with some enjoyment. I only have a small satchel, mind, but it was a thrill for me to shake the crumbs out and gather the fewest possible things for a journey.

When we got to London everything was made of the same colour as a big grey pigeon, all the stones and lintels and chimneys everywhere had all pigeon colours and pigeons were everywhere, with the odd purple and gold glint and lots of commotion, and the noise! And she got very excited before we even reached Covent Garden where Mary Lamb lived at number twenty Russell Street right across from the Drury Lane theatre with its big pillars and archways making me feel very small and countrified.

Miss, I says, will I find my own lodgings once you get settled away with Miss Lamb?

But she says no, James, and she catches my sleeve. Her hand is tiny but as strong as it always was. She suddenly struck me as a strong creature while here I was feeling lost in the big city of a London far grander than Manchester. Once in the Lambs' house I felt even smaller for there were cavernous rooms and a smell of old books and mysterious scents I had not smelled at Rydal. Different and again old, like smells from a lost time. Ye know how when ye enter a new house you sniff all its scents at once like any wild creature must when it meets a new place. The rooms were shady and full of stuff. I wanted more light and I yearned to follow the lad cleaning our boots to ask him where I'd sleep instead of waiting for Rotha or Mary Lamb to tell me, for those two were so caught up in one another they forgot I was there, hanging about like an extra broom.

When my eyes got used to the shadows I saw the place was a shambles—and why was Mary Lamb not accompanied by her brother? I'd heard she needed Charles beside her at all times. But it turned out he had gone to see their editor about an essay he was trying to write on dreams and witches and fears in the night, then he was off to a prize fight and after that somewhere else. He could be gone for days.

I told myself not to stay surprised at Charles Lamb's absence, for even if people claim one thing—such as you shouldn't leave your sister alone lest she come to harm—you find gaps where their plans get forgotten and they hope it won't matter. Real time is made up of more hours than they thought at first. They imagine they have all the time in the

world. But then other hours they thought would be there get snatched away.

The state of the place!

It was as if a great windstorm had thrust its way through the windows and doors and left everything in eddies and heaps. Books, papers, cups, forks, knives and spoons lay tumbled all over the floor and the furniture, and some of the chairs were upside down. The curtains trailed over plants and chairs like someone had trailed a tablecloth behind them over the fields on the way to a storm-wrecked picnic. One of the upside-down chairs had a straitjacket thrown over one of its legs, and I remembered I had heard Charles Lamb often had to bundle his sister in just such a jacket and walk her down the street to the madhouse. Yet there was a feeling of excitement in the room as if we had come upon the middle of something thrilling going on. It was a colourful room and a room without men if you didn't count me, for Charles Lamb had left no trace of himself.

I tried sitting on a cushion that had cat hair all over it but as I sat I got half-frightened I was doing the wrong thing and I jumped back up as Rotha and Mary Lamb started in talking about their teeth. How finally Mr. Demergue could mercifully see them both, for Miss Lamb had decided to get hers done at the same time so she and Rotha would have the carnage seen to once and for all. I couldn't understand the faith they put in Mr. Demergue or in the whole procedure.

I'll have to have quite a few pulled out before he can put any false ones in, says Miss Lamb, but I don't mind that one

bit. In fact, I'm dying to have them out as their place in my mouth is a fetid swamp!

It will release me, says Rotha, from my torture of being between young and old. A nothing place.

Aye, says Miss Lamb. I well know that in-betwixt nowhere.

But surely you're already out of that place, says Rotha. For Miss Lamb was ten years older.

That's what you might think, says Mary Lamb. It's what anyone'd think, looking at my silver hair or my fat middle which has got quite fetching over the last while, I am sure. And the two of them laugh about fat. But you don't have to worry about that, says Miss Lamb, being thin as a key all your life!

That is changing, says Rotha. And no matter how like a key I am, I cannot open just any door. In this state that straddles young and old I can have no lover. Nor, unlike my brother, do I have a following of people fascinated by my wisdom.

Aye, says Miss Lamb. A woman between youth and age is treated like a half-stale loaf. Not tender enough to devour, not dry enough to be cast into a pudding. Perhaps there's mould on her and she'll be tossed out! Not fit to feed hens. But I warn you, my having ten years on you is no use. You might imagine a sixty-year-old woman as being held in high regard but you'd be mistaken. I am not listened to and I fear this will never change.

This silenced Rotha.

I could not help interrupting!

I says, Misses, may I say that my mam—a woman between the ages of your two selves—has told me that for a man to

listen to her there has to be no one conscious left in the room, not even a housefly.

This got them laughing.

For if there is a housefly, I says, he will heed that fly before he heeds her. And Mam says it doesn't matter how old or young you are.

Your mam has that right, says Mary Lamb.

But, I says, Mam also says a few men lack the caul over their brains and can hear what women say, and you have to watch who you speak to and not waste your breath with the deaf ones.

But James, Rotha says—how does your mother tell the difference between the caul-brained deaf and men who can hear?

Aye, says Miss Lamb—has your mam got eyes in the back of her head?

My mam's second sight is elsewhere, I says.

I didn't know if I should keep talking or was I saying too much. But the two glanced at me, waiting very eager like, so I went ahead—it is like a stone, I says. In Mam's throat. And it has an eye that can see through her skin and into the head of any man speaking. Even a whole room full of men. And she can tell who is cauled and stupid or who has ears that can hear a woman.

Mary Lamb chortled very satisfied at this. But Rotha went quiet and her eyes looked like a pair of holes, and she says, William used to be like that . . . I felt in my throat, whenever I voiced anything—no matter how astonishing—my brother was never disbelieving. He never tried to dismiss me, and now—

Now? says Miss Lamb with a callous catch in her voice.

I was not sure whether I admired Mary Lamb or feared her.

I remembered what William had said about my not letting her draw Rotha into madness. Something lived in her tone as well as in her words. I was afraid it might leap out of Miss Lamb and into Rotha so that by the time Rotha's teeth were fixed and we got back to Rydal, her brother might not recognize her and he would certainly blame me. For my mam says you have to watch who you spend time with because any kind of madness is a spirit that'll jump out of one person and pounce right into the one next to them before they can do a thing about it. It's not that the madness rubs off on you gradual like, it's more like it makes a wily leap to inhabit two people instead of one. I wondered if Rotha was already catching the madness off Miss Lamb. I suddenly felt a tiny bit worried for my own sanity at number twenty Russell Street, to tell ye the truth!

Where is your little girl? says Rotha.

She is no longer really my little girl, says Miss Lamb. She is my brother Charles's little girl when all is said and done. Charles's very special little pet.

Then Miss Lamb shouts out in a bloodcurdling voice the name of the girl who William had assured me was real.

Emma!

The way she screamed it! I might have lived in the workhouse and my mam might have drunk a river of gin and struggled through a sea of troubles but I never heard the like of shrieking from one room to another in the house the way Miss Lamb summoned Emma.

And in comes a person who I can't call a little girl, not really, with an animal in her arms that was neither cat nor dog. I couldn't tell what it was but I caught a whiff off it and nearly choked for it smelled of piss. It couldn't possibly have been the girl herself stinking like that. That much I knew or hoped. How old was she? Eleven or twelve? Not thirteen, surely? She was thin and sullen with hair like a torn nest yet womanly in some perilous way. Her pet animal was long and slinky and I could hardly take my eyes off it. I felt certain it could fly at me and sink its teeth in my throat. It had a body like an eel, muscled and tense. But no one mentioned it. They talked to the girl as if the horrible thing was not squirming in her arms. So I did my best to pretend I was not on the alert.

Something stole over Miss Lamb in the girl's presence—Rotha had promised me that if anyone in the world had more sympathy than Miss Lamb, she had not met them. For Mary Lamb, says Rotha, is the essence of sympathy and understands me like no other. And I remembered what William had said: Mary Lamb had a fault, and the fault was that she was quicksand into which other people's feelings sank. She couldn't help it—she sucked in everyone else's feelings until they were her own and she could never, in the end, contain all the feelings she'd swallowed. Which was why she went mad and had to be carted off until she came to her pure single self again, with one person's feelings inside her instead of all the woes and shadows of her world. And I saw it. Before the girl Emma came in, Miss Lamb was a sheltered body of ground into which all the rain in the world might fall and

bring forth untold blossoms. Her eyes held such a promise I nearly felt like telling her my own troubles.

But when Emma Isola entered the room something quick and dark and invisible strangled all that promise.

And the child in her turn looked very much as if she did not want to be there. In fact she kept her back to Miss Lamb and faced Rotha as if facing a warm hearth, with Miss Lamb a freezing blast at her back.

How are you, Pet? says Rotha.

Very well thank you, Miss Dorothy, says the child in a voice waxen as a lily.

How I wish, says Rotha, as if remembering something blown away and lost, I could have brought mine and William's little boy Basil.

I knew that Emma's meeting Basil was impossible given the years that had passed. According to William, he and Rotha had looked after Basil thirty years before! Yet Rotha says to Emma, you and Basil would have made fantastic playmates, then looks around her as if Basil would pop out if she looked sharp, for he was only playing a crafty game of hide-and-seek. I watched her eyes sharpen to needles, glancing all around the room that was so disorganized a small lad could hide in it pretty easily.

I'm dying to go outside, Rotha said and she started for the door. I tensed, being ready to keep an eye on her as William had charged me. I didn't want to let her out of my sight, not in London. I battled the feeling I had no say in the matter. I felt invisible. No one had shown me a cot or any place to

put my bag and I had no idea what my place was supposed to be, unlike at Rydal where all was certain.

Wait! says Mary Lamb.

I can't wait, Rotha says. We must be outside!

I know we must, says Miss Lamb, who hoists herself with some difficulty off her chair and stares at Emma Isola and then at me as if I hold a key.

And Emma, with her eyes welling up, says, Aren't I coming?

No, you're going to stay here with Mr. Dixon, says Miss Lamb to my consternation.

When I get concerned like that, over matters beyond my control, a boiling tide wants to poach my heart like an egg. I get paralyzed.

Show Mr. Dixon what a lovely reader you are, Miss Lamb says.

You promised to take me to the Arcade!

We'll bring you an éclair from Gunter's, says Miss Lamb.

I want to come!

I'll fetch your doll from Mrs. Carruthers's with its new clothes on. Mr. Dixon will look after you, won't you, Dixon?

Miss, I—

He'll slice you a tomato from the greenhouse . . .

No!

. . . and he'll listen while you read him a story—

I don't care about my stupid doll or its clothes! You promised I could have a magic glass! Mr. Dixon doesn't want a story read to him. He's only a stupid servant.

Oh, Emma, he's not, not really, says Rotha. He loves having stories read to him, and your mother and I will bring you an éclair and we will not bother about the doll. But Miss Lamb and I are dying to go on a meander by ourselves—

He *is* only a servant! And he's only a man! Look at him. He doesn't even want to look after me. And I am the only girl in London without a magic glass!

Be kind, Emma, Rotha says. Miss Lamb and I need to catch up on everything we have missed in each other's thoughts. Besides, whenever she and I ramble in the city we climb a great many steep lanes and stairs and—

I climb better than both of you!

But Miss Lamb and I speak to each other without saying anything out loud for ages.

I don't care!

You would be worn out at the end of an hour, begging us to stop and have cake, and it is much better for us to explore in pure freedom and bring you the cake back in its own lemon-coloured box with a silver ribbon you can trim for your hair. And this might be our only day, for tomorrow we have to have very painful things done at Mr. Demergue's and we will be convalescing. Don't you care about our one day of freedom?

No and I don't care one bit about my hair! Emma Isola buries her face in the urine-smelly animal and wails fit to crack the windows. I'm terrified that before I know it I'll be left alone with this child. How am I supposed to look after her? Rotha's the one I'm pledged to watch, and if she has

her way she'll be rampant down every crooked street and up staircases and down narrow hills, forever on and on in a maze of alleys unfolding 'til the lamps are lit and me unable to account for her whereabouts!

Very well, says Miss Lamb. Put the ferret in its cage and tell Bernice to dress you and we'll take you and Dixon. He can carry our bags and mind you while Dorothy and I catch up on all we have to say to each other. Mind, you leave us alone and walk behind us and don't interrupt or whinge, or you come straight home, Dixon will see to it. And for heaven's sake bring a book to entertain yourself and Dixon instead of your whining to come home any time before dusk. *My legs are tired! I'm thirsty! I'm bored!* None of that. Do you hear? One word and you're bound for home.

I DON'T GET DAZZLED VERY OFTEN but I got dazzled in London. I wish I could tell ye all that was said and done on our day traipsing through all the best parts—Rowland's for face cream and Lock's for a hat band and cherry wine at Rudd's all very fancy I couldn't believe it, imagine me in all those places!

I had to keep an eye on Rotha while at the same time never letting the child Emma out of my sight, for she wanted to pop down every alley and in every sweet-shop asking for this and that confit and never letting up about her magic glass that she wanted. And Rotha and Miss Lamb were

heads-together talking the whole time and whatever they said got the two of them more and more excited until Rotha trembled as if lightning ran through her.

And if ye want to know all that happened in London, Rotha wrote her version in the red book and I'm soon going to read it to ye as I promised. I am.

For I've already read it and I can understand it in part, but I cannot explain it to ye in my own words. Rotha's own words are that different from mine, they're a kind of wilderness or foreign country, and you'll have to forgive me if I don't do a very good job reading them to ye out loud, they are too strange. Though I promise I'll try. But I'll tell ye, Rotha's time in London with Mary Lamb started something up in her, it made her different. Or it sped up a change in her that'd been happening. And there was I saddled with the lass, Emma, and struggling to keep up with Rotha, the one I was supposed to mind. Ye can't mind everyone or everything, for people have their own minds.

Certainly Emma Isola did have her own mind and as we were all about to leave the Arcade she says to me, They are leaving without getting me the magic glass they promised! Sure enough there's Rotha's and Miss Lamb's heads together as one, going off into the street and what does the little fiend do but dig her nails in my wrist making my flesh white then purple and she won't let go until I stop those two ahead and ask them about the glass.

All right Dixon, says Miss Lamb, Dorothy and I will nip in and get her the promised kaleidoscope but we are not

taking her with us for she will make the matter last all day, turning this one and that one to test the colours.

There was a tea shop at the end of the Arcade with black-and-white tables and Miss Lamb told Emma to sit and read me the book she had brought while they went to get the thing.

Once they were gone off Emma Isola glares at me and grumbles, You don't want a story at all, do you?

I felt as awkward as the back corners of a cow. I had no clue what to say so I says tell me the story of your last name, what is it again? Though I well remembered what her name was, it being so strange.

So she says it's Isola.

I says is it really? I says that's unusual for a name isn't it?

Isola, she says with her serious face, means isolation, and isolation means—

I ken what isolation is, says I in a tone I hoped she wouldn't find gruff though I must say I did not enjoy such a small person telling me what a word means. I says to her, it means lonely, but you're only making that name up because they wouldn't let you go to the magic glass shop with them. That can't be a real name. I says this to her for a kind of taunt, for I figured she enjoyed having an argument. And now here you are lonely with me, I says, for I'm a stranger no doubt about it. But you don't have to worry, I won't make you read me a story or do anything you don't feel like—and you don't have to tell me your real name if you don't want to.

No, she says! Emma Isola is my real name. She likes being in the right and me being in the wrong. She gets comfortable

with that arrangement, and she says do you want me to read you *The Tempest* or *The Taming of the Shrew*?

I said aye, read me *The Tempest* if you can, but Shakespeare is a bit hard for one as young as you, is it not? I know it's very hard even for me! I was secretly proud that she did not have to tell me Shakespeare had written the stories. I have a habit of paying attention to everything at Rydal, and that includes the bookshelves. But Little Miss Lonely had to argue with me on that an' all.

No, she says, taking the book out of her pocket, *The Tempest* is one Miss Lamb wrote especially for children.

But look here lass, I says, you're having me on again. That's one of William Shakespeare's plays. I might be only a servant of Miss Wordsworth but you needn't make a mockery out of me. I do know a few things about books, having lived with the little family for so long.

No, she says, I'm not mocking you! Mary Lamb made Shakespeare's book into a new book for children.

And she gets a look on her face I can only describe as honest and straight as a baby crow. And I like it. Strong and dark, like, ye know how young crows look—they are never without their glare that can seem a bit frightful even in the youngest bird. And she thrusts the book at me, See? she says. *Tales from Shakespeare*, it says on the front, *by Charles Lamb*. Only never mind it saying Charles Lamb, she says quick as anything. Mary Lamb wrote *The Tempest*. Only they put his name on the front and not hers. She writes all the time but nobody knows. Everybody thinks her brother writes it all. She licked her thumb and found the page quite professional like, as if she

was my little teacher in our classroom, and I had to stifle a laugh for Emma Isola would have hated to be laughed at.

Be quiet! And she starts reading it out clear as a bell:

> There was a certain island in the sea, the only inhabitants of which were an old man, whose name was Prospero, and his daughter Miranda, a very beautiful young lady. She came to this island so young, that she had no memory of having seen any other human face than her father's. They lived in a cave—

See, she says? Easy as anything!

In a cave! I says.

Yes, she says, and wait 'til you hear about Prospero's magic books, and Caliban and Ariel and the storm—and she reads me the whole thing and by heaven I do understand every word of it, *full fathom five thy father lies*, and *where the bee sucks, there suck I*, and the pitiful monster Caliban who is a servant like me and whose mam is enchanted but even more so than my mam, a witch, even. And something in Emma Isola's voice makes me feel caught up in it in a wonderful manner. So by the time we're done here's Rotha and Miss Lamb back already with the magic glass. Here was I thinking it'd drag on worse than a day hoeing turnips in the sleet. She was a right lively lass, Emma Isola.

But she did not ooh or ah over her magic glass for long. Took a look in it but was then back to her normal self which was like a bird on the lookout for some new pip or worm or shiny beetle. The one who took up looking in the glass—

completely taken by it—was Rotha. The thing as I could make out had mirrors all down the insides, and coloured pieces of glass inside, and when you look through the tube and swivel the end towards the light, well, Rotha says, it is like looking through her wee botanical glass into a cowslip or bluebell or some other field enchantment, only in the kaleidoscope you aren't seeing the real flower chambers ye lot know about.

No, she says, I've fallen in the world of a thousand blooms unknown to anything but the imagination!

Ye couldn't drag it away from her, and in my mind that was a blessing, for the very next day was to be the day of Mr. Demergue going at her gums and teeth with his knife and pliers, and I knew that day would be a sore day for Rotha and for Mary Lamb and I was worried both would come back hurt—I've noticed many times that when a person goes under a knife or any big remedy that involves sawing bone, yes the body heals. If you're lucky. But what nobody tells you is you come home stooped and battered with part of your spirit cut away, a bit you might never find again. Or if you get it back it can take years and you'll have changed and the lost piece of you cannot catch up.

Rotha had put great hope in Mr. Demergue.

I'd heard my mam talk about getting her roof fixed with something like the same hope. When I get the roof properly done, Mam said, I'll not have to worry no more. The damp'll never get in!

It was as if damp had infected Mam's own being and she hoped a new roof would not only make her house high and

dry but would banish mould or mildew or damp from her legs and her whole body and from her spirit. And that is how Rotha and Miss Lamb talked about what it would be like once Mr. Demergue fixed their mouths.

When we arrived back at Russell Street from our day traipsing the streets, Miss Lamb gave Rotha a chamber with white curtains and ferns on the sill, and I was given a cot in a room that was tiny but clean.

I'll recover while reading, says Rotha. I'll look at Emma Isola's kaleidoscope. I'll meditate on leaf and shadow and half-light. I'll write.

Bernice has covered your chair by the window in white, says Miss Lamb, and washed the curtains. You'll be able to lie down and recall yourself, feel all your membranes and the organs they contain. Dixon will open the window to let air in and shift your pillows won't you, James?

I'm good at fixing pillows, I says. For when I turn a pillow it is cool and sits under a person's head in all the right ways.

Rotha shuddered like a child that has had its complaints heard.

You'll convalesce in shade, says Miss Lamb, and see no lurid day nor eat food you have had to prepare yourself. James will look after us—won't you, James—I can tell you are intelligent.

I hope I can be useful, ma'am, I says.

And, Rotha, says Miss Lamb, you will find rejuvenation and pass from the agony of lost youth into an older, exultant place.

ONLY THE NEXT EVENING WHEN the two came back from Demergue's I saw nowt but despair.

The corners of Rotha's mouth had dried blood-flecks—Demergue had not bothered to warm a cloth and bathe her face, which is what I did immediately after I led her to the bed. Miss Lamb had hardly more spark either as Bernice helped her upstairs. I would have liked at that moment to locate Demergue and remove his own teeth for him. The amount he had charged!

For the first couple of days I hardly knew what to do except bring Rotha broth I had Bernice simmer from lamb bones—I asked her to cook it 'til the gelatin was extracted and the broth glittered with marrowfat. For only bone repairs bone, and our jaw is the foundation of our talking. It's the jaw that sets flight to our words, and her words were what Rotha needed to find. I was frightened she'd never utter another word with that butchered mouth.

And the pain!

But she says James, I'm used to pain. I have known pain all my born days.

I let her sup the bone broth from a spoon I held, and I did not ask her anything.

We were quiet.

She looked through Emma Isola's kaleidoscope, or she opened her red diary and wrote. Penned in it the thoughts of her convalescence, this notebook I have here on the basket for ye now.

Aye, the diary was closer to her in London than I had ever seen it. She lay upon it like a hen protecting its one warm egg not yet devoured by the weasel.

5

After summer merrily

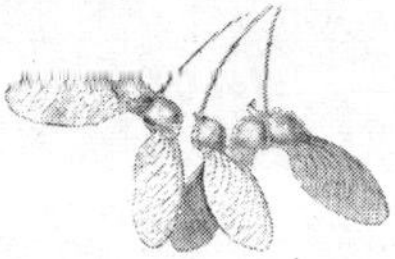

What can be more ordinary than my voice—wind through my branches, sap gurgling in my wood? Trees cover the earth, as common as stones! Inventors and poets scour their own minds for sparks of life, but Rotha perceived vitality in natural bodies. She knew life was a force no inventor can create, and even now her knowledge remains visible yet unseen, just as the word *real* indwells the word *realm*.

But invention! Progress! Machines to counterfeit myself, Sycamore, and other trees. Bee-sized apparitions to mimic bee work, humming and whirring ever faster, louder than Rotha's undersong of wind in wood, of fluttering wing, of hue atremble in corolla.

Common life will become uncommon. The ordinary will slip underground from whence it once flourished. Not dead, you understand, but in waiting.

fifteen

I WISH, JAMES, that I was a fairy, Rotha says to me, then I'd light on a leaf in your wheelbarrow and off we'd go to the fields and flowers and I could commune with our bees whilst you do your weeding and hoeing.

For by this time she was troubled often by her legs being what she called heavy as marble. Immobile. Every three or four days, like.

So I said Miss D, I can arrange a way for you to get around. For by now I was used to arranging many things for her. Anything you care to name, James Dixon could take care of it.

This was later, as ye know. I mean after London and then after the other time she tried going away to dig in. The last time of all. Digging in, she called it. Off to Whitwick to help William's son John set up his parsonage. And she lived with John alone, helped him write his talks, just like when she helped William with his poems at Dove Cottage. She was going to help John with his ideas. But the son's ears were parched as the father's! *Give me the goblet of your skull and I will drink my fill.* I saw her write that. John Wordsworth

drank from her mind as his father William had done until she fell very ill and had to come home, agony of the bowels and paralysis of the leg. And once she was sixty the family hardly understood what was going on with her at all. This understanding fell to myself and I did not find it hard. I deciphered things the others could not decipher or were not able to think about.

Dig in! I'm always digging for home, she says, and they couldn't understand it. You are home, said Mary and William. But I knew Rotha had no home.

What happened was I'd clean my barrow and haul Rotha to one spot one day and another the next. Always out of doors. And that's when she started making the maps. We covered miles. It looked to the others as if we were only going around the terraces like, but it was much farther. We were like ye—we flew. We revelled in ye and your ways and we saw things ye see. We always had. Not as clear as ye see, mind. I'm not saying that.

And she says remember, James, just treat the terraces and the distance you drag me around the lake, treat those yards like many miles. Every yard being a few miles. We're expanding space and time. We're making the most.

And I didn't know what she meant at first. Only that the terraces and the land outlying the house seemed to grow bigger in her mind than other people saw them.

Ye know what the terraces were to the Wordsworths when I first came to Rydal. Ye remember how I helped William build 'em, and they'd saunter, him and Rotha, up and down for hours, winding the miles. He wanted the ground carpeted

all mossy or lined with stones and the two of them trod from one end to the other, him composing, muttering, thinking out loud, and she writing down anything he said. She tried writing verses but—she despaired of hers amounting to anything. I am not a poet, she said. No. A different kind of word-making was hers. Aye they both traipsed the terraces in the old days.

And they wound their way along, down, up again, down, up, down—thread like a thread being wound on a bobbin. A gold thread making words. And a silver thread. Sun and moon. Night and day they wound. Frost and sun. Gold and silver. Light, moon, sun, frost.

Wind.

Ah, they wound, those two. Long time ago now. Winding round they wound the paths of the terraces. Up one end, up to the extreme last bit with its gooseberry bush and the plant that has leaves smelling like lemons, up to there and then they turned—like a pair of dancers—like the wheels in the cuckoo clock that so enchanted William. Ever whirring and turning. Wound, winding, sound, sighing, singing, thinking, composing, making. Their winding words. The winding thread. The terraces were the bobbins and on 'em they wound their words. William's in the poems everyone loves, Rotha's in her secret cocoon.

But now he was never with her like that. He was hardly outdoors at all.

We started off with my wheelbarrow and me giving her the few giddy rides in it until William says that has to stop, that is unseemly, my sister in a barrow, please. So I says to

him I'm sorry, it won't happen again, but would it be all right, Sir, if I built her a proper little cart?

Now look here, he says, we can't have my sister falling out of some contraption onto the ground. Her health! For he was very concerned about her bowels and her legs and her head and all the pain she felt, though whatever caused it was, he told me, a mystery.

I says Sir, you know me, I'll make sure Miss Dorothy is in no danger, will you leave it to me? And by this time William himself was past sixty for he's a year older than his sister, and he goes off and leaves my question hanging with neither a yes nor a no because he has a lot to do and his time is precious, so of course I maximize the situation and decide for everyone that the space between William's yes and his no is my own special place for me and Rotha.

Though her real place is she doesn't know where, for after London and then Whitwick she tries and tries to find it and cannot. No one has a spot for her in their plans. And they do not look at her writing any more. Oh she writes. She writes her Scottish book and makes copies and gives it to people and they claim to treasure it but I hear Mary Wordsworth tell their friends Mrs. Ellsworth and Mrs. Luff not to bother reading the whole thing. It has a bit, for instance, says Mary, about the flowers in a Scottish potato field! Those rustic insignificant flowers on a potato plant!

This is when ye lot perk up, isn't it. This is when ye remind me ye have been in on the story all along. Careful on me face!

Mary would go upstairs to Rotha's room and find her staring at the wall, or staring through more like it, that part

of the wall where the old window was concealed. Mary was perplexed, for Mary never gave a thought to that window.

Here, Dorothy, Mary says, a new book for you to read.

And Rotha says—Mary tells me this dumbfounded—she says Mary, I don't care to read. I need no new book, for I am busy with my own feelings. I'm on an edge.

Busy with her own feelings! Mary's astonished. On an edge! An edge of what?

And I fathom it better than Mary can, but all I says to Mary is, Mrs. Wordsworth, never mind, I'll take Miss Dorothy outside once the rain stops.

And Rotha won't need any book.

But I don't say that part.

The thing about being a servant is you can't let on you see something another member of the family is blind to. And we're funny blind things, people. Ye know that. Ye can see everything but we can see very little. For one thing, ye know about time past and time to come and together with the time we are in, it is for ye all one big golden day. It must be nice. I feel it as soon as I sniff ye'r honey, without a drop on my tongue.

Just the scent. It goes on forever. And that's where we'd go when I took Rotha outside in the little cart whenever the rain stopped. Out to your world.

Our faery phaeton she called it—our rude phaeton, its wheels my liberty—and you, James, my trusty steed.

Ye know our little cart. Ye've seen us traipse the land, me at the helm and Rotha alighting among your flowers. Really

your flowers lit on her, aye, dangling on her lap and falling round her shoulders like a garland for the queen of the fairies.

For she was to me a queen as your queen is to ye.

Was it spring of 1830 I built it? I know the year numbers mean nowt to ye. It was spring for we were coming out of the usual lingering sleet and dark. I modelled it on a rough but fairy-like cart she saw a tinker ride with his lass and his pots when she was still walking the roads herself forever on the move. I scrounged the wheels and various bits—the biggest job was only a matter of changing a fixed axle to a mobile one and it meant whittling a knob and reaming a nice deep groove so it'd hold over the rough bits of the terraces. But as it is with any common task that takes half an hour, you might go a week before you get a chance to do it, what with one thing and another demanding your attention. William had been all week trying desperately to write a poem about spring to send to his friend Bob Southey for inspection and he wanted to go through Rotha's notebooks to see what she had written about it first.

My sister has a rough way, he says to me, you can get a grip on that roughness like you would grip a well-knotted rope and clamber up it and spy the view she has—it's like the view I had a long, long time ago. When I was a youth, he says. Before I was even fifteen. Aye, I had what she has then. He says this with a kind of rage and his bad eye watered and his face went mottled like it gets when his head is killing him. Robert Southey is waiting for the poem, he says. Robert Southey was still the laureate that spring and William was

practising for when his turn came around. Every year the laureate is supposed to come up with something for the King and William had an awful time getting anything ready by a certain date. He found it was torture. I was still helping him find in Rotha's notebooks the things she had written that might suit him, for by then I knew where everything was in her notes. When you have always done something for a man, done it for years, how can you deny him? Even if you feel awkward about it.

But once I had William satisfied do ye think I could nip to my hut to fix Rotha's cart? No! Because all hell is breaking loose over a bloody chicken. Sometimes I felt like I was in a madhouse. No sooner am I clear of William than Mary Wordsworth needs me to help her get something off her chest about the same chicken she's been on about all the day before. Of all the family, Mary is the stable one. But I knew this made her wild inside with things she'd never mention to William. Instead she'd tell me. I have always been different things to different people in the family, and for Mary I have been a bare corner where she could unload burdens the others never suspected she was tired of carrying.

All Dorothy wants, says Mary, is more food! All last week asking for a whole chicken to be roasted only for herself! A whole chicken! For one small woman! No wonder she's getting fat. And she wants a fire in her room and will want it stoked through the middle of July. Mayflowers will pass. Daffodils will have come and gone. Bluebells will be here. Cows making butter unlimited! And all Dorothy wants is fire in the grate. A hundred degrees in her room, nobody can

breathe in it. Or she wants fried fish. Or porridge with butter in a molten puddle. She wants new knitting needles but never knits! You should see how much she ate last night, James—no wonder she has problems with her bowels. Then somebody has to clean up after her and who is that somebody? Not that I mind one little bit. Never will I be said to have minded! But mind you, she says, Dorothy with that chicken—it is pure greed.

I said to myself—not out loud—I says no, I don't think that's what it is at all.

The chicken was plump and studded wi' herbs all right, a gorgeous crackling skin—The smell of it filled the house and was tantalizing. I'd have devoured it alone in my hut and it wouldn't have taken me long either. It had fat little legs on it and crisped wings, and Mary knows as well as I do how smashing it is to fall on a well-browned wing and gnaw the crackling and the shreds of meat off it and wash it down with tea or cold, clear water.

I says to Mary I says it is true Miss Dorothy did devour it . . . I stifled a chortle to myself over Rotha's enjoyment of it—like a wolf. A real wild animal she was, feasting on that crisp and fragrant bird.

But, says Mary, it's not the way she devoured it that mystifies me. It's how she went on about wanting it all week until I couldn't stand talk of it anymore and had to get you, James, to go have Tom Sharp slaughter the thing. And no, it wasn't good enough we should share it—me, William, Dora or any of us—as I know how to stretch a chicken dinner amongst company.

I know you do, Ma'am.

Add a few parsnips, the last couple of sausages from Ambleside, Mary says. But no, Dorothy wants that chicken. For my own self, she says. What sort of desire is that, and William going right along with it? Everyone going along with her strange desires, day in and day out?

I mean, I'd hardly call that true. I would call that one of Mary Wordsworth's fantasies—we all have our illusions and I might say that one of Mary's is a perpetual notion of Rotha as a gaping scream. A loud demand. A clamour for more—the kind of lament you hear from one of the trapped hares on the mountain at night. The hunter far off asleep. The trap digging into the creature's foot so it can't move yet it won't die. No wonder the lament can never stop but for one thing alone.

Aye, Mary says, all Rotha wants is more food. But me, I say all she wants is human touch.

Aye. Ye look at somebody ye know over the minutes and hours and days and weeks and years and decades and ye look at how much human touch they're given. And eh, Rotha's little dog, Little Miss Belle . . . that dog clung close to her ankles every time she wrote. The dog knew she was writing. The dog knew that was when its mistress needed a warm body touching her skin, and the dog provided that, didn't it. Now the dog never clung. It wasn't a clinging dog. But it pressed itself against her ankles. She told me this. She laughed. She giggled like a girl and she said, I feel the dog's hot body against my skin as I write. It's lovely, oh it's lovely. And I had an eye on that.

Eating a whole chicken, well that's one way of having another hot body press against your skin from the inside, isn't it. And that's your throat. The ankles and the throat—the dog and the food. And then the fire she wanted. Never warm enough. Never often enough, the fire. The warm body of the wood with the sun's borrowed radiance as she called it. In the flames.

Aye, a warm touch. I could not provide that, other than the few times our little cart broke down. And I took her in my arms. Aye, I did. She weighed, even when she was plumper at the end, not very much more than—than a bird! I mean 'course she weighed more than a bird but, felt like, aye it felt to me like carrying a plump little bird that . . . sank into my embrace. Oh how she sank into my arms as I carried her. And she'd drape an arm over my embrace and gather a mugwort or henbane or a lovely little—sometimes we'd stop and I'd help her pick a rose without getting pricked. Or an iris. Oh she loved to gather blooms when she was in me arms and together we'd carry them home. Ha like a little bride and groom. Aye, I loved that. I loved it . . . I loved helping her to feel . . . cradled . . . Did she write about that? I had no way of knowing unless I looked for myself in her diary. Oh you look for yourself, don't you. You have a glance, looking for your name.

As for that roast chicken, just burstin' with lovely gold juices. The aroma alone set my mouth to watering an' all, I tell ye. You could not fault Rotha for getting enthusiastic about it. Even so, the mouthwatering appetizing part of it wasn't the real nourishment it gave her. No. It wasn't until

we were well into our travels in the phaeton that she told me what it meant.

It was all about the little maps. All the places she had travelled with William and Sam Coleridge on foot or in their own outlandish cart that people scoffed at all over Scotland. Draw me a pair of Scottish maps, she says to me, and we'll affix them to the inside of our cart. Each map had a key on it that she labelled Our Legend. I made one for the lowlands and another for the highlands. She'd pencil in the names of all the lochs and mountain horse-paths and trackless heaths, the castles or any inn where they'd stayed the night. No more than caves, some places they'd stayed, moonlight shining on the dripping roof like melted gems.

And here, she says, draw in the Trossachs, the hills around this lake called Ketterine—Coleridge and I were faint with hunger—look, here is where our boatman put us into a tub so leaky his wife had to ladle the water out—William was so nervous that when we got down the bay he stood up near shore and dropped our food bundle in the water! Spoiled the sugar and the coffee and the pepper-cake—but our roast fowls were intact! Sam and I fell upon them faint with hunger. How I've craved a roast chicken like those ever since, but nothing ever compares with our roast fowls in sauce made of the lake! William had run off—he explored the coast without us . . . Here . . . sketch the heather I stumbled through running after him. I found him sitting alone on a hilltop . . . Here she faltered.

Miss, I says, perhaps it's too much . . . these maps, remembering. You know how good you are at remembering. You

take yourself right back there again. I never said *right back running after William.* But I was thinking it. Always running after the one she loved, with Sam Coleridge not far behind. The three of them. And now with our maps she did it all again, through memory, like, and I was her horse. I dragged her wherever she wanted to go and we kept the maps up to date with each new journey we made. The rest of the family thought we never went beyond Rydal.

Thunder cracked her open as if she were sky. I saw it from the time she told me about William jumping ship. Thunder affected her as if it might kill her but then it did the opposite.

I've seen many an animal killed by lightning but there are some creatures that come to life after a thunderstorm strikes them. A pony my uncle Jim had revived itself after lightning struck it down and lived to be twice the age of any normal horse. He changed its name after that, from Blackie to Flash. I remember Flash being a lovely pony with one star glinting in her deep eye and I kept wishing lightning would come near her again, for Uncle Jim says to me son, if it happens again she'll sprout wings!

And thunder knew Rotha. It was forty years since she'd loved Coleridge under the winter boughs if you go by a calendar, but thunder and lightning know no time, like ye yourselves. Thunder told her Sam Coleridge was dying. She was out in our phaeton as lightning flared over Nab Scar. She went rigid with its white light and would not take shelter.

I cannot come inside! she says. I must feel it.

And up she stands in the phaeton, rain running down her face and soaking her clothes. William would be very angry.

Mary an' all, if they knew I let that happen. Three days that was, before the death of her beloved Sam. And when the letter came to say Sam had died, she had already felt him go, standing in our wild little cart in the wind and rain, the thunder crashing through our bodies like a nightmare. Only it was day. Her new kind of day where she's busy with all her feelings and the day crashes into her, full wind and rain.

She was the one that noticed the little gateways. All of a sudden on our rides around the terraces there'd be little gateways everywhere. She was the one—is that right? Or was it me that noticed first? Aye, I might have said it to her because I'm used to—with the rabbit snares—finding tiny—not human-sized but rabbit-sized gateways, and after that, other little ones that all the animals make. I noticed—aye—one in the reeds. Them big reeds that grow tall. People don't like them, frightened the reeds will choke small plants. But I like the way they whisper, and sometimes an animal will have gone in before you and made a—trod down a little area.

Yes it was one of them, leading down to the lake. I says, come on, Miss, look at this.

She says aye, it's a little gateway. And in we went. Yes that's it. I found the thing and she called it by the name.

And ye'll remember yourselves—that was when she stopped caring about all that went on *inside* the house. Stopped forever.

Aye, I don't think most people know about the little gateways. Once you go through them . . .

Rotha kept her microscope in a pocket at all times and let me look through it to see what she saw and what ye see

when ye go in the chambers of your blooms. Ah, she needed to read no book! Needed to write, yes. Not read.

She wrote plant names in a guidebook she had and started coming to see ye with her reports of where and when they bloomed. Heckberry! Crab blossom! Anemone! Speedwell! Aye they sped well, our four wheels. Only around the terraces mind, but on our map she covered all her old ground. Our map signified not only Grasmere and Rydal but all the ground she'd once trod with William and Sam. Helm Crag, Stone Arthur, Nab Scar, Loughrigg, Elter Water, Ambleside and up Kirkstone Pass—Geraniums! Gowans! Little star plants with no flowers, or flowers that only opened under the stars like white lights in the darkness leading their way home. Her and William and Sam. Rotha still surefooted as a goat.

I took her back to all that in our little cart.

She nearly forgot I was not William.

The gateways everywhere. We searched high and low. Here under the willows or there in the grasses. There'd be a gateway in the sycamores or in the rocks themselves.

She noticed any tiny difference in sound. I saw well enough but she heard an' all. I mean ye can hear it now, the wind in those reeds, listen . . . (wind sound, whispering reeds)

Aye, that was music to her ears. She loved that. Loved it if a natural sound gently overcame all the other sounds of the village . . . of someone hammerin' and workmen bellowing to each other about a step they were digging, or even William's din . . . he could make a racket when he was working on the terraces. She couldn't abide his mallet on the stone. We'd go through the little gateways and the rushes and

leaves softened all other sounds and she would become very peaceful.

Then she'd lie against my shoulder like somebody who—aye like a lass who'd—might I say gone to sleep on the breast of its mother? No. I was still a youngish man in my thirties and she old enough to be me own mam, yet . . .

Aye, in the phaeton we travelled, didn't we, through gateways. All through those late years she called down to me from her bedroom, and out we ventured in the wagon. Into a world far deeper than her brother's.

She'd tell me, Look, James, at that ash tree! Each of its leaves is a lantern. And look how each pendulous lantern is lit! Oh, James. And she'd get out of the cart and we'd run to it. Just her and me.

The others indoors. And she had no need of a cart then.

I had a wisp of Mam's magic in me, and I had my ears, with which I have listened to the wind and to ye and to Rotha through my faithful years. So I knew me and Rotha were in the world between worlds that I had always felt to be just out of grasp. Through her, standing there, our phaeton like something out of a fairy tale with the light catching its ordinary wooden wheels yet changing them—I saw her lamps lit throughout the ash tree.

But after a moment—not even a moment—the blaze faded and she said, crumpled like, so I had to catch her and seat her in the cart propped up by an old cushion, she said that's it, James—it has left us.

In clock-time indoors people saw her in agony, in her bed, trapped in a terrible state of mind. But ye know pollen!

Each golden speck seems as dust to the ordinary eye . . . yet any pinpoint of golden time I had with her in the cart went on forever for us just as pollen does for ye.

That's where my little cart took her and I was careful to keep its wheels oiled and the planks sanded for whenever she wanted to come outside.

No matter that once I'd drag her home and park it against the back of my hut, our cart looked for all the world no more elegant than a barrow with a board for a bench.

sixteen

AND WHAT ARE WE GOING to do with ourselves now she's gone, me an' ye lot? Ye bees and all the glory that surrounds ye?

And Mary.

Aye, Mary, alone on the stairs after they laid the body out. Ever alone, that one. A space around herself at all times.

Did ye know—ye must've—we all did—what Mary really was?

Aye, William's biggest poem of all, the daffodil one. Saying he wandered lonely as a cloud . . . yet he was with Rotha when they saw all the golden daffodils. I've told ye Rotha saw them first. And Rotha first wrote their glory, William used her eyes for his poem and her eyes were all he needed but for one detail.

The best line of all . . . where the great poet lies on his couch remembering the golden glory . . . William couldn't figure out how to write that part. How you hold onto a vision after it has gone. Rotha had no trouble letting it fly free. She never tried to capture it! But William would grope. Oh it drove him nearly insane.

How do visions work? William asked the fireplace. It did not answer.

But Mary, sewing in the corner, keeping quiet until she could hold it no more, the missing line growing bigger inside her till it burst forth—*They flash upon that inward eye which is the bliss of solitude!*

Aye, we all knew Mary made up the wisest line her husband ever wrote.

For solitude was what our wife Mary knew more than any of us! Yet she was content in hers.

Mary is that rare self-sufficient person.

And this morning on the landing Mary says to me, James, now that Dorothy has died, don't worry about losing your position with us.

Us, she says to me. As if anyone but herself remained.

And I minded how Mary had said those same words to me when William died five years before. John Carter had made no bones telling me there was only enough money to keep either myself or William's horse. And that horse was a favourite with Mary for it had known William well and Mary stood for a long time with her face against that horse's head after William's death. I nearly said, Mary, don't fret, keep William's horse. I can always find a job don't you worry. But I still had Rotha to think of then. So I said nowt and I stayed, and Mary did have to say goodbye to that horse.

But now this morning of Rotha's own death when Mary says to me, James, you have been faithful to us and I will be faithful to you, I says to her, I'm not a bit worried, Mrs.

Wordsworth. For as you know, I am here at your service if you need me, but only then.

And she looks right into me and I understand her as I have always understood Mary. I have always heard her as I have always listened to everyone here at Rydal and she knows that. Oh, she's a lone one, that one.

Sometimes ideas are struggling to be born. An idea thriving in one place is mebbe something everybody there has known about for ages. And somewhere else, not far away, that same idea or mebbe a similar idea is behind a membrane having a very hard time being able to pierce through, struggling for its life. Aye, I think all of life is like that, ideas struggling to be born. Oh the difficulty they have. And the stillborn ideas, and the maimed ideas, beautiful they would've been had they had a chance to beak or claw or scratch their way through that membrane and burst into full life . . . Mary Wordsworth!

I mean Mary was never one for gallivanting but she wanted to see people. She was not a pondering person. Not a person that needed to write poetry unless her husband was having an emergency. If it were left to Mary, Rydal Mount would be the most temperate and peaceful place on this earth.

But I cannot stay with Mary.

And neither will ye, my lovelies. Aye, I'll read ye the red diary now, today, before we leave, ye and me. And we'll do the thing that I promised Rotha I would do, at the last.

For she reckoned I'd been peeping in it—when I got the chance—I had to peep in the red diary to see if she had put down anything we did together or thought together. I was anxious for it, looking for the story of myself—myself

counting—in the whole story of the little family. My place in it. I kept leafing through the new bits looking for myself. As if Rotha Wordsworth would write about the likes of James Dixon. But I kept hoping.

One day she mentioned our little gateways!

Little gateways made of light
Naught of darkness told
Ephemeral Continuum
Inscribed with dust of gold—

And on the very day I read that part—I had been trying to find a time to confess to her that I had stumbled upon her book—but didn't she catch me holding it lovingly in my hands reading that verse over and over again!

Do you like my couplets, then, James?

She stood over me having moved soundless on her small feet.

I had warned myself about the soundlessness of those little feet. They could steal up on a fly or a midge or even a thrush. Not one of ye, mind. Ye'd know. She weighs no more than seven stone but she's spent that much time among ye I think she turned into one of ye at times, weighing no more than a bee herself. Going about on small wings like yours from here to there, now plunged in speedwell, now in the crab blossom, now in celandine—

Oh I felt terrible. A crawl of pure shame singed up from my chest to my neck over my face and closed around my scalp like a fish net closing over a fat trout that was my own stupid

head with a big innocent grin on it like, as if she could count on me to be both a dunce and a deceiver. Well I never felt so ashamed in all my life. I might as well have never abstained from drink, only become the village drunk. I would rather in that moment have been anything and anybody but James Dixon, faithful deceiver of Dorothy Wordsworth.

Well? she says—do you?

Bravado was not in me and I never said a word of an excuse for I had no such thing prepared. I knew I was found out.

But Rotha doesn't calculate things the way other people do.

It's all right, James, she says. No need for you to play rigid rabbit. What you've read can't be unread. But tell me, James . . .

She was struggling and I do not want to admit I felt some small power surge up in me like a blade.

Sometimes you cannot help feelings that arise in you. My mam said that. You can't help the feelings, the only thing you can do is watch yourself in how you act.

Quiet, I have discovered, is a good weapon against your own worst self. It feels like a useless thing but it is very useful. I keep a little piece of quiet folded up in my back pocket. I know that with it I have wiped away quite a few of my own mistakes before they spilled over the whole of my world and spoiled it.

I didn't make up the little couplets, you know, she says.

Didn't you? I leapt gentle as I could upon this topic—where she came up with her secret words—instead of the topic of why I was anywhere near them.

They came to me of their own will, she says.

I remained quiet.

Sometimes it works, she said, and sometimes it doesn't. Listening. Knowing which message is of freedom and which issues from the prison of my own smallness. That is why this book is secret. Only in this book do I dare write my own sorrows. Might you read some of it out loud to me, James?

Out loud, Miss?

What about this part? She took the book from me and found a section and handed it back, open.

I tried to argue but she says no, go on. I need to know how it sounds in the mouth of another person. For when William hears me speak in the way of the red diary, he warns me that I might yet join poor Mary Lamb. That I am mentally unwell. So read to me, please. I want to hear how it sounds, myself, with fresh ears.

So I says, Miss, don't mind my nose down in the book and my not looking up, for that is how I have to read, slower than you would do it yourself.

But she says never mind slow, James—I know my handwriting is bad. Read this part about the tree roots—

And I read a bit about roots reaching out like hands, but not reaching for her. There was nothing in their hands for her—and she says, Do you know what I mean by that, James? Do you?

And I says I think so, Miss. I've often felt the roots of trees were a bit like hands myself.

And she says go on then.

And I read as smooth as I could, like. She's right, her writing is slanted and squashed and some of her lines are like string pulled nearly straight with only a few kinks for letters.

I do the best I can and after I finish she says to me, Do you see? How a tree plunges its roots—her roots—like arms into the earth and her beautiful head is underground, and her trunk splits in two as her legs reach into the sky. The tree is an upside-down woman. Head buried in moss, James. Legs flung up like limbs of a great, petrified acrobat! Ears under the ground, unhearing. Mouth underground, unspeaking. One with that tree, James, I have heartwood instead of a human heart and there's nothing I can do to make it flesh. And now you've read it.

I have done, Miss, I'm sorry . . .

Stop it. What do you think? Do you think, as my brother does, that I need a few more drops of medicine?

How would ye lot have replied?

Look down the bank will ye—pieces of ice are floating past us on the lake. The water isn't disturbed enough to wrinkle, only ripple in spots—halves of circles colliding soft on a misty mirror—a mirror with polish smeared on it but no one's wiped the polish off yet with a cloth. Everything soft grey except the reeds, and they're that quiet gold. And snowflakes floatin'. And the old gold grasses bowed and swaying and all the leaves brown as dead mice.

Miss, I says, I'm not the one who'd know if you need more medicine.

No, she says, I suppose you're not. But you have known me a long time.

Aye, Miss, I says, I have. And I wondered then how many more rides in the cart we'd have, though I said nothing about that.

We've eaten quite a few blackberries together by now, you and me, she says. And drunk the juice.

Aye, Miss.

I had wiped purple dribbles off both our chins with my hanky.

Have ye ever eaten a purply-black bursting-with-sunshine blackberry sticking through somebody's fence? Have ye ever—o'course ye have! Ye lot feast and slurp on 'em, I've seen ye with my own eyes. Quaffing blackberry wine with the fairies! And so did we, Rotha and me over the summers. We grew hungry and thirsty with wandering and that's what we ate and drank.

Blackberry is made of a sky dull and leaden but cracking with lightning. A berry like that knows the flight of swallows and robins that've fledged then grown up near the bush—the berry only comes out once the robin has grown and learned its song. All that song and all that lightning and all that blackness and all that rich redness of the robin's breast is in that berry and ye know it—and Rotha did an' all. But more than only taste, she'd look in each drupe of that berry, the little mirrors . . . they were little mirrors, this is the thing. And Rotha knew they were gems. She was a gem-seer.

William and Rotha were once twins inside your world.

Ye'd think nobody like me could get in there. Really, I never thought I would.

It was well-brambled. It was hidden. It was secured from anyone that can't understand, but ye understand. Ye were born inside the columbines. Ye were born between the layers of the leeks. Ye were born in the bluest wings of the blackest bird . . . Ye know. Ye know the land where Rotha lived.

And her brother saw it. William. He knew where she lived, but some people see a thing and they can't abandon themselves to it. They're not wild enough. He wasn't wild enough. Aye, she was never tamed. He had the church. He went to church and so did Mary, but she couldn't. Now why couldn't she? The pain. Oh but the pain was not only medical pain. The pain was a thorny barricade that prevented her from entering the tame world. She wanted William to go the whole distance into the wild land but—he had a grain of caution, didn't he. He was the one that had the grain of caution.

But me—what would I be doing with caution?

Here's the diary, look—she stitched it herself like all her notebooks. The thing is, now like, I've got to do the right thing by this red one, haven't I. You can't just leave it lying around. Her other ones—with their shopping lists for this and that—sewing needles, special ingredients for the custard and bits of material to lengthen the curtains in the room downstairs, and on and on. A mustard spoon, all listed, and, heh, lovely bits and pieces of her day. Then they flip to her real song . . . or pieces of her song like bits of bread along the path or notes you hear of a bird's song. In all her tattered books she's scattering crumbs or taking down the notes from birds' throats as they sing. She's not changing the notes into

anything. They're the plain wild notes. And in those books there is no Dorothy. There is hardly ever an *I*. But the red diary is not like that . . .

Here ye go. Here it is . . . I will read it to ye because she asked me to read it out loud in the fresh air after she was gone. All her feelings. Disperse them out of doors once and for all, she says to me. And I'm here to not only read it to ye now, but to do the other thing she asked an' all.

Aye, ye lot won't be long here at Rydal and nor will I, not without Rotha.

Mary will not want ye in the sycamore without Rotha and Dixon to keep ye happy, to tell ye things, to tend ye.

I'm going to be gentle and I'm going to take ye with me. I promise ye that. And if a few wisps of smoke come in it's only me doing as Rotha wanted, ye understand. I'll smoke ye but I won't use much. Every one of her pages I'm about to read to ye now, I'll light each one and I'll blow the smoke in your hollow.

Don't mind it! I'll never harm ye.

I'm only burning the red diary as Rotha begged, for its ashes to fly with all her feelings to where only ye'll find them.

I've put a comb of your honey in my skep and ye'll be safe when the smoke comes in your sycamore, just crawl out into the skep and it'll hold ye.

I'll wait here for every one of ye. I'll wait here for your queen as I waited on my own queen all these years. And off we'll go.

Our wife Mary won't pay no mind and there'll be no harm to ye. For Mary won't be much longer following the

dead and then, aye, it'll be strange coming back to visit the little churchyard in Grasmere once I'm the only one left of the fam'ly.

Do ye know the first thing I'll buy with my railroad shares? A railing to place 'round the Wordsworth gravestones. So no one will disturb them, only lichen and moss. I'll bring my flask of tea and I will think about them and all the time we had together. And there'll be lots of visitors like that big spider with yellow stripes, look. Rooks and thrushes and the flowers she loved, and the church bells ringing.

And us.

Rest in peace they say and yes, she'll love that. Hated any hustle unless at the fair like. Oh she loved that all right, hawkers and the pie man, horse traders, lasses and lads at play. As long as she had only to nod to gypsies and children. None of the stifling talk regular people get on with. And she'd say after an hour, James, I've had enough! Take me home into the quietude. As if she was saying let's go to the willows where the cold moon shines. Or bulrushes where a duck might hide. Away from all glare or noise.

Aye, quietude. She said that word so many times it was like a brooch on her breast.

It's daft me talking about the fair in January isn't it. The wind's blown me hat right off. Hang on while I nab it—rolling like a wheel! That's 'im. Aye, the fair's nice. Summer's fine. But Rotha always loved frost and a cold moon. Not another soul about. Under frost glittering on the bare branches. She loved a winter tree.

The little family. Have they left each other desolate?

They tried not to. They tried, each one of them, not to abandon each other.

What will I do with the cloak William dropped in the grass the very first time I laid eyes on him and Rotha? He never knew I kept it. It was a dandy cloak then, but it's threadbare now. It's in shreds! I have it yet in my hut, wrapping up some of the tender bulbs all winter to keep them alive. Would ye like me to wrap our basket in it when we go?

When you see somebody for the first time and you're nowt but five and she's a white moth—away on the wind she flies after her brother, who has left his cloak on the grass in his big rush to meet the mail coach . . .

And you pick that coat up even though your mam says Eh, you shouldn't, but of course she doesn't stop you, your mam can't help but be a bit proud of your nabbing the cloak . . .

I had it for a blanket for a long time.

The red satin lining was the be-all and end-all in finery as far as I was concerned, even if it had been mended twenty times by the time William left it on the ground. Rotha was the one who mended it for him. She mended his everything.

And I never forgot that later day in Lady Wood, with the mushrooms and the blue flowers. She was still young and quick then, and yet so sad.

He had three fairies looking after him, didn't he. He had Mary and her sister Sarah and he had Rotha. People talked. How pampered he was. But he was the one who wrote, *The world is too much with us*—that was one poem he managed to write all by himself! *Getting and spending, we lay waste our powers*. That's what powerful people do with their powers

isn't it. Lay them waste. *Little we see in Nature that is ours.* That was his tragedy and we all knew it, and I wouldn't want anybody to think that I hold it against him.

His life was a sacrifice.

For Dorothy held the keys to the kingdom.

Oh, Lady, you held the keys.

Hang on, let's see if her pages will catch . . . I'll try one from the end with nothing on it, only a bit of blotted ink with the word *William* shining through—that's 'im—aye! The ash floats all right, just like that white moth she was on the first day I saw her. And now let me read ye the red diary before we leave Rydal. I've told ye a few bits, now here's the rest.

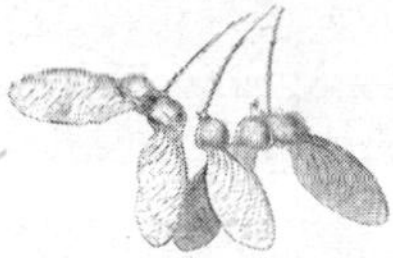

Motes, ash, softness. Dorothy's word transmute into these, her private pages dissolve and disperse in the air—no one to know them now but myself, Sycamore, and Rydal's bees, riding the wind.

Do you burn the pages because her voice is strange, James? Too strange for human ears and eyes? Is that what you fear?

Can that be the moon floating up already, while it is yet daylight? See how it hangs, caught in my top limbs, even before the sun has gone? Time!

Time is both late and soon, my friend James. Dorothy's death-day is growing late, and the sparks that will soon undo her pages burn with a strange, intense gold.

Her strangeness is my home.

Dispersal—as you know, James—is not disappearance. There was nothing dissoluble about our Rotha! *The naked seed pods shiver*, she wrote. *The pine trees rock from their base.* Comfortless was her world. Would you erase this truth? Innocent child, James Dixon, fulfilling the will of the enchanted housemaster.

Would you like me to say now, like the god of St. Oswald's, *Well done, thou good and faithful servant . . .*

Quietly, stoically
standing by
to pick up the pieces
as they fly . . .

For you were with the little household all along, weren't you, James, making things run as smoothly as humanly possible. While the others imagined that they did everything by themselves. Their imaginations were always the important thing.

But the truth I know is a stranger one. As strange as Dorothy's unspoken words.

All right, then, James. Speak Dorothy's words now, and set your fire to her pages. We in the garden will hold her feelings far beyond Rydal's years, into an age you cannot see.

I, Sycamore, feel the people listening even now, in the gold span outside our little day.

6

THE RED DIARY

Wm said no & I believed him. I wrote my recollections of Scotland five times by my own hand . . . & I fixed it up—oh—finding the memories & placing them in the correct locations . . . that was a monumental task. I mean I worked hundreds & hundreds of hours on it.

I never said it was for anybody other than our friends. It was not myself that contemplated publication. Was it?

But—I was asked . . . & I—I've always been the same as Wm & Sam—me on my rock & Wm on his & Sam Coleridge lying on the grass between us with a blade of hay in his mouth, chewing on it & thinking, & all of us thinking. All of us thinking with one mind.

All the same.

That was the promise.

It was the promise I was given: when Mary Wordsworth came it would not change—Wm & Sam & I were all one & the same. We were The Concern.

We were the same.

I was not different.

I did not marry a man & become a wife. That was the promise. I would not become anyone's wife. I would keep writing.

. . . & writing, & writing. So when I asked Wm . . . when I said I'd been invited to publish, it took a long time for me to realize—Wm was trying to find something to say, some reason why I shouldn't. I mean, he'd promised, had he not. We were all one & the same mind.

You won't like it, he said.

The limelight. You'll hate it. You, my dear Sister, who likes so much to hide in solitude. You'll wilt, he said, he the one that wrapped himself up in blankets & hid in the bottom of a boat. He the one that sequestered himself away in the terraces. He the one that wore that black cloak with the red lining—& wrapped himself up in it to be invisible in the night. He the one that groaned if Little Miss Belle barked for it meant unexpected visitors. People coming to see him. Gawk at me, he'd say. Watch me & look at me. I always

thought, if somebody wants to hide themselves, they will do it. No one needs to be encouraged into quietness. He had me convinced that writing & being a published writer were two different things. The first was all right but the second, he claimed he wanted nothing more in this world than to protect me from it.

That's the funny thing—it stopped my argument. For claiming no need of protection meant wanting. Wanting more. Wanting readers. Wanting what Wm had. There was a very dark, raven-like aspect to my brother that forbade my saying that I wanted what he had.

So it stuck in my gullet.

A knot at first.

A pain. A sickness. A stab. A mute agony that grew.

I couldn't eat.

Oh I could eat.

But I couldn't digest or be nourished.

I held my desire back—& it was never desire for the bodily love of any man, Wm or Sam or Hazlitt or any man, not Quincey, not any man's body, surely they knew that.

I held myself back from my own body—of published work.

I swallowed a big stone there, didn't I.

XXX

There is a me-shaped hole in the path—maybe it has a membrane. Maybe it has just been torn into the flesh of the garden & is skinless.

At night the hole is black & by day it is green. I am an empty space. Nevertheless, people call me by name. They offer food as to a me-shaped god made of light & darkness. Little sandwiches, an orange, buns of bread, a saucer of gooseberry jam.

If the hole that has replaced me speaks, it does so by a deep scream of one who is falling. No one can hear, for if they could, they would rush to the hole-edge, peer through, & be themselves in danger of disappearing.

But I have not disappeared—the me-hole is visible, it is present, it is my shape, it is defined, it is both a Missing Person & a definite shape of me. I am a hole. The hole is truly myself. The hole is horrifying. Is everyone a hole & am I the only one who doesn't mind? I don't mind because I am with Wm & Sam, who are, no, Wm & Sam Coleridge are not holes—they are jubilant glow-worms who have eaten into the leaf of the world & made the me-hole.

Before I was a hole, what was I?

Slugs have green blood. So I am not a slug.

But though I had red blood I was not a man, which I did not like & did not appreciate.

No. The opposite of that: I am a shy body with retractable claws all along my belly: I grow fatter & more substantial, & by the end of my growth I occupy a large part of the path & cannot be got around. Everyone must halt. They consult Wm. He does not want me bodily removed or rolled aside. He has made a vow to leave me as general obstruction. You will never hear from his lips a word of complaint. Mary has asked him to build a lightweight bridge over me out of thin sticks & bits of willow. He won't even consider it: he has secretly asked James to keep my little cart wheels & pegs maintained & ready for carriage at all times of the day or night. This does not please Mary. She would like to get a pair of shears & cut me in two halves.

I have never been beautiful.

We are—Wm & I—interested in roundness: the roundness of my shy-body which can be rolled up- or down-hill . . . & the roundness of wheels, small wooden ones, that can be placed under my body so I can be transported.

They have already started acting on this idea of me as a me-shaped hole. A cut-out, a silhouette, a cameo disappearance. Of course, nothing could be farther from the [illegible] The membrane is not cut but torn. If you look with the micro-vision of bluebottle or even thrush, perhaps even dog or cat—it has nothing to do with domesticity blinding one—I have never cooked a single meal to be eaten sitting indoors. All you need is clear sight—wash the windows for heaven's sake! Splash waterfall-ends into those eyes as do I.

I hurtle through.

All I need is to go outside, look into a green-lit space, go deeper into star-shaped bits of shade.

Into spider-house geometry.

Into gooseberry stripes.

Into measurements of one mountain against the next.

Around the bark of someone standing silent for its hundredth summer.

Into the veins of a leaf map or remnant of melted stone locked red within another stone. Fur inside reeds. Rampant extravagance of perfume in the dog-rose, look closer—be proboscis suspended by wing—be all eyes in a pile like the

beads of a blackberry which turn out to be fly-eye, buzz-vision, airborne Eye of membrane-held focus: the membrane made of something thin as thought.

The membrane is flesh's spit, blown into a bubble & cut & sewn by fingers of that Dorothy you thought had fallen down a hole, a green hole by day & a dark hole by night—Oh she did not fall down it! She is quite easy to see in there—out there—all you need is a massive eye where your hunger dwells . . . have you ever seen yourself with an eye, a massive eye, where your belly once sat? Some of us have replaced mortal hunger with a hunger for vision that renders us fearless, renders us without human love. For what is human love for, if not to see, together, the mathematical secrets within what dwells out-of-doors? I do not mean numbered mathematics, but umbrel & shoot as they slow-sizzle in the gas from water & sun & earth & air. Animals are quivering question-marks, like us: look at a velvet cow, how sad its peaceful restraint!

No—we plunged our noses into the ground & breathed ground's drug made of animate geometry. To meet the red-breast became an enregistration into the courts of the traveller-king.

Envoy, that's me.

XXX

On my Scale of Decrepitude which goes from zero (Beyond Utmost Decrepitude) to 13 (The Golden Streets), every Indoors is a blundering state of being below five, with dust or crumbling bits or general malaise for its energy & none can stop me longing to go wild.

& what of the Grim state of Manhood? First let me mention that the flowers who know Myself are, some of them, blue & tall. Others have been short & pale cream or yellow. Certain ones such as Bee Balm are red & bear fragrant leaves. All without exception have been varied & original in our conversations. People think that flowers cannot, for instancc, be acerbic. This is un-insightful. I have had frequent talks with Chicory, for instance, about the Grim state of Manhood in the neighbourhood.

As a matter of fact, there is one living in this house who would, were I to die, do all in their power to demolish every calyx, pistil, petiole, umbel, pod, anther & filament until the place be a mass of uprooted gore—this would hardly destroy the entities themselves, whose life exists in a Body that cannot be murdered.

This imperishable Body is known about by certain people. It is not Floral but extends to bird life as well as to the un-murderable States of animals, fish & minerals, the mineral Body being elemental as opposed to fluid-animate yet force-filled & in fact basic to all other imperishable Body-forms. (Basic in the sense that there is nothing without it.)

Red Potentilla.

Bell-like flowers lend a ready, listening ear—Nothing could, for instance, be more sympathetic than a Delphinium bending to listen to a question put to it by myself.

Of course, any question worth asking reverberates in a bell-ear for some timeless-time, as if it were a mouthful of mystery-wine lingering 'round the tongue of a vineyard-labourer who, in wind, sun, rain & time, has perceived more about wine's secrets than the most revered & sophisticated Sommelier.

But as with all forms, Delphiniums come with their particular gentle warning: Our colony slowly deteriorates with age & there is nothing you can do about it.

Alas?

No—triumph!

For what can be more relaxing than the certainty that there was nothing you could have done? No recrimination here in Delphiniums' world.

×××

Our wife Mary has thrown another Book on my bed admonishing me to read but I am too busy with my feelings

to open it & have been busy thus for years. People are so tiresome in their mad rush to avoid all feelings whatsoever, especially the literary souls all around me—the books! The poems. The endless words. Get me out of this room, out of any book, outside. Had I known when young the things I know now, I would not have married my brother Wm.

Oh, it was quite a wedding. He held onto the ring for ages, blessing it & walking with me & with it under the moon, itself an ever-changing ring trying to come into being: now broken, now filled with molten gold, never quite fitting on my finger because it was the moon & far bigger than any ring, farther away, & moving—always sailing around the stars & the clouds—why did I ever believe it could be made into a Husband ring & slipped on my own finger?

Oh Wm did slip it on, all right. The replica. The ring that has forever since our wedding night—or that morning after our wedding night when he tore it off me—or we both tore it off me—where it has nestled around the finger of our wife Mary ever since!

Mary, so perfect, like the perfect ring which is Not a perfect replica of the everchanging ever incomplete ever knowing moon.

I am sorry, everyone will have to wait if they want me to join the epidemic of reason, the queue of propriety, manacles of safety—no more of that for me. They will have to wait

outside the bars of my cage-not-cage. Only those who do not feel their feelings will look on my room, my bed, my posthumous life as some pathetic enclosure. We know—the inhabitants of my mind, & myself—me & my multitudinous winged companions, leafed companions, song-voiced familiars—we know we have bolted to freedom. It seems not thus, I know. It seems as if others are the sensible ones & I have gone somewhere inaccessible & restricted. Mary, you come to my bed with books! As if books could ever replace all amongst which I now run free.

Poems? Oh, Wm. Poems? With their structure & gait, they are like dark horses & you barely holding the reins, but holding on, vying for control. Everyone vying for control.

All are afraid of darkness, when all I want is for it to sweep down upon me so I can freely visit the splendours I find by following the light collected in my own mind—not imagined, no—but real sight—I always had it & that is why I found it impossible to enter a room of people chattering away about the things in that room. Arguing over tea-sets or the Turkish carpet or the curtains or who was coming down over the road in a new hat.

Take all that away!

I should have shouted this when I was—at what age did it become unbearable? For when we were young, Wm, Sam & I—there was no Turkish carpet, only the frost hung like

diamonds in the trees. Gems upon gems. They could see it. Once upon a time . . . & then something—did it blind them? What blinded them & did not blind me, so that I had to—I was the one who had to hold the gem-world fast when all around me, all the so-called faithful men around me, had become—Can I say faithless?

Oh I don't care anymore what I say to our wife Mary, to all proper ladies of the vale—give me Miss Barker. Give me the young men I loved, who were wild & not tame. My feelings might be too much with me but I'd rather that a thousand times than suffer the pallid consequence of focusing on a book Mary would have me read, or on any of the things coming out of people's pale & monstrous mouths. Laudanum! Oh yes it was convenient at first for me to take that, it shut me up & kept me quite happy, in their minds, didn't it. The poppy. The brandy. The diffusion of all sharp things. Well give me the sharp things now. Give me my sword. Get that nurse out of here or I will knock her on the head once more—yes I mean it. I do mean it. I do for once mean it. Oh yes.

XXX

What is love? You think I was a spurned lover? You think Wm's cracked wedding vow was about my not having a husband in the earthly sense? When will you know by looking into my eyes that nothing in me whatsoever is or ever has been or ever will be about earthly sense? How is it

you can't see? It's because the world is too much with you, yes, late & soon, yes late & soon & all time that is not time. Getting & spending you lay waste your powers, yes, you have given your hearts away, a sordid boon, amen. Little we see in Nature that is ours . . . We? No. Speak for yourselves. What happened to you? You crowd of lost traitors, bereft imbeciles—I am speaking to you now from my saddle on the back of a bat.

×××

Excuse me, what was it you wanted?

Have you people not learned how to get along without me yet? A button sewn on? A transcription of your latest thoughts for the papers?

Hello?

Have you not noticed something is different? It has been some time now since I felt able to pretend to care about any of that. As a matter of fact, it has been seventeen years, twenty-one days, two hours, thirty-seven minutes & seventeen seconds since I cared about your own personal situation. The children have long grown up, or at least they have ceased to need me the way you appear to still need me, or the facsimile of me that you have created for your . . . shall we call it your convenience?

I have been a convenient person to have around, loving as unreservedly as I do, or did. Forbearance has been important to me & I know you will agree it has helped this household. Funny that they call it a house-hold & not a house-drop. Not a house let-go. Not a house fallen downhill, & not a house released.

Hold me in your house.

Yes, you have done that, thank you.

You did it & I was supposed to find that sufficient. Was. I was a convenient person to have around, but now how things have changed.

×××

Womanliness!

What is womanliness? I thought I knew, or I thought I might know. Until Mary Lamb went mad from too much of it—let's see, what happened again? Ah, yes—her grandma died so Mary & her family could no longer go to the country & were stuck in a small London flat. Who did Mary Lamb, in all womanliness, look after? Her mother, paralyzed in her body, slept in bed with her like an unmoving log of hate. The mother who had never shown her any love, not even when she was a babe & her brother John had an accident & an infected fever which Mary Lamb tended because she loved

him, & her beloved brother Charles, like my own beloved Wm, was away away in the days, away from the little cramped flat. Away on his own important business. Though he said he loved her—& her father in the flat as well, completely demented, & she had to look after him & her grandmother dead so that the house in the country was no longer a place to which she could escape, & she the only source of an income for the household, sewing cloak after cloak amongst the rest of them & their clamour. Who would not have a temporary frenzy?

Was that womanliness? Or might womanliness mean when I went to Germany with Wm & kept our fire going whilst we both translated German to make pennies? The cold unbearable, & neighbours refusing to believe we were brother & sister, not man & woman living together unwed. We had no language, no friends, & no real fire, as I was—I must face it—a terrible fire-keeper, most unwomanly.

Is womanliness in my love of flowers? In my naming of them, my lying in grass on the soft earth who is, herself, womanly? But no—I left off naming, or I named wrong, or I concentrated on nameless curves, pistils, trumpets. I concentrated on a most unwomanly, piercing blue, for my favourite flowers were blue & they had about themselves something merciless.

Or might I have become womanly through having looked after enough children of other women, when those women

were away or ill or indisposed? Certainly like you, Mary Lamb, in your mothering of young Miss Isola, did I not mother my little Basil when Wm & I were still a couple? Taught him to read? Gave him jam & bread with cream? Did not suckle him with my breasts but lo, how could these small breasts suckle a whole child? I am such a small person! Still, some sort of woman, & not a man. Nobody has suggested I am a man.

Womanly, then, how?

You could say I have roasted a few chops so the fat glitters & drips & makes mouths of men water like crazy mouths do when they foam with lust.

Or you could say that when Sam Coleridge & I stood under the hanging birch bough gemmed with frost, I wore a bridal veil studded with heaven's jewels if there be a heaven, & Sam did not deny I was womanly, for if he had denied it, he would be denying the times we were together with ferocity, though frozen not hot—we had a frozen burning. But a frozen burning is perhaps not the womanly evidence for which I search.

I have a bosom, a bonnet, a lump of cheese in my pantry to share, a tart whose edge I crimped with my thumb, & that crimping extended the flesh of my thumb into the pastry of the tart before baking, so that the pastry itself was like a piece of my flesh—Here, this is my body to be

broken for you. This is my flesh for you to share. Eat it in memory of me.

No, apparently that is not womanly either.

& Whatever all the things might be that I have outlined, doesn't there always loom a time when they become defunct? A time of war, a time of men chasing their own fame, a time of famine or plague, a time of catastrophic cold or storms? When the details of womanliness, or all details whatsoever, become a thing of the past, or an extravagance, or—& this one is very womanly I have been told—a frill?

×××

Eye-skin. Endless intrigue—I have descended into the kaleidoscope. There is a hole leading to a staircase leading to an intricacy of streets with pieces of every colour glass you can name—pea-green, turquoise, garnet or gold—pieces of glass & when you come close you do not need William Withering's optical glass but can look through the transparencies with your bare eyes. Naked flesh has nothing on the naked eye-skin.

Naked flesh is fat & bread, lard & bun. But the skin on the eye is so thin as to be made of fish skin from the depths of the ocean. Eyeball membrane separates me from wonder & the separation is unmeasurably thin, thinner than glass or even than new-formed ice in November on the Lake's edge.

Thinner than thought itself is eye-skin, & who has ever peeled it or looked through it except the medical experts, the surgeons & body-thieves? I have my own eyes to look through in the streets of London with Mary Lamb. Together we name for each other the things we see, & what we see is not what our brothers see! The kaleidoscope is a gift for a young girl who already knows what we know but has not named it. Emma Isola, if only Mary Lamb & I'd had mothers as you have in us. We would have trusted far sooner the visions we saw through our own eye-skins.

×××

The gaping give-mouth in our skulls.

Mary Lamb is older than I am & she is completely porous when feeling my situation or anyone's. Her sympathy knows no bounds if she chooses to award it, & if she does you had better say yes. For Mary Lamb's sympathy has saved me.

I do not think she gives it to everyone, or that she could if she desired, because it takes something from her, much like the spark they say Christ felt depart from him once touched by a woman in a crowd. But Mary Lamb gave me more than the Lamb of God ever gave that woman in the book of—what book was it? I do not remember those books. That woman in that book did not then go on & proclaim her joy from the rooftops but here I am, writing down exactly what transpired for me when I had my fortnight with Mary

Lamb—ostensibly to get my teeth renewed—but in fact to renew my whole Self, through the power of Mary Lamb's own experience. Her womanhood. Her descent into what they call madness. Her murderous past, her matricide, & most important—two blessed weeks uninterrupted by the male members of our families.

Her first instructions came before my teeth were pulled & replaced. Why, I asked her, have I become exhausted in this perpetual & enervated manner that means I drag myself around like seven stones of flour in a sack?

The reason, she said, is the very gaping give-mouth in our skulls, whose openness is a perpetual asking of what we can do for everyone in the house, even when they have not asked us. It is the controlling force behind our every move on behalf of the mother, the father, the husband, the brother, & any baby or child in our sphere. What, asks our gaping give-mouth, do you need, & how may I present it to you? & there we go, walking miles into the village or the town, stooping to pick things dropped on the floor or the ground that might be in the way of our family members or of value to them. Moving this package here & that bottle there, this burden here & that burden there, carrying like a donkey every little scrap & morsel whether it is a jar of milk or a broken heart.

We carry it all, says Mary Lamb, & we carry it down the miles & when we sleep, or so-called sleep, there we are, still carrying gingerly so as not to lose or drop all that requires

carrying in our beloved families. So that by the time we are fifty as you are now, my dear Dorothy, you are left with your giving gape-mouth hanging on its hinge ready to wail with tiredness, & your shoulders are tired to the bone, & you are tired to the bone, yet what do you do but keep going, for you do not even realize you are tired, only that you hurt in a blinding way.

Blinding, yes, I said to Mary Lamb, for my vision itself is getting blurred at morning & at night with increasing labours & I cannot read as much as I should. I am losing my reading.

Reading, she cried! You wear your eyes out mending the shirts, all the little stitches for everybody, sewing not only their garments but their broken souls, sewing their weary thoughts with your comforting words but never hearing the one sentence that would quell the bleeding lining of your own perception.

& when Mary Lamb said the bleeding lining of your own perception I did not hesitate to know what she meant. For inside me is a layer like wet silk that lines my brain & heart & bowels & if I am honest it has a wet silken twin that lines my womb, & that one—that one!—has never been attended to. I told Mary Lamb this & she said yes, this is why you have to do as I say whilst you are here with me, while you wait to have your jaw renewed with its teeth & its hinges & its sadness that runs deep as oceans.

XXX

I don't know—it's as if someone whilst I slept peeled my skin off so I awaken all of a sudden skinned & raw with no knowledge of how I became thus. I look at the hills, & they have nothing to do with me but have turned their backs. Their shoulders are blue & their faces are turned against me. No hope of comfort there, best turn to the trees—but no, the trees also have become uninterested in me. Something has changed their sympathetic leaves which no longer contain green blood but are dry & swish like threshed hay, the green gone out of them & a greyness greeting me instead. Granted this happens more often in August than it does in winter or early summer.

Is it the late summer, then, that gives me this merciless feeling as if I am nothing to any of the beloved hills & fields that once held me in their regard?

I wake raw & peeled & bleeding. My emotions have all run to the surface of my limbs & they writhe there in agony like orphaned worms. The sky glares down at me with a merciless blaring blue. Where is the beloved & merciful rain? Where is mist or fog? Why am I caught in the lamp of the sun's stare, as if the sun wanted to witness me curling up & burning with arid fever?

But I lie. It can happen at any time of year. In the tenderest April shower or the newest froth-greened baby birch

half-leafed bowers, I can be this spectral lone wolf, this animal caught in mid-howl with a cold grimace for a face & a blind sleet-storm for tears, & no reason for any of it. No reason but being a crazy lonely soul with its skin peeled away & its muscle, blood & nerves pulsating purple & blue & garnet like a monstrous wound bound by a membrane thin as a berry's skin—oh but a word will puncture it & my blood will obliterate my world.

If only I were that lucky—if only I could end everything with a needle-prick. I would do it—it would appear like a sewing mishap or simple kitchen accident . . . She was one minute dressing the fowl, & the next, the tip of the blade merely pricked her thumb & she burst like a ripe fruit in the centre of the kitchen, & was whole no more, but shattered & scattered & spilled so that every bit of her became formless—there was a pool where our Sister once stood.

This is what happened in Mary Lamb's mind only it was her mother she pricked & the pricking was not small or incidental but massive, a slaughter. So it was not the same. Yet—if I could simply end my life by seeming to cut my finger with the point of the meat knife or the embroidery needle or the darning awl, then nobody could fault me & nobody need know about this torment I feel, this peeled, raw state that comes upon me in which I feel the cruel ache of having to move & stand & walk & be alive among other living beings, who do not seem to feel these torments at all. Except Mary Lamb, whose raw agony is even more excruciating than my

own. In fact, my own, next to hers, becomes insignificant, & that is what makes being with her a relief.

I wish I knew what causes the peeled state with its unbearable harshness. If it were aloneness then I would simply try to spend more time in company. If it were feeling overwhelmed by social demands, why, I could easily plead a headache or bad bowels—god knows I often do! If it were simply too much glaring sunlight I could stay in the shade of a willow or rest behind curtains like the lovely curtain Mary Lamb hung at my window during my convalescence there. But I sigh with incomprehension of my own self, for any of these things might set me off the wrong way one day yet bother me not at all the next. I do not know what it is that causes the light or the darkness to overtake me.

When it is at its worst I cannot even grieve or cry—my chest & throat & eyes become encased in a leaden shield. I go around like this for days or even weeks, not knowing what caused it or why it started, though I can always pinpoint the moment at which my joy departed . . . & then—a moment later & who can tell when it might happen—joy flies back into my body exactly like a wild bird that has been away & flown back of its own sweet accord!

I wish I could beckon it somehow when I feel ready to give up, when my body becomes immobilized, my legs wooden & my fingers dead, & my mind unable to remember the idea of any kind of future, let alone a beautiful one.

At home at Rydal of course I do not tell anyone this. I do not tell Wm, who would medicate me.

& I certainly do not mention it to our wife Mary, who would admonish me—who would say—who has said—For heaven's sake, woman, rise above it! Every woman's throat has a burning coal stuck red-hot in it. If we patiently endure as we should then the coal will eventually behave itself. The coal will tinkle & dwindle to grey & settle into words we can share with the people around us as if they were normal words. As if they had always been normal words & not a wild woman's incendiary wails—is what our wife Mary would say. Not out loud, of course. Never out loud.

XXX

Is London a dream?

Or is it real? I never know!

I dreamed not once but many times that I travelled its lanes, the back lanes behind the grand displays are the thing, places that begin in a narrow passageway then beckon with colour & sound just around the corner. A shout, a scrap of garment hung to dry, white that contains all colours or blue reflecting in a white garment from the sky above all the soot—blue filtering down or mauve filtering up from the shadows.

All the lanes, the little ones, the little busy ones, there they start all narrow & they last long & blossom out as if into fireworks, or the bloom at the end of a stem, or the fantastic scene at the end of this, the toy we found for Emma Isola—yes, your mother's friend has not forgotten it. But it is not a toy, inasmuch as every grownup in London has one in his hand & peers into it for dear life, to escape this world & join the indescribable glories of heaven.

I say I dreamed my London walks & I did dream them. I dreamed them in Grasmere & in Germany & I continue to dream them as I grow old in Rydal. For each night once my eyes shut upon the spangled fields where Dixon drags me in our cart, upon what should they open but sister-gems of the city! I doubt I only dreamed London's most beguiling streets. Yet I think—though I'm strangely never sure—that the most tantalizing, the mistiest streets, faint or lurid in equal measure, all jewel-clash like Emma Isola's new toy—the purest streets, the most dreamlike alleys with the best stories or fragments of tales—those I did dream. I walked them with these same feet that strode the Lakes.

I love London, when I am in it, every bit as much as I have loved my country home with all its flower gems, its lake-shimmer, its diamond crowns sparkling in hidden places, its cascades of silver, falling water. The city is all this & more once I am in it. It is only when listening to Wm that I forget & believe it dirty or fearsome or a place in which

I might get lost. Listening to Wm you would think we were a pair of fragile & new-hatched swallows unable to stand a smudge of chimney smoke or eat a Cheapside bun. Maybe Wm is that fragile.

XXX

It's wonderful how I can roam the streets invisible. A man lords it over a woman but once in the streets of London, hark! He is constantly seen as a mark—offered companionship or wagers or the latest swindle-toy or defunct pocket-watch—or offered nothing but the unseen hand filching from his trousers soft as a feathered bird that has no bones. Yet a woman past fifty can walk the streets for an hour & be seen by no one at all. As if by magic, she is unseen like the wind itself, known only by other women her age, for we see each other with special eyes that live all over our bodies.

Yes our bodies are covered in sensitive eyes.

Some of the eyes see in the way normal to ordinary eyes: they see form & hue & can read signs or tell when a thunderhead looms. But our other eyes can do all sorts of things. They can smell, only it is not a nose-kind-of-smell they know, but a sharp curling of the air from a doorway or back lane—we know if someone is being hurt or maimed or loved in the shadows—& some of our eyes can hear, only it is not an ear kind of hearing—it is more as if our skin has scales

like tiny herring scales except these are old woman scales, yes, we have them all over our skin & all we have to do is adjust them like miniature sails in this direction or that, & we can sense any sound through six walls, through an earthen roof over a work cellar, through a bell tower high over St. James's Street. And lies!

We have eyes lining our throats like keyholes, & where are the keys but in the raindrops or songs of street starlings & the keys tell these, our throat-eyes, all sorts of songs-of-the-day, such as how long it will be before anyone notices us noticing them, which is very long—in fact months & sometimes years or even forever.

We can, & this is the part Mary Lamb & I most enjoy in our fleet-footed romps around London, we can stare into the faces of all & sundry & we can, with our combined old-woman bodily eyes, read the fortunes therein, all the woes & waiting, all the hurt & betrayal, all the hope & lust, all the forlorn aloneness, all the greed or very occasionally greed's opposite which is a pouring-out of love so great no one but we can discern its end, for it has no end. This is something we see in the hardest places, where women older & more invisible than ourselves sit by themselves thinking no one can see them at all.

We can stare all we like, with all our eyes, at all these things, & nobody knows.

Our age & sex have drawn over each of our heads, Mary Lamb's & mine, & over the heads of any women like us in age or sensibility, a silken cowl.

XXX

The late, great Antoine Lavoisier, shouts Mary Lamb, finding his name in the Gazette after our egg bun, for they were comparing his discoveries with those of a new genius named Faraday. Dorothy, do you remember Lavoisier's most famed finding? *Rien ne se perd, rien ne se crée: tout se transforme.* Ha! I could have told the world that the moment I turned thirty. In Nature nothing is lost, nothing created: everything transforms . . . She shoved the paper in her bag to show her brother when he came back from the prize fight. She still showed Charles everything as I used to show Wm.

When we turn thirty, according to Mary Lamb, we become old in the sight of men. Then in our forties our blood runs like the gore of slaughtered pigs & each step squelches in a red flood & our bodies become suddenly changed—on some ordinary Wednesday our arms become someone else's arms. Our faces become those of our fathers. Our sense of smell alters. As a small person I have always smelled the ground as my nose is nearer it than Wm's nose. But now I sniff deeper in the ground & in the air high above it, for scents have whirled into a vortex whose point is attracted to my nose. Sardines! Earth! Feces! Carnations! Peppery &

coppery or stinking of sweet, rotting fish—all of London inhabits our noses.

Nothing created nor destroyed! Mary Lamb sings all the way down Bennett Street, euphoric.

I am not sure, she cries, that the Gazette realizes our former youthful hunger has but been transformed!

. . . & I knew what she meant. Late-summer air pressing my skin was now unbearable like the insistence of a lover when one is sated. The air itself our lover! The scent of rain our passion. Utterly sensual, the feeling of simply being alive; it can ache just to walk down the street. I am ransacked as the bee unpetals her late rose. By accident the passing bee unhinges the last pink flake . . . & then what? The swelling of the hip. The filling of the hip with paste, not liquid—orange, not pink. The sweet, pasty sugar & a gnarled star atop it all—oh nothing is destroyed, only transforms. This is a fact all women know before being told by Monsieur Antoine Lavoisier. Spring in a woman's body is hardly sensual compared to autumn & winter—when, against ice & snow & monochrome of black & white—against skeletal life in the waste ground along the Thames or the edges of our beloved Lakes—the fruited hip with its gnarled star is the fragrant rose transformed from soul to body in a transubstantiation not of church altar & not of the body of any man whether that man be young or old.

Matter, marvelled Mary Lamb as she hauled the Gazette out of her bag to examine it once more. Why only matter? Did Lavoisier think only matter matters & did he not realize how matter extends into feeling & perception?

I halted beside her while a man with pots dangling from his belt & a hen under each arm had a mind to crash into us on the downhill cobbles.

Mind where you stop, he says—a pair of right cows!

This is where you are wrong, Sir, said Mary Lamb, for I am a lamb & my friend here, she is your quintessential goat.

He spat at us but she deflected the gob with her newspaper & off he tromped with a page of it stuck to the rump of his fattest hen.

Dear Lavoisier, we wrote at thc Lotus Café on the bits of paper I was never without in case an idea came into my head in field or steeple of wherever I might walk in this life.

> *We, authors Mary Lamb and Dorothy Wordsworth, thought you might like to see our list of things which, besides matter, are neither created nor destroyed. We feel we owe it to Science to suggest the following additions, though our list is by no means exhaustive, we realize.*

Only look at us as one pair of observant women whose advanced Age allows us to imagine we have noticed a few things that behave like Matter and that we believe are of the same category, being of denser or more amorphous concentrations . . .

Our advanced age, laughed Mary Lamb, pleased with herself.

Allows us to imagine! I said, getting into the spirit.

Here, then, is our list of items which, like Matter, we Believe "ne se perd, et ne se creé," but only transform:

Tears
Love
Yearning
Hunger
Rage
Pain
Ecstasy
Thirst
Unknowing
Agony
Jealousy
Mourning
Humiliation
Triumph

Dream
Wind
Cloud
Rainbow
Abandonment
Companionship
Hatred
Terrible Mistakes

Together we compiled a list that was in danger of using up my entire store of spare pocket-paper.

Our list went on.

Our list could have been endless.

Over some entries we laughed & over others we cried.

I had not been prepared for the feelings our list would unleash & I did not realize until trying to sleep that night & thinking it over, that it was not the list that made me feel loss or gain or love or wrongness or any other feeling.

No, it was not the list.

But it was the making of the list, & it was the companionship of Mary Lamb during the making. For she was the one who saw so much that had, for me, remained unspoken for years.

Antoine Lavoisier's name, when you break it apart as I often do break words to see what falls from their cracks, contains the word *la*—feminine form of the—& *vois*—a form of the French word meaning to see.

. . . & I thought, as I broke his name in the lamplight filtering from Russell Street, how Mary Lamb herself was more of a she-who-sees, a seer—mad or not mad, I did not care what men called her—more of a seer than any eminent scientist.

Where will we send our letter? she asked me. To the celestial academy where Lavoisier is eating the fruits of his discoveries? He will be swallowing a heavenly profiterole at the moment, bless him, & perhaps washing it down with cognac . . .

In the end, we addressed our letter to the void.

×××

It has taken me a while to realize how insignificant I am to others.

I was propelled, in youth, not by beauty—I was never a beauty, far too intense & strange for that! But my lovers did not find me insignificant. Far from it! Quincey marvelled at my concentrated self which he said was as if a pinpoint contained the night. Both he & I were so small compared with the others in our lives—tiny, really, the two of us

weighing no more than one normal-sized man or plump woman, he said.

Night-time was for us the most wonderful invention!

. . . & I think it was because Darkness let us dissolve in it & become inky sources of our new wild thoughts. No need to fit expectations. Night covered our strange strength & those nights were the best I have known even if they are shattered now in our memory so that neither of us can be sure of their having passed.

I do not use the word insignificant—once my brother separated himself from me, once he became the husband of Mary Hutchinson—did I come loose from my own claim to being a person whose words were of worth?

Even before London, when only a few of my teeth were gone—I remember telling Mary Lamb, It's all finished now—meaning entanglement with men, even men small or strange. Yes, the teeth went & then it went—my significance. But I am not truthful here. Long before I became invisible did I not see a hundred women cast aside like lumps of old clothes, disconsolate, going about their unimportant business of kneading & needling & needing & keening & all the other insignificant things a lump of woman will do once men render her unseen? Once brother & lover have discounted her, as did her father before them?

Says Mary Lamb when I visited her in London to reconstitute my teeth: You must become felt to yourself. You will look out the window that I have dressed in a bridal curtain for your pleasure, & you will see the fern shines green against it, & the room reflects a projection of shadows from the street, & you will breathe & not succumb to the idea that you are supposed, once again, to find some way to pretend you are indispensable. For you are not indispensable.

What you are, says Mary Lamb, is something else. That something is what you need to find, & to find her, it is good to lie down & allow being, not working. This is nearly impossible I know, but it is your medicine. What happens in your chest-cave then in your bowels & even in your heretofore pronounced dead womb & its dormant orchid? Feel!

How did you do it? I asked Mary Lamb. How, without a friend like you are to me, did you navigate the sea between fifty & sixty so that you stand here intact & strong?

Oh, says Mary Lamb, you forget I have spent many months in a madhouse where for days & weeks & months on end, stretching, yea, into years, no one asked of me a thing. For I journeyed beyond the boundaries of their own desires. So I did not have to unpot a herring for any man, no herring of any sort did I have to provide . . . & in the place of all herrings with their silver scales & their concentrated smells & all else about them, in their place grew a bushel of silver scales for me alone, made of my own

vision, my own tolerance, my own feelings & desires. You do not even know what your own feelings are, do you, my dearest Dorothy?

. . . & I had to admit to Mary Lamb that she was right.

For two weeks I was like a sleeping maiden in her shadowy parlour.

She left me alone.

It is not, as some say, as if she polluted my mind with her insanities.

No.

The only insanities have been mine, made of layer upon layer of Unvoiced things that have piled up in my body since I was first the beloved of men who include my brother. In their gaze I was not myself. In their gaze my own layers, my geology, built up & towered flakes of silver & cream-coloured stone made—as stone is made—of components leaf-shaped & changeable & moist. Permeable to begin with, but in the end—though I do not want it to be my real end—impermeable slices nestled one upon the other like leaves of shale.

XXX

I remember—& of my two Marys, Wordsworth & Lamb, the latter would agree & the former would not—I remember being one of the men or at least akin to them in my own mind, for years. Sprawled on the ground, thinking. Marvelling & thinking all the complicated thoughts a writer thinks when confronted with the majesty of the world & the squalor—is life convoluted or harmonious? Will humans destroy the world or learn how to echo its spherical movement in the heavens' harmonious exultation? I thought along those lines as I tore our bread in three & shared it with Wm & Sam. Grass pricked our legs alike & shadows of the same willows shielded us from the sun. We heard the same crows caw & saw the same rainbow. Wm & Sam listened to me & my words mingled on our pages with their own & many times my words became their own. We all agreed. Our minds were more interesting than the holy trinity for none of us was separated body from spirit but manifested both. There ran transparent stairs from the cellars in our bodies to the resplendence of our minds, & our words were the light. I was lit & I was one of them.

No, says Mary Wordsworth—just because you & I were deprived of mothers does not mean we should not learn how to be proper women! Look around you. Remember correctly instead of in a longing daze. Who made the bread you tore in three?

When I knew I was no longer one of the men—once Wm married Mary & she became—everyone called her—I had

to call her—my sister—though Wm promised me—he promised on their wedding night she would be our wife. But the world called her my sister & Wm did not correct the world.

. . . & with my sister I was now suddenly left behind—I have never got over the shock of this.

Again it happened with Quincey. Oh he found me to be a wild boy with startling eyes! A boy small like himself, tattered & dissolved at our edges & fit only for the out-of-doors in a storm, along with the ragged leaves & all the things that were like us windblown—until he found the little farm-girl & married her! Then I became no longer Quincey's boy friend. I suddenly faded into the same woman I had become in the eyes of Wm & Sam . . . & this was the second shock from which I am still reeling, & which causes my bowels to shut down if I do not wrench myself with an effort far greater than anyone knows.

The first shock was realizing I was no longer one of the boys.

The second shock came after Wm & Sam stopped including me, & after Quincey also found a wife—what is it about their finding wives that made me obsolete? The second shock was that, No, I had never been one of them.

Not in our youth & not in our age. What had I been? They loved my thoughts, it is true, but did not hear me utter them. Rather, they imagined that my ideas had flown to them from the same invisible wind that flows to all men, & that my ideas counted among their discoveries.

Once married, they somehow remembered I too was feminine, like their wives.

Whereas before they were wed, I was a magic stick blown from a wild tree & accompanying them in their windblown travels. A pointer, a wand, a branch from the Tree of knowledge.

After their marriages Wm & also Sam & Quincey would listen for an hour to the yammering of the most menial servant—yes even James our poor manservant who grew up in & out of the workhouse, Wm regards as superior to me in matters requiring any decisiveness . . . hired him—a poor, simple soul, thinks Wm, but reliable enough to coax my beloved sister Dorothy out of her troublesome agitation here at home or in the house of Mary Lamb, a woman who has refused to swallow a thing. Mary Lamb, a dangerous influence!

Mary Lamb, with whom I am not one of the boys, have never been one of the boys, am not interested in the boys.

With Mary Lamb I knew this.

Not interested in the boys is the meat I chew on with my new teeth after our fortnight in London. This is the carnage I am damned if I will be prevented from swallowing & once I swallow it, I will work on digesting it for the rest of my life. My bowels will thrash like seaweed thrashing offshore, & the household here at Rydal will have to accommodate my wildness. James Dixon are you still reading this?

Are you with me?

You, who are different in some elemental way that my brother has failed to notice. You, who are also not one of the boys. You, who have built our little carriage in which we can travel wherever we want to go, without them.

×××

Of course, Mary Lamb is right again.

Our brothers do not worry in the least, upon waking, whether or not they are useful. They, no matter how old they grow, do not think, There is as if a layer of powder settling upon me & rendering me less & less useful not only to the outer world, but to myself.

They do not then ponder, & what is the entity I have just named Myself & why is it still lying down at noon?

Our brothers can sleep, geniuses as they are, through noon & on until ten o'clock at night with only a changed word in a second verse to show for it & perhaps not even this. Perhaps there is no change at all in their work, only a subtle change in their minds, a change bestowed by sleep, the sleep necessary to men of great thoughts & words. Men whose words are worth something or whose silence is worth even more & is different from the silence of their sisters.

The silence of sisters is reproachable! For should sisters not be talking of tasks, of errand lists & prices, of economies & time? Women face the clock-face unlike the way in which men face it. Men face the clock not to gauge where they have fallen short of time, but to note how long it might be before the next meeting with another man. Which meal is imminent & which visitor must be given sway? Get the sisters to set the table while we veer to the sill & gaze on distances & conclude, If this therefore that.

Whereas for sisters it is, If this, well then, *this* it is . . . & if that, then, simply that. Thus the world for sisters develops into myriad efflorescences; a panoply of surprises! Whereas our brothers must control each minute, & if their minutes prove uncontrollable, well, it is because they are forced to live in a maddening world containing sisters & trees & thunder.

So it is that on waking I am beset by forces, colours, sensations, crowding in on me & making it hard to get up while

at the same time making it impossible for me to remain lying down, or to claim reverie, or to—forbid this!—wonder what it might be like to let things be & not work each second of the day towards my life being considered worthwhile.

My brother, says Mary Lamb, is worthwhile simply by placing his silhouette against the window & resembling a dark poet. I could say the same thing of Wm if I dared.

Accomplishment, says Mary Lamb, is a woman's word. A man has no need of this word as he fulfills it by virtue of having been born & having not yet died. Simply by occupying space in his neutral-coloured garments that we have stitched with our thousand thousand tiny hand-stitches & clapped with our irons & bleached & starched & laid on the rocks to brighten in the sun with a brightness of angels . . . simply by donning this angel-white shirt & partly-covering it in a cloak so as to hide the brightness until needed in some important conversation . . . simply by being clothed in this bright & dark garb, by standing straight & tall, by gazing abstractedly into an inner poem . . . thus do our brothers outrace us while we labour toward accomplishing all they have set out for us to do by their mere existence. Accomplishment does not exist for them as a word, because for it to do so would imply that there is a time before perfect completion in themselves—a hole, if you will; a gap or a lack preceding the whole & complete man . . . & no such space exists.

But sisters are space embodied without form. We are the void. We are the gap, the hole, the time before. Accomplishment is our word & our reason for lying in agony for some time before rising, if we are able to rise at all. Accomplishment is for us inaccessible. Evasive. Always ahead. A state of being whole by gazing into our inner word that isn't a poem but is some other form of story or meaning—this is a wholeness that cannot exist for us as long as men stand like gnomons & define timelessness for themselves alone.

So says Mary Lamb.

Oh, she cautions, but we love our brothers.

We love them, she says, with a sick & pitiful persistence because we have been made to love them through a demon calling to us in the night whilst we sleep, & in the day we have been made to cry after that love, that nightmare, half-remembered yet wholly compelling—our disease of the soul.

. . . & Mary Lamb will soon go off again to the madhouse but I will not.

I hang on well enough to remain in the land of normal people. Wm, for one, could not bear to have me disappear into the place where Mary Lamb goes. Without my gay shadow at the hem of his days, he might not believe quite so hard in himself, in his genius, in his poetry. He might fall off the edge into a kind of bog with nobody, not even our

wife Mary, quite understanding what it is that he needs daily spooned for him to continue with his usual abilities.

One line after another, spoonful by tiny, exquisite spoonful, do I feed Wm the words the world thinks are created by himself alone.

Alone, for Wm, means Himself plus his insubstantial Sister.

Only in bed in the morning, in the ghastly time before I get up, do I dare imagine that my brother Wm & I are two, not one, not himself alone. Once I rise I cease to be Dorothy & recommence my twinship, my kinship, my death.

Oh but that is your voluntary death, insists Mary Lamb. Entirely up to you—& off she goes again to the madhouse to be wrapped in forgetfulness. Not her own forgetfulness. The madwoman does not forget. The world around her is the forgetful substance. She, on the other hand, is mad because she remembers.

Are you not angry? Mary Lamb asks me.

—& this is the question with which she leaves me, steeping in what she has named my unacknowledged rage. This, says Mary Lamb, is the poison causing your paralysis of the limbs, your agony in the bowel.

—& off she flies, light as a fairy, into her sanctuary.

XXX

I love Rydal when the sun slips onto the water at morning—even if the distant sound of the hammer begins & rings incessant through the mist—Sun & mist whiten the water. You cannot really see the mist. It's only sufficient to diffuse the light so the lake looks as if it is made of . . . crystal . . . milk . . . Sometimes there's a little bit of ice at the edge, just a little bit of ice & a few flakes floating white . . .

The sounds that infiltrate are getting worse & worse. The smells that infiltrate are getting worse & worse, stench & racket from industry & progress. But our sycamore with its serious beauty—it's not a nonchalant kind of tree, it's a—hear that echo, hear that hammer—the sycamore moves in the very slight breeze, its dry leaves uttering a whisper that—can it not remain on the—just on the—hopeful side of sombre?

The Terrace saves me. Sounds roar beyond it. Horrible buildings loom outside it. The new road snakes around it. Inside the Terrace sighs the influence of the trees, much like the influence of the stars in that book I hardly read—*Who can bind the sweet influences of Pleiades?*—Scripture can be beautiful but I admit I just don't have a taste for it when the air itself inside the Terrace is pregnant & alive—

& no, I have never been pregnant, but I have been alive, even now when the branches are nearly bare, winter a thing nobody loves enough. The architecture. Skeletons. Bones of

the trees, & the air clinging & dancing all around & hanging there grey & white, white & rain-coloured. Those are the colours of the living air in winter. Those are the colours of the Wordsworth siblings. The living air inside the terrace is like a mind. It is my mind teeming, slumbering, dreaming—flying, floating, hanging, moving in wind-riven play—

I must beg James to drag me out onto the Terrace again.

×××

But the wind!

The wind had scattered willow leaves on the moss & the moss caught them in perfect formation where they fell & clung. So that as Dixon dragged me by it in the cart, I saw the image of the willow tree on the moss, created by its cast-down leaves. There was something violent about them, yet each leaf retained its perfect oval beauty with its graceful elongation & points at each end. It was as if somebody had shed . . . their work. Someone had created work beautiful & alive, & had, in a fit, cast it on the ground—

& when I looked up at the naked willow, blackened leaves shivered on a single branch, the rest denuded.

The tree was aghast, its bark down below incised deeply.

At that moment it flung a few last leaves down—

& when a mere handful of leaves—dry & rattling in the storm—is cast upon your face with that much force, it stings like a rain of nails—

XXX

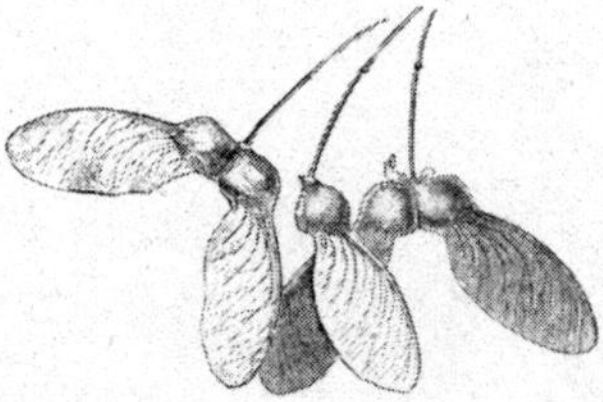

ACKNOWLEDGEMENTS

I thank my family, friends and colleagues, without whose help and support the research and writing of this book would not have happened. With special thanks to the following: Jean Dandenault and the Dandenault family, Helen Humphreys, Jeff Cowton and The Wordsworth Trust in Grasmere, Dr. Polly Atkin, Dr. Will Smith, Dr. Shelley Snow, Char Davies and the Reverie Foundation, Quebec Writers' Federation, Lynn Verge and the Atwater Library, Syd and Maureen Boulton, Barbara Muir Wight, Elizabeth Dillon, Brenda Keesal, Meredith Fowke, Elise Moser, Mini Carleton Group, Tiny House Farm, Michael Winter, T.L. Winter, Paul Winter, Christine Pountney, Margaret Spooner, Daniel Karrasch, Rebecca Krinke, Enid Stevenson, Arthur Griffin, Art Andrews, Anne Hardy, Ernest de Sélincourt, Susan Levin, James Dixon, Esther Wade and Juliette Dandenault. I thank my agent Shaun Bradley, assistant editor Rick Meier, copy editor Melanie Little, and designer Jennifer Griffiths. Very special thanks to my editor Lynn Henry, and to the land and living entities upon it that have nurtured and inspired Dorothy Wordsworth and all of us, especially trees, rock, water and plants. I thank Sufi my rescue dog, who has rescued me. And thank you, Dear Reader.

Courtesy of the author

KATHLEEN WINTER's novel *Annabel* was shortlisted for the Scotiabank Giller Prize, the Governor General's Literary Award, the Rogers Writers' Trust Fiction Prize, the Amazon.ca First Novel Award, the Orange Prize, and numerous other awards. It was also a *Globe and Mail* "Best Book," a *New York Times* "Notable" book, a *Quill & Quire* "Book of the Year" and #1 bestseller in Canada. It has been published and translated worldwide. Her Arctic memoir, *Boundless* (2014), was shortlisted for Canada's Weston and Taylor nonfiction prizes, and her 2017 novel, *Lost in September*, was longlisted for the International Dublin Literary Award and shortlisted for the Governor General's Literary Award. Born in the UK, Winter now lives in Montreal.

For Dorothy Wordsworth

VINTAGE CANADA EDITION, 2022

Published by Vintage Canada, a division of Penguin Random House Canada Limited, Toronto, 2022. Originally published in hardcover by Alfred A. Knopf Canada, a division of Penguin Random House Canada Limited, Toronto, 2021. Distributed by Penguin Random House Canada Limited, Toronto.

Vintage Canada and colophon are registered trademarks.

www.penguinrandomhouse.ca

Library and Archives Canada Cataloguing in Publication
Title: Undersong / Kathleen Winter.
Names: Winter, Kathleen, author.
Description: Previously published: Toronto : Knopf Canada, 2021.
Identifiers: Canadiana 20210143703 | ISBN 9780735278240 (softcover)
Classification: LCC PS8595.I618 U53 2022 | DDC C813/.54—dc23

Cover design: Adapted from an original by Jennifer Griffiths | Cover images: (flower) Glow Images / Getty Images; (painting) *Newburyport Meadows*, The Metropolitan Museum of Art, New York, Purchase, Mrs. Samuel P. Reed Gift, Morris K. Jesup Fund, Maria DeWitt Jesup Fund, John Osgood and Elizabeth Amis Cameron Blanchard Memorial Fund and Gifts of Robert E. Tod and William Gedney Bunce, by exchange, 1985.

Interior design: Jennifer Griffiths | Interior image credits: All images courtesy of The Internet Archive. Book images: (helicopter seeds) page 868 of "The natural history of plants, their forms, growth, reproduction, and distribution;" (1902), NCSU Libraries; (bee) page 376 of "The ABC and XYZ of bee culture; a cyclopedia of everything pertaining to the care of the honey-bee; bees, hives, honey, implements, honey-plants, etc." (1910), Smithsonian Libraries; (flower) page 531 of "Cyclopedia of American horticulture, comprising suggestions for cultivation of horticultural plants, descriptions of the species of fruits, vegetables, flowers, and ornamental plants sold in the United States and Canada, together with geographical and biographical sketches" (1900), Boston College Libraries; (owl) page 41 of "The British bird book" (1921), Cornell University Library; (bat) page 119 of "A comprehensive dictionary of the Bible" (1871), The Library of Congress; (dandelion) page 53 of "Dreer's garden book: 1904" (1904), U.S. Department of Agriculture, National Agricultural Library.

Printed in the United States of America

2 4 6 8 9 7 5 3 1

Penguin Random House
VINTAGE CANADA

Undersong

Kathleen Winter

VINTAGE CANADA

ALSO BY KATHLEEN WINTER

FICTION

boYs (2007)

Annabel (2010)

The Freedom in American Songs (2014)

Lost in September (2017)

NONFICTION

Boundless: Tracing Land and Dream in a New Northwest Passage (2014)

Praise fo

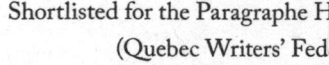

Shortlisted for the Paragraphe H

(Quebec Writers' Fed

"[A] lyrical meditation and character study of class, gender, and recognition. Drawing from varied sources, Winter's narrative captures the inner life of her protagonist with clarity, tenderness, and quiet psychological insight. The writing is nuanced and luminous in equal measure. . . . The novel, while set at the start of the Industrial Age, speaks urgently to contemporary readers: a deep adoration to our own small walks of woods, mountains, dirt and lake is what is required of us to cease the destruction of the earth and halt a planetary fire." —Jury Citation, Paragraphe Hugh MacLennan Prize for Fiction

"An engrossing delight. . . . Dorothy [Wordsworth]'s exuberant imagination blooms on the page. . . . A tantalizing glimpse into a life as it could have been." —*Literary Review of Canada*

"[In] rich prose . . . Winter's new novel takes an unconventional approach in its portrayal of the unconventional Dorothy Wordsworth, a talented nature writer here posited as the stalwart genius behind her brother William's poetry." —*The Globe and Mail*

"Kathleen Winter is a rare talent, a writer whose prose is rife with compassion and emotional intelligence, equally able to convincingly give voice to a misunderstood historical figure. . . . [Her] version of Dorothy Wordsworth's story reveals the rich, hidden life of a woman determined against all societal expectations to live on her own terms." —*Toronto Star*

"Consistently elegant and original. It is very much a book about language and atmosphere. Winter mimics period style beautifully, and she also infuses the novel with unconventional touches . . . that arguably conjure the idiosyncratic spirit of her heroine better than any first-person narration could have achieved." —*Quill & Quire*, starred review

"AAAHHH!"

I have no reflection. None. I'm looking straight into the glass, but absolutely nothing is looking back at me.

I drop my toothbrush and reel backwards. My shoulder blades slam into the towel rack on the wall behind me.

From this perspective, I can see the tarnished metal bar reflected in the mirror. The top of the faded pink towel that's hanging there. But no green eyes rimmed with my perpetual dark circles. No unruly mane of long auburn hair. No pale, freckled skin or heavy C-cups propped up by my navy-blue push-up bra.

And no expression of the complete shock and horror I feel.

Seriously, it's like I'm not even standing here.

Now, don't get me wrong: I'm used to being invisible. At 5'4" and a size that's often hidden away in some "special" section way in the back of the store, I don't exactly turn a lot of heads. But this? This is some kind of scary-ass, Bram-Stoker, straight-outta-Transylvania shit. Right?

Am I right?

I mean, I don't want to sound absurdist or anything, but either I'm a vampire or—

No.

No way.

There's got to be some other, more logical explanation. One that doesn't end with me living crappily ever after as some fictional night-stalking daughter of darkness.

Because that's what vampires are. Fiction. Like Bigfoot. Little green men. One-size-fits-all clothing.

And this? This isn't fiction. This is my life. My *real* life.

I inhale. Exhale. Ignore the icy river of panic that's rushing down my spine. At the risk of sounding like a meme, I need to keep calm and figure this shit out.

I stagger out of the bathroom and plop down at my tiny dining table that doubles as my tiny office. I fire up my laptop. The clock in the upper-right corner of the screen reads *Sunday 5:17 p.m.*

Not a.m.—*p.m.*

Okay, so that means I must have been passed out cold on the floor all day. And I must have woken up, um, *just after sunset?*

Another check in the vampire column. Except vampires are not real. Not. Real.

My hands are shaking as I connect to the free Wi-Fi from the deli next door. Trying like hell to keep my head on straight while I wrangle my unnatural thirst, I navigate to WebMD and launch a search of my ever-growing list of, well, *symptoms*: bloodlust + uncontrollable urges + fangs + no reflection + nocturnal.

And you know what comes up?

Nothing. No results found.

So much for that whole logical explanation thing.

Getting desperate, I try a few other medical websites. Google. Bing. My fingers attack the keyboard. My eyes scan screen after screen after screen, but it's all just Comic Con tickets and Dracula-themed bars and indie horror film fests.

I keep at it for a good hour before I finally give up and collapse back in my chair. I feel disoriented, like I just stepped off the bus in the middle of apeshit la-la land. I'm way past losing touch with reality. I've totally cut the cord.

Sensibly, I know this can't be happening.

And yet…

And yet.

I try to ground myself by focusing on the things I know to be true.

My name is Lily Baines. I'm twenty-five years old. I live on Bleecker Street in the West Village. I work as an overnight web editor…

And apparently, I'm a fucking vampire.

CHAPTER 2

A few minutes later, I'm hunting through my bag, searching for my phone—but not to order that burger. New change of plans. I've got to talk to Cat.

Why didn't I think of this earlier? I mean, I know we agreed to meet at Dos Rosas last night—and barring a natural disaster, my BFF would never just stand me up. So, assuming we were together, she should be able to fill in at least some of the gaps in my memory.

Plus, as a special added bonus, Cat is kind of a vampire geek. Legit. She's read every single one of those Twilight novels. She even owns the movies on DVD. Sometimes, I think she half believes the fantasy. So, you know, maybe she'll have some helpful insight into my current, um, *condition.*

Or maybe—just maybe—she'll call bullshit on my immortal bloodsucker theory, and the two of us can work out what's really going on.

A ghoul can dream, can't she?

I locate my iPhone at the bottom of the bag and dial Cat's mobile. As soon as I hear my bestie's voice, I'm sure I'll feel much better.

Only, I don't.

"Hi. This is Cat McMahon. Leave a message, and I'll get back to you."

Typical.

I swear, Cat is a certified computer genius, but she's completely inept when it comes to simple everyday stuff like keeping her iPhone charged. The thing goes straight to voicemail more times than not.

But as I hang up without even bothering to wait for the beep, an uncomfortable thought starts to niggle at the back of my mind. *What if Cat didn't just forget to recharge her phone? What if something happened to her last night too?*

A shudder runs through me as I recall how my body reacted to that pigeon. How I pounced and tried to attack it on instinct, before I was even aware of—

Oh, no! What if something happened to Cat…and I did it?

Okay. That settles it.

I've got to haul my undead ass uptown to Cat's place ASAP. I need to go check on my best friend and make sure she's okay.

• • • • •

So, just FYI, a crowded subway car is a bad place to be if you're a vampire.

Okay, correction: a crowded subway car is a bad place to be if you're a vampire who doesn't want to act like, you know, a *vampire*.

I'm sitting on the Uptown 1, and the car is unbelievably fragrant with the blood of my fellow passengers. I breathe in and their unique, individual scents—sweet and spicy and earthy and tart—mingle together in my nostrils in the most tantalizing way, teasing my new preternatural taste buds. The aroma is almost irresistible.

Luckily, I came prepared. I mean, I knew there was no way I could risk the trip to Cat's without a strategy for keeping my unnatural appetite in check. That whole business with the pigeon gave me the big hairy heads-up on just how quickly I could lose control. But after a lifetime of being bombarded with clickbait for weight-loss products and programs—and yes, sometimes taking the bait—I'm a walking Wikipedia of dieting tips and tricks.

So, before I left my apartment, I drank a ton of water to make me feel full. Then I popped a wad of sugarless gum into my mouth to avoid, um, *nibbling*. And now, as I sit here on the train chomping Dentyne, I'm playing solitaire on my iPhone to distract me from my cravings.

Go ahead and laugh—but you know what? This shit is actually working. As the brightly lit car goes speeding along, rattling through the pitch-black underground tunnel, I can feel my fangs receding.

To confirm this, I look back over my shoulder to examine my reflection in the subway car window—

But once again, I come up empty.

I turn away, slouch down in my hard plastic seat, and return to my game. Only now I can't help wondering what I'm *not* seeing. Because let's face it: after a typical Saturday night of drinking margaritas at Dos Rosas, I look like living death. So, last night, if I actually *became* living death…

Jesus. How scary must I look right now?

I chew my gum and try to concentrate on dealing the cards on my touch screen—but my focus is now irreversibly split. And the fissure is creating just enough space for an increased awareness of my surroundings to seep in.

I grow a little too cognizant of the middle-aged woman in the light-blue scrubs, hot-pink Crocs, and denim jacket seated across from me. I home in on the way the vein in her neck is pulsing in perfect rhythm with the Lady Gaga song I can hear leaking out from her little white earbuds. And I swear, the pumping of her heart is like a goddamn dinner bell.

Abruptly, my fangs extend again to their full length, nicking my tongue. The rich, slightly metallic flavor of my own blood fills my mouth, and all of a sudden, it's like… Well, you know how if you don't eat any potato chips at all, you're fine, but if you eat even one, then—*bam!*—you want the whole bag?

Okay. I need off this train. Like, right now.

We're pulling into the Fifty-Ninth Street/Columbus Circle station. It's still one more stop to Cat's place, but I can't take the chance. I don't trust myself in this enclosed, populated space anymore.

I jump to my feet. Just then, the subway jerks to a stop, and I lose my balance.

Out of nowhere, a strong hand is on my arm, steadying me.

"Are you okay?" asks a low, masculine voice. Considering my minor stumble, the heavy concern in his tone seems a little extra.

I peer up, and this outrageously gorgeous guy is hovering over me. I don't remember noticing him on the train before—and how I could have failed to notice *him*, I really don't know. But then, I guess I have been a little preoccupied with, um, *other* things.

Anyway, he certainly has my full attention now. Probably somewhere in his early thirties, he is long and lean, broad-shouldered and muscular. His clothes are clearly expensive but casually rumpled. His perfect features are kept from looking too perfect by a couple days' growth of stubble. He reminds me of a war correspondent—I mean, not the way they really look, all old and grizzled and battle-fatigued like on CNN or something. No, more like the way they look in the movies, all sexy and rugged and bad-boy dangerous. A young Clint Eastwood with Indiana Jones's styling. His indigo-blue eyes *twinkle*—I swear, they actually twinkle—as they gaze down at me from underneath a tousled mop of longish sandy-brown hair.

"Y-yeah. I'm fine," I say with difficulty. Partly because it's hard to talk without flashing my fully extended fangs. But also because—full disclosure, here—whenever I'm around a really good-looking guy, I get stupid. Totally stupid.

And this guy isn't just swipe-right good-looking. Honestly, I don't think I've been this attracted to anyone ever.

Except, well…my attraction isn't just about the way he looks—although, of course, that's a part of it. But mostly, it's about the way he's looking at me. It's like he sees me—really sees *me*—and not just my size. It's like he knows me. Or wants to get to know me. And I find that I want to get to know him.

I think maybe that's why the pressure of his hand, still grasping my forearm below my elbow, is driving me out of my mind. Why my skin is flushed and my breathing is accelerated. Why a slideshow of filthy fantasies is flashing through my brain, and it's pretty much all I can do not to throw myself at this man, right here and now.

"Do you need to get off?" he asks me.

I freeze.

Jesus. Does he already know me way too well?

Then he smiles, revealing a mouthful of perfect, pearly-white teeth, and inclines his head to indicate the subway's sliding doors.

It takes me a moment, but—*well, duh*. He's talking about getting off *the train*.

And here I am, so mesmerized by everything I'm reading into his twinkly indigo gaze that I'm actually entertaining the possibility that he might be hitting on me.

As if.

The doors open with a hiss—or is that just the sound of my ego deflating?

Whatever.

"Thanks," I mumble with a quick nod.

Then, mortified, I tear my arm out of his grip and make a hasty escape. A beat after my boots hit the concrete platform, the doors whoosh closed behind me.

But then—okay, I can't help it—I turn back to get one last glimpse of him through the subway car windows. Only…he's not there.

I blink. Blink again. My eyes scan the inside of the car as the subway brakes release with a groan and the train clatters off into the dark tunnel ahead. Still, I don't see him anywhere.

I look up and down the length of the platform. Maybe he exited the car too?

But no. He's not in the station either.

Somehow, just as mysteriously as he appeared, the guy has completely vanished.

CHAPTER 3

I head up Columbus Avenue and hang right onto West Sixty-Fifth Street—and what do you know? The combination of the brisk walk and the crisp night air does wonders to cool my bloodlust. Unfortunately, it doesn't do a thing to cool my *other* lust. The one for Mysterious Subway Dude.

I'm still thinking about him, about the way he looked at me. About the way it made me feel—and the way it's still making me feel, despite my misunderstanding. Did I really just imagine that connection between us?

With my body burning as hot as my curiosity, I ring the bell for Cat's apartment.

After a brief wait, my BFF's familiar voice crackles through the intercom. "Hello?"

Immediately, my romantic speculations are washed away by a flood of relief. Sounds like Cat is perfectly fine.

"It's me," I say into the box. "Lily."

"Hey!" Cat's voice crackles again. "Come on in. And come on up."

The buzzer buzzes in invitation, and I pull open the outside security door to my friend's building. Way nicer than mine, it's a quaint little prewar structure, its mere six floors tucked just around the corner from the newer, flashier high-rise residences on Columbus and Broadway.

I step through the vestibule, pull open the second security door, and enter the well-kept lobby. My boot heels click across the highly polished mosaic-tile floor as I bypass what I already know to be the slowest elevator in all of Manhattan and take the stairs up the single flight to Cat's second-floor one-bedroom.

Cat is already waiting for me in her doorway. Any last lingering fears for her safety are put definitively to rest as I see for a fact she's okay. Better than okay, actually.

So, I guess now is as good a time as any to mention that, in addition to being the code-writing superstar at an about-to-go-public tech firm, Cat could be a supermodel. While I look absolutely nothing like the tall, elegant flower I was named for, Cat looks, well...exactly like a cat. She's all long, lithe arms and legs with wide-set blue eyes and a black bob of hair so shiny and sleek you just want to reach out and pet it. Currently, she's rocking oversize red-flannel drawstring pajama bottoms slung low on her slim hips and a pinkish tank I'm betting used to be white because, um, sorting laundry is another one of those things that's way too mundane for Cat's advanced intellect to comprehend. But even dressed like this, she looks amazing.

"Wow," says Cat when she sees me. "What's the occasion?"

I assume she's referring to the unannounced drop-by. Not usually my thing.

"I tried to call," I say. I walk down the hall to where she's draped gracefully against her doorjamb. "Charge your fucking iPhone."

"No, I mean all this." She waves her hand at me, indicating my hair, my face, my outfit. "You look really great, Lil."

"Shut up," I say with a self-conscious tug at the bottom of my black sweater. Obvi, with (a) no reflection and (b) no idea if Cat was alive or dead or maybe even undead, I didn't spend a ton of time primping. I just washed my face, dragged a flat brush through my long tangle of reddish-brown hair, threw on a little Cherry ChapStick and a pair of jeans that did close around the waist, and hoped for the best. I'm pretty sure I've never looked worse.

But, hey, in the win column, at least my fangs have gone back into hiding.

"So, is this like a predate wardrobe check or something?" asks Cat. "Are you meeting that guy again?"

"Guy?" I shoot back. "What guy?"

"Duh," says Cat. "The guy you left Dos Rosas with last night."

"So, we were at Dos Rosas last night?" I ask, just to be sure.

"Of course, we were at—"

"And I left with a guy?"

Cat's perfectly arched eyebrows knit slowly together in concern. "You don't remember?"

No. I still don't remember. But suddenly, somehow, I *know*.

"This guy… Did he kind of look like Clint Eastwood and Indiana Jones had a superhot baby?"

Cat studies me long and hard. She knows me better than anyone, so she must see that I'm not entirely myself.

She must also see that, whatever my reason for showing up unexpectedly, it's not something I want to discuss out here in the hall.

She takes a step back, clearing her doorway, and waves me inside. "Get your butt in here. Sounds like we need to talk. Big time."

• • • • •

Cat's apartment is an eclectic mix of expensive state-of-the-art electronics and whatever furniture happened to be on sale at IKEA. The only decorative touch—if you can even call it that—is what I like to refer to as Cat's *doll collection*: shelf after shelf of mint-condition, mostly still-in-the-box action figures. There's Spider-Man, the Incredible Hulk—plus a lot I can't even name. Usually, I make fun of them. But tonight, as my eyes survey these fictitious little freaks of nature and science experiments gone awry, I feel an odd kind of kinship.

"Uh, Lily…?"

I turn to meet my friend's increasingly anxious gaze. I open my mouth to speak—but quickly, I close it up again. I clear my throat to buy a little time.

Now that I'm here, where do I even begin?

I take a deep inhale and try to organize my thoughts.

Then I take one more for courage.

"Cat," I say finally, "what do you know about vampires?"

• • • • •

Once we get past her initial confusion, Cat humors me by outlining the basics of the Dracula tale. And, guess what? The description is so spot-on it could be my new online profile.

Then she really gets into it, rattling on and on about other vampires in fiction and film with TED-Talk-level proficiency. The more I listen, the more I feel whatever slim tether I still had to my human life slipping away, sliding through my fingers like the string of a helium-filled balloon.

By the time Cat gets around to fangirling on Twilight, I figure I've heard enough. Lacking words of my own, I decide to just show her. Impulsively, I grab her by the hand.

"Hey! What are you doing?" she asks as I drag her into her bedroom and over to the sliding mirrored doors of her closet. "And why is your hand so cold?"

But when her big blue eyes get even bigger and her jaw goes slack with wonder, I know she must be seeing exactly what I see. Despite the fact that we are standing side by side and hand in hand in front of the glass, our reflection shows only Cat, grasping the empty air next to her.

"No way," she whispers. Her eyes dart back and forth between the mirror and me, the mirror and me. "No friggin' way."

"You said vampires cast no reflection," I say. "Right?"

"Is this a trick?" asks Cat. Her gaze settles on me and narrows. "Some kind of illusion or something?"

"Oh, please. Do I look like David Blaine?"

"Well, you don't look like Nosferatu."

I open my mouth, curl my top lip back, and show her my fangs.

"Holy shit!" She jumps away from me, pulling her hand out of mine.

"Sorry," I say.

"But…*how?*"

"I don't know," I say. "That's the thing. I don't remember. Actually, I was hoping maybe you saw something last night…?"

Cat shakes her head slowly. She's across the room now, on the other side of her unmade bed. Ever since she got an eyeful of my new dental work, she's been backing away from me, keeping her distance. I can't exactly say I blame her—but her reaction stings, all the same. Usually, she has more confidence in me than I do.

"I'm not going to hurt you, you know," I say quietly.

"I know you would never *intentionally* hurt me," she says. She's pressed up against the wall now, still scrutinizing me. "But in practically all the stories, newborn vampires are wildly unpredictable. They can't control their insatiable hunger."

"Amateurs," I say. "I'll bet not one of them ever tried Noom. You want to talk about insatiable hunger? Try living on twelve hundred calories a day. For a month solid, I was so fucking hungry I wanted to eat my own arm. But I managed to keep my appetite on lockdown then. I can do it again now."

Cat fixes me with a hard look. "If that's your plan, it sucks."

"Did you really just say 'sucks' to a vampire?"

"I'm serious, Lil. You can't deprive yourself forever. Literally, *forever*."

"You don't know that."

"Actually, I do," says Cat. "And you do too. Not only is it wildly unhealthy, but starving always leads to bingeing."

I hit pause and think about this. And, okay, I have to admit, my friend makes a fair point. Pretty much since puberty, I've been riding an unstable roller coaster of weight loss and gain: a month of wasting away on Noom followed by a week of unbridled munchies; a three-day organic juice cleanse followed by a late-night trip to Mickey D's and one of everything off the dollar menu; two weeks of strict paleo eating followed by—

"Oh," I say as realization settles like a big, heavy rock in my gut. "Oh, fart biscuits."

Okay, so maybe I do need to rethink my strategy for keeping the ol' bloodlust in check.

"Well," I say—and I can't even believe I'm about to ask this, but here goes: "What did the sparkly vampires do for blood? They didn't attack humans, did they?"

"No," says Cat thoughtfully. "Not the Cullens, anyway." The tension that's been keeping her body rigid eases up a little. "Instead, they wrestled big-game animals with their vampire superstrength and drank from them. Mostly grizzlies and mountain lions, I think."

While this seems totally fucked-up and not at all helpful to me, it seems to give Cat an idea.

"Okay," she says decisively. She takes a deep breath and walks back around the bed, her new reticence mostly disappearing. "First things first. We need to get you some proper nourishment before you do something you'll regret."

"How?" I ask. "How are we going to do that, exactly? Is there some trendy new restaurant I don't know about with O negative on the menu? And do you have connections to get us a table?"

Cat slides her bare feet into a pair of beat-up Converse sneakers. "We're not going to a restaurant."

A horrible thought crosses my mind. "Please tell me we're not going to the big-game exhibit at Central Park Zoo," I say. "Because, seriously, Cat, I don't think I have any vampire superstrength. And I definitely don't know how to wrestle."

She plucks a ratty old NYU sweatshirt that dates back to our college days off the top of her laundry basket and pulls it on. Just pulls it on right over her pajamas.

"Come on," Cat says. "Trust me."

And then, without even a teeny-tiny peek into the mirror to see how she looks, she grabs the brown-suede hobo-style bag hanging from her bedpost and strides past me, walking out of her bedroom and toward her front door.

I stare after her, flabbergasted. Her complete nonchalance about her appearance is, as always, incomprehensible to me. Maybe even more incomprehensible than my new thirst for blood.

Man, what I wouldn't give to be that casual and carefree about the way I look. For me, it's like the Holy Grail of attitudes.

"You coming?" she calls back over her shoulder.

Just then, a fresh wave of bloodlust washes over me, practically bowling me over.

Cat's right. I need to do something about this—before I do something I'll regret.

And if she has an idea? I'm in. After all, she's never given me any reason to doubt her. Not since we were randomly thrown together as freshman dorm roommates. I trust her with my life.

Unlife?

Whatever.

So, after my own compulsive but ultimately futile glance in the empty mirror, I get my ass in gear and follow my friend out the door.

CHAPTER 4

Thankfully, we don't head in the direction of the Central Park Zoo.

Instead, we walk over to Hell's Kitchen and stop in front of the entrance to an impressive brick and glass building. Its familiar logo glows red and white in the darkness.

"The American Red Cross?" I ask.

Cat nods.

A blood-bank heist? Seriously?

I swallow. Hang back a little. "So, we're, um, breaking in?"

"Don't be ridiculous," says Cat. She's already heading up the steps. "I have a key card."

"You have a key card?" I ask, trotting after her. "Since when?"

"Since I started volunteering here. About six months ago."

"You've been volunteering at the Red Cross?" I ask. "For six months?"

Cat shrugs like it's a total no-biggie. "I'm helping them update their computer system."

So, I'm not going to lie to you. I mean, I love Cat, and I'm all about the whole sisterhood thing. But still, it's extremely annoying to be blindsided by the fact that, in addition to being hotter and smarter and more gainfully employed than I am, my best friend is also a way better human being. And don't even get me started on how I'm not even, technically speaking, a human being anymore.

The only thing that makes me not want to just crawl into a hole and stay there for the rest of my immortal life is that Cat is currently swiping her volunteer employee key card with the magnetic strip facing in the wrong direction and wondering why the entrance isn't opening.

"What's wrong with this stupid thing?" she grumbles.

"Here," I say. "Let me." I take the card and flip it over. "You need to swipe it this way. Like the little icon shows." I swipe the card correctly, and the pinpoint red light turns to green. "See?"

I hand the card back to Cat.

"Oh. Duh." She pulls the door open and—

Whoa.

If this were a cartoon, the aroma of the blood from inside the building would have snaked toward me like a long, ghostly arm, lifted me right off my feet, and led me floating off blissfully in the direction of its source.

"It's this way—"

"No shit," I say as my fangs snap to their full attention, practically piercing my lip. Abandoning all civility, I push straight past Cat and enter the deserted interior.

The halls are dark, but that's not a problem. I follow my nose. It leads me straight to a room that looks like a cross between an industrial kitchen and a laboratory set on one of the CSI shows. Here, light from the street streams in through big, square windows, bathing the stainless-steel surfaces in an ethereal light. I reach for one of the gleaming handles of the supersized, wall-length refrigerator and—

"*Wait!*"

Cat's voice startles me. I've become so intoxicated by the scent of blood in the air that I pretty much forgot about her. I turn now to see her rushing into the room after me, all wide eyes and waving hands.

"No, no, no. Not from in there." She gives the fridge a short nod as she scurries past it. "From in here."

She indicates a plastic receptacle.

A fire-engine-red plastic receptacle.

A *trash* receptacle.

Okay, so this has got to be some kind of a joke. A bad joke.

"You want me to eat out of the garbage?" I ask.

"It's not garbage," Cat explains calmly. "It's hazardous medical waste."

"Oh. Gee. That sounds so much more appetizing," I say. "Um, *pass*."

"Well, you can't have the blood from the refrigerator," she insists. "Every bag in there is bar-coded and logged in the computer. If even one goes missing, they'll know." She holds up her key card. "And based on the entrance log, they'll know I had something to do with it."

"Yeah, but...can't you just work some of your computer magic so they won't know?"

"Lily!" She gives me an appalled look and points at the fridge. "That blood is meant to save people's lives."

Low blow, huh? Way to make the new evil being on the block feel, well...positively *evil*.

Reluctantly, I rein in my bloodlust and take a step back from the promised land. "Okay, okay," I say. "Tell me about this reject blood."

"Okay," she says. "Well, some of it tested positive for infectious disease—"

"Infectious disease?!"

"Well, nothing that'll kill you."

"How do you know?"

"If you're a vampire," she says, "you're already dead."

Her words hit me like a slap. What with the no-reflection thing and the gee-it-looks-like-I'm-a-vampire thing and the must-have-blood thing, it's a concept I haven't even stopped to consider.

Jesus. Am I dead?

As in I died? Bit the dust? Went to that great big house party in the sky?

Only, I didn't go anywhere.

My silence seems to hit Cat like I slapped her back.

"I'm sorry," she says quickly. "That was cold. I wasn't thinking. I mean, of course, you're not dead." She shakes her head vehemently. "You're *undead*. Undead isn't dead. Or else, how could you even be here?"

How, indeed?

I try to wrap my head around this, around this idea of my, um, *undeath*.

For some reason, I look down at my hands. They don't look dead.

I stretch out my fingers as far as they'll go, then curl them into tight fists. They don't act dead.

I extend my fingers back out. Turn both hands over, palms up.

Suddenly, Cat places her hands in mine and squeezes. "Ah, Lily," she says with a catch in her voice.

I feel a cry coming on—

But, no. I can't go there. I mean, between the powerful smell of blood that surrounds me and my own extreme thirst, I just can't right now. It's too much.

Without raising my eyes to meet Cat's, I pull my hands out of her grasp.

I swallow. Try to collect myself.

"Well," I say, clearing my throat, "dead or undead or whatever, I am not drinking infected blood."

"Wh–what?"

Feeling mostly composed again, I hazard a peek up at my friend. "You were telling me about the blood that tested positive for infectious disease," I remind her. "And I was telling you to forget it."

Cat opens her mouth to say something, to protest my emotional shutdown, I'm sure. But I give her a warning look—and she decides not to push.

I watch gratefully as she pulls it together for my sake, as her brain works to pick up the lost thread of our previous conversation.

"Right," she says when she finds it. "But it's okay. Really. I mean, I'm pretty sure you'd be immune to any infection from the donated blood. As far as I've read, human diseases do not kill vampires. Sunlight, fire, a wooden stake through the heart, decapitation? Yes. Syphilis? No."

"*Syphilis!*"

I swear, it would be just my luck to contract a sexually transmitted disease without even having sex. That would totally fit with the direction my love life has been going. Sadly, it's been dead a lot longer than I have.

A small smile starts to tug at the corners of Cat's mouth. "You know," she says, "for a bloodthirsty creature of the night, you really are kind of a wuss."

"Fuck you," I say. "For the last time, I am not drinking infected blood."

"Fine," says Cat. "Do you want to know why the rest of the blood was discarded?"

"I don't know," I say skeptically. I cross my arms and widen my stance. "Do I?"

"All red blood cells get tossed after forty-two days."

I wrinkle my nose. "So, it's like…spoiled?"

"Theoretically, yes," Cat says carefully. "But, well…you know how sometimes the milk is a day or two past the expiration date, but then you sniff it, and it's perfectly fine?"

I look at Cat, incredulous. "You want me to sniff the expired blood?"

For a moment, Cat just looks back at me sheepishly. Then she shrugs her assent.

Okay, this is starting to sound a little too familiar, like a replay of that situation with the orange beef. And considering how well that went? I'd rather not go there again.

I mean, I don't even like the five-second rule. I accidentally drop a Peanut M&M on the floor, I kiss the damn thing goodbye. So, the thought of dumpster diving for sustenance? Total gag city.

But then I hear Cat's words from earlier tonight echoing in my head: *Starving always leads to bingeing.* And, yes, okay, the consequences of me "bingeing" now could be a hell of a lot more catastrophic than just a few regained pounds.

"Fuck nuggets," I say with a sigh. I drop my arms to my sides in resignation. "Okay, okay. I'm in. But let's do this quick, before I change my mind."

• • • • •

After Cat finds a pair of disposable latex gloves and puts them on, she gingerly pulls a few pints of blood out of the gar—um, *hazardous medical waste*—bin. Then, she makes me wait with my fangs hanging out while she logs on to the nearest computer and checks the ID numbers.

The first pouch is positive for hepatitis B; the second, hep C. But the third? The third is the charm: forty-three days old.

"Here you go," says Cat. "Try this one."

I weigh the firm but slightly squishy bag of thick, red liquid in my hand. Then, cautiously, I put my nose to the plastic and take a big whiff.

"So?" asks Cat. "How does it smell?"

How does it smell? *How does it smell?* To my newly turned vampire self, it smells like hot buttered popcorn and cotton candy, like homemade chicken soup and freshly baked bread, like sugar and spice and everything nice—only *better*.

"Fine," I manage to croak out in a voice that sounds so rough and scratchy with desire I barely recognize it as my own. "It smells fine."

"Sweet," says Cat. "So, uh…dig in, huh?"

But still I hesitate. And not just because I can get a little self-conscious if someone is watching me eat.

See, while the vampire in me is all, "Yeah! Bottoms up," the me in me is all, "Ew! Blood."

I try telling myself it's just like a juice box. Only, not a box. And not juice.

"Straw?" I ask, stalling.

Cat stares at me, confused. "Shouldn't you just, you know, use your fangs?"

"Right," I say with a nod. "Right. My, um, fangs."

But okay, for reals: it's not just the idea of drinking blood that's got me squeamish. Fact is, I'm about to cross a line here. I mean, if I do this, that's it—you know? Then, there's no more denying what I am.

Only, if I am what I am, well…what other choice do I have?

So I, um, *vampire* up. I pull the surface of the pouch taut, close my eyes, and ever-so-tentatively sink my teeth into it.

The split second my fangs pierce the plastic and the first drops of blood touch my tongue, my new instincts take over. Unwavering, I suck in the sweet, red nectar, drinking it down in big, greedy gulps.

Almost immediately, I feel a warm sensation bloom deep in my core. Then, slowly, the warmth radiates outward. It spreads through me like an electrical current, like a full-body wake-up call.

I continue to drink, and the heat continues to surge, filling me up. And even when there's no more me to fill, it keeps flowing and flowing until I explode—and every inch of me is bathed in undulating waves of fully satisfied pleasure.

I may be undead, but I swear, I've never felt more alive.

I drain the bag dry, and my contented fangs recede.

I open my eyes again, and—okay, so you know how, after the tornado in *The Wizard of Oz*, Dorothy steps through the front door into Munchkin Land, and her black-and-white world is all lit up in Technicolor? Well, I'm all of a sudden seeing things in colors and details I never even imagined existed. And it's not just seeing. All my senses are supersharpened, ultra-heightened. I'm like Dorothy on acid.

"Lily," Cat says softly, "are you okay?"

She's watching me the way you watch a scary movie: a mixture of captivated interest—and pure terror. To her credit, though, she's managing not to grimace and peer at me through her fingers.

I meet her gaze, and I wonder if her big blue eyes were always flecked with silvery-gray like that. Was her flawless skin always so glowing and rosy and pulsating with life?

"Yeah," I say when I find my voice. "Yeah. I'm…I'm fine."

Only, that's not 100 percent true.

See, in addition to quenching my thirst and boosting my sensory perceptions, that dose of blood seems to be rebooting my memory.

The lost events of Saturday night are coming at me in a rush, tumbling toward me like an avalanche. Engulfing me. Burying me.

I feel like I'm suffocating.

"Lil?" says Cat. "What is it?"

Mentally, I claw my way up through the rubble, one recollection at a time. When I reach the top and resurface in the present, I inhale sharply.

"Lily?"

"I remember now," I whisper, wide-eyed, to my friend. "I remember how it all happened. I remember, um…*everything*."

CHAPTER 5

The Saturday night in question started with me wriggling and writhing around on the bed—but, um, not in a vampire-porn kind of a way.

The very unsexy truth is that, even after six days on a three-day celebrity detox cleanse, I still couldn't zip up the jeans I wanted to wear out for the evening. So, in order to squeeze my ass into this pair of vintage Levis I fell in love with at a neighborhood upcycle shop, I first had to squeeze said ass into some serious shapewear.

Twenty minutes later, I was sweaty, exhausted, and encased so tightly in reinforced spandex from my midsection down to my knees that I could barely breathe, barely walk. But twenty minutes after that, I was pulling open the door to Dos Rosas in—hello—the vintage Levis.

And yes, okay, even as I entered the Tex-Mex joint feeling pretty damn good about my accomplishment, deep down, I was conflicted. I mean, I could totally see how this kind of behavior would make an outside observer think they needed to dive in and save me from my fat-shaming self.

But seriously, it wasn't as if I liked having this adversarial relationship with my own body. I didn't enjoy beating up on myself. I wanted to stop. I wanted to make friends.

And I was trying—really, I was. I followed a bunch of body positivity activists on social media. I listened to their podcasts. I retweeted their words of wisdom, and I hearted their posts. I was all in on the healthy-at-any-size movement.

When it came to other people.

But when it came to me, well...it was one thing to know something. To agree with it. To believe in it, even. But, to feel it in your heart, in your soul, in your gut? That was another thing entirely.

So, I guess you could say that when it came to how I saw my own body, I was still a work in progress. A very uncomfortable, Spanx-wearing work in progress.

• • • • •

I looked around, scanning the bar area as the aroma of freshly made tortilla chips wrapped me up like a cozy Mexican blanket.

"Lily!" I heard Cat call above the chatter.

I turned in the direction of her voice, and she raised her frozen margarita to me in greeting. She was wearing a pair of ripped skinny jeans that she'd obviously just thrown on with a paint-splattered hoodie and a pair of brown suede Uggs—no industrial-strength undergarments required. And natch, she was already holding court.

"This is my friend Lily," she said to the two bearded, bespectacled, hipster-looking dudes flanking her at one of the high-topped bar tables when I joined them. "Lil, this is Max. And Ben."

Max and Ben each greeted me with an expression I'd only seen a gazillion times before: relief that I wasn't another guy mixed with dread that he might be the one stuck talking to *me* all night.

Welcome to my world.

Now, to be clear, I didn't resent Cat for any of this. She was literally the sweetest, kindest, best person I knew. She was unfailingly nice to everyone—including the Maxes and the Bens of the universe. Begrudging her for just being her beautiful self, inside and out, would have been a total asshole move on my part.

That said, it would have been nice if, just once in a while, the Maxes and the Bens paid me the same kind of courtesy and didn't look down on me for simply being me.

"Margarita," I said, flagging down a passing server. "Rocks, no salt."

As I settled in across from Cat, my glance darted from one guy to the other, then down to the basket of tortilla chips in the middle of our table. After almost a week of nothing but juices and water and detoxing tea, there was no contest which of the three I desired most.

Only, if I started chowing down on the chips, there was a good chance Max and Ben would look at me all judgy and disapproving. But, hey—it wasn't as if they were looking at me with any kind of approval now. In fact, they weren't looking at me at all. After their initial assessment, they'd both simply dismissed me and gone back to ogling Cat.

And besides, I was already blowing my detox with the alcohol.

So, I grabbed a chip, dunked it into the salsa, and officially started, um, retoxing.

• • • • •

An hour or so later, Cat was trying her best to include me in a passionate debate with her new admiration society about who would win if the Justice League fought the Avengers. I was having trouble following because (a) I kept confusing the Justice League with the Supreme Court; (b) I was nearly through my second margarita, so everything was getting a little fuzzy around the edges; and (c) the drinks—plus the body-hugging spandex pressing oh-so-tightly against my bladder—had created a distraction that was making it impossible for me to concentrate.

I knocked back the rest of my drink and leaned across the table, gesturing for Cat to meet me halfway. I positioned my mouth close to her ear. "I'll be right back."

• • • • •

Behind the locked door of the single-patron restroom, I took care of business. But then I made an unexpected discovery: what goes up comes down but, um, it doesn't necessarily go up again. See, between the cramped quarters of the restroom and my less-than-sober state, I couldn't maneuver my ample ass back into my smooth-and-shape bottoms.

I pulled and tugged, but the compression undies simply wouldn't go the distance around my curves. My skin broke out in a nervous sweat, which made things even worse. After several minutes of squirming and struggling, I'd managed to poke a fingernail through the Spanx—but I still couldn't get the damn things to budge past my thighs.

Eventually, someone waiting on the other side of the door jiggled the knob—the international signal for "Hurry up, you're not the only one who needs to pee."

"Just a minute," I called sweetly.

I tried grabbing the spandex waistband and jumping up and down.

"Ow!" I said as my knee slammed into the sink.

The knob jiggled again. "Are you okay in there?" asked a feminine voice through the door with faux concern. Translation: "Are you going to hurry up, or do I need to get the manager?"

"Yes, fine," I called back, trying not to panic. "Be out in a sec."

I took a deep breath and attempted to clear my tequila-fogged brain.

Okay, I thought. *Okay, so…I can just take the minimizers off and go commando. But then, there's no way I'll be able to zip up my jeans. My stupid, fucking, I-must-have-been-high-when-I-bought-them, too-small jeans!*

I wanted to scream and I wanted to cry.

I wanted to barricade myself in that restroom, living on just tap water until my waist wasted away to the actual size stamped on the tag. And I wanted desperately to not want that at all.

I wondered if this might be my version of hitting bottom.

In a fit of desperation, I opened my bag and peered in at its contents, searching for some way to MacGyver my current predicament. Could I possibly fashion a pair of pants that fit out of dental floss, Tic Tacs, and old ATM receipts?

Probably not.

Then I spotted the oversize safety pin I used as a key chain. Dawn broke, divine light shone, and a choir of angels sang a hallelujah chorus that echoed through the rafters of my skull.

Working quickly, I stepped out of my jeans and peeled off the Spanx. Then I put my jeans back on, shoved my loose apartment keys into the front pocket, and secured the waist with the safety pin—

"Ow!"

I pricked my finger, but there was no time to dwell on that—as yet another jiggle of the knob reminded me.

"Almost done!"

I left my shirt untucked to cover my makeshift fly. Then, I stood on my tiptoes to examine my improvised makeover in the mirror over the sink. I wouldn't be making anybody's best-dressed list tonight. But at least I wouldn't be wearing my jeans down around my ankles and getting arrested for indecent exposure.

I washed my hands, used the Spanx to dry them off, and tossed forty fucking dollars' worth of supposed hip-slimming magic into the wastebasket before I opened the door.

I was greeted by a line of three pissed-off women who seriously needed to piss. I wanted to explain the holdup—but really, what would be the point? A quick inspection of their trio of trim figures showed not so much as a muffin top among them. And yes, okay, maybe I wasn't giving them enough credit—or cutting myself enough slack—but I was pretty positive there would be no sisterhood of the too-tight pants here.

"All yours," I muttered.

Then, avoiding their eyes, I made a beeline for the bar.

• • • • •

"Margarita," I said about a hundred years later, when I'd finally managed to get the bartender's attention. "Rocks, no salt."

"Put it on my tab."

I turned in surprise toward the deep, masculine voice. It was Mysterious Subway Dude—although I didn't know him that way, or any way, yet. But he had the same twinkling, indigo-blue eyes, the same sexy, sand-colored bedhead—and the exact same two-days' growth of stubble he would have a full day later.

True to form, I got an eyeful of him and his molten good looks and immediately lost at least fifty IQ points. So, I figured I had to be missing something.

I glanced around, sure he must be making this move on some other woman, someone more in line with conventional standards of beauty. Someone more his equal. Except, all the likely candidates in the vicinity were otherwise engaged. And when I turned back, he met my gaze directly, staring at me like I was the only person in the room, leaving no doubt that his offer was intended for me.

My whole body simmered.

"Oh. Well, um, thanks," I stammered.

He grinned, way happier than he should've been for the privilege of dropping nine bucks on *me.* It made me paranoid that maybe he'd just won a bet or something.

I swept the bar area again, this time on the lookout for a table of conspiring, snickering bros—and found none. Of course. Because this wasn't some predictable rom-com. Unfortunately, it was just me being my predictably insecure self.

That made me think about those influencers I followed on social media, the ones who confidently shared photos of their curves of all sizes and shapes in bathing suits and sports bras and body-con dresses. When I scrolled through their pics, I didn't "like" them out of pity or some other ulterior motive. I genuinely thought they looked great. So, why was it so hard for me to believe that someone might look at me and think the same thing?

Why was it so hard for me to believe this guy might have looked at *me* and sincerely wanted to buy *me* a drink?

"Will you join me?" he asked. His delivery was supersmooth, like an old-timey matinee idol or something. If he weren't so gorgeous, the over-the-top gallantry might have been comical.

Only, he was. So. Gorgeous. He got up, and his tall, denim- and leather-clad physique unfolded, opening before me like the best gift ever.

"Please." He gestured at his barstool with a chivalry that seemed to belong to another era and, unbeknownst to me then, probably did. "Take my seat."

I wasn't used to being on the receiving end of this kind of attentiveness. And I have to say, I was liking it. My body heat rose to a boil, dissolving some of my defenses. So, mentally crossing my fingers that my safety-pinned-together fly would hold out, I tried to put my insecurities on the back burner and accepted his invitation.

I slid carefully onto his vacated stool, and he leaned casually against the bar next to me.

"Do you come here often?" he asked.

And I couldn't help it. I was nervous and a little tipsy, and the black-and-white movie vibes I was getting from his opening line were just way too much for me. I burst out laughing.

"Sorry," he said, looking a bit sheepish. "That was a terrible cliché, wasn't it?"

"Not so terrible," I said quickly. I hoped my reaction hadn't embarrassed him. "The truth is, I do come here often. This is kind of my local hangout. Only, I don't think I've ever seen you here before."

"No," he said. "But I was just across the street at an antique store—"

"As Time Goes By!"

"You know it?" He leaned down a little closer as he spoke so I could hear him over the bar chatter.

"I *love* it," I said with a heartfelt smile. Now that we'd found some common ground, I started to relax. "Secondhand shops are totally my jam."

"And why is that?" he asked, leaning closer still. And this time, I didn't think it was entirely because of the noise.

"I don't know," I said. "I guess I just like the idea that old things can still find a new life."

He smiled at that, almost wistfully. And although I couldn't imagine why he would have been nervous, it seemed like he relaxed too. "I like that idea as well," he said. "I like that idea very much."

We were silent for a moment, simply looking at each other and smiling—and if I hadn't just teased him about his hackneyed dialogue, I would have been tempted to ask an equally cheesy "Is it getting hot in here?" No joke, I was beginning to feel like somebody jacked the thermostat up to about a thousand degrees.

Luckily, the bartender plunked my frothy, ice-cold drink down in front of me on the colorful, Mexican-tiled bar top.

I reached for my margarita. But before I could lift the thick, bubbled, green-tinted glass to my lips, my new drinking companion touched my hand to stop me. In retrospect, his unnaturally frigid fingers—so much colder than my margarita on the rocks—should have given me a hint that something was off. Way off. But in that moment, all I could think about was the prospect of those icy-cool fingers touching other places on my body, bringing sweet relief from this agonizing heat—

"Does it hurt?" he asked.

I peered up at him, confused. "Wh-what?"

He oh-so-gently lifted my hand away from my glass and turned it palm up. "Your finger," he said. "It's been bleeding."

I lowered my gaze. There was a tiny speck of dried blood on my fingertip where I'd pricked it with the safety pin—but I wasn't about to give him a play-by-play.

"Oh, that?" I shrugged it off. "That's nothing."

I started to pull my hand away, but he held on, his eyes intent. Again, this should have struck me as weird. But sadly, in my view, the fact that somebody who looked like *him* was paying all this attention to *me* was already such an anomaly that the rest barely even registered.

I nodded down at my upturned palm, still cradled in his grasp. "So, um, are you planning on telling my fortune or something?" I asked.

He glanced up at me with a look of unexpected amusement.

"Okay, sure," he said. He dropped his eyes again to stare down at my hand, pretending to read my palm. "I see…nachos."

"Nachos?"

"Nachos," he said gravely. Then, he looked back at me, all suave and sincere. "I was thinking of ordering some. Do you want to share?"

Okay, so this was the point where I'd normally start to get uncomfortable, to overthink things, to wonder if his suggestion to split such an indulgent appetizer was some kind of subtle jab at my weight.

Except, he wasn't Max or Ben or any of the other nameless assholes I'd encountered in the past. The way he was looking at me didn't make me feel self-conscious. Or unworthy. Or inconsequential. It actually made me feel…*special.*

Oh, don't get me wrong—I wasn't feeling anywhere near as comfortable in my own skin as I wished I did. But, for once, I wasn't feeling totally uncomfortable either.

I guess I was just inebriated enough on tequila and lust to be having a good time. And I wanted to keep playing whatever game this was.

So, no way was I going to risk any of that by scarfing down a heaping platter of chips and cheddar and assorted toppings. Eating in front of him was totally off the table. Hard pass. I hadn't lost all my inhibitions.

I switched our grip so I was holding his hand. Then I peered down at his palm, imitating his little performance, deciding to poke some fun at him. "I see…extra cheese."

"On the nachos?" he asked. "Or is that a dig at me?"

My laugh came out like a bark. In truth, I wasn't expecting him to get my snarky double meaning.

"Oh, it's a dig," I teased with a grin. "But this time, I think you just managed to *under*cut the cheese."

He threw back his head, and his laugh was big and throaty and made me feel like I should have my own late-night TV talk show.

"So, chicken?" he asked when he regained his composure. "Or beef?"

I shook my head. "Thanks," I said. "But no, thanks."

His hand gave mine a gentle press that seemed to squeeze at my heart. "You're sure I can't tempt you?" he asked.

"No," I said. Only now I wasn't sure if we were still talking about the nachos. "I'm good."

A wicked glint flashed in his eyes, and he bowed his head even lower, so his mouth was almost grazing the shell of my ear. "I guess we'll just have to see about that."

CHAPTER 6

We drank and chatted. Well, *he* drank, nursing his bottle of Dos Equis, and chatted. I, on the other hand, guzzled my third margarita in about two seconds flat and stuttered and sputtered like I didn't know how to speak English. But Tristan—that was his name, Tristan Newberry—didn't miss a beat. It was like he had an inner Google Translator that automatically converted my inarticulate blathering to coherent conversation.

And I guess he wanted to keep the conversation going. Because after he got me a glass of ice water and settled the tab, he offered to escort me home.

He was the perfect gentleman as he guided me through the growing Saturday night throng, his hand resting lightly against my lower back. I felt all floaty walking out ahead of him, my tequila buzz mixing nicely with the buzz I was getting from his touch. I couldn't believe how well this was going!

But then I spotted Cat.

I stopped. I swear, I was such a spectacular shithead! In all the years of our friendship—and despite a plethora of opportunities—Cat had never once ditched me for a guy. Ever. But one drink with Tristan, and I'd completely forgotten about her. I'd broken the number one unbreakable rule of the girlfriend code.

But Cat just flashed me a grin. And indicating my companion with her eyes, she gave me a discreet thumbs-up. Then she made the shape of an old-school landline with her hand and waggled it next to her ear.

"Call me," she mouthed.

After a moment, I smiled back and nodded.

And so, with my best friend's stamp of approval, I let Tristan Newberry lead me out the door and into the night.

• • • • •

"So, um, Tristan," I said, trying to act all casual and nonchalant and sober as we strolled together toward my place. "What do you do? For a living, I mean."

"I read palms, obviously."

"No," I said. "Seriously. What do you do?"

"I write," he said after a pause. "I'm a writer."

I looked at him, a little thrown. I don't know what I was expecting him to say. *I model underwear*, maybe? *I race BMX bikes. I work as a personal trainer by day and cage fight at night.* While the solitary life of a writer suited me just fine, the idea of this glorious paragon of manhood spending most of his time hidden away, alone at a computer, seemed like a cruel act of deprivation aimed at everyone with eyesight.

"Really?" I said. "Me too."

"Really?" he said. "What do you write?"

"Well, eventually I want to write serious investigative pieces," I said. "Maybe some long-form nonfiction? But for now, I'm paying my dues. I work overnights at a website."

"So, you're nocturnal," he said.

"Pretty much."

This reply seemed to amuse him. A lot.

"What's the website?" he asked.

I considered lying, but I was frankly too tipsy to think up a convincing fib. Also, despite our short acquaintance, I felt uncharacteristically at ease opening up to Tristan and telling him the truth. "It's this totally tits-for-brains guide to New York City nightlife called, um—wait for it—Take-a-Bite-dot-com." I rolled my eyes. "I mean, I guess they were thinking *New York, the Big Apple, Take a Bite...*" I shook my head. "Weak, I know." I shrugged. "Basically, I write crap."

"Well, if you listen to some of my critics," said Tristan, flashing that killer smile of his, "then we have something else in common."

Now, my interest was totally piqued. "So, spill," I said. "What do you write?"

"Historical fiction," he said. "Mostly eighteenth- and nineteenth-century American, but some older, some European.

"I publish under a pseudonym, though," he continued. "Please, try not to laugh. My pen name is Delilah Manning."

Delilah Manning...Delilah Manning...

Why is that name so familiar?

Then suddenly I knew. In my mind's eye, I saw the piles and piles of paperbacks at my mother's house in Cherry Hill, New Jersey: their pages filled with references to heaving bosoms and engorged appendages, their covers adorned with corseted women and bare-chested men locked in torrid embraces, their well-creased spines bearing alliterative titles like *Passion's Prisoner* and *Fortune's Fire*—all written by Delilah Manning.

I stopped walking. Partly because we'd arrived at my apartment building. But mostly because I was so tickled by this new discovery.

"You write bodice rippers!"

Now his old-fashioned ways made a little more sense. Since I knew there was such a thing as a method actor, I figured maybe he was some kind of a method writer, all deeply immersed in his art.

"Actually," he said, "'bodice rippers' is a bit of a misnomer. It's true, sometimes the bodices in my novels are ripped off in the heat of passion. But more often, they're removed with excruciating slowness. To heighten the sexual tension."

And okay, his method was totally working on me. My own bosom was heaving. And I swear, if I had an appendage, it would certainly be engorged.

Talk about writing what you know!

I mean, at the time, I wasn't clued in enough to suspect Tristan might have been alive—or undead, at least—several centuries ago and therefore had actual hands-on experience with bodices. But even without that knowledge? I would have bet my last cent that he had a shit ton of hands-on experience heightening sexual tension.

Only, one thing didn't quite fit.

"So, you believe in happily ever after?" I asked.

He stabbed his hands into the pockets of his leather jacket and shifted his weight from one Doc Marten to the other. "'Ever after' is an awfully long time," he said finally, carefully. "I suppose I believe more in…happy for *now*."

And there it was: the shit that had always been headed for the fan, the other shoe that was bound to drop, the cards that were inevitably destined for the table.

Okay, so maybe I didn't yet know that, for him, *ever after* really was a looong time. But I wasn't exactly surprised to learn that a guy this charming and charismatic was a player.

Even so, I was a little thrown by the surge of disappointment I felt.

Points to him for being up-front with me, though.

"So, what's your backstory?" I asked lightly, trying not to let my discouragement show. As a teenager, I'd covertly sampled enough of my mother's romance library to know the conventions and tropes of the genre. "Broken heart? Tortured past? Or just like to sleep around?"

"Wow," he said with a small laugh. "I think you may have just covered every hero in my catalog."

"So, which are you?" I persisted, gazing up at him.

He shook his head, and something like sadness eclipsed the twinkle in his eyes. "I'm no hero, Lily," he said. "If you're looking for one, you should definitely look somewhere else."

There was a painful honesty to his words that made me speak honestly too. "Thanks," I said, "but I kinda like where I'm looking right now."

Our gazes locked, and time seemed to freeze. The twinkle in his eyes made a rousing comeback. "Does that mean you're going to invite me in?"

My stomach didn't just do a somersault. It did a full-on, Olympic-gold-medal-winning balance-beam routine.

Obvi, it wouldn't be forever. He'd basically told me as much.

Probably, it wouldn't be for more than this one night—which was not exactly my modus operandi. Let's just say that if someone said, "Never have I ever had a one-night stand," I didn't have to drink.

But then it wasn't as if I had men like Tristan wanting to get with me every night of the week. Or any night of the week. And I wasn't ready for this night to end.

Okay, and bottom line: I'm not sure I believed in happily ever after either. Not for me, anyway. If Tristan was no hero, I was surely no romantic heroine. I wasn't the type to inspire that kind of undying love. I wasn't strong and confident. I wasn't complicated and endlessly fascinating. Basically, I was the quirky friend who cracked jokes on the sidelines while other people fell in love.

"Lily?"

Still, the way he said my name made my body prickle all over with anticipation, and I let myself speculate about how happy-for-now Tristan Newberry might make me feel. How he might use those hands-on experienced hands on me, removing my shirt...and then my bra...and then my jeans—

Hold on. My jeans?

My way-too-tight, safety-pinned-together jeans?

"Are you—"

"No!"

To say Tristan looked surprised would be the understatement of the millennium. *No* probably wasn't a word he heard very often—especially not uttered quite so forcefully late at night at a woman's front door.

Only, as much as I wanted to say yes, I simply couldn't bear the humiliation of having my secret shame exposed. Being honest with words was one thing. But I was going to have to draw the line at the, um, *naked* truth.

"W-what I mean is..." I spluttered. "Well, you know, it's just... tonight—? Yeah, tonight's not really a good time for me."

CHAPTER 7

Tristan and I stood there together on the sidewalk, my smooth-as-sandpaper rejection hanging in the cool night air.

"Perhaps another time, then," he said eventually. He actually sounded bummed. "This was more fun than I've had in a while. And I really would like to get to know you better, Lily. If you'll let me."

He reached out his hand and pushed a stray curl out of my eyes. Then he focused the full, penetrating intensity of his gaze on me.

"Okay," I murmured. Okay to the promise of another night with him. And okay to what I thought he was going to do next. What I was dying for him to do next.

Only, instead of kissing me, he just kept staring at me. And staring. And staring some more.

What the fuck? I wondered. *Do I have cilantro in my teeth or something?*

Then, my not-so-old insecurities came rushing back with a vengeance.

Did I read this situation all wrong? Did he just buy me that drink because he felt sorry for me? Or because there really was some kind of a wager?

I was all set to say an uncomfortable good night and bail when—*finally!*—he leaned down and brushed his cool-to-the-touch lips against my cheek.

I shivered—but not from the coldness.

He wrapped me up in his long arms and let his mouth wander.

"So lovely," he whispered against my skin. "So very lovely." He kissed his way down my neck, his stubble tickling and teasing in such an enticing way that I started seriously rethinking how I'd shut him down.

Maybe I can invite him in, I thought as the kissing turned to licking. *Then, before things go too far, I can do that excuse-me-while-I-change-into-something-more-comfortable thing.*

I sighed softly against him as he pulled me closer.

Only, what would I change into? I thought as the licking turned to biting. *I don't exactly own dressers full of nice lingerie. And* comfortable *is supposed to be a euphemism for* sexy. *Not* ratty, old sweatpants—

Hey, wait a minute, I thought in a brain zap of realization. *Biting? BITING?*

Tristan had warned me he wasn't a hero, but *seriously?* This guy—or whatever he was—was actually sinking his teeth into my throat!

So, okay, I definitely hadn't signed up for this.

I wanted to protest, but I couldn't find my voice. I tried to pull away, but either I was getting weaker or Tristan was somehow getting much, much stronger. My body was locked against his, his face buried deep in the crook of my neck, his teeth buried deep in my flesh. My eyes darted around desperately, searching for help—but all I could see was Tristan's ear, hovering close in front of me.

Since flight wasn't an option, I chose to fight—the only way I could. I opened wide, inclined my head forward, and chomped down as hard as I could on his earlobe.

Tristan loosened his grip. He pulled back and looked at me, startled—no, more like *shocked*. Whatever. Lucky for me, his stunned reaction gave me the opening I needed.

Ignoring the taste of his blood in my mouth, I broke out of his hold.

• • • • •

"Hang on," interrupts Cat. We're back at her place, where I've been talking and Cat has been raptly listening for a while. "You bit a vampire?"

"Hey, he bit me first," I say. "And, by the way, without my consent."

My hand goes protectively to my throat, touching the skin over my jugular. It's totally mended now. Smooth. Not so much as a scab.

"Lily," says Cat with emphasis. "You *bit*. A *vampire*."

As the absurdity of my action sinks in, I start to laugh. A breath later, Cat joins me. Before I know it, we're both practically rolling around on her living room floor in hysterics. I know, I know, it's not really all that funny, but I guess we both need the release. And screaming with laughter seems like a better way to relieve the tension than just plain screaming.

When we're pretty much all laughed out, Cat wipes a tear from her cheek and looks at me somberly. "Okay, tell me the rest," she says. "What happened after the blood exchange?"

"Blood exchange?"

"The vampire tasted your blood, Lil," says Cat. She tucks her long legs up under her on the couch that IKEA calls "oatmeal" but has always looked vomit-colored to me. "Then, when you bit his ear, you tasted his. There was an exchange of blood. That's how he must have turned you. Sounds like it was unintentional. I mean, he can't have predicted you'd bite him back, but…" She frowns a moment. Then she asks, "Did he know what he did?"

On the other end of the couch, I lean back into the "oatmeal" cushions and think about this.

• • • • •

As soon as I was free of Tristan's embrace, I bolted for the front door of my building. As a result of my hot mess of a wardrobe malfunction, at least I didn't have to waste time fumbling in my bag for my keys. They were within easy reach, tucked into the front pocket of my jeans. Quickly, I retrieved them and let myself in.

"Lily!" Tristan shouted.

I turned around just as the outer glass door clicked shut, separating the two of us.

On the other side of the tempered glass, Tristan stared in at me. Those indigo eyes of his weren't so much twinkling as blazing. Oh, and his ear? Totally healed.

"Lily," he repeated. His voice was muffled by the door between us, but his distress was coming through loud and clear. "Invite me in. Please. You need me."

Oh, he knew what he did, all right. And okay, in hindsight, maybe he wanted to help me deal. *Maybe.*

But in the moment, I wasn't having any of it.

"Fuck you," I said, touching my hand to my own still-bleeding wound. The defenses I'd stupidly let slip earlier in the night were back—and they'd returned with some powerful reinforcements. "Don't flatter yourself. The last thing I need is whatever kind of weird-ass cannibal S-and-M shit you're into. Do me a favor and count me out."

Or, I think that's what I said. See, right about then, everything started to go sideways.

I had to use the wall for support as I turned my back on Tristan and stumbled my way down the dim, narrow hallway toward the back of the building, to Unit 1C. My heartbeat was racing, pounding so strongly in my ears that I worried it might be loud enough to make my neighbors call 911 and complain about the noise.

When I reached my apartment door, my vision was totally messing with me. I was surprised to see no less than three doorknobs, so it took me at least three tries to get the key inserted in the actual lock. By the time I picked a winner and made it inside, I was shaky and sweaty and so dizzy I could hardly stand.

I pulled the door shut behind me and collapsed back against it, eyes closed. I figured it must be the full force of the tequila finally hitting me.

I'm not sure how long I stayed like that. Maybe seconds. Maybe minutes. Maybe even longer.

When I felt my heart rate begin to slow, I decided to try to make it to the bed.

Using the bedside lamp I'd left lit as a guiding star, I walked unsteadily toward my queen-sized mattress. Along the way, I shed my bag, my shirt, my boots. Even managed to undo the safety pin joining the waist of my jeans. Only, my heartbeat wasn't just slowing down. It was stopping altogether.

Before I could wriggle out of my Levis, the room started to spin.

My last thought before I crumpled to the floor in a half-dressed heap was that for oh-so-many reasons, I really shouldn't have let Tristan Newberry buy me that third margarita.

CHAPTER 8

Knowing the full story of what happened to me makes me feel better. Bitter and vengeful and absolutely livid at that jackhole Tristan Newberry—but better.

Problem is, there's still so much I don't know.

I look at Cat as she curls back up on the opposite end of the sofa. Once I finished telling my tale, she got up, went to the kitchen, and poured herself a big glass of wine—and I swear, the fact that she managed to hold out as long as she did is a downright miracle. If she showed up at my door with fangs and a taste for human blood, I'd have been reaching for something a hell of a lot stronger than box chardonnay a hell of a lot sooner.

Right now, I'd totally join her for a glass or six, but I'm not sure if vampires are even supposed to drink alcohol.

Oh, I know, I know, Tristan had a beer when we met. But now that I think about it? I don't know if he was actually drinking it, or if he was just taking fake sips to blend in.

I suppose I could crack open one of the outdated donor units we pilfered from the American Red Cross. But since my bloodlust is currently at bay, I figure I should save my supply for whenever the next craving hits.

Still, I feel a little bad about making Cat drink alone.

"So," I say after a bit, "I guess I'm really a vampire, huh?"

Cat nods. "You're really a vampire." She takes a big gulp of her chard.

I decide maybe it's time to revisit the topic I couldn't bear to discuss earlier. "So, that means I'm, um, *dead*," I say. My voice sounds small.

"Undead," she corrects quickly.

I shake my head and blink back the tears that have probably been on the verge of falling for a while.

"Whatever that means," I say.

"It means you're not dead," she says.

But does it? I don't know…

Should I be planning a funeral for my mortal soul? Saying a formal goodbye to Lily 1.0? Would that bring me some kind of closure?

And if I do find a way to close the door on my past, what then? I mean, I've got literally no idea what to expect from this new future of mine.

"I'm scared," I hear myself confess.

"I know you are," says Cat.

"Like really scared."

"I know."

"And I don't even know what I'm scared of," I say. "It's, like, when it comes to this whole vampire thing, I don't know what I don't know. You know?"

Cat is quiet for a moment.

"I know," she says. She takes another big swallow of the white wine. "That's why we need to be smart. *You* need to be smart. You can't go and do anything stupid."

I let out a rueful laugh. "Like thinking a hot guy wanted me, you mean?"

"Stop," says Cat. "That's not what I mean at all, and you know it. Besides, I saw the two of you together. He was into you."

"Oh, please," I say. "Tristan wasn't into me. I don't think he even wanted to get into my pants. He just wanted to get into my veins. The only reason he treated me to a drink at Dos Rosas was so I'd return the favor. That bloodsucking fuck."

"Look, we can trash him later if you want," says Cat. "But right now we need to talk about *you*."

Her voice is different. Serious. Maybe more serious than I've ever heard her.

"Now you're really scaring me," I say.

"Sorry." She takes another drink. "It's just...I know how you are, Lily. You don't always take things seriously. You make jokes. But this? This is no joke. You need to be careful."

Her words make me squirm a little uncomfortably on the couch.

"Okay, I get it, but...careful how?" I ask. "Careful of what?"

"Well, for starters," she says, "you need to promise me you'll stay out of the sun."

"I'm a fair-skinned, freckled redhead," I say. "I always stay out of the sun."

"No," she says. "I mean, you can't go out in the daytime anymore. Ever."

I think about this. "Not even with SPF 50?"

"Not. Ever."

I give this idea a little time to settle. "So, I can seriously never see the sun again?"

"Correct."

It's my first night as a vampire, and I'm already over it.

Okay, so maybe I'm not the kind of artsy-fartsy romantic who marvels at the beauty of the sunrise on a regular basis. Legit, I can't remember the last time I even watched the sunrise. But the thought of never seeing it again? That just seems so, well, unfair. I feel like I've lost something I didn't even appreciate I had. And didn't know I could lose.

Then something occurs to me.

"Wait, wait, wait," I say. "In Twilight, they went to high school, right?" I smile, pretty pleased with my razor-sharp powers of deduction. "In the *daytime*."

Cat doesn't smile back, though. I notice she's already completely drained her wineglass. "Well, yes," she says with a sigh. "But they lived in Forks."

"Forks?"

"It's in Washington State," she says. "Apparently, it's like the cloudiest place on earth."

"So, I can go out when it's cloudy," I say.

"No!" says Cat.

"But—"

"No, Lily!" she says. "See? This is just the kind of thing I'm talking about. You can't go taking risks like that. You need to watch out for yourself. And that starts with no sunlight. No sunlight means *no sunlight*!"

That's when I pick up on it: Cat is crying. There are tears rolling down her cheeks.

It's a strange thing to witness. Partly because, with my blood-enhanced vampire eyesight, I can see the lamplight refracted by the streaks of salt water running down her face, so it literally looks like there are rainbows shooting out of my friend's eyes. But mostly because, well, I've never seen Cat cry before. Not like this, anyway.

"You're my best friend, goddammit," she says, barely above a whisper. "And I don't want to lose you."

A lump the size of a bowling ball rises in my throat.

"You're not going to lose me," I say hoarsely. "I'm immortal."

"Not if you don't listen to me and stay out of the friggin' sun!"

And I can't help it. That makes me laugh.

A moment later, Cat can't seem to help it either. She joins in and laughs too.

"If you end up dying on me, I'll kill you," she says through a combination of giggles and sniffles.

"Fair enough," I say with a chuckle.

Cat snuffles one last time and swipes her hand across her face, wiping away her rainbow-colored tears. And for a little while, it's all good.

Only, as my friend's weeping subsides, I suddenly feel my own tears start to well up again and spill over. My laughter quickly morphs into choking, hiccuppy sobs.

"Lil?" says Cat. "What is it?"

What is it? *What is it?* Here's what it is: the full meaning of what I said so glibly not a minute ago has just hit me.

"*I'm immortal!*" I howl.

"But that's a good thing," Cat says. "Isn't it?"

I shake my head. Because the true ramifications of living forever have just dawned on me.

"You're not going to lose me," I manage to say in between my blubbering. "But…but I'm going to lose *you*."

And not just her. I'm going to lose everyone I know. Everyone I love.

Everyone.

Seriously?

"But not for a long, long time," says Cat.

Her words are cold comfort. The future that lies ahead for me is suddenly all too clear. No sun. No friends. No family. Just me-myself-and-I, holed up all alone in the dark with whatever blood I can manage to beg, borrow, or steal.

Jesus. How am I ever going to deal with this?

Then I feel Cat wrap her arms around me. She is warm and soft and soothing, like my favorite fleece blanket just out of the dryer.

"Best friends forever," she whispers.

And then I know how I'll deal with it.

I hug her back. I know my icy-cold vampire flesh can't possibly feel anywhere near as reassuring to her, but she doesn't flinch.

Because that's the thing: when the shit gets real, best friends don't flinch.

"For fucking ever," I whisper back fiercely through my tears. "For fucking ever."

CHAPTER 9

I hang out with Cat until an hour or so before sunrise. Then, with my ugly cry mostly behind me and my BFF's final reminder to stay out of the sun still ringing in my ears, I head home with a reusable grocery bag full of the expired blood we swiped. And for the first time, I'm grateful that my crap-trap of a ground-floor studio apartment overlooks a back alley and gets pretty much zero sunlight.

As I step out onto West Sixty-Fifth Street and begin my short walk to the downtown subway station, my newly awakened vampire senses are on overload. I see the dewdrops glistening like tiny diamonds on the parked cars in the predawn light. I smell the sweet, buttery croissants baking in the café on the corner. I feel the bracing tingle of the cool autumn air on my skin. And despite my dark mood, I can't help but be overwhelmed by the miracle of it all—so much so that I barely even notice the elongated shadow inching up on me from behind.

"Lily?"

Tristan.

My whole body tenses up as my anger flares. Has he been lurking around, following me, watching me all this time?

I keep walking without looking back. "New York City has anti-stalking laws, you know."

"I'm not here to hurt you," he says. He falls into step next to me. "Just the opposite, in fact."

Proactively, I hang a *Do Not Enter* sign on the door to my heart. Double-check the locks for good measure. Then I stop and turn to face him.

To my human eyes, he was undeniably gorgeous. To my lately blood-born vampire vision, he is resplendent. Magnificent. Godlike.

And evil personified, I remind myself. *Bastard.*

But this time, at least I don't get tongue-tied by the sight of him. I'm too pissed off.

"Drop dead," I say. "Oh, too late for that, isn't it?"

He smiles sadly. "Too late for a lot of things," he says. "As much as I'd like to, I can't undo this. But now that it's done, I really do want to help you."

Oh, no. No, no, no, no, no. No way am I getting seduced by his old-school charm. Again.

"You've done more than enough already," I say. "Fuck the fuck off."

I walk away from him, but he refuses to stay in my dust.

"What is that awful smell?" he asks. He catches up to me and grabs the eco-friendly bag out of my hand. Before I can reclaim it, he peers inside, then reels back in what I can only describe as horror. "Do you really plan on drinking this prepackaged sludge?"

"Stop criticizing my diet," I say. I snatch back my shopping bag full of the post-fresh blood and quicken my pace. "You sound like my mother."

"I'm hardly your mother," he says, easily matching my stride. "Actually, I'm your master."

Hearing that one, my jaw practically hits the sidewalk. It's a moment before I can even find my voice.

"*Excuse* me?"

"A vampire who turns another is referred to as master," he explains. "I'm your master."

"The fuck you are."

"And as your master," he continues, either unaware or unconcerned that this might sound a tad offensive, "it's my duty to tell you that you'll never come into your full power unless you drink from the vein."

"Forget it," I say. "I'm not a predator like you."

"I'm hardly a predator," he says. He actually has the nerve to look insulted.

Is he kidding me?

"You *bit* me," I say.

"Because you said it was okay."

That makes me stop dead—um, *undead?*—in my tracks. "I most certainly did not!"

Tristan looks genuinely confused. "But I stared into your eyes," he says. "And you said 'okay.'"

"I—*what?*"

I take a moment to process this, to review my memory of what happened.

"Okay to maybe seeing you again," I admit grudgingly. "Okay to a kiss good night. Not okay to sucking the fucking life out of me."

The blood—*my* blood, probably—drains from Tristan's face. "But I asked you," he insists. "I asked if I could drink from you. I asked you with my influence."

"With your, um, *what?*"

"My influence," he says. "It's a kind of telepathy. A sixth sense that can be used on humans, to read them and to soothe them. I reached into your mind—"

"You were poking around in my mind?"

His eyes widen in a kind of horrified realization. "Apparently not," he says slowly. He shakes his head in disbelief. "Oh, no. Oh, this is just dreadful."

"Ya think?"

"Lily, I assure you, I would never have bitten you if I didn't think I had your permission."

"You know what? Save it, asshole."

I walk off, but once again he follows.

"It's just...in all the centuries I've walked the earth, I've never met a human who was capable of escaping a vampire's influence," he says.

"And yet, try as I might, I can't seem to escape you."

"I thought I had your consent to drink," he says, still not giving it up. "Truly. And I thought I'd transported you into a temporary state of euphoria while I took what I needed."

"Where'd you learn that move?" I snap. "The Bill Cosby playbook?"

He flinches at that. As if *he's* the wounded party here.

"No! God, no! It's not like that," he says. "For me—*for us*—it's all simply a matter of survival. It's how conscientious vampires have always operated."

"By forcing your way into people's private thoughts?" I ask. "Invading their brains? And manipulating their emotions? How can you think that's okay?"

And even though all I want is to get away from him as quickly as possible, I stop again. What I need to tell him is too important.

"It is not okay," I say. "It is not okay to cross someone's boundaries without being invited. It is not okay to manipulate any part of someone's body without permission. And it is not okay to use your power over someone less powerful. It is never fucking okay."

"I completely understand your point of view," he says. "But you also have to understand mine. This is how my own master taught me to subsist. This is how it's always been done. This is how I've managed to endure for nearly four hundred years—and how vampires have endured for millennia before me."

"Oh, yeah?" I say. "Well, this just in, dude. Time's up."

I stalk off again. I'm just a few feet away from the concrete stairs that lead down to the underground station. But before I can even descend the first step, Tristan is somehow in front of me, blocking my path. "Let me give you a lift home," he says.

I stare up at him, exasperated. "Oh. My. God. Exactly what part of 'fuck the fuck off' do you not understand?"

"Let me put you in a cab, then," he says.

"Get out of my way," I say. "I'm taking the subway."

"No. You can't," he insists. "The subway isn't safe."

Now he wants to be a hero?

"Give me a break," I say. "Since when are you so concerned about my safety?"

"Since your last subway ride probably put you—and me, by the way—in grave and potentially lethal danger."

That gets my attention. I search the vampire's face for signs that he's bullshitting me. But just like the night before, his expression is all sincerity.

I'm not sure which is more dangerous for me right now: believing him or not believing him.

"Okay," I say cautiously. "Tell me, then. How am I in danger?"

He glances up at the night sky before leveling a serious look at me. "It'll be daybreak soon," he says. "Let me drive you home, and I'll explain it all on the way."

I know, I know, I know. This has "bad idea" written all over it. I mean, I haven't forgotten what happened the last time I agreed to let Tristan Newberry escort me home.

But, um, here's the thing: although I haven't had the opportunity to put it to much use yet, I actually do have a BA in journalism. And my journalistic instincts are telling me there's a story here. A story I should at least hear out.

And, okay, for reals: I don't know dick about being a vampire. And I still have a lot of questions. And right now, my go-to source on the subject is getting a good chunk of her information from young adult fiction. So, if I really am in danger, well… It can't hurt to gather a little firsthand intel, can it?

Or hopefully, it won't hurt too much.

I narrow my eyes at Tristan. "You actually keep a car in the city?"

CHAPTER 10

Tristan tells me he's parked in front of the building I exited, so we turn around and walk together back toward Cat's.

Not wasting any time, I start in on my fact-finding mission. "So, what's the real deal with sunlight?" I ask.

"Sunlight?"

"Vampires and sunlight," I clarify. "Yes or no?"

He shakes his head. "Definitely no."

So, not the answer I was hoping for.

"But…what about Forks?" I ask.

He looks at me curiously. "Forks are fine," he says. "Spoons too. As long as they aren't wooden and used to stake you through the heart."

"No," I say. "I mean Forks, Washington. Or other places where it's cloudy. What's the story with vampires and overcast days?"

Those blue eyes of his start to twinkle in amusement. "Lily," he says. "Are you talking about Twilight?"

The question surprises me—until I remember that he's a romance novelist. So, of course he'd know all about the popular franchise.

"Well, it's not as if there's a how-to manual on being a vampire that

I can pick up at my neighborhood bookshop," I say. "My resources are kind of limited. I'm doing the best I can here."

Tristan stops walking, so I do the same. Then he fixes me with his gaze, a gaze full of concern and regret—and something else too. Something like what I saw when he looked at me on the train earlier tonight. And goddammit, even with everything this jugular-sucking jackass has done to me, I have the same reaction. I feel seen. Truly *seen*. It makes me light-headed and swoony and a little bit breathless.

"Make no mistake, Lily," Tristan says. "Sunlight, even filtered through clouds, is absolutely lethal for vampires. So, unless you have a death wish, I recommend avoiding it at all costs."

"Good to know," I say.

"Glad to help."

And because I don't have a death wish, I break eye contact with him before my sex drive kicks into overdrive.

We start to walk again. A little slower this time. A little more in sync.

It takes me a moment to remember my next question.

"So, um…what about food?" I ask finally. "And drinks? Besides blood, I mean. Do vampires eat and drink?"

"We don't require food or drink to survive," he says with a shrug. "But it seems silly to deprive ourselves of life's pleasures. Don't you think?"

He smiles at me, and my mind involuntarily fills with a whole catalog of pleasures that have nothing to do with eating and drinking.

Jesus. Why does he have this effect on me?

I force my mind to refocus as we walk on.

"Okay, so, back there," I say with a nod behind us, back toward the subway station. "You said you've been around for nearly four hundred years. So, how old were you when you became a vampire? Thirty? Thirty-five?"

"Twenty-three," he replies.

I look at him doubtfully.

He shrugs again. "Life was a lot harder then. People looked older. Aged more quickly. But if I understand what you're really asking," he says, "rest assured. No matter how many centuries pass, you'll still look as young and lovely as you do today."

My heart stops—or it would if it were still able to beat.

Because even though I'd really like to air-drop his vampire ass onto a sun-drenched desert and watch from the safety of a daylight-proof helicopter while he burns or melts or evaporates or whatever, I can't deny that a little thrill is rippling through my body right now at his compliment.

God, I hate Tristan Newberry. I really fucking do.

• • • • •

As it turns out, Tristan doesn't just have a car. He has a four-wheeled, two-doored, two-seated, motorized work of art. I'm not at all into automobiles, but even I can tell that this shiny, black sports coupe is the luxury ride of luxury rides. Seriously. As I sink into the plush, tan upholstery and inhale the scent of expensive leather, it's like I'm nestled inside a giant Hermès Birkin Bag. Looks like "Delilah Manning" does quite well for himself.

I wait until Tristan buckles in behind the wheel and gets the engine purring. Then, before I get too comfy and forget why I agreed to this ride in the first place, I resume my interrogation.

"Okay," I say. "So let's get down to the main event. You told me I'm in danger. How's that, exactly?"

Over the next few minutes, while we drive downtown and the cool night air rushes in through the open windows, Tristan prefaces his answer by giving me a crash course in vampire protocol—and oh my God, now I know why his historical romance novels are like a million pages long. Talk about verbose!

But, um, nutshell? Apparently, there are rules, and he's inadvertently violated the mother of them all: Thou shalt not turn a human without the prior approval of the Vampire Council.

"There's a Vampire Council?" I ask.

He nods. "We answer to the North American chapter, which is headquartered here in New York City. The chapter council is made up of the thirteen oldest living vampires on the continent—well, the ones who are still interested in those kinds of politics, anyway."

"Politics?" I ask. "So, this Vampire Council is, what? Like Congress?" Because, I swear, if they're anywhere near as dysfunctional as the Senate and the House, I'm pretty sure Tristan doesn't have anything to worry about. It'll take them forever, literally, to agree on any action against him.

"Not quite," he says. "See, our chapter of the council is led by our oldest vampire, Grand Master Gideon. And unless the other twelve members vote unanimously to override him, his interpretation of vampire law is…law."

"So, then it's kind of a dictatorship?" I ask.

"More or less," he says with a small shrug.

He turns off the West Side Highway, and I lean back in my seat to think about this.

Grand Master Gideon? The Vampire Council? Vampire law?

Boy, I really wish Cat were here. Partly because she would absolutely geek out over this kind of insider information. But mostly because I could really use another set of ears to help me keep it all straight—not to mention another perspective on whether or not to believe any of it.

I mean, granted, the story seems a little too intricate for Tristan to be making it all up on the fly—even if he is a storyteller by trade. Still, given everything that's happened? I don't know if I can trust what he says.

And unfortunately, I've got no independent way to fact-check his information. It's not as if I have a confidential informant on this Vampire Council or a paranormal expert on speed dial. I've got nothing to go on here but pure gut instinct.

I take a deep breath and continue with my questioning.

"Okay," I say. "So, if this Grand Master Gideon finds out you've violated vampire law by making me, what then? Will there be a hearing? Will I get a subpoena to testify?"

"Not a subpoena, exactly," says Tristan. "But if and when the grand master wants you to appear before the council, you'll know it."

I don't like the sound of that. I don't like the sound of that at all.

I try to shake off my uneasiness and keep grilling him.

"So, then what?" I ask. "There's a trial?"

"In most cases, yes," says Tristan. "But in this case, the problem is that Gideon and I have...*history*."

Okay, here we go. Now, we're getting somewhere. Just the way he says that, I can tell it's the truth. And I can tell it's not the good kind of history Cat and I have.

"I take it you're not BFFs?"

"Hardly," he says with a mirthless laugh. "Gideon's had it out for me for centuries. And when he learns I've made a newborn without the appropriate permissions? He'll jump at the chance to punish me to the full extent of vampire law."

"No offense," I say, "but how is that my problem?"

"Because he won't just punish me," Tristan says. "He'll punish you too."

Well, at least we've finally circled back around to the danger part. But…*seriously*?

"He'll punish *me*?" I ask. "What the fuck? Isn't being turned into a vampire punishment enough?"

"Gideon won't see your situation as a bad thing," he informs me. "Neither will the council. They view any transformation from human to vampire as an upgrade."

"So, what? They'll all just blame the victim?" These vampires need some major sensitivity training.

Then another question occurs to me.

"Hang on," I say. "Are any of these laws even written down anywhere? I mean, how does anyone know what they are? Is there like a vampire charter or constitution or something?"

"There's a book."

"A book?"

"The Book," says Tristan, and I can basically hear the capital T, capital B as he says the words. "When you're made, you sign your name in The Book. In your blood."

"That sounds like something from an episode of *The Sopranos*," I say.

"Not a bad analogy."

"So, you're saying I just joined the mob?" I ask.

"No," he says. "That's the problem. You didn't join. Not officially. Your making wasn't sanctioned by the Vampire Council. And you didn't sign The Book."

"So then," I say, seeing a possible escape hatch, "I can't be subject to its laws."

"Well, that would be entirely up to the grand master."

"Because his word is law?" I ask.

"Because his word is law."

We drive in silence while I chew on this for a bit.

"Yeah, but…this grand master and I don't exactly socialize in the same circles. So, unless you tell him—and I'm guessing you won't—how will he even know about me?"

"You rode the subway," says Tristan.

"So?"

"So, the tunnels are filled with our kind."

"There are *vampires* in the subway tunnels?" I ask, just to be sure I'm understanding him correctly.

"Think about it," he says. "If you need a dark, out-of-the-way place to spend the daylight hours, where better?"

Where better than a dank, smelly, rat-infested hole in the ground? News flash: Even my shithole apartment beats that. I say as much to Tristan.

"The vampires who inhabit the tunnels aren't so…particular," he says.

"Seriously?"

He shrugs. "They're the soldiers of the race. The enforcers, to continue with your organized crime comparison. They do the grand master's dirty work, and in return for their loyalty, Gideon looks the other way if they occasionally…slip."

I crinkle my brow. "What do you mean, um…'slip'?"

We brake at a red light, and Tristan turns to look at me. "Have you ever heard the urban legends about alligator attacks in the New York City subway system?"

Slowly, I nod.

"Well, the truth behind those attacks would be even harder for most humans to believe."

Frankly, I'm finding this all a little hard to believe. But, hey, if you would've told me a day or so ago that vampires are for real and I was about to become one? I wouldn't have believed that either.

So, as the traffic light blinks back to green and Tristan hits the gas again, I try to keep an open mind and consider the possibility that there really is a band of feral bloodsuckers stalking the MTA, preying on random, unsuspecting commuters.

I swear, my skull is about to burst.

"Our problem is," Tristan says, his eyes back on the road, "if Gideon's minions saw you—and we have to assume that at least one of them did—the grand master already knows there's an unsanctioned newborn running around Manhattan. And once he discovers who you are, and that I'm the vampire responsible for you, he'll—"

"Punish us both," I finish for him.

"Punish us both," he confirms.

Suddenly, the comfy leather passenger seat isn't so comfortable. I squirm a little. Swallow hard. Squirm a bit more.

I remind myself it might all be bullshit.

But then again, it might not be.

Regardless, a real journalist asks the tough questions. And keeps asking them until she gets to the truth, the whole truth, and nothing but the truth.

"So, what's the punishment?" I ask.

CHAPTER 11

Tristan doesn't answer me right away.

Instead, he concentrates all his attention on maneuvering the roadster into a space in front of my building. Normally, I'd be wondering how he managed to find a legal parking spot in my neighborhood at all—let alone one right smack at my doorstep. But at the moment, I'm a little preoccupied with a different question.

I wait until he shifts into park and kills the engine. "And I repeat," I say. "What's the punishment?"

Tristan leans back from the steering wheel and sighs. His leather seat cushion releases a burst of air, sighing along with him.

Yeah, so this definitely isn't going to be good.

"It can vary, depending on the circumstances." He turns slowly to meet my gaze, and his eyes are bleak. "But usually the punishment for both the rogue maker and the unsanctioned newborn is death."

My cold, undead body goes even colder. "I'm sorry. Did you just say 'death'?"

"Yes."

"Death?"

"Yes."

"'*Death?*'"

I'm shouting. I'm shouting and I'm shaking and I can't seem to stop—and no wonder. I mean, come on! I'm still grappling with the idea that I'm going to live forever. And now, he's telling me I'm as good as dead?

I don't know when Tristan put his arms around me and pulled me close, but I suddenly find myself wrapped up in his strong embrace. I feel the reassuring pressure of his hand on my back. The light touch of his chin resting on the top of my head. The muscles beneath the sleeves of his leather jacket as his arms encircle me.

And even though my nose is smashed awkwardly against his chest and the gearshift is jamming painfully into my abdomen, it feels good.

Really good.

Too good.

I somehow gather the resolve to shove Tristan away and settle back in the passenger seat. I need the distance from him so I can think. I've got to maintain my objectivity here. I can't necessarily accept everything he tells me as fact.

Only, nobody lies for no reason. And despite my distrust, I can't come up with a good reason why Tristan would be lying to me about all this.

Still, I swear there's something about this whole craptastic story of his that isn't landing quite right. Except I can't pinpoint what it is.

Then, all at once, it dawns on me.

I shoot him an accusing look. "If you've been in this grand master's crosshairs for hundreds of years," I say, "then why didn't he just order his subway squad to take you out ages ago?"

"For starters, he has his reign to think about," says Tristan, not missing a beat. "Using his position and his power to settle a personal score wouldn't exactly send a good message to the rest of the race, and he doesn't want an uprising. Plus, he has a sadistic streak. He likes to toy with his enemies before he strikes. I suspect Gideon has rather liked the idea that I've been looking over my shoulder all this time, wondering when and how he might finally take his revenge."

"So, what did you do to him?" I ask. "What burned his ass so bad it's been stinging for centuries?"

In answer, Tristan just stares at me. Or maybe he's staring through me at some memory from long ago. Or—

"Hey!" I say. "You're not trying to, um, *influence* me again, are you?"

"What?" He blinks at me. "No," he says. "No, of course not."

"Did you try to influence Gideon?" I ask. "Is that why he's still so pissed?"

Tristan leans back in his seat. He furrows his brow at me, and his eyes are searching. "Lily," he says. "Do you really think the mere act of trying to exert my influence would warrant a centuries-long grudge?"

And just like that, it seems we're not just talking about the grand master anymore.

I meet Tristan's gaze defiantly, ready to answer in the affirmative. I mean, I think I made my views on this topic pretty clear. But as we stare at each other across the gearshift, the same heat from last night starts to rise between us, and the locks that I so carefully secured on my heart start to melt. Suddenly, it's hard to remember my name—let alone why I'm so angry with him.

How on earth has this Grand Master Gideon been able to hold a grudge against Tristan for hundreds of years? I wonder. I've barely been able to keep mine going for the length of this car ride downtown.

"Influence only works on humans, by the way," Tristan says

quietly. Then, his lips curl into a small smile. "Well, *most* humans. Not vampires."

Good info, I guess.

But there's still so much I don't know.

"Okay," I say, trying to get this convo back on track. "Then, why the epic cat-and-mouse game with the vampire-in-chief? What did you do?"

"Look," Tristan says. "Everyone makes mistakes. And I've lived longer and made more mistakes than most. But what I did or didn't do before isn't the issue here. What's important," he adds emphatically, "is what I plan to do now."

Tortured past? I find myself speculating. *Is that his backstory?*

I mean, clearly, he's hiding something. I know an evasion when I hear one. Journalism 101.

And, hello? It seems to me that his past is *way* relevant here. If what he's telling me is true, his past is a major factor in both of our futures.

But…okay. I'm willing to put a pin in that subject for now. I figure if I keep him talking, I'll eventually get the full story. Or else I'll get him to trip up and expose his lies.

"Fine," I say, playing along. "Then what do you plan to do now?"

"Protect you," he says simply. "Now that I've saddled you with immortal life, I intend to make sure you keep it. And I'll do whatever it takes, Lily. I promise I won't let you die on my watch."

I open my mouth, but for once I don't have a smart-ass comeback. It's kind of hard to argue with that kind of out-and-out altruism.

He leans in closer, and I can't help wondering if he's going to kiss me.

My body is totally on board with the idea, all systems go.

But before I launch myself at him, my brain flashes back to the last time I thought he was going to kiss me. And all at once, I remember exactly why I'm so fire-ants-in-my-panties mad at him.

I pull back and give him a cold stare. "I don't need a bodyguard," I say. "Especially one I'm not so sure I can trust."

He stops where he is. Nods almost imperceptibly.

"Then what *do* you need, Lily?"

I gasp. Partly because the question is so heavy with innuendo. But mostly because there are all these things I suddenly do need very badly. The touch of his hands. The thrum of his fingers. The press of his lips against mine.

My breath is shallow. I lean closer.

Then I catch myself.

"I need to get the fuck out of this car," I say.

Amusement glints in his deep-blue eyes.

"You're right, of course," he says. "It's almost sunrise. You should get inside."

Then, instead of going in for a kiss, he leans across me and pushes my door open. His long arm just barely grazes my chest. I'm pretty sure the contact is accidental, but my nipples—*the little traitors*—tighten anyway.

I unbuckle my seat belt and gather my things. "And just so we're clear, I'm not inviting you in tonight either."

As I get out of the vehicle and shut the door behind me, I hear him laugh.

Annoyed, I hiss at him like a tabby in a bad mood and bare my fangs.

He laughs harder.

"You're a natural, you know," he tells me through the open window. He fires up the ignition again. "Vampire looks good on you, Lily."

And with that, he drives off.

I stand where I am by the curb.

Was he flirting with me? Or fucking with me? And seriously, why should I care either way?

I think about that as I watch his shiny black car disappear around the corner.

Then I think about everything he told me. Vampires in the subway tunnels. The council. Grand Master Gideon. The Book. Punishment. Death.

Then the morning light begins to tease at the horizon. And suddenly, I'm so drowsy I can't think about anything except getting into my apartment and hitting the sheets.

• • • • •

I drag my tired butt down the dimly lit hall, back toward my cave of a studio apartment. As I dig out my keys, I notice an oblong white box leaning against my door.

A florist's box.

Did Tristan send me flowers? I wonder, suddenly perking up.

Immediately, I chastise myself. Who cares if Tristan sent me flowers? As if giving me flowers could even begin to make up for everything he's taken from me, everything I've lost.

Still, like some lovestruck loser, I wonder if they're roses.

I've never had a boyfriend who sent me roses before. I mean, not that Tristan is my boyfriend or anything. Definitely not.

Only, that makes me think about my previous boyfriends. And honestly, I'm not so sure any of them were really, truly my boyfriend either. Which could certainly account for the no-roses thing.

First, there was Tom. We bonded in high school over our mutual love of *Absolutely Fabulous*, secondhand clothing stores, and boy bands. In retrospect, it seems ridiculous I didn't know he was gay. But in my defense, he didn't know either. He was in the process of figuring things out. Once he did, we broke up, obvi—but we stayed friends. He lives in Los Angeles now, but we continue to text and email. The frequency of our messaging spikes around the Met Gala or whenever Harry Styles drops new music.

Then, in college, there was Aidan. I guess you could say he was a boyfriend of convenience. See, he was roommates with this guy Jonathan, who was dating Cat. I don't think he was particularly into me, and I know I wasn't particularly into him—which is kind of sad, because I lost my virginity to Aidan. It was basically a non-event. As was our breakup. When Cat and Jonathan split, Aidan simply didn't come by our dorm room anymore. When I finally noticed, I didn't especially care.

Most recently, though, there was Joe. We met through a dating app—well, okay, a *hookup* app. And we hooked up. Repeatedly. Seriously, the sex was amazing. But it was more than that—or at least I thought it was. We also messaged each other in the app all the time—and it wasn't just sexting. Only, it never went anywhere—or, I should say, *we* never went anywhere. We never went to dinner or to the movies or…*anywhere*. I never met his friends, and he never met mine.

Hell, he never even gave me his phone number. He said it was easier for him to just use the app. When I pushed, he deleted his profile—and that was the end of that. Cat said he was probably married or engaged or else just not looking for anything serious, which, given the nature of the app, totally makes sense. Even to someone with my insecurities. But sometimes, when I hit an especially low point, I can't help but wonder… Would things have gone differently if *I* was different?

So, I guess all this is to say that long white boxes that could quite possibly contain roses do not exactly appear at my door every day.

Intrigued—and yes, okay, a little excited—I lean over, pick up the box, and remove the lid.

Nestled inside on a bed of green tissue paper is a single, perfect lily.

A lily. For Lily, I guess.

A little cheesy, but in a nice kind of way.

Absolutely the kind of old-school gift Tristan would send.

Smiling despite myself, I pluck it up by the stem to breathe in its perfume with my supersensitive vampire sniffer. Only, when I lift it, something's not quite right. The head of the flower lolls over drunkenly to one side.

On closer inspection, I realize the stem wasn't just accidentally bent or broken. The head of the flower has been neatly lobbed off, left hanging by just a few fibers.

A lily. With its head cut off.

Someone has sent me, Lily, a lily with its head deliberately sliced off.

Suddenly, I remember that laundry list Cat recited earlier, the list of all the things that could kill a vampire. Fire. Sunlight. A wooden stake through the heart.

And decapitation.

"Holy shit!"

Horrified, I drop the lily and all its wrappings, backing away. A small white card bounces out of the box and onto the scuffed hallway floor.

For a moment, I just stand there and stare at it.

Then, gingerly, I bend down and retrieve it.

It bears a short message, written in red ink. Or, at least I think it's ink.

SEE YOU SOON. XOXO GIDEON

Quickly, I sift through the filing cabinet in my mind, reviewing what Tristan told me about Grand Master Gideon. I pay special attention to the file marked "sadistic." He likes the chase, apparently. And he likes to toy with his prey before he attacks.

Then I think about what this creepy delivery from him must mean: (1) Gideon already knows about me, about my unauthorized transformation that flies in the face of vampire law; and (2) he wants me to know what the punishment is for the crime of my very existence—a punishment he and he alone has the authority to dish out.

Oh, sure—I suppose this could be some big, elaborate ruse on Tristan's part. Something he sent me to back up his story, to get me to believe him.

But...*why?* Why would he go to all the trouble?

No, in most cases, the simplest explanation is the right one. And right now, the simplest explanation is that Tristan has been telling me the truth.

The simplest explanation is that I have just received an actual fucking death threat from the grand master of the Vampire Council.

CHAPTER 12

"Lily…? Lily! *Lily!*"

On the next evening, with the sound of my own name ringing in my ears, I open my eyes—and see a terrifying, inanimate mask of features hovering over my bed.

Grand Master Gideon, I think immediately. *He's here to make good on his death threat.*

I want to scream, but no sound will come out of my mouth. I want to run, but I can't move my limbs.

"I've been buzzing and buzzing," says the frightfully frozen face—which I now realize is attached to a tiny, wiry, regularly Soul-Cycled body in a mint-green French-terry track suit. "Eventually, I just used my spare keys. It was getting dark, for heaven's sake!"

"Mom." I sigh with relief. I sit up in bed, wishing I could shed my bleariness as easily as the covers. I shake my head, trying to clear it. "Um, did you tell me you were coming to visit?"

"Didn't you check your phone? I texted you this morning that Dr. Andrews was able to fit me in late this afternoon for a tune-up." She frowns—or tries to, anyway. The Botox or collagen or Restylane or whatever cocktail of the above that Dr. Andrews has injected into my mother this time is making any kind of facial expression pretty much impossible. "Have you been sleeping all day?" she asks.

Translation: "Have you been lying around all day being lazy instead of going to the gym?"

"Don't be so judgy." Swinging my legs out of bed, I yank at the hem of my "Need More Sleep" nightshirt to keep my dimpled thighs hidden from her critical eye. "My body clock is on a different schedule. I work nights. Remember?"

"Mmm," says Mom. She swipes an index finger—freshly gel-manicured in an obnoxiously bright teal—through the fine layer of dust on my nightstand. "When does the cleaning lady come?"

"When I get paid enough to afford one."

Mom brushes her hands off. "I really wish you would get yourself a better job, sweetheart."

I stuff down one snide response after another, like so many Twinkies over the years. Does she seriously think that the *New Yorker* or the *New York Times* or even the *New York Post* is just waiting for the opportunity to hire me, but I stubbornly insist on working the graveyard shift at TakeABite.com?

"Actually, in this market, I'm pretty fortunate to have the job I have," I say finally as I get to my feet. And for once, I truly am grateful for the shitty overnight gig. Thanks to my nocturnal schedule, I can still go to work, still pay my bills. At least I'm not a vampire *and* unemployed.

"But you need to start thinking about your future," says my mom. "You won't be this young forever."

I'm about to contradict her—but I stop myself just in time.

No way can I let her know that (a) vampires really exist; and (b) I've just become one. I mean, she's already getting cosmetic procedures every couple of months in some desperate attempt to hang onto her waning youth. If she ever found out there was a one-and-done way to make time stand still, I swear, she wouldn't leave me alone until I found a way to turn her too. Then this Grand Master Gideon could be gunning for us both.

"How about some coffee?" I ask her to change the subject.

"How about a hug first?"

And before I know what's happening, Mom's arms wrap me up in a fierce squeeze. Now that I'm this close to her, even the heavy, sickeningly sweet, rose-scented perfume that she apparently bathes in can't camouflage the underlying smell of her blood.

All at once, my fangs jut out. I'm ravenous.

There have, of course, been many times over the years when I've figuratively wanted to kill my mother. But there's never been a time when I might literally have acted on the impulse—until now.

"Coffee," I mutter. I pull away from her, scurry down the length of my studio, and escape into my tiny kitchen.

I fling open the refrigerator door and grab a bag of the blood that Cat and I stole last night. Unflinching this time, I bite through the plastic and begin to suck down the viscous red liquid. The pleasure it gives me is no longer new, but no less intense. I drink deeply, enjoying surge after surge of blissful gratification—until I hear my mother's buzzkill of a voice right behind me.

"What are you eating?"

I freeze. "Um…nothing," I say without turning around.

"Are you sneaking carbs?" she asks.

Because, of course, carbs aren't something any self-respecting person would dare to eat in public. Ever.

"No," I say.

"You know, Lily, if you could just cut back on the carbs—"

"Oh, for fuck's sake," I say, spinning to face her. "I am not eating carbs. Okay?"

For once, my mother lets my use of the f-bomb go without comment. She looks slowly from my undoubtedly red-stained mouth to the nearly drained donor unit in my hand.

"Is that...*blood?*" she asks.

Okay, so it seems pretty pointless to deny it. But I give it a try anyway.

"No. No, of course not," I say. Thanks to the thirst-quenching infusion of post-fresh B positive, my fangs have receded, so I'm not literally lying through my teeth. "It's a...a new protein drink. Like a meal-replacement shake. Fortified with iron. Clever packaging, huh?"

Wide-eyed and statue-still, I stare at my mother, waiting for her reaction. With my blood-boosted vampire vision, I take in her bleach-damaged blond hair, her chemically plumped-up skin, and her intentionally paralyzed facial muscles. While last night I was noticing a whole new level of beauty in the world around me, I'm now noticing a whole new level of, um, *freaky*.

For the first time in a long time, I don't feel angry or annoyed or frustrated with my mom. Actually, I feel kind of sorry for her. If she could only look past her tiny lines and graying hair and see how naturally lovely she really would be without all the—

"I knew it!" she says, pointing one of those neon-teal nails at me. I watch as her absurdly puffy lips elongate into a misshapen smile, revealing her too-bright, artificially whitened teeth. "I thought you were looking a little thinner."

I don't know whether to be thankful or horrified that she actually buys my story. But then, why wouldn't she? Considering some of the other fad diets I've tried over the years—some with her recommendation, all with her blessing—the lie seems totally plausible.

Obvi, my mother is not a big supporter of the trend toward body acceptance. I doubt she even knows it's a thing. In her view, "accepting" a body that looks like mine would be tantamount to quitting. And, well, let's just say Mom didn't raise me to be a quitter.

"And I've got just the thing to keep you motivated on your diet," she says.

• • • • •

I follow my mother out of the kitchenette, back into the main room of my apartment. She grabs her leopard-print overnight bag, plops it onto my sleeper sofa, unzips it, and—

Hold the phone. Overnight bag?

I hadn't noticed that before.

How long is she planning to stay? I wonder. *How can I keep my dark secret from her if she's here? And how can I possibly keep her safe from my new enemies when I don't even know how to keep myself safe?*

"Don't you have to get back to the diner?" I ask. I hope I don't sound rude.

"I've been pulling double shifts since last Thursday," she says, riffling through the bag. "The other girls can cover while I spend a little time with my only—Ah, here we go!"

With a flourish, Mom pulls out…the most gorgeous little black dress ever. Truly. Even with her own insistence on dressing like a Carmela Soprano wannabe, my mother actually can have quite good taste in clothing when she wants to.

"It's Calvin Klein." She holds the dress up proudly for my inspection. "I found it on the clearance rack at T.J.Maxx."

I glance at the tag and frown. "It's too small for me."

"For now, maybe," she says. "But you can use it as inspiration to help you stay focused and reach your goal. You just need to lose a little more weight, maybe tone up a bit," she says like that's the easiest thing in the universe. "Then it'll be a perfect fit." She smiles her beaming, blinding-white smile, wholly satisfied with this plan.

FYI, my mother has been doing stuff like this since I was in middle school: surprising me with impossibly beautiful dresses and shirts and pants and skirts, always in what she likes to call "aspirational" sizes, hoping these gifts would encourage me to drop a few pounds. She even talked me into buying my senior prom dress in a size too small—a decision that led to me spending prom night locked in my bedroom with a lilac chiffon dress with a busted zipper, a pint of Ben & Jerry's Chunky Monkey, and a spoon.

Fucked-up, I know.

But seriously, here's the thing: I long ago made peace with the fact that Mom's actions in this regard, if horribly misguided, were at least well intentioned. She's always just wanted what's best for me, in her own way.

Only now, as I look at the exquisite but way-too-small LBD that my mother is dangling in front of me like a lovely designer carrot, it dawns on me that the circumstances have changed.

I'm a vampire now.

Admittedly, I don't know everything there is to know about being a member of the undead society. But I know a few things.

I know Tristan is nearly four hundred years old, but he apparently still looks the way he did when he was turned at twenty-three. And I know the stubble on his jaw has been the exact same length every single time we've met.

I know Tristan told me that, no matter how many centuries passed, I would always look "as young and lovely" as I do today. At the time, I was so swept up by the compliment that I didn't get the broader meaning.

But I get it now.

I will look like this—*exactly* like this—for all eternity.

And I know something else too.

I look at my mother, still holding up the LBD. "I'll never fit into that dress."

"Sure, you will," says Mom with her usual former-cheerleader enthusiasm. "If you keep drinking your protein drinks—"

"You don't understand!" I say in an unrestrained burst of emotion. In fact, until just this minute, I didn't understand it either. Not fully. "I'm going to have this body—these thighs, these hips, this belly, this ass—forever. *Forever!*"

The irrefutable truth has just hit me like a sucker punch to the gut. Because, as a vampire, I will never grow old, get wrinkled, or go gray. My appearance is permanently locked and loaded at twenty-five, at this moment in time.

But that also means I will never, *ever* lose weight. There is no diet that will reduce my curves. No exercise regimen that will reshape my figure.

"Lily, don't say that," says my mother. "Don't give up. With just a little bit of willpower and determination—"

"You know what?" I say, cutting her off. "I can't have this conversation right now. I need to get ready for work."

CHAPTER 13

I stand in the shower, close my eyes, and let the hot water cascade over my permanently cold body.

My permanently cold, permanently *plump* body.

I swear, this whole vampire thing really is just one giant kick in the tits after another. Every time I turn around, there's a new layer of shit getting piled onto the shit cake. And I can't even decide what's worse: the thought that Grand Master Gideon really does want to kill me, or the thought that I might actually have to live on indefinitely at my current weight.

No, that's a lie. Right now? I'm thinking it's got to be way worse to be relegated to the role of "fat friend" forevermore.

Forever. *More.*

I shouldn't care so much. I know I shouldn't. I should just accept it, accept my body, and move on.

But…*how?*

How am I supposed to embrace my size when everyone from so-called experts to my own goddamn mother has told me I should want to reduce it?

How am I supposed to walk away from the dream of being thin

when it's a dream I've literally had since childhood? Oh, I know it's not a particularly profound dream. Or even a healthy dream.

But it's *my* dream.

And yes, okay, it's not my only dream. I want other things too. I want the things everyone wants: success, happiness...love. But the thing is, if I ever dare to imagine my future self with a killer career and a committed relationship and an all-around wonderful life, I always imagine myself thin.

So, if I'm never going to be thin? I just can't see myself getting the rest.

Blindly, I reach for the shampoo, squirt a little Herbal Essences into my palm, and massage the fragrant gel into my hair and scalp. I inhale, hoping the aroma of rosemary and other herbs will help soothe me.

FYI, it doesn't.

Then it's lather, rinse—and seriously, does anyone ever bother to *repeat*?

I move on to washing my body, and I try to scrub my curves without actually looking at them. I mean, my figure was disappointing enough to my human eyes. I don't even want to know what I look like in vampire HD.

On the upside, though, at least I shaved before I went out Saturday night. So, given the consistent length of Tristan's beard, I guess I'll never have to shave my legs or my pits or my bikini line again.

I'll also never have a body that I think looks good in a bikini.

Jesus. I totally want to bawl my head off.

But I don't want my mother to hear.

So I just stand here, quiet and immobile, under the spray of the shower until the water gets cold and my fingertips start to prune and my mom is probably wondering what I'm doing all this time.

After I towel off, I swipe my hand across the fogged-up mirror above the sink before I remember there's no point. So, I just work a little de-frizzing serum through my long, damp hair and let it air-dry while I pull on panties, an old bra, and my boyfriend jeans.

And, by the way: *boyfriend* jeans? Who came up with that brilliant name? Like I said, I've had three "boyfriends" in my life so far, and even if I could've managed to squeeze my ass into any of their jeans, the fit definitely wouldn't have been relaxed or baggy or fashionably slouchy. I swear, everything in this whole goddamn world uses skinny women as the gold standard.

And now I will never be one of them.

Forever. *More.*

I swallow down the lump in my throat.

Don't cry, I tell myself. *Don't cry.*

I slip into an Old Navy graphic tee, a long black cardi, and a pair of black suede ballet flats.

Don'tcrydon'tcrydon'tcrydon'tcrydon'tcry...

And with this as my mantra, I try to hold it together as I reach for the knob of the bathroom door and prepare to face my mother again.

• • • • •

First, I smell the coffee. Mom must have brewed some while I was getting ready.

Then I hear the talking—followed by my mother's unmistakable, high-pitched laughter. I assume she's switched on the TV and found one of her shows, and as I walk past my rumpled bed and back into the main room of my studio, I wonder whether it's the Kardashians or the Housewives that are keeping her so entertained.

Turns out, it's neither.

Tristan.

I stop short when I see him sitting there like the lord of the manor in the only slightly worn dark-green wing chair that I picked up about a year ago at a charity thrift shop.

But, hey, at least I'm not on the verge of tears anymore. The sight of him making himself comfortable in my home fixes that. *The nerve!* I'm so angry it takes me a beat or two to find my words.

"What the fuck are you doing here?" I demand when I find them.

"Lily!" my mother practically shrieks. "Manners!"

I turn my anger on her. "How did he even get in here?"

"I answered the buzzer while you were busy doing I-don't-know-what in the shower." She's perched on the edge of the folded-up sleeper sofa, balancing a steaming mug of Starbucks House Blend on her knee and staring googly-eyed at our guest.

"Yes," says Tristan. He shifts in the chair and attempts an innocent smile—which, much to my annoyance, is also sexy as hell. "Your mother was kind enough to *invite* me in."

And just like that, I know three things with absolute certainty: (1) The rule that says a vampire needs to be invited into a place of residence is 100 percent true; (2) Since my mother has keys to my place, she was able to do the inviting; and (3) Thanks to her cluelessness, Tristan now has unfettered access to my personal space.

My anger ratchets up another notch. Apparently, since he can't barge into my brain, he's decided to barge into my apartment. Once again, this bloodsucking bastard has thoughtlessly sought to violate my boundaries. How dare he bulldoze his way in here and expect me to like it? I guess that's what happens when you're used to being able to control people with your mind.

Or with your beauty.

Because, I'm sorry… Even without exerting his vampire influence, I'm betting Tristan rarely has any trouble getting people to do exactly what he wants them to do. I mean, look at the way my mother is sitting here panting at him like a lovesick puppy dog, hanging on his every word. It's the same way guys are constantly tripping all over themselves around Cat.

Beauty is its own kind of influence.

Well, guess what? Tristan *can't* affect me with his vampire mind tricks. And I'll be damned if I'll let him manipulate me any other way.

"So, Lily," says my mom, "why didn't you tell me you have a new boyfriend?"

"I… What, now?"

"And such a famous one, to boot," she continues. "Wait 'til I tell my book club! My daughter is dating Delilah Manning! And Delilah Manning is a man! A man named—"

"Tristan Newberry is not my boyfriend," I say, cutting her off. I don't know what kind of fairy tale he's been spinning for her, but it ends right here, right now.

"Lily and I only just met, you see," adds Tristan, still smiling. The son of a bitch is enjoying this. "In all honesty, it's probably too soon to be assigning labels."

"Well, if I were you, young lady," says my mother, wiggling the fingers of her left hand at me in some weird parody of a Beyoncé music video, "I'd be trying to get him to put more than just a label on it."

"Mom!"

"Lock it down," she whispers—pointlessly, as Tristan, with his amped-up vampire hearing, is closer within earshot than I am. "Before he changes his mind and gets away."

In addition to being mortifying, her words hit a major nerve. I mean, if Tristan and I were dating—which, of course, we're not—I'm pretty sure it wouldn't take long for this hot AF, successful AF, charming AF vampire to realize he could do much better. It would just be nice if my own mother didn't think so too.

"Relax, Rose," Tristan interjects on my behalf—although I see he's already on a first-name basis with Mom. "I'm planning to stick around for a while."

A while, I can't help noting. *Not forever.*

Not when I'm forever *more*.

Clearly, his romance-writing ass is only here now out of some twisted sense of obligation to play the hero and protect me.

Well, fuck the fuck out of that.

I've gotten along just fine by myself up until now. I don't need him to protect me. Not from some flower-sending sadist of a grand master. And certainly not from my own mother.

"Stick around all you like," I say to Tristan. "I have to get to work."

"I'll drive you," he says, getting to his feet.

"Not necessary," I say. "In case you haven't noticed by now, I'm not one of your beautiful but helpless damsels in distress."

"But you have other fine qualities, sweetheart," my mother pipes in with an encouraging smile and a nod. I'm sure she thinks she's being helpful.

"I agree, Rose," says Tristan smoothly. He keeps his gaze fixed on me while he continues to address my mom. "Lily is that rare combination of beauty *and* strength."

And that's all it takes. Seriously. My body sizzles at the praise.

Only, now that our conversation is touching on his profession, it dawns on me that Tristan Newberry, a.k.a. Delilah Manning, has yet another tool of influence at his disposal: his words. He seduces people with them for his job.

So, I'd be living in a fantasy land to think that this compliment of his is anything more than some purple-prose ploy to bend me to his will. Obvi, the guy is a control freak.

Even so, I feel my insides go all gooey, like the center of a chocolate lava cake.

And, yes, okay, it's not lost on me that Tristan's words, truth or fiction, have just rendered my mother absolutely speechless. Her inflated lips hang open. Her artificially widened eyes now have the genuine look of surprise.

I feel some of my anger dissipate, and I bite my lip to suppress my smile. For sure, her reaction is the best thing that's happened since I woke up this evening.

"However," Tristan continues, eyes still locked on me, "your daughter is also a lot like those frustratingly independent heroines I sometimes encounter when I write. The ones who refuse to stay within the outline of my plot." He raises his eyebrows meaningfully. "Even when it's for their own good."

I bristle, especially at that last bit. Tristan doesn't even know me. So, who is he to say what's good for me? Pretty arrogant, if you ask me. I'm about to tell him to go back to the eighteenth century or wherever the hell he came from and leave me alone.

Except…what if he really has outlined some sort of a plot, one that could help me deal with this real and present threat from Grand Master Gideon?

I'm like a rope being pulled in two directions. There's a tug of war raging between my emotions and my reason, and I swear, I'm about to snap.

But in the end, my pragmatic side ekes out the win, and I figure it's probably in my best interest to go along with Tristan for now, pump him for more information, and get his take on last night's disturbing flower delivery. I'm not going to be too stupid to live.

Or to go on being undead.

Or…whatever.

"Okay," I tell him. "Wait here. I just need to get my stuff."

CHAPTER

14

Your mother seems—"

"Totally out of her mind?" I suggest.

Tristan laughs as we buckle ourselves into his sleek black auto—which, once again, has managed to find its way into a spot directly in front of my apartment building.

"Actually, I was going to say she seems rather devoted to you. In her own way, of course."

I shrug at his fairly on-the-nose assessment. "Yeah, well, it's always been just the two of us."

He looks at me across the gearshift. I can see the question in his eyes, the obvious one. But he tactfully refrains from asking me anything about my father.

Instead, he asks, "Where are we going?"

"Midtown," I say. I give him the address of the TakeABite.com offices, and he starts up the car.

Only now, as we begin to drive through the night, all the new questions I had for him about Gideon and the council and the menacing message that showed up at my door are being drowned out by the special paternity-test episode of *Maury* that's blasting in my brain.

Who is my biological father? I wonder for only about the zillionth time. *Why has he never wanted to be a part of my life? Or my mother's life?*

Hey, what do you know? Another happy-for-now guy.

Mom, for her part, has always flat out refused to discuss the subject with me. Kind of funny, considering how she can't seem to quit talking about most other things related to me, like my diet, my relationship status, and my unladylike language.

And believe me, I asked. My mother would say I badgered and harassed, but I never saw what the big deal was. I certainly wasn't the only kid in the neighborhood being raised without a father. And the other kids all knew their dad was a war hero who'd died in Afghanistan or a bum who'd left them for a dental hygienist in Haddonfield or an anonymous sperm donor who'd made it possible for their two moms to have a family. I just wanted to *know*.

So, once I got to be a teenager, I stopped asking and started investigating. In a weird way, I suppose I owe my interest in journalism to my absentee father. If they ever make a movie about me, the opening scene will surely show me digging around for information about his identity, honing my fact-finding skills at an early age—but, okay, now I'm getting off topic.

The thing is, eventually, I got the idea to look into my mother's banking records. And there it was, bold as balls, the lead I'd been searching for: regular monthly deposits, dating all the way back to a whopper of a six-figure deposit made two days after my birth.

Well, that certainly explained the upscale suburban lifestyle we enjoyed—despite the fact that my mother worked for minimum wage at a diner.

But get this—and, I swear, I'm not making it up. The payments were being wired from an offshore account. An *untraceable* offshore account. Seriously. It was like something straight out of a rerun of *Law & Order*.

I kept up my investigation for a little while, but apparently when it comes to untraceable offshore bank accounts, untraceable means really, truly *untraceable*. I hit dead end after dead end. So, ultimately, I decided to let it lie.

My best guess? My biological father is wealthy. Powerful. Maybe even a little shady. And, um, probably married to someone other than my mom.

"So, there's definitely been some chatter," says Tristan.

"Um, what?" For a millisecond, I think maybe Tristan has heard something about my bio dad.

"There's been chatter," he repeats. "About a newborn."

I drag my head out of my past and back to the here and now. This is no time to be getting caught up in my daddy issues. I've got way bigger issues.

"A newborn?" I ask. "Meaning me?"

"Meaning you."

"Are you sure?" I ask, even though I've got pretty solid evidence that the chatter has indeed been about me—and has traveled all the way up the vampire phone tree to the grand master's ears. I plan on telling Tristan about the lily, but I want to feel out what he knows first. "Maybe they were chattering about some other newborn. I mean, are freshly minted vampires really such a rare commodity?"

"They are, actually," says Tristan. "There hasn't been an approved transformation in decades. It's preservation of the species."

I let that new information roll around in my head for a second or two, examining it from all sides.

"That doesn't make any sense," I say. "If you want to preserve the vampire species, shouldn't you just, you know, make more vampires? Like, as many as possible?"

Tristan doesn't look at me. He keeps his eyes straight ahead, out the front windshield. There's a sudden downturn to his mouth, a sudden intensity to his gaze—an expression that suggests more than just concentration on the road.

"You'd think so, but no," says Tristan. And I swear, it's there: underneath his matter-of-fact tone is an undeniable note of sadness. Regret. Maybe even heartbreak. "See, much of our survival hinges on secrecy."

I want to pry and ask him what's wrong. Is it something to do with this centuries-long feud he's got going with Gideon?

Only, since he just respected my privacy in regards to my paternity, I feel like I should respect his in regards to, um, whatever *this* is.

So, instead, I just listen in silence while he goes on to vamp-splain why less is more when it comes to vampires. I'll spare you the long-winded lecture, but basically, these are the headlines: (1) Vampires are scared shitless that if word gets out about them, humans will want *their* blood; (2) An organized human offense targeting vampires in their daytime resting places, when they're at their most vulnerable, could wipe out the entire race; and (3) The more bloodsuckers there are, the harder it becomes for them to keep their existence under wraps, making it more likely for 1 and 2 to happen.

I frown. "And that's it?" I ask. "That's why there are all these rules around creating new vampires?"

He hesitates. Then he shrugs. "More or less," he says.

I think about this. And yes, okay, I guess that rationalizes why Grand Master Gideon might want to make an example out of Tristan and me. But really, the whole thing just makes me think vampires are a lot like a bunch of tween girls. Can't keep a secret to save their lives. Like, *literally*.

Tristan pulls up in front of my office building—and look! There's an empty space right in front. I'm about to ask him if this incredible lucky streak with the New York City street parking is due to some kind of vampire magic or just amazing coincidence. But then I figure I should stay on point.

"So, I got a little gift," I say.

"From your mother?" Tristan asks.

Yes, but I am so not getting into the whole too-small dress story and the realization it triggered. Not with him. Not ever.

"From Gideon," I say.

He snaps off the ignition and whips his head around to face me. "Excuse me?"

"It was a lily," I say. "With the head chopped off."

His eyes flash with anger—at the grand master, I assume.

"Why didn't you tell me sooner?" he demands.

That's when I realize the anger is aimed at me. Um…*seriously?*

"Chill," I say. "I'm telling you now."

"You have to tell me these things," he says. "Otherwise, how can I protect you?"

"Okay, first of all," I say, "I never asked for your protection. And second of all, I don't *have* to tell you shit. Especially when you're obviously keeping secrets of your own."

He frowns. But he doesn't deny it.

"You can be very frustrating," he says.

"Back at ya," I say.

Mulling over this latest complication, he leans back in the driver's seat. I see that's where he likes to be, both literally and figuratively. In the driver's seat. Control freak.

"So, a lily?" he asks.

"Yes."

"Without a head?" he asks.

"Yes."

"Well," he says, "it sounds like Gideon still has a flair for the dramatic."

"It came with this," I say. I reach into my pocket, pull out the card, and hand it to Tristan. "Do you think it's really from the grand master?"

Tristan sits up straighter and looks at the message, hand-lettered in red. His nostrils flare. "Yes."

"You recognize his handwriting?" I ask.

"I recognize his *scent*."

"Um...*what?*"

He looks back at me. "Every vampire's blood is unique," he says. "It's a special blend of their human blood and the blood of their maker. And it has a fragrance that's all its own."

Grimacing, I point at the card. "So, that's written in his, um—"

"Yes."

I shudder, more than a little creeped out.

"I'm sorry about this, Lily," says Tristan. He drops the card into the car's cup holder and runs a hand over the perpetual stubble on his jaw. "I know it's all my fault you're in peril. And I swear, I'm going to find a way to get you out of it."

"Or maybe *we* could find a way out of it," I say. "You know, together. Like equals. I mean, hey, if you've got any ideas, I'm open to discuss."

I sit back in my seat and look at him expectantly.

He looks back at me with that dreamy indigo gaze of his—and suddenly, I'm superconscious of how close we are, just the two of us sheltered together in the two-seated, leather-upholstered cocoon of his sports car.

My mouth goes dry. I try to swallow, but my throat muscles are apparently on strike, refusing to work. I know I should probably look away—but seriously, where am I supposed to look? His broad shoulders and long limbs seem to fill every last inch of the tight space.

"Well," he says, and I feel his breath sweep across my cheek like a lover's touch. "We could go underground."

"Underground?" I say, trying to focus on something other than the way all my nerve endings are perking up. "I, um, thought the subway tunnels were dangerous." Not to mention, *gross*.

"I was talking metaphorically," he says.

I take a beat to decipher that. "So, you want us to go into hiding?"

"I have connections," he says with a small shrug. "And I have means."

Briefly, I let myself consider this. I imagine us fleeing together. Running together through the night. Holing up together throughout the day. Attraction building between us over time until it finally explodes in an earth-shattering burst of wild—

Jesus. Now, *I* sound like a romance novelist.

I remind myself that we're not on some action-packed, enemies-to-lovers road trip to everlasting happiness. At best, it's an awkward rideshare through the bad part of town that we both just need to endure so we can go our separate ways and have a nice immortal life.

"But I have responsibilities," I say. "A job. A mother. Friends." I shake my head. "I can't just up and leave everything behind."

"What if I told you those things were all just ties to your former life?" he asks gently. "To your human life?"

"What if I told you to go fuck yourself?" I shoot back.

He laughs, but not in a laughing-at-me way. More like a laughing-with-me way. As if we share some private joke, some cozy little bond. Something more than just the pointy teeth and the liquid diet and the wooden stake that's apparently aimed at both our hearts.

I recall how we connected that first night we met. Before...*everything.*

And I wonder if maybe we do share something more—but I reject the idea before it can get settled in my cortex and claim squatter's rights.

"Okay," he says, nodding as though he expected my knee-jerk rebuff. As if he already knows me. "Okay. So, I guess that means we prepare to fight."

With a groan, I recall my one pathetic attempt at kickboxing. I broke a toe. Legit. "I really hope you mean *that* metaphorically."

"We'll see," he says. "But if we're going to have any chance of success at all, you need to be at your full power."

It doesn't take me long to put together what *that* means.

"Oh no," I say. "No, no, no. Forget it. I already told you, I am not drinking human blood straight from the source."

"Understood," he says. "But...there is another way."

Now he tells me.

"Go on," I say. I eye him warily. "I'm listening."

His eyes are doing that twinkling thing again. "If you want," he says, "instead of drinking from the vein of the living, you can drink from me."

CHAPTER 15

Drink from Tristan?

The suggestion alone stirs all kinds of desperate longings in me: dark, unnatural desires I don't fully understand but now desperately want to explore.

As if to underscore this, my fangs descend. And descend and descend and descend some more—or try to, anyway. It's like there's a tiny yoga instructor inside my mouth, pushing the little enamel daggers to stretch well beyond their physical limits and cross the short divide between my mouth and Tristan's flesh.

"So, what's the catch?" I ask around my achy, throbbing teeth.

"For a vampire," Tristan says slowly, being careful with his words, "the act of drinking from another vampire is, well, extremely intimate. Extremely...erotic. For a young vampire, it can be uncontrollably so."

"So, what?" I ask. "You think if I drink from you, I'll just automatically jump your bones?"

"I don't think it," he says. "I know it."

"Oh, please," I say. "Get over yourself."

Never mind that I've been on fire for Tristan pretty much since I first laid eyes on him. Thanks to his insufferable arrogance, my fangs begin to retreat.

"No, no… It's not about me," he insists. "It's simply our nature."

"Maybe it's *your* nature," I shoot back.

"Look," he says, "I'm telling you this because I don't want there to be any more misunderstandings between you and me. You need blood to be strong. I have blood that can make you strong. But if you consent to drink from me, I want to make sure you understand what else you're ultimately consenting to."

Okay, so maybe he is trying to do the right thing here. I get it. Except, if I'd be consenting in this scenario, then what exactly would he be doing? Submitting? Surrendering? Gritting his fangs and bearing it?

"Gee," I say, "you make it all sound so romantic."

My response is meant to be flippant. But once it's out, I realize that it also kind of nails my whole problem with this strange proposition of his. There's no, um, *romance* to it.

I mean, if this spontaneous vampire-on-vampire sex he's describing wouldn't be about him, then it wouldn't be about me either. It wouldn't be about him wanting *me*, desiring *me*. Choosing *me*.

I look at Tristan, and suddenly, it's as if I'm looking at all the guys who didn't choose me. All the guys who singled out Cat, or someone who looked like her, as their first choice—but then ended up settling for me.

"I could make it all sound very romantic," says Tristan. "But this isn't one of my novels. This is serious, Lily. It's you and me versus an alliance of the oldest, most powerful vampires on the continent."

"Way to take one for the team," I mutter.

"What?"

"Nice of you to be so willing to make the supreme sacrifice," I say more distinctly.

Tristan frowns at me in confusion for a moment. Then he leans back in his seat and pegs me with a look so superhot and smoldering I'm surprised the whole car doesn't burst into flames. "If you think having sex with you would be any sort of a sacrifice on my part," he says in a voice that's almost a growl, "then you haven't been paying attention."

FYI, if I wasn't paying attention before, I sure as shit am now. Every last molecule of my body is on red alert, amped up to DEFCON 1. Or is it DEFCON 5? Well, whichever DEFCON is the DEFCON where you're on the precipice of total annihilation, um, that's me. Once again, Tristan Newberry has me on the verge of spontaneous combustion.

And okay, maybe I don't think sleeping with me would be a *sacrifice* on Tristan's part, exactly. I mean, sex is sex, right? And sex—even so-so sex—is a hell of a lot better than a kick in the head.

Only, I'm a realist. I know people don't usually go hooking up outside of their league. And since vampires used to be people, I have to assume the same rule still applies.

That's when all the doubts I've had since we connected at Dos Rosas start running across my mind like a stock ticker.

Why was he so flirty with me that first night? I wonder. *Why did he turn on the old-timey charm and try so goddamn hard to seduce me? Was he really attracted to me, or was it simply about satisfying his own bloodlust? Was I just a means to an end all along? A way for him to scratch some supernatural itch?*

"Why me?" I find myself asking aloud, my voice barely above a whisper.

"What?"

"Why me?" I repeat a little louder.

"I heard you the first time," says Tristan. "I just don't understand the question."

"Why me? At the bar?" I ask. "Why did you target me?"

His eyebrows knit together. "I didn't 'target' you," he says. "You walked up next to me, and I offered to buy you a drink."

"Because you figured the fat girl would be an easy mark?" I ask—and now, I can't stop asking. "Because you thought someone like me would let you do whatever the fuck you wanted? Because you assumed I'd just be grateful for whatever attention I could get?"

"What?"

"I'm pretty sure you heard me that time too."

"I did. But I'm having a hard time with your choice of words, among other things," he says. "I saw a redhead with freckles and dancing green eyes who looked like she might be fun to talk to. So I offered to buy her a drink. With absolutely no agenda."

God, I want to believe him.

Only, how can I? I mean, he's a romance writer. His whole job is telling people what they want to hear. So, how can I know where Delilah Manning ends and Tristan Newberry begins?

How can I ever know?

Plus, I may not have a reflection anymore, but I know what I look like in the mirror. I know my most obvious physical characteristic is not my red hair or my green eyes or my freckles. And now, that's never going to change. Ever.

By now, my blood is boiling—and not in a, um, *sexual* way.

"Fuck you," I say.

Then he actually has the nerve to say, "I don't know why you don't see yourself for the beautiful, desirable woman you are."

Okay. That's it. That's got to be a line straight out of one of his novels.

"For starters, because I don't have a reflection anymore," I say—or rather, I shout at him. "Because somebody in this car turned me into a fucking vampire."

Tristan flinches but recovers quickly. "Now, I can see why my influence didn't work on you," he says. "You don't let anyone in, do you?"

I blink at him. "Excuse me?"

"Why do you put up these walls?"

"*Excuse* me?"

He moves closer, getting in my face. "Why do you insist on being the prickly heroine who pushes everyone away?"

Oh, no, he did not.

My boiling blood boils over.

As if I even need to push Mr. Happy-for-Now away. As if I ever needed to push any guy away from the time I was born. My absentee father didn't need any pushing away, did he?

At this point, the up-close-and-personal seating arrangements in this sports coupe aren't so much titillating as suffocating. I need out. Now.

"Fuck. The. Fuck. Off."

And before Tristan can say anything else, I'm up and out of the car, slamming the door hard behind me.

.....

I shove my way through the heavy revolving door of my office building without looking back. I swear, that vampire has some nerve. I mean, did it not even occur to that conceited son of a bitch that maybe I just want to push *him* away?

Besides, I let people in. I let Cat in. And, um...well...I let Cat in on *everything*.

And by the way, he's one to talk. He's not exactly an open book either. There's still a truckload of shit he's keeping from me.

"Asshole," I mutter to myself—or, that's my intention, anyway. Unfortunately, I mutter it just as the doors dump me into the lobby, and the expletive echoes off the marble walls and floor.

The security guard at the desk raises his sleepy eyes to give me a reproachful look.

Busted.

At the front desk, I flash my ID and sign in with an apologetic smile. "Sorry."

Then, shuffling across the well-buffed floor toward the elevators, I try to untangle the jumble of emotions knotting up my insides.

Anger. Because, well... *Tristan.*

Desire. For him. Still. Unwelcome and unwise, but undeniable.

Frustration. Exasperation. Confusion. Regret.

Hurt.

All because of that fucking bloodsucker.

I punch the up button repeatedly, a little harder than necessary.

Okay, a lot harder than necessary.

Okay. So hard it's a certified miracle I don't break my index finger.

Tristan Newberry bit me two nights ago. But when, exactly, did he start getting under my skin?

CHAPTER 16

When the elevator dumps me out on the seventeenth floor, I'm greeted by TakeABite.com's tacky-as-shit logo: a mouth, teeth bared, biting into a big, shiny-red apple emblazoned with the map of New York City. I step past the custom-painted graffiti-style eyesore on the hallway wall and enter the website's small, industrial-chic office space.

Caged light bulbs dangle from the ceiling above the big, reclaimed-wood reception desk. The desk, as usual, is unattended. I'm not sure if it's occupied during the day or not—and now, I guess I'll never know.

I turn the corner into the open-concept work space—all exposed bricks and concrete floors and metal tables and chairs on casters. The place always smells like coffee and various kinds of fast food, but tonight I also detect the unmistakable scent of my coworkers' blood. Good thing I downed that bag at home—and thought to pack a spare for later. I do not need to be getting hangry on the job.

I see the usual suspects are already gathered around the big table in the middle of the room, dammit. On top of everything else Tristan has done, he's made me late for work. I try to wrangle my emotions as I pick up my pace and join tonight's story meeting, already in progress.

Peter Sutton, the site's wiry, pasty-faced editor-in-chief and the sole fortysomething in this sea of twentysomethings, sits at the head of the table behind a KFC Fill Up and a large Pepsi. I swear, it's the definition of unfair that the guy indulges like this night after night and still stays so damn thin. Metabolism is such a fickle bitch.

"Lily," says Peter as he waves his extra-crispy drumstick in my general direction. "Nice of you to join."

"Sorry," I mutter. I slide into the only empty seat at the table and unpack my MacBook Air.

On my left, Gabby Park gives me a sassy wink from behind the red frames of the glasses. She covers the downtown art and club scene. Totally plugged-in. Totally cool.

On my right, Evan Knowles angles his seat away from me, toward Peter.

Okay, so, um, *Evan*.

Here's the thing: he's a good writer. He really is. His whole intellectual-nerd look with the closely shaved hair, the Buddy Holly specs, and the straight-from-Steve-Jobs's-closet black turtleneck isn't just a consciously cultivated image. He actually has the intellect to back up the look. In fact, I've often thought the two of us might make a good team. Except for one teeny-tiny little thing...

Evan Knowles hates my fucking guts.

Seriously. I don't know what I ever did to piss him off so thoroughly, but he never talks to me. He never even looks at me. If there's so much as a chance that our eyes might accidentally meet, he can't pivot away from me fast enough.

Case. In. Point.

But, hey—whatever. I'm used to the nightly brush-off. However, here's what I'm not used to: my unwelcome proximity is causing

Evan's heart rate to rise, poking the beast that is my new paranormal appetite. I watch as the vein at his temple pounds double time beneath his smooth, dark-brown skin. Instinctively, I drop my eyes to his turtleneck and start to imagine how his jugular must be throbbing.

Then I realize what I'm doing.

Now I have to look away too.

"So," says Peter through a mouthful of KFC mashed potatoes, "who wants to dazzle me first?"

One of the overeager interns, whose name I can't remember, immediately volunteers. As the college kid launches into a story pitch about a search for the city's best Moscow mule—probably because he wants to get drunk on the company's dime—I stare down at my laptop keys and try to think about something other than taking Evan's vein.

So, natch, I end up thinking about taking *Tristan's* vein.

What would that be like? I can't help wondering. I recall his invitation to drink from him and the sensual heat it created between us before things bubbled over in anger.

Now that I have the safety of distance from him, I indulge my thoughts, letting them roam freely. *Would drinking from him really be so over-the-top arousing that I'd completely lose my inhibitions?* I wonder. *And my self-control?*

And what if I did end up having sex with Tristan? Would it be as bone-meltingly satisfying as I imagine?

And what other superpowers would his blood unlock in me? Would they be powerful enough to fight off this Grand Master Gideon and the subway-prowling—

"Vampires."

The word, uttered in Evan's deep, resonant bass voice, jerks my attention back to the meeting.

"I'm sorry. What did you just say?"

Evan squirms under my direct gaze. He still refuses to make eye contact with me, but in front of the rest of the staff, he can't refuse to answer my direct question. Not without raising other questions.

"Vampires," he repeats to the table. "I want to do a story about vampires in New York City."

"*What?*" I practically scream.

Now everyone turns to me. Including Evan.

So, objectively speaking, Evan is a handsome guy. Kind of male-model-meets-news-anchor handsome. Even with him avoiding me at every turn, I'd managed to notice that long before today.

But now, I see his muscles tense up underneath his black turtleneck, and—

Muscles. He has muscles. *Huge* muscles.

That's new.

At least, I think it's new. Granted, it's not as if I've ever spent any time ogling Evan's body. But I swear, he wasn't this pumped when I saw him on, well, Friday. It's like all the biceps and triceps and whatevers just popped up out of nowhere over the weekend.

Then again, the last time I saw him, I didn't have the benefit of vampire supersight. So maybe that's why I'm suddenly seeing that TakeABite.com's resident Clark Kent is rocking a Superman bod?

I don't know.

Weird.

"Is that the extent of your feedback, Lily?" asks Peter dryly, interrupting my speculations. "Or would you like to elaborate?"

"Sorry," I say, using my indoor voice again. "It's just, I mean, um, 'vampires'?" I force a laugh that I hope sounds dismissive and not borderline psychotic. "I know we're a *night*life website, but…come on, Evan. Everybody knows vampires don't really exist."

"Everybody *thinks* vampires don't really exist," says Evan. "But I have information that indicates there's some kind of an undead society in the city. One that's very much alive and well."

"Who's your source?" I ask. "The boogeyman?"

My tone is dismissive, but my question is entirely sincere. How much has Evan been poking around already? And how much does he know? Because if vampires are all about secrecy like Tristan said, then investigating them cannot possibly lead to anything good. Not for Evan, not for TakeABite.com—and definitely not for Tristan and me. And we've already got enough trouble.

"I've been talking to some people in the city's Goth subculture," says Evan.

Club kids, then. All he's got are club kids.

I'm so relieved I could cry.

"Oh, please," I say. "Wearing black clothes and black eyeliner doesn't make you a vampire. If it did, most of the women in New York City would qualify. A lot of the men too."

"You didn't let me finish," says Evan. He sits up straighter in his seat, and the muscles in his upper body seem to get even bigger. "I'm hearing rumors about a small but significant subculture to the subculture. Goths who aren't just making a fashion statement or expressing their dark side while they dance to Evanescence and the Cure. Some say they have actual…fangs."

"Probably plastic. Left over from Halloween," I say. "Or else, some kind of freaky dental veneers. Body modifications." I look at the guy, searching. "Is that it?"

"Apparently, they also drink human blood." And if he had a mic, he would have dropped it.

"Doubtful," I shoot back—although I can't help thinking about the sack of expired, donated human blood stashed in my bag. "I'm sorry, Evan, but this all just sounds like some kind of elaborate cosplay. Or maybe some new role-playing game."

"Well, I intend to find out," says Evan.

"No," says Peter.

"No?" asks Evan.

"Actually, I'd like Lily to take this one on," says Peter. He smiles a self-satisfied smile as he takes a draw on the straw of his supersized soft drink. "It's nice to see her get so fired up about a story for once."

"Me?" I ask, hoping I didn't just hear what I think I heard. Does the boss seriously want me to investigate the same undead creatures who want to kill me?

I'm pretty sure this is what you'd call a conflict of interests.

But somehow, I don't think HR will understand.

CHAPTER 17

Okay, so I'm not going to make you sit through the rest of our meeting. All you really need to know is (1) Evan argued that the whole vampires-in-New-York-City thing was his idea, his story; (2) I argued that we weren't some tabloid that trafficked in fake news, so it shouldn't be a story at all; and (3) Peter overruled us both, stuck to his guns, and assigned the story to me.

By the time the drama was over, I needed a drink. Badly.

So here I am, locked in one of the stalls at the back of the ladies' room, sucking down some forty-four-day-old AB positive.

As I drain the last few drops of blood from the plastic donor bag, my iPhone rings—well, vibrates, actually. But with my freshly amplified vampire hearing, it might as well be screeching like a car alarm. I reach into my bag, pull out my mobile, and check the caller ID.

Cat!

I accept the call immediately. "Hey!"

"Lil," says the welcome voice of my BFF. "I've been thinking about you all day. Are you at work? Can you talk?"

"Yes. And yes," I say. "I'm just having a late-night snack in the ladies' room."

"It's not a lady," she asks, "is it?"

"Cat! Of course not!"

"Just kidding," she says—and I really do hope that's the truth. "So, how's, uh, everything?"

I think about how to answer, and I can't even believe how much has happened since I left her less than twenty-four hours ago.

Quickly, I fill my bestie in on the highlights. I start with my predawn face-off with Tristan and our eventual car ride home together. I recount what he told me about the grand master and the Vampire Council and the rogue blood-drinkers trolling the subway tunnels, and how turning me has apparently put a price on both Tristan's head and mine. I fill her in on the unsettling delivery from Grand Master Gideon himself, on the implicit death threat contained in the box.

I tell her about the unexpected visit from my mother. Then I describe tonight's drive to work with Tristan, his strange invitation to drink from him, and the angry way we parted. Finally, I wrap it all up with a play-by-play of my uncomfortable exchange with Evan and the perilous irony of my latest assignment for TakeABite.com.

"So, Tristan is your personal Uber now?" asks Cat.

"Seriously?" I say. "After everything I just told you, you zero in on *that*?"

"You like him," says Cat.

"What?"

"Admit it," says Cat. "You like him."

"I am not doing this right now," I say.

"Okay, okay." And it doesn't take any kind of supernatural hearing to pick up on the grin in my best friend's voice. "To be continued."

After we put that topic on ice, we discuss the more immediate, eternal-life-threatening matters. Cat's tone rapidly turns more somber. "Shit, Lily. What are you going to do?"

Ten minutes ago, I would have said, "Fuck if I know." But once again, the intake of blood has cleared my mind and sharpened my thinking. I can see a plan coming together, the pieces beginning to fall into place.

"I'm going to do what I'm good at," I say with growing confidence. "What I'm trained to do. I'm going to get to the bottom of the story."

"You mean the assignment? The vampire story? No way," says Cat. "I don't care if Peter is your boss. You can't go looking into that. It's way too dangerous."

"Or maybe it's my way out of danger," I say.

"I don't follow."

"Okay, listen," I say. "According to what Tristan told me tonight, the thing vampires fear the most is exposure, right?"

"Right," says Cat in reluctant agreement.

"And as a journalist, exposure is kind of my specialty." I start to get all amped up. "Think about it. I mean, Peter can't possibly be expecting me to turn in anything more than a fluff piece. Goth role-playing shit. So, if I can put together a solid exposé about this underground undead community, I can just dummy up a safe version for Take-a-Bite-dot-com. Then I can use the real story as a bargaining chip against the grand master: You don't kill me, I don't out you and your crew to the whole world. Threaten him back, you know?"

"You want to blackmail the friggin' grand master of the Vampire Council?"

"Brill, right?"

"Sure," Cat mumbles. "If he doesn't figure out what you're up to and chop off your head first."

"Come on! A little support here, please?"

On the other end of the wireless connection, Cat is silent for a few breaths. Then, she says, "What about this other writer? Evan?"

"What about him?" I ask.

"Do you really think he'll just let this whole vampire story go?" she asks. "Because if he keeps digging around, that could be trouble."

"Fuck nuts," I mutter. I hadn't really thought about that.

Okay, so I'm probably going to need to down a few more bags of red blood cells to work out all the details of my brilliant plan.

"You know, maybe you should talk this all over with Tristan," suggests Cat, trying to sound totally casual. "Get his take."

"So, we're back to Tristan?"

"Uh-huh."

I exhale and lean back against the bathroom-stall door. "He says I push people away."

"So, he's perceptive *and* hot," says Cat.

"Hey!" I say. "You're supposed to be on my side."

"I am on your side," she says. "Always. But honestly, it sounds like Tristan is too."

"Are you kidding me?"

"Look, I know you two started off on the wrong foot—"

"'Started off on the wrong foot'?" I say. "He *bit* me."

"He thought he had your consent," says Cat.

"He *changed* me."

"It was an accident."

"Yeah, well, it wasn't an accident when he tried to invade my brain in the first place," I say. "I mean, who does that?"

"A four-hundred-year-old vampire who needs to guard his secret from humans but also needs human blood to survive?"

The downside of having a computer genius for a best friend is that when she starts thinking with the logical side of her brain, it's nearly impossible to argue with her.

"So, what are you saying?" I ask. "I should just give him a pass?"

"Well, maybe you should just give him a *chance*. I mean, he's earned that much, hasn't he?"

I think about this. And okay, it's true that Tristan seems genuinely sorry for how things went down initially between us. And even though his chivalry act is way extra, he does seem to be trying to do right by me now, in his own way. And yes, okay, he did kind of stand up for me in front of my mother…

I know that lying to Cat is a no-go. Her BS detector where I'm concerned is pretty much infallible. But I'm not sure I can admit the truth to her. Or even to myself.

"Maybe I like him…a little," I say in a whisper so soft I wonder if it's even audible to Cat's human ears.

FYI, it is.

"I knew it!" she says.

"But…he's gorgeous," I say. "And I'm—"

"Gorgeous," she finishes for me.

"To you, maybe," I say. "You're my best friend. But—"

"No 'but.' Like I said before, I saw the two of you together at Dos Rosas on Saturday night," says Cat. "I saw the way he was looking at you. There was serious chemistry. Trust me, Lil. He's interested."

I don't believe her—although it's scary how much I *want* to believe her.

"So then do you think I should agree to drink from him?" I ask. "Considering the potential, um, *consequences*?"

Cat snorts a laugh. "Look," she says. "If you're going to stay safe, it seems like you need him. You need his help. And you probably need his blood. So, if you like him *a little*, and you can have some fun in the middle of this whole shitstorm…why not go for it?"

"He's got some outdated ideas about men and women," I say.

"So, teach him some new tricks."

"There's stuff he's still not telling me," I say.

"A little mystery can be a good thing."

"He's immortal, but he's not the forever type," I say. It's the last argument I can think of. "He's a player."

"So, play!"

I'm about to respond when I hear something. Well, okay, not *hear*, exactly. It's more like I *sense* something.

"Lily?" says Cat through the phone. "Are you still there?"

"Gotta go," I say quietly.

I end the call and slowly open the door of the stall. I peek out, but the ladies' room is empty. I'm completely alone. And obvi, not even my own reflection stares back at me as I walk along the row of sinks to the exit.

Silently, I scold myself for being so paranoid.

But then I spot something on the restroom floor, just inside, like somebody slipped it under the door.

It's a glossy picture postcard, the kind you'd find on a rack in your average, ordinary souvenir shop. Nothing overtly sinister about it. Totally innocuous.

Even so, my hackles go up. An overwhelming sense of dread seeps through my body.

I tell myself to get a grip. After all, it might not even be for me. Anybody could have accidentally dropped it there. Anybody. It's not necessarily anything bad.

Carefully, I stoop down and pick it up. My hand trembles as I flip it over.

Just as I feared, the brief message is written in the same hand as the card that came with the headless lily. In the same, um, dark-red fluid.

WISH YOU WERE HERE. XOXO GIDEON

I turn the postcard back over and look at the front again. It didn't quite register with me before, but now I see the picture shows a white-hot sun beating down on a beautiful black-sand beach.

Gideon wishes I were there. On the beach. In the *sunlight.*

Another way to kill a vampire.

Another death threat from the grand master.

I feel like I'm going to be sick.

Not only does Gideon know where I live. He also knows where I work. And while I've been hoping the vampires-need-to-be-invited-in rule can protect me at home, I don't know if that rule applies to public buildings like this one.

I'm thinking not.

Oh, and obvi, the grand master knows how to kill me. And he really wants me to know it.

I wonder... Is this all some kind of a creepy countdown? Is this bloodsucking bully planning to send me a nightly communication, each one taunting me with a different way I might meet my ultimate downfall, until he picks one and follows through?

Because if that's the case, I don't think I have a ton of time left. According to Cat, there are only two things remaining that can end a vampire: fire and a wooden stake through the heart.

Two days—or, um, nights? Could I really be gone in two nights?

If I was scared when I got that first message, I now feel absolutely petrified. Hell, if fright could kill a vampire, Gideon's death threats would already be a fait accompli.

Only this time, mixed in with my bone-deep horror, there's also a smidge of something else. Something like…anger.

Because, seriously, what is this asshole's problem? Who died and made him my judge, jury, and executioner?

I don't know exactly what his beef with Tristan is, but I'm tired of being caught in the middle of it. This has to stop. So, if that means fighting like Tristan said? Okay, bring it on. I'll fight.

And I'll do whatever I need to do—and drink from whoever I need to drink from—to make myself as strong as possible.

And I'll worry about my heart later.

Decision made.

I flip the card over again, back to the side where the note is scrawled. And remembering what Tristan told me, I bring the postcard up to my nose. Ignoring my revulsion, I make myself take a big inhale and memorize the scent. Because when Gideon finally has the balls to stop playing around and come at me, I want to know he's coming. And I plan to be ready for him.

Then I shove the postcard in my pocket and head back to work. Because, to paraphrase the saying, if you stop living your undead immortal life because of the threats, then the terrorists win.

And this terrorist is so. Not. Winning.

CHAPTER 18

When I return to the TakeABite.com work space, Evan is stuffing his laptop into his backpack. And it's kind of funny. After I just got myself all pumped up about facing off with the grand master, my first impulse when I see Evan is to make a u-ey and go back into the restroom and hide until he's gone.

But after everything that went down between us earlier this evening, I decide I should try to make nice—and make sure he's not going to keep poking around in vampire business, like Cat suggested he might.

So, before I lose my nerve, I walk up behind him.

"Evan?" I say. "Can we talk?"

The muscles of his shoulders go rigid, and once again, I'm struck by his powerful build. I swear, he wasn't always so ripped. How did he get so buff so fast? Out of habit, I wonder what his regimen is—and where I can sign up. But then I remember I'm eternally saddled with my body as is. There's no boot camp that can help me now.

"Sorry," he says without turning around—and without sounding sorry at all. "Thanks to you, I need to go dig up another story to pitch to Peter."

"Well, if there's anything I can do—"

"Don't you think you've done enough already?" he demands, turning on me.

I take a step back and put my hands up in a gesture of surrender. "Hey, I'm just trying to do my job," I say.

"No. You're trying to do *my* job." He zips up his backpack and slings it over one of his newly beefy shoulders. "Do you know how much time I spent looking into this story?"

Again, I wonder how much truth Evan has managed to uncover.

And I wonder if he'll share it with me.

"Well, you know," I say carefully, "that work doesn't have to be wasted."

His dark-brown eyes flash angrily behind his glasses. "Unbelievable," he says. "First, you steal my story. Now, you want to steal my research too?"

"Dude. Chill. We're not competing reporters—or at least, we shouldn't be," I say. "We're on the same side."

"Are you sure about that?"

His question is so blatantly aggressive I don't even know how to respond.

While I'm still working on a comeback, my colleague just takes his backpack and his transformed physique and his utter and total disdain for me and stomps straight past me. His bicep brushes lightly against me as he goes.

That's when I realize Evan's new bod isn't just hot. It's, um, practically on fire.

If my vampire flesh is unnaturally cold, then I swear, his is unnaturally heated—and that gives me pause. Seriously, the guy must be taking some dangerous combination of supplements, or worse, to be spiking that kind of fever in his quest for bigger muscles.

I turn and look after him with something like empathy. Maybe Evan and I have more in common than I ever realized.

• • • • •

With that postcard burning a hole in my back pocket—figuratively, that is—I complete the rest of my shift. But despite the constant reminder of my undeadly predicament, the next few hours pass without incident. Around 2:30 a.m., I've wrapped up my regular nightly duties, and I'm riding down alone in the elevator. Because of the hour—and yes, okay, because I'd be a fool not to avoid the subway now—I pull my iPhone out of my bag to request a lift.

There's no signal in the car, of course. My thumb hovers restlessly over the Uber app as I wait, watching the overhead numbers light up in their silent countdown to the lobby. That's when Cat's smart-ass question from earlier comes back to me.

So, Tristan is your personal Uber now?

Well, obvi, he's not.

I mean, okay, so maybe he popped up and played chauffeur a couple of times. But considering how we left things, it's not likely he'll show up again tonight.

Not likely at all.

The elevator bell rings, the car jerks to a stop, and the doors slide open—except now, it's as if the floor is Dubble Bubble, and I'm stuck. Looking down at my phone, I suddenly realize I have no Tristan app. No number to call or text. No way to contact the vampire at all.

And in the last few hours while I was working, anything could have happened. If I received a death threat, Tristan could have been captured by Gideon's underground brigade and dragged before the Vampire

Council to answer for his crimes. He could have been sentenced to death and executed by the grand master.

He could have decided that the overweight, sharp-tongued newborn simply isn't worth his time or his trouble.

My chest feels tight, and it's suddenly hard to breathe. *What if I never see him again?* I wonder.

In a flood, my half of the conversation with Cat comes rushing back to me.

Maybe I like him…a little.

The elevator doors start to close. Automatically, I reach a hand out to stop them. The doors chomp at my fingers before stuttering and springing back apart. When they're fully open again, I take a slow, deep inhale, pull up my big-girl panties, and make myself step out of the car.

Because, seriously, it's not as if I've been expecting Tristan to stick around for good. He's not the sticky type—and I'm not exactly the type to inspire stickiness.

And if I can't gain strength to fight my enemies by drinking his blood, so be it. I have a plan of my own now—or at least the beginnings of one. I can take care of myself. Always have.

The soft snores of the security guard dozing behind the front desk echo through the marble lobby. I sign out without waking the guy. Then I walk past him toward the revolving glass doors to the street. I glance down at my iPhone, still in my hand, and see the signal bars coming back to life. I'm about to open the Uber app when something tells me to look up.

So, I look up.

The first thing I see through the wall of glass before me is the now-familiar black sports coupe. *Again, with the primo parking*, I think with a smile.

But I don't think it for long. Because the second thing I see is Tristan, his long body leaning languidly against the back end of his car. And then I can barely think at all.

Tristan's eyes light up when he spots me—and my unbeating heart leaps. As embarrassing as it is to admit, I've got a case of the warm-and-fuzzy feels so bad it's like I've just watched a three-day marathon of cute kitten videos.

Without breaking eye contact, I stuff my phone back in my bag and push through the revolving doors until the cool night air hits my face. I emerge onto the sidewalk, deserted save for the two of us. But then, feeling uncharacteristically shy, I hesitate a couple of feet from Tristan.

"Hey," I say quietly.

"Hey," he says.

"Are you waiting for me?" I ask.

"No," he says.

For a moment, I feel utterly stupid—until the twinkle in his eyes tells me he's kidding.

"Asshole," I mutter. But there's no edge to my voice.

"You're right," he says. "I have been behaving like an asshole."

The insult sounds strange coming out of his mouth. I realize it's the one and only time I've heard him use foul language.

"It's just…I've been a vampire for so long." He drags a hand back through his thick, messy hair, mussing it up even more. "I guess I've forgotten what it's like to be human. I've forgotten how monumentally confusing the transition to vampire can be—especially when you've been blindsided by the whole thing."

His words are heavy with apology—and something more. It occurs to me that maybe he's speaking from experience. "Were you, um, *blindsided* too?"

He nods. "My master turned me to save my life—for which I'm eternally grateful. But in the beginning, the adjustment was a challenge, to say the least. And that was without the added layer of these new vampire politics. So, I'm sorry, Lily. Truly."

"Okay," I say quietly. It's all I trust myself to say.

"And just to be clear," says Tristan with a grin. "What are you saying 'okay' to?"

I grin back. "Make me an offer."

"Do you maybe want to go somewhere?"

That sends my head whirling, spinning my thoughts around like a blender on high. *Is Tristan asking me out? On a date? Or am I reading too much into his words?*

I swallow nervously. "Go somewhere?"

"To talk?" he says. Only, his eyes are saying something else.

Or am I reading too much into his look?

"Oh!" I say, suddenly remembering that I have a houseguest. "My mother—"

"Is surely asleep by now," he says. "Text her if you want. Let her know you're with me. I'm sure she won't mind."

No. She'll probably start sending out wedding invitations.

Then I recall the postcard tucked into the back pocket of my jeans.

"Are you sure it's safe?" I ask. "What with the grand master out there and all?"

"We'll be careful," he says. "Besides, I think we still have some things to discuss. About how we might prepare to deal with Gideon…together?"

His innuendo isn't lost on me. I know he's tiptoeing around the subject that triggered our earlier quarrel, and I appreciate his delicacy.

I squint at Tristan, trying to figure him out. While I still have a strong distaste for so-called vampire influence, I can certainly see the advantage of being able to snoop around in someone's head. But regardless, it's not an option here.

I'll never know for certain what Tristan is thinking, what he really wants.

I just have to decide what I want. And what I'm willing to risk to have it.

"So, what do you say?" asks Tristan.

CHAPTER 19

So, where are we going?" I ask Tristan as he starts up the car.

He turns to me with a playful grin that makes me remember why I was so attracted to him in the first place. "Have you ever been to the top of the Empire State Building?"

I press my lips together to smother my laugh, but it escapes through my nose like a snort. Of course, he would pick number one on the list of cheesy New York City date spots. Assuming this is even a date.

"I hate to break it to you," I say, "but I'm pretty sure the observation deck is closed at this hour."

He grins wider, and his eyes twinkle with mischief. "Lily," he says, "you really need to stop thinking like a human."

• • • • •

While I text my mom to let her know I'll be home later than usual, we find a parking space—where else? Directly opposite the Empire State Building.

As I get out of the car, I pull up the back of my jeans—and my hand brushes the top of the postcard sticking out of my back pocket. I have to tell Tristan about this new threat.

I probably should have told him during the drive. Only, I didn't want to derail our date—if it even is a date.

I promise myself I'll tell him. I just have to find the right time.

Standing on the sidewalk, I stare across West Thirty-Fourth Street at the towering, iconic landmark. At the top, its exterior is all lit up in pink—to commemorate Breast Cancer Awareness Month, maybe? But aside from a window here or there where someone is working after hours, the interior of the building is dark.

Tristan gets something out of the trunk, then joins me on the curb.

I'm about to give him my best I-told-you-so speech. But before I can even get the "I" out, he slips his hand into mine. When his icy-cold flesh meets my icy-cold flesh, the result is surprisingly warm.

Hot, even.

Okay. So, I'm saying this is a date.

"Ready?" he asks.

"R-ready?" I ask. "Ready to do what?"

"Jump."

My suspicions rise, and I shoot him a look. "Am I supposed to ask how high?" I ask, remembering his chauvinistic tendencies.

He laughs and aims his gaze across the street. "I believe it's eighty-six stories."

I know, from editing the entertainment listings for TakeABite.com, that the open-air observatory is on the eighty-sixth floor.

"You've got to be kidding me," I say.

"I assure you, I am not."

"I can't jump eighty-six stories."

"Possibly not, given your substandard diet of bagged blood," he says with a note of mock-scolding in his voice. "But I can. And I can take you with me."

"What?"

"It'll help if you bend your knees and push off the pavement."

"What?"

"On three," he says.

"*What?*"

He tightens his hold on my hand. "One…"

"Tristan…"

"Two…"

"I don't think this is a good idea."

"Three!"

"*Holy dick boogers!*" I scream as I clench Tristan's hand with all my strength and clamp my eyes firmly shut.

Then it's like I'm riding a roller coaster, climbing up, up, up along the steepest track ever. Only without the roller coaster. Or the track.

Or my stomach, for that matter. I'm almost positive I left that somewhere back on the Thirty-Fourth Street sidewalk.

Abruptly, the ride stops. And as I brace for the big drop, I figure I can quit worrying about Grand Master Gideon and his threats. Although it wasn't on Cat's list, I doubt even an immortal blood-drinker can survive an eighty-six-story fall.

"Lily," says Tristan softly. "Open your eyes."

That's when I realize that, miraculously, my feet are on solid ground. Slowly, I let my eyelids flutter open.

Like many people who actually live in New York City, I've never been to a lot of the popular tourist attractions. I've never seen the view from where I find myself standing now, on the observation deck of the Empire State Building. But even if I'd been here before, I'd never have seen *this* view.

I'm sure, to the human eye, the panorama is breathtaking. But as

I stare out into the clear, moonlit night and take in the city with my vampire eyes, I feel like I'm being transported.

We're on the north side of the building, facing uptown. Beyond the colorful lights of Times Square, Central Park unfolds before me like an enchanted forest in the middle of a mythical, magical kingdom. Its lush green meadows are laced with ribbons of pathways and decorated with colorful pom-poms of trees. Even without using the provided binoculars, I can detect the individual autumn leaves of red and rust and gold.

I have the urge to take out my mobile and snap a photo—only I know that even the latest iPhone technology can't match my high-powered vampire peepers. So, I do my best to take a mental snapshot and save it for later.

"Beautiful, isn't it?" asks Tristan.

I turn to look at him, and I swear, he's an equally beautiful sight. With his long hair blowing in the breeze and his indigo eyes shining in the moonlight, he looks like he stepped right off the cover of one of his Delilah Manning novels.

My throat gets tight and my heart grows full. Screw roses. He gave me this picture-perfect view! Legit, it's one of the nicest things anyone's ever done for me. Certainly, it's the nicest thing any *guy* has ever done for me. Immortal or otherwise.

Suddenly, his cheesy choice of a date destination isn't so cheesy at all. It's simply amazing.

I smile and nod. I find it's the only response I can muster. *Did my transformation amp up my emotions as well as my senses?* I wonder. *Is that why I'm feeling so seriously overwhelmed that tears sting at the corners of my eyes?*

Embarrassed, I spin away from Tristan, back to the view. I blink a few times to clear my vision. I swallow. Then, letting my hand slide out of his grip, I step forward to the railing at the edge of the observatory and slowly make my way around the 360-degree deck.

The East River. The Brooklyn Bridge. The Statue of Liberty. The Hudson. Each familiar sight is like a new revelation. By the time I complete the circuit and return to my starting point, I'm totally blown away.

"Would you like a drink?" asks Tristan.

Wow, I think. *That was fast.*

I mean, don't get me wrong. I've already decided I want to drink from him. And to sleep with him. But… Does he really want me to drink from him *now*? And then what? Does he expect us to just do it right *here*, on the top of the Empire State Building?

Wait. Actually, that sounds kind of hot.

I look over at him. He has indeed spread out a blanket—but, um, not for unbridled vampire sex in a public place. The blanket—red-and-white-checkered—is laden with assorted cheeses. Olives. Crusty baguettes. The old-fashioned picnic basket that he must have retrieved from the trunk before our jump lies off to the side, empty. And Tristan stands holding a bottle of wine in one hand and two plastic wineglasses in the other.

"Would I like a drink…of *wine*?" I ask.

Tristan frowns. "You don't like cabernet?"

I walk over to him slowly. "No, I do," I say. "I just thought, um…" I shake my head. "Never mind."

He offers me the glasses, so I take them. Then he twists off the bottle's screw-top cap.

"Funny," I say. "I would have thought you'd be a cork guy."

"Well, I'm not an early adopter, by any means," he says. "I resisted e-publishing for a while too. But, eventually, even I could see that some twenty-first-century technology has its advantages."

He fills the two glasses, recaps the wine, and puts the bottle down. Then he takes one of the glasses and raises it to me. "I hope you can see that being a vampire has its advantages too."

I glance around again at the gorgeous view, at the picnic. I still can't believe he did all this for me. It's so...*romantic*.

Then I realize what he's doing. He's giving me the romance that was lacking before, the romance that was missing when he first brought up the topic of drinking from him and, um, what would inevitably follow.

Unable to find words, I just smile and clink my plastic wineglass against his. Then I take a sip.

So, FYI, I'm not a big wine drinker. I mean, I'm certainly not opposed to a glass or two of red—especially with Italian—but I'm no connoisseur. When people start throwing around terms like oaky and full-bodied and buttery, when they claim to taste notes of chocolate or coffee or clove with hints of vanilla and fruit, I always figure they're just being pretentious AF.

But the cabernet hits my tongue—and what do you know? There really are all those notes and hints and shit! I swish the wine around in my mouth—and, yes, I actually *swish*, I can't help it—and I swear, it's like a nuclear explosion of flavor, of earth and air and *life*. I guess even my "substandard diet" of expired blood has dialed up my sense of taste.

"Um...good wine," I say after I swallow.

Tristan grins at what's clearly a massive understatement. "Shall we sit?"

As gracefully as I can, which I'm sure isn't very, I lower myself onto the blanket. But Tristan doesn't seem to notice any awkwardness on my part—and, for reals? I'm starting not to feel any. I even manage to arrange myself in a cross-legged position without spilling my wine.

Tristan settles similarly beside me, close enough that our knees almost touch.

"Would you like to try the Manchego?" he asks. He grabs a plastic knife and starts to slice me a hunk of the cheese.

Aaand, cue the awkwardness.

The specter of my old insecurity creeps over me, casting a dark cloud over our moonlit picnic.

"I–I shouldn't," I say automatically.

"Why not?" asks Tristan.

Because I've seen that look before, I think. *The disapproving look I sometimes get from people in restaurants if I order anything other than a salad—or, God forbid, dessert. And I just can't bear getting that look from you right now.*

Oblivious to my inner turmoil, Tristan breaks off a piece of the baguette, puts the cheese on top, and offers it to me. "You're an immortal now, Lily," he says. "You don't have to worry about human health issues, like your cholesterol. Or your blood pressure. Or your weight."

"What about my weight?" I ask, getting defensive.

Only, there's zero judgment in his eyes. His tone is totally matter-of-fact. "You simply are as you are," he says with a shrug. "Forever."

My head goes whirling. "So, I can eat whatever I want?" I ask. "As much as I want? And not gain any weight?"

"Of course."

Okay, so I've heard outrageous diet claims before. But Tristan's words have the strange ring of truth to them. And based on everything else I've learned about vampires in the past couple of nights, what he's saying does make sense.

Still, it's hard to wrap my head around the concept. The thing is, I'm not sure I've ever simply eaten what I wanted. More often, I ate what I unrealistically hoped would give me the body I wanted. I deprived myself, buying into the diet culture, opting for sugar-free, fat-free, carb-free—and largely taste-free—substitutes for the things I craved. Or else, I jumped onto the bandwagon of some unhealthy fad or other, sometimes eliminating whole food groups. Sometimes eliminating food itself. Can you say bad idea?

So, natch, when I did indulge, I overindulged. It was a vicious cycle.

But, now…

I look at Tristan. And even though I maybe shouldn't, I find that I don't just believe him. I trust him.

I trust Tristan.

So, I smile broadly and say those three little words to him that I've never said to any other guy before. Ever.

"Pass the Manchego."

And then, I do something I've never done with any other guy before either.

I actually enjoy a meal.

CHAPTER 20

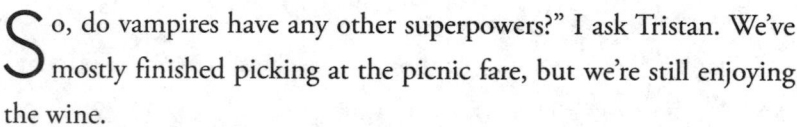

So, do vampires have any other superpowers?" I ask Tristan. We've mostly finished picking at the picnic fare, but we're still enjoying the wine.

"Superpowers?" he asks.

"You know," I say. "Like, how you flew us up here."

Tristan shakes his head. "I didn't fly. I just jumped—albeit, very high. And don't worry," he adds. "I can jump us back down with equal success."

"Or, we could just take the elevator," I suggest.

"But where's the fun in that?" he asks with a grin.

I grin back and take another sip of the cab.

"So," I say next, "what about other vampires? Are there any who can fly?"

"Not in the Superman sense, if that's what you're asking," he says. "But when vampires are very old and very powerful, their horizontal jumps can sometimes look like flying."

Cool.

"What else?" I ask. I'm kind of getting into this. "What else can vampires do?"

"Well, you've already noticed that your senses are heightened. We all have enhanced taste, hearing, vision, and so on."

"X-ray vision?" I ask.

He shakes his head and laughs. "Not that I'm aware."

I try to think of other superpowers to ask him about—but this is Cat's area of expertise, not mine. "Anything else?" I ask.

"Well," he says, "of course, there's influence."

"Stop," I say. "Please stop. Let's not go there and ruin this beautiful night. Okay?"

He's about to say something, but then—what do you know? He closes his mouth, smiles, and actually respects my wishes.

I smile back.

Then we just sit here, smiling at each other and sipping our wine. I become hyperconscious of my body—but not in a self-conscious way. I'm aware of the quickening of my breath. The tingling of my skin. The aching low in my belly.

"So, is that it?" I ask softly. "No other vampire superpowers?"

"Let's see," he says, thinking.

I'm aware of his body too. The way his fingers curl around the stem of his wineglass. The rise and the fall of his chest. The slight crinkle of his brow.

"Well, we do have amazing restorative powers," he says.

Right. I remember how quickly his ear healed over when I bit him. When I, um, first tasted his blood.

His blood...

"And we're all faster and stronger than humans," he says.

"How much faster and stronger?" I ask. Only now I'm finding it a little difficult to stay focused on our conversation.

"That depends," he says. "Vampires become more powerful as they age." He shifts on the blanket and looks at me seriously with that piercing gaze of his. "And so does their blood."

He continues to look at me, and I don't look away. I don't blink. Emboldened by the wine and the conversation and the, well, *everything*, I hold his gaze with my own.

"So, if I drank your blood," I ask, "would I have your powers?"

"Temporarily, yes," he says carefully. "But, as I told you before, there would be…"

"Consequences?"

After a moment, he nods. "Consequences."

"Um…Tristan?"

"Yes?"

I grin. "I am so totally down for the consequences."

For a moment, he seems a little thrown. And his surprise is, well, surprising. I mean, is he really such a Neanderthal that he doesn't know how to deal with a woman who takes the lead sexually? I wouldn't have thought it, considering that the heroines in the kinds of books he writes are usually pretty brazen and bold in that department.

But finally he laughs and grins back. "I am so very glad to hear it."

He puts his wineglass down, and he takes mine away too. Then, slowly, he leans toward me across the red-and-white checkered blanket.

I lean in as well, happy to meet him halfway.

Oh, did I say happy? Try dancing-on-the-ceiling ecstatic.

Finally! I think. Finally, we're going to have our first k—

THWACK!

Startled, I turn away from Tristan, away from the almost-kiss, and in the direction of the noise.

I gasp. There's an arrow. A *flaming* arrow. It's landed at the far edge of our blanket, and it's beginning to set fire to our picnic.

I stare in horror.

Fire. Another way to kill a vampire.

And this time, it's not a photo of fire. Not an abstract representation. It's actual fucking *fire*.

"Lily!" says Tristan.

He grabs my hand, pulling me up off the blanket and onto my feet—and just in time. A split second later, our lovely moonlight picnic goes totally up in flames.

Through the blaze, I see the dark silhouette of a tall, well-built male figure backlit by the moon, standing on the edge of the observation deck. He is accompanied by a few bigger, burlier figures, and he holds a bow in his hand. He raises it and gives us a jaunty little salute before he leaps right off the building. His entourage dives after him.

It's the kind of a jump that would be pure suicide—unless, of course, it was executed by a vampire. Or a band of vampires.

I sniff the air with my elevated vampire sense of smell. Mostly, I just smell smoke. It stings my eyes, my throat, my nostrils.

But it's there. Just the hint of something else—or, I guess I should say *someone* else.

Gideon.

I think I've just met the grand master and some of his subway-stalking thugs.

• • • • •

"You should have told me, Lily," says Tristan. "You should have told me about the postcard."

We're back in Tristan's sports car, headed back downtown to my place. He's been all snippy and snotty with me since I filled him in on the other threat I received from the grand master earlier tonight.

"Well, I was going to tell you," I say in my defense. "It just slipped my mind."

"That's no excuse," he says.

"I told you when it became relevant," I say.

"That's not good enough," he says.

"Oh, really?" I shoot back. "Then maybe you should tell me what caused all this bad blood between you and Gideon in the first place." And FYI, my pun is totally not intentional.

Tristan just presses his lips together in an unhappy line and keeps on driving.

"Right," I say. "How come I'm supposed to tell you everything, but you get to keep me on the need-to-know plan?"

"I'm just trying to protect you," he says.

"Well, congratulations," I say. "You're doing a real bang-up job of it so far."

Tristan reacts like I just kicked him in the nuts—and I admit, it was kind of a low blow. But seriously, his I'm-the-man-and-I'll-handle-it attitude is driving me straight up a wall.

"Sorry," I say. "But, I really don't have the time to coddle your fragile male ego."

"My ego notwithstanding," he says, "you do, in fact, have all the time in the world. But not if you keep making reckless decisions about things you don't understand."

"So help me understand, goddammit," I say. "If you'd actually bother to read me in here, maybe I could help."

He doesn't say anything.

"See, I have a theory," I say as we turn onto Bleecker. If he's not going to share, then I will. I'll show him how it's done.

I explain how I think Gideon might be running through some list of all the things that can slay the undead. And how I suspect he's going to go through the whole menu of mortal moves before he makes his coup de grâce. And how, after tonight's twofer, I can only think of one thing left that he hasn't threatened.

"So," I say, "besides a wooden stake through the heart, is there anything else that can kill a vampire?"

Tristan parks in front of my building, then turns to face me. "A woman with a mind of her own," he says.

It takes me a moment to get it. Then I grin widely. "Tristan," I say, "did you just make a joke?"

He tries not to smile back, but the corners of his mouth tick up anyway. His indigo-blue eyes are doing that twinkly thing. And the tension between us mostly lifts.

"Good night, Lily," he says softly.

I was going to invite him in tonight. Really, I was.

And given the fact that the intensity of Gideon's threats seems to be escalating, I could certainly use the extra strength I'll apparently get from drinking his blood.

But the arrow that interrupted our intimate picnic didn't exactly fan the flames of our passion. And the way I see it, our first time together should happen because of a desperate need for each other—and not just a need for fortification against an ancient homicidal bloodsucker.

Besides, as this romance writer told me the night we met, taking things slowly helps build the sexual tension. So, I decide to let it build.

Plus, I remember my mother is sleeping on my couch.

"Good night, Tristan," I say. "Sweet dreams."

CHAPTER 21

The next night, Cat and I stand in front of my refrigerator, loading it up with the additional donor units she brought over. Apparently, my BFF, God love her, went on a solo op to the American Red Cross to keep me well stocked with expired blood.

Cat tosses the last bag from her blood run onto the shelf. "So, you still haven't told me if you even need these," she says. She raises her eyebrows suggestively to make sure I get her meaning.

I shake my head. "I didn't drink from Tristan last night," I tell her. I close up the fridge. "And we didn't, um, you know."

"But you saw him?"

I give her the recap. I try to keep it to just the facts. But as I hear myself recounting the details of our skyscraper rooftop picnic, I realize that even just-the-facts sounds like a Hallmark Channel movie. If Hallmark did vampires, that is.

Well, at least it does until I get to the part where our evening crashed and, um, burned. Instead of being interrupted by the arrival of a small child or a cute dog or a doddering old relative, our first kiss was thwarted by the arrival of Grand Master Gideon, his goon squad, and a flaming arrow.

"Omigod!" says Cat. "Are you okay?"

I shrug. Nod.

"Lily," she says, shaking her head in concern, "I don't know. I think maybe you *need* to drink from Tristan."

"I will," I say. "I will. I just want to wait until the time is right."

"The grand master shot a ball of fire at you," says Cat. "I think the time is friggin' right."

"Not for the blood-drinking," I say. "For, you know, all the rest."

"Ah." Cat looks at me. "So, you're not that into Tristan?"

"No, I am," I say. "I am. I just want to be sure he feels the same way about me."

And I know, I know, after I got that menacing message in the restroom last night, I was totally amped up to just go for it. I was all set to juice myself up on some four-hundred-year-old vampire blood and, as my best friend put it, have a little fun in the middle of this whole shitstorm.

Only, after spending that evening together with Tristan, well... things are different. If my heart was at risk before, it's basically on life support now. This supernatural link between blood and sex has created quite the conundrum for me. Physically, it's true, I don't know if I can survive without Tristan's blood...and without the sex that's apparently destined to follow it. But, emotionally? Well, I'm just not sure I can survive a casual hookup with Tristan Newberry.

"Are you kidding me?" squeals Cat. "Tristan is so into you. I mean, look at what he did for you."

I grab the edge of the kitchen counter because, seriously, her words make me feel like I'm about to float away on a cloud of happiness. And I need to stay grounded. I have to maintain some perspective here. I've got to keep it real.

"It could've just been his way of apologizing," I say. "For the fight we had before."

"No way," she says. "He could've apologized in a thousand other ways. But instead, he carried you up to the top of the Empire State Building."

"Kind of like King Kong," I mutter. Which, now that I think about it, pretty much fits right in with his me-Tarzan, you-Jane inclinations.

"No," says Cat. "*Exactly* like Edward Cullen."

"What?"

"Lily," says Cat. "He gave you the full Edward Cullen treatment."

"The *what*?"

She gives me an impatient sigh, as if she's being perfectly clear and I'm somehow being deliberately thickheaded and refusing to get her meaning. "It's just like in Twilight, when Edward speed-carried Bella up into the treetops and showed her the view of Forks," she explains. And I swear, her hand is over her heart. Her eyes are actually getting misty. I'm a little worried she might, um, swoon.

"He's bringing you into his world," says Cat.

"I don't know," I say. "It doesn't feel like he's bringing me into anything."

"Edward was the same way," Cat assures me. "All closed off and careful and brooding. But then—*poof!* He opened up."

"Yeah, but this isn't some vampire romance," I say.

"Says the girl who's dating a vampire who writes romance," Cat says with a cheeky grin.

"We're not dating," I say. Because even though last night felt like a date, tonight I'm not so sure.

"Oh no?" she says. "Then what are you doing?"

Um…good question.

What am I doing?

As I drifted off to sleep at sunrise after that whirlwind night, I wasn't thinking about Grand Master Gideon or his threats or how I was going to defend myself against them. I was thinking about Tristan.

And not just about his off-the-charts good looks. No, I was thinking about *him*. About how his extra-cheesiness is also kind of charming. How his throwback chivalry is maybe just a little bit sexy. How he can be infuriatingly thoughtless, yes—but also incredibly thoughtful.

When I woke up at sunset, he was still on my mind. And since we finally traded digits the previous night, the first thing I did was reach for the phone on my bedside table to see if he'd texted. Or called.

He hadn't.

Of course, he hadn't.

And that's when my thoughts took a nosedive into a sea of negative self-talk. I proceeded to convince myself there was no way in hell Tristan could ever have woken up thinking about me. Because the Tristan Newberrys of the world simply do not fall for the Lily Baineses. They fall for the Cat McMahons.

I tell my bestie as much.

Cat gives me a strange look. "I don't know," she says. "I don't see any sexy vampires standing in line to whisk *me* up to the top of the Empire State Building."

"You know what I mean," I say.

"I do," says Cat. "And frankly, it's a little offensive."

For a moment, I'm speechless.

"What?" I finally say.

"Well, I'd like to think I'm more than just the way I look," says Cat, a little indignant. "And I'd like to think that one day I'll find a guy who sees that too."

At first, I think she's joking. But the seriousness in her eyes and in the set of her jaw says otherwise.

Then I don't know what to say. I'm too floored.

I mean, of course my BFF isn't just beautiful. She's the whole package. I never meant to imply otherwise.

But clearly I have.

Jesus, what is even wrong with me? I've gone and let my negative self-talk become actual talk. Now I'm not just being self-critical. I'm inadvertently criticizing Cat.

"I'm…sorry," I say uncertainly. "I didn't mean to insult you."

"But you do it a lot, you know."

"Insult you?" I ask, horrified.

Cat shrugs. "Not insult, exactly, but…I don't know. You act like just because I'm thin, my life should be perfect."

My gut instinct is to protest, tell her she's wrong. Only then I remember how I used to imagine my future self. How thinness and a happy life always seemed to go together.

"You act like because I wear a size small, I shouldn't have any problems," she continues. "Or if I do, I should just get over it."

"Oh my God," I say, my horror rising. "Do I make you feel like you can't tell me stuff?"

She's quiet for a moment. "Sometimes?" she says.

I feel nauseous. Absolutely nauseous.

"I mean, it's just…sometimes I'll have a crappy day at work, and I'll really want to talk about it. But then I'll call you, and you'll have some story about somebody fat-shaming you on the subway or something. And then I just figure you won't want to hear it."

"Cat," I say quickly, "I will *always* want to hear it."

She nods. But I'm not really sure she believes me.

Okay. Time to get real.

"Look," I say. "I know that when it comes to my body, I tend to get stuck in my own head. But…I'm trying not to be. Stuck. In my own head."

"I know," she says. "I know you are."

"And, I swear, I'd rather die than have my fucked-up relationship with my weight fuck up my relationship with you."

She smiles.

"And Jesus," I say, "I couldn't have gotten through these last couple of days without you. Seriously. You are the best. And not because you're thin. Because you're *you*.

"So, if you ever, ever feel like I'm not appreciating you or not listening to you or not *seeing* you, you have to call me on it. Because I always want to be there for you the way you're always there for me."

She looks at me for what feels like an eternity. Then she nods again. And this time I can tell she believes me.

"So, we're good?" I ask.

"Yeah," she says. "We're good."

I breathe a sigh of relief.

Then I hear the front door open.

"Hello!" calls my mother's voice. "I'm back."

• • • • •

When Cat and I join Mom, she's unpacking cartons of Chinese food on the coffee table. I feel a stab of guilt that she had to go out in search of her own dinner. Obvi, I'm the shittiest hostess ever. But seriously, between work and the death threats and not being able to leave home during the day, when am I supposed to go grocery shopping?

Still, it could be so much worse. At least she didn't go digging in the fridge and try one of my, um, *protein drinks*. That would have been seriously awkward.

"Cat!" Mom exclaims when she spies my bestie. Immediately, she goes in for a hug. "I was hoping I'd get to see you this visit."

FYI, my mother absolutely *loves* my best friend. And why wouldn't she? Cat really is the whole package. She's everything I'm not. And not just the things my mother values, like tall and thin and gorgeous. She's caring and supportive…and totally understanding and forgiving of my sorry ass, even when I don't deserve it.

"Good to see you too, Ms. Baines," says Cat with an easy smile, returning the squeeze.

"*Rose*," corrects my mom. "Please. Call me Rose."

Rose invites Cat to stay and have some food. We all sit, and she passes a paper plate and disposable utensils to Cat. *Not* to me.

"Lily's on a special diet," says my mom.

"No kidding," says Cat. She spears a steamed dumpling.

I shoot my friend a warning gaze, and she shoves the whole dumpling into her mouth to keep from laughing. If I did that in front of my mother, I'd never hear the end of it.

Just then, my iPhone—which I'm carrying around in the back pocket of my jean leggings like some lovesick teenager—*pings*. I'm ashamed to say how quickly I check it.

"Is it Tristan?" asks Mom.

It is.

I nod. I don't trust my voice, which will surely betray the pathetic mix of relief and outright joy that's currently coursing through my body.

"Well, what does he have to say?" asks my mother.

"If it's not too personal," adds Cat diplomatically.

It's not, actually. I read the text again. And again. Although Tristan pens romantic sagas, his message to me is fairly simple and straightforward. That helps me put a lid on my own flowery feelings.

"Um, 'Get to work safely,'" I say, reading aloud. "'Pick you up after.'"

"So, I guess that means you'll be out all night again," says Mom in a singsong voice.

"Oooh, I wonder what he has planned this time," says Cat.

But as my mother and my best friend continue to speculate about the pick-you-up-after part, I home in on the get-to-work-*safely* part.

I remember that my immortal life is still in danger. I remember how, last night at work, I actually had the beginnings of a plan to force a stalemate with Grand Master Gideon, a plan that didn't necessarily hinge on drinking from or sleeping with Tristan. But then when Tristan showed up and literally swept me off my feet, I got totally distracted.

And I recall how, in the immediate wake of my transformation, I vowed I wouldn't fall under Tristan's spell. But then I totally let him charm me. With his romantic words and his romantic gestures. With his yummy good looks and his yummy goddamn Manchego.

Well, I can't afford to let myself get sidetracked like that again. Not if I want to live. Or, unlive. Or—well, you know what I mean.

It doesn't matter if he's the whole package too.

I cannot—cannot—let myself go falling for Tristan Newberry.

CHAPTER 22

Cat and I share a cab uptown, and she drops me at the office.

I pause at the security desk to show my ID to the guard and sign in, and—

"Lily? Lily Baines?"

I turn in the direction of the chirpy, vaguely familiar voice. The only other person in the lobby is a blond around my own age and weight, sitting in one of the leather chairs. Her hair and makeup are perfect, and her outfit is to die for. It's like she stepped right out of an Instagram feed. Everything about her, from her sleek salon highlights to her patent-leather Louboutin pumps, gleams with the shine of wealth.

She pops up onto the signature red soles, all smiles at me.

I smile back uncertainly.

Then I place her. My smile tightens.

"Kelly," I say through gritted teeth. "Kelly Kohl."

I haven't seen Kelly Kohl since we graduated from NYU, since she let me know that her final GPA was one-tenth of a point higher than mine. And that was just the last one-up in a weird one-upmanship contest that she started day one of our first year.

Maybe it was because we were so much alike. Both journalism

majors. Both women—and curvy women, at that. Both taking the same classes and working toward similar career goals. But if I asked a smart question in lecture hall, she had to ask a smarter one. If I studied late, she had to pull an all-nighter. And I'm pretty sure she applied for an internship she didn't even want, just so she could beat me out of it.

And she did. Beat me out of it.

"It's so great to see you," she says.

And I can just imagine why.

Knowing I'd be seeing Tristan tonight, I dressed a little nicer than usual. Dark jean leggings tucked into black-suede over-the-knee boots. Fitted tank in a green color I like to think matches my eyes. Gauzy, black fly-front cardigan. But next to Kelly, I probably look like the biggest frump ever. She must be loving this unexpected opportunity to one-up me one more time.

Only…there's no smugness in her expression. Her smile actually seems sincere.

"Um, you too," I say. "Love the new hair."

"Oh, thanks," she says. "Yeah, I just wanted a change."

She lifts her hand to her formerly brunette locks and tucks a stray blond strand behind her ear. The glare off the enormous diamond solitaire she's wearing practically blinds me.

"You're engaged," I blurt out.

"What?" she says, confused. Then she looks at the rock on her finger, realizing. "Oh. Married, actually." And suddenly, her whole face lights up. "It's Kelly Matheson now. Palmer and I just tied the knot in August."

"Wait. You're married to *the* Palmer Matheson?" I ask.

FYI, Palmer Matheson is the man at the helm of Matheson Multimedia, a multibillion-dollar communications empire comprised mostly of conservative, "values-oriented" media outlets. In addition to being in his sixties at least, the mogul is stridently pro-family—and last I heard, long-married to somebody else.

Well, this isn't adding up, I think.

If the self-proclaimed "morality maven" had left his wife of forty-odd years for a much younger woman, the scandal surely would have made the news.

"No, sorry. Not Palmer. Palmer *Junior*," she says. "I met him when I was working as an editorial assistant at the *New Traditionalist* and, well, we just clicked." There's genuine affection in her tone. And she doesn't seem to be rubbing it in my face at all.

Okay, so this whole encounter is a little surreal. It's like I'm staring at my reflection in a fun-house mirror—but it's not my body that looks different. It's, um, everything else.

I mean here's Kelly, basically my same size, my same shape. But she doesn't seem to have any of my insecurities—which, I swear, used to be hers too. Now, she seems totally confident and happy. And way past our silly rivalry.

"Well, congratulations," I say. I'm talking about her new marriage, but I guess I could just as well be talking about this new attitude of hers.

"Thanks," she says.

"So, are you still at the magazine?" I ask, mostly just to have something to say.

She nods. "But now, I'm the features editor," she says. "And you?"

"Same," I say. "Features editor. And speaking of work…" I gesture at the elevator. "Night shift."

"Oh!" says Kelly. "Okay. Then have a good night." She smiles at me again. "And it really is good to see you."

"Yeah," I say slowly, thinking. "It's good to see you too."

• • • • •

I ride up in the elevator, and I can't get Kelly out of my head.

Kelly—with a great career and a great marriage and a great…*life*.

It's not that I'm jealous. I mean, it's not as if I'd actually want anything to do with her über-right-wing husband or her conservative media job or even her overpriced designer wardrobe. We have totally different values.

But there are things I do want. Things that, in my head, I've always associated with being thin. But there's Kelly. Not thin. And living her best life ever.

Just then, the doors glide open on the seventeenth floor and I find myself face-to-face with my current rival.

"Evan," I say. "Hey."

His long-sleeved black tee is stretched taut across his chest, clinging to the muscles beneath—and again, I'm struck by how his body seemed to change overnight.

He mutters something in return as he shoves past me into the car. Once again, his arm brushes lightly against mine. This time, though, the fleeting contact is like a pack of lit cigarettes being extinguished on my flesh.

Flinching, I grasp at my upper arm. I use my cold vampire hand like an ice pack to soothe what feels like a third-degree burn, and my head snaps back to look accusingly at Evan.

Our eyes lock. Behind the lenses of his glasses, his eyes are a deep, rich brown dusted with flakes of gold. He's glaring back at me, looking supremely annoyed. And defensive. And a little guarded. Basically, his resting I-hate-Lily face. So, no shockers there.

But then, suddenly, his guard slips and his eyes ignite with a rage so intense and primal it rattles me to the core. I swear, if I couldn't hear his heartbeat and smell his blood, I would say that this unprovoked wrath wasn't even human. That *he* wasn't even human.

Maybe he's a werewolf, I find myself thinking.

Now, if I'd had this same thought even a few nights ago, I would've thought I was losing my mind. But now that I know vampires are real, I figure it's at least possible that other paranormal peeps exist too.

And don't werewolves hate the vampires just because they're vampires? Kind of like the way Evan seems to hate me just because I'm me.

I make a mental note to ask Cat about it.

Or, hey—better yet, maybe I should just go straight to the source and ask Tristan.

Meanwhile, Evan's guard has gone back up, and the unearthly fury has disappeared from his gaze.

The elevator doors slide closed between us.

I stand where I am in the hallway, still holding my arm, staring at the doors. In my mind, I replay what I just witnessed.

Now, I wonder if maybe I just imagined it. Maybe I'm so caught up in my own supernatural drama that I'm starting to see eerie stuff everywhere?

But, no. The lingering feeling of absolute dread that permeates every microcell of my body tells me what I saw was 100 percent real.

• • • • •

When I check my mail cubby at work, I see that Evan—probably at Peter's prodding—has, in fact, left me copies of his vampire story notes. *Copies.* Which means he's still hanging onto the originals. Which means, as Cat suggested, he's probably still chasing down the vampire story on his own.

Awesome.

So, I settle in at one of the open workstations and think through my to-do list for the evening: (1) Go through Evan's research and see what he's uncovered about vampires; (2) Start writing a scathing vampire exposé that I can use to negotiate a literal cease-fire with Grand Master Gideon; and (3) Keep my vampire butt safe from said grand master, who definitely wants to kill me, and also from Evan, who might possibly be a werewolf.

Yeah, just another day at the office.

As I'm reading over the xeroxed pages to find out what Evan has dug up, Gabby walks by with a fresh face of makeup, undoubtedly on her way out to somewhere fab.

"Hey," I say, stopping her. "Do you know a place called, um…" I refer back down to Evan's notes. "The Crypt?"

Gabby nods. "Goth club down in the Bowery. Not far from where the old CBGB used to be." She grabs a chair, turns it around, and swings a camo-clad leg over it with an ease that suggests either a background in dance or a genetic connection to Wonder Woman. "The main club is pretty basic," she says, straddling the seat backwards. "But rumor has it there's a super-exclusive back room that stays open 'til almost dawn."

"'Rumor has it'?" I ask.

Gabby shrugs. "It's all weirdly secretive. I mean, usually, no matter how private your club is, you want word about it to get out. You want the unwashed masses to know they're not cool enough to get in. You want people to *want* to get in. Desperately. That way, the hopefuls continue to line up night after night, and the folks who do make it past the door feel special. But in this case?" She shakes her head. "I can't even confirm that there is a door, let alone get on the list."

We chitchat a little more before Gabby gets up and heads off, but I'm only half paying attention.

Super-exclusive back room? Open 'til almost dawn? Weirdly secretive?

Sounds like either the vampire impersonators are doing one hell of an impersonation, or Evan was—and likely still is—hot on the trail of the real thing.

CHAPTER 23

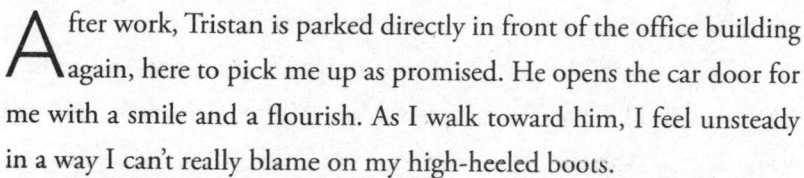

After work, Tristan is parked directly in front of the office building again, here to pick me up as promised. He opens the car door for me with a smile and a flourish. As I walk toward him, I feel unsteady in a way I can't really blame on my high-heeled boots.

Not falling for Tristan Newberry is a hell of a lot easier said than done.

"Lily," he says in greeting, and I swear, the fire that explodes in my loins—yes, my *loins*—should be fatal.

"Tristan."

I wrap my sweater around myself a little self-consciously as he closes me into the passenger seat.

He crosses around to the driver's side, and I stare at him through the front windshield like a fashionista staring at the window display at Saks. I imagine him rubbing up and down against my bare skin like some slinky satin dress.

Jesus. I have got to get a grip.

I mean, hello? There's the grand master and the Vampire Council. The feral blood-drinkers trolling the subways. They're all still out there, and unless something has changed, they're all still out to get us.

I try to ignore Tristan's old-fashioned manners, which are definitely growing on me. Instead, I focus on his old-fashioned thinking. And I remind myself that I'm not going to let him call the shots anymore. If we're both in danger here, then we're both going to come up with a way out of it—whether he likes it or not.

So, before Tristan is even settled in behind the wheel—and before he springs some other dream date on me and makes me lose my head again—I take control and set the agenda for tonight. I suggest that maybe we should go downtown and check out The Crypt.

"The Crypt?" says Tristan, frowning.

"It's a club. Down in the Bowery," I say. "I've heard it has a back room. That stays open late. For, um, vampires?"

"I know that," he says. "But how do you know that? And considering you and I are on the vampires' Most Wanted list, why would you want us to go there?"

I tell Tristan what I was too diverted to tell him last night, filling him in on my latest story assignment—and my master plan to use it to barter for our lives with the grand master.

"No," says Tristan.

"What do you mean, no?" I ask.

"I mean, I think it's a terrible plan and you should abort it immediately."

"Stop being a bag of dicks," I say. "I'm trying to come up with a way to save our asses."

"And I'm trying to be smart," he says. "Think about it. This assignment of yours? It sounds like some kind of a trap."

"How could it be a trap?" I ask.

"I don't know." He rubs at the stubble on his chin, and I try not to think about how delicious that eternal two-days' growth of beard would feel scraping against my own skin. "But it's awfully strange that your first job as an unsanctioned newborn is to investigate *vampires*." He looks at me, his eyes searching. "Is it possible that someone at the website has ties to the grand master?"

"I don't see how."

But then I remember Evan's skin burning like hellfire. And the CGI-worthy look that exploded tonight in his eyes.

"What?" asks Tristan. "What are you thinking?"

"Besides the vampires that stalk the subway tunnels," I say, "does Gideon by chance employ any, um, werewolves?"

"Werewolves?"

I nod.

Tristan bursts out laughing. "Lily," he says. "There's no such thing as werewolves."

"Well, how the fuck am I supposed to know that?" I ask. "Up until recently, I thought there was no such thing as vampires."

He's still laughing.

"And it's not as if you're so forthcoming with the information," I add.

I swear, he's laughing so hard he's almost crying.

"Trying to get anything out of you is like pulling fangs," I mutter.

He shakes his head and catches his breath and somehow manages to compose himself.

"Why on earth are you asking me about werewolves?" he asks.

Now that he's been making fun of me and all, I almost don't want to tell him. But then I decide I need his perspective. Even though he's almost four hundred years old, I guess it's up to me to be the mature one.

So, I tell him about Evan. About the muscles that grew out of nowhere. The otherworldly cast to his gaze. The searing-hot temperature of his flesh. And how, for some reason, we've always kind of been at odds with each other.

"Only, as far as the vampire assignment goes, I don't think Evan was setting me up," I say in conclusion. "He really didn't want me to have the story. It was his idea, actually. He wanted to keep it for himself."

I notice Tristan isn't laughing anymore. And I'm not so sure that's a good thing.

"What?" I ask. "What is it?"

Tristan sighs. He drops his hand from the keys in the ignition, leans back in his seat, and rakes his fingers through his hair. When he turns to look at me, his eyes are full of anguish.

"Lily," he says. "There's something I need to tell you."

And I know, I know, I literally just complained about him not telling me stuff. But now? I'm wondering if clear and honest communication might be overrated.

"Okay," I say, trying to ignore my mounting dread. "Tell me."

"From what you've just said," says Tristan, "it sounds like your coworker might be a vampire slayer."

• • • • •

Several minutes later, still sitting with Tristan in his parked car, I can't yet get my head around this latest little bomb-drop.

"A vampire slayer?" I ask him for the trillionth time.

"Yes."

"Like, um, Buffy?"

"Minus the cheerleader moves and witty dialogue. But essentially? Yes."

"Well, that's one hell of a coincidence," I murmur.

Tristan's body tenses. He looks seriously uncomfortable.

My eyes go wide in realization. "Shit," I say. "It's not a coincidence, is it?"

"You have to understand," he says quickly. "I didn't mention it before because it doesn't always happen."

Oh God, I think.

"And considering all you've had to deal with lately, I didn't want to worry you unnecessarily."

Oh God oh God oh God oh God oh God...

"But another reason why there are so many rules around making new vampires is that, sometimes, the creation of a new vampire triggers the creation of a new vampire slayer," he says. "And when it happens, it happens to someone in the new vampire's circle of acquaintance. Someone who's already something of an adversary."

OH GOD!

Normally, I'd already be berating Tristan for withholding this information from me. But right now, I'm too busy berating myself.

"So, Evan is a vampire slayer," I say. "And it's my fault."

"No," says Tristan emphatically. "It's *my* fault."

Except, I don't think that's entirely true. I mean, yes, okay, I didn't ask to be a vampire. I didn't ask to be changed. But what I'm hearing is that Evan changed because he and I didn't get along. And, um, that makes me at least partly to blame. If I'd made more of an effort to get to the bottom of our differences and resolve them, maybe he wouldn't have transformed.

Well, now I guess he has a *real* reason to hate me.

I think about Evan, about what he must be going through—and since I'm basically going through the same thing, it's not hard to imagine his struggle.

I wonder if he has a best friend to lean on. Is there some more experienced slayer out there to show him the supernatural ropes? Or is he just Netflixing old episodes of *Buffy* in a desperate attempt to understand his new fate?

I wish I knew a way to help him. I'd like to try to be his friend now.

Just then, Tristan fires up the ignition.

"Hey, did I miss something?" I ask. "Where are we going?"

"The Crypt," he says.

"The Crypt?" I say, surprised. "I thought you didn't like my plan for dealing with Gideon."

"I don't," he says. "But now, *I* have a plan for dealing with him."

His statement has the distinct whiff of my-plan-is-better-than-your-plan condescension, and I really don't care for it. But considering that (a) it sounds like he does have a plan; and (b) he's actually talking to me about it, I decide to cut him some slack.

"Well, don't keep it all to yourself. We're in this together. Share, please."

"Now that we know there's a slayer, we can use that information," he says. "We can use it at The Crypt to try to buy us some vampire allies."

• • • • •

We drive down to the Lower East Side, but I don't like this plan of Tristan's. I don't like his plan one bit. It feels wrong to be using Evan's new paranormal dilemma to our own advantage against the grand master.

"Lily," says Tristan. "You're still thinking like a human. And like *he*'s a human. But he's not. He's not just your coworker anymore. He's a vampire slayer. Which means he's now hardwired to kill vampires. Like you and me."

Oh. Right. I guess I hadn't exactly thought about that.

"Awesome," I say, slumping down in my seat. "Now, the grand master *and* Evan want us dead. It's like a supervillain BOGO."

Despite the grimness of our situation, the corner of Tristan's mouth ticks up in a smile.

"So…are slayers immortal?" I ask. "Like vampires?"

"I don't know."

I do a double take. "You don't *know*?"

"No," he says. "They don't exactly share all their trade secrets with us."

"You mean, there's something you don't know?" I tease. I can't help it.

"Lily—"

"So, you don't know everything," I say. "You just act like you do."

Tristan gives me an annoyed eye roll. But I can also see he's suppressing an amused grin as he drives on.

• • • • •

We pull up in front of what looks like an old abandoned church on Delancey Street, just off Bowery—and for once, I think Tristan hasn't been able to provide us with door-to-door service. But then I spot the sign above the run-down church's big, metal dungeon-like doors, and I realize that the former house of worship *is* The Crypt.

"It looks closed," I say.

"Only the main club is closed," says Tristan. "The human club. Not the back room."

After we lock my laptop bag in the trunk, Tristan leads me through the darkness, down a gravel path that cuts through a small, adjacent graveyard.

I listen to the little stones crunch-crunching under our feet and the wind whistling through the autumn-bare trees. I inhale the stench of mold and earth and decaying flowers. And I tell myself it's not creepy as shit at all.

"You okay?" asks Tristan.

He suddenly takes my hand, and I try to keep my thoughts on The Crypt and out of the gutter.

"Yeah," I say gruffly. "Yeah, I'm fine."

We walk on. The path loops back around to a side entrance mostly hidden by a pair of overgrown hedges. The door looks wooden, but when Tristan knocks on it once, twice, three times, it makes the sharp rap of knuckles against metal.

Then, hand in hand, we wait.

Just when I'm pretty sure nobody's home, a rectangular panel in the door I hadn't noticed in the dark slides open, all speakeasy-style. Through the opening, about six inches across and two inches high, a pair of eyes peers out at us.

Beautiful, dark, mysterious-looking eyes. With long, thick black lashes.

The eyes widen, flickering with recognition—and something else.

"Raven," says Tristan. "We need to talk."

CHAPTER 24

The eyes—*Raven's* eyes—flit from Tristan, to me, and back to Tristan. Then there's a muttered curse as the panel slams shut.

A beat later, the door flings open, and I get a gander at the rest of Raven. Creamy, pale skin. Pouty, red mouth. A cascade of luxurious, raven-black hair that reaches almost to her waist. And speaking of her waist? It's tiny, nipped in by a black corset that barely contains what have to be double-D cups, at least. A slinky black skirt, slit high up one side, reveals about eight hundred miles of shapely, fishnet-covered leg. Black patent-leather stilettos add five or six inches to her already statuesque height.

While Cat looks like she could be a high-fashion runway model, Raven looks more like a Goth wet dream.

Oh, and obvi, she's a vampire. So she gets to spend all eternity looking like this.

"I heard the whispers," says Raven, throwing Tristan some serious shade. "But I didn't believe them. You've done some foolish things over the centuries, Tristan Newberry, but I never thought you'd be foolish enough to defy Gideon and the council and make an illicit newborn."

"Raven Dupree," says Tristan, totally unruffled, "meet Lily Baines."

She raises one perfectly groomed eyebrow at him. "And you bring this abomination to my club?"

"Hey!" I say. "The 'abomination' is standing right here."

"But you shouldn't be," says Raven. She redirects her attention and starts throwing shade my way. "Neither of you should be. The last thing I need is trouble with the grand master."

Okay, so I'm going to go ahead and say I don't much like this Raven Dupree. And, I swear, it has nothing to do with the fact that she's forever gorgeous, and I'm forever more.

I'm sorry, but I don't like the way she's talking to me. Or to Tristan, for that matter. I don't like what she's saying.

But, okay, putting all that aside? I really don't like what she's, um, *not* saying. Because beneath her abrasive facade, I'm also picking up on some genuine, bone-deep fear. No doubt about it, she's scared of Grand Master Gideon and the Vampire Council.

A wave of oh-fuck washes over me.

Not that I haven't been scared before now. Only, I think there's also been a tiny corner of my mind that's been in some serious denial.

But now, here's Raven, a totally independent source. And her reaction basically confirms that Tristan and I are headed for vampire death row.

Oh—unless, of course, Evan gets to us first.

"There's a slayer, Raven," says Tristan, piling on this latest complication. "A new slayer."

Raven turns sharply back to Tristan. "The newborn triggered a slayer?"

"Apparently," he says.

She glances at me warily. "Someone she knows?"

"A male coworker."

"Well, sorry, but she can't hide from him in here," says Raven. She starts to close the door on us.

"Raven," says Tristan. "The slayer knows about The Crypt."

That makes her stop. Her eyes become dark slits as she scrutinizes Tristan for what seems like years. Then, she shakes her head of abundant black hair and expels a frustrated breath.

"Damn you, Tristan," she says. She opens the door back up and steps aside to let us in. "You've put me in uncomfortable positions before. But then, at least, it always ended in a mind-blowing orgasm."

My eyes pop. My jaw drops.

My surprised reaction is the first thing since our arrival that seems to please Raven.

As Tristan pulls me inside, her eyes fall to our intertwined hands, and her full, red lips curl into a catty smile. "Oh, I guess he didn't tell you," she practically purrs. "Tristan and I used to be lovers."

"About three hundred years ago," says Tristan.

Raven shrugs. "A mere blink of an eye in vampire time."

Now, on top of everything else, I feel like I just walked into a soap opera. *Like sands through the hourglass, so are* The Days of Our Immortal Lives.

Part of me wants to pull my hand out of Tristan's grasp and smack him silly for not giving me the heads-up that we were going to see his *ex*. Meanwhile, the other part of me doesn't want to give Raven the satisfaction.

And let me tell you, no part of me wants to think about the satisfaction Tristan and Raven must have given each other once upon a time.

No, if I start thinking about that, about Tristan being with someone who looks like Raven, then I'll inevitably start thinking about how he could never be satisfied with someone who looks like me.

Then, for the bazillionth time, I remind myself that I cannot let Tristan Newberry send my emotions into a free fall.

I end up leaving my hand where it is, just to piss off Raven. But I throw Tristan some shade of my own when she turns her back on us to shut the door.

He either doesn't notice, or he pretends not to.

"You might as well sit down," says Raven sourly. And I can only assume she's a more gracious hostess to her paying clientele.

She motions us into the small, windowless anteroom, over to a couple of overstuffed maroon velvet sofas. As Tristan and I take a seat on one and Raven drapes herself across the cushions of the other, I look around.

The walls and the floor are stone. Candlelight provides the only illumination—although, upon closer inspection, I see that the flames flickering from the two wrought-iron chandeliers hanging over us are faux. The candles in and above the white marble fireplace are also flameless.

No fire, I see. No wood. Nothing that could be used to lethally wound a vampire. It's like a bloodsucker safety zone in here. The whole place has been the undead equivalent of babyproofed.

"Do you want someone to drink?"

I gape at Raven.

Did I hear her correctly? I wonder. *Is she just trying to shock me again? Or...exactly what kind of place is this?*

I recall that whole vampire-influence thing Tristan described, and I shiver to imagine how she might be putting it to use here at her establishment.

"No, thank you," says Tristan, quickly shutting down the topic as well as my speculations. But I set a mental reminder to find out more about this later. "We only came to talk."

"So, start talking," says Raven. "How does the new slayer know about my club?"

Tristan gestures to me. I take his prompt and tell her about the website where Evan and I work, the story he was researching. The notes of his that specifically mention The Crypt.

Raven listens in silence. But if looks could kill a vampire, I'd totally be dead right now.

"So we wanted to warn you," says Tristan when I finish. "After all, our kind come to The Crypt as a refuge, to be safe. But if a slayer were to attack here—"

"Yes, okay, I get it," says Raven, sitting upright. "Even if everyone survived, it would be bad for business. I'll brief my security team and add reinforcements, and I thank you for the information." She raises her dark brows and eyes Tristan shrewdly. "But I suspect you're hoping for more than just my thanks."

"We came here in good faith to alert you to a potential threat," says Tristan with a shrug. "In your line of work, you hear things. I would hope that, if you heard about any kind of an imminent threat against Lily and me, you would return the favor."

"But my clients don't just feel physically safe here," she says. "They also feel safe to speak freely. And if they were to find out I betrayed their confidence—"

Just then, I hear a crash—we all do. The sound is startling but muffled, coming from somewhere behind the wall where the fireplace stands.

Raven leaps to her stilettos and travels across the room quicker than humanly possible—but of course, she's not human. Right on cue, as if to emphasize this, she pulls at the solid marble mantel with what must be her vampire superstrength. The fireplace swings open like a door, revealing a long, narrow passageway.

She might as well have opened up a portal into Hell. Unfiltered noises of unholy chaos—all underscored by the driving beat of techno dance music—blast out at us.

Vampire bar fight?

Or something way worse?

A single bloodcurdling shriek cuts through the clamor—then chokes off abruptly. I shiver.

In a flash, the club owner disappears down the passage.

I stay where I am, seated on the velvet sofa. Frozen in fear, I couldn't move if I tried.

Tristan, however, gets to his feet. He digs in his pocket and withdraws his car key, dangling the fob in front of me. "Take it."

"What?"

"Take my car key."

I reach up and do what he says. My hand is trembling.

"Drive yourself home. Lock the door. And don't, under any circumstances, invite anyone in. Do you understand?"

I hear someone whimper. I realize it's me.

Another earsplitting crash explodes down the hallway. I jump in my seat.

"Lily! Do you understand?"

I nod.

Tristan's indigo eyes sweep across my face. It's like he's trying to memorize my features.

Oh, no, I think. *Should I be trying to memorize his too?*

Then, suddenly, he swoops down toward me—not vampire-quick, but quickly and with a sense of urgency. For a second, his eyes lock on mine, and I swear, he sees straight down to my soul. And then—

He kisses me.

I'm unprepared—and yet it feels like I've been waiting for this since the beginning of time. Forgetting everything else, I close my eyes and savor the gorgeous crush of his mouth against my mouth, the delicious scratch of his beard against my skin. Our lips are hungry but a little hesitant until we find just the right angle, the right pressure, the right rhythm.

Tristan's long, deft fingers thread through my hair, and I tingle all over.

And for a few blissful moments, there's no slayer, no Raven, no grand master. There's no who-knows-what drama blowing up in the chamber beyond. There's just the two of us, joined together in this amazing lip-lock.

When Tristan releases me and draws away with a last teasing nip at my bottom lip, I want more. So much more.

I open my eyes. Only now, he's nowhere to be seen.

Just like he did on the subway, he's completely disappeared.

The ungodly symphony is still blaring from the next room. If anything, the commotion has become louder, more intense. But I can just detect Tristan's footsteps, rushing straight into the danger.

That's when I get the horrible feeling that our first kiss may have also been our last.

CHAPTER 25

I know I should do what Tristan said.

I should make serious tracks out of The Crypt and go hole up at home, pronto.

Except, that kiss—*that kiss!* It's left me feeling woozy and wobbly and light in the head. I swear, one little taste of Tristan Newberry, and it's like I'm totally drunk on him. I don't trust myself to stand upright, let alone flee. Let alone drive!

So, still sitting on the plush, deep-red sofa, I try to gather my wits. But as I will the clouds in my brain to clear, something else is becoming strangely clear.

I don't want to just up and leave Tristan.

He says he's not a hero—and maybe that was true, once. But since I've become a vampire—and despite my protests against his antiquated reasoning—he's done nothing but try to keep me safe. Safe from Gideon and his idea of vampire justice. Safe from my mother's hurtful comments. And safe from whatever's happening now.

There's a rush of activity coming toward me. A single-file line of men and women—mostly vampires, though I do pick up on a human heartbeat or two—streams out from behind the fireplace. The ones in the lead streak past me in a blur, almost too quick for me to track. But those in the rear move closer to human-fast.

There's no time to hide, but I don't need to. No one casts so much as a glance in my direction. They're all too panicked themselves, too intent on getting out the door.

I should probably take the hint.

I get a queasy feeling in my gut. This is no mere vampire skirmish. There's some kind of an active threat in the next room.

But what kind of a threat? What would compel immortals who can probably move slabs of marble with their little pinkie fingers to run for their everlasting lives?

Evan Knowles, vampire slayer?

After the last vampire in the line exits, I drop my gaze to Tristan's car key, still clutched in my hand.

The smart move is to follow the crowd. Like, immediately.

I get to my feet, knees shaky. But my eyes stupidly drift over to where I heard Tristan disappear down the hallway to hell.

Oh, I know it would be safer to go. Safer for my health. And way safer for my heart. Only, I don't think I want to play it safe anymore.

I recall how annoyed—insulted, even—I felt every time Tristan talked about wanting to protect me. I was so convinced his instinct to defend me just sprang from some deeply ingrained sexism or some misplaced sense of obligation. But now I'm not so sure.

Now, I'm thinking maybe it was about me. Maybe he just wanted to protect *me*.

Because now I find that I want to protect him too.

Am I really going to be like that dumb-ass girl in every second-rate horror flick? I ask myself. *The one who goes running into danger instead of away from it?*

I think about Tristan, about what he might be facing in the next room. Then I shove the key away in my pocket.

Yes, I decide. *Yes, apparently, I am going to be that dumb-ass girl.*

• • • • •

I move my dumb ass down the passageway, the recessed bulbs in the ceiling dimly lighting my way. The heels of my boots clack softly against the stone floor. I can hear my footfalls loud and clear because, aside from the techno music still playing, things at the other end of the hall have gone quiet.

Scary quiet.

I keep going, and the acrid scent of smoke begins to fill my nostrils. I blink as the burning haze stings my eyes.

Okay, so, where there's smoke, there's fire—*duh*. But fire in a club that's been completely purged of anything that could mortally wound a vampire? Not a good sign.

Also, the smoke is…*different*. Different than the smoke that rose last night from the burning remains of our picnic. Different than any smoke I've ever smelled before.

I reach the end of the corridor. The smoke is getting thicker, choking me. I suppress a cough as I peek around the stone wall, peering into the after-hours club within this club.

What a few minutes ago must have been a Gothic-cool private party space is now completely trashed. Heavy wrought-iron tables and chairs are overturned. Patrons who haven't been lucky enough to escape are crouched behind the furnishings, shielding themselves, cowering in fear. There's broken glass everywhere—and it's not just shattered bottles and glassware from the huge, carved-marble bar. One of the converted church's original stained-glass windows is totally smashed in. And some of the shards and jagged edges appear to be, um, melted.

I feel the heat emanating from the far end of the room—but *heat* doesn't even halfway describe it. It's like an inferno of rage made tangible. I swear, I can sense the burning hatred on my skin just as intensely as the blistering hotness.

I lean out farther into the smoke-clouded room, twisting my neck and squinting through the miasma so I can detect the source of the firestorm, and—

Evan.

It's Evan, all right.

His jeans and tee are torn in places, revealing patches of smooth, dark, muscled skin beneath. Behind his black-rimmed glasses, his eyes are blazing with that same supernatural wrath I glimpsed earlier tonight. And somehow, Evan is wielding a sword made entirely of, um, fire. Seriously. *Fire.*

So, it's not like I thought Tristan was lying or anything when he told me that my transformation to a vampire had triggered a sort of equal and opposite reaction in Evan. And I totally went along with him when he gave Raven the whole there's-a-slayer-who-knows-about-The-Crypt speech. But until this moment, I don't know if I actually believed it.

My work rival, Evan Knowles, is a fucking vampire slayer.

Evan is currently surrounded by Tristan, Raven, and three supersized vampires in head-to-toe black leather—two males, one female. The Crypt's security team, I'm guessing. Their fangs are all bared in anger, and I notice my own fangs have instinctively descended too.

Normally, I would say the five-against-one thing doesn't seem like a fair fight. But I have to say, the sword made of *fire* kind of levels the playing field.

Tristan lunges at Evan's back. Evan spins on Tristan—and my heart is suddenly in my throat. I don't want Tristan to get hurt, but I don't want him to harm Evan either. It's like I'm watching a wrestling match and rooting for the whole thing to just get canceled. I hold my breath as the slayer drives the vampire back with his flaming blade.

Drives him back. But doesn't wound him.

I exhale in relief. Tristan is unharmed. And so is Evan. It's a draw.

For now, anyway.

Next, Raven moves in. But Evan quickly swings at her, too, forcing her to retreat.

As the deadly dance continues like that, I inch out into the room. I hug the wall so closely I can feel the roughness of the stone through my clothing. I'm practically peeing my pants in fear, but I can't just stay here on the perimeter, waiting for the vampires to get incinerated. Or for my coworker to get obliterated.

After all, this mess is at least partially my responsibility. Evan is a slayer because of me. And as much as I'm not a big Raven fan, well…I did kind of bring this disaster to her doorstep. So, I've got to do *something*.

Desperate, I look around for a fire extinguisher.

Then I stop, chiding myself for thinking I could somehow douse this blazing weapon of otherworldly fury with a tool made to put out small kitchen fires. Problem is, like Tristan keeps saying, I've got to stop thinking like a human—

Hold on.

I'm still thinking like a human. Because I haven't been a vampire very long.

Just like Evan hasn't been a slayer very long.

So, maybe—just maybe—he's still thinking like a human too?

What if I can reach the part of Evan that isn't a vampire-killing machine?

I mean, I know I've never really connected with Evan before. So, I don't know what makes me think I might be able to connect with him now that he's like the Terminator. Except, apparently, we now have this actual supernatural connection…

Plus, it's the only idea I've got.

Suddenly, Evan slashes through the air, and his blade of fire glances across the cheek of one of the male security guards. And just like that, three hundred or so pounds of vampire muscle are reduced to a steaming pile of ash.

I gasp. The foul stench of death and decay nearly suffocates me.

"Evan!" I shout. Without thinking, I step away from the wall. "*Evan Knowles!*"

Evan shifts his eerie eyes in my direction—and he's not the only one. Across the room, through the smoke, Tristan's gaze finds mine. He shakes his head, and even at this distance, I know his eyes are telling me to get the hell out of here.

Probably excellent advice.

Ignoring it, I walk farther into the room. "Evan, it's me. It's Lily. Lily Baines."

With Evan focused on me, Raven makes another attempt to tackle him from the rear—but it's like he's equipped with the slayer equivalent of an SUV backup camera. Still looking ahead at me, he slices backhandedly at her, nearly skewering her in the abdomen. If her waist wasn't cinched in so tightly, she might be toast crumbs now too.

"Evan!" I repeat.

But it's not the Evan I know who's surveying me. It's like he's possessed.

"I know you're still in there somewhere," I say, hoping it's true. "And maybe you don't like me. Maybe you've never liked me. But I'm pretty sure you don't want to kill me."

As if to prove me wrong, he lets out a bloodcurdling roar and leaps out of the circle of vampires. Vaulting over their heads, he sticks a landing a few feet in front of me.

Tristan was wrong. He does have cheerleader moves.

Evan stands poised to attack me, the flames of his deadly sword reflected in the lenses of his nerdy-hip eyeglasses. This close, the combined heat of his weapon and his anger is painfully searing. Almost unbearable. It should horrify me—and I'm not saying it doesn't. I'm scared of him.

Only, I'm also scared *for* him.

Because the way this is going? This won't end well for anybody.

Now, I don't know what it's like to be a slayer. But I know what it's like to be a vampire. I know about the urges, the bloodlust. I know how it can all feel completely uncontrollable.

I also know it's possible to maintain control.

"Evan," I say with all the authority in my voice I can muster. "You don't have to do this. You don't have to be a mindless predator. You can still be you."

And what do you know? Something about my speech seems to jog something in him. His homicidal gaze falters as if the Wi-Fi connection to his livestream of murderous hate is buffering… buffering…buffering—

"Lily?" he croaks.

"That's right," I say. "It's me. Lily."

I remain immobile, barely breathing, while the eyes behind the lenses of Evan's glasses seem to channel surf, flipping from rage to confusion. Blind hatred to self-loathing. Purpose to regret.

I wonder what I'm going to end up watching—the Evan Knowles Network or Slayer TV.

Then I'm staring into Evan's eyes, his human eyes.

"Lily. I–I'm sorry."

His voice is laced with sadness. I'm not sure if he's apologizing for what he's done in the past or what he's doing right now.

"I'm sorry too," I say.

Then, he lifts his fiery blade—and for a moment, I'm afraid he might be apologizing for what he's about to do.

But instead of aiming the flaming sword at me, Evan raises it at the broken window. The fire extends in a blazing arc, reaching through the hole in the stained glass he must have created when he literally crashed the party. In a blink, his dark figure is up in the air, flying, following the glowing arch through the shattered glass and disappearing into the night.

A fraction of a millisecond later, Tristan is next to me, holding me fiercely to his side. Good thing too. As my limbs fill with relief, I barely have the strength to stand.

"That was reckless," he says into my hair. "You could have been killed."

"Look who's talking," I say into his chest.

"I told you to take my car."

"Yeah? Well, next time, maybe ask if I even know how to drive a stick."

His torso rumbles against me with a small laugh.

"Nevertheless, I told you to go."

"Fuck you," I say. "You're not the boss of me."

He squeezes me tighter. "Apparently not," he says after a moment.

Something in his voice makes me peer up.

Now that Evan is gone, his fangs, like mine, have retreated. His eyes are shining down on me, contemplating me. "Perhaps I've underestimated you a little," he says.

"'*A little?*'" I lift my eyebrows in challenge.

"Don't push it," he says.

It's not exactly enlightened, but I'll take it.

Just as I bury my face back in his chest and start to get comfortable, I hear the crush of glass underfoot. I try to ignore it, but the sound gets closer.

Oh, for chrissake, I think. *Now what?*

CHAPTER 26

Still wrapped in Tristan's arms, I raise my eyes.

As the smoke clears and the ash settles, I see Raven and what remains of her security squad walking over to us. In my peripheral vision, I spy the vampires who were hunkered down around the room beginning to get up and venture out of their hiding places. Slowly, a crowd forms around Tristan and me.

I can't tell if we're headed for some kind of ding-dong-the-witch-is-dead, all-hail-Dorothy moment or more of an angry mob situation.

My body tenses up in Tristan's embrace. I wouldn't have thought it was possible for him to pull me even closer, but it is. Because he does.

Raven looks from the muscular male vampire on her right to the equally ripped female vampire on her left. Then she focuses her dark, heavy-lashed gaze on me. And I see her fangs are no longer on display.

Good sign.

"You have a deal, Tristan," says Raven quietly.

She's addressing him, but she's still staring at me. There's something different in her eyes, something that wasn't there before. Something like...respect?

"The newborn helped us," the club owner continues, raising her voice so it carries throughout the room for everyone to hear. "So we'll do what we can to help her. And," she says, finally looking at Tristan, "I suppose we'll help you too."

Ding! Dong!

Tristan and Raven exchange a few more words, and then Tristan leads me off the floor. But before we even make it to the narrow hallway—

"Lily?" calls Raven's voice. "Before you go, could we have a little chat?"

I look back over my shoulder at her.

She gestures with her head toward a door at the far end of the room. "In private."

• • • • •

"I want to help you," says Raven.

I nod. "Like you already said."

We're alone together in the club owner's office. The decor follows the same gothic-hip style as the rest of The Crypt. Raven sits in a wrought-iron chair that looks like a cross between a throne and a medieval torture device, which somehow seems entirely appropriate. I opt to stand by the door.

Raven shakes her head of long, dark hair. "I'm not talking about helping you with the grand master and the council now," she says. "I'm talking about helping you with Tristan."

My eyes go wide and my shoulders go back. I stand up taller. "I don't need your help with Tristan," I say.

"Trust me," says Raven. "You do."

Trust her? I just met her. And while I seem to have won her over in some weird kind of a way, my jury's still out on her.

Okay, so maybe we're allies now. Vampires in arms. But we're certainly not besties. If Raven wants to talk strategy, fine, I'm all in. But I'm not really comfortable having a heart-to-heart here.

I want to turn around and leave. Only, I also don't want to jeopardize whatever tenuous alliance we've managed to forge here. I mean, between Gideon and Evan, the danger out there is real.

So, reluctantly, I pull up the chair in the room that looks the least threatening and settle in to listen to whatever she feels compelled to tell me.

"Look, I've been there," says Raven. "I've been with Tristan."

I squirm a little in my seat. Does she seriously feel the need to rub my nose in this again?

"Like you already said," I tell her.

"And from my experience," she says, "he's not so good at dealing with modern women."

I narrow my gaze at her. "You dated him three hundred years ago," I say.

"Exactly," she says. "And if an eighteenth-century woman was too much for him to handle, how will he ever handle you?"

Obvi, she's not telling me anything I haven't already observed. Except, since I've met Tristan, I've also witnessed some subtle shifts in his archaic attitudes. Baby steps, but we're making progress.

"I'll handle it," I say. "Is that all?" I start to get up.

"He's completely stuck in the past, you know," says Raven.

Again, this is nothing new to me. I sit back down with a sigh.

"I get that," I say. "I figure that's why he writes all those historical romances. Nostalgia for a time gone by and all."

"He writes all those historicals," says Raven with a knowing expression, "because he's trying to rewrite his own history."

I blink at her. Did I mention I don't want to be having this conversation? And yet, what she's said has piqued my interest.

"Rewrite his own history?" I ask against my better judgment. "Rewrite it how?"

"I never got the whole story," says Raven. She reclines back in her throne-slash-torture-device, and she somehow manages to look comfy. "But from what I could gather, there was someone special. She died suddenly. In a fire, I think. By the time Tristan got there, it was too late. He couldn't save her. And he's never gotten over the loss."

"So, he was in love with her?" I ask, even though I'm not sure I want to know the answer.

"Not just in love," says Raven. "Obsessed. And since he's still writing those romances, I'm betting he's still carrying a torch."

"He's still in love with her?" I ask. I hear my voice break just a little.

"And take it from me," says Raven, nodding. "There's no way to compete with a ghost."

"But not a literal ghost," I say. "Right?"

She looks at me, confused. "What?"

I shake my head. "Never mind," I say. I don't need her laughing her ass off at me too. "Forget it."

The thing is, as much as I don't want to believe it, her tale about Tristan tracks pretty well with the bits and pieces I know so far.

Is this why he doesn't think of himself as a hero?

Is this why he doesn't believe in happily ever after?

And is this why he's so balls-out determined to protect me?

"Tortured past," I mutter.

"Something like that," Raven says.

Except, why is she even telling me all this? I wasn't born yesterday—well, okay, I guess in vampire terms, I kind of was. But, um, what I mean is, it's more than a little strange that Tristan's ex would be sitting here offering me relationship advice.

Then, I remember to put on my journalist hat—which really should be mandatory dress code whenever I'm dealing with vampires from here on in.

"Wait, wait, wait," I say. "How do you even know all this? Did Tristan tell you?"

"Oh, please," she says. "Are you joking? When it comes to the strong, silent type, that vampire is the original model."

True dat, I think.

"Then how do you know?" I ask.

"I operate an establishment where vampires gather," she says. "And when vampires gather, they talk."

Do they, now? I think. *Hmm…*

"Do they ever talk about what caused the rift between Tristan and Gideon?" I ask.

"Sorry," she says. "I can't help you there."

Figures.

"Okay," I say. "So are we done now?"

Raven sits up straighter, and her expression gets a little haughty.

"You know," she says, "I really am trying to do you a favor here. The favor I wish someone would have done for me."

Then, all of a sudden, I get it. Three hundred years or so ago, Tristan must have broken Raven's heart.

Well, that kind of explains why she was so snotty to Tristan—and to me—when we first showed up at her back-room door.

But then I start to think about what this really means.

Raven and Tristan shared something. But ultimately, she wanted more than he could give her. And centuries later, the hurt is still there.

And I think about that kiss I shared with Tristan earlier, how it left me wanting so much more.

Only, if Raven—beautiful, shrewd, confident Raven—wasn't enough for Tristan…

"Look, I get the attraction," she says with a sad smile. "Who wouldn't? Tristan is gorgeous, and he's got that whole moody-broody vampire thing going on. And actually, when push comes to shove, he's a pretty decent guy. You saw how he jumped to the rescue tonight, here at my club." She leans forward, and her voice gets more forceful. "But, Lily—? I saw how *you* jumped to *his* rescue. So, just be careful. Be careful with your heart. Because his is already taken."

• • • • •

With Raven's words of warning ringing in my ears, I rejoin Tristan by the exit.

"So, what did Raven want to talk about?" Tristan asks me as we leave The Crypt together.

I think about how to answer. I decide to go with the truth—or an edited version of it, at least.

"You," I say. "She told me I shouldn't get involved with you."

He grins. "She's probably right."

It's basically what he told me that first night we met.

It's basically what I've been telling myself, on and off, ever since.

I grin back. "Yeah. She probably is."

Only, here's a little something about me: I don't much like doing what people tell me to do. Not Tristan. Not Raven. And apparently, not even me.

"Car key?" asks Tristan.

I dig it out of my pocket and hand it over. His fingers brush lightly against mine, and I suddenly go all warm and melty inside.

He unlocks the vehicle. "Let's get you home safe."

He opens the door for me, looking at me like I'm something precious, something dear. My limbs liquefy. I don't so much climb in as pour myself into the passenger seat.

Tristan gets in on the other side, and his sheer nearness makes me inhale sharply. The smell of smoke from the slayer's sword still clings to him, mixing with the musky, masculine scent that is 100 percent him. And totally intoxicating.

My gaze drifts to his perpetually messy sandy-brown hair. I'm not sure if I want to smooth it down or mess it up even more, but my fingers itch to touch it.

To touch him.

I swear, I've never wanted anyone this much, ever. Not my first boyfriend, Tom. Or my boyfriend of convenience, Aidan. Not even my hookup-app boyfriend, Joe.

Tristan slips the key into the ignition—something I've watched him do several times before. Only, this time, it makes me think naughty thoughts. Nasty thoughts. Thoughts about something else slipping into somewhere else. I wriggle a little in my seat, trying to alleviate the sudden ache in my groin, but the movement just makes it even worse.

When Tristan drops his hand to shift the car into drive, the sight of him palming the gear stick is so sexually suggestive, I swear I could almost die.

Of course, I did almost die. We both almost did.

We still could.

There's a vampire slayer out there who hates me. A grand master who's sending me death threats and has some kind of a centuries-old ax to grind with Tristan. And who even knows if this new alliance with Raven Dupree and The Crypt vampires will be enough to help us stand against them?

So, can you blame me for craving a little life-affirming activity?

Undeath-affirming…?

Whatever.

So what if Tristan has baggage? He's been around hundreds of years. I understand that he's got a past.

And so what if it doesn't last forever? I've never really seen myself living happily ever after with Tristan—or with anybody else.

Besides, right now, I'm not thinking about forever. I'm just thinking about tonight.

"I don't want to go home," I say huskily.

Tristan's deep-blue eyes dart over to me. I catch his gaze drifting down to my mouth, and I wonder if he's thinking about that kiss we shared earlier. Did it leave him wanting more too?

"You don't want to go home?" he says in a rough, rumbling voice that vibrates through me, seeming to stroke the most sensitive parts of me.

"No," I whisper. "I don't."

He looks back up to meet my gaze, and I can see that he does want more. So much more. Everything I'm willing to give him.

And in this moment, I'm willing to give him everything.

"Can we, um, go to your place?" I ask.

CHAPTER 27

Obvi, I suggest going to Tristan's place because my mother is sleeping at mine. Except, it's not just about privacy. It's also about safety. Her safety. Considering all the paranormal peeps who seem to want a piece of me, I figure the more I stay away from Mom, the better off she'll be.

Only thing is, if I spend the night with Tristan, I'll need to spend the day with him too. I can't go out in the sunlight. So, I'll be leaving my mother on her own for basically twenty-four hours.

Hopefully, she won't think I'm avoiding her.

I pull out my iPhone and send her a text.

Staying at Tristan's tonight. Dinner tomorrow?

Then, I remember she thinks I'm on a "special diet."

Or a movie maybe?

Then, I remember the blood in my fridge.

Please don't drink my protein shakes.

I put my phone away with a sigh.

Shittiest. Hostess. Ever.

• • • • •

Tristan and I get out of the car. And since he seems to have a gift for scoring the perfect parking space, I assume we're in front of our destination. I stare up in awe at the stunning Gothic-revival structure that dominates the corner of Seventy-Second Street and Central Park West, its gables creating a striking silhouette against the moonlit sky.

"You live in the Dakota?" I ask.

"Is that a problem?" he asks. He retrieves my bag from the trunk and slings it over his shoulder to carry it for me.

Slowly, I shake my head.

Problem? Hell, no. I mean, his building is only like the most coveted address in all of Manhattan. So exclusive that big-time celebs like Madonna and Cher were rejected by its co-op board. Sadly, it's also where John Lennon was gunned down by a crazed assassin—but if anything, that's kind of added to its mystique.

I'm rocking some serious apartment envy.

"So, how long have you lived here?"

Tristan doesn't answer me right away. Instead, he walks me over to the building's arched entranceway, where a dark-haired, gray-uniformed doorman stands guard beside an ominous sign that reads "Authorized Persons Only Beyond This Point."

"Hello, Joseph," says Tristan amiably.

"Mr. Newberry," says the doorman with a polite smile and a nod.

"Joseph, when did the Dakota first open its doors?"

"1884, sir."

Tristan turns to me as we walk through to the impeccably kept courtyard. "1884," he whispers.

"You were one of the original owners?" I ask. I also try to keep my voice down in case anyone is listening, but it's a definite struggle.

"Well, tenant back then," he says. "I didn't buy until the 1980s when the building went co-op."

"So, you've lived here for more than a hundred years?"

He leads me over to the waiting elevator in the southeast corner of the building. "On and off." We enter the car, and he presses the button for the ninth floor. "For obvious reasons, I relocate every decade or two, then return as my namesake descendant—a son or a nephew or a distant cousin." He grins playfully. "The people who still remember me say the family resemblance is uncanny."

The elevator doors close, we begin our ascent, and I think about this little glimpse into the practical reality of being an immortal living under the radar in a mortal world.

"I can teach you these things, you know," he says. "Things like how to periodically move around and reinvent yourself before people start to notice you aren't getting any older."

"No worries," I mutter to my feet. The first little seeds of doubt start to sprout in my head as I'm suddenly reminded of just how different I am from Tristan. "No one ever notices me."

"Impossible."

Tristan gently touches me under my chin, lifting my face until I'm staring straight into those deep pools of indigo blue.

"Lily," he says softly. "Don't you know? You're magnificent."

This time, his kiss doesn't take me by surprise—although, okay, I'm still a little stunned that someone like Tristan wants to kiss me at all. But this time, I see him coming. He moves toward me unhurried, almost in slow motion. His permanent two-days' scruff scratches at my skin as he brushes his cool, soft lips against mine.

Heat rips through my cold body.

No longer thinking, only wanting, I close my eyes, part my lips, and stroke his tongue with my own. Consumed with a desperate need for him, I grab his leather jacket and try to yank him closer to deepen the kiss. Only, Tristan's fingers slide skillfully from my chin back into my long hair. He clutches a big handful of my curls and holds me back, taunting me all the while with the featherlike touch of his lips, the barely there flick of his tongue.

It's torture. Delicious, exquisite torture.

I moan, and my cry echoes off the walls of the elevator.

In answer, Tristan finally goes for it. Pulling gently but firmly at my hair, he angles my head upward and takes our kiss to a deeper, more erotic place. Our tongues wrestle with each other, dancing together in a too-perfect rhythm.

I feel utterly boneless.

Before my legs go right out from under me, I lean closer to him. He folds his other arm around me, holding me tight against him. That's when I can detect the growing evidence of his own arousal pressing hard against me. And just like that, my burgeoning doubts are mowed down.

He wants me too.

As the elevator doors open, we reluctantly separate and come up for air.

Tristan stares at me like he wants to decimate me—but, um, in a good way. His gaze is so sizzling hot, I swear it's a wonder I'm not reduced to a pile of steaming ash.

But then, something occurs to me. Something I probably should have thought to ask him way before we got to this point. "Do we need, um, protection?"

Tristan looks at me questioningly. "Well," he says, "we've got Raven and her security team on our side now."

"What?" I ask. It takes me a moment to realize he went straight to the here-I-come-to-save-the-day connotation of *protection*. Of course, he did. "Tristan, I'm talking about safe sex."

"Oh!" he says, understanding dawning in his eyes. "No. No, vampires can't reproduce. And we can't transmit diseases. So, sex with a vampire is, by definition, safe."

So, no condoms, I think. *Good.* I don't have any with me, and I don't know where there's a twenty-four-hour pharmacy in this neighborhood.

Only, a breath later, the fuller meaning of what he just said lands with me.

So, no kids. Ever.

To be honest, I'm not sure how to feel about this. It's not as if I've ever really wanted children. I've never had any burning desire to become a mom. And I mean, considering how my own mother fucked me up so royally with her thin obsession and her fat phobia, I always figured it would probably be best to let the madness end with me.

Still, it's a little like the no-sunlight thing. Something else ripped right out from under me, leaving me struggling to find my balance again.

"But," says Tristan, misreading my hesitancy, "if it would make you feel more comfortable..."

"No," I say quickly. "No, I'm good."

He continues to look at me uncertainly, searching.

"I didn't want kids anyway," I say with a small shrug.

I watch as he processes my oblique explanation, as the pieces all click into place.

"Ah," he says, realizing. "I'm sorry."

"It's fine," I say, shaking my head. "*I'm* fine. Really."

He looks at me, trying to read me. Trying to decide if I really am fine, I guess. Then, tentatively, he wraps his arms around me again.

With a sigh, I collapse back against him.

He draws me close and hugs me tight—but this time, it's not in a sexual way. Now, it feels like he's comforting me. Consoling me.

And I know he's trying to be sensitive and give me what I need. Only, goddammit, this is so not what I need right now. Not what I want. Instead of dealing with the seemingly unending complications of being undead, I just want to do something that makes me feel really, truly alive.

I don't want this night with Tristan to be ripped from me too.

He pulls back a little so he can look me in the eye.

"What can I do for you?" he asks.

I notice the elevator doors have closed on us, but the car is still stopped on the ninth floor.

I hit the "door open" button and peer up at Tristan with a smile. "You can invite me in."

CHAPTER 28

This is not the first time I've gone back to a guy's place. But in my limited past experience, the place has almost always been strewn with empty pizza boxes and smelled like dirty socks and unlaundered gym clothes.

Not so Tristan's.

I step into the elegant, spotless foyer and breathe in the clean, welcoming scent of lemon furniture polish. Tristan drops my bag onto the gorgeous, gleaming mahogany floor.

"Would you like a tour?" he asks.

I smile, a little embarrassed. I guess it's pretty clear I have a hard-on for his apartment. But I don't want him thinking it even approaches the raging hard-on I have for him.

"As long as it ends in the bedroom," I say.

He takes my hand and leads me through his nine rooms—yes, *nine* rooms—every one looking like it popped straight out of a centerfold spread in *Architectural Digest*. Total home-and-living porn.

There are solid mahogany doors to match the floors. Original carved-wood fireplaces. A carefully curated collection of furnishings—some antique, but maybe new when he bought them; others more contemporary. The windows are all hung with heavy dark-velvet drapes drawn shut against the pending sunrise—a sad but necessary waste of what must be a truly spectacular view of Central Park.

As we stroll into room number nine, the master bedroom, Tristan flicks on a Tiffany lamp. No, not a Tiffany-*style* lamp. The real thing.

In the soft, diffused light, I drag my free hand across a classic Shaker bookcase. The impeccable lines of its shelves are packed with books—many of which, I notice, were penned by Delilah Manning.

"These are yours!"

Curious, I randomly grab one of the thick paperback volumes. Its title is *Forbidden Fantasies*, and something about it looks familiar. At first, I think it's because I must have spied a copy back at my mother's house.

But then I study the cover illustration. A tall, muscular, sandy-haired hero is burying his face deep in the neck of a stunning heroine, bending her over backwards. The guy's resemblance to Tristan seems pretty undeniable.

And then everything Raven told me comes rushing back. Does Tristan really write all these historical romances in an effort to rewrite his own history? Is it his way of reliving his own epic love story, of achieving the happy ending he was denied?

I shift my focus to the woman on the cover. She has waist-length blond hair that fans out behind her. White skin. Her heavily lashed eyes are closed, and her full, red mouth hangs open in ecstasy. There's a long, shapely leg peeking out from under the folds of her voluminous blue skirt. And her generous bosom strains against her tightly laced blue bodice.

Aside from the blond hair, the heroine is a dead ringer for Raven.

And I know, I know, she said she wasn't the love of Tristan's immortal life—and on that score, I believe her. But they were together. They both admitted that.

So, if Tristan is penning these novels about his one true love—and she looks exactly like one of his ex-lovers—then doesn't that mean Tristan has a type?

And if this is his type, then, um, where do I fit in?

Tristan reaches over, snatches the paperback from my grasp, and places it back on the shelf.

"What do you say we concentrate on our own romance tonight?" he says.

Taking a deep breath, I try to wipe these self-sabotaging thoughts from my mind and follow Tristan's suggestion.

It's what I want. If I'm honest, it's what I've wanted since he first bought me that drink and offered me his seat at the bar at Dos Rosas.

And he's here with me now, isn't he? Not Raven. Not some long-dead lover from his past. *Me.*

Plus, it's not as if I think this is really going anywhere. He's already told me he doesn't do the happily-ever-after thing. He's strictly the happy-for-now type. So, expectations managed.

"Lily?"

And after the nightmare of a night I've had tonight—hell, the past few nights—I deserve a little happy.

For now? Forever?

Whatever.

"Lily. Is something wrong?"

I think about those body-positive activists I follow, the ones with figures like mine. And I try to borrow some of their amazing confidence.

And I think about Kelly, so much lighter now—but not because she lost weight. Because she somehow managed to lose this toxic way of thinking about herself.

I'm not there yet, but maybe I can fake it until I make it?

I take another deep breath and look at Tristan.

"Something is very wrong," I say decisively. "You're still dressed."

I stuff down my anxiety and focus instead on the vampire standing in front of me. For the first time since I've known him, Tristan sheds his signature leather jacket, revealing a black T-shirt that's just fitted enough to hint at the chiseled chest and killer abs that must lie beneath it. As he tosses the jacket onto a Stickley chair, I try not to gawk at the long, powerful forearms and well-defined biceps extending below his short sleeves.

"Your turn," he says.

My turn?

Yes, okay. My turn.

I strip off my black cardigan and let it drop to the thick Persian rug under our feet.

Tristan ogles me, smiling a sinfully hot smile. Then, in one fluid move that could have come straight out of the Magic Mike movies, he pulls the tee off over his head and throws it on top of the jacket.

His body is sick. Beyond perfect. Like the *David* or something—only carved out of flesh.

But here's the thing: I'd want him whatever he looked like. I really don't want to jump his bones because he's hot. I want to jump his bones because he's Tristan.

My nipples pucker up, begging to be kissed. Wetness pools between my legs. My fangs descend.

That last one takes me by surprise. Up until now, only extreme thirst and extreme aggression have coaxed my new teeth out of hiding.

"It's a perfectly normal reaction for us," says Tristan, sensing my confusion.

Okay, so I guess extreme arousal also calls my fangs out to play.

And what do you know? His wicked grin reveals his own extended fangs. Which, okay, must mean he's into this too.

But then, as he continues to drink me in with his indigo eyes, I realize he's waiting. Waiting for me to reciprocate by removing my own top.

Suddenly, my borrowed confidence is on an express train back to its owners. So much for faking it.

My first instinct is to switch off the lamp, dive for the king-sized sleigh bed, and hide under the bazillion-thread-count covers to wriggle out of the rest of my clothing. Only, I'm the one who started this game.

So, trying my best to suck in—and wishing I didn't feel like I had to—I peel off my green tank. My move isn't nearly as smooth or as sexy as Tristan's. Feeling awkward as balls, I disentangle myself from my top and let it fall next to my cardi.

I stand before Tristan, naked from the waist up—save for an old stretched-out, beige-colored bra that does less than zero to enhance my bust. My belly and muffin tops are on full, unobstructed display.

Now, my desire for the vampire fights with my desire to shield my body from his view—and what I can't help fearing will soon be the look of major disappointment in his eyes.

Impulsively, before he can see too much, I launch myself at him. Lips against lips. Chest against chest. Bare flesh against bare flesh.

Without missing a beat, Tristan eagerly explores my mouth with his tongue. His hand grazes the curvature of my hip and traces a tantalizing path up to my waist.

And I want to enjoy this, dammit. I want to enjoy being with

Tristan. Only, as his fingers roam over my midsection, fresh thoughts of Raven Dupree invade my brain. And I start mentally comparing my body to hers all over again.

Tristan finds the fastenings at the back of my bra. But as he undoes the first hook and eye, I stiffen.

To his credit, he picks up on my reaction and stops. With his arms still encircling me, he breaks our kiss and pulls back a little to look at me.

"Do you want this?"

I do. I do want this.

And I want it even more because he's asking.

Why can't I just get the fuck out of my own way?

Because it's not Tristan. Every vibe I'm getting as we stand here says he wants me. *Me.*

And from Dos Rosa's to our endless car rides to the top of the Empire State Building, he's really never said or done anything to imply I'm any less because I'm, um, *more.*

It's me. It's all in my head.

If only it was possible to shake off these damn insecurities. To silence these negative voices. To shed my inhibitions like my tank and cardi and just go for it.

Then it occurs to me: maybe it *is* possible.

"I want to drink from you first," I say to Tristan. "Can I drink from you?"

CHAPTER 29

Tristan's blue eyes gaze at me. "You want my blood?"

"Yes," I murmur.

I recall what he told me. Not just that it would make me strong, but that it would make me lose control with him. And I want to lose control.

I choose to lose control.

I mean, Tristan keeps telling me to "stop thinking like a human"—and that's exactly what I want to do. I want to stop comparing myself to other women and thinking I somehow come up lacking. I want to enjoy the pleasure of my vampire body with Tristan's vampire body without my stupid human hang-ups getting in the way.

For a moment, he just looks at me without saying anything.

Then he asks simply, like it's the most natural thing in the world, "Do you want my wrist? Or my neck?"

The question gives me pause. I mean, sure, I've been thinking about drinking from Tristan since he first brought up the idea. Only, I've been thinking about it in the abstract. I've never actually considered the, um, mechanics of it.

Am I really going to do this? I wonder.

Just then, I think back to our skyscraper picnic and how much I enjoyed the meal. Not because I could eat without gaining weight, but because, for once, I could eat without *worrying* about gaining weight. I felt so free.

I want to feel free like that again.

"Neck," I say.

Obligingly, Tristan tilts his head back, baring his throat to me, making himself vulnerable. He gently presses my cheek to his bare shoulder until my head is nestled against him. It's somehow both comforting and arousing.

And confusing as fuck.

"I–I don't know what to do."

"Yes, you do," he says. "Just follow your instincts. Let your hunger guide you."

I almost laugh. I've spent so many years suppressing my hunger, trying to keep it in check. Now, I'm just supposed to *let it guide me?*

"Lily," he says. "It's okay. Relax."

He's right. I need to relax.

I take what I hope will be a calming breath. My nostrils fill with the seductive scent of the vampire. And his underlying blood.

I bare my fangs and let them hover over his jugular. But just before I bite, I stop.

"I don't want to hurt you," I whisper against his skin.

"You won't," he says. "I promise. This will give me every bit as much pleasure as it gives you."

"Right."

I close my eyes, open my mouth, and let the vampire inside me loose to do her thing. The razor-sharp tips of my fangs penetrate Tristan, first piercing his skin, then sliding home into his vein.

And who knew that teeth could be erogenous zones? I swear, the rush of rapture I feel when my twin canines are fully seated within my oh-so-willing victim practically sweeps me off my feet.

I get a taste of Tristan's blood—and instantly, I understand what he's been saying all along. The difference between drinking from the outdated donor units that Cat helped me swipe and drinking live on tap from a vampire's vein is like the difference between day-old leftovers and a freshly prepared gourmet meal. The rich, robust flavor of him fills my mouth, and I simply can't get enough.

"Drink," whispers Tristan. "Take what you need."

I suck. And suck and suck and suck, swallowing him down. His blood flows through my body like electricity, powering every inch of me until all my circuits detonate.

I feel gratified like never before—and yet, I still want more.

I need more.

But it's different than what I expected.

See, the way Tristan made it sound, I thought drinking his blood might turn me into some kind of a mindless sex fiend. Like I'd be nothing but nerve endings and libido and uncontainable urges. Only, I don't feel like I'm losing control at all.

Instead, I feel like I'm gaining control. Control over my body and my mind, my thoughts and my passions. Everything is sharper, clearer. It's as if there were ropes binding me—but they've all fallen away. And now I'm free to pursue exactly what I desire.

I ease my fangs out of Tristan's neck and lick my lips to get every last drop of him. Like magic, the double puncture wounds in his throat heal over almost immediately.

I move closer up against him, and the hard bulge of his erection teases me through his jeans. It's heavenly hell. Now that I've been inside of him, I want for him to be inside of me.

Unabashed, I tug at his waistband. The top button of his fly pops off, ricocheting off the wall and landing somewhere behind me with a *ping!* In some back room of my brain, I wonder how I could've pried off the rivet like that—but it's a fleeting thought, at best. I've got other things on my mind.

"Too many clothes," I say roughly.

"Race you?" asks Tristan with a grin.

I grin back. "You're on."

In a blur of activity, we remove our shoes and disrobe. And there's zero clumsy groping with zippers and other fastenings. Thanks to my new, blood-fortified speed and strength, my remaining clothing is gone in a New York minute.

I'm not sure who wins our race. I guess we both win.

"Lily," says Tristan in a husky voice. His indigo eyes rake over my naked body, blazing with a desire that matches my own. "You're so beautiful."

But I barely even register the compliment. I'm too enthralled by him. My breathing goes ragged. I step forward, not at all self-conscious. For once, I feel wholly in possession of my body. And I want to get my body with his.

I put my hands flat against the contours of his pecs and walk Tristan backwards to the bed. When the backs of his shins hit the box spring, I push him down onto the king-sized mattress. He falls back onto the fluffy covers, and his impressive erection bobs at me. Beckoning me forward.

"I hope you're going to invite me in now," he says with a wolfish grin.

I grin back.

Then, without any hesitation, I climb onto the bed and straddle him. He reclines back into the pillows, for once happy to let me take the lead. But he doesn't take his eyes off me. I know, because I don't take mine off him.

Kneeling over him, I grip the base of his thick cock firmly—and his breath hitches. It's a little heady, knowing I can affect him like that with just my touch. But when he lifts his large hands to my hips, I gasp, reacting just the same. Everything feels heightened. Incredibly intense. And I don't think it's entirely due to the vampire blood.

Tristan reaches around and cups my ass, caressing and squeezing, urging me on. Except, I hardly need the encouragement.

Bracing myself with one hand against his shoulder, I use the other to guide the long, hard, silken length of him inside me. Somehow, there's no awkwardness, no fumbling or faltering while we learn the contours of each other's bodies. It's as if we've always known each other.

He glides smoothly, so smoothly, into me. The sweet sensation as he fills me completely makes me cry out loud.

We both cry out.

We tumble together onto the big bed—a tangle of arms and legs, hands and tongues—and our bodies find a staggering rhythm. Tristan flips me over—he's on top of me now—but this isn't one of our battles for control. This is a joining of equals, a give and a take. Our pleasure is doubled by pleasing each other.

Tristan drives into me again and again and again.

It's both too much and still not enough.

Then, his mouth finds my breast and his fingers find my clit, and—

Oh. My. God.

Suddenly, I'm engulfed not so much by waves of pleasure as by a tsunami.

Several fucking tsunamis.

The spasms of my orgasms squeeze Tristan's cock, and I feel him find his release too.

Then, breathless and spent, I float back down to earth.

I curl my body into his, obnoxiously sated. He hugs me to his side. We snuggle together.

And just so you know, this is not my SOP. I'm not normally one to lie around basking in the afterglow. In the past—not that I've had much of one, sexually speaking—I've always been too busy searching frantically for a shirt to cover up. Or making up some excuse to get fully dressed and head out the door. But apparently being a bloodsucker has its privileges.

Or maybe it's just being with Tristan.

Whatever. For once, I'm too happy to start analyzing.

I feel rather than see the day dawn. As that now-familiar fatigue starts to pull me under, I yawn and cuddle closer, settling in next to Tristan for a long day's sleep.

But then, like it did that first time I drank blood, it happens.

A landslide of memories overwhelms me. Only this time they're not my memories. They're, um, *Tristan's memories?*

Blissfully unaware that his immortal life is currently flashing before my eyes, Tristan draws the covers up over us both and presses a tender kiss to my temple.

"Sleep well, dear Lily," he whispers.

And before I can process any of what I'm seeing in my mind's eye, I slip deep into an undead slumber.

CHAPTER 30

The next evening, I drift back into consciousness with a long, languorous stretch. The luxurious bedding caresses my flesh, titillating my ultra-sensitive vampire skin that's been made even more sensitive by Tristan's blood. Instinctively, my hand reaches out next to me, skimming between the sheets, searching. Only, the other side of the bed is empty.

I open my eyes. No Tristan.

Then, all at once—and with the force of a bullet train slamming into my cranium—I remember what I saw last night. What Tristan's blood revealed to me.

Centuries of memories flood my head. Way too much to comprehend. So, I concentrate on the one face that keeps repeating. The one image that never seems to be far from the surface. The one recollection that I can just about grasp and hold.

A woman.

Beautiful. Like an angel. But a vampire.

Blond hair. Sweet face. Petite.

Loved.

Gone. Long gone.

But still so very, very loved.

I've just had a rude awakening. Because it looks like everything Raven told me about Tristan is absolutely true.

He may have made love to me last night. But clearly, he is still *in* love with somebody else.

And it was one thing to hear it from Raven. To believe it, even. But to actually feel it in my veins? To literally *feel* his affection for another woman coursing through my body? To feel his complete and utter heartbreak at her loss? Jesus. That's another thing all together.

This just in: not all vampire sex is safe sex.

I bolt up to a sitting position. In the soft light of the Tiffany lamp, the sumptuous sheets slip away, revealing the slopes of my breasts.

My decidedly unperky breasts.

The silky bedding slips lower, baring my thick waist, my rounded belly.

Self-consciously, I pull the covers back up to hide my nakedness—even though there's no one here to see me.

Only, someone did see me.

Tristan saw me.

And, okay, yes, I know what the two of us shared last night. I was there. And, I mean, he was too. He was fully *there*. I don't really believe he was thinking about anybody else.

But now, the side effect of drinking Tristan's blood has waned, and my insecurities are returning with a vengeance. So, of course, I'm comparing myself to this woman from his past. And I can't help wondering if maybe Tristan is now too.

In the cold light of, um, night? Did he look over at me and decide that I was a poor substitute for the gorgeous, golden-haired nymph who has eternal dibs on his heart?

Wrapping the sheet around me, I jump off the mattress and pad over to the bookcase. I know it's a terrible idea, but I can't stop myself. One by one, I pull the Delilah Manning paperbacks off the shelves to inspect their covers before I drop them onto the floor. The majority of the cover girls are blonds, I notice. And each of them, in her own way, is reminiscent of the ghost whose lovely image is currently haunting my brain.

The rest are brunettes, like Raven, with a smattering of redheads. But even the gingers don't look like me. No, they look like my thinner, prettier, very distant ancestors. If I suspected it before, I know it now. Clearly, Tristan has a type—and I'm not it.

Last night, yes, okay, I let myself get swept up in a rush of I-nearly-got-slayed-but-lived-to-tell-the-tale adrenaline. I guess we both did.

But Tristan isn't available. Not really. And certainly not to someone like me.

If it weren't for this trouble with Grand Master Gideon, Tristan probably wouldn't be hanging out with me at all. He probably would've been up and out of my everlasting life just as quickly as he was up and out of this bed this evening.

And I'd be smart to remember that.

I don't need Tristan to protect me. I need to protect myself.

I need to get out of here.

Keeping myself wrapped in the sheet, I do a little recon work for my clothes. I'm happy to discover that, thanks to the previous night's hit of Tristan's blood, I've still got some superspeed of my own. In a flash, I gather my things off the floor.

Only, um, Houston? We've got a problem.

My tank and cardigan are fine. But my bra? My panties? My jean leggings? They're in absolute tatters. Way beyond distressed. Like, totally unwearable.

Last night, unaccustomed to the strength and speed that Tristan's blood unleashed in me, I didn't just get undressed quickly. I must have literally ripped the clothes right off my body.

Jesus. Another epic wardrobe malfunction.

I spy Tristan's jeans, also discarded on the floor, and I pick them up to examine them. They're missing the top button, which I vaguely remember being my doing. But otherwise, they're intact. I peer hopefully at the waist size stamped on the tag—but, no. That's not going to work.

I glance around the room in desperation. My gaze lands on a big, antique-looking dresser. I dart over and start opening drawers, rooting through them.

Socks…underwear…tees—sweats! Thank God!

I grab a pair of black sweatpants—and yes, they look stretchy and roomy enough to fit. Quickly, I pull them on under the sheet, going commando out of necessity for the second time in practically as many days.

Next, I turn away from the open bedroom door, drop the sheet, and throw on my tank and cardi.

But then I contemplate my boots. My black suede over-the-knee boots. They're still intact, but they'll look ridiculous with sweatpants. Only, what other option do I have? It's not as if I can borrow Tristan's Doc Martens—or any other shoes in his closet. I'd walk right out of them. My shoe size, at a 6, is the only petite thing about me.

With a frustrated sigh, I sit on the edge of the bed and start to pull the boots on over the sweats.

Just as I finish dressing, I hear the creak of the mahogany floorboards.

"You're extremely overdressed for breakfast in bed," says Tristan in a voice like warm butterscotch.

I look up to see him strolling into the room in a pair of black boxer briefs—and nothing else. He's carrying a covered silver tray. My mouth starts to water. Partly from the delicious aromas that suddenly fill the air. But mostly, dammit, from the mere sight of Tristan—and in his skivvies, no less.

"I, um, I had to borrow your sweatpants," I say as I get to my feet. I indicate the shredded remains of my jeggings.

"Yes," he says with a smile. "We were both rather enthusiastic last night."

"Yeah, well," I say. I shrug and try to play it cool. "What with the vampire blood and all…"

He gives me a look as he puts the tray—which I can now tell is genuine sterling silver—down on a table and removes the lid. Crispy bacon. Scrambled eggs. Buttery toast.

"You cooked?" I ask.

"You thought my talents were limited to the bedroom?" he says with a cocky grin.

His eyes drag over my body, practically searing my skin through the clothes. But that is so not happening again. I mean, self-preservation and all.

I pull my sweater around me to hide my bralessness.

Once again, I remember the last time we shared a meal, on top of the Empire State Building. I felt so relaxed and comfortable then.

Self-consciously, I pull my sweater tighter. I don't feel like that anymore.

"Thanks," I say, nodding at the food. "But, no thanks."

Tristan looks confused—and maybe a little hurt. His gaze cuts over to the pile of romance novels I discarded onto the floor. His brow furrows, but he doesn't say anything.

"I–I should go," I say quickly. "I, um, I need to get home. You know. My mother and all."

Not that I'm exactly anxious to get back to her. She'll have a million questions about Tristan, and I won't want to answer any of them.

But right now, I'd rather be with her than be here.

Tristan's eyes shift back to me. "Just give me a chance to get dressed," he says slowly and quietly, like he's talking to a skittish animal ready to run. "I'll drive you back down to the Village."

CHAPTER
31

The car ride downtown is a little awkward. Neither Tristan nor I say much.

As he easily finds a parking space you-know-where, I'm struck by the stark difference between my building and his. Yeah, we're not at the Dakota anymore.

"You don't have to come in," I say.

"Of course I'm coming in," he says.

I'm about to protest, but I let it go. Since my mother invited him in the other night, it's not as if I can keep him out. And besides, if he's with me, it might help curtail her inevitable criticism of my impromptu walk-of-shame attire.

I unlock the outer glass security door and lead Tristan down the hallway to my unit. But I stop a few feet short of 1C when I discover that the door is partially ajar.

Maybe my mother accidentally left it open?

"Let me go first," says Tristan, stepping out ahead of me. He says it calmly, but the undeniable undercurrent of concern in his voice makes my own concern spike.

With him in front, we creep the rest of the distance to my apartment doorway, doing our best TV-cops-on-a-raid imitation. I have the ridiculous impulse to make the shape of a gun with my fingers. I attribute the giddiness to nerves.

Tristan reaches out and gently pushes the door open. "Hello?" he calls.

No response.

In fact, my über-sensitive vampire ears don't pick up any sound coming from inside at all. Feeling emboldened, I walk past Tristan and enter my studio. "Mom?" I call. "Mom? Are you here?"

She's not.

I look around. Her stuff is still here. So, she hasn't gone back to Jersey yet. Maybe she—

My iPhone rings then, breaking the silence. I pounce on it, thinking the call might be from my mother—but the caller ID says otherwise.

"Cat," I say when I answer. "Hey."

"Lily! Thank God," she says. "You're not dead."

"Nope," I say. "Still undead."

"You need to check out the news," she says. Her voice is strange. Squeaky with urgency.

"Why?" I grab the remote and click on the TV. "What's up?"

"They found a body," says Cat. "An unidentified woman. In the subway. Attacked."

That gets my attention. "Subway?" I repeat. "Attacked?"

"Apparently, she was bitten. All over. Practically mauled."

As Cat continues to run down the details of the story, my flat-screen comes to life. Weirdly, it's tuned to MMN—Matheson Multimedia News. Definitely not my channel of choice. I guess my mother was watching, though I didn't know she was a fan of the ultra-conservative pundit pack. She probably just likes that the female anchors fit the physical mold she's always trying to squeeze me into.

Currently, one of the anchors is echoing a lot of what Cat just told me.

"And after everything you said about the grand master and his underground army," says Cat, "well, I was terrified it might be your body they found."

"No," I say. "Not me."

But I don't know where my mother is.

And the door to my apartment was open.

And since Gideon's threats have been getting closer to home, metaphorically speaking, it's not hard to imagine he might have forced his way into my literal home while my mother was here alone.

I told myself keeping my distance was safer for her. But now it looks like that was a lie.

My stomach begins to churn. It's a good thing I didn't eat any of the food Tristan prepared, because it would be threatening to make a return appearance now. I swallow hard to keep down the bile.

Is the grand master really sadistic enough to kill my mother, just to fuck with me? Just to antagonize Tristan?

I look at Tristan. With his amped-up vampire hearing, he's surely caught most of my convo with Cat. And he's definitely hearing the TV news report.

I hope he's going to allay my fears. Tell me I'm jumping to conclusions. Only, he meets my gaze with grave eyes. His mouth is a grim line, his body rigid. His hands curl into tight fists at his sides.

Obvi, we're connecting the same dots.

No. No, no, no, no, no. She can't be dead. She just can't be.

I start to make all sorts of deals in my head.

Just let my mother be alive, I think. *And I'll treat her better. Spend more time with her. Clean up my fucking language.*

But who am I even dealing with? The all-powerful, psychopathic leader of an undead army?

I throw up a little in my mouth.

"Lil?" says Cat. "Are you still there?"

I swallow again. "Yeah," I say darkly. "But, um, my mother is missing."

• • • • •

While I frantically call and text my mother—to no avail—Tristan pulls out his own phone, does a quick internet search, and determines that the unidentified female from the subway attack would have been brought to the city morgue over on the East Side.

"We're here," announces Tristan.

I don't really remember the drive—or even the walk from my apartment to his car. And I'm only vaguely aware of being shuffled out of the passenger seat, through the automatic doors of Bellevue Hospital, and down into its basement.

The long, subterranean corridor is gray in color but unexpectedly bright, lit by fluorescent ceiling fixtures. One of the bulbs flickers ominously on and off, buzzing overhead like a Jedi light saber, providing a spine-tingling soundtrack. With Tristan propelling me forward, his hand gently cradling my elbow, we arrive at the gunmetal-gray desk at the end of the hallway.

"May I help you?"

The gentleman who looks up at us is gray too. Gray hair, gray eyebrows, gray scrubs. I swear, even the guy's skin has a gray tinge to it. Seriously, it's like we've just walked into an old black-and-white horror movie.

I shiver.

Tristan releases my elbow and slides his arm around me. Without breaking eye contact with the attendant, he runs his palm in a comforting, warming gesture up and down my upper arm.

I shiver again—but, um, not for the same reason.

What kind of a horrible daughter am I? I wonder, steeling myself against the allure of Tristan's touch. *Am I seriously getting butterflies when my mother could be lying dead on a slab?*

"Tristan Newberry," announces Tristan. "And Lily Baines. We're here to identify the body from the subway."

After a beat, the attendant says, "Yes. Of course."

He gets to his feet and walks to a door labeled *Morgue*. We follow, waiting as he punches a key code into the numerical pad. The lock releases with a *pop*.

He pulls the door open, unleashing the stench of formaldehyde, bleach, and, well, death. When Tristan tightens his hold on me, I realize I'm swaying on my feet.

"Okay?" he asks. He looks down at me solicitously, eyes filled with concern.

I nod. Try to get a grip. Take shallow breaths through my mouth. I need to do this, goddammit. I need to do this.

The attendant leads us into the stainless-steel facility. We play follow-the-leader through the maze of examination tables—and thank Christ, they're all unoccupied. No grisly postmortems in progress. Our short trek ends in front of a wall of drawers.

Tristan holds up the hand that isn't busy supporting me. "Give us a moment, please."

The creepy guy stops cold, his hand poised on one of the drawer pulls.

"No, no. It's okay," I say. "I'm okay. Please. I just want to get this over with."

Tristan's eyes linger over me, assessing, before he acquiesces with a shrug. "As you wish," he says. He turns back to the morgue attendant, whom I've decided to call Igor. "Proceed."

Igor comes back to life and hauls the drawer open. Inch by inch, he reveals a grayish-white sheet draped over a form that's unmistakably a dead body.

My insides curdle.

Igor grips the top of the sheet and slowly folds it back. I see the top of a head of dyed blond hair begin to peek out from underneath. The hair is the same shade as my mother's. My heart drops.

The morgue worker continues to lower the sheet, exposing…*a face?* It's so badly marred with bite marks that, if it weren't framed by the blond hair, it would be hard to tell.

I want to look away, but I make myself focus. I try to look past the flesh wounds to the features.

Recognition shoots through me like a lance. Recognition—and confusion.

My mother looks at least twenty-five years younger. At first, I think maybe death-by-vampire-attack has done what Dr. Andrews and his battalion of chemical injections never really could…?

"It's okay, Lily," says Tristan. "It's not her."

I turn to him. "How—"

Then I remember. Duh. He met her two nights ago.

I look back at the body and blink a few times to clear my vision. Tristan is right, of course. It's not my mother. But there was a reason for my initial jolt of recognition.

Although it's not my mother, I do identify the victim.

"I know," I say. "It's Kelly." I turn to Igor. "It's Kelly Kohl, um, Matheson. This woman is Kelly Matheson."

CHAPTER 32

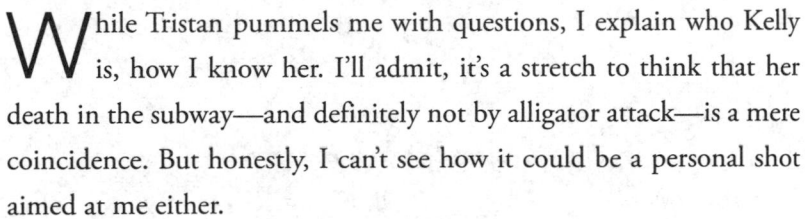

While Tristan pummels me with questions, I explain who Kelly is, how I know her. I'll admit, it's a stretch to think that her death in the subway—and definitely not by alligator attack—is a mere coincidence. But honestly, I can't see how it could be a personal shot aimed at me either.

"So, she wasn't a friend of yours?" asks Tristan.

"No," I say.

I feel the twinge of guilt as soon as I say it. I mean, it's true. Kelly and I were never close. Just the opposite, really. But it's in pretty piss-poor taste to be saying so—and so bluntly—right next to her corpse.

I stare back down at Kelly's brutalized body. And I wonder why the two of us weren't friends. On paper, we should have been. Really, we had more in common than not.

And then I realize maybe that's why.

When I looked at her, I saw myself. And since I was so at odds with myself, well, how could I have been friends with her?

"Okay, then," says Tristan. "We're done here."

I watch as Igor pulls the sheet back up and over Kelly's face, and I feel a genuine sense of loss. I wish we could have been friends back then.

I would've liked to have been friends now.

Tristan starts to lead me away—and at first, I let him. But then, something is off. Something is bugging me. I stop and stay planted where I am.

"Wait, wait, wait," I say. "Don't I need to fill out some kind of identification papers or something?"

"Right," says Tristan. "Just in case our enemies forget how to find you, let's leave them a paper trail."

"I wasn't asking you," I tell him. "I was asking, um…"

My voice trails off as I see the creepy morgue attendant pushing the human-sized file drawer back into the wall. I swear, he might as well be sleepwalking.

Sleepwalking…?

I spin on Tristan. "You're using your influence on him!"

Tristan doesn't even flinch. "Well, of course, I'm using my influence on him."

"Why would you do that?" I ask, astounded. "Why would you do that when you know how I feel about that?"

"To protect you," he says. His favorite comeback.

"And you know how I feel about *that*," I say. "I don't need your protection."

And just like that, it's as if all the progress we've made toward each other over the past few nights is wiped clean, and we're right back where we started. He's somewhere back in old-timey times, and I'm halfway up a tree.

Tristan gives me an exasperated look, like I'm the one being unreasonable here.

"If you would just listen to me—"

"If you would just talk to me—"

See? I swear, it's like we're caught in a loop.

He nods over at Igor. "This is for his protection, too, you know."

The thing is, in my head, I kind of do know that. Legit, the guy probably *is* safer if he has no memory of Tristan and me being here. Kelly's body is prime evidence of that.

And yes, okay, maybe I'm safer this way too.

But still, in my heart, I don't like it. I don't like this pathological need of Tristan's to protect me, a need that respects no boundaries.

I think about what Raven told me, about how the woman he loved died in a fire and he was too late to save her. Okay, so maybe he doesn't want another death on his conscience—but still, that's no excuse.

I start to work up a pretty good argument about the whole mind-invasion thing—although, if I'm honest, that's not even what's troubling me the most.

I look again at poor Igor. The eyes staring back at me are totally vacant. Is this what Tristan tried to turn me into that first night we met?

More to the point, is this what he'd really prefer me to be? Some empty husk of a person who won't trouble her pretty little head about anything. No independent thoughts, no ideas of my own. Compliant to his every whim.

Is that his type?

I think of the angelic, blond-haired beauty from the Tristan Newberry retrospective I saw last night, courtesy of his blood. I try to imagine her challenging his authority. Defying him at every turn. Telling him to fuck the fuck off.

Nope. I can't see it.

"Lily," says Tristan softly. "We should go."

I point at Igor. "But what about him," I argue.

What can I say? I can't be some Alexa or Siri who just does Tristan's bidding. Even if what he's bidding is probably the smart move.

"He'll be fine," says Tristan. "He'll come out of it after we go. But we have to *go*."

He looks at me sternly with those penetrating indigo eyes. I know he can't use his influence on me. But I have to wonder… *Does he wish he could?*

• • • • •

Back in Tristan's car, I pull out my iPhone so I don't have to talk to him. I don't really want to fight with him, but I don't know how *not* to fight right now.

Still no word from my mother, I see. I text her again.

Where r u???

Then, I remember I thought she might be dead.

Love u 😘😘😘

As long as I'm at it, I text my boss too. Obvi, I can't go into the office while my mother is still missing. I tell Peter I'm busy tracking down some leads on that vampire story. Not *exactly* a lie.

"You're awfully quiet," says Tristan after we've been driving a while.

"Yeah," I snap. "How do you like it?"

He frowns.

My phone pings. It's a text alert. Finally, a response from Mom.

I stare at the words, but they don't make any sense. I want to write it off as a bad case of autocorrect. Only…my gut is saying that it's something way worse.

"Pull over," I whisper to Tristan.

"What?"

"Pull over," I repeat. "Pull over! *Pull over!*"

He cuts me a questioning look but obediently swerves to the curb. Somehow, even on the fly like this, he finds a legal parking space.

"What's wrong?" he asks when we're stopped.

I hand over my iPhone.

Eyeballing the screen, he scans the words enclosed in the conversation bubble. Then, suddenly, it's like he has some kind of an internal vacuum that powers up and sucks all the ease out of his expression. Only sharp, chiseled lines remain.

"Gideon," Tristan hisses. He thrusts the phone back into my hands. "Gideon has your mother."

I peer down again at the text message. I make myself focus and reread the words. This time, I imagine that the sender isn't my mother, but the grand master of the Vampire Council.

Present yourselves, and I'll make a trade.

Tonight. Midnight. Track 61.

"So…Gideon kidnapped my mother?" I ask numbly. "And the ransom is—"

"Us." Tristan's voice is calm, but there's an undertone of anger. Cold, lethal anger. "This is his final move against me. He's using your mother as bait to ensnare us both."

I remember what Tristan told me that first night of my undead life, when I battered him with all those questions: *if and when the grand master wants you to appear before the council, you'll know it.*

New questions pop into my head—slowly at first, then all at once, like popcorn kernels exploding in a pan of hot oil.

Is my mother okay?

Does she know I'm a vampire?

How did Gideon's vampires find her?

Were they hunting for me?

If Tristan and I do what the grand master asks, will he really let my mother live?

Will he kill us?

And what the fuck is Track 61?

Apparently, I say that last one out loud.

"It's an abandoned underground train track in Grand Central Terminal," says Tristan. "Beneath the Waldorf Astoria Hotel. Back in the day, when train travel was the way to go, VIPs with private railway cars could bypass the station, pull up to the platform, and go directly up into the hotel through a special elevator."

Under different circumstances, I might be fascinated. Now? Not so much.

"The grand master is holding my mother hostage in an abandoned underground train tunnel?" I demand, horrified.

This is all my fault, I think. *My mother's life is in danger, and it's all my fault.*

"Lily," says Tristan. "I swear to you on my immortal life, I'm going to get her out of this safely. I'm going to get you both out of this safely."

He leans toward me, but I shrink back against the passenger side door.

"Don't make promises you can't keep," I say warily.

He balks a little at that but quickly recovers. "It's going to be okay."

"We save my mother," I say to Tristan. "Do you understand me? We do whatever it takes to save her."

And FYI, my commitment to this is 100 percent real.

Oh, I know I haven't exactly painted a rosy picture of my relationship with Rose Baines—and I'm not going to go back on it now. My mother is a huge pain in my ass. But you know what? I'm willing to bet that's true for almost everyone. Personally, I think any woman who says her mother is her best friend is totally full of shit.

Obvi, my mother is not my BFF. She's the one who makes me batshit. Drives me mad. Sets me off. She's the one who presses all my buttons—mostly because she's the one who programmed them all in the first place. But make no mistake: none of this means that I don't love my mother. Or that I won't do everything I can to get her back.

"We do whatever it takes," I tell Tristan. "Even if it means we both die."

"It won't come to that," he says.

"You don't know that!" I spit back at him. "Jesus. This isn't one of your historical romances where you control the narrative and everything comes up sunshine and rainbows and unicorns. If this doesn't end well, you can't just rewrite history."

Tristan blinks. Studies me for a moment. Then he asks carefully, "Did my blood show you something last night?"

The question catches me off guard. It brings up squishy, complicated emotions I don't really want to get into right now. Not while my mother is in jeopardy.

"Um, what?"

"My blood," says Tristan. "Did it show you something after you drank?"

Blond hair. Sweet face. Petite.

Loved.

Gone. Long gone.

But still so very, very loved.

I swallow. Nod.

"Something from my past?" he asks.

"Someone," I manage to say. "A vampire. A female vampire."

"Marianna?"

"Is Marianna kind of a mash-up of Marilyn Monroe and Little Bo-Peep?" I ask.

He smiles a little sadly. "Yes."

"Then, um, yes."

He frowns deeply. "So, is that why you've been so distant with me since you woke?"

"Is that why you don't believe in happily ever after?"

And don't judge me too harshly, but even now, with my mother's life on the line, I kind of want Tristan to reassure me. To tell me that last night meant something. That I mean something. Even if I'll never mean *everything*.

And the way he looks at me makes me think he's going to say what I want to hear.

Only, he doesn't.

But, at the same time…he does.

"I lost someone I loved deeply," he says. "But I won't let you experience the same kind of tragedy. I will save your mother. And you too, Lily. Whatever it takes."

CHAPTER 33

As we merge back into traffic, the clock on Tristan's dashboard reads 8:02 p.m. Less than four hours until Gideon's ominous deadline.

I push thoughts of Marianna aside and ignore my hurt feelings while I concentrate on how to deal with our current cluster. Only—surprise, surprise—Tristan wants to park me back at his place like some toddler at day care and handle things on his own.

"Fuck you," I tell him. "I'm not sitting around on the sidelines while my mother is in danger. If you have a plan, I'm in. And I'm coming with."

Tristan sighs. "Can't you just do what I ask for once?"

"Can't you just drop the patriarchal bullshit for once?"

"I'm trying to protect you."

"Again, I don't need you to protect me," I say. "I need you to respect me."

"We don't have time to argue—"

"So, stop arguing," I say. "My mother, my call."

The clock on the dash blinks. 8:03 p.m.

"So, where are we going?" I ask.

Finally, Tristan gives in. “To see Raven.”

“Raven?” I ask.

“After last night, she owes us,” he says. “She owes *you*. Time to collect.”

It makes perfect sense, I know. Really, it’s the logical move. It’s the whole reason we went to see her last night. Time to rally the allies and all.

Only, I don’t want to face her. Not now that everything she told me about Tristan—everything she *warned* me about Tristan—has turned out to be totally on the money. I mean, he’s all but admitted he’s still head over heels for Marianna. Hell, I can feel the proof of his love for her literally under my skin.

I swear, if Raven calls me into her torture chamber of an office for another fun chat and invites me to join the Tristan Newberry Ex Club, I’m going to hang myself in one of her scary chairs.

Question: Can you even be someone’s ex if you were never officially…together?

Oh, but I know, I know, I have to suck it up and deal. My mother has been kidnapped. I need the help. I need Raven’s help.

“I just want to make a quick pit stop at home,” I tell Tristan as I pull my cardigan tighter around me.

If we’re going to see Raven, I’m at least putting on a bra.

• • • • •

I’m not even surprised when Tristan pulls into an open spot right in front of my doorstep. But I am surprised—and in a good way—when I spy my bestie sitting on said doorstep, scrolling through her iPhone.

“Cat!”

I’m up and out of the sports car before Tristan even shifts it into park.

"Lil!" Cat shoves her phone into one of the big pockets of her utility jacket and jumps to her feet. She wraps me up in a big hug. This close, I get a major whiff of her blood—but after last night's feeding, the scent is more of a comfort than a temptation.

"Your mother?" she asks the top of my head.

"It wasn't her," I say. I bury my face in her shoulder, in the rough khaki fabric, and hug her back. "It wasn't my mother's body."

"Oh, thank God." Cat gives me one last squeeze before she lets me go. "So, did you find out where she disappeared to?"

Tristan joins us on the sidewalk. "Unfortunately, yes."

• • • • •

I make the official introductions as we head inside my building. Tristan greets Cat with the same kind of polite indifference guys usually aim my way. Jesus, he must really be hung up on the lovely Marianna if he's immune to Cat's obvious charms.

Whatever.

Once we're all inside my place, I let Cat in on the latest plot twists. Kelly Kohl Matheson, dead. My mother, kidnapped.

"Kidnapped?" she asks. "Lily…what can I do to help?"

Tristan pulls out his car key and offers it to her. "Can you drive a stick?"

"Oh, no," I say. I step between him and my friend, blocking the key exchange. "We've already been through this. Where you go, I go."

"Please," says Tristan. "Be reasonable. Let your friend drive you back to my place. Or to her place. Or to some other place where you'll be out of harm's way. You don't need to get mixed up in Gideon's personal vendetta against me."

"Against *you*? Who's been on the receiving end of the death threats?"

I ask. "Whose mother is being used to bait a trap? No." I shake my head vehemently. "Gideon might have unfinished business with you, but he made this personal against *me*. I want that asshole's blood. And not to drink."

Then I turn to Cat. "I'll be two secs. Don't let the vampire leave without me."

• • • • •

Obvi, I'm gone a little longer than two seconds.

Rounding the corner of my L-shaped studio, I'm careful to keep my speed to human-quick as I remove my cardigan, then my T-shirt. I mean, assuming I survive past midnight, I can't afford to replace my entire wardrobe.

I fling open my undies drawer and pluck up the first bra I see—a black sports bra. And after a beat of hesitation, I grab a pair of black panties too. I mean, in addition to not wanting to show up at The Crypt all basic and braless, I'd rather not have the distraction of Tristan's sweats rubbing up against my bare butt cheeks while I'm trying to kick some grand master ass.

Hopping up and down on one foot, then the other, I yank off my boots. Then, I drop trou and don the underthings. And since I'm already undressed, I figure I might as well replace my current ensemble with something a little more conducive to, um, ass-kicking.

I pull open another drawer and dig into my cache of workout gear. I wriggle into a pair of black Fabletics leggings. A black, long-sleeved, moisture-wicking Under Armour shirt. Then I step into my Nikes and find a ponytail holder to pull my wild curls blindly up into a topknot.

My transformation to badass vampire ninja warrior assassin takes three, maybe four minutes max.

But when I return, Cat is standing in the middle of my apartment, frowning down in confusion at the car key in her hand. And You-Know-Who is nowhere to be seen.

"Where did Tristan go?" I ask.

Cat looks up at me. She opens her mouth to say something—but then she just closes it again and shakes her head, dumbfounded. "I have no friggin' idea."

CHAPTER 34

I can't believe Tristan used his influence on Cat.

Seriously, we just talked about this—and I'm pretty sure I told him exactly how I felt. If I was angry about him using influence on a perfect stranger, how did he think I was going to feel about him using it on my best friend?

Obvi, he just doesn't care.

He doesn't care about my feelings or opinions or ideas. He just cares about being the all-knowing, all-powerful, all-up-in-my-business vampire master, calling all the shots for the silly little newbie.

As far as vampire masters go, he's like the helicopter parent from Hell.

Whatever.

If Tristan would rather go talk to Raven without me, let him. I wasn't exactly looking forward to seeing the club owner again anyway.

And now I have some time and space to maybe figure out a plan of my own to rescue my mother.

With a little help from my friend.

Cat is next to me, in the driver's seat of Tristan's car, circling her block for a parking spot. After she recovered her wits, she convinced me that since my mother probably invited her captors into my apartment, hers would be a safer place to, um, strategize. If we ever get there, that is.

See, in addition to not being able to find street parking, we've just stalled out for the third time.

"I thought you knew how to drive a stick," I tell Cat over the urban symphony of car horns erupting behind us.

"I do," she says a little indignantly. "I'm just out of practice, is all."

To get us moving again, my friend is working the gearshift with an indelicacy that I'm sure is doing some kind of permanent damage to Tristan's auto. Serves him right.

"I still can't believe that sneaky son of a bitch used his influence on you to get me out of the way," I say.

"He just wants you to be safe, Lil."

"He just wants me to be submissive."

"Well, that could be fun," she says. "You know, in a *Fifty Shades of Grey* kind of way."

I shoot her a withering look. I've already filled her in on last night's blood-fueled sex-capades with Tristan, including the greatest-hits medley that was the unexpected aftereffect of drinking from his vein.

At last, the car rumbles back to life.

"I just think it's a mistake to write Tristan off completely," says Cat, circling again. "I don't care what you think his blood showed you. There's got to be something you're missing."

"My mother," I remind her. "I'm missing my mother."

"And Tristan is totally on a mission to get her back for you," says Cat.

"Yeah," I say. "A solo mission."

"Still," she says. "It's so obvious that he cares for you."

"No," I say. "He doesn't."

He cares for Marianna. And it's not just because she's sweeter and lovelier than I'll ever be—although I can't help thinking that's part of it. But having died centuries ago, Marianna also escaped modern influence. Not *vampire* influence. Human influence. The suffragette movement. Feminism. #metoo. She left this world at a time when most women simply did what they were told.

It seems to me that Tristan is pining away for that time almost as much as he's pining away for her. I know Raven thinks Tristan is writing those historical romance novels to rewrite his own history. But me? I think he's writing them not so much to rewrite history as to revisit it. Relive it. Revel in it.

And not just Tristan. From the influence thing to the master thing to the whatever-Gideon-says-goes thing, it seems like all of vampirekind is seriously behind the times.

The dash says 8:55 p.m. About three hours until midnight.

Cat downshifts to turn the corner, and we start to stall again.

"You know what? Fuck it. Just park it in the bus zone," I say. It's pretty clear we're not going to have anywhere near Tristan's good luck finding a spot. "If the car gets towed, that's Tristan's problem. Let him influence his way out of *that*."

• • • • •

At Cat's, we try to talk through some options and come up with a plan, but nothing really gels. Once again, I bring up my idea of writing a scathing exposé of the vampire underworld and using it to barter with the grand master—this time, for my mother's life. But once again, Cat nixes it. And, admittedly, I'm not sure how scathing an exposé I can crank out before Gideon's midnight deadline.

"The pen isn't always mightier than the sword, Lil," says Cat.

"Sword?" I say as a light bulb goes off in my head. "As in…fiery sword, maybe?"

"What?"

My eyes drift over to those shelves upon shelves of Cat's action figures.

"Sometimes, they team up, right?" I hear myself asking.

"Huh?"

I get up from the couch and walk over to the display. Randomly, I pick up one of the boxed figures. It's a huge, rock-skinned hulk of a guy, one of the Fantastic Four.

My friend is next to me so fast it's almost like she has vampire superspeed. "What are you doing?" she asks, an uncomfortable edge creeping into her voice. She gently takes the box from me, uses her shirt to wipe off my fingerprints, and replaces it on the shelf.

I swear, if I manage to survive this night, I am so going to give her incredible amounts of shit for acting like she cares more about the Thing than about me. But right now, my brain is racing, remembering that stupid discussion from Saturday night with the downtown hipsters, the one about the Avengers versus, um, *not* the Supreme Court.

"Superheroes," I say. "Sometimes they join forces, right? Even when they don't necessarily see eye to eye. Because they want the same outcome. Like, the enemy of my enemy is my friend, right?"

"Uh, sure," says Cat. She starts to launch into a detailed analysis of *End Game*, but I cut her off. And not because of spoilers.

"I need to call Evan," I say. I go back to the couch, where I left my bag, and dig around inside for my phone.

"Evan?" says Cat. Her face scrunches up in confusion. "I'm pretty sure work can wait."

That's when I realize I haven't brought her up to speed about everything. What with my mother getting kidnapped, plus all the drama with Tristan, I've forgotten to fill her in on a key piece of the story.

"No, see… Evan is a vampire slayer," I say.

Cat's eyebrows shoot up and her eyes go wide. "Excuse me?"

Quickly, I top-line it for her. Evan's new muscles. Skin so hot you could fry an egg on it.

"Sounds like a werewolf," says Cat.

"Thank you," I say, feeling a little vindicated. "But, no."

I fill her in on the rest. The inhuman look in his eyes. The showdown at The Crypt. And how, apparently, his transformation is supernaturally linked with mine.

She just gapes at me. Open mouth. Speechless.

"Seriously," I say, nodding. "Like my own personal Buffy."

I find my iPhone. But before I can dial, Cat grabs it out of my hand.

"Hey!" I say. "Give that back."

Cat shakes her head. "You promised me you wouldn't go and do anything stupid."

"What are you talking about?" I ask.

"Lily," she says. "I hate to break this to you, but vampire slayers slay vampires."

"Exactly."

Obvi, I'm thinking about Grand Master Gideon and whatever other bloodsuckers are holding my mother captive.

"And, uh, *you* are a vampire," says Cat.

Aha! Now, I see what she's getting at.

"Sounds like you got lucky once," Cat says sternly. "Don't push it."

"No, no," I say. "See, I don't think it was luck. I mean, you know that saying about how there's a thin line between love and hate?"

Cat just looks at me, not sure where I'm going with this.

That kind of makes two of us, but I keep talking, trying to puzzle it all out.

"Well, I don't know… It's like Evan and I have this connection now. And it's supposed to make us enemies. But maybe it could also make us allies?"

My friend seems unconvinced.

"I mean, I'm a vampire, right? I'm supposed to drink blood from humans, from their veins. Only, I found a way around that.

"And yes, okay, Evan is a vampire slayer. *My* slayer. He's supposed to want to slay me. Only, he didn't at The Crypt. I found a way to reach him. So, maybe I can help him find his own path too?

"And then maybe we can both find a way to work together," I conclude. "Instead of killing each other."

Cat surveys me for a few moments, brows creased together in thought. "Lil," she says finally, "you're talking about blowing up centuries of vampire-slayer history."

I think about this. Slowly, a big grin spreads across my face.

"So, what do you say?" I ask. "You in?"

• • • • •

For my safety, Cat insists on meeting Evan in a public place. She figures he won't try to slay me in front of people, especially if there's a chance they could become collateral damage.

"Slayers protect humans," she informs me in her TED-Talk voice. "At all costs."

Since Evan hasn't tried to attack me in front of the TakeABite.com staff, I figure she might be on to something. So, I choose the popular diner a few blocks uptown, on Broadway, as our rendezvous point.

Cat and I walk in, and like all good diners, it smells of strong coffee and breakfast on the griddle—even though it's dinnertime. The aromas sweep me up in an unexpected surge of nostalgia. See, my mother waits tables in a diner that smells just like this one. Always has, as far as I know. I spent my prepubescent after-school hours doing homework in one of her booths. In my head, I can still see the cracks in its maroon upholstery, haphazardly mended over with silver duct tape. I used to sneak sugar packets with the state birds on them when Mom wasn't looking because she was already monitoring my daily caloric intake.

Weirdly, the memory warms me.

"You okay?" asks Cat.

I swallow and nod with renewed determination. Dammit, I'm getting my mother back.

We snag a booth by the window, sitting together on the same side, facing the door. Cat orders a hot chocolate. I order fries, French toast, and a double-chocolate shake. The server gives me *that* look, the judgmental one, but for the first time ever, I really don't give a fuck. I mean, I could *die* tonight. If this is my death-row meal, so to speak, I'm making sure it's a good one.

Just then, the door opens, and the bell above it tinkles.

I spot him before he spots me. I nod toward the door. "Evan," I whisper to Cat.

He pauses by the register and looks around. I know the exact moment he sees me because, for a nanosecond, the eyes behind his glasses do that retinas-on-fire thing.

"Hell's bells," murmurs Cat.

"Right?" I say. I assume she caught the same look I did.

As he walks over to our table, I wonder if I should have told him to leave the fire sword at home. But then I wonder if that would even be possible. I mean, is it like a lighter that he carries with him and flicks on and off? Or does he just manifest the thing as needed, straight out of thin air?

I think about asking him, but it seems like the kind of slayers' club members-only info he might not be allowed to share with a vampire. So, maybe I'll ask Tristan—if I ever decide to speak to him again, that is.

"Lily," says Evan by way of hello.

"Evan. Hey. Thanks for meeting me."

Things between us are a little stilted.

"Sit down," I say. "Please." I gesture at the red vinyl banquette opposite. "This is Cat, by the way," I add, indicating my BFF.

Evan barely glances at her as he slides into the seat across from us. The booth creaks under the weight of his large frame.

"I'm Cat," says my bestie—both unnecessarily and a little too loudly. At first, I think it's just because she's nervous. And really, why wouldn't she be? I mean, vampires and slayers and grand masters—*oh, my!*

But when I turn to her, I see that she's blushing.

Then I get it.

My best friend is basically fangirling on Evan. And given her fascination with fantasy, superheroes, and paranormal romance, I guess I shouldn't be surprised.

Meanwhile, Evan is beginning to look distinctly uncomfortable. Focused on me, he gestures in Cat's direction. "So, is this your, uh, *blood donor*?"

"What?"

Then I see what he's implying.

So, that's what's making him so uneasy!

"Cat is my *friend*," I say, setting him straight. "I don't drink from her. Or anyone, um, *living*."

I watch as he processes this.

"But don't you *have to*?" he asks.

The question is about me. Only, I get the feeling that the answer he's seeking is about him and his own impulses too. So, I figure this is my chance to launch my campaign for improving vampire-slayer relations.

"What I've discovered," I say slowly, "is that you don't have to do anything you don't want to do."

"But the urges—"

"Are real," I say. "But they can be controlled. Or satisfied in other ways."

We look at each other across the table. Then Evan nods. He seems to relax a little.

"Here we go."

The black-clad server returns with Cat's hot chocolate, my shake, and my heaping plates of carbs and sugar and fat. After he plunks it all down, he turns to Evan. "Ready to order?"

Evan looks from me to my food, then back to me. But there's no disapproval in his gaze. Rather, there's—dare I say it? Understanding.

Because, really, the pair of us are like two sides of the same supernatural coin.

And whatever happens tonight? He's got to be thinking there's a chance this could be his last meal too.

"Same," he says, pointing at my order.

I'm pretty sure it's the first thing we've ever agreed on.

CHAPTER 35

Truth is, I wasn't 100 percent sure Evan would show.

When I called and asked him to meet me, I tried to appeal to his new instincts as a slayer. I gave him the big picture of what I wanted to discuss, luring him with the opportunity to (1) protect my human mother and (2) kill her vampire abductors.

But even when he walked into the diner, I wondered why he was really here. Was he genuinely willing to hear me out? And maybe work with me? Or was he just playing along, waiting for an opening to whip out his flaming sword and barbecue my bloodsucker butt?

Now, as we eat and talk, I realize he does have an ulterior motive. Only, it's not the one I suspected.

"I think the vampires who are holding your mother are the same ones who killed Kelly Matheson," he says.

Cat and I exchange a look.

"You know about that?" I ask him. "You know Kelly?"

He nods as he takes a sip of his shake. "We grew up together. She's my oldest, closest friend," he says. "Or, she *was*."

At that, his eyes flare up again, and I worry that our little vampire-slayer summit might be in trouble.

But then Cat reaches across the table and places her hand on top of his. She doesn't have stars in her eyes anymore. She looks at him with genuine compassion.

"I'm so sorry," she says. "I'm sorry for your loss."

Her touch and her voice and I guess the sheer reminder of her presence—her *human* presence—seem to have a calming effect on Evan. When his eyes settle back to normal, they're still focused on Cat. He adjusts his glasses, and—*boom!* It's like he notices her for the first time.

And not just her beauty. Her kindness.

"Thanks," he says. His gaze softens.

"I only knew her a little," says Cat, and her eyes lock with his. "We all went to college together. I hadn't seen her in years. But Lily ran into her just last night."

"Yeah," I say, trying to reinsert myself into the conversation. I'm starting to feel a little like a third wheel. "I saw her in the lobby, on my way into work." Now, my strange chance encounter with Kelly makes more sense. "So, she was there to meet you?"

"She was," says Evan. He pulls his hand out from under Cat's and drags his focus away from her, readjusting himself in his seat. "I called Kelly after Peter gave my vampire story to you. Arranged to meet her the following night. What can I say?" He shrugs. "Losing that assignment pissed me off. So, I shared what I had with her. I figured Kelly and I could work on the story together, and maybe I could parlay our collaboration into a job at Matheson."

"You'd want to work at Matheson?" I ask. It's off topic, I know, but it just doesn't seem to fit.

"I thought it might be nice to work with a friend," he says in a way that sounds like it might be an insult at me.

So, I figure I should get back on topic, ASAP. "So, um, you and Kelly were following up on your story leads?"

After a moment, Evan nods. "The plan was, I'd take The Crypt and she'd check out the tunnels."

I recall the wounds on Kelly's lifeless face, and I start to imagine just what she found in those tunnels. I put my fork down. Suddenly, I'm not in the mood to eat anymore.

"And as for me, well, the closer I got to The Crypt, the less I was operating on journalistic instincts. And the more I was operating on these other instincts I didn't understand."

I feel his pain. He must be so confused. And have so many questions. "Do you at least have a mentor or something?" I ask. I stop myself before I add "like Buffy."

"Not that I know of."

"And you don't have a best friend anymore to lean on," adds Cat, all empathy.

"Do you have anyone you can talk to about your, um, situation?" I ask.

He laughs sadly. "Who would even believe it?"

"I would," says Cat. She glances over at me. "I mean, I did."

"Well, then," says Evan, "you must be a truly extraordinary friend."

He smiles at her shyly.

Cat beams back.

And yes, okay, I see what's going on here. And it's not as if I have anything against it. But—hello? This is so not the time for a meet-cute. Midnight is approaching.

I need to get this runaway train back on track. Fast.

But now I know that Evan's rage against these particular vampires isn't just a metaphysical instinct. It's personal—as personal as mine. So, maybe the enemy of my enemy really can be my friend.

"Okay," I say to Evan. "You want revenge for Kelly? Here's what I'm proposing. Meet me down in the subway tunnels. Help me get my mother away to safety. And if anybody tries to stop us? Feel free to slay away."

"I want to say yes," he says. "But you saw me at The Crypt. You saw how out of control I was. I may not be able to distinguish between vampires who want to hurt your mother"—he looks hard at me—"and vampires who don't."

I hear what he's saying. I do. I mean, he is *my* slayer, after all.

"But I stopped you at The Crypt before you could hurt me," I say. "I helped you gain control. So, maybe I could help you again?"

"Maybe," says Evan.

It's not exactly the ringing endorsement I'm hoping for.

But, hey, it is what it is.

And...yes, okay, it's a risk I'm willing to take. I figure my mother's chances of getting out of this alive are better with Evan than without him.

I glance over at the wall. Amid the collage of framed photos of celebrities, local celebrities, and pseudo-celebrities who've eaten here, there's a clock. 9:40 p.m. Just a little over two hours to go.

I turn back to Evan. "Okay," I say. "Let's get ready to slay."

• • • • •

I give Evan the where and the when of my meeting with Gideon. Cat pulls out her iPhone—which, by some kind of an early Christmas miracle, is still charged. She finds some online photos of the mysterious Track 61.

Oh boy! And my mother thought my apartment needed maid service?

We can't find any info about how to get down there, but Evan doesn't think that'll be a problem for him. Recalling how he got into The Crypt, I, um, have to agree.

Then there's nothing to do but settle the bill. I offer to take care of it, but Evan insists on splitting things right down the middle. I choose to take that as a good omen for our partnership.

Out on Broadway, we say our goodbyes.

"Midnight," he says.

I nod. "Midnight."

We walk off in opposite directions, him uptown, Cat and I downtown. But then something starts to nag at me. And it just won't quit.

Before we reach the corner, I turn back. "Evan?" I call after him. "Hold up a sec."

He stops and looks over his shoulder at me.

"Give me one minute," I tell Cat. I motion for her to stay where she is, and I do a light jog back toward him.

"Hey," I say when I arrive in front of him. "I need to tell you something."

I take a deep breath, knowing that what I'm about to say may give him second thoughts about helping me. But I figure the guy has a right to know his own origin story.

"Evan, I'm really sorry, but you're basically in this whole supernatural mess because of me."

Quickly, I tell him what Tristan said. How creating a new vampire can also create a new slayer. And how it's generally someone the new vampire already knows.

Some who's already an adversary.

Evan doesn't say anything.

And I've probably said more than enough.

Only, I keep talking.

"And, you know," I say, "it makes sense. Because even before I became a vampire and you became a vampire slayer, I always felt like you didn't like me very much."

He doesn't deny it.

I take another deep breath. This is my chance to finally get to the bottom of the mystery of why Evan Knowles hates my guts.

Only, asking this is hard.

I mean, I've always told myself that Evan despised me for no good reason. But…what if he has a reason? A good reason?

Okay. Now or never.

"Can I, um, ask why?"

He shifts his weight a little uncomfortably from one of his Vans to the other. But finally, he gives me a one-word answer. "Kelly."

I crinkle my brow, trying to make sense of this one word. "Kelly?" I ask.

Evan rocks back on his heels and regards me through narrowed eyes. "You don't remember the first time we met," he says. "Do you?"

"At work?" I ask.

"Before."

I met Evan before we started working together?

I shake my head.

"I came to visit Kelly for the weekend at NYU," he says. "We were in line in the cafeteria. You walked by, and Kelly introduced us."

All of a sudden, I *do* remember. Kelly made it sound like Evan was her boyfriend—or maybe I just heard it that way. Anyway, I thought it was yet another thing she was rubbing in my face, that she had someone and I didn't.

"We were getting pizza, I think," says Evan. "And you looked down at her tray and you made some comment. Something like, 'Oh, that looks good, but I need to hit the salad bar.' And I know, it sounds like such a small thing. But it had a big effect on my friend."

It does sound like a small thing. But if the roles were reversed? I would have felt judged. I would have felt fat-shamed. I would have felt like shit.

"You have to understand, Kelly had a hard time in high school. She was bullied about her weight. But once she got to college, it seemed like she was finally in a good place. She was coming into her own. And we were having such a great visit. But after running into you? After that comment? She was quiet and self-conscious and withdrawn again. It was like she was back in high school. And I didn't even know you, but I kind of hated you for it.

"And then, one night, I walked into work at Take-a-Bite-dot-com," he says. "And there was that girl who disrespected my best friend."

My first reaction is to try to explain, to defend myself.

Because, seriously, I'm the last person on earth who would disrespect another woman because of her size.

Except, well, that's not entirely true, is it?

Up until lately, I always thought my negative self-image wasn't hurting anybody but me. But just last night, I inadvertently insulted my best friend. And now it looks like back in college, I did the same to Kelly.

Jesus. How many other people have I unknowingly slighted? And for how long?

So, instead, I say, "Wow. I wish I knew how I made her feel. I wish she were still around so I could give her my apologies."

Evan looks at me. Not with his slayer eyes. With his human eyes. "Give her justice," he says. "Give her justice, and that'll make it right."

• • • • •

"So, Evan is kind of interesting," says Cat.

We're back at her place, and the clock on her DVD player says 10:15 p.m.—which may or may not be correct. I swear, Cat hooked up her entire high-tech entertainment wall in about two-and-a-half seconds flat, but she's never quite mastered that whole spring-forward, fall-back thing.

"I mean, he must be an incredibly strong person to be dealing with this slayer stuff all on his own," she says. "Don't you think?"

I see she's not going to give up on this topic.

"You're into him, aren't you?" I ask her. "You're into Evan."

I don't mean for it to come out like an accusation, but it kind of does.

Luckily, my BFF doesn't take my tone personally. She sees me keeping tabs on the time.

"Let's just get through tonight," she says. "We can sort out our love lives later."

I roll my eyes at her.

"Oh, come on. You and Tristan can still work it out," she insists.

Nice of her to think so. Only, I know the clock isn't just ticking down the time until my face-to-face with Gideon. It's also ticking down the time I'll be spending with Tristan.

I mean, even if the worst doesn't happen, even if we make it out of this otherworldly confrontation with our undead asses intact, um, where does that leave Tristan and me?

No place together, that's for sure. He's way too stuck in the past to be with me. And I hate to admit it, but I guess I'm too stuck in my own head to be with him—or maybe anyone.

"Nothing to work out," I say, more dismissive than I feel. "I'm really not his type, Cat—um, no pun intended."

"You know," says Cat, "you really shouldn't compare yourself to Tristan's old flames. You shouldn't let them make you feel small."

I don't want to say it—especially not after that private chat with Evan—but I swear, I can't stop the smart-ass, knee-jerk response that shoots out of my mouth. "They don't make me feel small," I say. "They make me feel huge."

"Ah, Lily. You really need to get over this obsession you have with looks," says Cat. "People are more than their friggin' looks."

"I know," I say. "I know."

"Do you, though? Do you really?"

And I'm not sure if it's the stress of the current situation or what, but suddenly it's like the dam breaks, the floodgates open, and the city walls are breached. My best friend is on a literal tirade.

"My God, when are you going to accept that your body is just your body? It's like the wrapping paper you throw away to get at what's inside. And Lily, there is so much good stuff inside you. You are such a goddamn gift! But it's like…I don't know. You're so messed up, you'd rather just go and exchange all the good stuff inside so you can get some different wrappings."

"Are you done?" I ask after a moment. "Because that was a truly terrible analogy."

"Shut up," she says. "I'm not a writer like you. And besides, you know I'm right."

I shrug. "It's just…I've been down on my body for so long."

"Well, now you have all eternity to turn it around."

"Like that's such a gift," I say.

"It could be," she says.

"Oh, please," I say. "Don't even get me started on my vampire body—and not just about being frozen in size. It's…all of it. Like now, on top of everything else, I'll never see the sun again."

"But you'll see centuries," she says.

"I'll never experience motherhood," I say.

"But you'll experience everything else with jacked-up senses," she says. "And besides, you don't even like kids that much."

That makes me crack a smile. She's not wrong about that.

"Plus," says Cat, "you'll be superfast and superstrong."

"But eventually," I say, "I'll also be super-alone."

"If you are," she says. "it'll have nothing to do with your size or your looks—and everything to do with your attitude. If you want someone to love and accept you, you need to love and accept yourself. Your whole self. Body, mind…and vampire."

I want to make fun of her little Oprah speech—only, I know she has a point.

Plus, tonight of all nights, I really can't let myself get caught up with negative thinking like this. I really can't.

I've got to stay focused on the positives. If I want to see another night—and see my mother again—I'm going to need to draw on all of my, um, *gifts*. Human and vampire.

Just then, Cat's door buzzer buzzes. She crosses over to the intercom and presses the talk button. "Hello?"

"It's Tristan." His deep voice hisses through the box. "May I come up?"

"Sure," says Cat with the hint of a smile. And before I can stop her, she buzzes him in.

CHAPTER 36

I don't even want to know how Tristan found me, how he always seems to find me.

"How did you find me?" I ask him after Cat invites him in. "How do you even know where Cat lives?"

Okay, so maybe I do want to know how he found me. Because I'm starting to wonder if maybe there's something even more nefarious than just stalking going on here. I mean, now that I'm aware of the whole vampire-slayer connection, I wonder if there's some kind of creepy connection between a maker and his, um, made? One that enables Tristan to keep tabs on me like some runaway dog that's been microchipped?

Tristan pulls out his phone and shows me the screen. "Find My Car Key app," he says with a grin.

"Oh!" Cat digs in her pocket and hands his key over.

Whatever.

"So, I spoke with Raven," says Tristan after we all take a seat around Cat's assemble-it-yourself IKEA dining table. His demeanor grows more somber. "I told her how we've been manipulated to appear before Gideon and the council. She says she'll honor her word to help us, and she'll bring along backup."

I frown. Suddenly, I think about this in light of the side deal I just made with Evan. Evan, the slayer who invaded her club. Evan, the slayer who killed her security guard. Evan, the slayer who can't totally control his, um, slayer. Now, bringing him to the fight without giving her fair warning seems like a really shitty thing to do.

"Do you believe her?" I ask Tristan, hoping the answer is no. "Do you believe she'll really follow through?"

"I'm not naive," he says. "But then, neither is she. She's quite a shrewd businesswoman. And she promised us her support—in front of her patrons. If she goes back on that promise now, and word gets out, it won't be good for her reputation. So—for now, at least—I believe she's a dependable ally."

I frown deeper. I have to tell him. I see that now. And not just so he can tell Raven.

For Tristan's own safety, I realize I have to tell him.

This is so not going to go over well.

"What?" says Tristan. "What is it?"

I look over at my friend. "Cat," I say. "Do you think you could give us a minute?"

As usual, my BFF knows just where my head is. She gives me an encouraging smile. "Take as long as you need," she says. She gets up, walks into her bedroom, and closes the door after her to give us some privacy.

Unfortunately, I can't take long. It's 10:27 p.m., according to my iPhone. The DVD player, as it turns out, is only a couple of minutes fast.

"Lily?" prods Tristan.

I get up, and the table's inexpertly assembled legs wobble. Again, that's Cat for you. Einstein's theory of relativity? No problem. Screw pole A in slot B? Incomprehensible.

"Lily?"

"Right," I say. "Well, here's the thing. While you were off talking to Raven, I secured us another supernatural ally."

"What?" says Tristan, genuinely stumped. "Who? Who do you even know?"

"Um, Evan," I say.

"Ev—the slayer?" demands Tristan.

I nod.

"The *slayer*?" he repeats.

"Uh-huh."

"THE SLAYER?"

Tristan gets to his feet, and suddenly, the logic of this whole idea seems as shaky as the IKEA dining table.

"Yes, the slayer," I say a little defensively. "Okay? The slayer. I made an alliance with Evan the vampire slayer. He's going to help me rescue my mother."

"Lily," Tristan says, practically apoplectic with rage. "You can't make an alliance with a slayer."

"There you go again," I say. "Telling me what I can and can't do."

His fury dials up another notch.

"I'm not saying you can't do it to be domineering," he says. "I'm saying you can't do it because it's an absolute impossibility."

"Says who?"

"Says every vampire and slayer who's ever walked the earth."

"Until now," I say.

I swear, I've never seen him this angry before. I didn't know anybody could even get this angry.

"This is bad, Lily," he says. "This is a mistake that could get us all killed."

Jesus. This is going over even worse than I thought.

I'm almost sorry I told him—but then, I remember why I did.

"So, are you going to warn Raven?" I ask in a small voice.

He runs his hand over his beard, back through his hair, trying hard to compose himself. "Yes," he says, somehow reining in his own volume. "Assuming I can catch her." He pulls out his phone. "If she's already underground, she may not have a signal."

I look at the clock. It's past 10:30 p.m.

"So, I guess we should, um, go?"

I brace myself for another argument. But he doesn't protest, doesn't tell me to stay while he goes off and handles it alone. It's like he can't even talk to me.

"Please give my apologies to your friend for the outburst," he says.

He scrolls through his contacts as he heads for the door. It's like he doesn't even want to be in the same room with me anymore.

"And say your goodbyes," he says. "I'll wait for you in the car."

Then, he's gone.

Wow.

A couple of ticks later, the bedroom door creaks open.

"Lil?"

I look over at Cat.

"You did the right thing," she says, walking over.

"Telling Tristan?" I ask. "Or making a deal with Evan?"

"Both, I hope."

Right.

Because, um, this is it.

Tristan told me to say my goodbyes—which, now that I think about it, has a disturbing ring of finality.

I realize that if things go south, this may be the last time I ever see my best friend. And I can tell from the way she's looking back at me that she's rocking the same kind of oh-shit in the pit of her stomach.

"I can't," I choke out. I shake my head. "I can't."

I can't let it out, not any of it. If I do, I'll lose it. And I can't afford a crying jag right now. My mother can't afford it.

Luckily, Cat gets it. Just like she always does.

She nods, blinks back the tears that are starting to well, and puts on a smile so oozing with confidence in me that I want to pack it up in a to-go box and take it with me for later.

"Just do you, Lil," she says. "Do friggin' you."

• • • • •

Somehow, Tristan's car hasn't been towed out of the no-parking zone. It hasn't even been ticketed. I swear, if we get through this, we should bottle his influence over the New York City Parking Authority and sell it on Etsy. We could make a fortune.

But who am I even kidding? It's not as if we'll be seeing each other after tonight.

Especially not now that he knows about the whole slayer thing.

Once we both get settled in his two-seater, I assume we're going to talk battle tactics. But instead, we drive mostly in silence through the night, heading toward Grand Central Station. I get the feeling he's not saying anything because he doesn't want to yell again.

"Did you reach Raven?" I ask finally, breaking the silence.

"I left a voicemail," he says, his voice clipped. "And texted. I haven't heard back."

We drive on again without speaking.

When we're almost there, Tristan finally says, "There's something else we need to discuss."

"Okay," I say.

Game time.

I sit up straighter in my seat, ready to get the final briefing on tonight.

"Before we go down into the tunnel," he says, "I think you need to drink again."

Dammit! I think. *I didn't bring any blood.*

But then, I realize Tristan isn't talking about drinking from my stash of stolen Red Cross donor units. He's talking about drinking from *him*.

Is he out of his mind?

Right now, he can't even look at me. He can barely talk to me. But he expects us to—

"No," I say.

"Lily—"

"No," I repeat. "That is not a good idea."

"You need to be strong," he says. "As strong as you can be."

Yeah, I think. *But at what cost?*

And it's not just because of the current tension between us.

I remember what happened the last time I took his vein. How the blood quashed all my insecurities and doubts. How it silenced all the negative voices, so I could just listen to what I really wanted and choose to take it.

Only now, my insecurities and doubts are my friends. They're what's keeping me safe, what's keeping my heart safe. Because unless I have all the negative voices to tell me otherwise, I know I will go and choose Tristan all over again.

And the more I have him, the more I'll want him.

Now, I'm no expert on immortality, but I'm pretty sure wanting what you can't have is no way to spend all eternity.

So, I need to stand firm here. My "no" has to be nonnegotiable.

Only, Tristan is finally looking at me. He's still angry. But he's still…him. And as he stares across the gearshift at me, I can already feel my resistance wavering.

"My blood will help you be strong for your mother," he says with quiet persuasion.

Seriously? He's playing the mother card?

"Yeah," I mutter. "But that's not all it'll do, and we both know it."

Tristan exhales a frustrated breath and leans back against the headrest, and I watch his long, fluid body slump down in the driver's seat. The leather of his jacket slides against the leather of the seat, making a sound like a frustrated whimper.

Or maybe that's me? Because, um…*yeah.*

"Look," he says to the roof of his vehicle, "after getting that window into my past, I understand why you may not want to be with me again." He pauses, then goes on with difficulty. "And I even understand why you may have gone to the slayer for help. I understand why you may not trust me to protect you." Still reclined, he turns his head toward me. "But my blood can at least offer you some protection."

I find myself sliding down in my own seat, slipping into an almost pillow-talk intimacy with Tristan while my resolve slips down even further.

Jesus. I haven't even drunk from him, and I'm already halfway to attacking him.

I decide to argue logistics.

"It's not practical," I tell him. "I mean, your car doesn't exactly give us privacy. And even if we drove somewhere out of the way, there's no room to, um…" My voice trails off as I glance around the tight space. I have to remind myself that I'm searching for a way to finish my argument, not for a way for us to pretzel our bodies together in these cramped quarters.

"We could get a room," suggests Tristan.

"What?" I say, sitting up straighter.

In answer, Tristan points behind me, out the passenger-side window. It just now dawns on me that we're stopped, and probably have been for a while.

I turn. We're parked directly in front of the ornate, canopied entrance to the Waldorf Astoria Hotel. The hotel that's just above Track 61.

"Are you fucking kidding me?" I ask.

"Lily—"

"This is why," I say, realizing. "This is why you didn't fight me about coming with you to face off with the grand master. You already made this secret little plan."

"You're hardly one to lecture me about a 'secret little plan.'"

Ouch. He's right, of course. But I don't care. Now I'm getting angry.

"Yeah? Well, at least I'm trying to help Evan gain control," I say. "I'm not trying to gain control over him."

"And what if Evan loses control?" says Tristan. "As slayers do. As slayers *always* do. Don't you think it would be a good idea to have the advantage of my blood?"

He's right again. I should drink from him. Only…

"I don't know."

"Dammit, Lily," says Tristan, banging his hand on the steering wheel.

The car horn blares, startling us both.

That's when I realize we have an audience. The doorman, a couple with luggage, and a trio of women grabbing a quick cig outside the hotel are all peering in at us through the car windows, watching our argument with curiosity.

I turn back to Tristan flustered. “Fine,” I say. “Whatever. Let’s get a room. We need to finish this discussion in private.”

CHAPTER 37

Just FYI, the Waldorf Astoria is not exactly the type of hotel that rents rooms out by the hour, which is about all we have 'til midnight. It's an old-school, strictly high-class establishment. Normally, I'd be transfixed by the elegance and grandeur of the recently renovated lobby. But nothing about this situation is *normal.*

With barely a glance up at the sky-high, mural-covered ceiling, I walk across the shiny, pink-marble floor. The soles of my Nikes squeak slightly when I pivot toward the impressive check-in desk to, um, check in. Only, Tristan reaches out a hand to stop me.

He flashes a key card that he pulls out of his pocket and motions me in the opposite direction, toward the elevators. "We can go right up."

It dawns on me that he was gone an awfully long time when he went to The Crypt to chat with Raven. Now, I see it's because he was also here, booking a suite. Presuming I'd simply go along with his idea.

"Planned ahead, I see."

He shrugs and presses the up button.

The doors of the first car glide open, we step inside, and suddenly, I'm absolutely furious.

Maybe it's irrational. I mean, Tristan is right, after all. I do need to be strong. And his blood will give me strength. All he's done here is have the forethought to make the necessary arrangements. But why is he always right in a way that feels so wrong?

Tristan slides the key card into the elevator panel and presses the button for the twelfth floor.

He can't use his influence on me. But I swear, it's like he's still trying to exert influence over me.

I glare across the otherwise empty car at him.

"You are such a hypocrite," I say.

He glares back at me. "Excuse me?"

"You don't like that I went to Evan behind your back," I say. "But I'm supposed to be perfectly okay with this little arrangement you made behind my back?"

"It's hardly the same thing."

"Fuck you."

"Lily," he says, "why does everything need to be an argument between us?"

I want to argue that it doesn't—but then I realize I'll be proving his point.

So, I just continue to stare him down. We stare at each other.

The thing is, I guess there is always some kind of heat swirling between us. Sometimes anger. Sometimes…something else.

There's anger between us now, for sure. But as we face off across the elevator, challenging each other in ways it seems only we can, there's also that other kind of heat. The kind that makes me feel as if I'm going to dissolve from the inside out.

Or…maybe I just have a thing for elevators?

But, no. The atmosphere between us prickles with something volatile. Animal. Irresistible.

And I simply can't resist it anymore.

"Fine," I say thickly. "I'll drink from you."

And we both know what else that means.

I've never had angry sex before. To tell you the truth, I've always thought it was some made-up convention. A thing that happens in romance novels to help move the story along—but not in real life. I mean, how could you possibly be turned on by someone you wanted to throttle with your bare hands?

But my fangs drop fully to confirm it. As angry as I am, I am also totally, ridiculously turned on by Tristan Newberry.

Lucky for him, throttling with bare hands, to my knowledge, is not on the list of things that can kill a vampire.

• • • • •

I don't know what our room looks like. Although under different circumstances I'd be dying to see the inside of one of these ritzy hotel suites, I don't bother to turn on the lights. Even before the door shuts completely behind us, I rush at Tristan, slamming his body up against the wall.

"Do it," he says—and in the darkness, I see the glint of his teeth, fully extended in ecstasy. He drops his head to the side, surrendering his throat to me. "Do it."

This time, there's no hesitation on my part. No preamble. I'm not concerned about hurting him. I kind of want to hurt him, to punish him for loving someone else. I zero in on his jugular and bite down hard, sinking my fangs unceremoniously into his flesh, into his vein.

Tristan moans a moan that skates that exquisite edge between pleasure and pain.

I drink from him with abandon, drawing his life force into me, gulping him down in deep, lusty swallows. The flavor is even more satisfying than I remember. It's intense and powerful and mysterious and complicated and—

Tristan.

It is uniquely Tristan.

And even though I know he holds things back from me, in this moment, he holds nothing back.

"More," groans Tristan. "Take more."

Things don't always flow easily between us, but this? This is somehow so easy. So right.

Such a taste of what things could be.

And that, more than anything else, is what sends me flying over the edge.

I withdraw from him, and for a moment or two, I'm spent. Like some half-drowned swimmer washed up on the shore.

Then it happens. It happens again.

Just like before, my mind becomes absolutely clear, and I know what I want.

I want Tristan.

Without all the drama—real or imagined—clouding my thinking, I have the glorious freedom to choose to do as I please.

With not even the pretense of gentleness, I move in to attack Tristan again—but this time, my target is his mouth. My kisses are like a wordless argument, expressing my needs. His lips reply to mine, not arguing back exactly, but not passive either. More…accepting. Accepting of me.

It's amazing.

So amazing, the rest of my body wants in.

Shamelessly, I lift my leg, opening my center to him, opening myself to him. I grind against him, demanding what I want. But with the difference in our heights, we aren't quite connecting.

Then I feel Tristan's clever hands on my ass, lifting me up off my feet—and suddenly, I feel weightless. Not weightless in the sense that I don't weigh anything at all, but weightless in the sense that my weight is of absolutely no consequence.

He lifts me higher, and I swear, I feel like I'm soaring. And then—

Fuck. Yes.

He positions my core over his erection. I circle my hips, dry humping him—only, okay, that's not quite accurate. Because I don't think I've ever been wetter.

I try to get closer—and we're so in tune, he understands. In a flash, he flips us around.

Now, my back is up against the wall, but I'm still the one driving this. He's listening, his body is listening to mine, so he knows I need that. And he submits to me.

It's not lost on me that, here and now, this unbelievable control freak is so willing to sacrifice control.

And there it is again. That taste of what things could be.

I wrap my legs around him and grab big fistfuls of his messy hair, yanking his head back as I piston myself against him. I want to tear off my clothes, tear off his clothes, and make this pantomime of intercourse the real deal. But despite my overwhelming arousal, somewhere in the back recesses of my brain, I'm still aware enough to remember what happened the last time I succumbed to this urge. I recall the shocking sight of my clothing on the floor in unwearable tatters. Tonight, I didn't bring a wardrobe change—and I really don't want to fight the grand master in a souvenir hotel bathrobe.

I want this to go on forever—but I know it can't, I know there's a clock ticking somewhere. And I won't last much longer anyway.

But when I feel myself shatter, it's like I can almost see forever stretching out ahead of me. It's almost like I can see *this* forever.

Us forever.

When I come back together, I'm wrapped in Tristan's arms.

And, God help me, I don't want to be anywhere else. Ever.

CHAPTER 38

Almost midnight.

I'm crouched down beside Tristan—and no, it's not Round 2 of Hot Angry Vampire Sex. We're on a deserted side street off East Thirty-Fourth, and I'm trying desperately to put Round 1 out of my head as I peer through a grate in the sidewalk.

"That's where it is?" I ask. "Track 61?"

"More or less," says Tristan.

"So, how do we get down there?"

In a single, effortless, clean-and-jerk-type motion, Tristan stoops down, threads his long fingers through the network of heavy steel, and rips it off its metal fastenings like it's no weightier than a gum wrapper.

Show-off.

I lean forward to get a closer look down into the dark depth. But even with Tristan's blood giving me the vampire equivalent of night vision, I don't see what I'm looking for.

"Stairs?" I ask him. I straighten up. "A ladder, maybe?"

"We'll have to jump," he tells me.

Was it just two nights ago that I took that leap of faith with him up to the top of the Empire State Building? If I were to look up from where we're standing now, I'd be able to see the skyscraper's observation deck, the site of our romantic moonlit picnic.

So, I don't look up.

I look down. "That's a three-story drop, minimum."

Tristan puts the grate down with a *clang* and smiles. "You can do it."

Can I? Two nights ago, I wouldn't have thought so.

But a lot has changed in those two nights.

"If you'd like, I can go first and catch you," he offers.

"No thanks," I say quickly.

With my enhanced vampire senses, I can still smell his musky, masculine scent on me. I can still smell the sharp, bittersweet scent of my own arousal. And God knows, it was hard enough prying myself out of Tristan's arms in that hotel room. I can't literally go falling back into them now.

Okay, so my heart doesn't beat anymore. But it still *feels*—maybe more than ever. So, it's just not smart to risk feeling things for someone who will never feel them in return.

And Tristan will never feel those things for me.

In the hotel room, I almost forgot that.

But now, thanks to that hit of his blood, I've got a fresh wave of his love for Marianna crashing through me, reminding me.

God, I just want this night to be over with.

I squint into the gloomy abyss, preparing to jump. "Any tips?"

"Believe," he says. "Embrace your power."

I look at him. It's not really something I'd expect him to say.

And it's a big idea. Almost too big. I mean, most of my life, I've felt powerless. But maybe that wasn't true.

Maybe I gave up my power. To the diet culture and the thin-is-best mentality. To my misguided mother and the Maxes and the Bens of the world.

Maybe my power was there all along. And I just needed to embrace it.

"And bend your knees when you land," he adds.

I can't tell if that's a joke or not.

Whatever.

Embrace my power, I think.

And before I can think any second thoughts, I close my eyes, breathe deeply, and dive into the chasm. Air rushes past me as I drop.

Believe, I think.

I *believe* I'm about to break both my ankles—but maybe they'll just mend again superquick with those amazing vampire powers of recovery?

Then something happens. It's as if time slows down. Or am I slowing time? Because now, I'm not so much dropping as floating. Opening my eyes, I look down and see the ground coming up to meet me—but it doesn't seem to be in any kind of a rush.

I can do this, I think.

And what do you know? I land on my Nikes, as sure-footed as a cat on its paws.

"Okay down there?" comes Tristan's voice from above me.

I raise one foot, then the other. Stretch out my arms, my fingers. Twist my torso. No broken bones. Not even a broken fingernail.

I look up. With my preternatural peepers, I see Tristan silhouetted against the midnight-blue sky. "Yes," I call back with not a little surprise. "All good."

• • • • •

Tristan lands beside me and points down the length of the long-abandoned train tracks. "It's this way," he says. "Track 61."

He starts to walk off, following along the tracks, but I reach out a hand and stop him.

He turns back. "What?"

"Is there anything I need to know?" I ask.

He looks at me blankly for a moment. "What do you mean?" he asks.

"What do I mean?" I demand. "I mean, I'm basically going in blind here, and my mother's life is on the line. Probably mine too. So, is there anything you need to tell me before we do this?"

"I already told you," he says. "I'll save your mother. And I'll save you too."

We're back to that? Seriously?

"Oh. My. God," I say. I don't want to argue with him. I really don't. I want to store up all my fight for the battle ahead. But if I don't get this stuff off my chest now, I may never have the opportunity again. "You just told me to embrace my power. Only, you don't want me to. Not really."

"That's not true," he says.

"Of course, it's true," I say. "Our whole relationship has been like one long episode of *Tristan Knows Best*."

"Funny," he says—but there's no amusement in his voice. "To me, it feels more like an episode of *Lily Knows Best*. I especially like the part where our heroine uses her good judgment to make an alliance with a slayer. Classic."

"Fuck you," I say. "At least I told you about that. You don't tell me anything."

"Would you listen if I did?"

"Listen? Absolutely," I say. "Obey? That's another thing entirely. And that's what you want from me."

"You have no idea what I want from you," he says.

"Because you don't tell me anything!" I say.

We eye each other. We came down into this tunnel to make our stand against the grand master. But now, it seems, we're making one last stand against each other.

"So, again," I say. "Anything you want to tell me?"

Tristan just compresses his lips together in an angry line.

"No? Okay. Well, if you're not going to talk to me, then I have a few things I want to tell you," I say. "The shit you pulled with the influence? First on that morgue guy, then on my best friend? Not cool. Giving me the silent treatment in the car on the ride over here because you were pissed about the slayer? And then springing the hotel room key on me? Not cool. Keeping me in the dark pretty much ever since we met? About things that have a direct effect on me? So. Not. Cool."

"I don't know what you expect me to say to that."

"Don't worry," I say. "I don't expect you to say anything at all."

Tristan shakes his head, blowing out a frustrated breath. "You act like I'm the bad guy," he says. "But everything I've done, I've done to protect you."

"Oh, please," I say. "When are you going to get it? I don't need you to be my hero, Tristan. Because I'm not a victim. Okay, so maybe I didn't choose to be a vampire. But I got here because of my choices. And I'm here now, by choice."

He doesn't say anything. Big surprise.

"You know, it's almost funny," I say. "You write all these romance novels as Delilah Manning. As a woman. From a woman's point of view. But you don't understand women. Not modern women, anyway. And you really don't understand me."

There's a lot going on behind those indigo-blue eyes of his, but I don't know what he's thinking.

So, what else is new?

"Well, if you don't have anything to say, we just should go," I say. "My mother is waiting, and I don't want to be late."

• • • • •

Together—well, physically together—Tristan and I head down the tracks, toward this notorious Track 61. I wish I wasn't still so pissed off at the vampire by my side. I wish he wasn't still silently fuming at me. But maybe we can channel some of the anger we're feeling toward each other and use it against our adversaries.

Unlike the hotel above us, there's been no recent renovation down here. There's no splendor, no opulence. We trudge over what must be decades of debris and muck, kicking up a low-hanging cloud of dirt and decay as we go.

And the smell—*good God, the smell!* If I were still human, the stench would be a horrific offense. But as a vampire—and a vampire whose senses have just been dialed up to ultra-supersensitive, no less, by that infusion of blood—the stink is a near-crippling assault.

The deeper we venture into the tunnel, away from the opening up to the street, the worse the assault to my senses. It's as if the thick, reeking air is pressing in on me, invading my pores and seeping under my skin.

"We're being watched," says Tristan in a low voice. "Do you feel it?"

I do.

I don't see them, but I know they're here: Gideon's underground army. Their eyes poke out at me like fingers, testing for my soft spots. Despite the lack of physical contact, I feel manhandled. Almost bruised.

I nod and try to shake it off. "How much farther?" I whisper.

Then, before Tristan can answer, big lights switch on overhead, flooding the dingy tunnel with white-hot illumination. It's blinding, at first—but my paranormal pupils adjust with lightning speed. A dozen or so yards ahead of Tristan and me, amid the flotsam and filth, sits an antique private railway car, its former luster well hidden beneath myriad layers of dust and grime.

My eyes start to shift to take in the platform, when a commotion emanates from inside the old train car. I stand on the tracks beside Tristan, both of us stopped in our, um, tracks. We watch as the car rocks back and forth, the rusted carriage creaking and groaning in objection. Then, the door is thrust open, and—

"Mom!"

Shoved out of the car, wrists bound, she falls to her knees in the waste. Usually impeccably groomed, she is now all mussed hair and smudged makeup, chipped nails and torn clothing. She looks exhausted. Disheveled. Broken.

My heart couldn't sink any lower if it were encased in cement.

I start to go to her, but Tristan holds me back.

"Careful," says Tristan. His voice in my ear is a warning. "She's alive. Let's keep her that way."

Even as I struggle against his hold, I see what he means. Two big, brawny male vampires in street wear emerge from the railway car behind her, standing over her. There's a murderous glint in their undead eyes; their mouths are twisted in bloodthirsty rage. Clearly, they'd love an excuse to strike.

I can't give them one.

"I'm chill," I say to Tristan. I ease back on my heels and try to meet my mother's unfocused gaze with a look of reassurance. "I'm chill," I repeat, hoping that'll make it true.

Just then, the grinding of gears and the whir of a motor comes from the direction of the run-down platform. I turn toward the cracked and crumbling block of concrete, toward the doors to the freight-sized elevator shaft that can't possibly be operational.

Flying in the face of all logic, the elevator doors begin to slide open.

"Still loves to make a big entrance," mutters Tristan.

"Who?" I ask. Only, I know the answer before he tells me.

"Gideon."

CHAPTER 39

Grand Master Gideon. The Vampire Council.

I've been bracing for this face-off for nights.

I can't say I've given any conscious thought to what it would look like—or more to the point, what *they* would look like. I got a glimpse of Gideon atop the Empire State Building, but the position of the moon kept his features in darkness. But, okay, I guess I've been imagining hideous monsters in long, black robes. Some vampiric Darth Vader and a shadowy army of acolytes.

I mean, these are my enemies we're talking about. The bad guys. Ancient bloodsuckers bent on my destruction. They're supposed to look like something straight out of Hell.

Not straight out of *Vogue*.

Only, when the enormous elevator doors open, it's like I've got a front-row seat at an elite runway show. A dozen elegantly dressed men and women—one more stunning than the other and each with the bored and detached expression of a high-fashion model—parade out of the cavernous car and take what seem to be their assigned places at the edge of the deteriorating train platform.

When they settle, there's an empty space remaining at the center of their lineup.

If you ask me, it's all a little extra.

"Here we go," whispers Tristan.

After a dramatic pause, the thirteenth vampire emerges from the darkness of the freight elevator with the confident swagger of a rock star. The most ancient one of them all appears to be about my age. In the overbright overhead lighting, his long pale-blond hair is a halo. The strong lines of his cheekbones and jaw are emphasized by hard shadow. And instead of concealing his tall figure beneath a shapeless, dark robe, he's flaunting his broad shoulders and trim waist in a perfectly tailored dark suit. Italian, if I'm not mistaken.

Apparently, the devil does wear Prada.

The unexpectedly beautiful Grand Master Gideon takes center stage and peers down at us with a smile that's both seductive and terrifying.

"Tristan," he says like some congenial host. "So kind of you to join us."

"Well, your invitation was quite compelling," says Tristan with a glance over at my mother.

"Was it? I wasn't sure it would be," says the grand master. "Given your…history."

My eyes shoot over to Tristan. It's clear to me that Gideon is baiting him in some way, taunting him about something from their mutual past. I search my head, but that last infusion of Tristan's blood hasn't given me any further insight into the source of his long-standing standoff with the grand master. It's just made his memory of Marianna—and of his love for her—even stronger.

But this is so not the time to be dwelling on that.

I see Tristan's jaw tic, but he doesn't take the bait. He stands otherwise immobile, eyes locked with Gideon's. After what seems like an eternity, the grand master blinks.

"Aren't you going to introduce me?" asks Gideon, refocusing his evil eyes on me.

I suppress a shudder and open my mouth to respond, but Tristan grabs my hand and gives it a cautioning squeeze.

"This is Lily," says Tristan.

"Lily," says Gideon. "A pleasure."

I pull my hand out of Tristan's and ignore his warning. "Fuck you," I say to the grand master. Probably not the wisest, but, I swear, I can't help it. "We're here. Like you wanted. Now, let my mother go."

The grand master looks at me with surprise. Then he laughs. "Such nerve," he says. He glances down the lines of council members to his right and to his left. "If only we were asked, we might have been persuaded to allow the transformation and invite her to sign The Book." His gaze comes back to Tristan and me, and his humor evaporates. "Only, we were not asked."

"And I'm the one who's accountable," says Tristan. "Not Lily. And certainly not her mother."

"You are accountable, Tristan," says Gideon. "And now you're going to pay."

The tension between the two of them is so thick, it would take way more than a knife to cut through it. I'm not even sure a chain saw would do the trick. There's something going on here. Something that's not entirely about me.

And then, suddenly, I know what it's all about.

"Marianna," I whisper.

But Gideon hears, of course. His head snaps toward me. "What did you just say?"

I can't discern any of the details, but I can feel the truth of it in my blood—or rather, Tristan's blood. And now I can see it in the grand master's eyes. "None of this is even about me," I say. "It's about Marianna."

"I don't know what lies your master has been telling you," says Gideon, "but we're not here to address the death of his master. We're here to address his recent violation of vampire law."

I turn sharply to Tristan. "Marianna was your master?" I ask.

Tristan looks back at me with confusion. "I thought you knew," he says.

"So…you were in love with your master?" I ask.

He blinks at me. Then, slowly, he shakes his head. "Not *me*."

"Enough!" shouts Gideon. His affable facade is cracking.

The vampires of the council, unmoving and unmoved until now, begin to exchange looks and whispers. I know I should keep my head in the game and use my vampire hearing to listen in on them, but my ears are still ringing with this unexpected revelation.

Is it possible? I think. *Was Marianna merely Tristan's master? And Gideon's lover?*

"I agree," says Tristan. "Enough. Enough of this charade. You didn't drag me here to answer for Lily's transformation. You want revenge for Marianna's death. Your quarrel is with me. So, punish me. But let Lily and her mother go free and in peace."

Gideon's lover, I repeat in my head. *Not Tristan's. NOT TRISTAN'S.*

Suddenly, Gideon is down off the platform and on the train tracks, standing right smack in front of us. Even with my blood-enhanced eyesight, his movement was too quick for me to follow.

Gideon points an accusing finger at Tristan. "You let my love die." Then he points at me. "Tell me why I should spare yours?"

I wait for Tristan to correct him, to tell him I'm not his love. Only, he's not the one who speaks up.

"Because she risked herself for us," comes a voice from behind us.

Raven?

I look over my shoulder, and there she is, in total Gothic-warrior-princess mode. It looks like she has indeed made good on her promise to have my back. And she's even managed to scare up a small entourage from the club to have hers.

Only, I have no idea if she made that choice knowing all the facts. I hope she got Tristan's messages about the slayer, and her decision to be here is an informed one.

And that makes me wonder: *Where's Evan?*

But before I can wonder too long, vampires drop to the ground from above, one after the other, surrounding us. They're Gideon's foot soldiers, the ones I felt watching our approach in the darkness before they switched on the floodlights. Although Raven still has numbers on her side, Gideon now seems to have the tactical advantage.

Unfazed by this latest development, Raven continues to defend me to the grand master. "The Crypt was attacked by a slayer," she says. "And the newborn drove him off."

"The newborn faced off with a slayer?" asks the grand master. The asshole doesn't even bother to conceal his skepticism. "And survived?"

I'm about to set him straight when, from out of the dark, Evan lands on the roof of the dilapidated train car, eyes ablaze, brandishing his sword of fire. And before you can ask WWBD—*What Would Buffy Do*—he takes a swing and scores a double, slicing neatly through the pair of fanged jailers standing guard over my mother.

As their steaming ashes rain down over her, Mom screams a scream so sharp it pierces my heart. Then she passes out, unconscious.

And that's when all hell really breaks loose.

CHAPTER 40

Before I say anything else, let me just say that the members of the Vampire Council are a bunch of crybabies. Seriously.

I mean, it shouldn't surprise me. The way this whole vampire leadership is set up, they're totally impotent. They've got zero power unless they all agree. And since you can't get a dozen *people* to agree on anything these days, I imagine vampires aren't much different.

But anyway, once Evan showed, the twelve of them couldn't get their well-dressed ancient asses back in that freight elevator fast enough. They were on their way up and out of here before the slayer even struck that first blow. Apparently, when shit gets real, vampire government officials are every bit as useless and motivated by self-interest as their human counterparts.

Meanwhile, the rest of us are ready for a fight. Only, with Evan's appearance, the battle lines aren't so clear anymore. Eyes dart around—my own included—assessing threats, reassessing alliances.

Oh, and here's another thing to add to this shitstorm we've got brewing: we're not at The Crypt anymore. Track 61 isn't fireproof—just the opposite, in fact. So when Evan cut down those two vampires, he also set off a handful of garbage fires. As if the tunnel doesn't reek badly enough already. So now, with these little bonfires of death burning all around, I, um, really need to watch my step.

"Let's use the confusion to our advantage," says Tristan. "I'll distract the slayer. You get your mother out of here."

"What? No!" I say, but I'm saying it to the empty air beside me. Tristan has already disappeared. In less than a blink, he touches down on top of the old train car to challenge Evan.

Without thinking, I take off after him.

I guess not thinking really is the key, because my new vampire superpowers propel me through the air and up onto the roof of the abandoned car, no prob. Somehow, I land squarely between Evan and Tristan.

"What are you doing?" I say to Tristan. "I told you. Evan and I made a deal."

Tristan looks past me and raises his eyebrows. "I think the deal is off."

I glance back at Evan—only, there's no sign of the Evan I know, the Evan I ate French toast with just a few hours earlier, behind the blazing eyes of the slayer. Being around all these vampires is clearly too much for him. He's reeling back, getting ready to strike again—and this time, Tristan and I are the ones in the line of, um, *fire.*

Before I can even try to get through to him, Evan takes another swing.

Tristan tackles me, pushing me out of the way.

As the arc of the slayer's flame whooshes past my back, my skin screams. Then I'm flying through the air again. Except, this time, I have no control over my trajectory.

I hit the ground hard on my butt, and the impact rocks my whole body. Hot pain shoots through my leg, and I wonder if Evan's sword has sliced me after all—but, no. It's just broken glass on the tracks that's cut through my leggings and the flesh of my thigh.

I look around me, struggling to gather my wits and get my bearings.

I'm alone, near the platform. Behind me, a wall of fire is erupting where Evan's blow landed, separating me from most of the other vampires.

Through the dancing tongues of flame, I spy Raven. Her dark eyes are lit with anger and betrayal. And all at once, I know that her keen supernatural ears picked up on me reminding Tristan about my double-dealing with the slayer. And clearly, that was the first she'd heard about it.

My insides shrivel with guilt.

I should have trusted Raven. I should have taken her at her word. If only I wasn't so intimidated by her, I probably wouldn't have been so quick to doubt her. And I might not have been compelled to make a side deal with Evan, a deal that's looking more and more like a big mistake.

As I lock eyes with her, I have the sick feeling that I may have just lost what could have been a true friend. And made what could be a new enemy.

With a last glare at me, Raven turns and signals to her paranormal posse. I watch through the flames as they vanish.

But then I notice the fire is spreading, inching toward my mother. My unconscious mother! And there's no way I can get to her without incinerating myself.

Desperately, I scan the area, searching for Tristan. For Evan. Hoping they haven't killed each other. Praying one of them can reach my mom before the flames do. Only, the smoke in the tunnel is growing thicker, making it hard to see.

My whole body seizes with panic.

The pain in my leg has receded, though, so I start to get to my feet. I need to find Tristan, find Evan. I need to do something.

But as soon as I stand up, a force like nothing else slams into me, knocking me back down to the ground. Backed by a couple of his soldiers, Gideon hovers over me, his foot on my chest, pinning me to the ground. With his fangs elongated and his beautiful features distorted in rage, he is now every inch the monster I imagined. And even with my vampire superstrength, I know I can't fight him off.

I recall Cat schooling me on the handful of ways to end a vampire's immortal life, and I stupidly wonder which of those the grand master is about to use to end mine. My money is on decapitation. Although Gideon could easily kick me into the encroaching flames behind me, he looks like he's going to bite my head off. Legit.

I glance over at my mother. The fire is getting nearer.

I make a dying wish that, if I can't save her, someone else can. Then I brace for the grand master's death blow.

Only, something shifts. Gideon's nostrils flare…and his expression softens.

"Marianna?" he whispers, eyes wide.

At first, I think he must be hallucinating.

Then I really hope *I'm* not the one who's seeing things, because Tristan has materialized next to the grand master. I'm so relieved I could cry—until I realize that, if he's on this side of the fire wall, he can't save my mom either.

Then I really do want to cry.

Tristan's eyes dart from me to Gideon. The grand master is focused intently on the slice in my leg—or rather, where my leg had been sliced. The gash is now completely mended over, healed. But my blood still soaks the torn fabric of my leggings.

Tristan puts it all together, and I see him calculate a plan.

"Lily shares Marianna's blood," he says carefully.

That's when I realize that the grand master is literally standing here smelling my blood.

A shudder runs through me.

"Think about it, Gideon," Tristan continues. He speaks to the grand master like a hostage negotiator, trying to talk him down—but now he doesn't take his eyes off me. And I know from his look that if these negotiations falter, he won't hesitate to use force to save me.

"Marianna made me, after all," says Tristan. "And I made Lily. Marianna's blood lives in Lily. Do you really want to kill a part of your mate that still survives?"

I hold my breath, waiting to learn the answer to Tristan's question. Is Gideon going to kill me? Or let me survive?

I look over at my mother. The flames are mere inches from her.

Then, Evan—or rather, his slayer—arrives out of nowhere. He raises his sword, preparing to take a swing at the grand master. And I can't say I really want to stop him.

Except, he's the only one who's not a vampire.

He's the only one who can safely negotiate the fire.

He's the only one who can get to my mother.

I look into his violently burning slayer eyes.

"Evan! No!" I scream. "My mother! Save! My! Mother!"

And then I'm looking into the eyes of, well, maybe not my *friend.* Not yet. But not my mortal enemy.

Our eyes meet for less than a second. Then he glances over toward the railway car, where my mother is passed out, and does one of his Buffy moves. I watch as he lands next to her and scoops her up—just in time.

Then an arc of fire shoots up from where the train car is parked. And like he did before at The Crypt, Evan rises into the air, riding that flaming wave up, up, and away. Only this time, he has my mother in tow, cradling her gently.

My mom is safe.

I breathe a sigh of relief.

That's when I realize Gideon's foot is no longer on my chest.

I look up. All the vampires, the grand master included, are staring down at me with something like awe.

"Fascinating," says Gideon.

I get quickly to my feet. And for the first time tonight, I feel my body relax.

Only, just when I think things might be looking up, Gideon leaps back onto the platform, reclaiming his position as grand master. Then, indicating Tristan and me, he addresses his bloodsucking subway squad. "Restrain the lawbreakers, please."

And just like that, there's a huge vampire on either side of me, holding me. I look over and see that Tristan is similarly restricted.

What the fuck?

"Now that the disturbance is over," says Gideon, "we can get back to the business of sentencing you two for your crimes. As you know, the punishment—"

"Gideon," says Tristan, just as flummoxed as I am, "Lily just saved your life. Are you really not going to spare hers?"

Gideon shrugs helplessly, as though the decision isn't totally and completely up to him. "Vampire law is—"

"Bullshit," I say.

"Pardon?" says Gideon.

"Vampire law is bullshit," I say.

Because, seriously? I've had it. And if we're back to trial by Gideon, then I'm making my argument. I've got nothing left to lose.

"I mean, these laws have been on the books—or, um, in The Book—for how long?"

"Centuries," says Gideon.

"Right," I say. "So, they're totally outdated. They need to evolve." I peer around me, from the grand master to his henchmen—and finally to Tristan. "You all need to evolve."

I turn back to Gideon. "Look. You have all these reasons for not creating new vampires. But the reasons don't apply anymore.

"I mean, okay, so when you create a new vampire, there's a chance that you also create a new slayer. But if slayers can be controlled—like you just saw me control mine—then that's not such a big threat anymore.

"And the fear of humans finding out about you? Please. My best friend knows all about you, and I guarantee she's not out there organizing a human army to attack you. She fucking loves vampires. Everybody loves vampires. Seriously, have you never heard of Twilight?"

I look at Gideon's soldiers, the two that are holding me. "Okay, maybe you guys haven't heard of Twilight. Because you *literally* live underground. But what's with that, anyway? Do you really want to live down here? In the subway tunnels? Or do you just do it because that's what's been done in the past?"

The goons exchange looks.

Then, one of the vampires restraining me drops his hold. "Why do we live in the tunnels?" he asks.

The others shrug. They don't let go of Tristan and me, but they do loosen their grip.

Gideon is starting to look nervous. He must be feeling like his grip is loosening, too, his grip on what have been his loyal vampires. He can't like the idea of his power slipping away.

Just then, I recall what Tristan told me about a million years ago, it seems. One of the reasons the grand master didn't move against Tristan sooner is that he doesn't want to appear to be using his position to settle a personal grudge. He doesn't want a revolt.

So, I stand up straighter and deliver my final pitch for, um, revolution. "I think it's time to do things differently," I say. "To throw out the old rules and smash the old ways. I think it's time for vampires to let the past be the past, embrace the present, and build a new undead future!"

"I do too," says Tristan.

I look over. He's smiling at me, eyes twinkling—no, more than twinkling. It's like there's a full-on fireworks display going off in his gaze, all in celebration of me.

I smile back.

Gideon clears his throat, bringing the attention back to him. "The newborn makes some interesting points," he says carefully. "It seems there is much to consider here. Much for *me* to consider here," he adds, reasserting his authority. "So, I believe the wisest course of action is to adjourn for now while I take this all under advisement." He motions at the three vampires who are still controlling Tristan and me. "You may release them."

They do what he says. But now I'm not so sure they're going to want to continue to do what he says. And clearly, neither is Gideon.

Not my immediate concern.

"So, we're free to go?" I ask the grand master.

He turns from me to Tristan, then to me again. The look in his eyes is definitely *not* a celebration of me. "For now."

And with that, Gideon disappears, his goon squad vanishes after him, and it seems like the danger is over.

For now.

CHAPTER 41

I'm sitting in the passenger seat next to Tristan, and I don't know what to say.

Okay, correction: I do know what to say—but there's so much to say, I don't even know where to begin. And for once, I really don't want to fuck it all up by saying the wrong thing.

"I didn't know Marianna was your master," I eventually blurt out. "Your blood… It showed me her face. It made me feel your bond with her. Your, um…" I make myself say it. "Your *love* for her. But that's all."

Tristan stares ahead out the windshield, watching the road. His fingers *tap-tap-tap* the steering wheel as he thinks. I hold my breath while I wait to hear how he'll respond.

If he'll respond.

"I did love her," he says finally. But before my heart plunges too low, he adds, "It was never a romantic kind of love, though. Gideon was her lover. But she was like family to me, as I was to her—even though I started out as her employee. In my human life, I worked as her driver."

"Hold on," I say. "You were her driver?"

Tristan nods.

"Her *driver*?" I repeat. "Seriously?"

"What?" he asks, adorably clueless.

I think about him being, as Cat coined, my personal Uber. And his infallible luck with the street parking.

I shake my head and suppress a laugh. "Nothing," I say. "Go on. Please."

It takes him a moment, but he does.

"It was horses and carriages back then. Not cars. Rough backwoods roads instead of paved streets or highways. And, of course, Marianna, being what she was, only traveled in the dark. So, it was probably inevitable that, one night, we'd be attacked by highwaymen."

"I thought there weren't any highways," I say.

"Sorry," says Tristan. "It's what we called robbers back then."

"Right," I say. *Duh.*

"You see, as her human driver, I thought Marianna was exactly what she appeared to be: a wealthy and lovely but rather fragile woman. So, when one of the bandits pulled a knife on her, I felt it was my duty to intervene and protect her. I didn't know her true nature, didn't know that a knife wound wouldn't kill her. There was a struggle, and I was stabbed in the chest."

"Shit," I murmur.

"Indeed," he says, a wry smile tugging at the corners of his mouth. "I would have died if Marianna hadn't turned me. I owed her my eternal life. But for centuries, I've felt like I let her down."

I think about how Tristan has been there for me these past few days, even when I tried my damnedest to push him away. "I find that hard to believe," I tell him.

"Believe it," he says. "You see, when she took my blood and gave me hers, one of the robbers saw her. And he remembered. Then, a few years later, he was arrested for another crime and would have been hanged—but he used the information about the rich lady vampire to barter for his life. One night, I woke in my quarters by the stables to find her house burning. It was set on fire by an avenging mob—with her inside."

It's the "house fire" that Raven talked about—but so much worse than I could have imagined. A shiver runs through me to think of Marianna's horror. And Tristan's.

"I'm so sorry," I say.

"Gideon was absolutely devastated," says Tristan. "As a result, he added the law to The Book that said no new vampires could be created without the council's approval. Ever since, transformations have been conducted in guarded secrecy, far away from potential discovery by human eyes. Only…he's never gotten over her. And he's never forgiven me."

"Tristan," I say, "from what you've just told me, Marianna's death wasn't your fault."

"But for centuries, I thought it was," he says. "After all, she was exposed because she saved my life. And I just stood by helplessly while she lost hers."

I see why, that first night we met, Tristan told me he wasn't a hero. He's been carrying around the burden of guilt for Marianna's demise for nearly four hundred years. I can't even imagine the torture.

And now, okay, I guess I kind of understand why he's been so hell-bent on protecting me—even when I fought him, um, *fang* and nail, to back off. I think about all those novels he writes, romances about rogues finding their redemption. And I hope, finally, he's found his.

"But seriously, Tristan, you should have told me about all this. You should have told me way before tonight."

"I've made so many mistakes with you, Lily," he says. "And I know I can't change my past behavior. But I can do things differently starting tonight.

"It's clear now," he continues, "even to me, that you can take care of yourself. And what you said to Gideon is true. *I* need to evolve. It's time for *me* to let the past be the past, embrace the present, and build a new future."

We've arrived at my building. There's an empty spot in front, of course. But rather than pulling into it, Tristan just stops the car and puts on his flashers.

"You're not coming in?" I ask.

He shakes his head. "I don't think so."

I'm floored, to say the least.

But then I wonder if this is his way of doing things differently, of finally respecting my autonomy. Evolving.

Maybe he's waiting for something.

An invitation, maybe?

I've withheld it all this time. I've just felt so insecure. About my body. About my worth. About…everything. But now that I know his heart isn't eternally stamped *Property of Marianna*—

"You're invited," I say quickly, before I wuss out and change my mind. "I mean, I'm inviting you in. You can come in, um, if you want to."

"Thank you for that," he says.

He stares at me across the gearshift, sexy and intense, and I'm such a hot mess, I turn to liquid Jell-O. I swear, it's a wonder I'm not dripping and oozing all over his leather seats.

"But now that we seem to have settled matters with Gideon," he continues, "I think I owe it to you to honor your wishes and do what you've wanted me to do all along."

"I don't understand," I say.

"I'm going to respect the boundaries you've been trying to maintain," he says to clarify. "I'm going to stop inserting myself into your life. I'm going to leave you alone."

"You're going to…leave me alone?" I ask.

"I'm done selfishly pushing my way into your world."

No. No, no, no, no, no. This is not happening.

"You know how to find me if you need me, of course," he continues. "And I'll always be there for you if you need me."

I want to tell him I need him now. In my bed. And in my, um, everything. But I can't form the words.

I can't form any words.

Then he looks at me. And it's *that* look. The one that sees me and knows me and understands me.

He opens his mouth to say something, and I think it's going to be okay.

He hesitates.

Then, he says, "Be well, Lily."

Be well? BE WELL?

I'm about to cry. Or scream. Or maybe throw up.

So, before I do any of that, I just nod dumbly and get out of the car.

CHAPTER 42

I wake the next evening to see my mother perched on the edge of my bed.

"Mom!"

I bolt up into a sitting position and wrap her small figure up in a big embrace. My nostrils fill with the scent of her—her heavy rose perfume and her underlying blood—and my whole body fills with relief.

Not letting go, I pull back and survey her at arm's length. Incredibly, she's all made-up and neatly coiffed, dressed in some ghastly suburban-mall nightmare of an outfit: giraffe-print leggings and a matching brown tunic with a sparkly giraffe appliquéd on it. I swear, you'd never know she just survived a supernatural abduction.

"You're okay?" I ask her. "Really?"

"Lily," she says. "I've dealt with tough customers my whole life."

I gape at her.

"Mom," I say, "these 'tough customers' didn't just send back undercooked eggs."

"Well, that's true," says my mother. "No sooner did I buzz them in—"

"You buzzed them in?"

"Sweetheart, they said they had a delivery for you," she says. "So, of course, I told them to come in. Next thing I knew, I woke up in some grisly old train."

"So," I say carefully, "you don't remember everything?" I've been wondering if the vampires holding her used their influence on her. Maybe even hoping they had.

"I remember enough," she says. "I remember that very handsome young man dropping me off at the emergency room. And I figured it was best not to contradict his story that I'd taken a tumble down the subway stairs."

"Does that mean you know the real story?" I ask.

"You mean that you're a vampire?" she says.

Well, there it is. I nod, grimacing.

Incredibly, she smiles. "I guess I really should have seen through that ridiculous business about the protein shakes."

I have to say, she's taking my new undead status a hell of a lot better than I did.

Maybe she's still in shock?

And obvi, she's not putting it all together. Just like I didn't, at first.

"So, you understand…I'm always going to look like this," I say.

"Lucky you," says my mother with a wink. "Think of all the money you'll save on Botox and hair dye."

"Right, but, um, I'm never going to be *thin*," I say.

Mom shrugs. "There are more important things."

I gawk at her for a moment. "Who are you, and what the fuck have you done with my mother?" I demand.

"Lily!" she says, horrified. "Language!"

"Ah! There she is," I say with a teasing grin.

"Oh, you!" she says. She scoffs and gives me a dismissive wave of her hand. I note that her gel manicure is now an obnoxiously bright purple. God love her, she must have gone straight from the hospital to the nail salon.

I'm about to give her a little grief about that when I see that her expression has grown serious. She takes my hand in hers. "You know, Lily," she says, "if I ever made you feel anything less than beautiful just the way you are, I'm sorry. Truly."

It shouldn't matter. It really shouldn't. Like I've already told you, I'm over my mother and her misguided priorities.

Only, maybe that's not 100 percent true. Because her words set off such a powerful wave of emotion in me that, for a while, I can't even speak.

And I know, I know. This speechlessness is becoming a seriously boring habit.

"I'm sorry too," I finally say. "I should have told you everything, straight off. But I kept it a secret, and that put you in danger."

"Well, you and I have a history of secrets, don't we?" she says. She raises her eyebrows and gives me a prodding look.

Still, it takes me some time to understand what she's getting at. I mean, if you ask me, my mother has always been a little too free with her opinions. The only thing she's ever kept to herself is the identity of my fa—

But, no. That can't be it. After all these years of staying mum on the topic, she can't possibly be ready to open up about my paternity? Can she?

"I know you've always been curious about your father."

Holy shit! She *is* ready.

I don't move. I don't even breathe. I'm terrified of doing anything that might quash this sudden urge of hers to share.

"And I've had my reasons for staying silent," she continues. "But Lily, from what I've seen, this new lifestyle of yours is dangerous. You have enemies. Powerful ones. So, I'm thinking you might need someone with some muscle to back you up."

Is my biological father a pro wrestler? I wonder. *A prize fighter? An assassin?*

"Do you know who Palmer Matheson is?" my mother asks.

"Of course," I say. "Everyone does."

I figure she's going to tell me that my father is his bodyguard. Part of his security team. Maybe his head of security. Only, when she doesn't say anything else, it hits me.

Wealthy.

Powerful.

Maybe a little shady.

And probably married to someone other than my mom.

Check. Check. Check. And, um, check.

Nice to see my journalistic deductions were right on the money.

Hell, I probably inherited my nose for news from him.

"My father is Palmer Matheson?" I ask. "The media mogul?"

"And family is very important to him," says my mother.

"All evidence to the contrary," I mutter.

"Lily!" she says. "That's not fair. He's always made sure you had everything you needed."

Now, I remember the monthly deposits to my mother's bank account. The house in Cherry Hill that she couldn't possibly have afforded on her salary from the diner. Still.

"Not *everything*," I say.

"No," she admits after a pause. "Not *everything*. I guess we both know that money can be a poor substitute for love."

I look at my mother. I try to see beyond the mom I know to the woman I never much considered. Has she seriously been pining away for Palmer Matheson—*Palmer fucking Matheson*—all these years?

I think back, and, okay, I can't remember her dating anyone. Um, ever. It never struck me as strange before, but…yeah. It was always just her and her stacks upon stacks of paperback romances.

"But the thing is," my mother continues, "he does have money. And connections. And influence. And if you found yourself in trouble again, honey, I know he would use all that and more to help you."

I want to piss all over that blatant bit of candy-coated delusion. I mean, give me a break. Obvi, Palmer Matheson cares about one thing and one thing only: protecting Palmer Matheson.

Only, my mom's eyes are shining with such absolute belief and trust in what she's said, I don't have the heart to contradict her.

• • • • •

So, after all these years, I finally know who my biological father is: the multibazillionaire king of conservative media.

I let that fact run around in my brain as the spray from the shower runs over my body.

I mean, it's sweet that Mom thinks Palmer Matheson, a.k.a. dear old Dad, will have my back. But I'm not so naive. The views expressed by the guy's media outlets don't exactly celebrate the other, the different. If he ever learned that his dirty little secret of an illegitimate daughter was also a vampire, I'm pretty sure he wouldn't be fighting in my corner. More likely, he'd be leading the charge to have my head and the head of every other bloodsucker in America on a silver platter. He'd probably consider it his patriotic duty to God and country.

Despite my argument to the grand master that everyone loves vampires, maybe the undead have reason to fear exposure after all.

Whatever.

I reach for the loofah, pump out a couple of pumps of shower gel, and start to wash. Only, I'm still so preoccupied with pondering this jaw-dropper of a who's-your-daddy revelation that I forget to avoid looking at my body.

I find myself staring down at my shape—the shape that, for so long, has been, well…not what I wanted it to be. Except now, I see it through new eyes. Sharper eyes. Vampire eyes.

All this time, I've been fearing my figure would appear even more flawed under the undead microscope. But, um, that's not exactly the case.

My gaze travels over my pale freckled skin, my plump curves glistening with water and suds. And, to my surprise, I don't cringe. I don't flinch. I don't turn away.

I keep looking. I blink a few times to clear my vision, but that's not really necessary. My vision has never been clearer.

Now, I'm not looking at myself from my mother's perspective. Or society's perspective.

For once, I'm not comparing myself to anyone else. There's no ideal to measure up to. No judgment.

And guess what? This new way of looking at myself isn't just because I'm a vampire.

Over the past few nights, I've changed in so many more ways than that. Yes, I've faced some of my worst fears, but I've also faced some of the worst aspects of myself. I've fought undead bullies who wanted to kill me, but I've also fought the voices in my head that kept me from living a full life. I've had to accept immortality…but along the way, I've also ended up accepting myself.

And finally, I see. And I just see…*me.*

My body.

And I recognize it for what it is: the vessel of skin and bone, flesh and muscle—and, yes, blood too—that connects me to everything around me. It's how I touch and how I feel. It's how I taste and smell and hear. It's how I embrace my loved ones and battle my enemies—and, oh so much more.

For the first time, I see that I *am* so much more.

I am more than the way I look.

Obvi, I always was.

And now, I always will be.

Forever. *More.*

And yes, okay, maybe I'll still hit a road bump or two as I go forward. But I've definitely turned a corner with how I see my body—and I'm not going back. And I've got all eternity to get where I want to be.

And no, I am not crying. Those are so not tears running down my face. Like I said, I'm standing under the goddamn shower spray.

CHAPTER 43

So, I figure there's no avoiding work tonight. Not if I want to keep my job.

My mother promises to stick around, though. For another day or two, at least. We've still got some things to talk about.

Oh, and she also promises to stay away from the door buzzer and not invite anyone else in. Just in case.

I throw on some brown cords and a peasant blouse, grab my denim jacket, and tell Mom not to wait up.

And, you know what? I'm out the door and halfway to the office before I realize I didn't even try to check my nonexistent reflection in the mirror.

• • • • •

I spend most of my shift at TakeABite.com keeping to myself, head buried in my laptop, cranking out a vampire exposé that exposes absolutely nothing. When I'm done, Peter sees it for the piece of shit it is and promptly kills the story.

So, mission accomplished.

"Uh, Lily?"

I look up, and an uncomfortable Evan stands over me. His hands are shoved deep in the pockets of his jeans and his big shoulders are slumped down beneath his plaid flannel shirt, perhaps in some demonstration of submission.

"Can we maybe talk?" he asks, avoiding my gaze like he did in the old days.

I glance around the room. It's still dotted here and there with our coworkers, but assuming no one else at the website is rocking supernatural powers of hearing, they're all well out of earshot.

"Pull up a chair," I say.

He hesitates a moment, then drags one over. The scrape of the metal legs against the concrete floor is like nails-on-a-chalkboard on steroids, and I kind of wish I wasn't rocking those supernatural powers of hearing either. I sit on my hands to keep from clamping them over my ears.

Then we sit in silence—which, at first, is a welcome break. But soon, the me-staring-at-him thing and the him-staring-at-the-floor thing starts to get weird. Way weird.

"Okay, I'll go first," I say. "Thank you."

He looks up at me with a start. There's surprise in his eyes, but no flash of that otherworldly fire. *He's gaining control over his slayer,* I think.

"You're not mad at me?" he asks.

"Are you kidding?" I say. "You saved my mother's life. I owe you."

Unconvinced, Evan frowns and shifts around in his seat. "Even though I, uh..."

"Tried to slay me?" I supply.

He winces.

I just laugh it off.

"Dude, forget it," I say. "That's part of the package now."

"But—"

"Take the win," I say. "I'm still undead. My mother's alive. So, you and me—? We're cool."

He takes a little time to process that.

Then his handsome features screw up in a shy expression, and a blush rises on his dark skin.

"How cool?"

• • • • •

"Evan asked me for your number," I tell Cat on my iPhone. I'm back in that stall in the ladies' room that's lately become my unofficial office.

"Oh, uh…did he?" She's trying to play down how pleased she is—but FYI, that infallible BS detector goes both ways with us.

"I told him you weren't interested," I say with a grin.

"*What?*"

"Easy, tiger," I say. "Obvi, I gave him your mobile. Along with a lecture about how, if he ever hurts you, I'll rip him a new one. You know, I could literally do that now."

"I really do hope you're joking," she says.

"He's lucky," I say. "Because you are seriously the most spectacular woman I know." My voice cracks a little. "Inside and out."

"Back at ya," she says after a moment. And her own voice breaks up in a way that has nothing to do with the wireless connection. And everything to do with *our* connection.

We smile at each other through the phone for a beat as only BFFs can.

"So, when are you going to see Tristan again?" she asks.

I've already filled her in on everything—except, um, *that.*

To tell the truth, I haven't wanted to talk about it. I haven't even wanted to think about it. And up until now, I've had enough distractions to keep the subject safely tucked away from too much scrutiny in a walled-off corner of my brain.

But now that my bestie has mentioned Tristan's name, that wall starts to crack. Crumble. Collapse. And suddenly Tristan Newberry forces his way into every inch of my consciousness. Just like he's been forcing his way into my world, accidentally or on purpose, ever since the night we met.

"Lil?" prods Cat. "What's going on with Tristan?"

"Inconclusive," I say.

"What does that mean?" she asks.

"Uncertain," I say. "Unclear. Unsure—"

"I know what 'inconclusive' means," she says. "Stop it with the thesaurus imitation. What aren't you telling me?"

I'm starting to crack.

"Nothing."

"Bullshit."

I'm crumbling.

"No, really," I say, trying to keep my shit together. "There's nothing to tell. Because there's nothing happening between Tristan and me. Ever."

"I don't understand."

I'm collapsing inside.

"He's going to steer clear and leave me alone," I explain.

"What?" ask Cat. "I don't get it. Why?"

"Because I fucking told him to," I explode at her, finally. "I've been telling him to fuck the fuck off all along. And now, goddamn him, he's actually decided to listen!"

My words echo back to me, reverberating off the bathroom walls and fixtures, and suddenly, I hear what I'm not saying.

I love Tristan Newberry.

And never mind that I've known him less than a week.

I fucking love him. I love his dry sense of humor and his over-the-top sense of honor. I love talking with him and sparring with him. I love the way he gets on my nerves, and I love the way he just, um, gets *me*. I want to spend all my nights with him, all my days sleeping by his side.

Only, I've lost him.

And I've got no one to blame but me.

All this time, I thought the problem was that Tristan just couldn't accept me for me.

Turns out, I was the one with that problem. I was the one who couldn't just accept me for me.

"You know what I think," says Cat, softly.

"What?" I whisper hoarsely.

"I think Tristan couldn't stay away from you if he tried," she says. "In fact, I'd be shocked if he wasn't parked out at the curb, waiting for you, right now."

• • • • •

Cat's right, I tell myself as I ride down alone in the elevator. *Of course, she's right.*

Since he turned me, Tristan's been all up in my business. Seriously, why would he bother to respect my boundaries now?

Because he doesn't need to prove he's a hero anymore, says a little voice inside me.

The elevator bell dings, the car bumps to a stop in the lobby, and the doors slide open.

Moment of truth, I guess.

I step out of the elevator and cross over to the front desk to sign out. The other night, I thought I'd pushed Tristan away for good too. But there he was, with his twinkling blue eyes and his sexy, sardonic grin and his fancy black car parked right in front of the building. My personal Uber.

Are things really so different now?

Yes, says that stubborn voice inside me. *Yes, they are.*

Ignoring it, I walk across the marble floor and push through the revolving glass door.

Only, this time, when I step out onto the dark, deserted street, all that's waiting for me is an empty parking space. Right smack in front of the building.

And that's exactly how I feel. Totally, utterly empty.

CHAPTER 44

Okay, yes, I am crying now. Ugly crying. Total waterworks.

By the time I get home, I'm sniffling and sobbing like some ridiculous drama queen on a reality television show. I try to suppress my blubbering as I creep past the sleeper sofa where my mother is sacked out—but it's no use. Mom flicks on the lamp next to her and squints at me with bleary eyes.

"Lily!" she says when she sees me. "What on earth is the matter?"

She's got some kind of night cream smeared all over her cosmetic-free face, and her blond hair is sticking up and out at odd angles. For once, she looks real.

My old reflexes kick in, and I'm about to lie to her. Tell her it's nothing. She should go back to sleep.

Only, the last time I lied to my mother, she ended up as a pawn in a paranormal power play. And all those years of her withholding the identity of my biological father certainly didn't do me and my ego any favors.

No more secrets, I decide on the spot. *Time for us both to be real.*

So, I flop down into the patchy, dark-green wing chair. I swipe my hand across my dripping nose and tear-streaked cheeks. And I pour my unbeating heart out to her.

• • • • •

"Oh, for heaven's sake, sweetheart," my mother says all matter-of-factly when I finish. "Tristan writes romance novels."

"Yeah," I say slowly. "So?"

"So," she says, like it's the most obvious thing on the planet, "there's a structure to these things. I think he just needs you to make a grand gesture."

"Come again?" I say.

"You've been pushing him away all this time," she says patiently. "So, now it's your move. You need to do something that makes a big, bold statement. To win him back."

All at once, every stupid-ass, over-the-top marriage proposal I've ever seen posted on social media flashes before my undead eyes.

"What, like skywriting?" I say, making a face. "Or a flash mob? Or a message on the jumbotron?"

Jesus. I can't even tell you how much I hate that shit. Seriously.

"Well," says my mom, reading my expression, "maybe you could come up with something else. Something that's a little more, you know...*your* style."

I think about this advice. And I have to admit, it's not half-bad. It certainly beats the hell out of suggesting that I purchase my prom dress in a size too small.

"Thanks," I say. And I mean it. "I'll sleep on it."

With a yawn, I drag my ass up and out of the chair so I can change and get to bed before the dawn, um, dawns.

"And, Lily—?" Mom says.

I turn back to her. "Yeah?"

"I know you've got all eternity ahead of you," she says. "But when it comes to love, don't wait too long."

I continue to look at her. I think about her with all those romance novels—but no romance of her own.

"Is that what you've been waiting for?" I ask. "A grand gesture?"

"Maybe," she says with a sad smile. "Maybe I have."

Huh.

• • • • •

The next night, I hail a taxicab to take my mother to Penn Station so she can catch the New Jersey Transit train back home to Cherry Hill. We stand together on the curb.

"Don't be a stranger," she says to me.

Obvi, it's just an expression. But in so many ways, we really have been strangers to each other. I feel like we're just getting to know each other now. I mean, she's still the mother I've always known. But she's also, um, *more*.

There's more to her too.

"I won't," I say, hugging her. "I won't."

"And let me know how it goes," she says as she slides into the cab's back seat. "With Tristan."

"I will."

I close the door and wave as the yellow cab heads up West Broadway.

Only, before I try to make things right with Tristan, I need to try to smooth things over with somebody else.

CHAPTER 45

After work, I take an Uber down to the Bowery and follow the creepy, twisty path around to the clandestine door of The Crypt's back room. And I knock.

A beat later, the panel concealed in the door slides open, and Raven's dark, thick-lashed eyes are looking out at me.

"Hey—"

The panel slams shut before I can even get a full sentence out.

Well…*fuck.*

I knock again.

And again.

She's not going to make this easy for me.

I keep knocking.

Eventually, the panel slides slowly open once more. The club owner's eyes stare out at me coldly.

"What's the password?" she asks.

There's a password? I think.

"I'm an asshole?" I try.

No reply. Her eyes just continue to glare at me.

"I should have considered my alliance with you before I made my pact with Ev—um, the slayer?" I try. "And I should have been more sensitive to the fact that he killed one of your crew?"

Nothing.

"Um...*sorry?*"

She still doesn't say anything, but her gaze warms by a micro-degree. Then, the peekaboo panel closes quietly.

I mentally cross my fingers and wait.

Finally, the door opens just enough to reveal Raven Dupree in all her Goth splendor.

"You were right the first time," she says dryly. "You are an asshole."

But then she opens the door wider to let me in.

• • • • •

Raven agrees to talk. As she leads me back to her office, I see that the damage Evan did the other night has already been repaired. I just hope I can repair things between the two of us.

She gets settled in her throne-meets-torture-rack thing. This time, I pull up one of the room's more ominous-looking chairs. I figure I don't deserve to be comfortable here. Not yet.

"So," I say. "Turns out Tristan *has* been stuck in the past."

"Like I already said," she says—and yes, I totally pick up on the way she's mocking how I responded to her the last time we sat here.

"And," I say, "he *has* been obsessed with someone."

She gives me a bored look and acts like she's trying not to yawn. "Like I already said."

"But," I say, "it's not *exactly* like you said."

I let my words sink in for a moment. Then I offer her the olive branch that I'm hoping she won't be able to resist: "Do you want to know the whole story?"

I see the interest flicker behind her disinterested expression.

"Go on," she says, feigning casualness.

So, I do. I fill her in on what I've learned. How the woman Tristan couldn't save all those years ago wasn't his lover at all, but his master. How she was actually Gideon's soul mate, and that's been the source of their ages-old conflict. And how the two of them seem to have reached a tentative truce.

"And so," I say, "it looks like all our undead asses get to live to fight another, um, *night*."

Raven takes it all in for a breath or two. Then she looks at me. "So, where does that leave you and Tristan?" she asks.

I sigh, frustrated. "I don't know," I say. "On the plus side, he finally gets that he doesn't need to hang around and protect me. But on the minus side, now he thinks he shouldn't be hanging around at all."

"Idiot," Raven mutters, shaking her head.

"Yeah, well…" I shrug. "The thing is, you really did try to do me a favor that first night we met. And you tried to do me another favor down in the tunnels. I should have trusted you more. So I really am sorry."

Raven takes a few moments to digest this. Then she says, "Do you want a drink?"

At first, I figure that's her way of saying apology accepted. But a beat later, I wonder if maybe she's still messing with me.

"You mean, like, a person?"

She shrugs. "If you want."

"So, that's really a thing, then?" I ask.

"Most of my immortal customers make their own arrangements," she says. "But I keep a few donors on retainer, just in case."

"And they're voluntary donors?" I ask.

"Well, of course they're voluntary donors," she says. "What kind of a place do you think I run?"

"Sorry," I say quickly. "I–I just didn't know."

She nods. And this time, I'm pretty sure she has accepted my apology.

But then I have to ask it: "So, they, um, enjoy it?"

"Different strokes for different folks," she says.

"Huh."

"But I also stock blood that's already been donated," she says. "What's your pleasure? A? B?"

I think about this.

"Actually," I say with a smile, "you got any tequila?"

CHAPTER 46

It's nearly 3:00 a.m.

I'm carrying what's left of the José Cuervo that Raven and I shared. Nervously strangling the neck of the bottle, I approach the doorman at the Dakota. It's Joseph, the same dark-haired attendant who was on duty a few nights ago. Although the vampire in me has been invited in previously, the rest of me still needs to get past *him*.

"Hi," I say uncertainly. "I'm, um, Lily Baines." I gesture at myself. "I'm here to see Tristan Newberry."

I expect Joseph to give me the high-class brush-off. Inform me that he can't possibly buzz a resident at this ungodly hour.

Only, maybe he's familiar with Tristan's nocturnal schedule. Because he picks up the phone and dials.

I hold my breath.

I try not to squeeze the bottle's neck so tightly with my vampire strength that I break the glass.

There's a brief conversation in hushed tones—but not so hushed that my vampire ears can't hear. I exhale with relief and relax my hold on the bottle. Tristan said to send me right up.

Joseph directs me to the elevator in the southeast corner of the courtyard.

"He's on nine," says the doorman.

"I remember."

• • • • •

"Lily!" says Tristan. He flings open his door before I can even knock. He's barefooted, wearing worn jeans and a white tee, and his sandy hair is especially unkempt. IMHO, he's never looked hotter.

His indigo eyes survey me up and down. "What's wrong?" he demands. "Are you okay?"

Obvi, my sudden appearance has made him suspect the worst.

"Oh, um, yeah," I say. I wave off his concerns. "I'm great. Are you busy?"

He frowns at me, confused. "What?"

"What are you doing right now?" I ask.

"Uh, writing," he says.

"Another historical?" I ask.

"A contemporary, actually," he says.

"*Really?*" I ask.

He shrugs. "I felt…inspired."

"How's it going?" I ask, genuinely curious.

He runs a hand back through his messy hair. "It's quite challenging for me," he says. "But I plan to stick with it."

I take this as a positive sign.

"Well, can you take a break?" I ask. I hold up the Cuervo. "Buy you a drink?"

"What?"

"Well, you bought me one that first night. So, I thought I'd just, you know, return the favor?"

His gaze fills with bewilderment. "What?"

"What's the matter?" I say. "You don't like tequila?"

He just gapes at me, gobsmacked.

He's cute when he's gobsmacked.

"Oh, for fuck's sake," I say. I walk straight past him, through his elegant foyer and into his equally tasteful living room. I plop down on the ginormous brown-leather chesterfield sofa and plunk the José Cuervo down onto the antique-looking coffee table that's probably worth more than all my furnishings put together.

"Well, don't just stand there," I tell him. "Get us some shot glasses. We're going to play a drinking game."

• • • • •

A few minutes later, we're seated shoulder to shoulder on the edge of the sofa, with the bottle of tequila and a couple of gold-rimmed shot glasses in front of us. "Have you ever played Never Have I Ever?" I ask.

Tristan wrinkles his brow at me. "No. I don't believe I have."

"Okay. Then I'll go first." I unscrew the cap and pour us each a shot as he watches. "Here's how you play. I'll say something I've never done. Like, 'Never have I ever gone skiing.' Or, 'Never have I ever been to Paris.' Or, 'Never have I ever tried turnips.'"

"You've never tried turnips?" he asks.

"Whatever," I say. "The thing is, if you've never done what I've never done, you don't do anything. But if you have done it, you have to drink." I put the bottle down. "Got it?"

"No."

"Seriously?"

"The phrasing is a little convoluted," he says. "My editor would flag that for revisions in a heartbeat."

Jesus. This is going to be even tougher than I thought.

"All right, all right. How about if we do a practice one?" I say. "Never have I ever, um…written a romance novel." I look at him expectantly.

"But I have?" he says, like he doesn't know the answer.

"Yes!" I say. "So, what do you do?"

He thinks for a moment, then tentatively picks up his glass.

"Well, go on," I say.

He hesitates. Then he knocks back the tequila.

"Excellent," I say. "Now, let's play for reals."

I refill his glass. Then, on impulse, I knock back my own shot. I've already had a couple with Raven, but I don't think alcohol has the same effect on vampires as it does on humans, because I still feel stone-cold sober. The amber-colored liquid burns a trail down my gullet, and the warmth spreads through my limbs. I think maybe it eases my nerves ever so slightly.

"Wait," he says. "Why did you just drink?"

Courage, I think.

"Level playing field," I say. "I want us to start off as equals."

I refill my own shot glass and take a deep breath.

Okay, I think. *Here goes, well…everything.*

I look at Tristan. "Until recently, never have I ever felt good about my body."

His mouth drops open. "I don't understand," he says.

I roll my eyes. "Have you ever felt good about your body?" I ask.

"I don't know," he says with a shrug. "I suppose. I've never really thought about it before. But why wouldn't you—"

"So, what do you do?" I ask, cutting him off.

"But—"

"*What do you do?*" I ask again, louder.

Okay, so maybe I yell it.

Tristan reels back a little. Eyes me like I'm some sort of wild animal, ready to attack. Then, without taking his wary gaze off me, he reaches for his shot glass slowly, like any sudden movement might set me off.

He drinks.

"Okay." I've managed to dial down the volume. "Okay, good." I refill his glass with shaking hands. Some of the tequila sloshes onto the wooden surface of the expensive table, but he doesn't seem to notice. He's watching me. "Still my turn," I say.

"Why is it still your turn?" he asks.

"Because it is," I say.

"But why?" he persists.

"Oh my God," I say. I throw up my hands in frustration. "I'm trying to make a grand gesture here, and you're totally fucking it up."

All of a sudden, it clicks for him. Understanding glimmers in his brilliant blue eyes. A smile threatens at the corners of his mouth.

"Sorry," he says. He relaxes back against the tufts of the sofa and gestures at me. "Proceed."

Now, you'd think that would make this easier. Only, I've got no muscle memory for sharing my feelings like this. For the longest time, I've barely been able to share my feelings with myself.

I have the overwhelming urge to down all that remains of the tequila. Or wuss out and run for the door. But that's not going to get me what I want. What I really want.

I tell myself it's just a game. Only, I know it's not. Because if I lose—

"Lily?" says Tristan softly.

"Never have I ever thought anyone would want me for just me," I blurt out. "So, yeah. You were right. I push everyone away."

We gaze at each other a moment. The atmosphere between us crackles with electricity.

"I think you should drink," I say, nodding at his glass.

"I don't know about that," he says. "Not if I'm understanding this game correctly. After Marianna's death, I felt responsible. For the longest time, I didn't feel worthy of being wanted. And when my blood showed you my past, and you pulled away from me, I took that as a confirmation."

I shake my head. "Like I said, I didn't see any details. I only saw… her. And that you loved her. I pulled away because she was so gorgeous. And I'm…"

"Lily—"

"No." I hold my hand up to stop him from speaking anymore. "I get one more turn."

This is it, I think. *This is it.*

"Never have I ever loved anyone so much," I whisper. "Until now."

I hold my breath and wait. He reaches for his shot glass, and legit, I want to die on the spot. If he drinks, it means he doesn't love me. Not the way I want him to love me. Not the way I love him.

But then, with a deliberate and exaggerated motion, he pushes the glass away from him.

He pushes it away!

And all at once, the body I've always thought was way too big seems much too small to contain my happiness.

"Is it my turn now?" Tristan asks with a lift of his brows and a twinkle in his eyes.

I feel light-headed and giddy—and not from the tequila.

"Go for it," I say.

"In nearly four hundred years," he says, "never have I ever met anyone quite like you." He reaches out his hand and touches my face, and I swear, it's a miracle I don't explode from sheer joy. "I write about romantic heroines, but Lily, you are *my* heroine." He strokes his thumb across my cheek, and my whole undead being springs to life. "You are more beautiful, more courageous, and yes, my darling, more maddening than anyone I could ever have imagined. And never have I ever loved anyone the way I love you."

I'm not sure if I tackle him or if he tackles me, but soon enough, we're horizontal, intertwined on the massive leather sofa. Together, our cold bodies ignite.

I claim Tristan's mouth with mine. He tastes of the tequila we just shared and something else, a flavor that's his and his alone—and decadently delicious.

As I feast on his mouth, my nipples harden, straining almost painfully against the soft lining of my bra. Thankfully, Tristan's clever hands find their way under my shirt and undo the front clasp. His palms cup my breasts while his fingers stroke and rub and tweak.

My pussy is all liquid heat. My fangs drop.

Jesus, I want to devour him. I want to taste every inch of him. I want to binge on him like pasta. Or Netflix. Or pasta and Netflix.

I begin to kiss and lick my way down his jaw, down to his throat.

"Do you want to drink?" he asks me.

"No," I murmur against his skin. "Drinking game's over. I win."

"I don't mean drink," he says. He tilts his head back and bares his throat to me. "I mean *drink*."

His offer takes me aback. On top of him, I sit back a little so I can look him in the eye.

So, okay, yes, the first time we made love, drinking from Tristan was the only way I could get past my insecurities about my body. But now, as Tristan's hands continue to skim over the curves of my flesh, I don't feel shame or fear or doubt. Instead, I feel aroused. Loved. Positively worshipped.

"I don't want your blood," I tell him. "I don't need it." I flash him a mischievous grin as I grab at the neck of his white tee and rip it clean down the middle to expose his bare chest—um, just because I can. "All I need is you."

EPILOGUE

About a week later, I stand in front of my open closet, peering down at the vintage Levis I was wearing when this whole adventure began. With a sigh, I fold the jeans up and add them to the green plastic garbage bag full of all the clothes I've been hanging on to. All the clothes that will never, ever fit my eternally larger-sized body.

I'll be honest: it's not easy letting them go. It feels a little like I'm admitting defeat.

But when I got my courage up to post about it on social media—just the body acceptance part, not the vampire part—I got forty-three likes. Not that I care so much about what other people think these days. But still.

And when I look up and see the uncluttered racks, the unstuffed shelves, I know it's actually a win. I mean, when you let go of the things that squeeze and poke and pinch at you, it opens up room for all kinds of other things to come into your life. Better things. Things that really do fit.

"All done?"

Tristan comes up behind me and slides his arms around me. I lean back against him and let my eyes drift shut, reveling in the amazing way our bodies fit so perfectly together.

"Mmm-hmm," I moan as his one hand cradles and fondles my breast over my gray ribbed turtleneck. His other hand glides down my belly and starts to find its way beneath the drawstring waist of my black joggers—until I remember we're not alone.

"Stop!" I say. I open my eyes and slap his hands playfully away. "Cat'll hear us."

"I can't hear a thing," calls Cat from the main room of my studio.

Tristan and I exchange a grin.

"I'll take care of this," he says, tying up the garbage bag. Like the personal Uber that he is, he's offered to drive the clothes over to a Goodwill donation drop, so that my old things can get a new life. He gives a nod in Cat's direction. "You take care of that."

He tosses the big bag over his shoulder, and I walk with him to the door.

"Good to see you, Cat," says Tristan.

"Liar," says my bestie, clicking away at my laptop keyboard. "But don't worry. I'll be gone by the time you get back."

Tristan gives me a quick but nonetheless toe-curling kiss that sets my cold body on fire.

And then, it's just me and my BFF.

"Okay," says Cat. She looks up from my laptop. "You're all good to go here."

"Awesome." I join her at my microscopic dining table, dragging the other chair around next to hers so we can both stare at the screen.

See, over the past week, I've been busy with more than just cleaning out my closet. Busy with more than just, um, Tristan. I've also been writing.

After I cranked out that fake vampire exposé for TakeABite.com—the one Peter rejected—I got to work on the real thing. I wanted there to be a record of my story, my true story. Something that could maybe give me leverage against Gideon in case he decides to cause trouble again.

Oh, I know, I know, I told the grand master that the whole vampires-need-to-hide-from-humans thing was outdated—and I still believe that. Only, not all humans are so progressive in their thinking.

So, I asked my best friend to use her mad computer skills to fix it so that, unless I log in by midnight every night to stop it, my story will automatically be emailed to Palmer Matheson at Matheson Multimedia.

I figure if he sees that the email is from me, he'll open it. Oh, I don't imagine he'll be thrilled to discover his daughter is a vampire. Or even care if I'm in danger. But if he learns there's an unholy army of undead bloodsuckers out there who have already claimed the life of his daughter-in-law? Well, I'm thinking he'll use the power of his platforms to spread the word. And I'm hoping the threat of that happening—and the events it could set in motion—may be just enough to keep my supernatural foe in line.

FYI, I have no plans to contact my biological father otherwise. Maybe my mother still has a soft spot for him, but I'm not my mother. Screw him.

"So," says Cat. She rattles off a string of technical stuff I don't understand. Then she shows me a password-protected log-in screen.

"I need you to pick a password that's at least seven digits long," she says. "It should contain at least one number, one uppercase letter, one lowercase letter, and one special character."

I think about this for a moment. "Got it," I say with a nod.

"Okay," she says. "You'll need to type it in, then type it in again to confirm."

She tactfully averts her eyes from the screen to give me privacy.

"Seriously?" I ask.

She shrugs. "It's safer if I don't know," she says. "Especially if Evan and I, um…"

Right. I almost forgot about Evan.

He and Cat have been talking. And texting. And they're supposed to have dinner together soon. She seems happy about it, so I am. But I guess I'd be one naive vampire to think that my bestie dating a slayer won't create some complications.

"Right," I say.

So, as my friend looks away, I stare at the screen, at the blinking cursor. Then I type it twice and hit Enter.

4Ever_More

"All done," I tell Cat.

Except, I'm not done. I feel like I'm just beginning. And now that I don't have my insecurities holding me back anymore, there's so much I want to do.

Good thing I have all eternity.

ACKNOWLEDGMENTS

This is my first novel. Even now, as I look at it, I can't believe I actually did it. But here's one thing I do believe down to my soul: I absolutely could not have done it without the support of some amazing people.

Thanks to the team at Bookcase Literary Agency—and especially to my agent, Maria Napolitano. You will never know how beyond thrilled I was when you called to offer me representation. And from the day I said yes, you have been a wonderful partner, advisor, cheerleader, sounding board, and friend.

Thanks to the team at Sourcebooks Casablanca—and especially to my editor, Mary Altman. You saw the potential in this book and helped me see it too. You made me push past the jokes and get to the emotional truth of things—and the story is richer because of it.

Thanks to my romance reading and writing buddy, Diana. If not for you, I would probably never have read a romance or gone to a romance writing conference—and I would never have known all the fun I was missing.

Thanks to novelist Liz Moore and everyone in the Exton and Philly sessions of the Palumbo Park Writing Workshop. Your feedback on my early chapters was such a gift. And your enthusiasm gave me the encouragement to keep writing to the end.

Thanks to my BFF, Joan, and her husband, Lee. Even when I was stressed out and panicked and deep down the writing rabbit hole, you made me stop and celebrate every milestone along this incredible journey.

And finally, thanks to my parents, Gloria and Duke. You always encouraged me to go after my dream. I only wish you were still here to see me achieve it.

ABOUT THE AUTHOR

Gloria Duke is a pen name for Gloria Ketterer, a WGA Award–winning radio writer, TV sitcom writer, and brand advertising copywriter. *When Life Gives You Vampires* is her first novel.

WHAT'S NEXT FOR GLORIA DUKE?

You thought life was hard for a vampire?
Keep your eyes peeled for the new Slayer on the block...

Meet Carrie Adams. Serious. Disciplined. Focused. But as an aspiring actress, she's at the mercy of casting directors who barely glance at her headshot before making snap judgments about her talent based solely on her looks. She feels powerless...until one night she goes from snarling at her obnoxiously attractive coworker (musician-slash-bartender Nick Stokes) to wanting to kill him. Literally.

Turns out Nick has become LA's latest vampire, and she is his chosen Slayer...a decidedly unwelcome job that comes with a super-bodybuilder-buff physique, the ability to conjure a sword made of fire, and a new gang of supernatural enemies out for her blood. Nick swears he'll help her. Carrie swears she'll figure out how to help herself.

But in a Hollywood-bright world of typecasting and body obsession, what's a new Slayer to do?

Keep an eye out for the next book by Gloria Duke, coming soon from Sourcebooks Casablanca!

FIX-IT WITCHES

Charming paranormal rom-coms from *New York Times* and *USA Today* bestselling author Ann Aguirre

Witch Please

A modern witch finds herself falling for an adorably earnest baker…much to the displeasure of her very traditional family.

Boss Witch

A modern witch goes toe-to-toe with a witch hunter determined to make a name for himself in her small Midwestern town.

Extra Witchy

A modern witch and a slacker afraid to dream thought they would never find love…until they found each other.

"Sheer happiness in a book."

—Courtney Milan, *New York Times* and *USA Today* bestselling author, for *Witch Please*

For more info about Sourcebooks's books and authors, visit:
sourcebooks.com